江苏大学国家级一流专业"英语"专业建设成果
教育部人文社会科学研究规划基金项目(19YJA752016)、
江苏大学教改项目(2021JGYB023)、江苏大学重点教材建设项目成果

LITERATURE AND SCIENCE
SELECTED READINGS IN ENGLISH AND AMERICAN LITERATURE

文学与科学
英美文学选读

主　编　毛卫强
副主编　来岑岑　刘晓春
编　委　(按姓氏音序排列)
　　　　来岑岑　李新朝　刘晓春
　　　　马风华　毛卫强　万雪梅
　　　　吴　燕　吴媛媛

东南大学出版社
SOUTHEAST UNIVERSITY PRESS
·南京·

内容提要

本书借鉴了文学与科学交叉研究领域的成果,并在梳理自然科学各主要分支方向的基础知识、其文学表征的现状、学界的研究进展等情况的基础上,通过讨论英美文学中相关代表作品所表征的科学知识、其建构的科学精神及其传递的人文思想,进而为如何推进新文科建设背景下英语语言文学专业的学科发展与内涵建设提供案例。

本书探讨了文学与自然科学之间的紧密关系,可以为如何深化英语语言文学专业的改革、拓展其学科内涵明确方向。本书不仅可以用作参考书,为新文科建设背景下英语语言文学专业的学科建设和专业发展提供参考思路,而且可当作教材,用于新文科建设背景下英语语言文学专业本科及以上层次人才的培养。

图书在版编目(CIP)数据

文学与科学:英美文学选读/毛卫强主编.

南京:东南大学出版社,2024.8. -- ISBN 978-7-5766-1485-5

Ⅰ.I561.06;I712.06

中国国家版本馆 CIP 数据核字第 202484JJ90 号

责任编辑:刘 坚(liu-jian@seu.edu.cn)　　责任校对:张万莹
封面设计:王 玥　　责任印制:周荣虎

文学与科学:英美文学选读
Wenxue Yu Kexue:Yingmei Wenxue Xuandu

主　　编	毛卫强
出版发行	东南大学出版社
出 版 人	白云飞
社　　址	南京市四牌楼2号(邮编:210096　电话:025-83793330)
经　　销	全国各地新华书店
印　　刷	广东虎彩云印刷有限公司
开　　本	787mm×1092mm　1/16
印　　张	26
字　　数	582 千字
版　　次	2024年8月第1版
印　　次	2024年8月第1次印刷
书　　号	ISBN 978-7-5766-1485-5
定　　价	69.00元

本社图书若有印装质量问题,请直接与营销部调换。电话(传真):025-83791830

江苏大学国家级一流专业"英语"专业建设成果出版编委会

总 主 编：李崇月
编委会成员：张明平　王　蕾
　　　　　　李加军　李　霞

总 序
FOREWORD

　　江苏大学是2001年8月经教育部批准,由原江苏理工大学、镇江医学院、镇江师范专科学校合并组建的重点综合性大学,是江苏省人民政府和教育部、农业农村部共建高校,也是首批江苏省高水平大学建设高校。

　　江苏大学英语专业的起源可追溯到1958年原镇江师范专科学校开设的英语教育(专科)专业和原江苏工学院1984年开设的英语师资班。历经几十年的建设,以英语语种为主体的外国语言文学学科已获得了长足的发展:2003年获批"外国语言学及应用语言学"二级学科硕士学位点,2018年获批"外国语言文学"一级学科硕士学位点,2021年获批"MTI英语笔译"专业硕士学位点;在近三年(2020、2021、2022)"软科中国最好学科排名"中,江苏大学外国语言文学学科稳居江苏省内高校前六位;得益于外国语言文学学科的有力支撑,近年来,江苏大学英语专业"四级"和"八级"一次性通过率远超全国平均水平;近三年来,本科毕业生考研录取率达35%;毕业生专业教学满意度在全校30多个文管类专业中连续多年位居前列;英语专业特色鲜明,专业建设成绩显著,2021年获批"国家级一流专业建设点"。

　　目前,江苏大学英语专业师资力量雄厚。近30位教师中,有教授10人、副教授10人。师资队伍中除了有多位英语语言文学博士外,还有传播学博士、外交学博士和逻辑学博士各1人。师资结构有力支撑了英语专业"国际事务与沟通"特色方向的建设。在新文科建设背景下,英语专业教师结合自己的教学及研究专长,紧扣一流专业建设目标,在教师发展研究、课程教材资源开发、教育教学研究等方面取得了一系列成果,现以专著或教材的形式由东南大学出版社出版。《社会文化理论视角下高校英语教师学习叙事案例研究》(李霞著)基于社会文化理论,对高校英语教师学习经历、学习过程及学习影响因素进行深入系统的探讨,为推动高校英语教师发展提供参考和建议。该研究成果有助于增进学界对高校英语教师学习的了解,激发教师反思自身学习,优化教学实践,实现科学、高效、持久的专业发展,从而进一步推进一流本科英语专业内涵建设及人才培养的高质量发展。

英语文学教材《文学与科学:新文科英语文学》(毛卫强主编)吸纳英语文学跨学科研究方面的成果,在介绍英语文学如何表征、传播甚至参与建构自然科学领域的研究及发现的同时,结合第一手文献资料和具体案例,培养英语专业学生利用自然科学领域相关知识来批判性解读英语文学作品的能力,发展学生的跨学科意识,拓展学生的科学人文素养。

英文教材《翻译简史》(李崇月、张璘主编)从中国学者的视角,以翻译文本类型(如宗教、科技、文学、社科等)和翻译的方向(译入、译出)为经,以历史上有影响的翻译事件和翻译思想为纬,勾勒中外翻译实践和翻译思想的发展脉络,在中外参照对比中突出中国丰富的翻译实践及其对中国文化发展的贡献。教材从总体框架设计、具体史料选择及对翻译事实的解读上都做到了宏观与微观结合、史实与史识相融,囊括了翻译史的主要内容,为我国翻译史的研究和教学提供了新视角。

《世界经典寓言童话故事选读》(叶富莲编著)的选材来自世界经典寓言童话作家的作品,教材从题材、人物、结构、修辞、主题、语言、同类比较等方面对寓言和童话进行了系统化的说明和阐释,各单元包括文本、注解、练习、讨论和写作等内容。本教材一方面可以提高英语专业学生的语言实践能力,另一方面可以引导学生利用相关语言材料进行英语语言教学的模拟实践。

《如何清晰、理性地思维:逻辑与批判性思维能力培养教程》(闫林琼编著)提供了适合中国高校尤其是理工科院校英语专业学生、融合思政要素并且难易度适中的逻辑与批判性思维能力培养教材。教材包括英语专业学生逻辑与批判性思维能力培养的紧迫性,如何提问,如何论证,如何在多种课程教学中培养逻辑与批判性思维能力等内容,有利于弥补英语专业学生逻辑思辨能力的不足。

《中国参与联合国大会人权议程设置的论辩话语研究》(候璐莎著)从中国参与联合国大会人权治理进程的不同阶段出发,考察中国参与联合国大会人权议程设置多边谈判之中影响论辩策略的因素,阐明了中国运用论辩策略来提高谈判说服力、议程设置能力以及国际人权话语权的研究路径。本书有助于培养英语专业学生的批判性思维、国际沟通与应变能力,增强学生用英语合理且有效地表达自己观点的论辩与谈判能力,有助于使其成为具有全球视野、跨文化交际能力的一专多能复合型英语人才。

《镇江文化外宣》(万雪梅编著)体现英语一流专业建设的地方特色,致力于讲好江苏大学所在地镇江的故事。本书提炼镇江文化的精神标识和精髓,从镇江历史、山水、文物、教育、文学、艺术、科技、饮食、对外人文交流等方面展开,呈现可信、可爱、可敬的镇江形象,助推中华文化更好地走向世界。

《唐宋诗撷英新译》(万雪梅、弗雷德里克·特纳编译)选译了李白、杜甫、王维、范仲淹、苏轼等53位唐宋诗人的148首诗作。所选作品皆为唐宋诗中的经典之作,既有哲学意蕴,又有诗学之美。且诗中体现的儒释道情感与精神能够激发起读者和译者的共鸣,对中华优秀传统文化的阐释和传播颇有裨益。

《学术英语能力及其标准建设研究》(钟兰凤编著)收录学术论文13篇,旨在通过对英文学术话语进行分析,兼采用实验法和调查法,探讨学术英语能力标准建设的主要构件:学术英语能力表现研究、学术英语能力培养的路径及影响因素、学术英语能力标准建设的基本路径和设计原则。本研究成果可以直接应用于英语专业必修课"英语学术论文写作"的课程内容改革及教学方法改革。

  以上是即将出版的英语专业建设成果，这些成果为江苏大学国家级一流专业"英语"的专业建设作出了极大贡献。我代表江苏大学外国语学院衷心感谢付出辛勤劳动的、从事英语专业教学的同事们，也要感谢教育部外国语言文学类专业教学指导委员会和英语专业教学指导分委员会多位委员长期以来对江苏大学英语专业建设的关心和指导，感谢江苏大学校领导和教务处对英语专业建设的关心和支持，感谢东南大学出版社刘坚老师编辑团队的默默付出。

江苏大学国家级一流专业"英语"专业点建设负责人
李崇月
2023 年 7 月 1 日

序言
INTRODUCTION

这部由毛卫强任主编、来岑岑和刘晓春任副主编的《文学与科学:英美文学选读》即将付梓出版,可喜可贺!

文学与科学是人类认知世界的两种重要方式:文学以美求真,科学以真求美。两者之间既有差异又有共性。从人类发展历史来看,两者经历了从融合共生到分离发展再到互补融通的发展路径。不管是涵盖文学、天文学、物理学、伦理学等古希腊百科全书式的哲学家亚里士多德的作品,还是涉及了哲学、政治、天文、文学等学科知识的中国的《易经》都表现出文学与科学的融合共生。古今中外出现了不少对文学和科学都感兴趣的作家或者科学家,如中国有张衡、徐霞客,林语堂等,西方有伽利略、歌德、雪莱、法布尔、罗素等。

西方现代科学直到 15 世纪后期才逐渐形成,由于科学在促进生产力方面的巨大作用,西方逐步形成体系严密但相对独立的各学科知识的专业领域。然而,科学的发展在一定程度上加剧了人与人之间的隔阂、人与社会的疏离,文学与科学之间的差异性日益凸显。直到 20 世纪后半叶,大量出现的学科交叉研究现象才使得文学与科学重新回到相互融通的境地。人们开始重新审视文学与科学的复杂关系并深入探讨文学与科学在想象力等方面的共通性,重视文学与科学的深层次、宽领域、多元化以及多学科之间的互补融通。《文学与科学:英美文学选读》正是一部探讨英美文学与自然科学之间关系的书,旨在引导读者深入思考跨学科融通能力、比较意识以及文学与科学的互动关系。

在当今全球化的背景下,外语学习已经不再局限于语言技能的培养,而更加强调跨学科融通能力和比较意识的培养。本书旨在通过文学与科学的结合,促进学生在外语学习过程中培养批判性思维和创新能力,使他们能够更好地适应多元文化的挑战。同时,通过探讨文学与科学的关系,本书也希望激发学生对不同学科之间相互影响的兴趣,为他们未来的学术和职业发展打下坚实基础。

该书的独特之处在于其突出展示了文学与科学之间的交叉点和相互影响。通过英美文学作品中所表征的自然科学,彰显其建构的科学精神和人文思想,拓展了文学创作和研究的维度。本书每章节选取自然科学中的地质学、化学、医学、遗传基因、信息通信、人工智能、农学和气候学等8个学科门类。他们通过精心挑选的英美文学作品,试图揭示文学作品中所蕴含的科学元素,以及科学进展如何激发文学创作的灵感。这种独特的视角不仅拓展了读者的学术视野,还培养了他们的跨学科思维能力,帮助他们更好地理解文学与科学之间的联系。本书每章节首先提供相关科学背景知识、文献传真,还提供了相关学科的文学作品导读和选读,以及文学作品的补充阅读,同时每节都提供了思考题供读者思考。

随着社会的不断发展,新文科建设已经成为高等教育领域的重要议题。本书的推出正是为了响应这一趋势,促进文学与科学之间的融合,为新文科建设贡献力量。通过培养学生的综合素养和跨学科能力,我相信本书将有助于培养具有跨学科能力和国际视野与创新精神的人才,也为英美文学教学提供了新的路径。

乔国强
2024 年 4 月于上海

前 言
PREFACE

习近平总书记指出,一个没有发达的自然科学的国家不可能走在世界前列,一个没有繁荣的哲学社会科学的国家也不可能走在世界前列。在此背景下,大力推进新文科建设,构建具有中国特色的哲学社会科学学科体系、学术体系及话语体系,促进人文社会科学与自然科学的交叉融合和均衡发展,是我国教育界和社科界为建设中国特色的社会主义提供的方案。做到这点,就必须以科学精神来指导人文科学的发展,以人文情怀来丰富自然科学的研究视域。具体到人才培养方面,就是要在夯实专业素质的基础上,重视科学素养和人文素养的均衡发展,既要使人文社会科学领域的人才具有良好的科学素养,了解自然科学领域的基本知识和最新发展成果,学会用科学原理和方法来解释、处理工作和生活中常见的问题,也要使自然科学领域的人才具有扎实的人文素养,树立准确的世界观和人生观,充分认识到自己的科学使命和社会责任。为了培养这种高规格的人才,必须重视学科发展和教材建设,深化教育、教学改革,加强自然学科和人文社会学科的交叉合作,真正做到自然科学和人文社会科学的均衡发展。为此,人文社会科学领域的学科发展与教材建设应当融入自然科学领域的发展成果,在发展该学科领域人才的专业素养的同时,多方位提高其科学素养;同时,也为如何提高自然科学领域人才的人文素养提供借鉴,在向其介绍和传授人文知识和文化思想的同时兼顾其学科专业特征。

《文学与科学:英美文学选读》正是在上述原则指导下编写的,将英语文学知识,主要是英美文学和自然科学结合起来。

文学与科学这两个学科领域的差距看似巨大、无法弥合,实际上却存在千丝万缕的联系。文学作品比如《简爱》(*Jane Eyre*, 1847)、《米德尔马契》(*Middlemarch*, 1872)和《美丽新世界》(*Brave New World*, 1932)等,不仅是一种文化载体,记述并传播自然科学领域取得的成就,而且也为自然科学的创新和发展提供了思想实验的场所,构想未来社会的科学进步及其建构的文明。因此,文学与科学关系的研究备受学界关注,特别是20世纪80年代以来,西方社会的人文社科研究出现了文化转向,越来越多的学者开始研究文学与科学在世界观、文化和话语体系、人类经验范畴、人类认知能力等方面的共性。经过30多年的发展,该交叉研究领域取得了丰硕的成果,不仅出现了诸如《第三种文化:文学与科学》(*The Third Culture: Literature and Science*, 1998)、《19世纪的文学与科学》(*Literature and Science in the Nineteenth Century: An Anthology*, 2002)、《文学、科学与新人文科学》(*Literature, Science, and a New Humanities*, 2008)、《文学与科学:剑桥指南》(*The Cambridge Companion to Literature and Science*, 2019)等标志性成果,其学科地位也得到学界普遍认可,牛津大学、剑桥大学、哈佛大学等欧美知名大学都设立了相关专业和研究方向,各种研究机构和期刊杂志也应运而生。

在编写过程中,本书借鉴了上述提及的文学与科学交叉研究领域的成果,并在梳理自然科学各主要分支方向的基础知识、其文学表征的现状、学界的研究进展等情况的基础上,通过讨论英美文学中相关代表作品所表征的科学知识、其建构的科学精神及其传递的人文思想,进而为如何推进新文科建设背景下英语语言文学专业的学科发展与内涵建设提供案例。本书共由八个章节构成,每章对应自然科学的一个分支,包括地质学、化学、医学、遗传学、信息通信、人工智能和人工生命、农学和气候学。每章均由相关学科知识及其与文学的关系、作品选读和补充阅读三个板块构成。其中,相关学科知识及其与文学的关系板块由背景知识和文献传真两部分构成,文献传真设有配套思考题。作品选读部分由作品导读和作品选读两部分构成,而作品导读又由作者简介、作品介绍和作品赏析三个部分组成。作品选读配有思考题,旨在引导读者思考文学和科学的关系,发展其科学精神和人文素养。补充阅读则节选与各章对应的自然学科分支相关的文学作品,鼓励读者通过广泛阅读来加深对相关话题的理解,实现本书的编写目的。

  本书具有如下几方面的用途:本书探讨了文学与自然科学之间的紧密关系,可以为如何深化英语语言文学专业的改革、拓展其学科内涵明确方向。本书不仅可以用作参考书,为新文科建设背景下英语语言文学专业的学科建设和专业发展提供参考思路,而且可当作教材,用于新文科建设背景下英语语言文学专业本科及以上层次人才的培养。对英语语言文学专业的学生而言,本书有助于巩固其学科专业知识,引导其用科学精神来分析和批评文学作品,探讨文学作品在解决自然科学带来的社会问题方面的作用。同时,本书也可用于其他专业本科甚至硕士阶段学生外语拓展课程的教学。对人文社科方向的学生来说,鼓励其结合本书介绍的科学知识,探讨所选作品反映的科学精神,借此发展和提高其科学素养。对自然科学方向的学生来说,鼓励其结合本书所选作品反映的人文思想和社会文化,探讨与自然科学相关的社会问题,借此发展和提高其人文素养。因此,本书可以满足不同专业爱好英美文学的学生的需求,发展其科学和人文素养,训练其跨学科意识,促进其整体能力水平的提高。

  本书各章编写情况如下:第一章、第五章和第六章由毛卫强、来岑岑共同编写;第三章由李新朝、吴燕共同编写;第二章、第四章、第七章、第八章编写人员分别为吴媛媛、马凤华、万雪梅和刘晓春;本书统稿、格式校对人员为毛卫强、来岑岑。

  本书是江苏大学教育部一流本科专业(英语)、教育部人文社科基金项目(19YJA752016)、江苏大学教改项目(2021JGYB023)和江苏大学重点教材建设项目的部分成果。本书从选题、设计到定稿,均得到了上海外国语大学乔国强教授、江苏大学吴鹏教授的指导和帮助,本人在此深表感谢。在编写过程中,本书也得到了江苏大学外国语学院院长李崇月教授的帮助和支持,在校对过程中也得到了江苏大学蒋萍老师的帮助,在此一并感谢。

另外感谢:Routledge 出版社授权使用 *The Routledge Companion to Literature and Science* 部分章节(各章节"文献传真"部分内容),Tracy Chevalier 授权使用其作品 *Remarkable Creatures* 小说部分章节(第一章第二节"作品选读"部分),Richard Powers 授权使用其作品 *Gain*(第二章第二节"作品选读"部分),Julian Barnes 授权使用其作品 *The Sense of an Ending*(第五章第三节"补充阅读"部分)以及 Kim Stanley Robinson 授权使用其作品 *Fifty Degrees Below* 部分章节(第八章第二节"作品选读"部分)。

鉴于水平有限,本书可能存在一些问题,真诚希望同行专家和广大教师不吝赐教。

毛卫强
2023 年 7 月

目 录 CONTENTS

第一章 文学与地质学(Literature and Geology) ……… 001

第一节 地质科学的文学表征 ……… 001
- 背景知识 ……… 001
- 文献传真 ……… 016
- 思考题 ……… 023

第二节 《奇妙的生物》与地质科学 ……… 023
- 作品导读 ……… 023
- 作品选读 ……… 029
- 思考题 ……… 051

第三节 补充阅读《石灰岩赞》 ……… 052

第二章 文学与化学(Literature and Chemistry) ……… 057

第一节 化学的文学表征 ……… 057
- 背景知识 ……… 057
- 文献传真 ……… 064
- 思考题 ……… 071

第二节 《盖恩》与化学 ·· 072
- 作品导读 ·· 072
- 作品选读 ·· 078
- 思考题 ·· 099

第三节 补充阅读《胎记》 ··· 100

第三章 文学与医学（Literature and Medicine） ················ 116

第一节 医学的文学表征 ·· 116
- 背景知识 ·· 116
- 文献传真 ·· 120
- 思考题 ·· 132

第二节 《米德尔马契》与医学 ··· 132
- 作品导读 ·· 132
- 作品选读 ·· 140
- 思考题 ·· 161

第三节 补充阅读《古舟子咏》 ··· 161

第四章 文学与遗传学（Literature and Genetics） ··············· 174

第一节 遗传学的文学表征 ··· 174
- 背景知识 ·· 174
- 文献传真 ·· 177
- 思考题 ·· 182

第二节 《美丽新世界》与基因工程 ··································· 182
- 作品导读 ·· 182
- 作品选读 ·· 187

- 思考题 ······ 205
- 第三节　补充阅读：莎士比亚十四行诗两首 ······ 206

第五章　文学与信息通信技术（Literature and ICT） ······ 208
第一节　信息通信技术及其文学表征 ······ 208
- 背景知识 ······ 208
- 文献传真 ······ 212
- 思考题 ······ 218

第二节　《在笼中》与电报通信 ······ 218
- 作品导读 ······ 218
- 作品选读 ······ 224
- 思考题 ······ 243

第三节　补充阅读《终结的意义》 ······ 243

第六章　文学与人工智能/生命（Literature and AI/AL） ······ 250
第一节　人工智能与人工生命的文学表征 ······ 250
- 背景知识 ······ 250
- 文献传真 ······ 253
- 思考题 ······ 257

第二节　《弗兰肯斯坦》与人工生命 ······ 257
- 作品导读 ······ 257
- 作品选读 ······ 263
- 思考题 ······ 284

第三节　补充阅读《机器中的达尔文》 ······ 284

第七章　文学与农学（Literature and Agriculture） ············ 289

第一节　农业科学的文学表征 ············ 289
- 背景知识 ············ 289
- 文献传真 ············ 293
- 思考题 ············ 297

第二节　《德伯家的苔丝》与农业科学 ············ 297
- 作品导读 ············ 297
- 作品选读 ············ 302
- 思考题 ············ 315

第三节　补充阅读《愤怒的葡萄》 ············ 315

第八章　文学与气候科学（Literature and Climate Science） ············ 324

第一节　气候的文学表征 ············ 324
- 背景知识 ············ 324
- 文献传真 ············ 327
- 思考题 ············ 334

第二节　《零下五十度》与气候变化 ············ 334
- 作品导读 ············ 334
- 作品选读 ············ 341
- 思考题 ············ 375

第三节　补充阅读《人生四季》 ············ 375

参考书目 ············ 377

第一章

文学与地质学(Literature and Geology)

第一节 地质科学的文学表征

背景知识

地质学的英文名称"geology"来源于希腊语"geología",它由"geo"和"-logía"两部分构成,在希腊语中分别表示"地球"和"关于的话语或研究"①。因此,地质学从字面上来看是研究地球的科学,隶属地球科学(earth science),主要探究地球的物质组成、形貌结构、地球起源及其演化历史②。一般说来,地质学可以分为普通地质学(physical geology)和历史地质学(historical geology)两大传统研究领域。普通地质学主要探讨地球的物质组成,力图了解地球外在形态、内部构造,阐明其特征、形成条件与变化规律,其分支学科包括矿物学、岩石学、矿场学、地球化学、构造地质学、区域地质学、地球物理学等③。历史地质学主要研究地球演变的历史及规律,研究内容涉及地球的形成,地球生命的起源,生物的演化,古地理的变迁,板块的离合以及地球不同圈层之间的相互作用,其分支学科包括古生物学、地史学、岩相地理学、第四纪地质学等④。另外,地质学还与生产和生活实践相结合,形成了一些应用学科分支。比如:以地下水的分布、找寻、开发和利用为目的的水文地质学;与铁路、公路、大坝、桥梁、隧道、城市工程等基础建设地质条件有关的工程地质学;与地震发生的地质背景、分布规律以及地震预报服务相关的地震地质学;与煤炭、石油、天然气、各种金属与非金属矿产等各种资源的开发利益及其对环境的影响相关的应用学科等。近年来,地质学研究还出现一个交叉综合的趋势,与地球科学的其他分支、其他星体研究、新材料开发研究、人文艺术研究等领域相结合而形成一些新的领域,比如行星地质学(planetary geology)、地质新材料(new

---

① Geology[Z/OL]. [2023-06-22]. https://en.wikipedia.org/wiki/Geology.
② 拉更斯,塔巴克. 地球科学导论[M]. 7版. 徐学纯,梁琛岳,郑琦,等译. 北京:电子工业出版社,2017:2.
③ PLUMMER C C, CARLSON D. Physical geology[M]. 15th ed. New York: McGraw-Hill Education, 2016: 8.
④ MONROE J S, WICANDER R. Historical geology[M]. 6th ed. Belmont: Brooks/Cole, 2010: 4. 另参见舒良树. 普通地质学[M]. 3版. 北京:地质出版社,2010:2.

geo-materials)研究、地质人文研究(geo-humanities)等①。

地质学从其萌芽到现当代跨学科综合发展大致经历了四个发展阶段,具体如下:

(一) 早期萌芽阶段(远古—1450 年)

从远古时期到中世纪,中国、希腊、印度等世界古代文明等都记述了人类如何在生产实践中探索地球的奥秘。中国古代的地质学知识由地球构成和起源、地质结构及变迁、矿物资源的开采和利用这三大方面组成。《周易》《尚书·洪范》中的"阴阳说"和"五行说"是中国早期关于地球物质构成和起源的假说。地质变化包括地壳运动、海陆变迁等。《诗经·小雅》中描述的"高岸为谷,深谷为陵"实际上是关于地壳变动的描述。《神仙传》中描述的"东海三为桑田"则是关于海陆变迁的记载。《竹书纪年》中记载的中国 3800 年前的地震,是世界上该方面最早的记录。宋代的沈括(1031—1095)和朱熹(1130—1200)在各自著述中都试图科学解释地质变迁或地壳变化现象。作为四大文明古国之一,中国在利用矿产资源、发展生产发面累积了不少经验。《山海经》《禹贡》《管子·地数》《汉书·地理志》等地学典籍都记载了丰富的岩矿知识,涉及金属、天然气、石油、煤和盐的开采和利用。南朝梁代的《地镜图》记载了如何寻找铅、铜、银等矿物。沈括在《梦溪笔谈》中根据太行山地区观察到的沉积岩的隆起、土壤的流失、沉积的泥沙、海洋生物化石等地质现象,提出了一种地质变迁理论,此外,他还在石油的命名及开采方面提出了独到的见解②。阿那克西曼德(Anaximander,611—546 BC)是古希腊最早绘制世界地图的天文学家之一,他猜想宇宙起源于原生质内部相反运动的分裂,认为地球呈圆筒状,其中心是地中海。亚里士多德(Aristotle,384—322 BC)认为地球是圆形球体,它是宇宙的中心,由空气、火、水和泥土四种物质构成,指出地震的产生是因为"地球内部捕捉的风能的释放",表明化石是"曾经存在过的生命的遗骸",河流会干涸,海洋会消失或地理位置会发生变化。除了这些关于地球的构成、变化等方面的观点,亚里士多德还探讨过矿物的成因,认为地球内部干热的烟气和湿冷的水汽共同作用产生了各种矿物。亚里士多德的同事及继承人泰奥弗拉斯托斯(Theophrastus,371—287 BC)在《论岩石》中详细讨论了各类岩石、矿物的构成、属性及其可能存在的位置,这为如何开采这些矿物资源提供了重要的参考依据。古印度吠陀时代(1300—300 BC)流传的《往世书》(The Puranas)提出了以十亿年为地质单位的地质创世说和毁灭说。后来的印度数学家阿里亚哈塔(Aryabhata,476—550 AD)认为地球的自转使得星星似乎在运动,指出日食是由

---

① 舒良树. 普通地质学[M]. 3 版. 北京:地质出版社,2010:2. 关于行星地质学参见 Planetary geology[Z/OL]. [2023-06-17]. https://en.wikipedia.org/wiki/Planetary_geology. 关于地质新材料参见 YASUHARA K. Development of new geomaterials[J]. Tsuchi to Kiso, 2007, 54(12):6-7. 关于地质人文参见 GeoHumanities forum[Z/OL]. [2023-07-10]. https://geohumanitiesforum.org/about/.

② 地质学发展史[Z/OL]. [2018-07-24]. https://www.sohu.com/a/242923299_650579. 另参见 JAN Z. Geology: a very short introduction[M]. Adobe Digital ed. New York: Oxford University Press, 2018:39-40.

于月亮遮挡住太阳而形成,并精确计算出日食发生的时间。在中世纪的欧洲,由于宗教禁锢,地质科学发展遇到了极大阻碍。在阿拉伯,情况则有所不同。比如,比鲁尼(Al-Biruni, 973—1048)以岩层中存在的化石为依据,提出海陆变迁的观点。另外,他还就矿物资源的分布和识别编著了相关专著①。

(二)学科奠基阶段(1450—1750年)

14世纪到17世纪欧洲的文艺复兴将自然科学从宗教神学的禁锢中解放出来。在此背景下,地质学知识告别了早期阶段朴素经验的记录,日趋系统化和科学化。在这个阶段,学界对地球的起源持有两种假说:其一是地球是自然界物质发展的结果,其二是地球起源于《圣经·创世纪》中的大洪水。法国哲学家笛卡尔(René Descartes, 1596—1650)在1644年提出了一种旋涡模型宇宙,由发光的、透明的和不透明的三种不同性质的粒子构成,这些物质不断运动和碰撞,进而形成了太阳系,其中星星由体积最小的发光粒子构成,地球及其他星球由密度较大的灰暗物质构成②。1696年,英国人惠斯顿(William Whiston, 1667—1752)在《地球新论》(*A New Theory of the Earth*)中从基督教的框架论证说明《圣经》中的大洪水确实存在,指出地球岩层是大洪水的结果。鉴于17世纪基督教的影响力,惠斯顿的理论受到当时人们的推崇③。在1749年,法国人布丰(Georges-Louis Leclerc, Comte de Buffon, 1707—1788)提出了彗星与太阳相碰撞而形成地球以及其他所有行星的观点,随后,他使用灼热铁球冷却的时间来推测地球的年龄④,从科学和宗教两个路径来讨论地球的起源,激发了当时的人们对地球产生更加浓厚的兴趣。同时,学界对地层的划分也变得更加系统化。达·芬奇(Leonardo da Vinci, 1452—1519)通过研究化石和岩石,发现地球的历史远比《圣经》所说的地球的历史要久远,认为自然界最强大的力量是水,是水塑造了地球的风貌;另外,他指出地球由多个岩层构成,地壳的运动导致岩层的上升,将含有化石的岩层抬到高处⑤。在《地球和天体的自然史》(*An Essay toward a Natural History of the Earth and Terrestrial Bodies, Especially Minerals*, 1695)中,伍德沃德(John Woodward, 1665—1728)指

---

① 地质学发展简史[Z/OL].[2023-07-05]. https://www.zgbk.com/ecph/words?SiteID=1&ID=49148&SubID=78317. 另参见 Al-Biruni[Z/OL].[2023-06-24]. https://en.wikipedia.org/wiki/Al-Biruni.

② Physical astronomy for the mechanistic universe[Z/OL].[2023-07-10]. https://www.loc.gov/collections/finding-our-place-in-the-cosmos-with-carl-sagan/articles-and-essays/modeling-the-cosmos/physical-astronomy-for-the-mechanistic-universe.

③ William Whiston[Z/OL].[2023-07-08]. https://en.wikipedia.org/wiki/William_Whiston.

④ ASHWORTH W B. Science of the day: George-Louis Leclerc, Comte de Buffon[Z/OL].[2018-09-07]. https://www.lindahall.org/about/news/scientist-of-the-day/georges-louis-leclerc-comte-de-buffon-2. 另参见地质学发展史[Z/OL].[2018-07-24]. https://www.sohu.com/a/242923299_650579.

⑤ JONES J. Leonardo da Vinci's earth-shattering insights about geology[Z/OL].[2011-11-23]. https://www.theguardian.com/artanddesign/jonathanjonesblog/2011/nov/23/leonardo-da-vinci-earth-geology. 另参见 NICOLAUS S. Tag archives: Leonardo da Vinci fossils[Z/OL].[2020-07-13]. https://www.geological-digressions.com/tag/leonardo-da-vinci-fossils/.

出,地球表面的岩石可以分层,认为岩石中包含的化石最初形成于大海。人们普遍接受他的这一观点,但他关于岩石形成的方法却经不起任何推敲,因而备受争议①。在这个时期,丹麦学者斯泰诺(Nicolas Steno,1638—1686)深受笛卡尔地质思想的影响,质疑了当时有关化石的来源以及岩石形成过程的说法,提出了地层学的一些重要原理,如"叠置律""原始连续律""原始水平率"对地质学的发展产生了深远影响,因而被认为是现代地层学和地质学的奠基者之一②。1667—1700年,胡克(Robert Hooke,1635—1703)在英国皇家实验学会做了系列报告,探讨化石的本质、地震的成因、大陆的形成等话题,提出了关于大陆形成的"移动的地轴"(wandering poles)理论,认为英国曾靠近赤道,地轴可能发生过倾斜。尽管胡克收集的一些化石、撰写的地质学理论手稿以及设计的一些研究工具已经遗失,他的一些思想却被后来的地质学家传递了下来③。

在这一阶段,岩石及矿物研究也得到了长足发展,出现了一些重要成果,促进了地质相关学科的发展,也为社会生产对矿物资源的需求提供了重要保障。比如,1556年德国矿物学家阿格里科拉(Georgius Agricola,1494—1555)出版了《论金属》(*De Re Metallica*,1556)一书,不仅提出了矿石、矿脉和矿床的生成理论,而且详细描述了如何探矿、开矿、试金、洗矿、冶炼、分离不同金属以及矿场的管理和经营,此书成为随后两百多年矿物研究和矿物开采方面的权威理论著作④。在中国明代,矿物的研究及其开采也取得了巨大成就。明朝医学家李时珍所撰写的《本草纲目》(1578)不仅是一部中医药方面的旷世巨著,而且也是一部重要的矿物学著作,记载的矿物的种类不仅较前代增多,而且更加系统全面、分类更加精确。这个时期涉及矿物研究和开采的另一部科学巨著是明朝科学家宋应星于1647年刊发的《天工开物》,涉及煤炭的开采烧制、金属的开采冶炼、珠宝玉石的来源和开采等⑤。

(三)学科确立与发展成熟(1751—1900年)

从18世纪中期到20世纪初,西方经历了两次工业革命,科学技术快速发展,生产力得到了极大的提高。随着矿产资源在资本主义社会经济发展中起着越来越重要的作用,越来越多的专家学者开始系统地探究地球的起源及构成,研究矿物的形成、分布及开采。在该阶段,地质学不仅注重野外实践调查,而且重视理论体系的建构。在1755年,德国哲学家康德(Immanuel Kant,1724—1804)提出了关于宇宙起源的假说,认为包括地球在内的整个太阳

---

① John Woodward[Z/OL]. [2022-09-05]. https://en.wikipedia.org/wiki/John_Woodward_(naturalist).
② History of geology[Z/OL]. https://en.wikipedia.org/wiki/History_of_geology#17th_century. 另参见 VAI G B. The Scientific Revolution and Nicolas Steno's Twofold Conversion[J]. Memoir of the Geological Society of America, 2009(203): 187-208.
③ The geological observation of Robert Hook[Z/OL]. [2016-01-18]. https://paleonerdish.wordpress.com/2016/01/18/the-geological-observations-of-robert-hooke/.
④ MA C, RUBIN A E. Meteorite mineralogy[M]. Cambridge: Cambridge University Press, 2021: 3.
⑤ 天工开物[Z/OL]. [2023-01-07]. https://zh.wikipedia.org/wiki/天工开物.

第一章 文学与地质学(Literature and Geology)

系是由气体星云冷凝而成。这在一定程度上回应了1749年布丰提出的星云假说,质疑了当时关于地球年龄的宗教神学,标志着地球研究开始抛弃先入为主的宗教立场而转向理性和科学①。随着科学研究方法及规范的使用,地质学开始成为一门独立的科学研究领域。一方面,在1777年德鲁克(Jean-Andre Deluc,1727—1817)首次正式使用"geology"这一术语,借此表示有关地球方面的研究,翌年索绪尔(Horace-Benedict de Saussure,1740—1799)将"geology"作为一个固定术语来推广介绍,这标志着地质学开始成为一个科学研究领域②。

另一方面,随着18世纪末有关岩石和岩层成因的水成论(Neptunism)和火成论(Plutonism)之间争论的展开,地质学也开始从宇宙起源论、博物学和古老矿物学中分离出来,最终成为一个独立的学科。德国地质学家维尔纳(Abraham Werner,1749—1817)及其学生是水成论重要代表,认为原始地球全部由海洋构成,地球上所有岩石(包括火成岩)均是由化学或物理积淀的结果(chemical or physical precipitation),在其重要理论著作包括《化石的外部特征》("On the External Characteristics of Fossils",1774)和《不同山脉的分类与描述》(*The Classification and Description of Different Styles of Mountains*,1878)中,维尔纳根据矿石的颜色、外形、光泽、硬度等外部特征对岩石进行分类③。火成论认为地核由液态岩浆构成,岩石则是地下热能的变化造成的。该理论最早由意大利地质学家摩络(Abbé Anton Moro,1687—1764)于1750年提出。在《地球理论》(*The Theory of Earth*,1788)中,被誉为现代地质学之父的英国地质学家赫顿(James Hutton,1726—1797)发展并完善了火成论观点,认为整个地球就像一台不断加热的机器,地下熔岩温度的升高导致地球外层的扩张,使得海底被挤压的沉积物抬升成新大陆④。水成论和火成论对18世纪末、19世纪初地质学的发展影响深远。

对该时期地质学发展有着重要影响的另一历史事件是有关地球表面形态变化以及地球生命演变的灾变论(Catastrophism)和均变论(Uniformitarianism)之间的争论⑤。法国地质学家居维叶(George Cuvier,1769—1832)是灾变论的重要代表,在研究巴黎盆地不同地层中的古生物化石时,他发现不同的地层含有不同的化石,地层越古老,化石中所含生物就越简

---

① ANGELO J A. Encyclopedia of space and astronomy[M]. New York: Facts on File Inc., 2006: 327. 1796年,法国科学家拉普斯(Pierre-Simon Laplace,1749—1827)发展完善了康德星云说(Kant nebular hypothesis)。另参见 Nebular hypothesis [Z/OL]. [2023-06-21]. https://en.wikipedia.org/wiki/Nebular_hypothesis. 另参见 WHITROW G J. Pierre-Simon, marquis de Laplace [Z/OL]. [2023-05-29]. https://www.britannica.com/biography/Pierre-Simon-marquis-de-Laplace#ref29401.
② CHAUHAN L K. Basics of geophysics[M]. Lunawada: Redshine International Press, 2017: 4.
③ GOHAU G. A history of geology[M]. New Brunswick: Rutgers University Press, 1990: 102. 另参见 CHAUHAN L K. Basics of geophysics[M]. Lunawada: Redshine International Press, 2017: 7-8.
④ RAFFERTY J P. Geological sciences[M]. London: Britannica Educational Publishing, 2012: 12-13.
⑤ VEITH W. The genesis conflict[M]. Delta: Amazing Discoveries, 2002: 56.

单。在有些地层中,古生物化石会突然消失,直到较长时间后的地层中才再次出现。在1813年发表的《论地球理论》(Essay on the Theory of Earth)中,居维叶指出造成地层中古生物化石断层的原因是突发的灾难如大洪水、地震等。在此基础上,他提出地质史上发生过多次灾变并造成生物灭绝的观点①。均变论的重要代表是赫顿(James Hutton,1726—1797)和莱尔(Charles Lyell,1797—1875)。赫顿是最早提出均变论思想的地质学家,他认为地貌是缓慢变化的②。莱尔正式使用该理论,阐述岩石起源于地貌变化,在1830—1833年推出的三卷本《地质学原理》(The Principles of Geology)中,他提出了"将今论古"的原则,即"用当下的自然法则来阐述所有的地质现象,灾变论在地质史上没有存在的必要性";莱尔不仅认为当今的地质现象能说明过去的地质事件,而且认为地质变化的强度和规模在过去和现在都保持不变③。《地质学原理》的出版,特别是"将今论古"原则的提出,完善了地质学的理论体系,标志着地质学学科最终确立。

在古生物研究方面,居维叶的《四足兽化石的研究》(Researches on Quadruped Fossil Bones,1812)提出了"器官相关律"(Principle of the Correlation of Parts),为重构化石、科学鉴定地层时代提供了依据④。在《化石鉴定地层》(Strata Identified by Organized Fossils,1816—1819)中,英国地质学家史密斯(William Smith,1769—1839)提出了地层鉴定法则,认为地层中包含了不同的生物的化石,可用于匹配不同地区的岩石⑤。在《无脊椎动物自然史》(Histoire Naturelle des Animaux sans Vertèbres,1815—1822)中,法国地质学家拉马克(Jean- Baptiste Larmarc,1744—1829)提出了生物根据需要而进化发展出某种特征,进而奠定了无脊椎古生物学和进化论思想⑥。在岩石、矿物研究方面,英国地质学家霍尔(Sir James Hall,1761—1832)多次进行石灰岩转化为大理岩的加热实验,开创了实验地质学和岩石学实验研究⑦。尼科尔(William Nicol,1770—1851)在1815年发展了岩石薄片加工技术,并在1829年发明了偏光显微镜,这两个技术促进了显微岩石学(petrological microscope)的快速发展⑧。1837年,美国地质学家丹纳(James Dwight Dana,1813—1895)发表了《矿物学系统》(The System of Mineralogy),根据矿物的化学性质、原子结构,对352种矿物进行系统分

---

① RUDWICK M J S. George Cuvier, fossil bones, and geological catastrophes: new translations and interpretations of the primary texts[M]. London: The University of Chicago Press, 1997: 263.
② RAFFERTY J P. Geological sciences[M]. London: Britannica Educational Publishing, 2012:56.
③ O'HARA K D. A brief history of geology[M]. Cambridge: Cambridge University Press, 2018: 18 - 20.
④ DAWSON G. Show me the bone: reconstructing prehistoric monsters in nineteenth century[M]. Chicago: University of Chicago Press, 2016: 322.
⑤ 同②253.
⑥ 同②59 - 60.
⑦ 同②111.
⑧ 同③77 - 78.

类。这标志着经典矿物学的成熟①。在地壳运动方面,赫顿发现了岩层"不规整"(unconformities)现象,认为这是大陆运动的结果,这在一定程度上构成了20世纪大陆漂移理论的基础②。至此,经过近一百年(1751—1840年)的发展,地质学学科体系基本形成,它由探讨地球历史的古生物学和地层学、探讨地球物质构成的岩石学和矿物学、探讨地球运动的构造地质学三大领域构成。

在19世纪后半叶,地质学进入了快速发展和成熟期。达尔文(Charles Darwin, 1809—1882)《物种起源》(On the Origin of Species, 1859)的发表,确立了古生物学研究的进化论发展方向。在英国地质学家赫胥黎(Thomas Huxley, 1825—1895)、德国地质学家威斯曼(August Weisman, 1834—1914)和海克尔(Ernest Haeckel, 1834—1919)等人的努力下,进化论逐步取代了宗教神学,成为解释物种起源的主要科学理论。赫胥黎的贡献在于他将进化论与古生物学和比较解剖学结合起来,运用于人类生命的起源的解释,为人类和类人猿有着共同的祖先这一假设提供了有力的证据③。威斯曼的贡献在于他区分了生殖细胞(如精子和卵细胞)和身体细胞,表明遗传只通过生殖系发生作用,进而奠定了遗传生物学的理论基础④。海克尔在形态学与胚胎学基础上重构了生命的进化史,对进化生物学和人类学的发展做出了贡献⑤。在19世纪后半叶,地质学在岩石与矿床研究方面也取得了长足的发展。一方面,德国的福格尔桑(Hermann Peter Joseph Vogelsang, 1838—1874)、齐克尔(Ferdinand Zirkel, 1838—1912)和罗森布施(K. H. F. Rosenbusch, 1836—1914)各自发表了显微镜下岩石矿物方面的著作,奠定了显微岩石学基础。英国地质学家巴罗通过对苏格兰高地变质岩的研究,在1893年首次提出了变质带概念。地质学界对矿产及其开采的系统研究始于19世纪末。1854年,美国地质学家惠特尼(Josiah Dwight Whitney, 1819—1896)讨论了矿床的次生富集(secondary supergene sulfide enrichment/secondary enrichment)作用,据其实地调查结果撰写的《美国金属矿物财富》(The Metallic Wealth of the United States: Described and Compared with That of Other Countries, 1854),成为矿物开采方面的标准文献⑥。1873年,美国地质学家纽伯利(John Strong Newberry,

---

① RAFFERTY J P. Geological sciences [M]. London: Britannica Educational Publishing, 2012: 15.
② 同①13. 另参见JOHN R. Missing links: in search of human origins [M]. New York: Oxford University Press, 2011: 16.
③ COSANS C E. Owen's ape and Darwin's bulldog: beyond Darwinism and creationism [M]. Bloomington: Indiana University Press, 2009: xx.
④ BROWN V A, BRYANT C. Cooperative evolution: reclaiming Darwin's vision [M]. Canberra: Australian National University Press, 2021: 64.
⑤ VEITH W. The genesis conflict [M]. Delta: Amazing Discoveries, 2002: 205
⑥ MCPHEE J. Assembling California-I [Z/OL]. [1992-08-30]. https://www.newyorker.com/magazine/1992/09/07/assembling-california-part-i. 另参见RABBITT M C. Minerals, lands, and geology for the common defence and general welfare [M]. United States Government Printing Office, 1980: 6-7, 55, 297.

1822—1892)提出了生油层(source rock)、储集层(reservoir rock)和盖层(cap rock)这三个石油基本构造要素,推动了石油地质学研究①。

在地质构造方面,地壳重力均衡模型(isostasy)及地槽-地台(geosyncline-platform theory)理论的提出使得该时期的地壳运动研究达到了巅峰。英国数学家普拉特(John Henry Pratt, 1809—1871)及艾里(George Biddell Airy, 1801—1892)分别在1854年与1855年提出了地壳重力均衡模型,认为地壳物质海平面以下部分支撑了海平面以上的部分,因而地球存在一个在任何地方单位面积重量都相等的深度,此即补偿深度(the depth of compensation)②。该理论模型的提出为20世纪60年代地球板块构造理论的发展提供了重要依据。地槽-地台理论是地质构造理论之一,最初由美国地质学家霍尔(James Hall, 1811—1898)和丹纳(James Dana, 1813—1895)分别在1859年和1873年研究美国阿巴拉契亚山脉时提出。地槽是地壳上最不稳定的构造带,地台则是大陆自形成以来未遭受褶皱变形的稳定地区。地槽-地台理论认为,地槽是两个大陆边缘或之间巨大狭长的下叠(downward fold)或海底下沉床,来自周边的沉积物不断地堆积在那里,在空间上形成了周边高、中间低的凸镜状。在地槽边缘巨大压力的挤压下,这些沉积物折叠抬升构成褶皱山,比如美国的阿巴拉契亚山脉、欧洲的阿尔卑斯山和亚洲的喜马拉雅山脉③。1885—1901年,奥地利地质学家修斯(Eduard Suess, 1831—1914)出版了三卷本巨著《地球面貌》(*Das Antlitz der Erde*),总结了19世纪地质学研究的成果,提出了南半球曾存在一个统一的大陆即"冈瓦纳大陆"(Gondwanaland)的假说,从全球的角度来研究地壳运动,奠定了古地理学和板块构造理论的基础,预示着20世纪地质学的到来④。

(四) 现当代发展阶段(1901年至今)

1901—1945年,尽管爆发了两次世界大战,社会生产力和科学技术仍取得了巨大进步,地质科学向纵深发展。首先,化学理论及研究方法被引入地质科学,形成了地球化学这一交叉学科,取得了不少成果。比如,克拉克(Frank Wigglesworth Clarke, 1847—1931)在专著《地球化学数据》(*The Data of Geochemistry*, 1908)中探究了岩石圈、水圈及大气圈的化学分析值,研究成果影响深远,因而被誉为"地球化学之父"⑤。霍姆斯(Arthur Holmes, 1890—1965)运用放射性铀矿来测量矿物的年代并出版专著《地球的年龄》(*The Age of the Earth*, 1913)。另外两位重要代表是戈尔德施密特(Victor Moritz Goldschmidt, 1888—1947)和菲

---

① WALTERS C C. The origin of petroleum[C]//HSU C S, ROBINSON P R. Practical advances in petroleum processing. Vol. 1. New York: Springer, 2006: 79-101.
② GUPTA H. Encyclopedia of solid earth geophysics[M]. Dordrecht: Springer, 1989: 627-633.
③ RAFFERTY J P. Geological sciences[M]. London: Britannica Educational Publishing, 2012: 22.
④ MARSHAK S. Plate tectonics[M]. New York: Chelsea House Publishers, 2009: 23.
⑤ COBB A B. Earth chemistry[M]. New York: Chelsea House Publishers, 2009: 70.

尔斯曼(A. Ye. Fersman,1883—1945),前者在1929年研究了地球化学元素的分布、分类和迁移[1],后者在20世纪30年代通过对伟晶岩矿的研究,提出了地球化学元素的迁移、循环概念[2]。其次,地质学与物理学交叉融合,取得不少重大发现。比如,在1897年,英国地质学家奥尔德木(Richard Dixon Oldham,1858—1936)使用地震仪首次测定了P波和S波,开启了用地震波来研究地球内部结构的新时代[3]。在1909年,莫霍洛维奇(Andrija Mohorovičić,1857—1936)发现了地下30千米处将地壳和地幔分割开来的莫霍面。在1914年,古登堡(Beno Gutenberg,1889—1960)发现了地下2900千米处地幔与地核的交界的古登堡界面,莱曼(Inge Lehmann,1888—1993)则在1935年发现液态地核内部存在着固态的内核[4]。在这一时期,岩石研究也成果斐然。葛利普(Amadeus William Grabau,1870—1946)和裴迪庄(Francis J. Pettijohn,1904—1999)在各自研究中均对沉积岩的成因进行了分类[5]。赛德霍姆(Jakob Sederholm,1863—1934)在1934年提出用"混合岩"来专门命名介于花岗岩与片麻岩之间的岩石[6]。另外,里德(Herbert Read,1889—1970)在二十世纪四五十年代发表多篇论文,探讨花岗岩变质的成因[7]。

在20世纪上半叶,古生物研究也取得了重要进展。1911年,乌登(Johan August Udden,1859—1932)使用微体化石(microfossil)来研究地层年代,为微体古生物学(micropaleontology)学科地位的确立打下了坚固基础[8]。在1953年,辛普森(George Gaylord Simpson,1902—1984)推出专著《进化的主要特征》(*The Major Features of Evolution*),总结生物演化的系谱和方式。辛普森是最早将数理方法用于古生物研究的学者,同时他也是综合研究进化论和古生物学的地质学家之一。作为美国微体古生物学的创始人,库什曼(Joseph Augustine Cushman,1881—1949)在1928年出版的专著《有孔虫》(*Foraminifera*)中推介使用有孔虫来研究地层。此外,库什曼提出了一种分类法,使得有孔虫首次被用于钻孔寻找石油,为油勘探做出了巨大的贡献[9]。地层及地质构造研究在该时期也取得重要发展。葛利普(Amadeus

---

[1] GLASBY G. Goldschmidt in Britain[J/OL]. Geoscientist, 2007, 17(13): 22-27. https://www.geolsoc.org.uk/Geoscientist/Archive/March-2007/Goldschmidt-in-Britain.

[2] BRUNO A. A eurasian mineralogy: Aleksandr Fersman's conception of the natural world[J]. Isis, 2016, 107(3): 518-539.

[3] SEN S. Earth: the planet extraordinary[M]. New Delhi: Allied Publishers, 2007: 52.

[4] GUPTA H. Encyclopedia of solid earth geophysics[M]. Dordrecht: Springer, 2011: 145-163.

[5] FRIEDMAN G M. Classification of sediments and sedimentary rocks[C]//FAIRBRIDGE R W. Encyclopedia of sedimentology. Dordrecht: Springer, 1978: 202-216.

[6] TANNER V. Jakob Johannes Sederholm[M]. Helsinki: Tilgmann, 1937: 24.

[7] YOUNG D. Mind over magma: the story of igneous petrology[M]. Princeton: Princeton University Press, 2003: 365.

[8] 地质学发展简史[Z/OL]. [2023-07-05]. https://www.zgbk.com/ecph/words?SiteID=1&ID=49148&Type=bkzyb&SubID=78317.

[9] GUPTA B K S. Modern foraminifera[M]. New York: Kluwer Academic Publishers, 2002: 12-13.

William Grabau,1870—1946)出版了《地层学原理》(*Principles of Stratigraphy*,1913)、《中国地层学》(*Stratigraphy of China*,1924)等重要著述,发展了地层研究的理论和方法,引入了沉积旋回概念,提出了脉动学说,认为地层的发育、古地理的变迁与生物演化有一定的周期性①。魏格纳(Alfred Lothar Wegener,1880—1930)在《大陆的起源》(*The Origin of Continents*,1912)和《海陆的起源》(*The Origin of Continents and Oceans*,1915)中提出的大陆漂移思想②、乔利(John Joly,1857—1933)的"放射性热循环说"(1925)③、霍姆斯(Arthur Holmes,1890—1965)的"地幔对流说"(mantle convection)④、杜多瓦(Alexander du Toit,1878—1948)的"大陆船说"(1937)等关于地质构造的争论是影响20世纪地质学界的重要事件⑤。

第二次世界大战后,社会生产力的稳步发展促进了地质学的纵深发展。一方面,新学科分支应运而生;另一方面,以现代化新技术、多学科交叉融合和全球化视野为特征的现代地质学知识体系开始形成。20世纪60年代,赫斯(Harry Hammond Hess,1906—1959)提出了海底扩张说。从这个路径来探讨洋盆、海底地貌、海底断层等现象的有迪茨(Robert Sinclair Dietz,1914—1995)、瓦因(Frederick Vine 1939—1981)和马修斯(Drummond Matthews,1931—1997)等。1968年,勒皮雄(Xavier Le Pichon,1937—)、摩根(William Jason Morgan,1935—2023)和麦肯齐(Dan Peter McKenzie,1942—)联合发表《海底扩张和大陆漂移》("Sea-floor Spreading and Continental Drift")一文,标志着板块构造学说(plate tectonics)的诞生,这使得许多重要地质问题得以从新的角度得到解释,地质学自此进入一个新的发展阶段。比如,杜威(John Frederick Dewey,1937—)于1970年最先将大陆造山带与板块学说结合起来,迪金森(William R. Dickinson,1931—2015)于1974年阐述了板块构造与沉积作用,康迪(Kent Condie,1936—)于1976年结合板块学说对地壳演化进行了综合论述。20世纪80年代后,着眼于全球地质、全球地层、全球气候、全球构造的一系列国际研究合作蓬勃展开。进入21世纪后,地质研究大国都将地球科学的研究与社会发展的需求结合起来,在地质灾害预测、环境保护、全球气候与区域响应等方面展开了深度合作。当前,信息技术、航天技术、生物技术等新技术的应用进一步促进了地质学与其他学科的融合,有力地支撑了现代地质学的发展。

---

① KUSKY T M, CULLEN K E. Encyclopedia of earth and space science[M]. New York: Facts on File Inc, 2010: 346 - 347.
② GUPTA B K S. Modern foraminifera[M]. New York: Kluwer Academic Publishers, 2002: 153 - 155.
③ BHARATDWAJ K. Physical geography: introduction to earth[M]. New Delhi: Discovery Publishing House, 2006: 210 - 214.
④ YOUNG D. Mind over magma: the story of igneous petrology[M]. Princeton: Princeton University Press, 2003: 155.
⑤ BRUNO A. A eurasian mineralogy: Aleksandr Fersman's conception of the natural world[J]. Isis, 2016, 107(3): 630 - 631.

第一章 文学与地质学（Literature and Geology）

中国近现代地质学研究始于辛亥革命后。此前，虞和钦、鲁迅、顾琅等人曾分别编写过《中国地质构造》(1903)、《中国地质概略》(1903)和《中国矿产志》(1906)。1912年，国民政府成立地质科，翌年章鸿钊与翁文灏等人创办地质研究所。1922年，中国地质学会成立，地质专刊《中国地质学会志》也开始发行，地质学在古生物研究、岩石矿物研究、地质构造及变化研究等方面都取得了不少成就。比如，李四光从1926年起，出版了《中国地质学》《地球表面形象变迁之主因》等著作，创建了地质力学理论。翁文灏于1927年发现并确定东亚地质史上的重要造山运动，1930年他建立了中国第一个地震台。黄汲清在1945年出版《中国主要地质构造单位》，系统论及中国及邻近地区大地构造单元划分及演化特征，提出了多旋回构造造山运动说。新中国成立为地质学科各分支的快速发展带来了契机。为了保障社会生产对能源、矿产的需求，国内学者结合相关理论，研究中国石油、金属、稀土元素等矿产矿物的分布规律，在推进中国地质科学学科研究的同时，为国家和社会发展做出了巨大贡献。20世纪50年代，李四光、黄汲清、谢家荣等先后根据板块构造和沉积理论提出了符合中国地质特征的成油条件及油田分布规律。在60年代，侯德封提出了核子地球化学观，引导稀有金属、稀土元素矿床学等地球化学研究。在60—70年代，涂光炽提出沉积再造矿观点，对华南花岗岩、地球化学及成矿规律进行研究，出版了《层孔矿床地球化学》等重要著作。同时期，刘东升倡导并展开环境地质化学研究，在古气候与全球变化等方面取得了一定成果。1986年，杨遵仪、程裕淇、王鸿祯合作出版英文版《中国地质学》，向国际地质学界系统介绍中国地质构造发展史及研究成果。在该时期，中国地质学界积极参与国际合作，在青藏地质、前寒武纪地质、生物成矿等领域取得了重要突破，研究成果跻身国际前列。

在当前跨学科综合研究中，一个重要层面就是人文视角下的地质研究。2002年，克鲁岑(Paul J. Crutzen, 1933—2021)在《人类地理学》("Geology of Mankind", 2002)一文中正式提出"人类世"(anthropocene)这一概念，将之作为地质时代第四纪的延续和发展，认为自1784年瓦特改良蒸汽机以来的人类活动对地球的影响远大于自然变化的影响[①]。人类世学说主要探究人类对地质岩层的影响，"旨在发展一个世人皆认可的战略，使生态系统可以持续地抵御人类造成的压力，而这将是人类未来的重大任务"[②]。尽管该学说的提出和发展意味着反人类中心主义，强调以一种得体的方式处理人类、其他形式的生命和地球环境之间的

---

① 地球历史可大致分为天文时期(46亿~35亿年，地球上基本未保留这一时期的地质体)、隐生宙时期(35亿~6亿年，地质体在部分地区有保留，已有原始生命出现)和显生宙时期(6亿年至今，此期地质体遍布全球)三个时期。地球历史年表主要按地质体时间划分，最大间单位是宙(eon)，宙下为代(era)，代下是纪(period)，纪下为世(epoch)，世下分期(age)，期下为时(chron)。以代来分，地球历史最新地质时代为新生代，它从6400万年前恐龙的灭绝、中生代的结束为标志，一直持续至今。新生代又分为古近纪、新近纪、第四纪，纪下包含七个世，它们是古新世、始新世、渐新世、中新世、上新世、更新世和全新世。参见"人类世"来了[Z/OL]. [2019-06-17]. https://www.cgs.gov.cn/xwl/kxjs/201906/t20190617_484443.html.

② SHAW D. Anthropocene[Z/OL]. [2018-10-10]. https://criticalposthumanism.net/anthropocene/.

关系,但这并不意味着必须反对人文主义精神或在地质科学研究中摒弃人文主义视角。惠廷顿(Jerome Whittington)指出,"人类世"概念是一种"不公正或脆弱的文化工程",认为克鲁岑对人文主义的理解过于狭隘,强调除了应当坚守傅里叶(Joseph Fourier,1768—1830)在19世纪探讨地球温度时所表达的"地质人文主义"(geological humanism)外,还应当发扬该时期人文学者比如巴尔扎克(Honoré de Balzac,1799—1850)在其作品《驴皮记》(La Peau de Chagrin,1831)和《人间喜剧》(La Comedie Humaine)中理解、接受地质深层时间和进化论过程中所表现出来的开放性和多元性[1]。实际上,恰如卡斯特里(Noel Castree)指出的那样,应当将"人类世"作为机遇,推进地质研究和人文研究比如环境人文主义的结合[2]。在《人类时代的阅读:地质时代的文学史》(Anthropocene Reading: Literary History in Geologic Times,2017)的序言中,曼尼利(Tobias Menely)和泰勒(Jesse Oak Taylor)指出,自然科学与社会科学密不可分,人类世学说为文学研究检验和改进其方法提供了机遇,同时,地质历史的表征也是一种叙事,受到文学样式或文类的影响。更重要的是,文学叙事是一种媒介,不仅记述人类在地质研究方面的发现和学说,也记述和解读人类活动在地球上留下的印记。本雅明(Walter Benjamin,1892—1940)在《讲故事者》("The Storyteller",1936)中指出,地形的缓慢上升或沉淀就如文学样式的变迁。本雅明的比喻在泰勒看来与时间尺度无关,相反,它与叙事在形式组织层面的作用相关,即地质形貌的变化与叙事样式的变化相似,就如岩层与叙事在时间组织方面的相似性一样——"岩层是一种中介,反映了人类如何看待自我。故事讲述者从矿物中看到了人类现实:'矿物是石化的、没有生命的自然世界的哲学——这种预言同样也适用他所生存的历史世界[3]。'"因此,地质学与文学密不可分。一方面,文学叙事为地质历史特别是人类世的地质历史的表征提供媒介方法。另一方面,地质时期及地质历史也为理解文学叙事样式、叙事模式、人类经验组织方式的变迁提供方法和语境。因此,我们既可以把人类世当作叙事来理解,也能从地质史的维度来解读文学史。比如,1610年莎士比亚(William Shakespeare,1564—1616)的《暴风雨》(The Tempest)发表的时间,不仅标志着"超经典剧本"(hypercanonical play)文类的出现,也标志着哥伦布交换(Columbian exchange)带来的全球地质环境变化的巅峰。另外,库切(J. M. Coetzee,1940—)的小说《等待野蛮人》(Waiting for the Barbarians,1980)给人造成"某种阅读的'逼迫'(duress)感,此即不同时间尺度上人类和自然力量之间冲突的阐释过程……而'逼迫'的

---

[1] WHITTINGTON J. Geological humanism [Z/OL]. [2020-09-22]. https://culanth.org/fieldsights/geological-humanism.

[2] CASTREE N. The anthropocene and the environmental humanities: extending the conversation [J]. Environmental humanities, 2014, 5(1): 233-260.

[3] MENELY T, TAYLOR J O. Anthropocene reading: literary history in geological times [M]. University Park: The Pennsylvania State University Press, 2017: 9-36.

第一章 文学与地质学（Literature and Geology）

本源指地层经受的持久的压力"①。这两个文学案例表明,人类时代的地质历史可以置于文学语境中来解读,阅读文学作品就如挖掘和表征人类在地质层留下的足迹。

诺威克(Stephen A. Norwick)在《地质学》("Geology")一文中声称,文学与地质科学的关系至少可追溯至17世纪欧洲启蒙运动期间现代科学的诞生之际②。然而,文学与地质学的关系源远流长。在宗教神话或早期文学作品中,往往有一些关于地球起源、地貌特征、地质事件的描述,它们是早期人类在认识地质相关方面知识的尝试。比如,《圣经》记载的大洪水,它在一定程度上印证了西方关于地貌形成的灾变说。在荷马(Homer)的《伊利亚特》(*Iliad*, 1598)中,有一些古希腊地貌特征的描述,它与斯特雷波(Strabo, 63/64 BC—43 AD)地理著作中的描述惊人的一致,因而被学界用来推断荷马时代古希腊海岸的地质特征③。在《诗经·小雅》《山海经》《神仙传》等早期文学作品中,也有一些关于海陆变迁、地貌特征、矿物矿产的描述,这说明古代人类在生产生活中借用文学叙事来记述他们对地质现象的认识。这些文学作品建构的地质学知识,不是为所描述的事件提供场景,就是简单呈现地质现象,就事论事,未能深入地解读这些地质现象在地质历史中的地位或作用。比如,英国文艺复兴时期的名剧《浮士德博士》(*Doctor Faustus*, 1592)在最后部分描述了一场风暴,在主人公浮士德的几个好友看来,该风暴充其量只是说明浮士德因为出卖灵魂而接受命运审判时的恐怖场景或氛围。尽管当下人类世这一地质学视角下的解读,不仅揭示了英国殖民者在掠夺新大陆物质资源的过程中如何影响了地质气候,而且抨击了"早期帝国主义和原始科学意识形态",但无论对于该剧作者马洛(Christopher Marlowe, 1564—1593)来说,还是对于文艺复兴时期的英国受众而言,这种解读未免显得过于超前了④。他们既不理解这种地质影响的相关理论知识,也没有接受过必要的道德训诫,因而根本无法在民族主义高涨的背景下来抨击英国早期在海外的殖民扩张。在18世纪末到19世纪30年代,彭斯(Robert Burns, 1759—1796)、布莱克(William Blake, 1757—1827)、华兹华斯(William Wordsworth, 1770—1850)、雪莱(Percy Bysshe Shelley, 1792—1822)、拜伦(George Gordon Byron, 1788—1824)、梭罗(Henry David Thoreau, 1817—1862)和爱默生(Ralph Waldo Emerson, 1803—1882)等英美浪漫主义作家也都描述过地质地貌,但他们在描述地质现象时既无地质学理论知识的支撑,也无意建构或传播地质学相关知识。在描写地质地貌时,这些作家特别关注岩石矿物,因为

---

① LARSEN T B. A Review of anthropocene reading: literary history in geological times, edited by Tobias Menley and Jesse Oak Taylor[J]. Universitas: journal of research, scholarship, and creative activity, 2018, 13(1): 1-8.

② STEPHEN A N. Geology[C]//CLARKE B, ROSSINI M. The Routledge companion to literature and science. London: Routledge, 2011: 135.

③ THOMAS N. Geology corresponds with Homer's of ancient Tory[Z/OL]. [2003-03-03]. https://www1.udel.edu/PR/UDaily/2003/troy030303.html.

④ ROSE M. "Anthropocentric signatures": writing natures in Doctor Faustus[J]. Early modern culture, 2018, 13: 188-198.

浪漫主义文学与地质学都起源于"以岩石作为首要审美客体的景观美学",毕竟"在越来越多地用地质学视角来审视客观环境的情况下,该审美话语已在人们意识中占据了一席之地"①。以岩石矿物为核心的景观美学思想深入人心,其根本原因在于18世纪工业革命的发展扩大了对矿物的需求。受此驱动地质学快速发展,研究岩石矿物的分布、开发和利用,借此提高生产力。在此背景下,岩石矿物成为英美浪漫主义文学的一个重要元素。

文学与地质学的相互影响在英国维多利亚时期(1837—1901年)达到了空前的高度。随着恐龙、翼龙等史前生物化石的大量发现并在英国各地博物馆的展出,地质学引起了人们的广泛关注,成为社会各界人士的业余爱好或职业追求。尽管地质科学在19世纪日趋理性和客观,它却与虚构性文学叙事紧密地结合在一起:一方面,许多作家积极地参与地质相关话题的讨论,并通过创作来介绍、传播地质学理论发展方面的成果及其社会影响;另一方面,一些地质学家也借用文学体裁来表征其地质研究成果,甚至还有些地质学家直接从事以地质研究为主题的文学创作。乔治·艾略特(George Eliot,1819—1880)、拉希金(John Ruskin,1819—1900)、丁尼生(Alfred Tennyson,1809—1892)、金斯利(Charles Kingsley,1819—1875)、柯南·道尔(Arthur Conan Doyle,1859—1930)、狄更斯(Charles Dickens,1812—1870)和哈代(Thomas Hardy,1840—1928)等是维多利亚时期的重要作家,他们的成长过程都见证了该时期地质研究方面的重大发现及发展成果,特别是居维叶的灾变论、莱尔的均变论和达尔文的进化论②。在创作过程中,他们通过类似于解读地层历史一样的方法,来解读人类历史,将人类时间变成地质深层时间。在叙事结构和情节配置上,这个时期的历史小说、侦探小说、现实主义小说甚至科幻小说都或多或少地受到化石考古的影响,通过对类似化石一样的遗留物来还原或建构现实,借此表达人类的基本关切。对文学创作在主题、内容和技巧上影响最深远的地质学思想当属达尔文的进化论了。比如,在《弗洛斯河上的磨坊》(*The Mill on the Floss*,1860)、《亚当比德》(*Adam Bede*,1859)等作品中,艾略特模仿了达尔文提出进化论时所使用的叙事技巧③。在《达尔文的情节:达尔文、艾略特和19世纪小说中的进化论叙事》(*Darwin's Plot:Evolutionary Narrative in Darwin,George Eliot and Nineteenth-Century Fiction*,1983)中,比尔(Gillian Beer,1935—)系统分析了《物种起源》对19世纪小说的影响。此外,她还分析了它如何在语言和叙事风格上受到了浪漫主义文学传统的影响④。因此,文学与以地质学为代表的科学在维多利亚时期并未真正分离开来:不仅

---

① HERINGMAN N. Romantic rocks, aesthetic geology[M]. New York: Cornell University Press, 2004: xv.

② O'CONNOR R. Geology and paleontology[C]//DENISOFF D, SCHAFFER T. The Routledge companion to Victorian literature. Abingdon: Routledge, 2020: 401 – 413.

③ O'CONNOR R. The earth on show: fossils and the poetics of popular science[M]. Chicago: The University of Chicago Press, 2007: 436, 447.

④ JONES G. Book reviews: Darwin's plot: evolutionary narrative in Darwin, George Eliot and nineteenth-century fiction[J]. Isis, 1985, 76(1): 93 – 94.

第一章 文学与地质学(Literature and Geology)

诗歌、小说、散文等不同体裁的文学作品可以像地质学一样来建构并传递自然和社会真理,而且地质学也可以像文学作品一样来建构和传递道德价值和美学思想。除了达尔文、莱尔、巴克莱(William Buckland, 1784—1856)、金斯利、休厄尔(William Whewell, 1794—1866)等其他地质学家在其地质研究中也借用了文学叙事来表征其理论立场①。

在表征地质科学时,维多利亚时期的文人学者也反思了科学进步给人类信仰造成的冲击。史前生物化石的发现颠覆了《圣经》中关于地球只有6000多年历史的假说。另外,物种的灭绝、生命的演变进化也颠覆了上帝创作万物的假说。因此,19世纪的地质的发现动摇了当时人们对上帝的信仰。马修·阿诺德(Matthew Arnold, 1822—1888)、丁尼生、艾略特、哈代甚至柯南·道尔等作家都参与了当时科学与宗教这两种文化之间关系的讨论,他们的作品在介绍地质发现以及理论建设成果的同时,也都在一定程度上分析讨论了当时的信仰危机。虽然阿诺德没有直接探讨地质学与19世纪的信仰危机的关系,他的传世诗作《多佛海滩》("Dover Beach", 1867)中的岩石、海床沉降、气候变迁、信仰危机等都在一定程度上反映了当时地质科学的研究发现及其对人类信仰的影响②。20世纪60年代以来逐渐兴起的新维多利亚小说(Neo-Victorian fiction),比如《法国中尉的女人》(*The French Lieutenant's Woman*, 1969)、《占有》(*Possession*, 1990)、《天使与昆虫》(*Angels and Insects*, 1992)、《猎骨人》(*The Bonehunters*, 2006)、《达尔文的射手》(*Mr. Darwin's Shooter*, 1998)、《奇妙的生物》(*Remarkable Creatures*, 2009)、《永远》(*Everafter*, 2018)等作品延续了这类作品的主题,以20世纪现代人的视角,重新审视维多利亚时期地质发现带来的信仰危机。格兰德宁(John Glendening)的专著《新维多利亚小说中的科学与宗教:鱼龙化石之眼》(*Science and Religion in Neo-Victorian Novels: Eye of the Ichthyosaur*, 2013)也对上述作品进行了深入分析,通过讨论科学技术快速发展背景下维多利亚时代人们的信仰问题,反思当下社会人们所面临的同样问题,试图协调自然科学与人文科学这两种文化之间的关系,为人类更好地理解自我并克服社会发展过程存在的问题提供一些参考③。

文学作品如化石一样,记述了人类世背景下地球的变迁历史。从地质学视角来跨学科地解读文学作品,特别是与地质历史相关的文学作品,不仅能够反映人类如何认识地球构造及其演变,揭示地球生命的起源及进化史,而且能够揭示人类活动如何影响了地质地貌,进而为如何协调人类生产发展与地质环境之间的关系提供一些建议。诺威克的《地质学》一文

---

① BUCKLAND A. Novel science: fiction and the invention of nineteenth-century geology[M]. Chicago: The University of Chicago Press, 2013: 26.
② KLAVER J M I. Charles Lyell's churches and the erosion of faith in Matthew Arnold's "Dover Beach"[J]. Linguae & Rivista di lingue e culture moderne, 2014, 13(1): 21-34.
③ GLENDENING J. Science and religion in neo-Victorian novels: eye of the ichthyosaur[M]. New York: Routledge, 2013: 228.

揭示了文学与地质学之间的关系,但未就如何展开深入讨论提供一些方法论的建议。地质学研究中的人类世转向,特别是 2015 年国际人类世工作小组(International Anthropocene Working Group, IAWG)将 1945 年美国三位一体核试验(Trinity Test)视作人类世新纪元的标志以来,学界开始构建人类世文学批评理论和方法,各种文献大量涌现出来,比如《人类世小说》(Anthropocene Fictions, 2015)、《边缘生态批评:作为阈值概念的人类世》(Ecocriticism on the Edge: The Anthropocene as a Threshold Concept, 2015)、《人类世的诞生》(The Birth of Anthropocene, 2016)、《人类世女性主义》(Anthropocene Feminism, 2016)、《人类世阅读:地质时代的文学史》(Anthropocene Reading: Literary History in Geologic Times, 2017)、《人类世诗学》(Anthropocene Poetics, 2019)、《现代主义人类世美学:乔伊斯、朱娜·巴恩斯和伍尔夫小说中的生态创新》(Modernist Anthropocene Aesthetics: Ecological Innovation in Novels of James Joyce, Djuna Barnes and Virginia Woolf, 2019)、《文学与人类世》(Literature and the Anthropocene, 2020)、《剑桥文学与人类世指南》(The Cambridge Companion to Literature and the Anthropocene, 2021)、《叙述非人类空间:超越人类世的形式、故事和经验》(Narrating Nonhuman Spaces: Form, Story, and Experience Beyond Anthropocene, 2022)。这些研究文献为我们如何从人类世视角来解读文学与地质学的关系提供了理论框架和批评方法。

文献传真

阅读《地质学》("Geology"),思考文末问答题。本文节选自《劳特利奇指南:文学与科学》①。

Geology

Stephen A. Norwick

[…]

We can see a pervasive interplay between geological, linguistic, and literary forms. Whereas the general language strongly influenced a great geological innovator such as Hutton to break through the dominant theories of his day, many writers also believed that different landscapes and climates produced different personality types, that the minerals, rocks, soils, and landscapes, without the mediation of scientific theories, inspired the genius of some authors. For example, the limestone valleys of central

---

① NORWICK S A. Geology[C]//CLARKE B, ROSSINI M. The Routledge companion to literature and science. London: Routledge, 2011: 135 – 144.

第一章　文学与地质学（Literature and Geology）

England weather into low, smooth, gently undulating plains that inspired the flower-filled, sweet, rural poetry of England such as poems by William Cowper. In the same way, the open lowlands of Scotland inspired James Thomson. In the twentieth century, W. H. Auden included numerous geological references in his poetry. Raised on the limestone of Yorkshire, he associated the dissolution and smoothing of this rock with the changes that happen to memories. Auden's "In Praise of Limestone" is partly about the environmental determinism by which landscapes developed over granite, clay, gravel, or limestone produced different types of plants, animals, and people.

The more varied rock types that make the rugged coast of Ayrshire, Scotland, produced high hills from which most streams flow rapidly into low, coastal plains. These streams became a major part of the poetry of Robert Burns, in which the streams are often symbols for the feelings of the poet or his characters.[①] Burns was a major influence on John Muir, who was both a geologist and a fine writer, who wrote that the structural weaknesses in the Sierra Nevada rocks "predestined" the paths of the glaciers, leaving "Nature's poems carved on tablets of stone".[②] Thus, the Scottish landforms inspired the poet who inspired the scientist who interpreted a completely different landscape, the Sierra Nevada of California.

As we have already noted, minerals, rocks, soils, and landscapes became common subjects of Romantic authors and influenced literature in many ways. Throughout the nineteenth century, science's influence on popular language grew stronger. Though dead by the Romantic period, Hutton was responsible for the creation of a new holistic trope of nature, the image of the self-modulating earth, often referred to as "the globe" or "the planet." This image spread slowly through the English-speaking world during the Romantic period, and until the late 1960s when NASA photographs of the Earth from space or from the surface of the moon popularized both visual and verbal images of planetary totality. Hutton's most important popularizer was another Scotsman, Sir Charles Lyell, whose *Principles of Geology* was the most-read geology textbook of his century. Calling this concept "uniformitarianism," Lyell emphasized Hutton's theory

---

① ARCHIBALD G. Types of scenery and their influence on literature: the Romanes lecture 1898 [M]. New York: Kennikat Press, 1898: 25.

② JOHN M. The mountains of California [M]. New York: The Century Co., 1898: 48.

that major changes in the earth are usually due to ordinary processes like weathering and erosion over very long periods of time. Many important literary figures read Lyell's Principles. Tennyson owned a copy and incorporated Hutton's "deep abyss of time" and rock cycle into his poetry: "The moanings of the homeless sea, / The sound of streams that swift or slow / Draw down Aeonian hills, and sow / The dust of continents to be". ①

Some geological concepts have accompanied major intellectual controversies in Europe. The notion that nature or society is improving, or degenerating, or static, can sometimes have apowerful influence over public feelings toward the Earth. Although they had a generally positive attitude toward nature, the ancient Greeks believed that the Earth was degrading. During the Enlightenment, the increasing knowledge of paleontology showed that life had changed markedly over geologic time. The rock record seemed to show dynamic but not directional changes, and this indeterminate status confused many authors, including Sir Charles Lyell, who passed this confusion on to Emerson and Thoreau, William Cullen Bryant, Victor Hugo, and many other nineteenth-century authors who wanted to find progress in nature but who only saw undirected change.

However, many writers used the fossil record to support their contention that nature was improving. In addition, the Huttonian notion that continents and mountains are continuing to rise in our day accorded with positive Romantic feelings that God was still at work in nature, and promoted mountains in particular. Byron left England for more adventurous mountainous terrain: "England! thy beauties are tame and domestic, / To one who has rov'd on the mountains afar: / Oh! for the crags that are wild and majestic, / The steep, frowning glories of dark Loch na Garr". ② At the same time, geological influences were often less powerful than other ideas. For example, William Wordsworth was well read in earth science but mildly anti-intellectual and opposed to "mechanic laws." His love of mountains was more likely a nostalgia for the low

---

① ALFRED T. In memoriam[Z/OL]. [2021-10-11]. https://en.wikisource.org/wiki/In_Memoriam_(Tennyson). 另参见 SUSAN G. Early Victorian science writers and Tennyson's "In Memoriam": a study in cultural exchange: part II[J]. Victorian studies, 1975, 18(4): 444.

② George G B. Lachin y gair[Z/OL]. [2023-07-10]. https://internetpoem.com/george-gordon-lord-byron/lachin-y-gair-poem/.

第一章 文学与地质学(Literature and Geology)

mountains of the English Lake District where he was born, as well as the high mountains of Switzerland that he visited. Wordsworth himself believed that the high places of the Earth corresponded to high moral character and so climbing mountains could literally elevate a person's character as well as their body.[①] Similarly, Fenimore Cooper's novel The Crater reflects Lyell's description of the formation and destruction of a volcanic island. The rise and fall of a utopian colony parallels the history of the volcanic island on which they are living.

Scientific practices strongly influenced the development of new popular literary forms. During the nineteenth century, the realistic and naturalistic novel, and especially the detective story, became popular because they enacted fictive scenes and behaviors that paralleled the scientific interests of the age. Most novels are like science in that they have realistic physical and social settings and a causal narrative. Edgar Allen Poe's pioneering detective, C. Auguste Dupin, behaved scientifically in the way he observed ordinary things in extremely fine detail and in his careful deductive logic. Like most scientists, Dupin loved puzzles, was deeply rationalistic, and strongly against magic and superstition.

However, detective literature owes more to field sciences like geology than to the laboratory sciences of chemistry and physics. The field sciences are usually actualistic, that is, they see their own patterns in the natural world without reference to the laboratory sciences' fundamental particles and forces. For example, Arthur Conan Doyle's Sherlock Holmes was strikingly actualistic.

As with geologists, he could not usually solve his cases by using the first principles of physics, chemistry, or mathematics. Instead, for instance, like the geologists who looked at sand deposits in rivers, beaches, lakes, and deltas and then inferred the origins of different sandstones, Holmes smoked and closely observed the butts and ash from all the cigars available in Western Europe, and then used this knowledge to catch criminals who left cigar ash at crime.

In the twentieth century, literary criticism began to use geological tropes to describe its ownoperations. For example, if there are several early versions of a famous text,

---

① ARCHIBALD G. Types of scenery and their influence on literature: the Romanes lecture 1898 [M]. New York: Kennikat Press, 1898: 55.

scholars can write a history of the choices that the author made to create the book, for example, Thoreau's *Walden*. Sometimes it is known that an earlier version has been lost. For example, Jane Austen's *Sense and Sensibility* started as an epistolary novel that she read aloud to her siblings. The original has never been found, so scholars have looked for "fossils" in "deposits" of earlier traces of the epistolary version in the present text. Such an analysis is called a "geologic study". ①Similarly, the deep study of a text has been called "geologic" by critics. Levine likened another critic's "shallow" understanding of Conrad's Marlow in *Heart of Darkness* as "lateral and surface topography—a map perhaps," as opposed to "geology" that is "deep". ②

The practice of science changed society in ways reflected in literature. The sciences of the earth, sea, and sky developed rapidly throughout the late nineteenth and early twentieth centuries and this had practical impacts on European cultures and European colonies around the world. Scientific mineral exploration was able to discover vast deposits of metals and ores of industrial minerals that had been overlooked by prospectors who were not aided by theory. Oil exploration would have been impossible without Hutton's insights into the age of the earth and the interpretation of earth materials. Geological engineering made possible giant hydroelectric dams. At the beginning of the twentieth century, these activities generated imaginative literature in which heroic geologists and engineers created vast works, making the new industrial European world, such as the boys' stories *Tom Swift and His Big Tunnel*, *Tom Swift and His Great Oil Gusher*, *The Young Engineers in Nevada—or, Seeking Fortune on the Turn of a Pick*, *The Young Engineers in Mexico—or Fighting the Mine Swindlers*, and the romantic novel *Soldiers of Fortune*, by Richard Harding Davis. ③

Academic studies of scientific influences on literary figures often involve personal connections. While there is a serious academic disagreement over whether William Blake had much direct exposure to geology or was just responding to popular ideas, Thomas Hardy claimed to have read the famous textbook by Sir Charles Lyell. However, he did

---

① FREDERICK P L. The geology of sense and sensibility[J]. Yearbook of English studies, 1979, 9: 246-255.
② GEORGE L. The novel as scientific discourse: the example of Conrad[J]. Novel: a forum on fiction, 1998, 21: 220-227.
③ CECELIA T. Shifting gears: technology, literature, culture in modernist America[M]. Chapel Hill: University of North Carolina Press, 1987: 117-134, 187.

第一章 文学与地质学(Literature and Geology)

not have a copy in his library, and it has been shown that Hardy owned and closely paraphrased a much more common and popular book, *The Wonders of Geology* (1848) by Gideon Algernon Mantell. [1] Henry Adams must have had more geologists for friends than any other literary figure in European or American letters. He knew Sir Charles Lyell well. Clarence King, first director of the U. S. Geological Survey, was a close friend, and Adams knew many other geologists from traveling as a journalist with a geological party surveying the length of the 40th parallel. However, the influence of geology on Adams was not positive. In his famous autobiography (1918) he recorded his disappointment: he had expected science to tell him some great truths, but it seemed very undecided.

In the middle of the twentieth century, the earth sciences were revolutionized by the idea that the continents are floating around on the surface of the earth. Although this idea has altered almost every form of geology, it has not influenced literature, unless one includes the five rather journalistic but Pulitzer Prize-winning books by John McPhee, which are based on interviews during long field trips with geologists: *Basin and Range* (1981), *In Suspect Terrain* (1983), *Rising From the Plains* (1986), *Assembling California* (1993), and *Crossing the Craton* (2000).

The clearest of all cases of the influence of earth science on literature occurs when the author practices both the science and the art. Important writers who were practicing geologists include Novalis, Goethe, and John Muir. Novalis, the founder of German Romanticism, was manager of several salt mines. He had studied at the Mining Academy of Freiberg with the great Neptunian, Abraham Gottlob Werner. Novalis took as one of his poetic tasks to harmonize science and poetry so as to rejuvenate the relationship of humans to nature. Neptunism was a static, historic view that believed that the main processes of earth formation had been caused by ancient catastrophes. However, Novalis did not agree with his teacher; rather, he agreed with James Hutton, the Plutonist, uniformitarian, and "founder of modern geology," that the earth was still being formed slowly by everyday processes. Novalis's sense of the otherness of the inorganic earth came from geology and contributed to the Romantic conception of the

---

[1] PATRICIA I. Hardy and the wonders of geology[J]. Review of English studies, 1980, 31: 60-61.

sublime.

Goethe was a skilled practicing mineralogist. The very common mineral and pigment Goethite, FeO (OH), is named for him. A Neptunist and catastrophist, Goethe was opposed to Plutonism. He believed that God made granite, as in "Über den Granit" (1784). In Faust, the Devil advocated Plutonism (of course), the school that believed that granite began as flaming liquid rock, although he knew that the theory was based on a vast hallucination. For his part, Muir left books full of marginalia, as well as his University of Wisconsin transcripts that show he studied glaciology with Ezra Carr, who in turn had studied with the great glaciologist Louis Agassiz at Harvard. Muir was the first to realize that glaciers carved Yosemite Valley. Then he discovered active glaciers in the Sierra Nevada, and finally he filled his popular books with rich figurative language about the Ice Age.

In contemporary literature, Sarah Andrews is a geologist who also writes murder mysteries, starring Em Hansen, forensic geologist. Intended to introduce the general public to geology and geologists, each of her novels takes up a different application of geology: soil pollution, paleontology, petroleum engineering, mineral deposits, seismic safety, etc. Geologist, historian, and poet Susan Cummins Miller is the author of four geological *Frankie McFarlane* mysteries. Linda Jacobs is a petroleum geologist who has written a series of steamy as well as geological, historical, and award-winning adventure stories set in the region of Yellowstone and Grand Teton National Parks.

We have seen that Indo-European languages motivated the development of earth science that created the present industrial world. We can also see that rocks, soils, and landscape without theoretical mediation have inspired many popular tropes in modern English. We have seen that the earth sciences were an important part of the Romantic project to give value to nature, and that science, particularly actualistic earth science, inspired the popularity of the prose novel and short story, especially detectivefiction. Perhaps surprisingly, we can see that some of the most powerful ideas in geology—the rock cycle, uniformitarianism, continental drift, and "The Great Abyss of Time"—have had little influence on popular culture or high literature since the Romantic period, but the macrocosm/microcosm analogy has been revived as modern Gaia science.

思考题

1. How did the general language related to the Fall of Nature influence the science of landscape?
2. What are Neptunism and Plutonism respectively? How are they different from each other as far as the formation of rock is concerned?
3. How did Romantic literature and geology interact with each other?
4. What influences did James Hutton have upon the development of literature and geology?
5. How was the new literary form of detective fiction influenced by the science of earth?

第二节 《奇妙的生物》与地质科学

作品导读

1. 作者简介

《奇妙的生物》是旅英美裔作家崔西·谢瓦利埃(Tracy Chevalier, 1962—)的代表作。她1962年出生在美国华盛顿,父亲是《华盛顿邮报》(The Washington Post)的摄影师。1984年从奥伯林学院(Oberlin College)毕业后,她就旅居英国伦敦,从事出版编辑工作。1993年,她到东英格兰大学攻读创意写作方向的硕士学位,师从小说家布拉德布里(Malcolm Bradbury, 1932—2000)、特雷曼(Rose Tremain, 1943—)等人。自1997年处女作《纯洁的蓝色》(The Virgin Blue, 1997)问世以来,谢瓦利埃迄今共发表10部长篇小说,1部中篇小说,2部编著,6部文集。《戴珍珠耳环的少女》(Girl with a Pearl Earring, 1999)是其成名作,它以荷兰画家维米尔(Johannes Vermeer, 1632—1675)的同名画作为基础,想象其生平、该画的创作过程以及他与该画作女模特格里特(Griet)之间的情感故事。通过强调视觉层面的细节、人物在情感层面的自制力,该小说与其说揭示了画家与女模特之间的私情,不如说凸显了17世纪荷兰社会下层女性的无助与卑微。格里特虽有一定的艺术天赋,但她只能成为维米尔的助手。她无法掌控自己的命运,只能任由父母甚至雇主的摆布和剥削。另外,虽然维米尔在世时已享有一定声誉,但其创作过程十分缓慢,作品数量有限,加上常使用昂贵的颜料,因而经济上比较拮据,去世时欠下大笔债务。由于贫穷,维米尔必须依靠权贵的资助,在经济甚至在肉体上遭受其剥削。通过历史重构,《戴珍珠耳环的少女》揭示了17世纪欧洲社会广泛存在的阶级剥削和性别歧视。《奇妙的生物》延续了该主题，但同时将笔触伸至女性的职业、阶级与地质科学之间的关系等层面。

2. 作品介绍

《奇妙的生物》主要讲述玛丽(Mary Anning，1799—1847)及好友伊丽莎白(Elizabeth Philpot，1780—1857)这两位女性的故事，她们在地质考古及古生物研究方面取得一些重大发现，推动了英国19世纪上半叶地质学的快速发展。玛丽父亲生前为木匠，其手艺不甚精湛，但却漫天要价，吓跑了简·奥斯汀等顾客，因而业务凋零，只得靠捡取化石，卖给涌入莱姆(Lyme Regis)海滩的游客，借此补贴家用。玛丽11岁时，父亲不幸酒后摔伤，不久便辞世，留下了大笔债务。为了帮母亲养家糊口，同时偿还家庭债务，以免被送进济贫院，玛丽将寻找化石作为其职业，成天在海滩翻找各类化石。常在莱姆海滩找化石的还有伊丽莎白，由于父母去世时留下的钱财只能为4个女儿中的一个提供必要的嫁妆，她和另外两姐妹只能终身不嫁。为了节省开支，她们在身为律师的哥哥约翰(John)的安排下，由伦敦迁居莱姆海滩。伊丽莎白及其姐妹每年有150多英镑的生活费，无须为了生计而担忧①。为消磨时光，她迷恋各种鱼类的化石，姐姐露易丝(Louise)喜欢植物，妹妹玛格丽特(Margaret)喜欢社交。

在找寻化石的过程中，玛丽和伊丽莎白跨越阶级鸿沟，结成忘年交。玛丽对化石有天然的洞察力，熟知菊石、海胆、粪化石、脊髓化石等多种类型化石的结构特征，能在海滩上迅速发现别人无法辨识出来的化石。这种技能让伊丽莎白叹为观止，甚至有点嫉妒她。伊丽莎白有丰富的理论知识，阅读居维叶的解剖学、莱尔的地质学等理论著述，每当找到一个化石后，都将根据林奈分类法对之进行命名，并记载找到化石的时间、地点及其所在的地层等信息。在伊丽莎白的影响下，玛丽参加了周末教会的学习班，在学会读写之后，阅读了相关地质学理论著述，能够像伊丽莎白一样对化石进行分类、命名，并用标签记载每个化石的出处、特征信息等。在理论知识的加持下，玛丽在寻找化石方面变得更加专业、高效。她发现了人类历史上第一具完整的鱼龙化石、第一具完整的蛇颈龙化石。1811年第一具鱼龙化石被发现时，其头部由于山体滑坡，少部分裸露在外。伊丽莎白帮助玛丽雇佣几名石匠，并为其垫付了工资，开挖了该具化石的头部，而身体其余部分尚在山体内，直到一年后才被开挖出来。当地贵族亨利(Henry Hoste Henley，1766—1833)在从玛丽的母亲莫莉(Molly)手上买走该鱼龙完整的化石后不久，便将之转卖给伦敦私人藏家巴洛克(William Bullock，1773—1849)，而巴洛克在展出该鱼龙化石时却将其发现者标注为亨利。在参观巴洛克博物馆时，

---

① 伊丽莎白于1805年迁入莱姆地区，当时150多英镑的生活费相当于2022年的14 391.47多英镑。1805年，英国一般体力劳动者收入大约38英镑/年、学校教师大约43英镑/年、警察51英镑/年、政府低级职员52英镑/年、棉纱纺织工65英镑/年、政府高级职员151英镑/年、律师340英镑/年。伊丽莎白三姐妹，平均每人约50英镑/年，虽谈不上生活何等的富裕，但在莱姆小镇应当能够生活得相当舒适了。关于1805年英镑的价值，参见 https://www.in2013dollars.com/uk/inflation/1805? amount=150；关于1805年英国各行各业平均年收入，参见 http://www.nws-sa.com/rr/Inequality/Lindert.pdf。

第一章　文学与地质学(Literature and Geology)

伊丽莎白发现了亨利欺世盗名的丑陋行径，回到莱姆后她当面质问亨利。亨利非但不道歉，反而恶意中伤伊丽莎白及玛丽，认为女性只是男性的附属品，必须由男性来代表女性发声。

虽然玛丽的成就未能获得学界认可，但其发现鱼龙化石的消息不胫而走，许多男性科学家及化石爱好者慕名而来，希望借助她的帮助找到各自的鱼龙化石。随着玛丽的成熟，她开始对那些前来找她帮助的男性绅士感兴趣，希望能够攀附上某位有钱的贵族，摆脱自己及家人贫困的处境。1817年，她迷恋上了前来找她帮忙的布茨(Thomas James Birch, 1768—1829)中尉，并将所有找到的化石都送给了他，其中包括一具完整的鱼龙化石。在被布茨抛弃后，玛丽失去了寻找化石的兴趣，加上布茨在莱姆期间她既未收取任何服务费，也没带回家任何化石，玛丽一家随即陷入经济困境。尽管玛丽因爱情冲昏了头脑，不听伊丽莎白的告诫——"跨阶级的婚姻在简·奥斯汀的小说中不能，在现实中更不可能了"——并与其决裂，但伊丽莎白出于同情和心底对友谊的珍惜，帮忙邮寄了玛丽母亲向布茨索要金钱回报的信件。在伦敦大英博物馆参观化石时，伊丽莎白遇见了布茨，指责他如何薄情，告诉他玛丽一家如何深陷困境，劝诫其归还玛丽的化石并做出补偿。布茨对于玛丽的情感也许真实，但由于自己经济地位窘迫，无奈只能和一名贵族寡妇结婚。为了补偿玛丽，他于1820年5月公开拍卖了玛丽给他的化石，连同他自己收藏的化石，将筹集到的400英镑(相当于2022年的34000英镑)全部赠给玛丽。有了这笔钱，玛丽不仅清偿了家里全部债务，而且还用余款购置了一些家具和衣物。由于是公开拍卖，玛丽名声倍增，过去厌恶化石、认为化石带来厄运的莱姆居民也一改过去鄙视玛丽一家的眼光。布茨拍卖带来的变化，让玛丽感激涕零，坚信他是真爱，尽管无法与其结婚，但她以身相许，并在随后将找到的化石都通过他进行买卖。

1823年冬天，玛丽找到了世界上第一具完整的蛇颈龙化石，激起了学界更广泛的兴趣和讨论，各地博物馆都竞相购买该化石。牛津大学的地质学家巴克莱前来恳求伊丽莎白，希望她能说服玛丽将它卖给伦敦地质协会，以方便其展开相关教学和研究活动。由于玛丽早已和她断交，伊丽莎白只能从报纸或他人口中了解玛丽的最新动态。当巴克莱告诉她玛丽新近的发现后，她趁玛丽一家去教堂祷告之际，潜入玛丽工作室，不仅被蛇颈龙化石的精美所震撼，为她的发现感到骄傲，而且被她阅读摘录地质研究文献时严谨和认真的态度所打动。不久后，玛丽母亲再次前来求助，告诉伊丽莎白说玛丽曾写信给法国地质学家居维叶，信中附上了蛇颈龙的解剖图，希望他能够购买该具化石。由于居维叶的地质理论尚不完善，无法解释蛇颈龙的解剖结构，因而回信指责玛丽，斥责她将两个不同物种的化石拼凑在一起，虚构了一个新的物种。由于居维叶是当时地质学界的权威，一旦他斥责玛丽的话流传出去，地质学界将再也不相信玛丽，她寻找到的化石将再无买家，这意味着她全家将再次陷入经济上的困境。为了补救她们之间的友谊，同时捍卫玛丽在地质学界的名声，伊丽莎白在寒冷的夜晚只身乘船前往伦敦地质协会。到达伦敦后，她不听哥哥的劝阻，乘其不备，带着侄儿小约翰(Johnny)，前往伦敦地质协会。由于女性不准进入地质协会，伊丽莎白在侄儿的帮助下，迫使门卫转告准备召开大会并朗读有关蛇颈龙化石论文的巴克莱和柯尼贝尔(William Conybeare，1787—1857)。见到伊丽莎白后，柯尼贝尔十分不悦，毕竟从未有女性跨过地质协会的大门。当她恳请巴克莱在大会上为玛丽发声时，尽管此前他曾多次得到过玛丽的帮助，不仅仅是寻找化石，而且在解剖学理论和实践上也深受其益，但巴克莱拒绝了。直到小约翰跑上地质协会楼梯，威胁说如果不替玛丽发声，他将告诉楼上所有参会的地质学家居维叶对玛丽的指责，如果这样，将引发学界的地震。最后，巴克莱只得同意捍卫玛丽的名声，但强调这绝不能记入伦敦地质协会的备忘录。伊丽莎白由此感叹，女性的一生只能不断地妥协，屈服于男性的权威。在伊丽莎白等人的努力下，居维叶认识到自己的错误，通过助手，告知玛丽他对蛇颈龙化石不再抱有疑虑。当玛丽得知伊丽莎白为了捍卫其声誉，不畏惧强权，突破了当时中上层女性在无人陪伴下决不能独自外出的社会禁忌，更不用说在夜晚独自乘船去伦敦并穿梭于伦敦街头后，因而对自己以往如何诅咒她及其姐妹感到十分懊悔。小说最后，玛丽与伊丽莎白和好如初，一起到海滩找化石，一直相互扶持，至死不渝。

3. 作品赏析

《奇妙的生物》在讲述玛丽及伊丽莎白这两个历史人物在19世纪上半叶的地质考古发现的同时，也反思了女性在地质科学中的地位、史前生物的化石与地球历史的关系、地球生命的演变与宗教神话的关系，以及文学叙事在表征地质科学方面的功能。

玛丽和伊丽莎白是19世纪早期活跃在莱姆地区的女性科学家。1805年迁至英国莱姆海滩后不久，伊丽莎白便去找玛丽，希望她的父亲能为其制作陈列找到的鱼类化石的展柜。当时，玛丽向她展示了自己找到的精美化石。所以，她初次踏上海滩寻找化石的时间，最晚应在1805年。作为地质学发展史上的标杆事件，伦敦地质协会的成立则在两年后，而地质学正式成为一门独立的学科，必须等到1832年莱尔发表《地质学原理》。在此之前，玛丽和伊丽莎白是莱姆海滩上两位最出众的化石勘探者，她们的发现为男性科学家如巴克莱、柯尼贝尔、康尼格(Charles Konig, 1774—1851)、贝什(Henry De La Beche, 1796—1855)、莱尔、居维叶和阿格西斯(Louis Agassiz, 1807—1873)等人的研究发现和理论主张提供了依据。但是，这些男性科学家在利用她们发现的化石来著书立说时却根本不提她们的名字。在他们看来，女性只是助手。甚至，就如第一具鱼龙化石买家亨利所说的那样，女性只是配件，必须由男性来代表女性。毫不奇怪，当得知玛丽写信给居维叶，甚至画了一张蛇颈龙化石的解剖结构图，柯尼贝尔难以置信，认为玛丽几乎是文盲，真是无知者无畏。

不仅玛丽和伊丽莎白得不到男性科学家的认可，她们的名字无法载入伦敦地质协会的备忘录，她们长久以来也得不到所在社区居民的认同。一方面，莱姆居民认为化石肮脏，不是淑女贵妇应当追求的爱好。像19世纪大多数人们一样，莱姆地区的居民坚信地球只有《圣经》所说的6000多年的历史，认为地球形状及地球生命与最初上帝创造万物时一样，根

第一章 文学与地质学（Literature and Geology）

本不可能有物种已经灭绝了，更不可能存在史前生物，认为化石是上帝惩罚恶魔的肮脏物件。由于这个原因，他们力图与玛丽和伊丽莎白保持距离，认为玛丽的父亲在酒后摔伤是上帝惩罚他的结果。另一方面，由于伊丽莎白是来自伦敦的中产阶级女性，而玛丽为下层工人阶级的女儿，她们地位悬殊，但却一直厮混在一起，甚至当着莱姆小镇居民的面，拥抱在一起，因而常常遭受到莱姆人的讥讽。由于伊丽莎白三姐妹不顾惜自己的名声，连莱姆地区最贫穷的石匠也看不起她们，他们宁可打光棍，也不愿高攀这几个来自伦敦的老处女。更为甚者，由于玛丽找到了世界上第一具完整的鱼龙化石，惊动了整个地质学界，许多男性地质学家和化石爱好者前来莱姆海滩寻找化石，经常向玛丽和伊丽莎白求助，这使得莱姆居民更加鄙视她俩，认为她们是"某些绅士的妓女"。玛丽与布茨的恋爱更是让整个莱姆人嗤之以鼻，而伊丽莎白也经常与他们在一起，因而她们一直是莱姆小镇流言蜚语的对象。

尽管如此，玛丽和伊丽莎白不畏世俗，她们相互学习，取长补短，不仅勘探化石，而且对化石进行分类和研究。玛丽在寻找化石方面累积了丰富的经验，知道去什么地方找化石，如何甄别化石，如何挖掘并清理化石，这些实践技能让伊丽莎白自叹不如。伊丽莎白理论基础扎实，阅读了居维叶等人的地质学专著，并且将这些理论知识传授给玛丽，因而她是玛丽的地质学理论知识的启蒙者。受伊丽莎白影响，玛丽找到化石后，都会结合林奈分类法以及居维叶解剖学方面的理论知识，对之进行命名，另外，她还学习伊丽莎白，记录化石发现的时间、地点，地层特征等信息。更重要的是，她会结合居维叶解剖学知识，对比所找到的化石的结构特征，借此判断该化石是否为居维叶所记载的生物的化石，还是未知生物的化石。比如，当她发现第一具完整的鱼龙化石时，她认识到该化石的头骸骨在长度、形状等方面，特别是眼睛的大小完全不符合鳄鱼的尺寸，因而向伊丽莎白坦陈说这不是鳄鱼。虽然畏惧当时的宗教学说，她不敢公开表达自己的怀疑，但她却试图向巴克莱探求真相。从这个意义上来说，玛丽，同样也包括伊丽莎白，她们不再是男性的助手。她们不仅具备丰富的实践技能，能够帮助男性科学家寻找化石，而且她们具有扎实的理论知识，能够对化石进行独立的研究并得出自己的结论，因而是严格意义上的科学家。玛丽在找到蛇颈龙化石后制作的解剖结构图、伊丽莎白在玛丽找到第一具鱼龙化石后对之进行的理论反思，都充分说明了这一点。

玛丽和伊丽莎白找到的各种史前生物的化石，充分说明地球绝非只五六千年的历史。当发现鱼龙化石不同于居维叶解剖图中的任何生物时，伊丽莎白便怀疑它是否由于不适应生存环境已经灭绝了。这不仅表明她具有敏锐的科学意识，还说明她不再相信物种从不变化、进化或灭绝的传统宗教学说。为验证自己的发现，她决定试探亨利。亨利认为玛丽找到的鱼龙化石是上帝的早期模型，认为上帝造出了更好的鳄鱼替代了它。亨利的回答无法消除她的困惑。为弄清化石与上帝的关系，伊丽莎白转向牧师求证。当听到鱼龙化石这是上帝抛弃的早期模型后，牧师惊骇万分，坚称我们看到的任何东西都和上帝创造世界时的景象一样。伊丽莎白指出，既然每块岩石和上帝创造它时一样，动物残骸又如何进入岩石而变成化石？她对牧师的驳斥,不仅说明她不畏惧宗教权威,还表明她已认识到传统宗教无法阐释为何存在古生物化石。由于不敢公然亵渎上帝的权威,她认同了波茨的观点,即上帝无须关注所有生物的发展,因为上帝最关心人类。伊丽莎白模棱两可的态度充分说明,19世纪的科学发现已对宗教信仰造成不小的冲击,而传统宗教也在一定程度上成为阻止女性追求科学真知的障碍。

史前生物化石的发现让伊丽莎白和玛丽开始思考地球生命的起源。正如伊丽莎白认识到的那样:"当玛丽发现鱼龙化石时,不知道自己的发现促成一种认识世界的新方式。人们从未看到过鱼龙,并且它似乎不再存在,已灭绝了。这种现象让人们认为世界或许一直在缓慢地变化,不像过去认为的那样一成不变。与此同时,地质学家研究不同的岩层,思考地球如何形成,推测地球生命的历史。很长一段时间,人们一直想弄清,地球是否只有6000多年的历史。哈顿认为,地球寿命远非那么简短……有人认为是由洪水造成。一些地质学家吸纳了这两种观点,认为地球是由系列灾变造成,最近一次则是诺亚方舟经历的大洪水。鱼龙化石的存在表明它不是唯一灭绝的物种,或许存在许多已灭绝的生物,进而证明地球不断地变化①。"虽然伊丽莎白未能阐明科学与宗教之间的关系,她不想亵渎上帝的态度却表明,她仍期待在《圣经》框架内探求生命的起源。这说明,在科学尚不发达的19世纪早期,人们力图在宗教和科学之间寻求某种平衡,以解释当时的地质发现。另外,伊丽莎白对化石作用的认识,表明她试图打破从字面来阐释《圣经》的传统,她对灭绝论的接受,更颠覆了传统宗教认为世界不变的观点。再次,玛丽和伊丽莎白发现的各种恐龙及鱼类化石,让人们认识到地球上不仅生物种类繁多,而且地球上的生命远早于《圣经》记载的大洪水。这使得一些地质学家完全否定了诺亚方舟的现实性,进而动摇传统宗教信仰的根基,造成了19世纪的信仰危机。

谢瓦利埃在《奇妙的生物》的后记中指出:"小说中许多事件与真实时间、地点并不完全吻合。此外,我也虚构了许多。比如,玛丽与巴克莱和波茨之间的绯闻并不存在证据,这恰是小说家才能涉足的地方②。"不管存在记载与否,谢瓦利埃的虚构性叙事让我们重新认识了19世纪上半叶地质学的发展史,特别是女性地质学家如何克服阶级和性别方面的阻碍,渗入男性的职业领域,并做出巨大贡献。因此,小说是谢瓦利埃从当代视角来重新审视英国维多利亚时期的女性在地质科学发展史上的贡献的重要媒介。正出于这一考虑,《奇妙的生物》力图还原维多利亚时期的男性如何依靠女性科学家的发现在地质学方面做出建树。下面请阅读小说节选部分,并回答相关问题③。

---

① TRACY C. Remarkable creatures[M]. London: Harper Collins Publishers, 2010: 126-127.
② 同①147-148.
③ 毛卫强.《奇妙的生物》中的博物学书写[J]. 国外文学, 2022(4): 141-149.

作品选读

Remarkable Creatures
Tracy Chevalier

Chapter 8
An Adventure in an Unadventurous Life

It is rare for anything reported in the *Western Flying Post* to surprise me. Most are predictable stories: a description of a livestock auction in Bridport, or an account of a public meeting on the widening of a Weymouth road, or warnings of pickpockets at the Frome Fair. Even the stories of more unusual events where lives are changed—a man transported for stealing a silver watch, a fire burning down half a village—I still read with a sense of distance, for they have little effect on me. Of course, if the man had stolen my watch, or half of Lyme burned down, I would be more interested. Still, I read the paper dutifully, for it makes me at least aware of the wider region, rather than trapped in an inward-looking town.

Bessy brought me the paper as I rested by the fire one mid-December afternoon. I did not often fall ill, and my weakness irritated me so that I had become as grumpy as Bessy normally was. I sighed as she set it on a small table next to me along with a cup of tea. Still, it was some diversion, for my sisters were busy in the kitchen, making up a batch of Margaret's salve to go in Christmas baskets, along with jars of rosehip jelly. I had wanted to include an ammonite in each basket, but Margaret felt they did not invoke a festive spirit and insisted on pretty shells instead. I forget sometimes that people see fossils as the bones of the dead. Indeed, they are, though I tend to view them more as works of art reminding us of what the world was once like.

I paid little attention to what I read until I came across a short notice, wedged between news of two fires, one burning down a barn, the other the premises of a pastry cook. It read:

On Wednesday evening Mary Anning, the well-known fossilist, whose labours have enriched the British and Bristol Museums, as well as the private collections of many geologists, found, east of town, and immediately under the celebrated Black Ven Cliff, some remains, which were removed on that night and the succeeding morning, to undergo an examination, the result of which is, that this specimen appears to differ widely from any which have before been discovered at Lyme, either of the Ichthyosaurus or Plesiosaurus, while it approaches nearly to the structure of the Turtle. The whole osteology has not yet been satisfactorily disclosed, owing to its very recent removal.

It will be for the great geologists to determine by what term this creature is to be known. The great Cuvier will be informed when the bones are completely disclosed, but probably it will be christened at Oxford or London, after an account has been accurately furnished. No doubt the Directors of the British or Bristol Museums will be anxious to possess this relic of the "great Herculaneum".①

Mary had found it at last. She had found the new monster that she and William Buckland had speculated must exist, and I had to find out about her discovery in the newspaper, as if I were just anyone and had no claim on her. Even the men producing the *Western Flying Post* knew about it before me.

It is difficult to have a falling-out in a town the size of Lyme Regis. I had first learned that when we Philpots stopped seeing Lord Henley②: we then managed to run into him everywhere, so that it became almost a game dodging him on Broad Street, along the path by the river, at St Michael's.③ We provided the town with years of gossip and amusement, for which we ought to have been thanked.

[...]

The rapping on our front door interrupted us as we were eating. It was so sudden and loud that we all three jumped, and Margaret upset her watercress soup.

Normally we let Bessy go to the door in her own ponderous fashion, but the knocks

---

① Herculaneum 赫库兰尼姆是一个古老的城镇,位于现代意大利坎帕尼亚的埃尔科拉诺市镇。公元 79 年维苏威火山爆发时,赫库兰尼姆被埋在火山灰和浮石之下。与庞贝城一样,赫库兰尼姆也是少数几座或多或少完好无损的古城之一,因为覆盖该镇的灰烬也保护了它免受抢劫和自然灾害的侵害。
② Henley 是莱姆小镇的富绅,他购买了玛丽找到的第一具鱼龙化石。随后,他高价将之卖给伦敦私人收藏者 William Bullock。
③ 莱姆小镇的基督教教堂。

were so urgent that Louise sprang up and hurried down the passage to answer it. Margaret and I could not see whom she let in, but we heard low voices in the passage. Then Louise put her head around the door. "Molly Anning is here to see us," she said. "She has said she will wait until we have finished eating. I've left her to warm by the fire and will get Bessy to build it up."

Margaret jumped up. "I'll just get Mrs Anning some soup."

I looked down at my own soup. I could not sit and eat it while an Anning waited in the other room. I got up as well, but stood uncertain in the doorway of the parlour.

Louise saved me, as she often does. "Brandy, perhaps," she said as she brushed past with a grumbling Bessy in tow.

"Yes, yes." I went and fetched the bottle and a glass.

Molly Anning was sitting motionless by the fire, the centre of all the activity around her, much as she had been when she came to see us with her letter to Colonel Birch. Bessy was poking the fire and glaring at our visitor's legs, which she perceived to be in the way. Margaret was setting up a small table at her side for the soup, while Louise moved the coal scuttle. I hovered with the brandy bottle, but Molly Anning shook her head when I offered it. She said nothing while she ate her soup, sucking at it as if she didn't like watercress and was eating it only to please us.

As she mopped her bowl with a chunk of bread, I felt my sisters' eyes on me. They had played their parts with the visitor, and were now expecting me to play mine. My mouth felt glued shut, however. It had been a very long time since I had spoken either to Mary or to her mother.

I cleared my throat. "Is something wrong, Molly?" I managed at last. "Are Joseph and Mary all right?"

Molly Anning swallowed the last of her bread and ran her tongue around her mouth. "Mary's taken to her bed," she declared.

"Oh dear, is she ill?" Margaret asked.

"No, she's just a fool, is all. Here." Pulling a crumpled letter from her pocket, Molly Anning handed it to me. I opened it and smoothed it out. A glance told me it was from Paris. The words "plesiosaurus" and "Cuvier" popped out at me, but I hesitated to read the contents. However, as Molly seemed to expect me to, I had no choice.

Jardin du RoiMusée National d'Histoire Naturelle Paris

Dear Miss Anning,

Thank you for your letter to Baron Cuvier concerning a possible sale to the museum of the specimen you have discovered at Lyme Regis, and believe to be an almost compete skeleton of a plesiosaurus. Baron Cuvier has studied with interest the sketch you enclosed, and is of the opinion that you have joined together two separate individuals, perhaps that of the head of a sea serpent with the body of an ichthyosaurus. The jumbled state of the vertebrae just below the head seems to indicate the disjuncture between the two specimens.

Baron Cuvier holds the view that the structure of the reported plesiosaurus deviates from some of the anatomical laws he has established. In particular, the number of cervical vertebrae is too great for such an individual. Most reptiles have between three and eight neck vertebrae; yet in your sketch the creature appears to have at least thirty.

Given Baron Cuvier's concerns over the specimen, we will not consider purchasing it. In future, Mademoiselle, perhaps your family might take more care when collecting and presenting specimens.

Yours faithfully,
Joseph Pentland Esq.
Assistant to Baron Cuvier

I threw down the letter. "That is outrageous!"

"What is?" Margaret cried, caught up in the drama.

"Georges Cuvier has seen a drawing of Mary's plesiosaurus and has accused the Annings of forgery. He thinks the anatomy of the animal is impossible, and says that Mary may have put together two different specimens."

"The silly girl's taken it as an insult to her," Molly Anning said. "Says the Frenchman has ruined her reputation as a hunter. She's gone to bed over it, says there's no reason to get up and hunt curies now, as no one'll buy them. She's as bad as when she were waiting for Colonel Birchto write." Molly Anning glanced sideways at me, gauging my reaction. "I come to ask you to help me get her out of bed."

第一章　文学与地质学（Literature and Geology）

"But—" Why ask me, I wanted to say. Why not someone else? On the other hand, perhaps Mary had no other friends Molly could ask. I had never seen her with other Lyme people of her age and class. "The trouble is," I began, "Mary may well be right. If Baron Cuvier believes the plesiosaurus is a fake, and makes public his view, it could cause people to question other specimens." Molly Anning did not seem to respond to this idea, so I made it plainer. "You may find your sales will fall as people wonder whether Anning fossils are authentic."

At last I got through to her, for Molly Anning glared at me as if I had suggested such a thing myself. "How dare that Frenchman threaten our business! You'll have to sort him out."

"Me?"

"You speak French, don't you? You've had learning. I haven't, you see, so you'll have to write to him."

"But it's nothing to do with me."

Molly Anning just looked at me, as did my sisters.

"Molly," I said, "Mary and I have not had a great deal to do with each other these last few years—"

"What is all that about, then? Mary would never say."

I looked around. Margaret was sitting forward, and Louise was giving me the Philpot gaze, both also waiting for me to explain, for I had never provided a sufficient reason for our break. "Mary and I… we did not see eye to eye on some things."

"Well, you can make it up to her by sorting out this Frenchman," Molly Anning declared.

"I am not sure I can do anything. Cuvier is a powerful, well-respected scientist, whilst you are just—" a poor, working family, I wanted to finish, but didn't. I didn't need to, for Molly Anning understood what I meant. "Anyway, he won't listen to me either, whether I write in French or English. He doesn't know who I am. Indeed, I am nobody to him." To most people, I thought.

"One of the men could write to Cuvier," Margaret suggested. "Mr Buckland, perhaps? He has met Cuvier, hasn't he?"

"Maybe I should write to Colonel Birch and ask him to write," Molly Anning said. "I'm sure he would do it."

"Not Colonel Birch." My tone was so sharp that all three women looked at me. "Does anyone else know that Mary wrote to Cuvier?"

Molly Anning shook her head.

"And so no one else knows of this response?"

"Only Joe, but he won't say anything."

"Well, that is something."

"But people will find out. Eventually Mr Buckland and Reverend Conybeare and Mr Konig and all those men we sell to will know that the Frenchman thinks the Annings are frauds. The Duke of Buckingham might hear and not pay us!" Molly Anning's mouth started to tremble, and I feared she might actually cry—a sight I didn't think I could bear.

To stop her I said, "Molly, I am going to help you. Don't cry, now. We will manage."

I had no idea what I would do. But I was thinking of the crate full of fossil fish in Mary's workshop, waiting for me to thaw, and knew I had to do something. I thought for a moment. "Where is the plesiosaurus now?"

"On board the Dispatch, heading for London, if it ain't already arrived. Mr Buckland saw her off. And Reverend Conybeare is meeting it at the other end. He's addressing the Geological Society later this month at their annual dinner."

"Ah." So it was gone already. The men had charge of it now. I would have to go to them.

Margaret and Louise thought I was mad. It was bad enough that I wanted to travel to London rather than simply write a forceful letter. But to go in winter, and by ship, was folly. However, the weather was so foul, the roads so muddy, that only mail coaches were getting through to London, and even they were being delayed, and were full besides. A ship might be quicker, and the weekly one was leaving when I needed it.

I knew too that the men I wanted to see would be blinded by their interest in the plesiosaurus and would not attend to my letter, no matter how eloquent or urgent. I must see them in person to convince them to help Mary immediately.

第一章 文学与地质学（Literature and Geology）

What I did not tell my sisters was that I was excited to go. Yes, I was fearful of the ship and of what the sea might do. It would be cold and rough, and I might feel sick much of the time, despite a tonic for seasickness that Margaret had concocted for me. As the only lady on board, I could not be sure of sympathy or comfort from the crew or other passengers.

I also had no idea if I could make any difference to Mary's predicament. I only knew that when I read Joseph Pentland's letter, I was consumed with anger. Mary had been so generous for so long, to so little gain—apart from Colonel Birch's sudden, madcap auction—while others took what she found and made their names from it as natural philosophers. William Buckland lectured on the creatures at Oxford, Charles Konig brought them into the British Museum to acclaim, Reverend Conybeare and even our dear Henry De La Beche addressed the Geological Society and published papers about them. Konig had had the privilege of naming the ichthyosaurus, and Conybeare the plesiosaurus. Neither would have had anything to name without Mary. I could not stand by and watch suspicions grow about her skills when the men knew she outstripped them all in her abilities.

I was also making amends to Mary. I was at last asking her to forgive me my jealousy and disdain.

There was something else, though. This was also my chance for an adventure in an unadventurous life. I had never travelled alone, but was always with my sisters or brother or other relatives, or with friends. As secure as that had felt, it was a bind as well that sometimes threatened to smother me. I was rather proud now as I stood on the deck of the Unity—the same ship that had taken Colonel Birch's ichthyosaurus to London—and watched Lyme and my sisters grow smaller until they disappeared and I was alone.

We sailed straight out to sea rather than hug the coast, for we had to clear the tricky isle of Portland. So I did not get to see up close the places I knew well—Golden Cap, Bridport, Chesil Beach, Weymouth. Once past Portland we remained out at sea until we had gone around the Isle of Wight, before finally coming closer to shore.

A sea voyage is very different from a coach trip to London, where Margaret, Louise and I were packed with several strangers into a stuffy, rattling, jolting box that stopped constantly to change horses. That was a communal event, uncomfortable in ways that as I grew older took days to recover from.

Being on board the Unity was much more solitary. I would sit on deck, tucked out of the way on a small keg, and watch the crew at work with their ropes and sails. I had no idea what they were doing, but their shouts to one another and their confident routines soothed my fears of being at sea. Moreover, the cares of daily life were taken out of my hands, and nothing was expected of me but to stay out of the men's way. Not only did I not feel ill on board, even when it was rough; I was actually enjoying myself.

I had been anxious about being the only lady on the ship—the three other passengers were all men with business in London—but I was mostly ignored, though the Captain was kind enough, if taciturn, when I joined him to dine each night. No one seemed at all curious about me, though one of the passengers—a man from Honiton—was happy to talk about fossils when he heard of my interest. I did not tell him about the plesiosaurus, however, or of my intended visit to the Geological Society. He knew only about the obvious—ammonites, belemnites, crinoids, gryphaea—and had little of use to say, though he made sure to say every word of it. Luckily he could not bear the cold, and most often stayed belowdecks.

Until I boarded the Unity, I had always thought of the sea as a boundary keeping me in my place on land. Now, though, it became an opening. As I sat I occasionally saw another vessel, but most of the time there was nothing but sky and moving water. I often looked to the horizon, lulled into a wordless calm by the rhythm of the sea and by ship life. It was oddly satisfying to study that far-off line, reminding me that I spent much of my life in Lyme with my eyes fixed to the ground in search of fossils. Such hunting can limit a person's perspective. On board the Unity I had no choice but to see the greater world, and my place in it. Sometimes I imagined being on shore and looking out at the ship, and seeing on deck a small, mauve figure caught between the light grey sky and dark grey sea, watching the world pass before her, alone and sturdy. I did not expect it, but I had never been so happy.

The winds were light, but we made steady if slow progress. The first I saw of land was on the second day when the chalk cliffs to the east of Brighton came blinking into

第一章　文学与地质学（Literature and Geology）

view. When we made a brief stop there to unload cloth from Lyme's factory, I considered asking Captain Pearce if I might go ashore to see my sister Frances. However, rather to my surprise, I felt no real urge to do so, or to send her a note saying I was there, but was content to remain on board and watch the residents of Brighton on land walking back and forth along the promenade. Even if Frances herself had appeared, I am not sure I would have called out to her. I preferred not to disturb the delicious anonymity of standing on deck with no one looking for me.

On the third day we had passed Dover with its stark white cliffs, and were coming around the headland by Ramsgate when we saw a ship off our port side run aground on a sandbar. As we drew nearer I heard one of the crew name it as the Dispatch, the ship carrying Mary's plesiosaurus.

I sought out the Captain. "Oh yes, that be the Dispatch," he confirmed, "run aground on Goodwin Sands. They'll have tried to turn too sharp." He sounded disgusted and entirely without sympathy, even as he called for the men to cast anchor. Soon two sailors set out in a boat to cross over to the listing vessel, where they met with a few men who had by now appeared on deck. The sailors talked to them for just a few minutes before rowing back. I leaned forward and strained to hear what they shouted to the Captain.

"Cargo was taken to shore yesterday!" one called. "They're taking it overland to London."

At this the crew jeered, for they had little respect for travel by land, I had learned during the trip. They saw it as slow, rough and muddy. Others—coachmen, for instance—might retort that the sea was slow, rough and wet.

Whoever was right, Mary's plesiosaurus was now somewhere in a long, slow train of carts grinding through Kent towards London. Having left a week before me, the specimen would now probably arrive in London after me, too late for the Geological Society meeting.

We reached London in the early hours of the fourth day, docking at a wharf on Tooley Street. After the relative calm on board, all now became a chaos of unloading by torchlight, of shouts and whistles, of coaches and carts clattering away full of people and cargo. It was a shock to the senses after four days of Nature providing her own constant rhythms. The people and the noise and the lights reminded me too that I had come to London for a reason, not to enjoy anonymity and solitude whilst eyeing the wider horizon.

I stood on deck and looked out for my brother at the quayside, but he was not there. The letter I had posted at the same time as I left must have got stuck in the mud en route and lost its race with me. Though I had never been before, I had heard about London's docks, how crowded and dirty and dangerous they were, especially for a lady on her own with no one expecting her. Perhaps it was because the darkness made everything more mysterious, but the men unloading the Unity, even the sailors I had got to know on board, now appeared much rougher and harder.

I hesitated to disembark. There was no one to turn to for help, though: the other passengers—even the cocksure man from Honiton—had hurried away in ungentleman-like haste. I could have panicked. Before the journey I might have. But something had shifted in me while I spent all that time on deck watching the horizon: I was responsible for myself. I was Elizabeth Philpot, and I collected fossil fish. Fish are not always beautiful, but they have pleasing shapes, they are practical, and they lead with their eyes. There is nothing shameful about them

I picked up my bag and stepped off the boat amidst a score of bustling men, many of whom whistled and shouted at me. Before anyone could do more than call out, I walked quickly to the Customs House, despite swaying with the shock of being on land again. "I would like a cab, please," I said to a surprised clerk, interrupting him as he ticked items on a list. He had a moustache that fluttered like a moth over his mouth. "I shall wait here until you fetch me one," I added, setting down my bag. I did not stick out my chin and sharpen my jaw, but gazed steadily at him with my Philpot eyes.

He found me a cab.

The Geological Society's offices in Covent Garden were not far from my brother's house, but to get there one had to pass through St Giles and Seven Dials, with its beggars and thieves, and I was not keen to do so on foot. Thus on the evening of the 20th February, 1824, I waited in a cab across from 20 Bedford Street, my nephew Johnny beside me. There was snow on the street, and we huddled under our cloaks against the cold.

第一章 文学与地质学(Literature and Geology)

My brother was horrified that I had come all the way to London on a ship because of Mary. When he was woken in the middle of the night to find me at the door, he looked so ill with surprise that I almost regretted I had come. Being quietly tucked away in Lyme, my sisters and I had rarely given him cause to worry, and I did not like to do so now.

John did everything he could to persuade me not to go to the Geological Society, bar expressly forbidding me. It seemed he was only willing to indulge me in unusual behaviour just the once, when he had escorted me to Bullock's to view Colonel Birch's auction preview. Mercifully he had never found out I attended the auction itself. He would not help me with something so odd and risky again. "They will not let you in, for you are a lady, and their charter does not allow it," he began, using first the legal argument. We were in his study, the door closed, as if John were trying to protect his family from me, his erratic sister. "Even if they let you in they would not listen to you, for you are not a member. Then," he added, holding up a hand as I tried to interrupt, "you have no business discussing and defending Mary. It is not your place to."

"She is my friend," I replied, "and no one else will take her part if I don't."

John looked at me as if I were a small child trying to convince my nurse I could have another helping of pudding. "You have been very foolish, Elizabeth. You have come all this way, making yourself ill en route—"

"It is just a cold, nothing more."

"—ill en route, and worrying us unnecessarily." Now he was using guilt. "And to no purpose, for you will gain no audience."

"I can at least try. It is truly foolish to come all this way and then not even try."

"What exactly do you want from these men?"

"I want to remind them of Mary's careful methods of finding and preserving fossils, and to convince them to agree to defend her publicly against Cuvier's attack on her character."

"They will never do that," John said, running his finger along the spiral of his nautilus paperweight.

"Though they may defend the plesiosaurus, they will not discuss Mary. She is only the hunter."

"Only the hunter!" I stopped myself. John was a London solicitor, with a certain way of thinking. I was a stubborn Lyme spinster, with my own mind. We were not going to agree, nor either of us convince the other. And he was not my target anyway; I must save my words for more important men.

John would not agree to accompany me to the meeting, and so I did not ask, but turned to an alternative—my nephew. Johnny was now a tall, lanky youth who led with his feet, had a residual fondness for his aunt and an active fondness for mischief. He had never told his parents about discovering me sneaking out of the house to go to the auction at Bullock's, and this shared secret bound us. It was this closeness I now relied on to help me.

I was lucky, for John and my sister-in-law were dining out on the Friday evening of the Geological Society meeting. I had not told him when the meeting was to take place, but allowed him to believe it was the following week. The afternoon of the supper I took to bed, saying my cold was worse. My sister-in-law pursed her lips in clear disapproval of my folly. She did not like unexpected visitors, or the sort of problems that, for all my quiet life at Lyme, I seemed to trail behind me. She hated fossils, and disorder, and unanswered questions. Whenever I brought up topics like the possible age of the earth, she twisted her hands in her lap and changed the subject as soon as it was polite to.

When she and my brother had gone out for the evening, I crept from my room and went to find Johnny and explain what I needed from him. He rose to the occasion admirably, coming up with an excuse for his departure to satisfy the servants, fetching a cab and hurrying me into it without anyone in the house discovering. It was absurd that I had to go to such lengths to take any sort of action out of the ordinary.

However, it was also a relief to have company. Now we sat in the cab on Bedford Street across from the Geological Society house, Johnny having gone in to check and found that the members were still dining in rooms on the first floor. Through the front windows we could see lights there and the occasional head bobbing about. The formal meeting would begin in half an hour or so.

"What shall we do, Aunt Elizabeth?" he demanded. "Storm the citadel?"

"No, we wait. They will all stand so that the meal can be cleared away. At that moment I will go in and seek out Mr Buckland. He is about to become President of the

第一章 文学与地质学（Literature and Geology）

Society, and I am sure he will listen to me."

Johnny sat back and propped his feet up on the seat across from him. If I had been his mother I would have told him to put his feet down, but the pleasure of being an aunt is that you can enjoy your nephew's company without having to concern yourself with his behaviour. "Aunt Elizabeth, you haven't said why this plesiosaur is so important," he began. "That is, I understand that you want to defend Miss Anning. But why is everyone so excited about the creature itself?"

I straightened my gloves and rearranged my cloak around me. "Do you remember when you were a small boy and we took you to the Egyptian Hall to see all the animals?"

"Yes, I recall the elephant and the hippo."

"Do you remember the stone crocodile you found, and I was so upset by? The one that is now in the British Museum and they call an ichthyosaurus?"

"I've seen it at the British Museum, of course, and you've told me about it," Johnny answered. "But I confess I remember the elephant better. Why?"

Well, when Mary discovered that ichthyosaurus, she did not know it at the time, but she was contributing to a new way of thinking about the world. Here was a creature that had never been seen before, that did not seem to exist any longer, but was extinct—the species had died out. Such a phenomenon made people think that perhaps the world is changing, however slowly, rather than being a constant, as had been previously thought.

"At the same time, geologists were studying the different layers of rock, and thinking about how the world was formed, and wondering about its age. For some time now men have wondered if the world isn't older than the 6,000 years calculated by Bishop Ussher. A learned Scotsman called James Hutton even suggested that the world is so old it has 'neither a beginning nor an end,' and that it is impossible for us to measure it." I paused. "Perhaps it would be best if you didn't mention any of what I'm saying to your mother. She doesn't like to hear me talk of such things."

"I won't. Carry on."

"Hutton thought the world is being sculpted by volcanic action. Others have suggested it has been formed by water. Lately some geologists have taken elements of both and said a series of catastrophes has shaped the world, with Noah's Flood being the latest."

"What does this have to do with the plesiosaurus?"

"It is concrete evidence that the ichthyosaurus was not a unique instance of extinction, but that there are others—maybe many extinct creatures. That in turn supports the argument that the earth is in flux." I looked at my nephew. Johnny was frowning at the light snowflakes swirling about outside. Perhaps he was more like his mother than I realised. "I'm sorry—I didn't mean to upset you with such talk."

He shook his head. "No, it's fascinating. I was just wondering why none of my tutors discuss this in lessons."

"It is too frightening for many, for it challenges our belief in an all-knowing, all-powerful God, and raises questions about His intentions."

"What do you believe, Aunt Elizabeth?"

"I believe..." Few had ever asked me what I believed. It was refreshing. "I am comfortable with reading the Bible figuratively rather than literally. For instance, I think the six days in Genesis are not literal days, but different periods of creation, so that it took many thousands—or hundreds of thousands of years—to create. It does not demean God; it simply gives Him more time to build this extraordinary world."

"And the ichthyosaurus and plesiosaurus?"

"They are creatures from long, long ago. They remind us that the world is changing. Of course it is. I can see it change when there are landslips at Lyme that alter the shoreline. It changes when there are earthquakes and volcanic eruptions and floods. And why shouldn't it?"

Johnny nodded. It was a relief to say such things to a sympathetic ear and not be judged either ignorant or blasphemous. Perhaps he could be so open-minded because he was young.

"Look." He pointed at the windows of the Geological Society house. Figures were blocking the light as the men got up from their tables. It was time for me to lead with my eyes. I took a deep breath and opened the cab door. Johnny leaped out and helped me down, excited to be acting at last. He strode to the door and knocked boldly. The same man answered as had the first time, but Johnny treated him as if he had never spoken to him before. "Miss Philpot here to see Professor Buckland," he announced. Perhaps he thought such confidence would open all doors.

The doorman, however, was not taken in by youthful assuredness. "Women are not allowed in the Society," he replied, not even glancing at me. It was as if I did not exist.

He began to shut the door, but Johnny stuck his foot on the jamb so that it wouldn't close. "Well, then, John Philpot Esquire here to see Professor Buckland."

The doorman looked him up and down. "What business?"

"It's to do with the plesiosaurus."

The doorman frowned. The word meant nothing to him, but it sounded complicated and possibly important. "I'll take up a message."

"I can only speak to Professor Buckland," Johnny replied in a haughty tone, enjoying every moment.

The doorman appeared unmoved. I had to step forward, forcing him at last to look at me and acknowledge my presence. "As it is to do with the very subject of the meeting that is about to start, it would be wise of you to inform Professor Buckland that we are waiting to speak to him." I looked him straight in the eye, with all of the steadiness and resolve I had discovered in myself on board the Unity.

It had its effect: after a moment the doorman dropped his eyes and gave me the briefest of nods. "Wait here," he said, and shut the door in our faces. Clearly my success was limited, for it did not overcome the rule that women were not allowed inside, but must stand out in the cold. As we waited, snowflakes dusted my hat and cloak.

A few minutes later we heard footsteps clattering down the stairs, and the door opened toreveal the excited faces of Mr Buckland and Reverend Conybeare. I was disappointed to see the latter; Reverend Conybeare was not nearly as easy and welcoming as Mr Buckland.

I think they were a little disappointed to see us as well. "Miss Philpot!" Mr Buckland cried. "What a surprise. I did not know you were in town."

"I only arrived two days ago, Mr Buckland. Reverend Conybeare." I nodded at them both. "This is my nephew, John. May we come in? It is very cold outside."

"Of course, of course!" As Mr Buckland ushered us in, Reverend Conybeare pursed his lips, clearly unhappy that a lady was being allowed across the threshold of the Geological Society. But he was not President—Mr Buckland would become so in a moment—and so he said nothing, but bowed to us both. His long narrow nose was red, whether from wine, a seat close to the fire, or temper, I couldn't guess.

The entrance to the house was simple, with an elegant black-and-white tiled floor and solemn portraits hanging of George Greenough, John MacCulloch, and other Society Presidents. Soon a portrait of William Babington, the retiring President, would join the others. I expected to see something displayed that would indicate the Society's interest: fossils, of course, or rocks. But there was nothing. The interesting things were hidden away.

"Tell me, Miss Philpot, do you have news of the plesiosaurus?" Reverend Conybeare asked. "The doorman said you might. Will its presence yet grace our meeting?"

Now I understood their excitement: it was not the Philpot name but mention of the missing specimen that had brought them racing down the stairs.

"I passed the grounded Dispatch three days ago." I tried to sound knowledgeable. "Its cargo is now being brought by land, and will arrive as quickly as the roads allow."

Both men looked discouraged at hearing what was not news to them. "Why, then, Miss Philpot, are you here?" Reverend Conybeare said. For a vicar he was quite tart.

I drew myself up straight and tried to look them in the eye as confidently as I had the clerk at the wharf and the Geological Society's doorman. It was more difficult, however, as there were two of them gazing at me—and Johnny too. Then, too, they were more learned, and confident. I might hold some power over a clerk and a doorman, but not over one of my own class. Instead of fixing my attention on Mr Buckland—who as future President of the Society was the more important of the two—I stupidly looked at my nephew as I said, "I wanted to discuss Miss Anning with you."

"Has something happened to Mary?" William Buckland asked.

"No, no, she is well."

Reverend Conybeare frowned, and even Mr Buckland, who was not a frowner, wrinkled his brow. "Miss Philpot," Reverend Conybeare began, "we are about to hold

第一章 文学与地质学 (Literature and Geology)

our meeting at which both Mr Buckland and I will be giving important—nay, even history-making—addresses to the Society. Surely your query about Miss Anning can wait until another day while we concentrate on these more pressing matters. Now, if you will excuse me, I am just going to review my notes." Without waiting to hear my response, he turned and padded up the carpeted stairs.

Mr Buckland looked as if he might do the same, but he was slower and kinder, and he took a moment to say, "I should be delighted to talk with you another time, Miss Philpot. Perhaps I could call around one day next week?"

"But sir," Johnny broke in, "Monsieur Cuvier thinks the plesiosaurus is a fake!"

That stopped Reverend Conybeare's retreating back. He turned on the stairs. "What did you say?"

Johnny, the clever boy, had said just the right thing. Of course the men did not want to hear about Mary.

It was Cuvier's opinion of the plesiosaurus that would concern them.

"Baron Cuvier believes that the plesiosaurus Mary found cannot be real," I explained as Reverend Conybeare descended the stairs and rejoined us, his face grim. "The neck has too many vertebrae, and he believes it violates the fundamental laws that govern the anatomy of vertebrates."

Reverend Conybeare and Mr Buckland exchanged glances.

"Cuvier has suggested the Annings created a false animal by adding a sea serpent's skull to the body of an ichthyosaurus. He claims they are forgers," I added, bringing the discussion to what concerned me most.

Then I wished I hadn't, for seeing the expressions my words ignited on the men's faces. Both registered surprise, giving way to a degree of suspicion, more prominent in Reverend Conybeare's case, but also apparent even in Mr Buckland's benign features.

"Of course you know that Mary would never do such a thing," I reminded them. "She is an honest soul, and trained—by your good selves, I might add—in the importance of preserving specimens as they are found. She knows they are of little use if tampered with."

"Of course," Mr Buckland agreed, his face clearing, as if all he needed was a prompt from a sensible mind.

Reverend Conybeare was still frowning, however. Clearly my reminder had tapped into a seam of doubt.

"Who told Cuvier about the specimen?" he demanded.

I hesitated, but there was no way around revealing the truth. "Mary herself wrote to him. I believe she sent along a drawing."

Reverend Conybeare snorted. "Mary wrote? I dread to think what such a letter would be like. The girl is practically illiterate! It would have been much better if Cuvier had learned of it after tonight's lecture. Buckland, we must present our case to him ourselves, with drawings and a detailed description. You and I should write, and perhaps someone else as well, so Cuvier will hear about it from several angles. Johnson in Bristol, perhaps. He was very keen when I mentioned the plesiosaurus at the Institution at the beginning of the month, and I know he has corresponded with Cuvier in the past." As he spoke, Reverend Conybeare ran his hand up and down the mahogany banister, still rattled by the news. If he hadn't irritated me with his suspicion of Mary, I might have felt sorry for him.

Mr Buckland also noted his friend's nerves. "Conybeare, you are not going to withdraw your address now, are you? Many guests have come expressly to hear you: Babbage, Gordon, Drummond, Rudge, even McDownell. You've seen the room: it's packed, the best attendance I've ever seen. Of course I can entertain them with my musings on the megalosaurus, but how much more powerful if we both speak of these creatures of the past. Together we will give them an evening they will never forget!"

I tutted. "This is not the theatre, Mr Buckland."

"Ah, but in a way it is, Miss Philpot. And what wonderful entertainment we have prepared for them! We are in the midst of opening their eyes to incontrovertible evidence of a wondrous past world, to the most magnificent creatures God has created—apart from man, of course." Mr Buckland was warming to his theme.

"Perhaps you should save your thoughts for the meeting," I suggested.

"Of course, of course. Now, Conybeare, are you with me?"

"Yes." Reverend Conybeare visibly donned a more confident air. "In my paper I have already addressed some of Cuvier's concerns about the number of vertebrae. Besides, you have seen the creature, Buckland. You believe in it."

第一章 文学与地质学(Literature and Geology)

Mr Buckland nodded.

"Then you believe in Mary Anning as well," I interjected. "And you will defend her from Cuvier's unjust charges."

"I do not see what that has to do with this meeting," Reverend Conybeare countered. "I mentioned Mary when I spoke about the plesiosaurus at the Bristol Institution. Buckland and I will write to Cuvier. Is that not enough?"

"Every geologist of note as well as other interested parties are upstairs in that room right now. One announcement from you, that you have complete confidence in Mary's abilities as a fossil hunter, will counter any comments from Baron Cuvier that they might hear of later."

"Why should I want to cast doubt in public on Miss Anning's abilities, and indeed—and more importantly, I might add—doubt on the very specimen I am just preparing to speak about?"

"A woman's good name is at stake, as well as her livelihood—a livelihood that provides you with the specimens you need to further your theories and your own good name. Surely that must matter to you enough to speak out?"

Reverend Conybeare and I glared at each other, our eyes locked. We might have remained like that all evening if it weren't for Johnny, who had become impatient with all of the talk and wanted more action. He ducked behind Reverend Conybeare and leapt onto the stairs above him. "If you don't agree to clear Miss Anning's name, I shall go and tell the roomful of gentlemen upstairs what Cuvier has said," he called down to us. "How would you like that?"

Reverend Conybeare made a move to grab him, but Johnny leaped up several more steps to remain out of reach. I should have scolded my nephew for his bad behaviour, but instead found myself snorting to hide laughter. I turned to Mr Buckland, the more reasonable of the two. "Mr Buckland, I know how fond you are of Mary, and that you recognise how much in debt we all are to her for her immense skill in finding fossils. I understand too that this evening is very important to you, and I would not want to ruin that. But surely somewhere in the meeting there is room for you to express your support of Mary? Perhaps you could simply acknowledge her efforts without mentioning Baron Cuvier specifically. And when his remarks are at last made public, the men upstairs will understand the deeper meaning of your declaration of confidence. That way we will all be satisfied. Would that be acceptable?"

Mr Buckland pondered this suggestion. "It could not be recorded in the Society's minutes," he said at last, "but I am certainly willing to say something off the record if that will please you, Miss Philpot."

"It will, thank you."

He and Reverend Conybeare looked up at Johnny. "That will do, lad," Reverend Conybeare muttered. "Come down, now."

"Is that all, Aunt Elizabeth? Shall I come down?" Johnny seemed disappointed that he could not carry out his threat.

"There is one more thing," I said. Reverend Conybeare groaned. "I should like to hear what you have to say at the meeting about the plesiosaurus."

"I'm afraid women are not allowed in to the Society meetings." Mr Buckland sounded almost sorry.

"Perhaps I could sit out in the corridor to listen? No one but you need know I am there."

Mr Buckland thought for a moment. "There is a staircase at the back of the room leading down to one of the kitchens. The servants use it to bring dishes and food and such up and down. You might sit out on the landing. From there you should be able to hear us without being seen."

"That would be very kind, thank you."

Mr Buckland gestured to the doorman, who had been listening impassively. "Would you show this lady and young man up to the landing at the back, please. Come, Conybeare, we have kept them waiting long enough. They'll think we've gone to Lyme and back!"

The two men hurried up the stairs, leaving Johnny and me with the doorman. I will not forget the venomous look Reverend Conybeare threw me over his shoulder as he reached the top and turned to go into the meeting room.

Johnny chuckled. "You have not made a friend there, Aunt Elizabeth!"

"It doesn't matter to me, but I fear I have put him off his stride. Well, we shall hear in a moment."

第一章 文学与地质学(Literature and Geology)

I did not put off Reverend Conybeare. As a vicar he was used to speaking in public, and he was able to draw on that well of experience to recover his equanimity. By the time William Buckland had got through the procedural parts of the meeting—approving the minutes of the previous meeting, proposing new members, enumerating the various journals and specimens donated to the Society since the last meeting—Reverend Conybeare would have looked over his notes and reassured himself about the particulars of his claims, and when he began speaking his voice was steady and grounded in authority.

I could only judge his delivery by his voice. Johnny and I were tucked away on chairs on the landing, which led off of the back of the room. Although we kept the door ajar so that we could hear, we could not see beyond the gentlemen standing in front of the door in the crowded room. I felt trapped behind a wall of men that separated me from the main event.

Luckily Reverend Conybeare's public speaking voice penetrated even to us. "I am highly gratified," he began, "in being able to lay before the Society an account of an almost perfect skeleton of Plesiosaurus, a new fossil genus, which, from the consideration of several fragments found only in a disjointed state, I felt myself authorised to propound in the year 1821. It is through the kind liberality of its possessor, the Duke of Buckingham, that this new specimen has been placed for a time at the disposal of my friend Professor Buckland for the purpose of scientific investigation. The magnificent specimen recently discovered at Lyme has confirmed the justice of my former conclusions in every essential point connected with the organisation of the skeleton."

While the men were warmed by two coal fires and the collective bodily heat of sixty souls, Johnny and I sat frozen on the landing. I pulled my woollen cloak close about me, but I knew sitting back there was doing my weakened chest no good. Still, I could not leave at such an important moment.

Reverend Conybeare immediately addressed the plesiosaurus' most surprising feature—its extremely long neck. "The neck is fully equal in length to the body and tail united," he explained. "Surpassing in the number of its vertebrae that of the longest necked birds, even the swan, it deviates from the laws which were heretofore regarded as universal in quadrupedal animals. I mention this circumstance thus early, as forming the most prominent and interesting feature of the recent discovery, and that which in effect renders this animal one of the most curious and important additions which geology has yet made to comparative anatomy."

He then went on to describe the beast in detail. By this point I was stifling coughs, and Johnny went down to the kitchen to fetch me some wine. He must have liked what he saw down there better than what he could hear on the landing, for after handing me a glass of claret he disappeared down the back staircase again, probably to sit by the fire and practise flirting with the serving girls brought in for the evening.

Reverend Conybeare delineated the head and the vertebrae, dwelling for a time on the number in different sorts of animals, just as Monsieur Cuvier had done in his criticism of Mary. Indeed, he mentioned Cuvier in passing a few times; the great anatomist's influence was emphasised throughout the talk. No wonder that Reverend Conybeare had been so horrified by Cuvier's response to Mary's letter. However, whatever its impossible anatomy, the plesiosaurus had existed. If Conybeare believed in the creature, he must believe in what Mary found too, and the best way to convince Cuvier was to support her. It seemed obvious to me.

It didn't to him, however. Indeed, he did just the opposite. In the middle of a description of the plesiosaurus' paddles, Reverend Conybeare added, "I must acknowledge that originally I wrongly depicted the edges of the paddles as being formed of rounded bones, when they are not. However, when the first specimen was found in 1821, the bones in question were loose, and had been subsequently glued into their present situation, in consequence of a conjecture of the proprietor."

It took me a moment to realise he was referring to Mary as proprietor, and suggesting she had made mistakes in putting together the bones of the first plesiosaurus. Reverend Conybeare only bothered to refer to her—still unnamed—when there was criticism to lay at her feet. "How ungentlemanly!" I muttered, more loudly than I had intended, for a number of the row of heads in front of me shifted and turned, as if trying to locate the source of this outburst.

I shrank back in my seat, then listened numbly as Reverend Conybeare compared the plesiosaurus to a turtle without its shell and speculated on its awkwardness both on land and in the sea. "May it not therefore be concluded that it swam upon or near the surface, arching back its long neck like the swan, and occasionally darting it down at the fish which happened to float within its reach? It may perhaps have lurked in shoal water along the coast, concealed among the sea-weed and, raising its nostrils to a level with the surface from a considerable depth, may have found a secure retreat from the assaults of dangerous enemies."

He finished with a strategic flourish I suspected he'd thought up during the earlier part of the meeting. "I cannot but congratulate the scientific public that the discovery of this animal has been made at the very moment when the illustrious Cuvier is engaged in, and on the eve of publishing, his researches on the fossil ovipara: from him the subject will derive all that lucid order which henever has yet failed to introduce into the most obscure and intricate departments of comparative anatomy. Thank you."

In so saying, Reverend Conybeare linked himself favourably with Baron Cuvier, so that whatever criticism arose from the Frenchman would not seem to be directed at him. I did not join in with the clapping. My chest had become so heavy that I was having difficulty breathing.

An animated discussion began, of which I did not follow every point, for I was feeling dizzy. However, I did hear Mr Buckland at last clear his throat. "I should just like to express my thanks to Miss Anning," he said, "who discovered and extracted this magnificent specimen. It is a shame it did not arrive in time for this most illustrious and enlightening talk by Reverend Conybeare, but once it is installed here, Members and friends are welcome to inspect it. You will be amazed and delighted by this ground-breaking discovery."

That is all she will get, I thought: a scrap of thanks crowded out by far more talk of glory for beast and man. Her name will never be recorded in scientific journals or books, but will be forgotten. So be it. A woman's life is always a compromise.

I did not have to listen any longer. Instead, I fainted.

思考题

1. In what ways is Mary Anning not just a fossil hunter but a scientist with expertise in paleontology?
2. Why is Elizabeth Philpot so eager to see the new geological find by Mary after

several years of severing with her?

3. Why should Elizabeth volunteer to defend Mary when Cuvier claims that she might have jumbled the fossils of two creatures to make up a new species?

4. Have women scientists like Mary Anning and Elizabeth Philpot been given due respect and recognition in the Victorian period for their geological discoveries? Why are women denied the right to cross the threshold of the Geological Society? How could Buckland refuse to record Elizabeth's request to defend Mary in the Geological Society's minutes even though he has made a name for his studies on the fossils found by Mary and has received tremendous help from her while making field studies on the beach of Lyme Regis?

5. How do the ordinary people in the story respond to the discovery of fossils? What lessons has Elizabeth taught her nephew Johnny on geology especially as far as the shape and age of the earth are concerned?

6. Can you name some women scientists in China whose contributions have not been recognized when alive?

第三节　补充阅读《石灰岩赞》

阅读奥登(Wystan Hugh Auden, 1907—1973)的诗歌《石灰岩赞》("In Praise of Limestone", 1948),思考它与地质科学的关系,特别是奥登眼中的人类城市与生命的进化和地质历史的关系。

In Praise of Limestone[①]

W. H. Auden

If it form the one landscape that we, the inconstant ones,
Are consistently homesick for, this is chiefly
Because it dissolves in water. Mark these rounded slopes
With their surface fragrance of thyme and, beneath,

---

① AUDEN W H. "In Praise Of Limestone"[Z/OL]. [2023-07-25]. https://allpoetry.com/In-Praise-Of-Limestone.

第一章　文学与地质学（Literature and Geology）

A secret system of caves and conduits; hear the springs
That spurt out everywhere with a chuckle,
Each filling a private pool for its fish and carving
Its own little ravine whose cliffs entertain
The butterfly and the lizard; examine this region
Of short distances and definite places:
What could be more like Mother or a fitter background
For her son, the flirtatious male who lounges
Against a rock in the sunlight, never doubting
That for all his faults he is loved; whose works are but
Extensions of his power to charm? From weathered outcrop
To hill-top temple, from appearing waters to
Conspicuous fountains, from a wild to a formal vineyard,
Are ingenious but short steps that a child's wish
To receive more attention than his brothers, whether
By pleasing or teasing, can easily take.

Watch, then, the band of rivals as they climb up and down
Their steep stone gennels in twos and threes, at times
Arm in arm, but never, thank God, in step; or engaged
On the shady side of a square at midday in
Voluble discourse, knowing each other too well to think
There are any important secrets, unable
To conceive a god whose temper-tantrums are moral
And not to be pacified by a clever line
Or a good lay: for accustomed to a stone that responds,
They have never had to veil their faces in awe
Of a crater whose blazing fury could not be fixed;
Adjusted to the local needs of valleys
Where everything can be touched or reached by walking,

Their eyes have never looked into infinite space
Through the lattice-work of a nomad's comb; born lucky,
Their legs have never encountered the fungi
And insects of the jungle, the monstrous forms and lives
With which we have nothing, we like to hope, in common.
So, when one of them goes to the bad, the way his mind works
Remains incomprehensible: to become a pimp
Or deal in fake jewellery or ruin a fine tenor voice
For effects that bring down the house, could happen to all
But the best and the worst of us...

That is why, I suppose,
The best and worst never stayed here long but sought
Immoderate soils where the beauty was not so external,
The light less public and the meaning of life
Something more than a mad camp. "Come!" cried the granite wastes,
"How evasive is your humour, how accidental
Your kindest kiss, how permanent is death." (Saints-to-be
Slipped away sighing.) "Come!" purred the clays and gravels,
"On our plains there is room for armies to drill; rivers
Wait to be tamed and slaves to construct you a tomb
In the grand manner: soft as the earth is mankind and both
Need to be altered." (Intendant Caesars rose and
Left, slamming the door.) But the really reckless were fetched
By an older colder voice, the oceanic whisper:
"I am the solitude that asks and promises nothing;
That is how I shall set you free. There is no love;
There are only the various envies, all of them sad."

They were right, my dear, all those voices were right

And still are; this land is not the sweet home that it looks,

Nor its peace the historical calm of a site

Where something was settled once and for all: A back ward

And dilapidated province, connected

To the big busy world by a tunnel, with a certain

Seedy appeal, is that all it is now? Not quite:

It has a worldy duty which in spite of itself

It does not neglect, but calls into question

All the Great Powers assume; it disturbs our rights. The poet,

Admired for his earnest habit of calling

The sun the sun, his mind Puzzle, is made uneasy

By these marble statues which so obviously doubt

His antimythological myth; and these gamins,

Pursuing the scientist down the tiled colonnade

With such lively offers, rebuke his concern for Nature's

Remotest aspects: I, too, am reproached, for what

And how much you know. Not to lose time, not to get caught,

Not to be left behind, not, please! to resemble

The beasts who repeat themselves, or a thing like water

Or stone whose conduct can be predicted, these

Are our common prayer, whose greatest comfort is music

Which can be made anywhere, is invisible,

And does not smell. In so far as we have to look forward

To death as a fact, no doubt we are right: But if

Sins can be forgiven, if bodies rise from the dead,

These modifications of matter into

Innocent athletes and gesticulating fountains,

Made solely for pleasure, make a further point:

The blessed will not care what angle they are regarded from,

Having nothing to hide. Dear, I know nothing of

Either, but when I try to imagine a faultless love
Or the life to come, what I hear is the murmur
Of underground streams, what I see is a limestone landscape.

May 1948

第二章

文学与化学(Literature and Chemistry)

第一节　化学的文学表征

背景知识

化学(chemistry)是自然科学的一个分支。从远古时代起,人类便使用化学手段来提高生产工艺和技能。从青铜时代的铁匠到古埃及的祭祀,从中国的方士到波斯的炼金术士,人类积累了很多提炼、蒸馏、归类物质的经验。因而化学在人类史上从未缺席过,但直到17世纪才成为一门独立的学科。科学家自此开始认识到,无论在自然界,还是日常生活中,许多物质的变化都是化学反应。另外,化学也是物质具有各种不同特性的原因。因此,化学研究的对象就是物质的特性和表现,主要目的就是探索物质的构成、结构、属性、形态变化以及该变化过程中伴随的能量变化[①]。于是,研究各种物质的组成,它们之间的反应,以及对这些反应的应用是这门学科的主要任务[②]。

化学的发展历史一般可划分为四个时期。第一个时期是上古时代工艺化学时期,这时的人类从生产和生活的实际经验中得到直观的启示,并通过化学手段来制陶、冶金、酿造和染色。这应该说是化学知识的萌芽时期[③]。古代人类在挖坑煮食的过程中,观察到火与泥土相接触后的变化,被烧过的土质地变硬,遇水不化,生成了某种复杂的硅酸盐,这是人类最早接触到的硅酸盐化学。当然,从看到这些变化到慢慢懂得烧制砖、瓦、陶器,经历了漫长的时间。远古人类从使用石器到开始掌握金属工具又经历了大约几十万年岁月。根据考古发现,人类对金属的加工和使用开始于新石器时代晚期。这个时期,人们在不断改进石器和寻找、开采石料的过程中偶然发现了夹杂在铜矿石中的自然铜——红铜。经过剥离和捶打,发现红铜有很好的延展性。由于当时烧制陶器的技术已经相当成熟,这就有可能对天然铜加热锻打以至熔铸,并逐渐过渡到用矿石来冶炼铜及其他金属。

---

① BROWN T L. Chemistry: the central science[M]. 13th ed. London: Pearson, 2015: 2.
② LOWE D B. The chemistry book[M]. New York: Sterling Publishing, 2016: 1.
③ 赵匡华. 化学通史[M]. 北京: 高等教育出版社, 1990: 3.

酒、醋、酱的酿造也是古代主要的化学产品。埃及人大约在公元前三千年前开始有意识地酿造麦酒。而在我国大约四千年前的龙山文化遗址中,发现了大量酒器,说明那时的人们已经会酿酒①。可以想象,在原始社会开始农业生产后,收获的粮食若没有很好的粮仓来存储,雨淋后会产生部分发芽的情况,这时麦芽糖就生成了。发芽的粮食经过蒸煮并放置一段时间,就会慢慢产生出酒来。而且谷物受潮后,发芽与发霉经常会同时发生,发霉的谷物中同时含有能使淀粉水解的糖化酵素和能分泌出酒化酵素的酵母菌,经过水浸后也会自然发酵成酒②。使用含有大量微生物及其酶的发酵剂来酿酒,是古代生物化学的一项重大成就。

化学发展的第二个时期是中古时代的炼丹术、炼金术与医药化学时期,也包括上古工艺化学的延续③。这时人类社会的生产力比远古时期有了大幅的提高,物质生活的改善和商品经济的出现使得人们对"发财致富"和"长生不老"的追求开始萌芽。金丹术成为封建帝王、贵族追求骄奢淫逸,梦想长生不死的重要手段。金丹术士可以说是最早的化学实验工作者,他们通过当时可能进行的各种化学实验,试图通过烧铅炼汞,变化五金八石,制取神丹妙药。虽然常常以失败告终,但他们为后世化学的发展积累了相当丰富的经验,也制备了很多有价值的化学药剂和合金。中国的金丹术流行了1000多年,从公元前175年一直持续到公元1000年左右。中国的方士们炼制神丹妙药、烧炼黄白的一些指导思想可以概括为以下三个方面:(1) 用金石炼制出的丹药可能使人长生不死;(2) 对物质变化规律的认识;(3) 对物质从低级到高级演进的见解以及金丹术的设计。中国金丹术为后世留下了丰富的化学遗产,但可惜的是,经过两千年的反复实践,它并没有像在欧洲那样汲取失败的教训,最终走向近代化学,而是陷入了神秘主义的泥沼④。

西方的炼金术实践起源于公元前400多年古希腊的亚历山大里亚(Alexandria),直到公元7世纪左右才随着伊斯兰教的入侵被阿拉伯金丹术取代。阿拉伯金丹术既继承了古希腊的炼金术,认为物质基本概念就是冷、热、干、湿四要素,也融入了中国金丹术的一些理念⑤。公元8世纪之后的500年里,最伟大的炼金术士都来自伊斯兰世界。直到公元12世纪,随着伊斯兰势力的衰弱,阿拉伯金丹术的手稿被译成拉丁语,欧洲的炼金术开始了。之后,炼金术在欧洲实践了500年,成为现代化学的序章⑥。在这500年间,炼金术士们学会了如何将手上的物质进行提炼、蒸馏和归类,在不知不觉中为现代化学打下了基础。大约在17世纪,在炼金术暮光之中,现代化学的太阳开始冉冉上升。随着新时代的自然科学家们开始掌

---

① 张运明. 化学·社会·生活[M]. 南宁:广西科学技术出版社,2002:1-2.
② 赵匡华. 化学通史[M]. 北京:高等教育出版社,1990:18-19.
③ 同②3.
④ 同②34.
⑤ 同②47.
⑥ HUDSON J. The history of chemistry[M]. New York:The Macmillan Press Ltd., 1992:16.

第二章 文学与化学（Literature and Chemistry）

握了能系统进行的、可重复的实验方法后，一个又一个新发现不断刷新了人们的认知。18世纪的科学发现，使得之前几千年所有的"术"黯淡无光，而19世纪的发现更远超于18世纪[①]。

化学在第三个发展时期，即近代发展时期，被确立为一门独立的学科[②]。一般认为，该时期始于拉瓦锡燃烧氧学说的确立以及近代化学元素论的奠定。1770年到1790年是化学经历最彻底变革的20年。在1770年之前，几乎所有的化学家都认为燃素说是科学界的统一法则，即使有些事实与燃素说不相符，将之进行一些修正和完善即可。然而到了1790年，不仅大部分化学家都接受了氧气燃烧理论，而且化学术语的命名法也发生了改变，现代元素的概念终于确立起来。这一切主要都归功于拉瓦锡（Antoine Laurent Lavoisier, 1743—1794）[③]。他提出"元素"的定义，命名了氧与氢，并且预测了硅元素的存在。经过努力，他使得化学研究由定性转为定量，并使用定量分析的方法，验证了质量守恒定律。他创立了氧化学说，用以解释燃烧现象，指出动物的呼吸本质上是一个缓慢氧化的过程。拉瓦锡坚信元素物质的存在，并意识到辨明化学元素对化学研究的重大意义，还为此设计了分解与合成的科学实验方法。当然，由于实验条件的限制和认识上的局限，拉瓦锡对化学元素的认识仍有模糊和错误的地方。但从拉瓦锡开始，建立在燃素学说基础上的化学从此被纠正过来，走上正确航向；近代化学元素学说的奠立，明确了化学的任务，使化学领域发生一场真正的革命[④]。

拉瓦锡在奠定了化学元素说时，未专门探讨原子论问题。与他同时代的爱尔兰化学家希金斯（William Higgins, 1763—1825）在《燃素论与反燃素论观点的比较》（*A Comparative View of the Phlogistic and Antiphlogistic Theories*, 1789）一书中阐述了原子概念，指出各种元素的终极粒子各具有一定的重量，在变成化合物时仍保持不变。但他未及时用分析实验来确证此设想，更未计划求出各原子的相对质量[⑤]。19世纪初，道尔顿（John Dalton, 1766—1844）将元素说与原子论统一起来，形成有机的整体，使化学成为一门真正独立的学科[⑥]。

化学发展的第四个时期是随着物理学上电子和辐射的两大发现开始的。20世纪初，物理学和化学同时迈入现代发展时期[⑦]。尤其当原子结构理论与量子化学打开微观世界的大门时，化学研究从宏观领域进入了微观领域。这一时期，化学研究主要体现在五个方面：（1）原子结构、分子结构和晶体结构的研究；（2）原子核结构和核内微粒运动规律的研究；（3）化学键本质研究——由于化学变化是以原子为不变单位的分子变化，但原子结构研究

---

① LOWE D B. The chemistry book[M]. New York: Sterling Publishing, 2016: 1-2.
② 赵匡华. 化学通史[M]. 北京:高等教育出版社,1990:4.
③ HUDSON J. The history of chemistry[M]. New York: The Macmillan Press Ltd., 1992: 61.
④ 同②85.
⑤ 同②99.
⑥ 同③19.
⑦ 同②4.

尚未接触到化学反应,要想掌握化学变化的规律性,就需要以原子结构为基础,进而认识到分子结构及其质变运动的规律,化学键本质的研究因而成了该时期最为重要的内容;(4) 合成化学及其机理的研究;(5) 化学分析测试技术和应用①。这些方向说明现代化学从物质的宏观研究过渡到微观研究,建立了微观与宏观相结合的化学理论体系。现代化学在纵向发展的同时,也与其他学科横向交叉发展。热力学、电化学、有机化学、核化学、天然产物化学、胶体化学等分支的兴起和发展使得化学这棵大树枝叶繁茂,形成一个大家庭。如今,现代社会生产生活的各方面都离不开化学学科的发展和应用,化学与现代人的生活也息息相关。

化学和文学虽然分属两个完全不同的学科,它们之间却有着较紧密的关系,且这种关系与化学学科的发展史以及人们对之的认知过程交织在一起②。英国文艺复兴时期的剧作家马洛(Christopher Marlowe, 1564—1593)、莎士比亚和琼生(Ben Jonson, 1572—1637)③,17 世纪英国资产阶级革命时期的诗人弥尔顿(John Milton, 1608—1674)④和邓恩(John Donne, 1572—1631)⑤、革命后期以及新古典主义时期的诗人德莱顿(John Dryden, 1631—1700)和蒲柏(Alexander Pope, 1688—1744),18 世纪的小说家笛福(Daniel Defoe, 1660—1731)和斯威夫特(Jonathan Swift, 1667—1745)等⑥,都在各自作品中或多或少地探讨了所在时代的化学研究方面的发现或成果。18 世纪末 19 世纪初,随着现代化学之父拉瓦锡燃烧理论和元素概念的提出,化学进入了快速发展期⑦。它不仅成为自然科学领域的一门前沿学科,而且也成为社会生活的一个重要话题,一些文人学者开始关注并讨论化学对社会生活的影响⑧。在 19 世纪,化学是实验科学的典型代表。想要描绘当代科学发展的作家们也自然而然地把创作的重心转移到化学上来。英国化学家、诗人亨弗莱·戴维(Humphrey Davy, 1778—1829)是将拉瓦锡的新化学与文学联系起来的第一人。作为好友,他甚至用自己的实验和作品影响了浪漫主义诗人柯勒律治(Samuel Taylor Coleridge, 1772—1834)、华兹华斯等人⑨。在戴维的时代,

---

① 邢润川. 关于化学史的分期[J]. 科学技术与辩证法, 1990(5): 32.
② 关于文学与化学科学的关系, 参见 LABINGER J. Chemistry[C]//CLARKE B, ROSSINI M. The Routledge companion to literature and science. London: Routledge, 2011: 51 - 62.
③ SIEDLECKI B. Two scientific manifestos: discourses on science in Jonson's the alchemist and Marlowe's doctor Faustus [D]. Edmonton: The University of Alberta, 1985: 104. 另参见 Shakespeare through the eyes of a chemist [Z/OL]. https://nextmovesoftware.com/blog/2013/10/28/shakespeare-through-the-eyes-of-a-chemist/.
④ MORSE K. Milton's ideas of science as shown in "Paradise Lost"[J]. The scientific monthly, 1920 (2): 150 - 156.
⑤ Contemporary science in John Donne's poetry[Z/OL]. https://www.englishliterature.info/2021/06/science-in-john-donnes-poetry.html.
⑥ JONES R F. Science and criticism in the neo-classical age of English literature[J]. Journal of the history of ideas, 1940(4): 381 - 412.
⑦ 不列颠百科全书公司. 不列颠简明百科全书(英文版)[M]. 上海: 上海外语教育出版社, 2008: 939.
⑧ SHARROCK R. The chemist and the poet: sir Humphrey Davy and the preface to *Lyrical Ballads*[J]. Notes and records of the royal society of London, 1962(17): 76.
⑨ KNIGHT D M. The physical sciences and the romantic movement[J]. History of science, 1970(9): 54 - 75.

第二章 文学与化学(Literature and Chemistry)

文学与科学的分界线还不是那么清晰。像他的诗人好友一样,戴维本人也经常写诗,涉及自然、想象和崇高理想等主题,同时记录他的化学实验过程和感受。他的讲座和专著甚至对《弗兰肯斯坦》(*Frankenstein*, 1818)的创作产生了重要影响。他的跨界和巨大影响力,使得化学不再是神秘的"法术"。虽然在柯勒律治等伟大的诗人看来,与严肃的诗歌艺术相比,化学只是令人放松的消遣①,但文学作品表征的化学已不同于"炼金术",而逐渐演变成一门严肃的学科。

19世纪早期,英国之外与化学有关的文学作品中最引人注目就是歌德(Johann Wolfgang von Goethe, 1749—1832)的《亲合力》(*Elective Affinities*, 1809)了。在这部小说里,歌德用化学反应来比喻人际关系。该作品的灵感源自瑞典化学家贝格曼(Torbern Bergman, 1735—1784)的同名著作《亲合力》所揭示的化学规律:自然界中的某些物质和元素喜欢结合在一起,而另外一些物质和元素则会互相排斥②。在某些化学反应中,只要一个催化剂,本来结合紧密的两种元素就会因为另外两种元素的加入而分离,并分别与另外两种元素相结合,产生"亲合力"。用公式表示就是:

$$A-B+C-D \rightarrow A-D+B-C$$

歌德借用化学亲合力的公式描写了小说中四位主人公之间错综复杂的关系。拥有一座大庄园的男爵爱德华年轻时与夏洛蒂相爱,但遭到父母反对,未能成婚。多年后,原配妻子去世,他才得以与夏洛蒂结合。婚后他们虽然和睦相处,但内心已无法燃起年轻时炽烈的情感。婚后不久,爱德华邀请朋友奥东上尉来庄园小住,夏洛蒂也把养女奥蒂利请到家里来度假。四人按照物质组合的"亲合力"原理玩起了游戏,结果夏洛蒂爱上了奥东,而爱德华爱上了奥蒂利。然而现实并不按他们希望的那样发展,游戏酿成了悲剧③。

19世纪文学对化学的兴趣经久不衰。欧美作家中创作主题带有一定化学特征的有巴尔扎克、福楼拜(Gustave Flaubert, 1821—1880)、霍桑(Nathaniel Hawthorne, 1804—1864)、艾伦·坡(Edgar Allan Poe, 1809—1849)、狄更斯、屠格涅夫(Ivan Turgenev, 1818—1883)和托尔斯泰(Leo Tolstoy, 1828—1910)等④。霍桑的短篇小说《胎记》("The Birth-Mark", 1846)描绘了一个对科学痴迷成瘾的主人公艾尔默(Aylmer)。他对于科学的执着,让他对

---

① JONES R F. Science and criticism in the neo-classical age of English literature[J]. Journal of the history of ideas, 1940(4): 60.

② 《文学与化学:亲合力》(*Literature and Chemistry: Elective Affinities*, 2013)也借用了贝格曼化学著作《亲合力》的标题,并在序言中结合歌德的小说《亲合力》,探讨了19世纪初文学与化学的亲密关系。参见 HAGEN M, SKAGEN M V. Literature and chemistry: effective affinities[M]. Nordre Ringgade: Aarhus University Press, 2013: 17.

③ GOTHE J W V. Elective affinities[M]. Washington, D.C.: Henry Regnery, 1963: 1-305.

④ SCHUMMER J. Historical roots of the "mad scientist": chemists in nineteenth-century literature[J]. Ambix, 2006(2): 99-127. 另参见 VARVOGLI A, VARVOGLIS A. Chemists as characters and as authors in literature[J]. The chemical intelligencer, 1995(2): 43-46, 55. 另参见 SCHATZBERG W, WAITE R A, JOHNSON J K. The relations of literature and science: an annotated bibliography of scholarship, 1880-1980[M]. New York: Modern Language Association, 1987: 1-458.

妻子有着严格的要求。他认为，妻子脸上的胎记破坏了她的美感，于是就想尽一切办法来除掉才甘心，即便是搭上妻子的性命也在所不惜。科学实验成了他清除妻子脸上胎记这一大自然的象征的手段①。霍桑对于这种盲目追求科学知识的危险倾向提出严重警告。借助该短篇小说，霍桑表达了对人与自然、人与科学之间关系的高度关注，同时也暗示了文学作品中科学主题由炼金术向化学的转变。虽然这个短篇未把化学当成新科学并残留炼金术的影子，但无论如何，化学在19世纪的文学作品中占有一席之地。即便该时期的作家对化学学科的理论发展和发现缺乏深入思考，他们已感知到现代化学的广阔前景，并对它表达了浓厚的兴趣。

到了20世纪初，情况发生了变化。20世纪的上半叶是物理学和生物学飞速发展的时代，人们的目光不断被新兴的概念吸引，如"相对论""量子""DNA""遗传密码"等。跟这些学科相比，化学的发展显得相当局限，人们认为它仅仅是一门"合成"技术，缺乏对于宏大主题的深度思考②。当然，化学并没有从20世纪的文学作品中消失，但跟数学、物理、生物等学科相比，它出现的身影相对较少。在人们眼中，现代化学成了一门居于物理和生物之间的，无法产生大师级人物的蹩脚学科③。虽然"化学改变生活"的口号很诱人，但20世纪的很多化学发现却带来了让人意料不到的可怕后果，文学作品中甚至出现了"化学恐惧症"（chemophobia）主题。提到该主题，人们最先想到的可能就是侦探小说或推理小说中的情节，在这类小说里化学总是隐晦又巧妙的下毒手段的来源。阿加莎·克里斯蒂（Agatha Christie，1890—1976）的小说中就有这样的例子：一系列超自然现象导致的离奇死亡事件实际上是铊中毒的结果，或者某个犯罪现场的神秘气氛其实是由磷化物毒药造成的④。侦探小说中对化学有着最详尽的描述无疑当属塞耶斯（Dorothy L Sayers，1893—1957）和尤斯塔斯（Eustace Robert Barton，1854—1943）合著的《涉案文件》（The Documents in the Case，1930）了。小说中一名男子因误食大量有毒菌类中毒而死，死状可怖，尸体嘴角挂着诡异的笑，身旁还放着一盘毒蘑菇。而这表面上看来是误食毒菌造成的死亡，其实是因为凶手将人工合成的毒蕈碱加入无毒的食物中⑤。最后，凶手的杀人手段因化学发现而暴露：剩余蘑菇中的毒素因为是人工合成而不具有旋光性，而自然毒物是有旋光性的。这部小说还曝光了毒蕈碱的合成路径和化学配方，并提到了分子的旋光性、手征性等化学概念，尽管存有一定错误，

---

① HAWTHORNE N. The birth-mark[C]//WAGGONER H H. Nathaniel Hawthorne: selected tales and sketches. 3rd ed. New York: Holt, Rinehart and Winston, 1970: 264-281.
② BALL P. Chemistry and power in recent American fiction[C]//SCHUMMER J. The public image of chemistry. Hackensack: World Scientific, 2007: 98.
③ LASZLO P. On the self-image of chemists, 1950-2000[C]//SCHUMMER J. The public image of chemistry. Hackensack: World Scientific, 2007: 335.
④ CHRISTIE A. Poirot loses a client[M]. New York: Dodd Mead and Co., 1962.
⑤ SAYERS D L, EUSTACE R. The documents in the case[M]. New York: Harper Paper Backs, 1995.

第二章 文学与化学（Literature and Chemistry）

但显得十分专业。20世纪后期，随着冷硬派和警察程序派侦探小说的流行，化学逐渐退居为法医学的助力，甚至消失不见。

化学在文学作品中的形象变得越来越负面，一个重要原因就是一战期间的毒气战让人谈化学而色变。德国化学家哈伯（Fritz Haber, 1868—1934）是毒气的主要研制者，备受争议，出现在很多作品中，最值得注意的就是托尼·哈里森（Tony Harrison, 1937— ）的《方轮》（*Square Rounds*, 1992）。该作品以哈伯（Haber）为主人公，揭示了很多化学实验的细节，但并未站在道德制高点上反化学。通过对比毒气战与枪弹，哈里森探讨了何种武器更加反人类、更为残忍，同时也强调了化学对社会生活的积极贡献。在作品中，哈里森用了如下一首诗歌来探讨化学的作用：

> Nitrogen fixation giving ammonia NH3
> Makes fertilizers, yes, but also TNT.
> Nitrogen as nitrates could make all Europe green
> But it blasts in even blacker as tri-ni-tro-to-lu-ene.
> The nitrogen you brought from way up high
> Now blows the men you saved into the sky.
> Those nitrates you produced for fertilizer
> Now serve the warlike purpose of the Kaiser.[①]

在介绍化学的"善"与"恶"的同时，哈里森将哈伯一生的功与过浓缩在短短几行诗句里。化学的"双刃剑"作用也成了20世纪后期文学作品中常见的主题。各种讨论环境恶化、健康问题甚至全球性灾难的警示性故事，都将矛头指向了化学。

20世纪末欧美文坛出现了一些以世界末日为主题的小说。在这些作品中，最为人熟知且与化学有关的就是美国作家冯尼古特（Kurt Vonnegut, 1922—2007）的《猫的摇篮》（*Cat's Cradle*, 1963）了。小说主人公是一位参与制造原子弹的物理学家，对现实生活和人类命运漠不关心。他研制了一种叫作"冰-9"（ice-nine）的水同位素，它能在常温下让水分子瞬间凝固。他的三个子女同样孤僻，在其去世后分别得到一部分冰-9物质。为了换取高位，子女中的一个将冰-9献给了加勒比海岛国的一位统治者。表面上该国统治者和宗教领袖势不两立，实际上却互相利用，目的就是要使社会处于巨大恐怖之中。他们设计了一起飞行表演事故，使得宫殿"意外"坠海，散落的冰-9造成了世界的毁灭[②]。另一部广为人知的小说是《赢利》（*Gain*, 1998），作者是普利策奖得主理查德·鲍尔斯（Richard Powers, 1957— ）。

---

① HARRISON T. Square rounds[M]. London: Faber and Faber, 1992.
② VONNEGUT K. Cat's cradle[M]. New York: Holt, Rinehart & Winston, 1963.

该作品运用了平行叙事策略（contrapuntal narrative strategy）将一个化工企业的发展史和一个死于卵巢癌的女人的故事交织在一起。第一条线索沿"劳拉·博迪患癌——化疗——去世"铺开，节奏明快逼真。小说没有将劳拉之死归因于克莱尔集团造成的污染，而是以近乎残忍的笔触描写她被癌症步步紧逼，迅速走向死亡。第二条线索用大量亦真亦假的"史料"，探寻虚构的化工企业克莱尔公司的发展史。小说暗示化学合成品既可能是导致癌症的有毒废料的污染源，也可能是治愈癌症药物的来源①。

20世纪后期，一些化学家投身文学创作，冲淡了化学恐惧症带来的阴影。犹太裔意大利化学家、小说家普里莫·莱维（Primo Levi，1919—1987）是纳粹大屠杀的幸存者，曾被关押至奥斯维辛集中营11个月。他的自传体短篇小说集《元素周期表》（*The Periodic Table*，1975）将化学和集中营的经历巧妙地结合在一起，每一个小故事的灵感都来自一种化学元素②。20世纪后期还有两位作家也是化学家出身，他们是罗德·霍夫曼（Roald Hoffmann，1937— ）和卡尔·杰拉西（Carl Djerassi，1923—2015）。霍夫曼曾于1981年获诺贝尔化学奖。他在一本探讨科学与犹太传统关系的书里，追溯了手征性的起源；在另一本书中，他阐述了化学人工合成的积极意义，强调其创造性而非人为性③。杰拉西将他的小说和戏剧称为"科学小说"（science-in-fiction）④，既关注科学家的工作和生活方式，又关注科学本身。霍夫曼和杰拉西还合作过一部戏剧《氧》，剧本假设诺贝尔基金会决定创立一个"追认诺贝尔奖"，以表彰一百年前那些在诺贝尔奖设立之前的伟大发现，并最终决定表彰氧气的发现者。现代化学之父拉瓦锡、普利斯特利（Joseph Priestley，1733—1804）和舍勒（Carl Wilhelm Scheele，1742—1786）都是被提名者。剧中关于优先权和伦理问题的讨论十分有趣又引人深思。正如剧中对话所述，"没有氧气的发现就不会有化学革命，现代化学就不会存在"⑤。这类作品的出现终于让化学在迈向21世纪时有望被文学作品当作一个严肃的主题来讨论，在一定程度上挽回了化学的声望。

文献传真

阅读《文学中的化学：文学反应》，并思考文末问答题。本文选自2008年11月27日的《化学世界》⑥。

---

① POWERS R. Gain[M]. New York：Farrar, Straus and Giroux，1998.
② LEVI P. The periodic table[M]. New York：Schocken Books，1984.
③ HOFFMANN R. The same and not the same[M]. New York：Columbia University Press，1995.
④ DJERASSI C. NO[M]. Athens：University of Georgia Press，1998：ix.
⑤ DJERASSI C, HOFFMANN R. Oxygen[M]. Weinheim：Wiley-VCH Verlag，2001：28.
⑥ BALL P. Chemistry in fiction：literary reactions[J]. Chemistry World，2008(12)：46-49.

第二章 文学与化学(Literature and Chemistry)

Chemistry in Fiction: Literary Reactions

Philip Ball

Chemistry makes occasional appearances in fiction but rarely takes centre stage. Philip Ball unearths chemistry's fictional roles.

C. P. Snow's 1959 Rede lectures on the breakdown of communication between 'the two cultures' of science and the humanities now sound in many ways like the gripes of another era. While science may have been disdained by the literary giants of Snow's time—and even that is not universally true—today it is seized avidly by many novelists as a source of metaphor and inspiration. Ian McEwan weaves cosmology into *The Child in Time*, Martin Amis reverses time in *Time's Arrow*, Jeanette Winterson incorporates grand unified theories into Gut Symmetries, and Margaret Atwood portrays a biotechnological dystopia in *Oryx and Crake*.

But who writes about chemistry in novels? True, you can find ample passing references in science fiction, from H. G. Wells' toxic compounds of argon concocted by Martians in *War of the Worlds* to Neil Stephenson's diamondoid nanotechnology in *The Diamond Age*. But these are not conceptual elements of the plot.[①] Does chemistry have anything to offer the modern writer beyond a means of bumping off characters in crime thrillers?

Chemical Marriages

Discussions of chemistry in fiction invariably begin with Johann Wolfgang von Goethe's 1809 novel *Elective Affinities*, and with good reason: seldom has a chemical metaphor been made more explicit. The story centres on four characters. Eduard and Charlotte languish in an affluent but stultifying marriage of convenience on a country estate, and invite to live with them 'the Captain', a childhood friend of Eduard's, and Ottilie, a beautiful young woman who is the orphaned daughter of Charlotte's dead friend. You don't need to be clairvoyant to anticipate what happens: it is a kind of human double displacement reaction, as Eduard falls in love with Ottilie while the

---

① Diamondoids are cage-like, ultra stable, saturated ringed hydrocarbons, which have a diamond-like structure consisting of a number of six-member carbon rings fused together. Adamantane is the cage compound prototype and the simplest diamondoid molecule.

Captain develops a relationship with Charlotte.

The 'affinities' of the title refer to the pre-eminent theory of the time for chemical reactivity, which was ascribed to precise but differing degrees of affinity between the elements. Eighteenth century chemists drew up 'affinity tables' summarising what was known about the laws of chemical composition. Affinity was often imagined as a kind of chemical force akin to Newtonian gravitation, giving chemistry the appearance of a unified and exact science. Goethe, whose own scientific interests are widely known, made laborious use of this metaphor.

It has been debated whether Goethe in fact intended all this as mere metaphor, or whether he thought there really were fateful forces that governed the relationships between people. Certainly the sociologist Max Weber, who read Goethe's work, used the term 'elective affinity' in the early twentieth century to describe specific attractions that he perceived in social phenomena, for example between Protestantism and capitalism.

But Goethe's use of chemical analogies in literature wasn't as new as is sometimes implied, since alchemy had long been a source of inspiration to artists, writers and poets. It's been suggested that alchemical imagery lies at the core of several of Shakespeare's works, most notably *King Lear*, where the tribulations of the king can be seen as symbolising the transformations in alchemy that were supposed to produce the 'Red King', a substance en route to the Philosophe's Stone. Alchemical metaphors for romance were particularly common in the Elizabethan age—two of Shakespear's sonnets are based on imagery connected to the Aristotelian quartet of elements—and in some ways Goethe's tale could be regarded as updating, to the science of his day, the old notion of the chemical marriage—the unionthat was supposed to take place in the alchemical crucible between 'male' and 'female' principles to create the fictitious Stone. John Donne wrote of *Love's Alchymie*, and he draws on the sexual union of the chemical marriage in his poem *The Comparison*, written in the 1590s:

> Then like the Chymicks masculine equall fire,
> Which in the Lymbecks warme wombe doth inspire
> Into th' earths worthlesse durt a soule of gold,
> Such cherishing heat her best lov'd part doth hold.

('Lymbeck' here is the alchemist's salembic.) Donne and Shakespeare both wrote during the age of chemical philosophies'—entire world views based on alchemical theories—when it seemed natural to interpret all worldly events in chemical terms in a manner that went beyond mere metaphor.

Curiously, the alchemical quest to make gold often becomes substituted, in more recent fiction, with a quest to make diamonds—as though, with the demise of alchemical theories of metals, this instead became emblematic of chemistry's quest to surpass nature. The German writer Jean Paul provided perhaps the earliest example of the diamond-maker in his book of 1820–1822, *Der Komet Oder Nikolaus Marggraf*, and H. G. Wells' eponymous hero in *The Diamond Maker* (1894) is the stereotype of the medieval alchemist, who almost ruins himself in his obsessive quest and fails to profit from it even when it succeeds. Even Primo Levi used this trope in his short story *Order on the Cheap*.

A Faustian Legacy

Elective affinities was not the beginning of any trend; it remains an oddity, a more or less unique attempt to create modern fiction from chemical themes. If we seek chemistry in literature between then and now, we generally tend to find it used much more straightforwardly, as a bit of science that somehow serves the plot—as in, to take a random example, the art forger's chemical art in Robertson Davies' *What's Bred in the Bone* (1985). One could even say this is true of Mary Shelley's *Frankenstein*, published just a few years after Goethe's novel, where it's easy to forget that it is chemistry that brings the monster to life. 'Chemistry,' says Victor Frankenstein's mentor Dr. Waldmann of the University of Ingolstadt, ' is that branch of natural philosophy in which the greatest improvements have been and may be made. ' It is clearly implied that a form of galvanic electrochemistry, a hot topic when Mary Shelley wrote the book around 1816, is what infuses 'a spark of being into the lifeless thing'.

But there is more to the chemistry in *Frankenstein* than a bit of vogueish science. The story is basically a retelling of the Faust myth, in which a hubristic knowledge seeker unleashes powers he can't control. It was Goethe himself who gave this myth a modern face, making Faust a tragic figure rather than, in the earlier medieval tradition, a bungling charlatan. And Faust always uses what is perceived as the most powerful science of his time, which is why Christopher Marlowe's Faust, in his 1594 play which was again a product of the chemical philosophies, is interested in alchemy, while Shelley's is a chemist. The twentieth-century retellings of hubristic scientists, meanwhile, such as Dr. Strangelove and the faceless lab coats whose botches create B-movie monsters, make them nuclear scientists; today's Fausts and Frankensteins are biotechnologists and geneticists (think of *Jurassic Park*). For better or worse, chemistry soon disappears as the central plot device in this particular strand of science in fiction.

But there is one notable exception. Thomas Pynchon's *Gravity's Rainbow* (1973) is almost without parallel in the way it engages with the place of chemistry in the modern world. Admittedly, it's no mean feat to discover this, because Pynchon's huge novel is one of the densest, most labyrinthine and peculiar works of the late twentieth century. If you're used to a coherent plot with a beginning, middle and end, and to literary staples such as character development, you're in for a shock. The story, such as it is, is almost impossible to summarise, but revolves around the journeys of US army lieutenant Tyrone Slothrop through Europe at the end and in the aftermath of the second world war, as he stumbles over the genesis and the intended future of the German V2 technology. A more conventional and less informed writer would doubtless have bound all this up with nuclear physics and the start of the Cold War. But Pynchon instead makes the architect of rocket technology a shady, trans-national industrial-military complex centred on the German chemical cartel IG Farben, manufacturer of the notorious poison gas Zyklon B. Its ominous schemes were set in motion by a chemist named Laszlo Jamf, an intellectual descendant of August Wilhelm Hofmann, who seems to have been a specialist in organic and polymer chemistry.

Jamf is the mad scientist in his icy Dr Strangelove guise. He is said to have invented a mysterious polymer called Imipolex G, a material that seems to change its properties in response to electrical stimuli and become, wickedly, erectile:

> Under suitable stimuli, the chains grow cross-links, which stiffen the molecule and increase intermolecular attraction so that this Peculiar Polymer runs far outside the known phase diagrams, from limp rubbery amorphous to amazing perfect tessellation, hardness, brilliant transparency, high resistance to

temperature, weather, vacuum, shock of any kind.

This was to be the smart skin of a new type of rocket bomb that is almost creepily intelligent.

In *Gravity's Rainbow*, Pynchon feels no need to ensure that his readers will follow all the science. Indeed, it is arguably part of the point that they won't, making it all the more apparent that IG Farben possesses occult knowledge that gives it the power to manipulate history. Pynchon pulls this off (in my view) because he himself knows what he is talking about: he studied engineering physics at Cornell in the 1950s, and later worked at Boeing.

Chemistry for Better Living?

All this might dismay the chemist who is sick and tired of being cast as the callous enemy of public health and safety. But I don't believe that Pynchon intended any such simplistic diatribe. His target was the military-industrial complex, not the science per se. And he had the insight to see that chemistry was central here, precisely because it is such an applied science.

A rather similar picture is presented by American author Don DeLillo in his 1984 novel *White Noise*, where the life of the Gladney family in middle-class Middle America is permeated and dominated by the textures and products of modern chemistry, from pills for every imagined ailment to synthetic fabrics with cryptic names like Mylex. The story pivots around a chemical accident, an 'airborne toxic event' involving a carcinogen called Nyodene D.

Again, this is no anti-chemistry diatribe, but a study of the almost mythic dimension that the products of modern chemistry have acquired. That too is a theme of Richard Powers' 1998 novel *Gain*, which has dual narrative strands. One tells of the origins and evolution of a chemical company called Clare, from its beginnings as a candle- and soap-making business of two Irish immigrants in Boston to a multinational rival of Lever and Procter & Gamble. The other describes the decline and death of a real-estate agent in Illinois called Laura Bodey, whose ovarian cancer may or may not be linked to the proximity of Clare's chemical works.

Even more than Pynchon, Powers embellishes his account with chemical details, to the extent of showing the reactions of the Leblanc process for converting sodium chloride into soda, and a diagram depicting the various uses of Glauber's salt (sodium sulfate). And again the message is complex, for chemistry is shown as a saviour as well as a potential killer—Laura is prescribed semi-synthetictaxol, and her son becomes an expert on protein folding for drug development. The message is not about the evils of chemistry, but about the double-edged sword of a consumer society. 'People want everything,' whispers the terminally ill Laura. 'That's their problem.'

Chemistry's Poet

Set against all of this is the writer who, along with Goethe, is bound to crop up in discussions of chemistry in fiction: Primo Levi. He is now virtually the patron saint of chemistry writing, whose 1975 book *The Periodic Table* is credited with making chemistry accessible to countless readers who would otherwise have run a mile from the subject. *The Periodic Table* is not a novel as such, but a series of vignettes and sketches, many of them autobiographical, that are somehow based around a chemical element. The last of these is explicitly pedagogical, but poetic enough never to feel that way: in Carbon, Levi traces the progress of that element through its natural biogeochemical cycle.

To my mind, Levi's novel *The Monkey's Wrench* (1978) contains a considerably more explicit and elegant depiction of what chemists do: 'we rig and dismantle very tiny constructions'. His chemist narrator relates how difficult it is to get all the parts in the right place, and how crude many of the shake'n' bake methods are. He fantasises about having delicate tweezers' that now sound remarkably like the atomic-probe microscopes, invented only a few years after the book was written, which can pick up atoms and push bits of molecules into shape.

The book is rather less compelling as fiction, however, perhaps because its autobiographical elements are more filtered and disguised. Nothing can equal the narrative and moral power that Levi brings to his accounts as a survivor of the concentration camps, glancingly in *The Periodic Table* but in detail in *If This Is a Man*. It was his training as a chemist that saved his life when he was selected to work as an assistant in IG Farben's Buna-Werke laboratory at Auschwitz, making synthetic rubber in an eerie resonance with Pynchon's fable.

Levi's stories in *The Periodic Table* delight in the materiality of chemistry: sodium, he explains ' is neither rigid nor elastic; rather it is soft like wax; it is not shiny or, better, it is shiny only if preserved with maniacal care'. The book is unique in actually explaining some chemistry, which should ordinarily never be the reason for putting science into fiction. Oliver Sacks achieves a similar interweaving of chemistry and humanity in his autobiographical *Uncle Tungsten* (2001).

Not Just a Villain?

An optimistic reading of these diverse examples of chemistry in fiction would suggest that they offer a more nuanced vision of chemistry than that perpetuated in media scare stories about the terrible things that chemicals' in our environment threaten to do to us. To my mind, linking chemistry to modern culture, with all its consumerist excesses, is potentially a good rather than a bad thing: it allows a writer like Richard Powers to show that the problems stem from the way applications are chosen and implemented, and moreover that evils' such as toxic spills and contamination of remote ecosystems are the flip side of the immense benefits that chemistry has conferred on society. Fiction offers opportunities for exploring these complex issues without resort to the polarities and simplifications typical of journalism.

But science in fiction can surely do more than provide a vehicle for debating its applications. Physics and biology appear to offer rich sources of literary metaphor, poetic imagery and allusion. Goethe and Levi have made the case that chemistry can do so too, yet they are unusual in that, if not perhaps unique. No doubt readers of Chemistry World would welcome books in which chemists are the heroes and not the villains. But how much nicer it would be to find the ideas of chemistry take centre stage, as alchemy did in some Elizabethan poetry. Who will take up the challenge?

思考题

1. The author refers to Mary Shelley's *Frankenstein* as a legacy of the Faust myth. In what ways do you think is the story of *Frankenstein* linked with the Faust myth?
2. According to the author, is it a good or bad thing to link chemistry to modern culture, with all its consumerist excesses? Why?

3. What are the major changes of the role of chemistry in literary works in the 20th century?

第二节 《盖恩》与化学

作品导读

1. 作者简介

理查德·鲍尔斯是当今美国实力派后现代作家。大学入学时,鲍尔斯主攻物理学专业,但选修了非常有魅力的施耐德(Robert Schneider)教授开设的课程。施耐德教授使其相信,文学是"高瞻远瞩之人的理想之地"①。受此影响,鲍尔斯对文学产生了浓厚的兴趣,在大学第一学期尚未结束时就转入英语文学系,并在本科毕业后攻读了文学硕士学位。在研究生期间,他被普鲁斯特(Marcel Proust, 1871—1922)、乔伊斯(James Joyce, 1882—1941)和托马斯·曼(Thomas Mann, 1875—1955)等欧美现代派作家的作品所吸引,对他们复杂的叙事结构非常感兴趣。同时,他也喜欢上了哈代的情感戏剧。他将自己置身于"高度实验化的现代主义小说理念"和传统现实主义叙事之间,在前者"自我辩解式的逻辑结构"和后者"强迫读者培养一种对世界本身洞察力的理念"的交替洗礼中陶冶了情操②。研究生毕业不久后,鲍尔斯前往波士顿,白天从事电脑程序员工作,晚上及周末广泛阅读包括文学、诗歌、历史、社会学和政治等各种题材的读物。由于住在波士顿美术馆附近,他经常在周六上午免费开放期间去那儿参观。某个周六,他看见了正在展出的桑德(August Sander, 1876—1964)拍摄的黑白照片,其中有一张的标题是"三个去舞会路上的韦斯特瓦尔德(Westerwald)农场男孩"。在那一刻,他觉得"之前所有的阅读都凝聚在照片中——20世纪的出生照"。他的感触如此之深,两天后便辞职,开始创作其第一部小说《三个农民去舞会》(*Three Farmers on Their Way to a Dance*, 1985)③。自1985年该作品问世以来,鲍尔斯几乎每隔一年就推出一部作品,迄今共出版小说13部。此外,他还发表了大量短篇小说和文学随笔。

鲍尔斯兴趣广泛,除了文学,还对计算机、政治、医学等方面都有比较深入的研究。在多部作品中,他将科学知识和文学作品天衣无缝地结合起来,创造出一种充满想象力的信息小说,也可以说是科学小说,涉及化学、分子生物学、神经科学、遗传学、制药和人工智能等领

---

① DEWEY J. Richard Powers[Z/OL]. https://www.richardpowers.net/biography/.
② 同①.
③ 同①.

域,同时关注人与电脑的同步和交互发展,以及后人类、非线性科学、想象力的本性与文学、小说的价值①。他也一直因为在诡异的小说世界里探索复杂的科学问题的能力而备受赞誉,其作品受到了学界和普通读者的一致好评。由于其独特的创作题材、卓越的叙事艺术,他的作品获奖无数,其中包括1985年美国艺术与文学学院颁发的罗森塔尔奖,1999年的詹姆斯·库珀最佳历史小说奖(James Fenimore Cooper Prize for Best Historical Fiction),2003年的道斯·帕索斯文学奖(Dos Passos Prize)和 WH 史密斯文学奖(WH Smith Literary Award),2004年的大使图书奖(Ambassador Book Award),2006年凭《回声制造者》(*The Echo Maker*, 2006)获得了美国国家图书奖,2019年凭《上层》(*The Overstory*, 2018)获得了普利策文学奖等。

2. 作品介绍

《赢利》是鲍尔斯的第六部作品,出版次年获得詹姆斯·库珀最佳历史小说奖。整部小说由两个平行部分以及穿插其间的各种拼贴材料构成:其中一部分描绘了克莱尔化学工业公司的发展史,另一部分则讲述了女主人公劳拉(Laura Bodey)的故事。作者将两条看似孤立的故事主线平行展开,让读者穿梭于历史与现实之间,不断循着小说的叙事轨迹,构建故事之间的微妙联系。住在雷斯伍德(Lacewood)小镇的单身母亲劳拉在常规体检时发现自己患上了癌症,癌细胞吞噬着她的身体,使她日渐衰弱。与当地众多患者一样,她的发病原因与小镇上的一家跨国化工制药企业克莱尔公司(Clare International)造成的环境污染有关。这家公司本来是一家生产肥皂的家族企业,秉承着给千家万户送去"清洁"的宗旨,依靠技术研发,利用印第安人的神秘药草,研制出一款药皂,期望清洁人体污垢的同时更能洗去人们心灵的污浊。随着化工技术的发展,克莱尔公司迅速壮大成为一家跨国企业,但在生产出多种化工产品如消毒剂、化妆品、医药、杀虫剂、化肥和建筑材料等的同时,它也造成了环境污染,使劳拉所居住的雷斯伍德小镇及其周边地区都遭到侵害。化学工业的发展成了一把双刃剑:杀虫剂等高科技化工产品确实消灭了害虫,消毒剂清除了污垢、杀灭了病菌,药品也达到了治病救人的目的。但是它们在为人们带来短期的、表面的福音的同时却潜藏着巨大的、长久的隐患,即化工产品造成了致命的环境污染。尽管小镇人们针对克莱尔公司对当地居民的健康和环境造成的巨大危害发起了诉讼并赢得官司,但克莱尔规模宏大、影响力深远,最终逃脱法律的制裁,成为"人类无法驾驭的怪物"②。

3. 作品赏析

作者追溯了雷斯伍德小镇与高科技的象征、现代化工巨子——克莱尔公司之间长达一

---

① 段军霞. 鲍尔斯小说的道德回归[J]. 殷都学刊, 2016(1): 84.
② Gain[Z/OL]. https://medhum.med.nyu.edu/view/1451.

百五十多年的爱恨情仇。克莱尔公司的农业分部总公司选址于雷斯伍德这个美国中西部小镇,一度曾使小镇的居民们兴奋不已,因为这意味着这个僻远小镇从此迈入工业化时代,腾飞的前景让每个人为之欢欣鼓舞。果然,该公司在此后的多年里都是小镇的经济支柱和当地人就业的最大雇主。克莱尔公司的化学产品从最初的蜡烛和香皂到后来日常生活处处可见的日用品,应有尽有。克莱尔公司的经营范围在几十年间不断地扩大,产品的生产过程也日趋复杂。起初生产的蜡烛和香皂所需要的资源都有赖于其他地方供应。为了提高产品的质量和销量,克莱尔公司充分利用本(Ben Clare)在南太平洋小岛上发现的植物块茎,开发出一款气味独特的香皂,一举成名,度过了公司最艰难的时刻①。在生产过程中,克莱尔特别注重提高生产技术和招募人才。雷瑟夫(Resolve Clare)所雇佣的爱尔兰工匠恩尼斯(Ennis)在生产过程中极大地促进了克莱尔香皂和蜡烛的生产和销售,最终"克莱尔的儿子们发现了恩尼斯怎样才生产出这样一种神奇的产品,而售价却如此之低"②。与此同时,克莱尔充分利用生产过程中的废品来生产新的产品,这样做并不是出于环境保护的目的。在发展初期,工业和人类社会的发展都依赖于自然的恩赐,因此克莱尔公司产品的生产在很大程度上要依靠大自然,要取决于自然所能提供的原料。然而,随着生产工艺的提高,克莱尔逐渐利用已掌握的技术来回收生产过程中的副产品,通过化学作用循环利用这些副产品,并合成新的化学产品。克莱尔甚至宣称:"在世界存在之前我们已经实现循环利用③。"自此,克莱尔便利用技术上的优势,扩大生产规模,降低生产成本,在激烈的市场竞争中占据优势。克莱尔在与自然和对手的竞争中取得了决定性的胜利。但是克莱尔为了发展,开始不择手段,比如修改产品的科学检测结果,采取不正当的营销手段,扩大宣传,攻击对手。通过兼并和重组,克莱尔的规模不断扩大,成为综合性的跨国企业。扩张后的克莱尔不仅摆脱了对自然的依赖还沉浸在征服自然所带来的满足感中。

然而,克莱尔在取得各种成绩的同时,也将自身置于生态和舆论危机中。在克莱尔总部所在地的莱斯伍德,小镇居民开始抗议克莱尔为越战军队提供落叶剂,同时也开始怀疑小镇居民患病的原因是否与克莱尔的产品有关。环境污染引起了大家的警惕:"有一天,美国人民突然发现,他们最大的湖泊正在死亡或者已经死亡。导致这种现象的原因在于富营养化……富营养化在某种程度上已开始加剧这一过程,千年才能完成的过程在十年之内就完成了。民众由此推断,导致这种现象的物质正是克莱尔公司生产的香皂及其同类产品磷酸除臭剂④。"一些居民发现自己患上了不同种类的疾病,有的甚至患上了癌症,主人公劳拉就

---

① KARNICKY J. Fascinated disgust in Richard Powers[J]. Contemporary fiction and the ethics of modern culture, 2007:73.
② POWERS R. Gain[M]. New York: Farrar, Straus & Giroux, 1998: 2.
③ 同②174.
④ 同②335.

第二章 文学与化学(Literature and Chemistry)

是其中一例。虽然作者并没有明确指出克莱尔公司是居民患病的直接原因,但是这些病人都曾在克莱尔公司工作过或者居住在克莱尔公司附近。克莱尔坚决否认这些指责,并通过科学证据来证明其产品中所使用的物质是安全的。而克莱尔的竞争对手也开始利用克莱尔面临的危机趁机进行扩张。正如一些学者所言,当今生态危机的根源在于"人与自然的对抗"以及"人类内部的利益争夺":人类在科学技术进步和社会繁荣的号召下,"试图通过改造自然而获得人类的自由,结果却将人类自身置于生态危机的困境之中"[1]。无处不在、无所不能的现代工业文明将人类包裹其中,既带给人类奇迹和利益,又带来危险甚至灾难。

小说的另一部分以劳拉癌症的治疗、恶化直至死亡为叙事主线。围绕这一主线,小说叙述了她与花园,两个孩子艾伦(Ellen)和蒂姆(Tim)、前夫唐(Don)、情夫肯(Ken)和克莱尔之间的故事。劳拉是一名房地产经纪人,为克莱尔公司工作。在生活中她是一位普通的母亲,受过良好的教育。她虽整日忙忙碌碌,但生活简单富足,与两个未成年的孩子享受着快乐的生活,既享受过前夫唐的宠爱,也曾和情人共沐浪漫的斜阳。她与邻居和睦相处,时常接济不宽裕的人。她有教养,有爱好,尤其喜欢打理花园。在花园里,她可以享受自然,感到身心放松,愉快接受着这个世界给予的一切,觉得每天都如此美好,死亡她对来说是遥不可及。就像克莱尔集团为化工行业的发展而欢欣鼓舞一样,劳拉也整日为虚无缥缈的梦想而春风满面。劳拉和克莱尔一样在假象中忙碌着:

> 但是莱斯伍德镇的人从未抱怨过。如果没有克莱尔集团,小镇的发展可能会一直停滞不前。如果不是时兴复古旅游,小镇可能永远偏远落后而无人问津。有了克莱尔集团,小镇才声名鹊起,成为集团遍布十多个国家的36个生产基地之一。"您的梦我来圆"是集团流行的广告语。人们对克莱尔愈加依赖,克莱尔简直就是第二个自然。劳拉每周至少三次开车驶过克莱尔集团农业部。离开克莱尔集团,莱斯伍德镇连玉米都煮不熟。集团几乎包揽了镇上全部生活消费,占据报纸头条,甚至决定学校何时举行升旗仪式。集团派人在新婚典礼上演奏口风琴,新婚夫妇蜜月旅行之时帮他们在下雨时抢收玉米,为医院培养员工,给尚未出生的胎儿做超声波检查[2]。

她本人对克莱尔化工公司充满了信心,这使得她对自己的生活充满了幻想。然而这种幻想同克莱尔公司的繁荣一样,是表面上的,在虚假繁荣的表面之下危机早已潜伏。小说接着叙述了劳拉被诊断出癌症,通过化疗的方法治疗癌症,直至死亡这一过程。作者用很大的篇幅来叙述劳拉患上癌症和治疗癌症,以及劳拉的前夫劝说劳拉加入起诉克莱尔团体中的

---

[1] 胡铁生. 生态批评的理论焦点与实践[J]. 吉林大学社会科学学报, 2009(5):79-86.
[2] POWERS R. Gain[M]. New York:Farrar, Straus & Giroux, 1998:5-6.

情节,暗示造成她癌症的部分原因是克莱尔化学公司对环境保护的无视。自从罹患癌症,劳拉就开始了她短暂而痛苦的抗争,"(她)双膝着地,细细揉搓着她50平方英尺的小花园的每一粒土壤……清晨她拼命地拔草",注意到死亡每时每刻都在吞噬花园里的生命,消磨着劳作的欢乐,也消磨努力与梦想①。她的一举一动都让她沉思过去,思虑即将来临的一切。实际上,她之前的工作也是在不经意间为未来的叵测岁月做着准备,是在为黑暗和不可逃脱的死亡做准备。这个准备的过程几乎耗尽了她的力量,销蚀了她的快乐,也挫败了她的意志。她一边打理花园,一边想起了阵亡将士纪念日,想起了逝去的生命。行将结束的20世纪会带走一切。死亡渐渐向辛勤劳动的劳拉逼近:她给刚冒出的嫩叶上喷洒大量的柠檬汁,杀死那些啃咬笋瓜和黄瓜芽的鼻涕虫,这些鼻涕虫、甲壳虫等真是无孔不入②。

劳拉赶走了那些害虫——"她的无草无虫的50平方英尺的花园,正如鲍尔斯之前作品《甲壳虫变奏曲》(*The Gold Bug Variations*, 1992)中描写的博物馆和电脑中心一样,是人们躲避外部环境的避难所"③。使用大剂量杀虫剂清除顽固的荒草和害虫后,花园显得干干净净,生机勃勃,宛如世外桃源。但好景不长,过不了几天,这些害虫就会卷土重来:"这样,害虫和荒草绝迹的花园,只是脆弱人类的错觉而已,一种人类可以设计和控制自然的假象,一个伊甸园④。"罹患癌症之后,花园成了劳拉心灵的慰藉:

> 只有园艺能使她身心放松。她全神贯注地打扫、浇水,只有偶尔听到鸟鸣声。摘黄瓜、采辣椒这些小事,尚可做到伸手即来。她想把水仙花的块茎插在水里等待来年春天再次发芽。侍弄花草似乎可以延迟死亡。可是疾病还是来得太快,她已弯不下腰,手也摸不到地面了⑤。

花园象征着自然本身,也是人类最后的家园。被害虫破坏的花园正是遭受人类破坏的自然。但见"害虫在咬噬园内的西葫芦芽和豆苗",这最后的家园已不再是伊甸园了⑥。

小说暗示克莱尔公司对劳拉之死负有一定的责任,同时也暗示劳拉作为克莱尔公司产品的消费者对自己的死亡也应负有一定的责任。劳拉本人既参与了克莱尔给莱斯伍德带来的生态悲剧,也参与了自己的悲剧。劳拉享受着克莱尔产品给生活带来的舒适,房间里满是工厂生产的化工产品:"从卧室走到厨房就好像是经过一场展览会一样。地板是杰姆·加德(Germ-Guard)公司生产的。窗户是科利尔·特鲁公司(Cleer-Thru)生产的。桌子是克劳尼尔·考特公司(Colonial-Cote)生产的……她还能生活在哪里呢……她生活的每时每刻都要

---

① POWERS R. Gain[M]. New York: Farrar, Straus & Giroux, 1998: 7.
② 同①5 – 7.
③ DEWEY J. Understanding Richard Powers[M]. Columbia: University of South Carolina Press, 2002: 113.
④ 同③.
⑤ 同①85.
⑥ 同①7.

第二章 文学与化学(Literature and Chemistry)

依赖于这些她数都数不过来的企业①。"

作为消费者,劳拉间接成为制造生态危机的化工工业的帮凶。临死前,劳拉想象到:"克莱尔来到家里,带她出去共进晚餐,一起跳舞。他已过中年,英俊潇洒,体格健壮,对她满含真情。来的时候,他带了一束花,这是很用心的一份礼物,甚至可以说是一首情诗。他一次又一次地来到她的家里,总是能在家里找到她。然而,浪漫的舞蹈之夜最终都会变成令人绝望的欺骗,变成一场残酷的袭击和强奸②。"虽然克莱尔公司的产品是导致劳拉患癌的元凶之一,但公司对她的影响已无处不在。

讽刺的是,劳拉因滥用高科技化工产品而饱受癌症折磨,而她的儿子却得益于科技的发展。他是早产儿,如果没有现代医疗技术,不可能存活。而且他打算与朋友合建一家公司,意欲利用他们痴迷的电脑软件去寻找抗癌秘方,但谁又能保证他们的公司不会带来相应的负面效应呢?劳拉在服用抗肿瘤特效药顺铂(Cisplatin)时对高科技的神奇更是深信不疑,"任何否认现代进步的人一定从未经历过目睹父母因无法医治而死亡的痛苦"③。劳拉的前夫唐也意识到,"即使我们想,我们也已经无法回到过去。而且又有谁真的想要退回到过去呢?尤其是我们已经因为使用那些超级杀虫剂培育出了一批新的超级害虫,现如今谁能离得开那些神奇的添加剂和超级杀虫剂而活下去呢"④?故事的最后劳拉拒绝参加对该公司的集体诉讼,"她不能起诉克莱尔公司,它并没有入侵她的房子。是她自己按自己的选择把这些消费品带进家的。如果让她再选择一次,她也还会这样做,而且是不得不这样做"⑤。而且,劳拉和她的家人都承认他们已经回不到过去,因为克莱尔公司如果倒闭,小镇多人将会失业,经济支柱坍塌,市场萧条,其连锁反应无法估量。

最后,劳拉去世的场景令人印象深刻:鲍尔斯为劳拉的离世创造了一个温馨的环境,这里,再重要的事情也是过往云烟,甚至死亡也不过是一道填空题,像修手指甲一样稀松平常。人去世后,比身体更大的东西留了下来,永传后世。人本源自泥土,当回归泥土。劳拉终将明白,死亡是人类与自然最终融合的过程:"生命是伟大的,无可厚非的,也是意料不到的。生命存在的意义非以稀缺论贵。生命的存在打破了供求关系。运行不畅的都会走向消亡,而生命仍将继续⑥。"从这个角度来看,尽管劳拉自己和家人、好友遭受了极大的痛苦,但劳拉的死只是自然界进行自我补充更新、永恒运动的一部分。

鲍尔斯运用化学隐喻,揭示人类在开发和利用自然过程中所面临的矛盾:对自然资源急

---

① POWERS R. Gain[M]. New York: Farrar, Straus & Giroux, 1998: 303.
② 同①344.
③ 同①114.
④ 同①258.
⑤ 同①304.
⑥ 同①344.

功近利地开发,既能带来意想不到的利益和便捷,也能带来危险甚至灾难。化学"既是毒药又是治病良方"的双重性在小说中展露无遗①。人类滥用化学这门本应是用自然元素的分离重组为人类谋福利的艺术,将它变为干预自然、掠夺自然的工具。克莱尔集团的崛起就是一则人类干涉自然的寓言故事:人类自以为是地认为,通过改变自然秩序、利用化学产品,就能"净化"世界、逃避死亡,然而,在不断占有自然资源、恣意破坏环境的过程中,沦为企业追逐"赢利"而必须承受生命代价的牺牲品。下面请阅读小说节选部分,并回答相关问题。

作品选读

Gain

Richard Powers

Day had a way of shaking Lacewood awake. Slapping it lightly, like a newborn. Rubbing its wrists and reviving it. On warm mornings, you remembered: this is why we do things. Make hay, here, while the sun shines. Work, for the night is coming. Work now, for there is no work in the place where you are going.

May made it seem as if no one in this town had ever sinned. Spring unlocked the casements. Light cured the oaks of lingering winter doubt, lifting new growth from out of nothing, leaving you free again to earn your keep. When the sun came out in Lacewood, you could live.

———

Lacewood's trace began everywhere: London, Boston, Fiji, Disappointment Bay. But everywhere's trail ended in this town, where folks made things. Some mornings, when the sun shone, history vanished. The long road of arrival disappeared, lost in the journey still in store.

At first, the town subsisted on the overhauled earth. Wild prairie weeds gave way to grain, a single strain of edible grass, grown on a scale that made even grass pay. Later, Lacewood graduated to human wizardry, thrived on alchemical transformation. Growth from bone meal and bat guano. Nourishment from shale. Breakthroughs followed one upon the other, as surely as May followed April.

There must have been a time when Lacewood did not mean Clare, Incorporated.

---

① HEISE U. Toxin, drugs, and global system: risk and narrative in the contemporary novel[J]. American literature, 2002(4): 747-778.

第二章 文学与化学(Literature and Chemistry)

But no one remembered it. No one alive was old enough to recall. The two names always came joined in the same breath. All the grace ever shed on Lacewood flowed through that company's broad conduit. The big black boxes on the edge of town sieved diamonds from out of the mud. And Lacewood became the riches that it made.

Forever, for anyone who would listen, Lacewood liked to trot out the tale of how it tricked its way into fortune. At its deciding moment, when the town had to choose between the sleepypast and the tireless nineteenth century, it did not think twice. With the ease of one born to it, Lacewood took to subterfuge.

The townsfolk felt no qualms about their ruse, then or ever. If they felt anything, it was pride. They laid their snare for the fifth Mr. Clare, the namesake president of an Eastern firm that had lately outgrown its old markets. Clare Soap and Chemical was heading West, seeking new hosts.

Douglas Clare, Sr., secretly preferred the aroma of Lacewood to the scent of Peoria. Lacewood smelled clean and distilled. Peoria was a little too unctuous and pomaded. He liked this place for a number of reasons. But he kept mum, sporting the indifference of a cagey suitor.

The fifth Mr. Clare could not say exactly what he was looking for in a future site. But he always claimed he'd recognize the place when he laid eyes on it. Even that most resourceful businessman could not call this location central. But the country's growth would yet center it. Lacewood sat on train lines connecting St. Louis, Indianapolis, and Louisville. It lay a reasonable freight haul away from Chicago, the West's lone metropolis. And land in this vacancy was still dirt cheap.

Lacewood decided to doll itself up, to look like what it thought Clare wanted. Weeks before the visit, the town began papering over its crumbling warehouses with false fronts. Every boy over ten turned builder. The mayor even had two blocks of plaster edifices erected to fatten out anemic Main Street.

For the duration of the company tour, the town rented an old Consolidation locomotive. It ran the engine up and down the line at frequent intervals, rearranging the consist for the sake of drama. The freight even discharged a much fussed-over load at the suspiciously new station.

Ten hours later, it returned from the other direction and hauled the crates of gravel away.

Clare and his advisers saw through the whole charade. One glance told the Easterners that the decaying antique hadn't seen service in over a decade. Peoria had run much the same stunt. And its fake facades had been fancier.

But necessity drove Lacewood beyond Peoria's wildest invention. Long in advance of its August inspection, Lacewood dammed up its sleepy little stretch of the Sawgak, just upriver of town. Ordinarily, the pathetic trickle didn't even dampen the dust on a muskrat's whiskers. But for four glorious days in the heat of late summer, the town council built itself a junior torrent.

At key intervals, Lacewood posted several fishers who passed as either entrepreneurs or sportsmen, depending on the light. With uncanny regularity, the anglers struggled to land a series of mighty northern pike: fat from off the land, food from nothing, from honest labor.

The fact that Esox lucius, the species these men pulled like clockwork from the synthetic rapids, had never on its own accord strayed south of Minnesota touched Mr. Clare. He admired the industry, the pathos in the stratagem. He could work with these people. They would work for him.

He glowered throughout the length of the inspection. He shook his head continually. At the last instant before heading back to Boston in his private Pullman—whose builder, up in Pullman, Illinois, had recently created an ingenious live-in factory town that supplied all his employees' needs—Clare acquiesced. Sighing, he accepted the massive tax concessions proffered him in perpetuity, and closed the deal.

And that's how Clare Soap and Chemical came to stay.

Years later, just in time to stave off the worst of the Great Depression, the globe's largest producer of earth-moving equipment dropped its world headquarters down in Peoria. Caterpillar played for more than fifty straight profitable years and ran up its annual sales to over $13 billion by the game's twilight, at century's end.

But Lacewood never complained. Without Clare, the town would have dozed forever. It would have stayed a backwoods wasteland until the age of retrotourism. With Clare, Lacewood grew famous, part of an empire of three dozen production facilities in

第二章　文学与化学（Literature and Chemistry）

ten countries, "making answers, meeting needs."

Lacewood joined the ride gladly, with both feet. It got the goose it bargained for, and more. For over a century, Clare laid countless clutches of eggs whose gold only the niggling would stoop to assay.

> WELCOME TO LACEWOOD. POPULATION 92,400.
> ROTARY, ELKS, LIONS. BOYHOOD HOME OF CALE
> TUFTS, OLYMPIC LEGEND. SISTER CITY OF
> ROUEN, FRANCE, AND LUDHIANA, INDIA. SITE OF
> SAWGAK COLLEGE. NORTH AMERICAN
> AGRICULTURAL PRODUCTS DIVISION
> HEADQUARTERS, CLARE INTERNATIONAL
> 　PLEASE BUCKLE UP

———

May, just before Memorial Day, just this side of millennium's end. Up on North Riverside, on the good side of the river, a Lacewood woman works her garden. A woman who has never thought twice about Clare.

Sure she knows it: the name is second nature. Traders on the Frankfurt Burse mouth "Clare" at the mention of Lacewood, the way they point and go "bang" whenever they meet someone from Chicago. Teens in Bangkok covet anything bearing the company's logo. Whole shipping-container sunrooms in Sao Paulo are emblazoned with it. The firm built her entire town, and then some. She knows where her lunch comes from. Which side of her bread bears the non-dairy spread.

She drives past Clare's Agricultural Division headquarters at least three times a week. The town cannot hold a corn boil without its corporate sponsor. The company cuts every other check, writes the headlines, sings the school fight song. It plays the organ at every wedding and packs the rice that rains down on the departing honeymooners. It staffs the hospital and funds the ultrasound sweep of uterine seas where Lacewood's next of kin lie gray and ghostly, asleep in the deep.

She knows what it makes as well as anyone. Soap, fertilizers, cosmetics, comestibles: name your life-changing category of substances. But still, she knows Clare no better than she knows Grace or Dow. She does not work for the corporation or for anyone the corporation directly owns. Neither does any blood relation or any loved one.

The woman kneels in her garden, kneading her fifty square feet of earth. She coaxes up leaves, gets them to catch a teacupful of the two calories per cubic centimeter that the sun, in its improvident abundance, spills forever on the earth for no good reason except that it knew we were coming. Some nasty bug has already begun to nibble her summer squash in the bud. Another goes after her beans. She responds with an arsenal of retaliations. Beer to ward off slugs. Lemon-scented dish soap in solution, spritzed liberally to counter beetle insurgencies. Home remedies. Stronger measures when strength is needed.

She transplants flowers outdoors from their starter beds. The work is play; the labor, love. This is the afternoon she slaves all week for. The therapeutic complement to the way she makes a living: moving families from starter homes into larger spreads.

Spring releases her. The early oriental poppies unwad like her children's birthday crepe. The alpine columbine spread their two-toned trumpets, an ecstatic angel choir. Every growing thing looks like something else to her. Her mind hums as she weeds, hungry to match each plant with its right resemblance.

Tight, hard globes of Christmas ornament relax into peonies. Daisies already droop their tutus like sad, also-ran, Degas dancers. Bleeding hearts hang in group contrition. She urges them on, each to its colored destiny. No human act can match gardening. She would do it all day long, if she could.

The ballet school sponsors. The ones who pay for the TV that nobody ever watches. The annual scholarships for the erector-set kids at the high school. The trade-practice lawsuits she hasn't the patience to follow, and the public service announcements she never entirely understands. The drop-dead-cute actress who has the affair with the guy next door in that series of funny commercials that everyone at the office knows by heart. The old company head who served in the cabinet during World War II. She hums the corporate theme song to herself sometimes, without realizing.

Two pots in her medicine cabinet bear the logo, one to apply and one to remove. Those jugs under the sink—Avoid Contact with Eyes—that never quite work as advertised. Shampoo, antacid, low-fat chips. The weather stripping, the grout between

第二章 文学与化学(Literature and Chemistry)

the quarry tiles, the nonstick in the nonstick pan, the light coat of deterrent she spreads on her garden. These and other incarnations play about her house, all but invisible.

This woman, forty-two years old, looks up into the gathering May sky and wrinkles her nose. Yesterday's Post-Chronicle predicted azure. But no point in second-guessing yesterday, with today coming on like there's no tomorrow. Her seedlings are further along than Memorial Day could have hoped. A dollar twenty-nine, two spritzes of lemon dish soap, and a little loving effort can still keep one in squash all summer.

The woman's name is Laura Rowen Bodey. She is the newest member of Next Millennium Realty's Million Dollar Movers Club. Her daughter has just turned seventeen, her son is twelve and a half. Her ex-husband does development for Sawgak College. She sees a married man, quietly and infrequently. Her life has no problem that five more years couldn't solve.

A woman who has heard, yet has not heard. And on this day, no one but the six people who love her gives her a moment's thought.

Business ran in the Clares' blood long before the first one of them made a single thing.

That family flocked to commerce like finches to morning. They clung to the watery edge of existence: ports, always ports. They thrived in tidal pools, half salt, half sweet. Brackish, littoral. They lived less in cities than on the sea routes between them.

Clare was, from the first, transnational. Family merchants traded in England for the better part of a century, specializing in a bold shipping commerce that ruined and made their fortunes several times a year. Each generation refined the gamble. Jephthah Clare drank in gambling with his mother's milk. He gambled the way he breathed.

Jephthah fled the mother country in a hurry, on a wager gone wrong. He left in 1802, the year the aristocrat du Pont, escaping the French turmoil, set up his gunpowder mill in Delaware. Jephthah Clare ran from a more prosaic chaos: not wrongdoing, exactly, but failure to share inside knowledge of a collapse in sugar beet prices with an excitable trading partner upon whom he had just settled a considerable shipment. After his house in Liverpool burned, Jephthah thought it wise not to await further repayment.

He, his wife, and three small children sailed unannounced. They stowed away on one of Clare's own packet traders. For the length of the crossing, the family slept on a cargo of Wedgwood Egyptian stoneware. The pain of the passage eased as soon as they and the plates disembarked upon India Wharf, in Boston, America. That thorny pallet of freight paid the family's way toward a comfort that outlasted all memory of the uncomfortable voyage.

The greatest meliorator of the world is selfish, huckstering Trade.
——EMERSON, "Works and Days"

[...]

Soap appealed to Samuel because it put the purchaser next to godliness. Resolve liked it because the purchaser used it up.

Scavenging what they could from the North End candle works, the brothers and their Irishman rebuilt the workshop on a larger scale. They moved the equipment out to Roxbury, closer to supplies of rendered fat. The new factory combined candle and soapmaking, feeding the scraps of the one to the other's maw.

Resolve and Samuel commissioned a huge, iron-bottomed soap kettle. They built the best crutcher, tanks, frames, and drying racks they could. All three men scorned false economy, each for his own reason. Profit depended on the efficiency and quality that only superior equipment would give.

The plant's dedication was a select affair, involving just the three of them. Ennis allowed himself half a flute of the christening champagne and sang a song his wife had loved, called "May Fortune Smile." Samuel prayed for the Lord's benediction, then set a modest production goal for year's end. Resolve, surveying with pleasure the first fruits of their labor, looked out over the new equipment and cackled a joke about Mrs. Whitney and her husband's interchangeable parts.

Saponification was a complex affair, a delicate marriage of science and idiosyncrasy. The four-day boiling process involved much poking, prodding, and tasting on Ennis's part. He determined the exact ratios of lye to red oil with a mix of algorithm and whim. He killed and caught the stock, steering the kettle back and forth between alkali and fat the way the old Clare captains navigated the Strait of Magellan.

第二章 文学与化学 (Literature and Chemistry)

He gauged the soapy strings adhering to his stirring paddle, awaiting the exact moment when the soap grained and salted out. He cut the steam and drew off the salt lye and glycerin, letting his broth set like a temperamental souffle. He lyed and boiled, boiled and lyed, awaiting strong change, the moment when the mass turned transparent and became another animal.

When the curds rose up like polar bergs, he cooled the mixture for several days and again decanted it. The batch settled into a parfait of soap, caustic nigre, and sedimented lye. In this standing rainbow, each crudeness floated to its own level. He skimmed the soap off the surface like scum off a pond. He washed off the impurities, pitched and finished the purified mass.

Until this point, he let no Clare near the broth. One cook: that's all that the world itself had taken. One skilled pair of eyes and hands, one nose, one tongue. Out of the kettle and into the crutcher, the soap became public domain. Only then did Ennis trust the others to mix and frame and dry and slab and cut. For by then the recipe was done.

The resulting slabs were a mystery to behold. Here was a substance, grease's second cousin. Yet something had turned waste inside out. Dirt's duckling transformed to salve's swan, its rancid nosegay rearranged into aromatic garland. This waxy mass, arising from putrescence, became its hated parent's most potent anodyne.

To make their first run, they paid cash for a quantity of fine rendered fat.

Thereafter, they sought suppliers who would trade good tallow for excellent soap, a pound for a pound. As their process made two pounds of soap for each pound of introduced fats, they would have half their run left over to pay for alkali, keep the equipment repaired, and put bread on their own tables.

Only when Resolve gazed upon that first readied ton did he consider their odd position. Their own customers would be their chief competition. Caked soap was still an expensive substitute for the slippery paste that every home could yet make as a matter of course. The Clares' soap had to teach thrifty New England how smelly, difficult, and undependable home soapmaking had always been.

To distribute their wares, Samuel and Resolve resorted to their old handlers. But these ancient family associates turned a deaf ear to the fledgling firm. The distributors knew the Clare family only as good merchants. Not one trusted such a late-day change of life, this willful descent to the mechanical ranks.

Weeks passed while the three men waited for some jobber to step forward and purchase any chunk of their stock, even on credit or commission. Desperate, Samuel drew up, at his dinner table, a crude advertisement which he ran in several trade circulars as well as the Boston Directory. The square of print bore much the same message as the wooden sign that hung upon the side of their shop:

J. CLARE'S SONS

JUSTICE AND SPRING STREETS, ROXB.

2ND DOOR NORTHWEST

MANUFACTURER & WHOLESALER OF ALL IMAGINABLE

SOAPS AND CANDLES

UNGUENT TO CLEANSE THE MULTITUDES LIGHT TO LIGHTENTHEM

HIGHEST PRICES PAID FOR TALLOW

Chemistry is the art of separating mixt bodies into their constituent parts and of combining different bodies or the parts of bodies into new mixts... for the purposes of philosophy by explaining the composition of bodies... and for the purposes of arts by producing several artificial substances more suitable to the intention of various arts than any natural productions are.

——WILLIAM CULLEN, c. 1766

[...]

She's still asking that first question, years later, when she wakes with tubes all over her. Which side is the cancer on? As if it mattered. As if Don or the doctor or anyone else cares. As if her ovaries know her right side from her left.

But her right side knows why her left asks. She woke in a panic, not for the disaster already handed to her, but for the one still hidden. Cancer: okay. She half expected it, going in. Too clean; too reassuring. A 2 percent chance of catastrophe.

She remembers bobbing up from the truth serum milkshake—thiopental sodium, fentanyl, tubocurarine, halothane—in a state perilously close to knowledge. The

第二章　文学与化学（Literature and Chemistry）

concoction left her with a continuous sense of micro-dejd vu. She heard the word "cancer" a good two seconds before the surgeon pronounced it. Maybe it was still the drugs, but she found herself thinking,

"All right. I can deal with this. I'm an adult." And for a second or two, she thought it might even be true.

She digested the horror with all the ease of downing nouvelle cuisine. It's the aperitif she gags on. She woke from her long nausea sure she'd fallen into one of those amputation stories where they misread the X-ray and take the wrong leg. Laura Somebody-else, a stranger's chart accidentally switched with her own. While she let her attention slip, ignorant medical personnel were busy committing colossal mistakes on her.

All the magazines agree: health care is now the patient's business.

Responsibility falls squarely on the care receiver. And there she was, sleeping on the job.

Her nose now sprouts a tube, like one of Tim's Star Wars creatures. It itches; she picks feebly at it like some declawed cat. She vomits up the last of the anesthesia, convinced that they've taken the good cyst and left the bad one inside her. She badgers the nurses until one of them checks the chart. "Mrs. Bodey, everything was bad. They've taken everything."

Someone sponges her off. Another gets her into a clean gown. Still a third—or maybe it's always the same nurse, recycled—hooks her up to sugar water and electrolytes, with a little anti-nausea chaser. Order of narcotic on the side. Self-administering, they call it. Hit this button every time you think you need some morphine.

She pretty much keeps her thumb locked on the joystick. Like Tim strafing Warsaw. But some sadist has disabled the flow, rigged it to deliver a new trickle only at ten-minute intervals. Patient-administered, but machine-approved.

Whenever the machine thinks she's ready for another thimbleful, it beeps.

After an hour, the beep itself is enough to give her a little imitation rush.

But the rushes don't last. She asks a nurse to check if there's been some mix-up. "Are you sure there's really morphine in the bag? I don't know. Maybe it's 7022's supper."

The smallest movement makes her wish for death. She never imagined that pain on this scale existed.

She keeps asking anyone in white what she's supposed to do now. But apparently she's just supposed to wait. "Just rest up," someone tells her.

"The doctor will come explain everything tomorrow."

After two hours, they come force her to walk. Something about her staples, possible peritonitis. She can make no more than token motions. Get upright, grab the rolling IV hat tree. Gag, retch, collapse, prop herself back up, take two baby steps. Mother, may I? Yes you may.

After four hours, they try her again. This time, she can get to the door of the room and take three steps down the hall before circling back around and crashing.

The kids drift in. She tries to rally herself, joke with them. "Your mother the cancer patient. You'll never have to turn in homework on time again."

Don's there, too. Every ten minutes, she tells him he can go home if he wants. Every time the morphine machine beeps. Finally he does. And finally the pain goes home a little, too.

Long after nightfall, she has the impression of Ken hovering by the bed.

Saying what he always says: "I can't stay long."

Laura tells him what she always tells him. Go before anyone sees you. A few minutes later, the visit vanishes into hallucination.

She lurches asleep. In her dream, Nan, Ellen's dead girlfriend, comes back home to get her annual height measurement. Her mother stands her up against the inside of the kitchen doorframe and makes another pencil mark. Only this one is lower than last year's.

They wake her up every couple of hours to get her vitals and check the catheter.

The next morning she waits some more. Waiting: the one skill you get worse at with practice. At eight, the nurses tell her, "The doctor usually makes rounds at nine." At ten, they say, "She's sometimes as late as six or seven." Someone checks; Dr. Jenkins is operating again today. Somewhere, another woman is waking up surprised.

They give her a plastic respiration toy. An accordion plug that bobs up and down

第二章 文学与化学（Literature and Chemistry）

when she blows into it. She is supposed to blow into it as often as she can. Something about pressure on the diaphragm, keeping her insides from gunking up. It makes her think of those carnival tests of strength.

Don takes off from work to come by. "So, what's happening?"

"I've got cancer," she tells him. "That's what's happening."

"That's all? That's all you know? I have some questions here. When is the doctor supposed to come?"

"Somewhere between three hours ago and eight hours from now."

"I'm going to go find someone who can give us a little satisfaction."

Laura groans. "What do you mean, Don? 'Can I speak with your manager, please?'" The way it works in his organization. In all the organizations he is used to dealing with.

"Yeah. What's wrong with that?"

She says nothing. She squeezes the button. The button does nothing.

"You think this place isn't a business?" Don asks her.

"Not that kind of business." "Not what kind of business?"

Not the kind that cares what its customers think, she would say. If she cared enough to say it.

They throw silence back and forth at each other until the gyny surgeon comes in. She has traded her scrubs this morning for a short, canary-yellow dress. Gorgeous, shocking, in this ward. Cheery to the point of obscene.

Laura has forgotten that yellow exists. She wonders if maybe it's okay to be reminded.

She looks over at Don. He's got this helpless, fretting look on his face. Fighting off the salivation reflex. Poor man. Life is way too complex for some souls. He's going to die without ever knowing what hit him.

"How's it going?" Dr. Jenkins greets Laura as if they're old sewing circle friends. Which they are, now.

Laura tries to grin. She holds up the morphine button, toasting with it as if it were stemware topped off with champagne.

"Good. Let's just have a look at that belly." Jenkins eyes Don. "Could you step outside a moment?"

Laura snorts. Mirth rips through her, canceling all pleasure.

The wound is fine. Hurting like hell. Doing what comes naturally. The doctor fetches Don, who comes back in without a peep.

"Well, the operation went very well," the beautiful canary says. "No visible signs of malignancy remaining in the abdomen."

"You mean she's clean?" Don asks.

Dr. Jenkins smiles at him. This semester's precocious kid, trying to trip her up with the old teaser about the three travelers splitting the hotel room and losing a dollar somewhere along the way.

"There's no visible tumor left after debulking. That doesn't mean that there isn't occult disease loose somewhere in the system."

Laura isn't keen on having her system referred to in the third person while she's still in the room. And occult disease doesn't sound all that hot to her either. She's still not crazy about the ordinary kind.

"How can you tell?" Don asks.

"Tell what? If the disease has gotten loose somewhere else? I took the omentum and peritoneal washings. They're in the lab right now. If they come back positive, then we can figure that some cells have gotten loose."

Laura's eyes close. "I have an omentum?"

"Not anymore." Dr. Jenkins laughs.

"Do you expect them to come back positive?" Don sounds like Laura's lawyer.

"I think it's likely."

"How likely?"

"I'd say there's a 90 percent chance that one or the other will come back positive."

Laura feels the thought flash through Don's mind. But he declines to make the kill. Probably can't kill anything yellow. Instead, he asks, "You're sure you got the whole tumor?"

Massively professional: "Quite sure."

"Say the washings come back positive," Don says. As if he knows what "washings" are. Maybe it's just as well. Left to herself, Laura would not ask anything.

第二章 文学与化学（Literature and Chemistry）

This way, she learns more than she wants, and doesn't have to take the blame for discovering.

"Let's say some cells are loose," Don says. "What does that mean?"

"That means the cancer is Stage Three."

"And if not?"

"Then it's a Stage One. Stage One C, technically."

"What happened to Stage Two?"

The man is hopeless. Laura bleats. But she still doesn't open her eyes.

When she does, Don is sitting across from her vacuum drain, scribbling everything down into a legal pad the color of the surgeon's dress. Asking how to spell "serous cystadenocarcinoma." Trying to keep his eyes off the pretty hemline. Poor soul. She's going to have to remind him, soon, tomorrow. They're less than friends, now. The contract's been canceled. He owes her nothing.

Jill Jenkins leans lightly against the empty bed next to Laura's. She seems to be telling Laura to wait some more. Longer. Wait for the lab tests.

Wait until tomorrow. Tomorrow: the only lever long enough to dislodge today.

"You'll need a few months of chemotherapy," the doctor says. A handful of system-wide poisonings. Half a year of vomiting and hair loss. "The specialist in Indy will decide what chemicals you will get. How much, and how often. Maybe your doses will include that new drug everyone's so excited about," Jenkins chirps. "The one they're making from tree bark. One hundred percent natural."

Laura can't keep from staring at this woman's legs, either. They remind her of the waxed fruit in that upscale food boutique in Next Millennium's office park. A dollar an apple, catering to young professionals who would never stoop to anything so déclassé as packing a lunch. How old can Dr. Jenkins be? How long will she stay ripe without refrigeration? How old should you be before you get really sick?

Outside, a freight runs past the new hospital parking expansion whose construction Laura fought. The train heads north, through the rotting neighborhoods Millennium never deals with. She begins to imagine herself in another life, indigent, penniless, victimized. But well.

Silence interrupts her fantasy. Jenkins has stopped explaining things. The doctor is waiting.

Laura hears herself speak, from inside a shortwave radio set. "What is the cause?" She cannot say of ovarian cancer. She cannot say of this. "Is it genetic?"

She just wants to know how much of this is her fault. Whether she should have done something. Might still do something. Whether she would have had to go through this even if she lived better. Whether Ellen.

"Sometimes." The doctor frowns. "Nobody really knows for certain."

Laura feels Don's fury, even through her sedatives.

"Which is it? Sometimes, or Nobody knows?"

"There was nothing wrong with me," Laura interrupts. "A little tenderness."

No warning signs at all. How could that be? she wants to ask. But she doesn't know what a warning sign looks like. Something like in the midnight reruns, when the pretty girl coughs while skipping rope, which means she'll be history by the next commercial break.

She wants to ask, how long do I have to live? But the words seem rude.

You can't embarrass the physician that way.

"What are my numbers?" she says, instead. The phrase sounds calm.

Almost sophisticated, once it's out in the open.

"Laura. Listen. People with ovarian cancer die of ovarian cancer."

What does that mean? Can, might, must? She tries to remember what exactly she needed to know. Should she quit her job? Forget about building that deck? Get the gutters cleared out as quickly as possible?

Don starts asking about prognosis. About five-year survival rates if she's a One versus if she's a Three. How does he know to ask these things? He must have prepared. He must have expected the worst, long before she knew what the worst was.

"Is there anything we can read that might help?" The man sounds like a brownnosing student. The topic interests him way too much. Laura doesn't want to read about it. She just wants it gone.

The doctor summons a nurse, who produces a couple of pathetic hospital pamphlets: Diet and Cancer. Chemotherapy and You. Dr. Jenkins also recommends a memoir written by a celebrity actress, one that sold well, even before the comedienne's death.

Disgust plows Don's forehead. A comedienne's memoir: worse than worthless. They need facts. Medicine.

"So." The surgeon taps Laura's chart. "Anything else I can answer for you?"

What do you mean, else?

"Are we asking the right questions?" Don asks. "Is there anything we should ask you that we haven't?"

Dr. Jenkins grins again. "You're doing just fine. I would give your questions... an A minus." She excuses herself. She leaves the room, a blazing flower, off to give more people the same message.

As soon as the surgeon disappears, Don starts in. He's got everything planned. Indianapolis. Medline searches. Second opinions. Dietary supplements. Second-look surgery.

"Don." *Go home*, she wants to say. I can't deal with you and this at the same time. "Don. I appreciate what you're trying to do. But I'm not your wife."

He flings his hands up-fine. He holds that wronged gesture in the air, as if he's playing a tree in the grade-school play. When he brings his paws back down, it's to shove the scribbled-over legal pad into his attache case and close it quietly. He rises, chilly, at a great distance.

"You're still the mother of my children."

[...]

LIFE AFTER CHEMISTRY

No, there's nothing wrong with this picture. There's nothing wrong with your magazine or its printers either. We just thought you'd like to see what life would look like without those life-threatening chemical processes you read so much about these days.

The thing is, all those exposes that you read are printed in high-quality inks on treated paper. Illustrated with four-color photochemically separated pictures. You flip through them lying on your no-stain couch in your favorite freshly laundered robe while sipping a diet lemon-lime...

We could go on forever, but you get the picture. And a good, clear picture, too. Life without chemistry would look a lot like no life at all.

Civilization has had growing pains, to be sure. It always will. That's no reason to throw in the no-iron, synthetic-fiber towel. We just need to choose what kind of world we want to live in, and then build that place.

And to do that, whatever our dream world looks like, we'll need the right building blocks.

Less knowledge is not the answer. Better knowledge is. Chemical processes are not the problem. They're the rules of the game.

It's elementary: your life is chemistry.

So is ours.

The Industrial Processes Group
CLARE MATERIAL SOLUTIONS

[...]

She gets a letter stamped "Personal and Urgent." Her address is typed right on the heavyweight bond envelope, so rare with her mail anymore. The return address is also typed: the Cancer Research Institute. Her first, frightened thought is that they want her to go to Houston or New York or Bethesda, some monstrous facility for special treatment.

But it couldn't be that, she thinks; it can't. Her doctors here would have told her about any plans on her behalf. Then she realizes: it must be this lawsuit.

The news has started to spread. The big, national groups must be trying to make a test case of it, for some reason. Don has sent them her address.

They must be trying to get all the local cancer cases to turn out in support.

To do their bit for the collective health.

She opens the envelope, her fingers shaking. Already, she is writing the apologetic response letter in her head. She's not the woman they're looking for. They need someone else, someone who knows what's what, who understands what's going on. Someone who can speak well. Someone who can say what everybody in this town is feeling.

Dear Mrs. Bodey, she reads.

第二章 文学与化学(Literature and Chemistry)

She plunges into the first paragraph. But right away, she has to turn around for a second read. Please send $25. Or anything you can afford.

It doesn't make sense. Solicitation letter. Why would they single out cancer patients? What kind of fund-raising drive is this, where they pass the hat not for the victims but to them?

It takes her a minute. A full, real minute, a pretty considerable unit of time these days. She's not being singled out. It's the same old list. The master database. The mass mailing to everybody.

She flips back to the envelope, the typewritten return address. A trick to make this piece seem like real mail. Hide all the tracks. Get the thing opened at least. Keep it from being pitched in the trash sight unseen. Maybe a letter that looks like first-class mail increases the chances of a contribution by another one percent. And one percent, on the scale things get done now, must come to millions.

A whole new art form: the protectively disguised bulk envelope. Like that one she got last week, a torn magazine page, pinned with her exact color Post-It note. "He-+y, Laura! Check this out! Susan." And she spent all afternoon tossing on the sofa, trying to reassure herself that she'd never had a friend named Susan in her life. Convinced that the cancer, the chemo, the rays were getting to her memory.

Avoid meat and fat. Don't smoke or drink. Limit the time you spend in the sun. Don't expose yourself to toxic chemicals at home or at work. Do not indulge in multiple sexual partners. And send twenty-five dollars.

Well, she's had sex with three men in her life, and one had trouble with intercourse. Sure, she drank a lot in college, with the girls. But these days, she could probably have had half a dozen more glasses of red wine a week and still come in under the guidelines. She smoked for maybe three years, now and then after dinner, just to be sociable. But, ludicrous or no, she never really inhaled. Her diet's not perfect, but because of the kids, she's always been more careful than anyone else she knows.

Don't expose yourself to toxic chemicals at home or at work. There's the catch. They might as well say: Don't get cancer. Well, she hasn't exposed herself. She hasn't, knowingly or otherwise, as far as she knows. She hasn't even been exposed. No Love Canal under the house. No Three Mile Island just across the river. Whatever she's getting by chance or proximity is no more than anyone else in the known world is getting.

She looks over the simple list of dos and don'ts, counting in her head all the things she's done wrong in her life. All the little carcinogenic amenities, the dangers she's known but risked anyway, because the odds seemed so small or so hard to work around. From hair spray to charred barbecued burgers. The paints and paint strippers. The hair color treatments, so crucial to her self-image. The maraschino cherries she used to reward herself with, for being so good. All the diet sodas, which she loved, because they made her feel that she could drink as much as she liked while burning more calories consuming them than she was consuming.

She sends Ellen to the library, and tells her to ask for Marian. Ellen comes home with a book called Shopping for Safety. Laura reads it in tiny increments, in those moments when her head is clear and her eyes can focus. As far as she can make out, nothing is safe. We are all surrounded. Cucumber and squash and baked potato. Fish, that great health food she's been stuffing down the kids for years. Garden sprays. Cooking oils. Cat litter. Dandruff shampoo. Art supplies. Varnish. Deodorant. Moisturizers. Concealers. Water. Air. The whole planet, a superfund site. Life causes cancer.

Lying awake at nights, afraid to take even those universally prescribed milligrams to help her sleep, she thinks about going clean. Cold turkey. Here is all the checklist anyone needs. With it, she could learn to buy only those goods that are above reproof. How hard could it be, to change a few habits? No beef, no chemical toothpastes, the right brands of polish... Nothing she would miss. Buy her way back to health, by choosing the recommended items.

The brief fanatical fantasy dissolves on her like pixie dust. She'd need a lot more health than she has to pull it off. And every plastic bottle of water she bought would just spew poisons somewhere else.

Another letter arrives to take her mind off the first. This one's not really to her, either. It's an open letter, a larger database. It takes up a quarter page in the Sunday Post-Chronicle. In the Public Notices column of the Classifieds. To anyone living in the area bounded by Base Line, Kickapoo, McKinley, and Airport Road-pretty much all

第二章 文学与化学(Literature and Chemistry)

Lacewood and Kaskaskia Heights, and most of the little farm towns and tax-evading subdivisions that hug them.

If you are suffering from any ailment that you or your physicians believe might have an environmental basis. If you have an interest in the current class action suit being lodged against the area's largest manufacturer. If you would like to be considered for inclusion in this suit. Please respond to the following post office box no later than March 21.

It has the look of some paid advertorial. Serious text in a black box, the kind that Laura sometimes mistakes for public service announcements. Mass tort, punitive damages: the kind of products that her edition of Shopping for Safety fails to rate for danger. It's the law firms' best product anymore, so of course they're going to hawk it. One efficient and profitable institution against another, both competing within the rules of the game that have made everyone rich.

She clips the open letter. She puts it up on the fridge so she won't forget the due date. After two days, she gets sick of looking at it. She moves it to the ceramic letter holder on the hutch, wedges it in next to her quarterly payment vouchers. But she's afraid she might forget about it there. She puts it on the dining room table, where no one has eaten for months. It keeps blowing off each time the kids walk past, so she weights it down with the money cowry shell that Ken gave her when she broke into the Million Dollar Movers Club.

[...]

Lacewood's sole moment of legatee's doubt came during the summer of 1932. Men gathered in barbershops and soda shops, forgoing haircuts and Cokes, for such frills had long disappeared into luxury. Women milled about at the A & P or at the fountain in front of the courthouse, each scared soul searching the other for explanations and shushing any brave individual who dared to speak the unspeakable.

But a few folks did say what everybody else wondered: Lacewood was better off without the damn factory. Better off before people had come off the land. The town was no better than a bunch of domesticated rabbits, living it up and praising the good life until the fattening hand came down on you with a club. That's what the "free" in free enterprise meant. Free to be the stooge of any enterprising crook who knew the system.

Others gainsaid the gainsayers. Depression wasn't Clare's fault. If it was, why were all those dust bowl Okies pouring off the land and heading here? Two score more of them every day, lining up in front of the Lacewood factory gates. Philo, Homer, Mantooga—all the neighboring farm towns were bellying up even worse than Lacewood. Farms failing left and right, all by their lonesome. At least the factory gave Lacewood some buffer, a little bit of mooring in the cyclone.

Debate went on throughout that summer and fall. Half the town damned the company and the other half fled in fear from the words that, spoken out loud, would surely bring down a realcurse upon them. Those who lifted their eyes past the town's borders saw that the source of their damnation had, if anything, spared them half the misery of the wider world.

By Independence Day, four fifths of the wealth traded on the New York Stock Exchange had vanished into the thinnest of atmospheres. The Jazz Age took a quick refresher course in the imaginary value of equities. Clare's stock tracked this average drop downward with all the tenacity of a bloodhound puppy. By summer's end, the worth of the entire, far-flung manufacturing empire was less than the book value of the Illinois factories four years before.

Alone among the corporate brass, William Clare had seen the shape of things to come. The careful financier knew all about bookkeeping by mass hypnotism. Throughout the twenties, he sold off his shares in steady, disciplined lots. By the peak, he'd gotten far more than fair market value for his portion. When all hell broke loose, he dumped the rest of his worthless paper, enjoyed a year of ship-spotting off Nantucket, and returned to business to serve briefly on the board of Gillette just before his happy death as a traitor to his family in 1931.

Douglas II was less hurt by the plunge in his net worth than by the reception of his monograph, The Dream of the Romanesque. Scholars laughed at the work because it was written by a businessman. And businessmen by and large failed to read it because it appeared to be about old stones. Douglas retired from the firm to the Greek island of Soundetos. There, in comfortable if reduced circumstances, he took to financing his own amateur forays into classical archaeology.

Everyone else whom the company bound together went to the cleaners. And the folks in the khaki shirts got cleaned longest and hardest of all. All the sorters and sifters and gauge-tenders and packers and haulers who had been forced into buying company shares at a discount now watched helplessly as their precious nest eggs cracked into the national omelet. Workers who had built their retirements for forty years came up empty-handed, the victims of the distributed pyramiding swindle of capital.

The Clare Guarantee of Full Employment worked right up until the moment that it stopped guaranteeing anything. Direct sale no longer absorbed overproduction, for there were no longer any buyers with credit left to absorb direct sales. Ten by ten, then hundreds by hundreds, workers got their walking papers. Each salary that disappeared cut by another small fraction the disposable income that might have lifted Clare from its slump.

Prosperity turned back into potash, on no provocation except whiplash and mob psychology. Those who lost their jobs, who were now losing their balloon-frame homes, began to wonder how else disaster could have happened if not through the faults of ownership itself. The map in the Lacewood Titles Office had been filled in. The world had gone fully professionalized. And the result was a third of the adult male population sporting sandwich boards that read "Will Work for Food," in the middle of the richest cropland in the world.

思考题

1. How does Lacewood bond with the Clare, Incorporated?
2. How does Laura deal with bugs in her garden? What do you think the symbolic meanings of "garden" and "bugs" are?
3. What does the author mean by saying that "business ran in the Clares' blood long before the first one of them made a single thing"? What are the characteristics of the Clare family?
4. What is the reaction of Laura and her family when they get to know that she has got cancer?
5. As one of the Clare's major products, soap is mentioned several times together with the word "clean". What do you think soap has brought to residents of Lacewood? Is it cleanness?
6. What do you think of the sentence "your life is chemistry" in the announcement of Clare Company on a magazine page? Do you think your life is chemistry?

第三节 补充阅读《胎记》

阅读霍桑的短篇小说《胎记》的选段,结合主人公艾尔默和妻子的对话,思考"胎记"的象征意义以及艾尔默试图用化学方法消除妻子脸上胎记的原因。

The Birth-Mark[①]

Nathaniel Hawthorne

In the latter part of the last century there lived a man of science, an eminent proficient in every branch of natural philosophy, who not long before our story opens had made experience of a spiritual affinity more attractive than any chemical one. He had left his laboratory to the care of an assistant, cleared his fine countenance from the furnace smoke, washed the stain of acids from his fingers, and persuaded a beautiful woman to become his wife. In those days when the comparatively recent discovery of electricity and other kindred mysteries of Nature seemed to open paths into the region of miracle, it was not unusual for the love of science to rival the love of woman in its depth and absorbing energy. The higher intellect, the imagination, the spirit, and even the heart might all find their congenial aliment in pursuits which, as some of their ardent votaries believed, would ascend from one step of powerful intelligence to another, until the philosopher should lay his hand on the secret of creative force and perhaps make new worlds for himself. We know not whether Aylmer possessed this degree of faith in man's ultimate control over Nature. He had devoted himself, however, too unreservedly to scientific studies ever to be weaned from them by any second passion. His love for his young wife might prove the stronger of the two; but it could only be by intertwining itself with his love of science, and uniting the strength of the latter to his own.

Such a union accordingly took place, and was attended with truly remarkable consequences and a deeply impressive moral. One day, very soon after their marriage, Aylmer sat gazing at his wife with a trouble in his countenance that grew stronger until he spoke.

---

① HAWTHORNE N. The birth-mark[C]//WAGGONER H H. Nathaniel Hawthorne: selected tales and sketches. 3rd ed. New York: Holt, Rinehart and Winston, 1970: 264-281.

第二章 文学与化学（Literature and Chemistry）

"Georgiana," said he, "has it never occurred to you that the mark upon your cheek might be removed?"

"No, indeed," said she, smiling; but perceiving the seriousness of his manner, she blushed deeply.

"To tell you the truth it has been so often called a charm that I was simple enough to imagine it might be so."

"Ah, upon another face perhaps it might," replied her husband; "but never on yours. No, dearest Georgiana, you came so nearly perfect from the hand of Nature that this slightest possible defect, which we hesitate whether to term a defect or a beauty, shocks me, as being the visible mark of earthly imperfection."

"Shocks you, my husband!" cried Georgiana, deeply hurt; at first reddening with momentary anger, but then bursting into tears. "Then why did you take me from my mother's side? You cannot love what shocks you!"

To explain this conversation it must be mentioned that in the center of Georgiana's left cheek there was a singular mark, deeply interwoven, as it were, with the texture and substance of her face. In the usual state of her complexion—a healthy though delicate bloom—the mark wore a tint of deeper crimson, which imperfectly defined its shape amid the surrounding rosiness. When she blushed it gradually became more indistinct, and finally vanished amid the triumphant rush of blood that bathed the whole cheek with its brilliant glow. But if any shifting motion caused her to turn pale there was the mark again, a crimson stain upon the snow, in what Aylmer sometimes deemed an almost fearful distinctness. Its shape bore not a little similarity to the human hand, though of the smallest pygmy size. Georgiana's lovers were wont to say that some fairy at her birth hour had laid her tiny hand upon the infant's cheek, and left this impress there in token of the magic endowments that were to give her such sway over all hearts. Many a desperate swain would have risked life for the privilege of pressing his lips to the mysterious hand. It must not be concealed, however, that the impression wrought by this fairy sign manual varied exceedingly, according to the difference of temperament in the beholders. Some fastidious persons—but they were exclusively of her own sex—affirmed that the bloody hand, as they chose to call it, quite destroyed the effect of Georgiana's beauty, and rendered her countenance even hideous. But it would be as reasonable to say that one of those small blue stains which sometimes occur in the purest statuary marble would convert the Eve of Powers to a monster. Masculine observers, if the birthmark did not heighten their admiration, contented themselves with wishing it away, that the world might poses one living specimen of ideal loveliness without the semblance of a flaw. After his marriage, —for he thought little or nothing of the matter before, —Aylmer discovered that this was the case with himself.

Had she been less beautiful, —if Envy's self could have found aught else to sneer at, —he might have felt his affection heightened by the prettiness of this mimic hand, now vaguely portrayed, now lost, now stealing forth again and glimmering to and fro with every pulse of emotion that throbbed within her heart; but seeing her otherwise so perfect, he found this one defect grow more and more intolerable with every moment of their united lives. It was the fatal flaw of humanity which Nature, in one shape or another, stamps ineffaceably on all her productions, either to imply that they are temporary and finite, or that their perfection must be wrought by toil and pain. The crimson hand expressed the ineludible gripe in which mortality clutches the highest and purest of earthly mould, degrading them into kindred with the lowest, and even with the very brutes, like whom their visible frames return to dust. In this manner, selecting it as the symbol of his wife's liability to sin, sorrow, decay, and death, Aylmer's sombre imagination was not long in rendering the birthmark a frightful object, causing him more trouble and horror than ever Georgiana's beauty, whether of soul or sense, had given him delight.

At all the seasons which should have been their happiest, he invariably and without intending it, nay, in spite of a purpose to the contrary, reverted to this one disastrous topic. Trifling as it at first appeared, it so connected itself with innumerable trains of thought and modes of feeling that it became the central point of all. With the morning twilight Aylmer opened his eyes upon his wife's face and recognized the symbol of imperfection; and when they sat together at the evening hearth his eyes wandered stealthily to her cheek, and beheld, flickering with the blaze of the wood fire, the spectral hand that wrote mortality where he would fain have worshipped. Georgiana soon learned to shudder at his gaze. It needed but a glance with the peculiar expression that his face often wore to change the roses of her cheek into a deathlike paleness, amid which the crimson hand was brought strongly out, like a bass-relief of ruby on the whitest marble.

Late one night when the lights were growing dim, so as hardly to betray the stain on the poor wife's cheek, she herself, for the first time, voluntarily took up the subject.

"Do you remember, my dear Aylmer," said she, with a feeble attempt at a smile, "have you any recollection of a dream last night about this odious hand?"

"None! —none whatever!" replied Aylmer, starting; but then he added, in a dry, cold tone, affected for the sake of concealing the real depth of his emotion, "I might well dream of it; for before I fell asleep it had taken a pretty firm hold of my fancy."

"And you did dream of it?" continued Georgiana, hastily; for she dreaded lest a gush of tears should interrupt what she had to say. "A terrible dream! I wonder that you can forget it. Is it possible to forget this one expression? — 'It is in her heart now; we must have it out!' Reflect, my husband; for by all means I would have you recall that dream."

The mind is in a sad state when Sleep, the all-involving, cannot confine her spectres within the dim region of her sway, but suffers them to break forth, affrighting this actual life with secrets that perchance belong to a deeper one. Aylmer now remembered his dream. He had fancied himself with his servant Aminadab, attempting an operation for the removal of the birthmark; but the deeper went the knife, the deeper sank the hand, until at length its tiny grasp appeared to have caught hold of Georgiana's heart; whence, however, her husband was inexorably resolved to cut or wrench it away.

When the dream had shaped itself perfectly in his memory, Aylmer sat in his wife's presence with a guilty feeling. Truth often finds its way to the mind close muffled in robes of sleep, and then speaks with uncompromising directness of matters in regard to which we practise an unconscious self-deception during our waking moments. Until now he had not been aware of the tyrannizing influence acquired by one idea over his mind, and of the lengths which he might find in his heart to go for the sake of giving himself peace.

"Aylmer," resumed Georgiana, solemnly, "I know not what may be the cost to both of us to rid me of this fatal birthmark. Perhaps its removal may cause cureless deformity; or it may be the stain goes as deep as life itself. Again: do we know that there is a possibility, on any terms, of unclasping the firm gripe of this little hand which was laid upon me before I came into the world?"

"Dearest Georgiana, I have spent much thought upon the subject," hastily interrupted Aylmer. "I am convinced of the perfect practicability of its removal."

"If there be the remotest possibility of it," continued Georgiana, "let the attempt be made at whatever risk. Danger is nothing to me; for life, while this hateful mark makes me the object of your horror and disgust,—life is a burden which I would fling down with joy. Either remove this dreadful hand, or take my wretched life! You have deep science. All the world bears witness of it. You have achieved great wonders. Cannot you remove this little, little mark, which I cover with the tips of two small fingers? Is this beyond your power, for the sake of your own peace, and to save your poor wife from madness?"

"Noblest, dearest, tenderest wife," cried Aylmer, rapturously, "doubt not my power. I have already given this matter the deepest thought—thought which might almost have enlightened me to create a being less perfect than yourself. Georgiana, you have led me deeper than ever into the heart of science. I feel myself fully competent to render this dear cheek as faultless as its fellow; and then, most beloved, what will be my triumph when I shall have corrected what Nature left imperfect in her fairest work! Even Pygmalion, when his sculptured woman assumed life, felt not greater ecstasy than mine will be."

"It is resolved, then," said Georgiana, faintly smiling. "And, Aylmer, spare me not, though you should find the birthmark take refuge in my heart at last."

Her husband tenderly kissed her cheek—her right cheek—not that which bore the impress of the crimson hand.

The next day Aylmer apprised his wife of a plan that he had formed whereby he might have opportunity for the intense thought and constant watchfulness which the proposed operation would require; while Georgiana, likewise, would enjoy the perfect repose essential to its success. They were to seclude themselves in the extensive apartments occupied by Aylmer as a laboratory, and where, during his toilsome youth, he had made discoveries in the elemental powers of Nature that had roused the

第二章 文学与化学 (Literature and Chemistry)

admiration of all the learned societies in Europe. Seated calmly in this laboratory, the pale philosopher had investigated the secrets of the highest cloud region and of the profoundest mines; he had satisfied himself of the causes that kindled and kept alive the fires of the volcano; and had explained the mystery of fountains, and how it is that they gush forth, some so bright and pure, and others with such rich medicinal virtues, from the dark bosom of the earth. Here, too, at an earlier period, he had studied the wonders of the human frame, and attempted to fathom the very process by which Nature assimilates all her precious influences from earth and air, and from the spiritual world, to create and foster man, her masterpiece. The latter pursuit, however, Aylmer had long laid aside in unwilling recognition of the truth—against which all seekers sooner or later stumble—that our great creative Mother, while she amuses us with apparently working in the broadest sunshine, is yet severely careful to keep her own secrets, and, in spite of her pretended openness, shows us nothing but results. She permits us, indeed, to mar, but seldom to mend, and, like a jealous patentee, on no account to make. Now, however, Aylmer resumed these half-forgotten investigations; not, of course, with such hopes or wishes as first suggested them; but because they involved much physiological truth and lay in the path of his proposed scheme for the treatment of Georgiana.

As he led her over the threshold of the laboratory, Georgiana was cold and tremulous. Aylmer looked cheerfully into her face, with intent to reassure her, but was so startled with the intense glow of the birthmark upon the whiteness of her cheek that he could not restrain a strong convulsive shudder. His wife fainted.

"Aminadab! Aminadab!" shouted Aylmer, stamping violently on the floor.

Forthwith there issued from an inner apartment a man of low stature, but bulky frame, with shaggy hair hanging about his visage, which was grimed with the vapors of the furnace. This personage had been Aylmer's underworker during his whole scientific career, and was admirably fitted for that office by his great mechanical readiness, and the skill with which, while incapable of comprehending a single principle, he executed all the details of his master's experiments. With his vast strength, his shaggy hair, his smoky aspect, and the indescribable earthiness that incrusted him, he seemed to represent man's physical nature; while Aylmer's slender figure, and pale, intellectual face, were no less apt a type of the spiritual element.

"Throw open the door of the boudoir, Aminadab," said Aylmer, "and burn a pastil."

"Yes, master," answered Aminadab, looking intently at the lifeless form of Georgiana; and then he muttered to himself, "If she were my wife, I'd never part with that birthmark."

When Georgiana recovered consciousness she found herself breathing an atmosphere of penetrating fragrance, the gentle potency of which had recalled her from her deathlike faintness. The scene around her looked like enchantment. Aylmer had converted those smoky, dingy, sombre rooms, where he had spent his brightest years in recondite pursuits, into a series of beautiful apartments not unfit to be the secluded abode of a lovely woman. The walls were hung with gorgeous curtains, which imparted the combination of grandeur and grace that no other species of adornment can achieve; and as they fell from the ceiling to the floor, their rich and ponderous folds, concealing all angles and straight lines, appeared to shut in the scene from infinite space. For aught Georgiana knew, it might be a pavilion among the clouds. And Aylmer, excluding the sunshine, which would have interfered with his chemical processes, had supplied its place with perfumed lamps, emitting flames of various hue, but all uniting in a soft, empurpled radiance. He now knelt by his wife's side, watching her earnestly, but without alarm; for he was confident in his science, and felt that he could draw a magic circle round her within which no evil might intrude.

"Where am I? Ah, I remember," said Georgiana, faintly; and she placed her hand over her cheek to hide the terrible mark from her husband's eyes.

"Fear not, dearest!" exclaimed he. "Do not shrink from me! Believe me, Georgiana, I even rejoice in this single imperfection, since it will be such a rapture to remove it."

"Oh, spare me!" sadly replied his wife. "Pray do not look at it again. I never can forget that convulsive shudder."

In order to soothe Georgiana, and, as it were, to release her mind from the burden of actual things, Aylmer now put in practice some of the light and playful secrets which science had taught him among its profounder lore. Airy figures, absolutely bodiless

第二章 文学与化学(Literature and Chemistry)

ideas, and forms of unsubstantial beauty came and danced before her, imprinting their momentary footsteps on beams of light. Though she had some indistinct idea of the method of these optical phenomena, still the illusion was almost perfect enough to warrant the belief that her husband possessed sway over the spiritual world. Then again, when she felt a wish to look forth from her seclusion, immediately, as if her thoughts were answered, the procession of external existence flitted across a screen. The scenery and the figures of actual life were perfectly represented, but with that bewitching, yet indescribable difference which always makes a picture, an image, or a shadow so much more attractive than the original. When wearied of this, Aylmer bade her cast her eyes upon a vessel containing a quantity of earth. She did so, with little interest at first; but was soon startled to perceive the germ of a plant shooting upward from the soil. Then came the slender stalk; the leaves gradually unfolded themselves; and amid them was a perfect and lovely flower.

"It is magical!" cried Georgiana. "I dare not touch it."

"Nay, pluck it," answered Aylmer, — "pluck it, and inhale its brief perfume while you may. The flower will wither in a few moments and leave nothing save its brown seed vessels; but thence may be perpetuated a race as ephemeral as itself."

But Georgiana had no sooner touched the flower than the whole plant suffered a blight, its leaves turning coal-black as if by the agency of fire.

"There was too powerful a stimulus," said Aylmer, thoughtfully.

To make up for this abortive experiment, he proposed to take her portrait by a scientific process of his own invention. It was to be effected by rays of light striking upon a polished plate of metal. Georgiana assented; but, on looking at the result, was affrighted to find the features of the portrait blurred and indefinable; while the minute figure of a hand appeared where the cheek should have been. Aylmer snatched the metallic plate and threw it into a jar of corrosive acid.

Soon, however, he forgot these mortifying failures. In the intervals of study and chemical experiment he came to her flushed and exhausted, but seemed invigorated by her presence, and spoke in glowing language of the resources of his art. He gave a history of the long dynasty of the alchemists, who spent so many ages in quest of the universal solvent by which the golden principle might be elicited from all things vile and base. Aylmer appeared to believe that, by the plainest scientific logic, it was altogether within the limits of possibility to discover this long-sought medium; "but," he added, "a philosopher who should go deep enough to acquire the power would attain too lofty a wisdom to stoop to the exercise of it." Not less singular were his opinions in regard to the elixir vitae. He more than intimated that it was at his option to concoct a liquid that should prolong life for years, perhaps interminably; but that it would produce a discord in Nature which all the world, and chiefly the quaffer of the immortal nostrum, would find cause to curse.

"Aylmer, are you in earnest?" asked Georgiana, looking at him with amazement and fear. "It is terrible to possess such power, or even to dream of possessing it."

"Oh, do not tremble, my love," said her husband. "I would not wrong either you or myself by working such inharmonious effects upon our lives; but I would have you consider how trifling, in comparison, is the skill requisite to remove this little hand."

At the mention of the birthmark, Georgiana, as usual, shrank as if a red hot iron had touched her cheek.

Again Aylmer applied himself to his labors. She could hear his voice in the distant furnace room giving directions to Aminadab, whose harsh, uncouth, misshapen tones were audible in response, more like the grunt or growl of a brute than human speech. After hours of absence, Aylmer reappeared and proposed that she should now examine his cabinet of chemical products and natural treasures of the earth. Among the former he showed her a small vial, in which, he remarked, was contained a gentle yet most powerful fragrance, capable of impregnating all the breezes that blow across a kingdom. They were of inestimable value, the contents of that little vial; and, as he said so, he threw some of the perfume into the air and filled the room with piercing and invigorating delight.

"And what is this?" asked Georgiana, pointing to a small crystal globe containing a gold-colored liquid. "It is so beautiful to the eye that I could imagine it the elixir of life."

"In one sense it is," replied Aylmer; "or, rather, the elixir of immortality. It is the most precious poison that ever was concocted in this world. By its aid I could apportion the lifetime of any mortal at whom you might point your finger. The strength of the dose would determine whether he were to linger out years, or drop dead in the midst of a breath. No king on his guarded throne could keep his life if I, in my private station, should deem that the welfare of millions justified me in depriving him of it."

"Why do you keep such a terrific drug?" inquired Georgiana in horror. "Do not mistrust me, dearest," said her husband, smiling; "its virtuous potency is yet greater than its harmful one. But see! here is a powerful cosmetic. With a few drops of this in a vase of water, freckles may be washed away as easily as the hands are cleansed. A stronger infusion would take the blood out of the cheek, and leave the rosiest beauty a pale ghost."

"Is it with this lotion that you intend to bathe my cheek?" asked Georgiana, anxiously.

"Oh, no," hastily replied her husband; "this is merely superficial. Your case demands a remedy that shall go deeper."

In his interviews with Georgiana, Aylmer generally made minute inquiries as to her sensations and whether the confinement of the rooms and the temperature of the atmosphere agreed with her. These questions had such a particular drift that Georgiana began to conjecture that she was already subjected to certain physical influences, either breathed in with the fragrant air or taken with her food. She fancied likewise, but it might be altogether fancy, that there was a stirring up of her system—a strange, indefinite sensation creeping through her veins, and tingling, half painfully, half pleasurably, at her heart. Still, whenever she dared to look into the mirror, there she beheld herself pale as a white rose and with the crimson birthmark stamped upon her cheek. Not even Aylmer now hated it so much as she.

To dispel the tedium of the hours which her husband found it necessary to devote to the processes of combination and analysis, Georgiana turned over the volumes of his scientific library. In many dark old tomes she met with chapters full of romance and poetry. They were the works of philosophers of the middle ages, such as Albertus Magnus, Cornelius Agrippa, Paracelsus, and the famous friar who created the prophetic Brazen Head. All these antique naturalists stood in advance of their centuries, yet were imbued with some of their credulity, and therefore were believed, and perhaps imagined themselves to have acquired from the investigation of Nature a power above Nature, and from physics a sway over the spiritual world. Hardly less curious and imaginative were the early volumes of the Transactions of the Royal Society, in which the members, knowing little of the limits of natural possibility, were continually recording wonders or proposing methods whereby wonders might be wrought.

But to Georgiana the most engrossing volume was a large folio from her husband's own hand, in which he had recorded every experiment of his scientific career, its original aim, the methods adopted for its development, and its final success or failure, with the circumstances to which either event was attributable. The book, in truth, was both the history and emblem of his ardent, ambitious, imaginative, yet practical and laborious life. He handled physical details as if there were nothing beyond them; yet spiritualized them all, and redeemed himself from materialism by his strong and eager aspiration towards the infinite. In his grasp the veriest clod of earth assumed a soul. Georgiana, as she read, reverenced Aylmer and loved him more profoundly than ever, but with a less entire dependence on his judgment than heretofore. Much as he had accomplished, she could not but observe that his most splendid successes were almost invariably failures, if compared with the ideal at which he aimed. His brightest diamonds were the merest pebbles, and felt to be so by himself, in comparison with the inestimable gems which lay hidden beyond his reach. The volume, rich with achievements that had won renown for its author, was yet as melancholy a record as ever mortal hand had penned. It was the sad confession and continual exemplification of the shortcomings of the composite man, the spirit burdened with clay and working in matter, and of the despair that assails the higher nature at finding itself so miserably thwarted by the earthly part. Perhaps every man of genius in whatever sphere might recognize the image of his own experience in Aylmer's journal.

So deeply did these reflections affect Georgiana that she laid her face upon the open volume and burst into tears. In this situation she was found by her husband.

"It is dangerous to read in a sorcerer's books," said he with a smile, though his countenance was uneasy and displeased. "Georgiana, there are pages in that volume which I can scarcely glance over and keep my senses. Take heed lest it prove as detrimental to you."

"It has made me worship you more than ever," said she.

第二章 文学与化学 (Literature and Chemistry)

"Ah, wait for this one success," rejoined he, "then worship me if you will. I shall deem myself hardly unworthy of it. But come, I have sought you for the luxury of your voice. Sing to me, dearest."

So she poured out the liquid music of her voice to quench the thirst of his spirit. He then took his leave with a boyish exuberance of gayety, assuring her that her seclusion would endure but a little longer, and that the result was already certain. Scarcely had he departed when Georgiana felt irresistibly impelled to follow him. She had forgotten to inform Aylmer of a symptom which for two or three hours past had begun to excite her attention. It was a sensation in the fatal birthmark, not painful, but which induced a restlessness throughout her system. Hastening after her husband, she intruded for the first time into the laboratory.

The first thing that struck her eye was the furnace, that hot and feverish worker, with the intense glow of its fire, which by the quantities of soot clustered above it seemed to have been burning for ages. There was a distilling apparatus in full operation. Around the room were retorts, tubes, cylinders, crucibles, and other apparatus of chemical research. An electrical machine stood ready for immediate use. The atmosphere felt oppressively close, and was tainted with gaseous odors which had been tormented forth by the processes of science. The severe and homely simplicity of the apartment, with its naked walls and brick pavement, looked strange, accustomed as Georgiana had become to the fantastic elegance of her boudoir. But what chiefly, indeed almost solely, drew her attention, was the aspect of Aylmer himself.

He was pale as death, anxious and absorbed, and hung over the furnace as if it depended upon his utmost watchfulness whether the liquid which it was distilling should be the draught of immortal happiness or misery. How different from the sanguine and joyous mien that he had assumed for Georgiana's encouragement!

"Carefully now, Aminadab; carefully, thou human machine; carefully, thou man of clay!" muttered Aylmer, more to himself than his assistant. "Now, if there be a thought too much or too little, it is all over."

"Ho! Ho!" mumbled Aminadab. "Look, master! Look!"

Aylmer raised his eyes hastily, and at first reddened, then grew paler than ever, on beholding Georgiana. He rushed towards her and seized her arm with a gripe that left the print of his fingers upon it.

"Why do you come hither? Have you no trust in your husband?" cried he, impetuously. "Would you throw the blight of that fatal birthmark over my labors? It is not well done. Go, prying woman, go!"

"Nay, Aylmer," said Georgiana with the firmness of which she possessed no stinted endowment, "it is not you that have a right to complain. You mistrust your wife; you have concealed the anxiety with which you watch the development of this experiment. Think not so unworthily of me, my husband. Tell me all the risk we run, and fear not that I shall shrink; for my share in it is far less than your own."

"No, no, Georgiana!" said Aylmer, impatiently; "it must not be."

"I submit," replied she calmly. "And, Aylmer, I shall quaff whatever draught you bring me; but it will be on the same principle that would induce me to take a dose of poison if offered by your hand."

"My noble wife," said Aylmer, deeply moved, "I knew not the height and depth of your nature until now. Nothing shall be concealed. Know, then, that this crimson hand, superficial as it seems, has clutched its grasp into your being with a strength of which I had no previous conception. I have already administered agents powerful enough to do aught except to change your entire physical system. Only one thing remains to be tried. If that fail us we are ruined."

"Why did you hesitate to tell me this?" asked she.

"Because, Georgiana," said Aylmer, in a low voice, "there is danger."

"Danger? There is but one danger—that this horrible stigma shall be left upon my cheek!" cried Georgiana. "Remove it, remove it, whatever be the cost, or we shall both go mad!"

"Heaven knows your words are too true," said Aylmer, sadly. "And now, dearest, return to your boudoir. In a little while all will be tested."

He conducted her back and took leave of her with a solemn tenderness which spoke far more than his words how much was now at stake. After his departure became rapt in musings. She considered the character of Aylmer, and did it completer justice than at any previous moment. Her heart exulted, while it trembled, at his honorable love—so pure and lofty that it would accept nothing less than perfection nor miserably make itself

第二章 文学与化学(Literature and Chemistry)

contented with an earthlier nature than he had dreamed of. She felt how much more precious was such a sentiment than that meaner kind which would have borne with the imperfection for her sake, and have been guilty of treason to holy love by degrading its perfect idea to the level of the actual; and with her whole spirit she prayed that, for a single moment, she might satisfy his highest and deepest conception. Longer than one moment she well knew it could not be; for his spirit was ever on the march, ever ascending, and each instant required something that was beyond the scope of the instant before.

The sound of her husband's footsteps aroused her. He bore a crystal goblet containing a liquor colorless as water, but bright enough to be the draught of immortality. Aylmer was pale; but it seemed rather the consequence of a highly wrought state of mind and tension of spirit than of fear or doubt.

"The concoction of the draught has been perfect," said he, in answer to Georgiana's look. "Unless all my science have deceived me, it cannot fail."

"Save on your account, my dearest Aylmer," observed his wife, "I might wish to put off this birthmark of mortality by relinquishing mortality itself in preference to any other mode. Life is but a sad possession to those who have attained precisely the degree of moral advancement at which I stand. Were I weaker and blinder it might be happiness. Were I stronger, it might be endured hopefully. But, being what I find myself, methinks I am of all mortals the most fit to die."

"You are fit for heaven without tasting death!" replied her husband. "But why do we speak of dying? The draught cannot fail. Behold its effect upon this plant."

On the window seat there stood a geranium diseased with yellow blotches, which had overspread all its leaves. Aylmer poured a small quantity of the liquid upon the soil in which it grew. In a little time, when the roots of the plant had taken up the moisture, the unsightly blotches began to be extinguished in a living verdure.

"There needed no proof," said Georgiana, quietly. "Give me the goblet I joyfully stake all upon your word."

"Drink, then, thou lofty creature!" exclaimed Aylmer, with fervid admiration. "There is no taint of imperfection on thy spirit. Thy sensible frame, too, shall soon be all perfect."

She quaffed the liquid and returned the goblet to his hand.

"It is grateful," said she with a placid smile. "Methinks it is like water from a heavenly fountain; for it contains I know not what of unobtrusive fragrance and deliciousness. It allays a feverish thirst that had parched me for many days. Now, dearest, let me sleep. My earthly senses are closing over my spirit like the leaves around the heart of a rose at sunset."

She spoke the last words with a gentle reluctance, as if it required almost more energy than she could command to pronounce the faint and lingering syllables. Scarcely had they loitered through her lips ere she was lost in slumber. Aylmer sat by her side, watching her aspect with the emotions proper to a man the whole value of whose existence was involved in the process now to be tested. Mingled with this mood, however, was the philosophic investigation characteristic of the man of science. Not the minutest symptom escaped him. A heightened flush of the cheek, a slight irregularity of breath, a quiver of the eyelid, a hardly perceptible tremor through the frame,—such were the details which, as the moments passed, he wrote down in his folio volume. Intense thought had set its stamp upon every previous page of that volume, but the thoughts of years were all concentrated upon the last.

While thus employed, he failed not to gaze often at the fatal hand, and not without a shudder. Yet once, by a strange and unaccountable impulse he pressed it with his lips. His spirit recoiled, however, in the very act, and Georgiana, out of the midst of her deep sleep, moved uneasily and murmured as if in remonstrance. Again Aylmer resumed his watch. Nor was it without avail. The crimson hand, which at first had been strongly visible upon the marble paleness of Georgiana's cheek, now grew more faintly outlined. She remained not less pale than ever; but the birthmark with every breath that came and went, lost somewhat of its former distinctness. Its presence had been awful; its departure was more awful still. Watch the stain of the rainbow fading out the sky, and you will know how that mysterious symbol passed away.

"By Heaven! It is well-nigh gone!" said Aylmer to himself, in almost irrepressible ecstasy. "I can scarcely trace it now. Success! Success! And now it is like the faintest rose color. The lightest flush of blood across her cheek would overcome it. But she is so pale!"

第二章 文学与化学(Literature and Chemistry)

He drew aside the window curtain and suffered the light of natural day to fall into the room and rest upon her cheek. At the same time he heard a gross, hoarse chuckle, which he had long known as his servant Aminadab's expression of delight.

"Ah, clod! Ah, earthly mass!" cried Aylmer, laughing in a sort of frenzy, "you have served me well! Matter and Spirit—Earth and Heaven—have both done their part in this! Laugh, thing of the senses! You have earned the right to laugh."

These exclamations broke Georgiana's cep. she slowly closed her eyes and gazed into the mirror which her husband had arranged for that purpose. A faint smile flitted over her lips when she recognized how barely perceptible was now that crimson hand which had once blazed forth with such disastrous brilliancy as to scare away all their happiness. But then her eyes sought Aylmer's face with a trouble and anxiety that he could by no means account for.

"My poor Aylmer!" murmured she.

"Poor? Nay, richest, happiest, most favored!" exclaimed he. "My peerless bride, it is successful! You are perfect!"

"My poor Aylmer," she repeated, with a more than human tenderness, "you have aimed loftily; you have done nobly. Do not repent that with so high and pure a feeling, you have rejected the best the earth could offer. Aylmer, dearest Aylmer, I am dying!"

Alas, it was too true! The fatal hand had grappled with the mystery of life, and was the bond by which an angelic spirit kept itself in union with a mortal frame. As the last crimson tint of the birthmark—that sole token of human imperfection—faded from her cheek, the parting breath of the now perfect woman passed into the atmosphere, and her soul, lingering a moment near her husband, took its heavenward flight. Then a hoarse, chuckling laugh was heard again! Thus ever does the gross fatality of earth exult in its invariable triumph over the immortal essence which, in this dim sphere of half development, demands the completeness of a higher state. Yet, had Alymer reached a profounder wisdom, he need not thus have flung away the happiness which would have woven his mortal life of the selfsame texture with the celestial. The momentary circumstance was too strong for him; he failed to look beyond the shadowy scope of time, and, living once for all in eternity, to find the perfect future in the present.

第三章

文学与医学(Literature and Medicine)

第一节 医学的文学表征

背景知识

医学(medicine)是人类与恶劣环境和疾病长期斗争的结晶,医学的定义随着历史文明的进程、经济科技的发展、社会自然的变化以及医学本身的探索而形成和变化。古代中国对医学有"仁术"的概括;古希腊"医学之父"希波克拉底(Hippocrates,460—370 BC)在《希波克拉底箴言》(*Hippocratic Oath*)中写道:"生命短暂,医术长青,机遇难逢,经验常谬,确诊实难",后来古希腊人把它定义为"医学是至圣的健康之术①。"20世纪,美国医学家罗希(G. H. Roche)在《医学导论》中指出:"医学科学以疾病为研究对象。医术以维护和恢复健康为目的②。"《牛津大辞典》对医学的定义为:"医学是预防与治疗疾病的艺术和科学③。"进入21世纪,医学发展与时俱进,其定义是:通过科学技术手段处理各种疾病或病变,促进病患恢复身心健康,适应自然社会的一门专业学科。从医学定义的演变,我们不难发现医学所独具的特点:医学既可以是宏观概括,也可以是具体解释;既是一项专业技术,也是一种崇高事业,不限于用一个完整、确切的定义来解释④。

作为一门学科,医学主要分为中医宏观体系和西医微观体系,中医讲究自身调理,西医着重外部干预。而医学的漫长发展大致经历了原始医学、古代经验医学、近代实验医学和现代医学几个阶段。原始医学随着人类的起源而诞生,人类诞生之初是在极其恶劣的环境中生活,采食果实、茹毛饮血。在这样的生存状态下人们逐渐知道了植物的营养、毒性和治疗作用;也意识到一些动物的内脏、血液等可以治疗某些疾病。这些活动都是最原始的、被动感知的"经验医学"。而古代经验医学持续时间相对比较长,这一时期的医学带有浓郁的宗

---

① 苏佳灿,黄标通,许金廉,等. 医学起源与发展简史[M]. 上海:上海大学出版社,2020:1.
② 沈胜娟,王悦. 医学导论[M]. 上海:第二军医大学出版社,2010:6-8.
③ 同①1.
④ 同①6-8.

第三章 文学与医学（Literature and Medicine）

教色彩，出现了所谓的"巫医""神医"①。当然这个时期古代东方医学也积累了许多有价值的治病经验，出现了一些有指导意义的医学论著，如：扁鹊（约前407年—约前310年）的望、闻、问、切四诊法，中国最早的医学典籍《内经》，秦汉时期的《神农本草经》、张仲景（约公元150~154年—约公元215~219年）的《伤寒杂病论》，唐代医学家孙思邈（541年或581年？—682年）的《千金方》以及明朝医药学家李时珍（1518—1593）的《本草纲目》等②。而在西方，希腊医学是欧洲医学发展的基础，其代表人物为"医学之父"希波克拉底。希波克拉底最大的贡献在于医生的职业化、理解自然并利用自然对付疾病的医学体系，此外他还受到希腊自然哲学家思想的影响，发展、完善并形成了"四体液学说"理论，从而使医学理论从哲学框架延伸出来，成为一门独立的学科；"四体液学说"理论认为人体内有四种基本的体液：血液、黏液、黄胆汁和黑胆汁，分别储藏于人体的心、肝、脾、脑，与自然界的空气、火、土、水相对应，表现出易怒、温润、冷静和忧郁气质③。根据这一理论，疾病就是人体体液失衡的结果，而这一理论也体现了希腊医学的整体观思想。此外，《希波克拉底文集》中很多地方都涉及医学道德问题，著名的有《希波克拉底誓言》，这是所有医学生入学时必须宣誓的④。

西方近代医学是指文艺复兴以后逐渐兴起的医学，一般包括16世纪至19世纪的欧洲医学。医学史上所谓的"医学革命"，指的是现代医学的诞生，是欧洲文艺复兴时期的科学发展的产物。17世纪由于物理、化学和生物学有了长足的进步，医学家不满意过去的医学学说，出现了一些新的派别。其一是物理学派，其代表人物是哲学家和数学家笛卡尔（René Descartes，1596—1650），主张用物理原理解释一切生命现象和病理现象。化学派代表是希尔维厄斯（Franciscus Sylvius，1614—1672），认为血液是中枢，一切病理过程都由血液产生，对所有疾病都用化学原理来解释和治疗。其二是活力派，代表人物是格奥尔格·恩斯特·施塔尔（Georg Ernst Stahl，1659—1734），认为疾病的原因在于生命力的减少，而其消失就是死亡⑤。18、19世纪生产力大大提高，自然科学和技术飞速发展，细胞病理学、细菌学、药理学、实验生理学、诊断学、外科学、预防医学、护理学等相继诞生并快速发展⑥。到了20世纪，近代医学与现代科学技术紧密结合，发展为现代医学。早期的突破是卡尔·兰德施泰纳（Karl Landsteiner，1868—1943）对于血型的研究，这有助于各种急救和手术。1921年和

---

① 卡尔格-德克尔. 医药文化史[M]. 姚燕，周惠，译. 北京：生活·读书·新知三联书店，2004：1-2.
② 苏佳灿，黄标通，许金廉，等. 医学起源与发展简史[M]. 上海：上海大学出版社，2020：3.
③ PORTER R. The greatest benefit to mankind: a medical history of humanity[M]. New York: W. W. Norton & Company, 1997: 58. 另参见卡斯蒂廖尼. 医学史[M]. 程之范，译. 桂林：广西师范大学出版社，2003：119-123.
④ GARRISON F H. An introduction to the history of medicine[M]. Philadelphia: W. B. Saunders Company, 1917: 93. 另参见卡斯蒂廖尼. 医学史[M]. 程之范，译. 桂林：广西师范大学出版社，2003：115. 另参见高晞. 医学与历史[M]. 上海：复旦大学出版社，2020：27-29.
⑤ 同②14.
⑥ 帕克. DK医学史：从巫术、针灸到基因编辑[M]. 李虎，译. 北京：中信出版集团，2019：163-230.

1922年,弗雷德里克·班廷(Frederick Banting, 1891—1941)和他的团队在多伦多开始用胰岛素治疗糖尿病。20世纪70年代以来,CT(电子计算机断层扫描)、MRI(磁共振成像)和其他电脑医学扫描仪造就了新一代的人体图像①。1978年,随着罗伯特·爱德华兹(Robert G. Edwards, 1925—2013)和帕特里克·斯特普托(Patrick C. Steptoe, 1913—1988)成就了第一个试管婴儿,生命的开始也有了新的方式。可见,现代医学的特点是微观和宏观的有机融合,分子医学和系统医学齐头并进;学科体系上,学科分立和学科之间的交叉融合。医学研究的国际化倾向日益明显,一些先进技术也在快速发展,但21世纪也面临着新的威胁和挑战,如:耐抗生素的细菌大量传播,新型病毒传染病引起的瘟疫大流行,恶性肿瘤以及痴呆症的异常增加②。因此,随着社会需求的不断变化,医学与时俱进,当下的尖端研究也会演变成将来具有实用性的医学技术,这是一个长期、艰苦的过程,只要坚持不懈,一切皆有可能。

文学作品对于医学发展成就的表征古已有之。虽然就学科分类而言,医学与文学"风马牛不相及",但文学与医学是生命救赎的两个重要支撑点,如果从文化层面进行分析,这两个学科都是将人作为研究对象,医学救人、文学树人,"以人为本"促成了这两个学科的完美融合和统一③。医学为文学提供了丰富厚重的创作素材;医学素养也丰富了文学创作的思维模式和艺术方法④。美国哥伦比亚大学"叙事医学"(narrative medicine)创始人丽塔·卡伦(Rita Charon, 1949—)在《叙事医学:尊重疾病的故事》(Narrative Medicine: Honoring the Stories of Illness, 2006)一书中也认为,哲学、医学、心理学和文学都是对自我的关注,只是视角不同⑤。因此,医学和文学既有各自独特的学科归属与研究范式,又有着极具默契的通性,在特殊的语境下宛如并蒂而生的双生花,同根同源存在着天然的亲近感⑥。

古希腊诗人赫西俄德(Hesiod)在长诗《工作与时日》(Works and Days)中最早描述了潘多拉打开魔盒放出各种罪恶的情节,疾病便是这诸罪之一。在中国传统文化的早期阶段,无论是诗歌、民歌、民谣还是市井小调,都是医学重要的传播载体。如大家耳熟能详的《诗经》,其中就有大量关于医学内容的描写,开启了以文传医的先河。一些古典文学作品,如《左传》《庄子》《吕氏春秋》《三国演义》等,也蕴含了丰富的医学思想以及疾病的描述。《红楼梦》中"两弯似蹙非蹙罥烟眉,一双似喜非喜含情目",对林黛玉的病情进行了生动刻画,而且林

---

① 帕克. DK医学史:从巫术、针灸到基因编辑[M]. 李虎,译. 北京:中信出版集团,2019:241.
② 卡特赖特,弗雷德里克. 疾病改变历史[M]. 陈仲丹,译. 北京:华夏出版社,2020:247-259.
③ 郑民,王亭. 文学与医学文化[M]. 济南:山东大学出版社,2015:1-6,26.
④ 同③6-7.
⑤ 常宇,蔡敏. 以叙事医学为突破口,诠释医者人文情怀:打造医学非虚构文学文本提升医院品牌形象[J]. 叙事医学,2020,3(2):98-100.
⑥ 薛守瑞. 文学与医学的天然亲近感:兼论鼠疫题材小说中的医疗书写[J]. 中国医学人文,2021(2):16-19.

第三章 文学与医学(Literature and Medicine)

黛玉的性情和命运,也跟病情有着千丝万缕的联系①。在西方文学史上,众多作家也在作品中讨论了医学相关的话题。比如,乔万尼·薄伽丘(Giovanni Boccaccio,1313—1375)在《十日谈》(*The Decameron*,1349—1352)中以大瘟疫作为引子,点明社会现状,为作品提供时代底色。莎士比亚的剧作中也存有诸多医学元素,展现了大量关于精神崩溃、睡眠障碍、癫痫等精神疾患的场景,增添了剧情的跌宕起伏和美感;而莎士比亚也被称为"社会精神病理学家"②。在英国维多利亚时代,一些小说将社会医学作为特定的主题,如夏洛特·勃朗特(Charlotte Brontë,1816—1855)的《呼啸山庄》(*Wuthering Heights*,1847)和艾略特的《米德尔马契》(*Middlemarch*,1872)。在美国作家凯瑟琳·安·波特(Katherine Anne Porter,1890—1980)的《灰色马,灰色的骑手》(*Pale Horse, Pale Rider*,1939)中,疾病情节贯穿于始终,小说男女主人公的恋爱虽是故事的主要事件,但在结构上却服务于疾病体验的传达。该小说想象了1918年的大流感,它是两次世界大战之间美国文学文化领域几近缺场的灾难事件,值得医学、文学等各领域学者进行深入探究③。

文学对医学的发展也有着重要的影响。始于意大利的文艺复兴运动可以说是近代西方文明的一个转折点,知识分子思考的焦点开始从"天上"转到"人间",对社会形成一种质疑、探讨的精神,不再盲目地迷信神的权威。这一时期天文学、物理学、化学等科学知识快速发展,人民对于自然界不再惧怕、不再恐惧,转而穷尽自然的法则,以求征服自然。正是在这个背景下,才有瑞士医学家帕拉切尔苏斯(Paracelsus,1493—1541)向传统道德规则和盲目崇拜发出了挑战,指出人体的生命过程是化学过程;也才会有达·芬奇解剖许多尸体,并留下150多幅人体解剖图,借此研究人体比例。另外,达·芬奇通过向气管中吹气,证明了人体心肺没有连接;通过对心脏的仔细研究,了解到心脏瓣膜有阻止血液回流的作用。这些关于人体心血管的研究,为医学的后续发展打下了坚实的基础。在达·芬奇逝世仅仅24年之后,安德烈·维萨里(Andreas Vesalius,1514—1564)就完成了巨作《人体构造》(*De Humani Corporis Fabrica*,1543),这是人类第一次精确地认识到自身的机体。不仅文学思潮为医学的发展提供了必要的探索精神,文学作品在医学教育和临床实践方面也起着重要的作用。一方面,文学作品所描述的疾病,能为医护人深入探究疾病的症状及治疗方案提供具体的案例;另一方面,文学作品如艾略特《米德尔马契》中关于医学的作用以及医护人员扮演的角色的思考,让医护人员及相关研究者认识到他们肩负的使命;甚至文学作品中的医学叙事,也

---

① 郑民,王亭.文学与医学文化[M].济南:山东大学出版社,2015:12-137.另参见孙玮志.中国传统医学与古典文学[N].光明日报,2018-08-13(13).

② EDGAR I I. Shakespeare's psychopathological knowledge: a study in criticism and interpretation [J]. The journal of abnormal and social psychology, 1935(1): 70-83.

③ 骆谋贝.医学人文学视角下《灰色马,灰色的骑手》中的疾病叙事[J].外国文学研究,2021(2):153-164.

为医学研究者和医护人员如何描述疾病提供了参考①。因此,文学研究及文学批评理论的发展能为医学的发展提供一种新的视角。通过阅读和研究表征医学发展成就、探讨疾病诊治及其影响的文学作品,医学研究者及医护人员就能够对医学窥见一斑。正如西格里斯评述的那样,关注医学的作家"用文学作为画布,然后在上面绘画出医学的全景"②。在第二次世界大战后,西方在医学研究领域取得了重大突破,但人们也越来越意识到人的价值和尊严正经受着前所未有的挑战,科技理性的发展正在背离人文伦理的需求③。针对这些问题,医学界的有识之士意识到这些"价值取向的偏差",需要借助文学的广阔视野。20世纪90年代,西方学界叙事医学(narrative-based medicine,NBM)的兴起再次改变了文学和医学的发展方向。2001年,丽塔·卡伦正式提出"叙事医学"的概念;叙事医学"由叙事能力所实践的医学",充分挖掘了个体的叙事能力,在很大程度上整合了医学的专业性与普及性,为科学与人文之间的交流开辟了通道④。

文献传真

阅读《医学》("Medicine"),思考文末问答题。本文节选自《劳特利奇指南:文学与科学》⑤。

Medicine

George Rousseau

The sub-discipline of literature and medicine arose after World War II, when it became evident that the two halves of its terrain shared common ground. Its genesis was stimulated by C. P. Snow's controversy with F. R. Leaves over the "two cultures"⑥, and further invigorated by far-flung discussions of these debates, resulting two decades later in the view that "one culture" represents the historical status of knowledge more accurately.⑦Peter Medawar, the British Nobel Laureate in Medicine, who also delivered the BBC Reith Lectures in 1959, entitled *The Future of Man*, and heightening sensitivity

---

① CHARON R, BANKS J T. Literature and medicine: contributions to clinical practice[J]. Annals of internal medicine, 1995(8): 599–606.
② 李媛. 医学与文学的相遇[J]. 云南行政学院学报, 2013(6): 182–183.
③ 郭莉萍. 从"文学与医学"到"叙事医学"[J]. 科学文化评论, 2013(3): 5-22.
④ ROUSSEAU G. Medicine[C]//CLARKE B, ROSSINI M. The Routledge companion to literature and science. London: Routledge, 2011: 170–171. 另参见郭莉萍. 从"文学与医学"到"叙事医学"[J]. 科学文化评论, 2013(3): 5–22.
⑤ ROUSSEAU G. Medicine[C]//CLARKE B, ROSSINI M. The Routledge companion to literature and science. London: Routledge, 2011: 169–178.
⑥ LEAVIS F R. Two cultures? The significance of C. P. Snow[M]. Richmond: Pantheon, 1963.
⑦ LEVINE G. One culture: essays in science and literature[M]. Madison: University of Wisconsin Press, 1987.

to the overlaps of literature and science and medicine, further stimulated the post-war growth of the sub-discipline. Nevertheless, the aftermath of all these debates made clear that literature and medicine bore an uneasy relation to its parallel discourse, literature and science, owing to the relatively steady state of the anatomical human body.[①]

The last point is consequential: science amounts to a vast body of advancing knowledge (*scientia*) perceived to be forever in a state of progress and is usually thought to improve the world; the human body, like the planet Earth, remains more or less constant and has been so from pre-Homeric times. This glaring discrepancy informed both sub-disciplines. Also complicating their uneasy relation was the old debate about whether medicine is an art or science; yet few philosophers of science have ever sustained any argument that science is primarily an art. Therefore, if literature and science and literature and medicine were conceptualized as discrete, developing sub-disciplines forming parts of the huge, complex canvas of knowledge, their differences were seen as being as great as their similarities, and a strong case developed after the 1980s that they had no more in common with each other than with other sub-disciplines such as literature and anthropology, literature and the law, literature and religion.

Framed otherwise, literature and science is the study of ever-advancing sets of relationships in which one half of the equation—the body of knowledge called "science"—never stands still, whereas literature and medicine focuses on the relation of two relatively stable categories: *literature* and *medicine*—neither of which can meaningfully claim to "progress" in the way scientific knowledge does. It would be odd to discuss literature in terms of progress—progress since Shakespeare's plays or Shelley's poetry? —yet much medical diagnosis is not "scientific" in the sense that rigorously tested, and peer-reviewed scientific hypotheses are. Medicine, even empirically based contemporary medicine, relies on scientific knowledge but embraces other, non-scientific components to compose its totality.

Even if imaginative, canonical literature itself does not "progress," scientific theory *about* literature does. And if the theory wars of the last generation have resolved anything, it is the degree to which much contemporary theory aspires to be "scientific"

---

① TALLIS R. Newton's sleep: the two cultures and the two kingdoms[M]. Basingstoke: Macmillan, 1995.

and in many instances attains its. Literary theory can be as scientific as other types of theory under controlled conditions. Compounding this propensity is the fact that at least since the 1970s the rotund cupola of literature—including imaginative canonical literature from Beowulf to Virginia Woolf and all other forms of written and verbal discourse—has embraced literary theory. Therefore, both literature and medicine and literature and science can seem to be in scientific parity only when the literature component of their cupola designates literary theory.

Something tantamount to this parallel state occurred in the late twentieth century when stimulated by the development of neuroscience, whose main concern then prioritized memory: a category of unusual interest to literature from time immemorial whose stock rose after World War II.① The difference now (after c. 1945) was that neuroscience was privileging memory. Within just a few decades all sorts of questions about memory arose, as did journals of memory studies. Was memory an action, a metaphor, or both? Were its defects symptomatic of illness, as in other somatic ailments, or a metaphor for something psychological run amok in the personality?② Was memory primarily biological, physiological, or psychological? Was it individual as well as collective? These and other difficult questions filtered into bread-and-butter literary theory debates, raising literature and medicine to a new threshold of relevance.

Concurrently, the 1990s rise of narrative-based medicine (NBM) changed the direction of literature and medicine yet again. NBM originates from a pointing which most "medicine" is presumed to be contemporary and affirms that doctor-patient interactions in all medical fields are primarily verbal; that the outcome of both diagnosis and therapy depends partly on the narrative experience of each party. Questions such as "how do doctors think?" and "how do patients talk?" assume current-day patients and doctors in contemporary settings. The pre-1950 past is expunged or relegated to "history."

NBM arose out of an accompanying agenda to transform the domain of current medical practice. With much justification its enhancements in communication aimed at altering the kingdom of patientdom: the patient was no longer an anatomical body to be

---

① SCHACTER D L, SCARRY E. Memory, brain, and belief[M]. Cambridge, Mass.: Harvard University Press, 2000.
② SONTAG S. Illness as metaphor [M]. New York: Random House, 1979.

diagnosed, surgically excavated, and clinically treated, but a word-making individual sensitive to the discursive exchanges between doctor and patient who wished to augment the story he told himself about himself.

Some doctors resisted but others willingly participated in these inflections. The collective medical self-image gradually altered and soon doctors were receiving instruction in the complexities of narrative interchange and re-educating themselves in literary analysis. Likewise patients were taught to construe their responsibility as more robust than earlier: fully to explain themselves to doctors and include the affective components. Some doctors reached out from medical practice to the community in the belief that medicine had grown too insulated, while others "wrote out" their illnesses-pathographesis-as they routinely had in the early modern world when geography dictated the pressing need for written accounts among absent patients. Pre-1800 travel was arduous; pathographies were sent to physicians who would never see their patients.[①] More recently the authors of pathographies have written for public audiences: to share their experience of illness. By the 1990s writing oneself out of sickness, both through and without publication, became a wide-spread activity, as if the act of "writing one's self out" were coevally a cleansing and healing.[②] Some renamed their writing "life writing" for its biocritical suggestion of healing.

In 1982–1983 the first journal for the study of literature and medicine appeared: *Literature and Medicine*. Initiated by Americans, it was intended for North American academic audiences but its contents also captured the attention of medical practitioners elsewhere. In its first decade its contents included historical topics such as the relevance of medical history to the developing literature and medicine field and discussion of figures who had been doctors-writers (Rabelais, Thomas Campion, Goldsmith, Smollett, Keats, Chekhov, William Carlos Williams); but after the 1990s this historical component largely dropped out and the focus turned increasingly to NBM salted with calls for feminist and minority reform in the medical interchange (*Literature and Medicine*, 1992–1999). A few papers appeared on Chaucer, Tudor plague, Montaigne,

---

① CALDWELL J M. Literature and medicine in nineteenth-century Britain: from Mary Shelley to George Eliot[M]. Cambridge: Cambridge University Press, 2004.
② HAWKINS A. Reconstructing illness: studies in pathography[M]. West Lafayette: Purdue University Press, 1993.

Georgian gout, Blake, and Keats, but these were buried under the mountain of general commentary about pain, stress, disability, intersubjectivity, and ethical concern as found, for example, in the thought of philosopher Emmanuel Levinas. In 1990 the *Journal of Medical Humanities* published its first issue, but its concerns were even less canonical and historical than its counterpart's and more bioethical(*Journal of Medical Humanities*, 1990–1999).

If we pause momentarily we can reflect on why literature and science could not then have had an equivalent academic journal: its field is significantly larger, especially if readers expect it to cover both literature and science from the Greeks forward. *Configurations*, a journal first published in 1993 and sponsored by the Society for Literature and Science, itself evolved from a group debating the interconnections of literature and science, aimed to fill some part of this gap. But while it was eloquent on theoretical aspects of postmodern thought it wisely made no claim to include the historical component of the sub-discipline literature and science. Historical coverage was left to the individual period journals devoted to the Renaissance, Enlightenment, Romantic, Victorian, American literature and so forth. Instead *Configurations* addressed, and still probes, the theoretical issues and leaves tradition, influence, biography, and especially the place of the history of science and medicine in the development of the sub-disciplines literature and science and literature and medicine to other outlets.

Despite these differences of literature and medicine and literature and science, it is curious the degree to which the pre-1900 literary canon, as well as the deep-layer analysis of the rise of these sub-disciplines, has been neglected. Typical treatment proceeds as if a scientific or medical moment were more or less static, without the far-flung context necessary to explain why it is problematic in the first place. There is little impulse to stretch backward in time. For example, the case study or pathographic propensities of the last generation: many secondary studies have discussed pathographesis as if its curve began in the twentieth century rather than by consulting the longue durée to demonstrate changes in the sub-genre. Or consider broader reflections on the development of the sub-discipline literature and medicine, the subject of this chapter: few studies treat it as a developing field over the long haul—from the

第三章 文学与医学(Literature and Medicine)

Renaissance forward. When they do, the contextual component is often absent.

Moreover, a further reason for the reduction of similarity and difference in literature and medicine is that, prior to the twentieth century, cure formed only a small province of medicine's activity. Today we take cure for granted as intrinsic to medical practice, but its rise is recent. Joseph Addison's famous quip that doctors "kill more than they cure" was a common perception throughout the nineteenth century. Only since the twentieth century has medicine's primary remit been to cure. Withhold cure from its domain, and medicine becomes a more amorphous territory than otherwise, extending to many realms of human life. The impact on literature and medicine is apparent: what do the two components of literature and medicine—literature and medicine—amount to if medicine has altered in this way? You need a considerable amount of history of medicine to unpack the changes to literature and medicine's development.

Here the Romantic movement has been crucial. By the late eighteenth century, British literature—especially the prose novel—was quickly absorbing medical content, while medical practice was being transformed to an unprecedented degree. By the time Coleridge and Wordsworth added the 1802 preface to their revolutionary *Lyrical Ballads*, with its famous passages about the poet's unending attraction to the discoveries of science and medicine, writers were more medically knowledgeable than they had been.[1] Poets and artists, moreover, were fashionable if seen as ailing.

But the Romantics' absorption in matters medical was not limited to their own often-sick bodies. They were also drawn to medicine's theoretical quandaries, especially the mind-body debates that had heated up since the era of Hobbes and Locke and culminated in the fictional sallies of Sterne in *Tristram Shandy* (Mulvey and Porter, 1993: 84 - 100; Richardson, 2001).[2] The Enlightenment emphasis on a complex nervous system (the animal spirits, fibers, nerves, the brain) in preference to the midriff zone redirected attention to the head and brain. As Romantic writers and artists debated such thorny concepts as character, personality, and temperament they increasingly wondered what role the brain played. The formation of pictures in the

---

[1] VICKERS N. Coleridge and the doctors, 1795 - 1806[M]. Oxford: Clarendon Press, 2004.
[2] MULVEY M, PORTER R. Literature and medicine during the eighteenth century[M]. London: Routledge, 1993: 84 - 100.

mind, and the production of dreams, especially, attracted them. By the decade of Byron's and Shelley's maturity in the 1820s, mind and body were being combined in ways unknown to earlier empiricists and ongoing mind-body debates had extended to groups exceeding the sphere of empirical philosophers. To be a Romantic poet or artist, whether a conservative Wordsworth or revolutionary Blake, was to engage in these debates.

The Romantics were also the first generation to recognize widely the importance of factitious diseases: imaginary maladies lodged in often hypochondriac patients. These maladies were sometimes as fictitious as they were factitious, and the differences of complete invention versus partial concoction based on ambiguous symptoms preoccupied those diagnosing them. Prose treatises began to appear distinguishing the two types. You could claim these writings for either literature or medicine—either domain—but they resided more accurately in the interstices, in a common ground belonging to both spheres.

The distance from hypochondria and factitious malady to mental illness is not far. The Romantics also recognized that the patient claiming to suffer from conditions no doctor can identify may be mentally ill. Writers before c. 1800 had recognized the possibility and commented upon it (Tobias Smollett's *Lancelot Greaves* is a classical locus) but the Romantics amplified it into a veritable subgenre in its own right. Writers had portrayed mad characters from the time of ancient Greek tragedy and playwrights like Shakespeare depicted them (*Hamlet*, *Ophelia*, *Lear*, *Macbeth*) in detail so exquisite that it would be folly to argue that the Romantics' representations were original. The difference now—after 1800—is that the writing is medically informed: imaginative literature is demonstrably being influenced by particular medical texts. Shakespeare's allusions to medicine, for example, are prolific but it is difficult to pinpoint the influence of specific medical writings on particular plays.

One facet of medicine eluded the Romantics: its status in a socially progressive era. Children of war and revolution, they could not envision medicine's role in a peaceful, progressive society, nor the way its concerns are represented among different class groups in different geographies and countries, or the diverse patterns of its prefiguration in the social fabric of culture. Such representation included, of course, the depiction of its practitioners—doctors, nurses, apothecaries, surgeons, patients—as well as ideas about its sociological function. The modern discipline known as the sociology of medicine deals with this domain when the setting is an advanced hegemonic society (American, British, French), as does medical anthropology in more primitive societies. Both have burgeoned for a half century, but in the nineteenth century they were nascent. The Victorians tapped into social medicine in their novels, privileging it as the theme of particular works, as in Charlotte Brontë's *Wuthering Heights* and Eliot's *Middlemarch*.

"Middlemarch" is a typical English country town, and the novel named for it focuses on two couples, one of whom is Rosamond and Lydgate, the town doctor, a new kind of general medical practitioner who combines the function of the older apothecaries and surgeons. Born well, Lydgate arrives in Middlemarch dreaming to build a modern hospital for the poor but is suspiciously viewed by the medical establishment. He gets few referrals, earns little, his savings quickly depleted by the high-flying, ostentatious Rosamond. Unexpectedly, Lydgate receives a loan from Bulstrode, a wealthy landowner, only to discover that Bulstrode has been charged with murder and Lydgate named as an accomplice. Disgraced by the accusations, Lydgate becomes helpless and surrenders his medical dreams. Instead he panders to rich patients and forgoes the possibility of establishing a medical practice for the poor. His revolutionary aspirations evaporate and he dies a broken man at 50, neither rich nor poor, an unmoored social outcast. Eliot could not have constructed her novel without immersing herself to this degree in the social history of medicine then: its concerns for the developing Victorian medical profession, as well as the doctor-patient relation. But she would not have described so vividly Lydgate's sense of himself as a failure without these contexts. Her wide reading in contemporary medicine, in several languages, demonstrated how notions of professional success were being transformed in her generation. What was success to Lydgate would not have been earlier in the world of Daniel Defoe or Jane Austen.

Soon afterwards, twentieth-century literature surrendered deep-layer probing of medicine's social tentacles and turned inward to the interior lives of its victims: sufferers and providers, those ailing and those caring for them. The impulse was not romantic regression—to revive the artist as invalid—but pierced instead to the heart of private lives in the state of sickness; to what it meant to be a patient in the modern world. It did this against the grain of developing national health systems (the NHS in the U. K., state health in Canada, and so forth), as well as the deep frustration of those countries (the U. S. A., Latin and South America) being unable to provide one. Some of its primary literature captured these social elements as minor themes, but most remained focused on the self and its plight.

Patient narratives and personal pathography's of the twentieth century were usually set in present time. When they demonstrated a nostalgic turn, the plot still evolved in relatively recent time but was rarely more than a generation or two behind. It is as if the novelist were insufficiently *au fait* with medical history to deal with past medicine.[①] But none could imagine such a stunning fiction about the consequences of a "plague of white blindness" attacking a whole country as Portugese Nobel Laureate Jose Saramago.[②] Medical students read his novel and relished its insights in the 1990s. Once exposed to fiction and encouraged to study creative writing, the landscape of literature and medicine changed again and young doctors invented plots set in previous times. They knew their medicine sufficiently well not to fret about the medico-historical background.

This education occurred in programs arranged around the "medical humanities," by the 1980s a sub-field taught in medical schools. It developed in medical schools and was driven by the contemporary critique that medical education, especially its omission of medical ethics, which was defective. Assuming that the modern world was composed of soul-denying Western societies, medical humanities claimed to be appalled by the lack of cultural critique of medicine, and judged medicine as far too serious a matter— literally of life or death—to leave to doctors only. Their point was strong. In self-defense the doctors retorted that they had little time for such pursuits. The indictment was nevertheless put and the field developed: first as an interdisciplinary module and then as a major. Programmatic glances were made at the humanities (literature, philosophy, ethics, history, religion), social sciences (anthropology, cultural studies,

---

① LOXTERKAMP D. A measure of my days: the journal of a country doctor[M]. Hanover: University Press of New England, 1997.

② SARAMAGO J, PONTIERO G. Blindness: a novel[M]. London: Harvill, 1985.

psychology, sociology), and arts (literature, theater, film, visual arts). But particular emphasis was placed on the utility of such approaches to medical education and, eventually, to medical practice. The early rationale was that such interdisciplinary vision would produce a crop of humane doctors. In practice, close reading and creative writing played minor roles in these courses, with little of it ever cast further afield than to twentieth-century literature.

During the 1980s and 1990s this rationale about the present deepened, abetted by publications in the journal *Literature and Medicine*, discussed above. Presentism developed along lines that while the humanities and arts provide insight into the human condition, pain and suffering, selfhood, personhood, depression, mental illness, and our ethical responsibility to each other, the medical humanities can offer physicians a deepened perspective on medical practice. It was further claimed that attention to literature and the arts nurtures skills of observation, analysis, empathy, and self-reflection—much needed for humane medical care. If the social sciences enable understanding of how bioscience and medicine take place within socio-cultural contexts, the medical humanities—so the claim went—taught much about the interactions of the individual experience of illness, especially the ways individual patients responded.

It was much less clear what such an ambitious agenda could do for the humanities—in particular for literature. That is, art has usually been decoupled from social reform. Its components are fundamentally aesthetic, philosophical, moral, and even vicarious but it is not ranked according to its ability to reform, or improve, society. Even so, "literature" is an ambiguous word. If "literature" designates all discourse, then many approaches offer something of value. If, instead, delimited to contemporary imaginative writing, then it is clear that such skills can focus the narrator's eye in the face of the perennially perplexing human condition and in relation to suffering, selfhood, and the moral responsibility human beings bear to each other. But it was less evident what this approach could do for literary criticism and literary history, fields of long pedigree. During prior epochs when medical concerns loomed, as in Victorian England, the medical humanities could alert the reader to medical content. But for other periods when medicine was less absorbed into the tissue of mainstream culture, it was far from clear what was to be gained. For example, medicine was relatively low on the pecking order of content for writers from Beowulf to Chaucer and Dante to Milton, and to most writers in the seventeenth century (excepting Thomas Browne). The distinction might also be narrowed to authors rather than historical periods: such as the Renaissance or Enlightenment, or, to change the axis again, to moderns and postmoderns, structuralists and anti-structuralists. By our time all these fields display well-developed literary histories incapable of persuasion that they can benefit from an infusion of medical humanities. Nevertheless, some critics have demonstrated how wrong they are.

The obvious retort to the academicians ought to have been that all epochs rely on medicine: how could it be otherwise when medicine measures pain thresholds and helps to sustain human life? But clarifications were rarely mounted, perhaps because they required scholars and critics au fait with the history of both literature and medicine in the pre-1900 world. This was the state of affairs circa 1990. Since then a technological revolution based on high-speed and hyperlink connection has changed the field—literature and medicine—again. When everything connects to everything, and when you can locate those connections with the stroke of a key, the parameters alter: the past becomes more accessible and historical negotiation less arduous than it was in the days of three-by-five cards and snail mail. If you can acquire the knowledge you need about a particular historical topic in one day, rather than one year, you will be less reticent to pursue an historically grounded literature and medicine. There is considerable evidence that this is happening in the field.

The trend is laudable but still leaves a sub-discipline in partial disarray gravitating to the contemporary scene, with myopic vision, if not misprision, of the past. Survey the girth of literature and medicine, and you find it splintered into camps of critics and scholars, theorists and historians, and now do-gooders eager to reform the practice of medicine, especially for patients. The theorists immerse themselves in models and systems, often leaving primary literature and primary medicine behind, while scholars focus on narrow domains sometimes embracing no more than a generation or single figure. The field eschews totalizing discussions that reflect on its past or meditate its future.

The matter is not the remedy, as if the sub-discipline of literature and medicine were ailing, but rather how to bring the contemporary technological revolution into the

第三章 文学与医学(Literature and Medicine)

service of this further developing field. Hyperlink realism and algorithmic mindsets are here to stay: everything is already being connected to everything else. Nor does need exist any longer for the old incantatory rhetoric about working alone in the wilderness or needing folk "to talk to": if only we could bring together the medical and literary camps. ... That was the last generation's desideratum; in reply to its cries the interdisciplinary mandate arose. The new hyperlink realism, in contrast, has rendered the past more readily accessible than it was even a decade ago. The issue now is whether our postmodern mindsets will harness the past in the service of an already developed field configured according to a narrow set of premises, or continue to evolve as a visionary sphere apart from lived history.

Put more simply, the matter is whether a literature and medicine whose materials stretch as far back as literature itself can have equal footing with postmodern theoretical discussions. If they cannot, then another "two cultures"—a veritable third culture—will arise within the already small sub-discipline: one group historical and approaching most of its critical tasks historically; another theoretical, grounded in the present, and not even persuaded that pre-1900 canonical literature falls within its remit; and a third hands-on and concerned with medical practice. If this further schism develops it will seem there are "three literature and medicines" within "two cultures," while everything points to only one. And then we are back to square one; roughly where we were around 1959 when literature and medicine gathered momentum, and C. P. Snow and F. R. Leavis were attacking each other.

It remains to notice that, since 1959, literature and medicine has developed mainly on American soil. The sub-discipline entrenched itself in academia there in cultures weighted toward the present. This fact has taken its toll and recently literature and medicine has not been attracting those already interested in the literary canon from Moses to Thomas Mann—the Mann whose *Magic Mountain* remains the seminal text for literature and medicine—with the exception of a few figures (George Eliot, Chekhov, William Carlos Williams). Hence difficult questions arise. Will literature and medicine always be limited to current-day concerns? Does literature and medicine have significant space for pre-1900 stories evolving in major Western traditions? Why is literature and medicine attracting so few students of canonical literature, in any languages, when it professes to deal with universal categories of primal significance: grief, loss, sickness, pain, suffering, and the great leveler, death?① Is it too ambitious to expect literature and medicine to embrace realist literary history and medical history as well as theory? Are its written productions recognizable as different from other types of social critique? Why does literature and medicine resist argument and counterargument about the kind of field it is? Literature and medicine must address questions like these if it wishes to be reinvigorated.

思考题

1. Why did literature and medicine bear an uneasy relation to its parallel discourse, literature and science?
2. In what ways has the rise in 1990s of narrative-based medicine (NBM) changed the direction of literature and medicine? And what is its agenda?
3. Why has Romantic movement been crucial to unpack the changes to literature and medicine's development? In what ways is Romantic imagination about mental illness different from earlier representation as found in Shakespeare's plays? Is it objective in envisioning medicine?
4. What are medical humanities? What rationales do they hold onto and what do they teach?

第二节 《米德尔马契》与医学

作品导读

1. 作者简介

《米德尔马契》是英国女作家乔治·艾略特创作的长篇小说。乔治·艾略特,原名玛丽·安·伊万斯(Mary Ann Evans),是19世纪英语文学最有影响力的小说家之一,与萨克雷(William Makepeace Thackeray, 1811—1863)、狄更斯、勃朗特三姐妹齐名。艾略特的文学创作生涯始于翻译。她自幼喜欢研究语言,通晓拉丁文、法文、德文、意大利文、希伯来文、希腊文等语言。1846年,她翻译了大卫·斯特劳斯(David Strauss, 1808—1874)的《批判性

---

① SCARRY E. The body in pain: the making and unmaking of the world[M]. New York: Oxford University Press, 1995.

第三章　文学与医学（Literature and Medicine）

审视耶稣的生活》（*The Life of Jesus, Critically Examined*, 1835）。1854年，她翻译了费尔巴哈（Ludwig Feuerbach, 1804—1872）的《基督的本质》（*The Essence of Christianity*, 1841）。这两部作品中的自由思想深深影响了艾略特日后的小说创作①。

1849年父亲去世后，艾略特随布雷一家旅居瑞士。1850年回到伦敦后，她担任了《西敏寺评论》（*The Westminster Review*）杂志的编辑，并在此期间认识了一生的挚爱刘易斯（George Henri Lewes, 1817—1878）。在刘易斯的鼓励下，艾略特年近四十岁时才开始小说创作，并于1859年发表第一部长篇小说《亚当·比德》（*Adam Bede*, 1859）。该作品一年内再版八次，其受欢迎程度不言而喻。随后两年，她出版了《弗洛斯河上的磨坊》（*The Mill on the Floss*, 1860）和《织工马南传》（*Silas Marner*, 1861）两部作品，它们确立了艾略特在英国文坛的地位。之后，艾略特还创作了《罗慕拉》（*Romola*, 1863）、《菲力克斯·霍尔特》（*Felix Holt the Radical*, 1866）、《米德尔马契》（*Middlemarch*, 1872）、《丹尼尔·德龙达》（*Daniel Deronda*, 1876）等作品，成就非凡。1878年，刘易斯去世，艾略特在悲痛中完成了爱人的遗作。两年后，艾略特下嫁小她二十岁的克劳斯（John Cross），并于同年十二月病故，结束了平凡却又丰富的一生②。

艾略特的创作素材来源于英国历史和现实生活。在19世纪的英国，资本主义经济快速发展，传统农耕文明逐渐走向没落。该时期的科学发现、技术变革和工业革命加剧了工人阶级与资产阶级的矛盾、农村与城市的对立、传统宗教与进步思想之间的冲突。在成长过程中，艾略特耳闻目染了这些社会矛盾：她是"农家女"，出生在沃里克郡（Warwickshire）乡村阿伯里庄园（the Arbury Estate Hall）的农场，父亲替纽迪吉特家族（the Newdigate Family）管理阿伯里庄园，母亲则是当地磨坊主的女儿。艾略特曾在阿伯里庄园农场当过牛奶女工，懂得农村生活的艰辛，深谙农民的疾苦③。1841年母亲去世后，艾略特便随父迁居考文垂，在那里结识了自由思想家查尔斯·布雷（Charles Bray, 1811—1884），并在他的介绍下认识了思想更加激进的大卫·斯特劳斯和费尔巴哈。在这些激进思想家的影响下，艾略特开始广泛阅读包括地质学、生物学、进化论、解剖医学等方面的书籍，进而对19世纪的科学话语和进步思想有着较深刻的认识。由于曾在宗教气息浓厚的学校就读过，艾略特受宗教影响颇深。在接触进步思想后，艾略特便开始质疑宗教神学，并在创作中反思传统宗教造成的社会问题④。在艾略特看来，宗教问题是一种社会疾病，而整个英国社会就像一具充满各种"病痛的人类躯体"⑤，现实主义小说家则必须担当起维多利亚时期科学家一样的使命，通过创

---

① 马建军. 乔治·艾略特研究[M]. 武汉：武汉大学出版社, 2007：72.
② 曹巍, 魏晓红. 乔治·艾略特小说的创作思想[J]. 大家, 2014(12)：1.
③ Victorians were obsessed with the idea that George Eliot had two different-sized hands[Z/OL]. https://crimereads.com/victorians-george-eliot-hands/. 另参见 George Eliot[Z/OL]. [2023-07-10]. https://en.wikipedia.org/wiki/George_Eliot.
④ 同①68.
⑤ MCCORMACK K. George Eliot and Victorian intoxication: dangerous drugs for the condition of England[M]. Berlin: Springer, 2000：1-2.

造性想象和细致的观察,拓展人类对那些"不为人知的悲剧"成因的感知能力,揭示潜藏在社会表象之下的真理,特别是"社会身体的自然历史"①。显然,艾略特将作家视为医生,借助酒精、鸦片等喻指"社会身体疾病"的隐喻,同时结合生活和阅读中所累积起来的医学知识,剖析"社会身体"的机理及其病因,进而探寻医治这些社会痼疾的良方②。

艾略特对社会疾病的探讨几乎贯穿其所有作品,它与虚构人物的生理疾病和心理疾病有机融合在一起,医学叙事因而构成其创作的一个重要特征③。艾略特的医学书写表征的社会疾病包括阶级、政治、经济、医疗、教育、宗教、婚姻等方面的问题,特别是其所熟悉的英国乡村的各种社会问题④。通过生动翔实的描述,并借助具有代表性的人物,艾略特的小说忠实反映了19世纪英国乡镇普通百姓生活的动荡与变迁⑤。艾略特不仅擅长描写人物的外貌,而且擅长描写人物的内心⑥。毕竟,"生理心理学认为心理疾病与生理疾病相互影响,而心理疾病与身体疾病则反过来影响到健康和社会问题之间的因果关系"⑦。因此,艾略特的心理描写不仅剑指身体疾病,而且披露社会政治问题。另外,这些细致入微的描写也把她的人物一下子拉到读者的面前——真实而亲切⑧。劳伦斯(D. H. Lawrence,1885—1930)曾讨论过艾略特心理描写的作用,将她视为"第一个把行为放进人物心理的作家"⑨。

在写作中,艾略特始终坚持艺术形式与道德内容的结合,美学与伦理的高度统一,其塑造的人物具有极高的艺术价值⑩。她认为"如果艺术不能扩展人们的同情心,就没有任何道德意义……"⑪在1866年写给哈里森(Frederic Harrison,1831—1923)的信中,艾略特说道:"我认为美学教育是最高层次的教育,因为它涉及的是最复杂的人生状况。但是如果它是唯

---

① LOGAN P M. Conceiving the body: realism and medicine in Middlemarch[J]. History of the human sciences,1991(2):207.
② MCCORMACK K. George Eliot and Victorian intoxication: dangerous drugs for the condition of England[M]. Berlin: Springer,2000:11.
③ CALDWELL J M. Literature and medicine in nineteenth-century Britain: from Mary Shelley to George Eliot[M]. Cambridge: Cambridge University Press,2004:143-70. 另参见 KENNEDY M. Revising the clinic: vision and representation in Victorian medical narrative and the novel[M]. Columbus: The Ohio State University Press,2010:119-147.
④ 艾略特认为婚姻问题是一种疾病,并将女性在婚姻中的不幸的原因与眼疾联系起来。在她看来,宗教问题、阶级问题、教育问题等都是社会疾病。参见 MCCORMACK K. George Eliot and Victorian intoxication: dangerous drugs for the condition of England[M]. Berlin: Springer,2000:159-182.
⑤ 曹巍,魏晓红. 乔治·艾略特小说的心理描写艺术[M]. 上海:外语教学与研究出版社,2015:12.
⑥ HARDY B. Readings in George Eliot[M]. London: Peter Owen Limited,1982:10.
⑦ 同②28.
⑧ 马建军. 乔治·艾略特研究[M]. 武汉:武汉大学出版社,2007:72.
⑨ 同②12.
⑩ 同②86.
⑪ CROSS J. George Eliot's life[M]. London: Blackwood,1885:279.

美的,如果它不是斑斓的色彩线条就是单调缺乏的数据信息,那它就成了最令人讨厌的教育①。"艾略特的这种艺术观受到了马修·阿诺德"平凡的自我"观点的影响,认为艺术创作在拓展同情心的同时,能帮助个体发展"最完美的自我",摆脱"狭隘的阶级私利的蒙蔽",进而意识到"人类的共同利益"②。显然,艾略特在人物塑造方面注重的是艺术感染力,她出色的人物塑造技巧使她在一定程度上实现了创作目的。一百多年过去了,学界对艾略特的研究方兴未艾,其医学书写也得到了国内外学界的重视。为更好地了解这位英国女作家并领略其作品的艺术魅力,特别是她如何借助写作来诊断英国社会疾病并寻求其疗治途径,则有赖于读者的悉心阅读和专家学者的深入讨论。下面以《米德尔马契》为例,通过介绍该作品在表征和解决19世纪英国社会医疗相关问题方面所做的努力,探讨艾略特医学书写的意义和价值。

2. 作品介绍

《米德尔马契》是乔治·艾略特成熟期的作品,代表其最高艺术成就,是维多利亚时代的一部史诗。作品以虚构小城镇米德尔马契(Middlemarch)为缩影,以两组爱情故事为主线,即思想深刻的多萝西娅(Dorothea)和学识丰富的卡苏朋(Casaubon)之间的爱情,以及青年医生利德盖特(Tertius Lydgate)与肤浅自私的罗莎蒙德(Rosamond)之间的爱情故事。这两组爱情都出现了灵与肉的严重冲突,两对恋人对未来都怀有美好的期盼,但个人性格和周围环境却一再扼杀了他们的理想。小说以这两个爱情故事为核心,运用朴实无华的叙述语言,同时塑造了一百五十多个人物角色,生动形象地展示了时代脉搏,以不同的视角和生动的细节披露了当时社会在婚姻、个人理想及事业、医疗改革以及女性教育等方面的问题。

多萝西娅是故事的中心人物之一,天性虔诚热烈,对生活的理想化认识激励着她追求崇高的理念和深奥的道理。她认为婚姻对象就如同人生导师,可以让自己认识更大的世界,愿意心甘情愿地为对方的事业和梦想付出一切。在她看来,以完成《世界神话索隐大全》(Index of World Myths)为终身志业的古典学者卡苏朋牧师是其理想丈夫。所以,当年龄比其大26岁的卡苏朋出现时,多萝西娅不顾亲友的反对,放弃了在财富、地位和家世更胜一筹的同龄追求者切特姆(James Chettam),在19岁时便与卡苏朋结为伉俪,认为这样的男人可以指引其通往更高的道德境界。然而,卡苏朋的冷漠和迂腐,使得多萝西娅倍感失望,因而冲突不断。卡苏朋在精神上的强大成为她肉体上的负担,她渴求自由体贴却得不到满足。对多萝西娅而言,婚姻生活的失落尤其难以忍受,因为这段婚姻承载的不只是她的家庭梦

---

① SCHRAMM J. George Eliot and the law[C]//ANDERSON A, SHAW H E. A companion to George Eliot. Hoboken: Wiley-Blackwell, 2013: 309.

② LOGAN P M. Conceiving the body: realism and medicine in Middlemarch[J]. History of the human sciences, 1991(2): 208.

想,也有她对有意义人生的追求。将个人追求寄托在另一个人身上,一开始就很危险。卡苏朋也有自己的困境:他在狭小的斗室和曲折的楼梯之间徘徊,在学术道路上找不到前进的方向。当意识到丈夫不如先前想象的那样博学多才,多萝西娅所剩下的只是对他纯粹的怜悯和忠诚了。当卡苏朋的侄子拉迪斯劳(Will Ladislaw)到访后,多萝西娅发现他与自己有诸多共同语言,找到了心灵上的依靠,然而她无法抛弃丈夫。但艾略特的高明之处在于她设计了卡苏朋的病逝,使得多萝西娅再次有机会来追求合适的爱情。因此,当丈夫病逝后,她放弃了遗产,选择与拉迪斯劳共度余生。

利德盖特来自伦敦,出身高贵,却从不炫耀其社会地位,是一个胸怀大志的青年医生。他初来乍到,参加了卡苏朋和多萝西娅的婚礼,首次踏入米德尔马契的医生圈子。此前,他曾在巴黎学习,回国后决计远离伦敦的勾心斗角,到外省当一名普通医师,引进现代医学,推行医疗改革,改进当地的医疗水平。这是他来米德尔马契时的初心。可悲的是,这个小城镇极端保守落后,对医疗改革不予认同,对他解剖尸体的研究嗤之以鼻,因而其改革实践进展缓慢。但是才华横溢的利德盖特成了当地少女梦想中的伴侣,时年二十七岁的他本不急于结婚,但他经受不住镇长貌美温柔的女儿罗莎蒙德的追求,将其视作完美女人的化身,却没看到其内心的自私冷酷与爱慕虚荣。婚后,罗莎蒙德不仅对他的事业毫无兴趣,还挥霍无度、奢侈浪费。为了满足妻子对物质的追求,利德盖特债台高筑,疲于应付各种债务。罗莎蒙德不愿同甘共苦,将家庭重担扔给了丈夫利德盖特。而此时,他的医疗改革事业也由于缺乏切实可行的计划和米德尔马契其他医生的不合作甚至阻挠而举步维艰。随着负债的增多,这对新婚夫妻的矛盾也逐渐加深。利德盖特走投无路,为了金钱而陷于医院金主布尔斯特罗德(Bulstrode)设置的圈套。最后,利德盖特名誉扫地,在米德尔马契的行医事业也难以为继。多萝西娅十分同情利德盖特的处境,积极地为他洗清罪名。此后不久,利德盖特被迫放弃医疗改革的理想,举家搬到伦敦。为了生存,他不得不在富人面前阿谀奉承,并继续与罗莎蒙德同床异梦的婚姻,在五十岁的时候就离开了人世。可见,利德盖特事业追求的失败,还归因于他在处理爱情和家庭事宜上的草率态度①。

《米德尔马契》的情节结构安排得错综复杂。在女主人公多萝西娅结婚前,小说呈现在读者面前的是未来美好的前景,而婚后又转折为夫妻的隔阂和猜忌,围绕他们的生活又穿插了利德盖特和罗莎蒙德的矛盾和小说中其他人物的悲欢离合,各种人物、事件和关系被作家安排在特定的舞台上进行表演。《米德尔马契》通过作家在细节上的精心设计,最后将小说高潮推到全书的结尾,使故事中相关人物和事件巧妙地联系起来,个性分明的人物跃然纸上,从外部的观察到内心的省视,独见作者艾略特深厚的人物刻画功力,而其洞察力也把维

---

① 温晶晶. 19世纪英国女性文学生态伦理批评[M]. 北京:国防工业出版社,2015:219-221.

多利亚时代的农村生活刻画得淋漓尽致①。

3. 作品赏析

英国维多利亚时代，医学科学、医疗技术和医疗事业取得很大的发展，它不仅加速了医学领域内的标准化、职业化、专业化的进程，给社会带来了许多福祉，而且还给小说家们提供了丰富的创作题材。许多小说家以其特有的敏感和社会责任感，将这类题材引入到他们的小说，因而勾勒出一道独特的文学景观。艾略特的《米德尔马契》就反映医学伦理问题的深度和广度而言，维多利亚小说中无出其右者。艾略特在小说中对伦敦及外省小镇医德现象与医德关系的叙述绘制了一幅维多利亚时期英国风云变幻的医界全景图；通过批评医学从业人员将个人权势利益凌驾于患者利益之上的医学道德滑坡现象，赞赏有志之士推动医疗改革的勇气与毅力，肯定社会、科学与医学发展之间的相互影响作用；同时也指出违背伦理、盲目迅猛的医学发展和医学实验可能引起的严重后果；并通过关注、探讨医学伦理学问题，强调医学伦理学在保障医疗实践活动顺利开展过程中的重要作用②。

在维多利亚时期的小说中，医生这一人物形象并不鲜见，但以医生作为主要正面人物之一，《米德尔马契》尚属首例。小说详细描述了年轻医生利德盖特在外省小镇米德尔马契开业行医、推行医疗改革、参与新医院设计管理、进行医学科学实验等起起落落的过程。利德盖特是个医术精湛的医生，自小立志从医，辗转在伦敦、爱丁堡、巴黎等地，接受了当时最为先进的医学教育和专门训练，他不仅医术精湛，还掌握了最前沿的医学知识。当踌躇满志的利德盖特从法国巴黎学成后，来到米德尔马契，而当时这个小镇的医疗状况，用利德盖特的话来说："1829年末，大部分医疗工作仍在老路上，趑趄不前，故步自封。这方面的科学研究仍然得从比夏(Marie Francois Xavier Bichat, 1771—1802)的终点开始。"这也正是当时英国医疗现状的真实写照，医疗机构建设资金严重缺乏，医疗体制条件落后；医学教育还存在明显的误区和盲点③。因此，富有改革精神的利德盖特，雄心勃勃，立志借助推行医疗改革和进行科学实验来提高小镇的医疗水平，同时实现个人名垂医学青史的梦想。19世纪上半叶，各种流行传染病在英国各处肆虐。在利德盖特的指导建议下，小镇米德尔马契建立了新热病医院，开辟供医学实验的研究室和隔离病房，同时推行医药分家的医改举措，这在当时的外省小镇无疑是进步之举。但后续医院董事会为了独揽大权操纵选举致使医生罢工、医院险些濒临停业。加之，在维多利亚社会金钱崇拜风气的熏染下，个人私利高于公众利益，医生为牟取暴利而大量开处方药，因而使得医药市场极度混乱。加之米德尔马契的医生闭塞

---

① ELIOT G. Middlemarch: an authoritative text, backgrounds, criticism[M]. New York: W. W. Norton & Company, 2000: Ⅱ-Ⅷ.

② 同①3. 另参见李增. 英国维多利亚时期的医学伦理小说：以乔治·爱略特的《米德尔马契》为中心[J]. 江西社会科学, 2017,37(4): 86-96.

③ 马建军. 乔治·艾略特研究[M]. 武汉：武汉大学出版社, 2007: 123.

保守,按资排辈,对于利德盖特的学识、思想和医术持不屑一顾的态度,行医者之间又互相排挤、嫉妒打压。最终,利德盖特的医疗改革举步维艰,新热病医院改革也以失败告终,这看似小镇大人物之间的权力博弈之争,实质上是作者在批判当时医疗界自私自利的行为,违背了以患者利益至上的根本原则。

作为一名医生,利德盖特没有贵贱贫富之分,医者仁心,值得称道。在行医过程中,他每次总能够耐心听取患者对于其病情的叙述,结合他自己的判断诊断病情。对待病人时无论是牧师卡苏朋、镇长公子弗莱德、女佣南希,还是流浪醉汉拉弗尔斯,利德盖特都能态度友好诚恳并认真仔细地诊治。通过反复检查,利德盖特方才确定卡苏朋患有心脏病;为了避免其情绪波动并引起心脏病发作,他没有将真实病情告知卡苏朋,而是通知其妻子病情的严重性。他细心观察出弗莱德伤寒病的早期症状,及时对症下药挽救了他的性命。当女佣南希来医院做肿瘤切除手术时,心存疑惑的利德盖特再次认真排查,并耐心地听南希讲述她的种种症状,根据其讲述推翻了内科医生明钦关于肿瘤的诊断,并连续半个月登门为南希诊治痉挛直至她痊愈。他在为醉汉检查病情时也极为细心,仔细询问了病人的姓名和病史后才确诊开药,这也体现了利德盖特的工作认真、心系患者、医术精湛。但是,利德盖特怀疑南希所患并非肿瘤而是痉挛时,却未及时联系主治内科医生进行会诊以明确诊断,而是私自更改治疗方案,固然他的诊断正确,使得南希免受手术之苦,但是整个过程却违背职业道德。

伴随19世纪科学技术的发展和医学进步,在医患、医际、医社关系之外,医研关系(医学科研中产生的道德关系)被称为医学伦理学研究的另一个医德关系[1]。在医研关系中,医学科研活动以人为实验对象,并涉及人体实验和尸体解剖等与传统理念完全相悖的活动;而医学的快速发展在很大程度上都依赖于医学实验和研究,过去的实验大都是利用病人,伦理问题在医学史上也绝非少见[2]。小说中的青年医生利德盖特不仅医术精湛,而且观念先进,进取心较强,对医学科学研究表现出浓厚的兴趣,并立志沿着维萨里(Andreas Vesalius, 1514—1564)、比夏等大师的足迹从事科学研究,在病理学方面有所突破。在巴黎医学院求学时,他终日沉浸在实验室里做电流治疗实验(galvanic experiments),并在导师的指导下进行尸体解剖、记录伤寒病症状。在米德尔马契行医之余,他继续追踪伤寒病等各种热病的病原理论和治疗方法的研究,跟进心脏病研究的最新发现,利用最新发明的医疗器械如听诊器和体温计等对疾病进行诊断、监控,在新热病医院开展科学实验并保留详细的实验记录。尽

---

[1] CORNFIELD P J. Power and the professions in Britain between 1700 and 1850[M]. London: Routledge, 1995: 8. 另参见李增. 英国维多利亚时期的医学伦理小说:以乔治·爱略特的《米德尔马契》为中心[J]. 江西社会科学, 2017, 37(4):86-96.

[2] BRAZIER M. Exploitation and enrichment: the paradox of medical experimentation[J]. Journal of medical ethics, 2008 (34):180-181. 另参见李增. 英国维多利亚时期的医学伦理小说:以乔治·爱略特的《米德尔马契》为中心[J]. 江西社会科学, 2017, 37(4):86-96.

第三章　文学与医学（Literature and Medicine）

管利德盖特勤奋刻苦、积极进取，但他入行时间短、经验尚浅，在医患、医际问题的处理上却有违反医生保密、尊重同道等伦理原则之嫌。此外，他为人真诚，却对米德尔马契这张尔虞我诈、错综复杂的关系网缺乏认识，因而无意中得罪同行甚至病人，招致记恨与报复。比如卡苏朋突然离世，病中修改遗嘱一事成为米德尔马契茶余饭后的谈资。利德盖特在家里同妻子讨论卡苏朋的病情以及卡苏朋修改遗嘱的传闻，他深知这有违医生行医保密原则，因此反复叮嘱妻子不许对外讲，但他的行为却有泄密之嫌①。从这个意义上来讲，虽然利德盖特仁心济世，但在医疗和科研过程中泄露病人隐私，因而违背了"保密、尊重同道"的医学伦理戒律。

此外，尽管利德盖特从事医学实验是纯粹为了科学研究，但其中仍不乏有悖于医学伦理的情形。在劝说拍卖商特郎布尔先生（Borthrop Trumbull）参与的肺炎临床前实验便是一例。为了说服他同意参加实验，配合实验人员记录和监视病情发展，利德盖特主动献殷勤并费尽口舌，不厌其烦地解释实验原理和过程。他跟特郎布尔先生交流时，故意选用一些医学术语，避重就轻地重点阐述参与实验能够带来的种种益处，而对实验中可能出现的风险性却只字未提。而当时肺炎属于严重急性病，即使在当今发达的医疗条件下，也可能出现因治疗不当或不及时而酿成大祸。一旦成功便可造福人类，但也存在伤害实验对象性命的危险。纵然特郎布尔先生身体强壮、实验过程中会有医护人员的全程监视，也并不能确保不会出现意外。因此，利德盖特没有将实验的风险、意外以及严重后果告知实验对象，无疑存在故意隐瞒危险的嫌疑，在患者并不完全知情的条件下进行实验，无疑是对患者权益的侵犯，因此，违背了"不伤害、患者利益至上"的医学伦理原则。艾略特的笔尖也委婉地流露出对利德盖特肺炎实验的不赞同态度，同时也质疑此次科学实验的正当性。

以《米德尔马契》为代表的小说通过叙述医生在行医过程中的所见所闻，给我们展示了良莠不齐的医生群体、唯利是图的医疗体系以及举步维艰的医疗改革的画面，洞见了维多利亚时期城镇的医疗现状。整个作品反映出作者对维多利亚时期医患、同行、社会和科学之间医学伦理关系的深刻思考，虽然讲述的是一个半世纪前的故事，但其中的医学伦理学问题却具有一定的普遍性，所蕴含的医学伦理精神、职业道德操守仍然值得我们借鉴②。

---

① LOGAN P M. Conceiving the body: realism and medicine in Middlemarch[J]. History of the human sciences, 1991 (2): 217. 另参见 FURST L R. Struggling for medical reform in Middlemarch[J]. Nineteenth-century literature, 1993(3): 343, 359.

② CALDWELL J M. Literature and medicine in nineteenth-century Britain: from Mary Shelley to George Eliot[M]. Cambridge: Cambridge University Press, 2004: 143-170.

作品选读

Middlemarch

George Eliot

Chapter X

"He had catched a great cold, had he had no other clothes to wear than the skin of a bear not yet killed."— FULLER.

[...]

Already, as Miss Brooke passed out of the dining-room, opportunity was found for some interjectional "asides."

"A fine woman, Miss Brooke! an uncommonly fine woman, by God!" said Mr Standish, the old lawyer, who had been so long concerned with the landed gentry that he had become landed himself, and used that oath in a deep-mouthed manner as a sort of armorial bearings, stamping the speech of a man who held a good position.

Mr Bulstrode, the banker, seemed to be addressed, but that gentleman disliked coarseness and profanity, and merely bowed. The remark was taken up by Mr Chichely, a middle-aged bachelor and coursing celebrity, who had a complexion something like an Easter egg, a few hairs carefully arranged, and a carriage implying the consciousness of a distinguished appearance.

"Yes, but not my style of woman: I like a woman who lays herself out a little more to please us. There should be a little filigree about a woman—something of the coquette. A man likes a sort of challenge. The more of a dead set she makes at you the better."

"There's some truth in that," said Mr Standish, disposed to be genial. "And, by God, it's usually the way with them. I suppose it answers some wise ends: Providence made them so, eh, Bulstrode?"

"I should be disposed to refer coquetry to another source," said Mr Bulstrode. "I should rather refer it to the devil."

"Ay, to be sure, there should be a little devil in a woman," said Mr Chichely, whose study of the fair sex seemed to have been detrimental to his theology. "And I like them blond, with a certain gait, and a swan neck. Between ourselves, the mayor's daughter is more to my taste than Miss Brooke or Miss Celia either. If I were a marrying man I should choose Miss Vincy before either of them."

"Well, make up, make up," said Mr Standish, jocosely; "you see the middle-aged fellows carry the day."

Mr Chichely shook his head with much meaning: he was not going to incur the certainty of being accepted by the woman he would choose.

The Miss Vincy who had the honour of being Mr Chichely's ideal was of course not present; for Mr Brooke, always objecting to go too far, would not have chosen that his nieces should meet the daughter of a Middlemarch manufacturer, unless it were on a public occasion. The feminine part of the company included none whom Lady Chettam or Mrs Cadwallader could object to; for Mrs Renfrew, the colonel's widow, was not only unexceptionable in point of breeding, but also interesting on the ground of her complaint, which puzzled the doctors, and seemed clearly a case wherein the fulness of professional knowledge might need the supplement of quackery. Lady Chettam, who attributed her own remarkable health to home-made bitters united with constant medical attendance, entered with much exercise of the imagination into Mrs Renfrew's account of symptoms, and into the amazing futility in her case of all strengthening medicines.

"Where can all strength of those medicines go, my dear?" said the mild but stately dowager, turning to Mrs Cadwallader reflectively, when Mrs Renfrew's attention was called away.

"It strengthens the disease," said the Rector's wife, much too well-born not to be an amateur in medicine. "Everything depends on the constitution: some people make fat, some blood, and some bile—that's my view of the matter; and whatever they take is a sort of grist to the mill."

"Then she ought to take medicines that would reduce—reduce the disease, you know, if you are right, my dear. And I think what you say is reasonable."

"Certainly it is reasonable. You have two sorts of potatoes, fed on the same soil. One of them grows more and more watery—"

"Ah! like this poor Mrs Renfrew—that is what I think. Dropsy! There is no swelling yet—it is inward. I should say she ought to take drying medicines, shouldn't you? —or a dry hot-air bath. Many things might be tried, of a drying nature."

"Let her try a certain person's pamphlets," said Mrs Cadwallader in an undertone, seeing the gentlemen enter. "He does not want drying."

"Who, my dear?" said Lady Chettam, a charming woman, not so quick as to nullify the pleasure of explanation.

"The bridegroom—Casaubon. He has certainly been drying up faster since the engagement: the flame of passion, I suppose."

"I should think he is far from having a good constitution," said Lady Chettam, with a still deeper undertone. "And then his studies—so very dry, as you say."

"Really, by the side of Sir James, he looks like a death's head skinned over for the occasion. Mark my words: in a year from this time that girl will hate him. She looks up to him as an oracle now, and by-and-by she will be at the other extreme. All flightiness!"

"How very shocking! I fear she is headstrong. But tell me—you know all about him—is there anything very bad? What is the truth?"

"The truth? He is as bad as the wrong physic-nasty to take, and sure to disagree."

"There could not be anything worse than that," said Lady Chettam, with so vivid a conception of the physic that she seemed to have learned something exact about Mr Casaubon's disadvantages. "However, James will hear nothing against Miss Brooke. He says she is the mirror of women still."

"That is a generous make-believe of his. Depend upon it, he likes little Celia better, and she appreciates him. I hope you like my little Celia?"

"Certainly; she is fonder of geraniums, and seems more docile, though not so fine a figure. But we were talking of physic: tell me about this new young surgeon, Mr Lydgate. I am told he is wonderfully clever: he certainly looks it—a fine brow indeed."

"He is a gentleman. I heard him talking to Humphrey Cadwallader. He talks well."

"Yes. Mr Brooke says he is one of the Lydgates of Northumberland, really well connected. One does not expect it in a practitioner of that kind. For my own part, I like a medical man more on a footing with the servants; they are often all the cleverer. I assure you I found poor Hicks's judgment unfailing; I never knew him wrong. He was coarse and butcher-like, but he knew my constitution. It was a loss to me his going off so suddenly. Dear me, what a very animated conversation Miss Brooke seems to be having with this Mr Lydgate!"

"She is talking cottages and hospitals with him," said Mrs Cadwallader, whose ears

第三章 文学与医学(Literature and Medicine)

and power of interpretation were quick. "I believe he is a sort of philanthropist, so Brooke is sure to take him up."

"James," said Lady Chettam when her son came near, "bring Mr Lydgate and introduce him to me. I want to test him."

The affable dowager declared herself delighted with this opportunity of making Mr Lydgate's acquaintance, having heard of his success in treating fever on a new plan.

Mr Lydgate had the medical accomplishment of looking perfectly grave whatever nonsense was talked to him, and his dark steady eyes gave him impressiveness as a listener. He was as little as possible like the lamented Hicks, especially in a certain careless refinement about his toilette and utterance. Yet Lady Chettam gathered much confidence in him. He confirmed her view of her own constitution as being peculiar, by admitting that all constitutions might be called peculiar, and he did not deny that hers might be more peculiar than others. He did not approve of a too lowering system, including reckless cupping, nor, on the other hand, of incessant port-wine and bark. He said "I think so" with an air of so much deference accompanying the insight of agreement, that she formed the most cordial opinion of his talents.

"I am quite pleased with your protégé," she said to Mr Brooke before going away.

"My protege? —dear me! —who is that?" said Mr Brooke.

"This young Lydgate, the new doctor. He seems to me to understand his profession admirably."

"Oh, Lydgate! He is not my protege, you know; only I knew an uncle of his who sent me a letter about him. However, I think he is likely to be first-rate has studied in Paris, knew Broussais; has ideas, you know—wants to raise the profession."

"Lydgate has lots of ideas, quite new, about ventilation and diet, that sort of thing," resumed Mr Brooke, after he had handed out Lady Chettam, and had returned to be civil to a group of Middlemarchers.

"Hang it, do you think that is quite sound? —upsetting the old treatment, which has made Englishmen what they are?" said Mr Standish.

"Medical knowledge is at a low ebb among us," said Mr Bulstrode, who spoke in a subdued tone, and had rather a sickly air. "I, for my part, hail the advent of Mr Lydgate. I hope to find good reason for confiding the new hospital to his management."

"That is all very fine," replied Mr Standish, who was not fond of Mr Bulstrode; "if you like him to try experiments on your hospital patients, and kill a few people for charity, I have no objection. But I am not going to hand money out of my purse to have experiments tried on me. I like treatment that has been tested a little."

"Well, you know, Standish, every dose you take is an experiment—an experiment, you know," said Mr Brooke, nodding towards the lawyer.

"Oh, if you talk in that sense!" said Mr Standish, with as much disgust at such nonlegal quibbling as a man can well betray towards a valuable client.

"I should be glad of any treatment that would cure me without reducing me to a skeleton, like poor Grainger," said Mr Vincy, the mayor, a florid man, who would have served for a study of flesh in striking contrast with the Franciscan tints of Mr Bulstrode. "It's an uncommonly dangerous thing to be left without any padding against the shafts of disease, as somebody said, and I think it a very good expression myself."

Mr Lydgate, of course, was out of hearing. He had quitted the party early, and would have thought it altogether tedious but for the novelty of certain introductions, especially the introduction to Miss Brooke, whose youthful bloom, with her approaching marriage to that faded scholar, and her interest in matters socially useful, gave her the piquancy of an unusual combination.

"She is a good creature—that fine girl—but a little too earnest," he thought.

"It is troublesome to talk to such women. They are always wanting reasons, yet they are too ignorant to understand the merits of any question, and usually fall back on their moral sense to settle things after their own taste."

Evidently Miss Brooke was not Mr Lydgate's style of woman any more than Mr Chichely's. Considered, indeed, in relation to the latter, whose mind was matured, she was altogether a mistake, and calculated to shock his trust in final causes, including the adaptation of fine young women to purple-faced bachelors. But Lydgate was less ripe, and might possibly have experience before him which would modify his opinion as to the most excellent things in woman.

Miss Brooke, however, was not again seen by either of these gentlemen under her maiden name. Not long after that dinner party she had become Mrs Casaubon and was on her way to Rome.

第三章 文学与医学(Literature and Medicine)

[...]

Chapter XXVI

"He beats me and I rail at him: O worthy satisfaction! would it were otherwise—that I could beat him while he railed at me."—*Troilus and Cressida*.

But Fred did not go to Stone Court the next day, for reasons that were quite peremptory. From those visits to unsanitary Houndsley streets in search of Diamond, he had brought back not only a bad bargain in horseflesh, but the further misfortune of some ailment which for a day or two had seemed mere depression and headache, but which got so much worse when he returned from his visit to Stone Court that, going into the dining-room, he threw himself on the sofa, and in answer to his mother's anxious question, said, "I feel very ill: I think you must send for Wrench."

Wrench came but did not apprehend anything serious, spoke of a "slight derangement," and did not speak of coming again on the morrow. He had a due value for the Vincy's house, but the wariest men are apt to be a little dulled by routine, and on worried mornings will sometimes go through their business with the zest of the daily bell-ringer. Mr Wrench was a small, neat, bilious man, with a well-dressed wig: he had a laborious practice, an irascible temper, a lymphatic wife and seven children; and he was already rather late before setting out on a four-mile drive to meet Dr Minchin on the other side of Tipton, the decease of Hicks, a rural practitioner, having increased Middlemarch practice in that direction. Great statesmen err, and why not small medical men? Mr Wrench did not neglect sending the usual white parcels, which this time had black and drastic contents. Their effect was not alleviating to poor Fred, who, however, unwilling as he said to believe that he was "in for an illness," rose at his usual easy hour the next morning and went downstairs meaning to breakfast but succeeded in nothing but in sitting and shivering by the fire. Mr Wrench was again sent for, but was gone on his rounds, and Mrs Vincy seeing her darling's changed looks and general misery, began to cry and said she would send for Dr Sprague.

"Oh, nonsense, mother! It's nothing," said Fred, putting out his hot dry hand to her, "I shall soon be all right. I must have taken cold in that nasty damp ride."

"Mamma!" said Rosamond, who was seated near the window (the dining room windows looked on that highly respectable street called Lowick Gate), "there is Mr

Lydgate, stopping to speak to someone. If I were you I would call him in. He has cured Ellen Bulstrode. They say he cures everyone."

Mrs Vincy sprang to the window and opened it in an instant, thinking only of Fred and not of medical etiquette. Lydgate was only two yards off on the other side of some iron palisading, and turned round at the sudden sound of the sash, before she called to him. In two minutes he was in the room, and Rosamond went out, after waiting just long enough to show a pretty anxiety conflicting with her sense of what was becoming.

Lydgate had to hear a narrative in which Mrs Vincy's mind insisted with remarkable instinct on every point of minor importance, especially on what Mr Wrench had said and had not said about coming again. That there might be an awkward affair with Wrench, Lydgate saw at once; but the case was serious enough to make him dismiss that consideration: he was convinced that Fred was in the pink-skinned stage of typhoid fever, and that he had taken just the wrong medicines. He must go to bed immediately, must have a regular nurse, and various appliances and precautions must be used, about which Lydgate was particular. Poor Mrs Vincy's terror at these indications of danger found vent in such words as came most easily. She thought it "very ill usage on the part of Mr Wrench, who had attended their house so many years in preference to Mr Peacock, though Mr Peacock was equally a friend. Why Mr Wrench should neglect her children more than others, she could not for the life of her understand. He had not neglected Mrs. Larcher's when they had the measles, nor indeed would Mrs Vincy have wished that he should. And if anything should happen…"

Here poor Mrs Vincy's spirit quite broke down, and her Niobe-throat and good-humoured face were sadly convulsed. This was in the hall out of Fred's hearing, but Rosamond had opened the drawing-room door, and now came forward anxiously. Lydgate apologised for Mr Wrench, said that the symptoms yesterday might have been disguising, and that this form of fever was very equivocal in its beginnings: he would go immediately to the druggist's and have a prescription made up in order to lose no time, but he would write to Mr Wrench and tell him what had been done.

"But you must come again—you must go on attending Fred. I can't have my boy left to anybody who may come or not. I bear nobody ill-will, thank God, and Mr Wrench saved me in the pleurisy, but he'd better have let me die —if— if—"

第三章 文学与医学(Literature and Medicine)

"I will meet Mr Wrench here, then, shall I?" said Lydgate, really believing that Wrench was not well prepared to deal wisely with a case of this kind.

"Pray make that arrangement, Mr Lydgate," said Rosamond, coming to her mother's aid, and supporting her arm to lead her away.

When Mr Vincy came home he was very angry with Wrench, and did not care if he never came into his house again. Lydgate should go on now, whether Wrench liked it or not. It was no joke to have fever in the house. Everybody must be sent to now, not to come to dinner on Thursday. And Pritchard needn't get up any wine: brandy was the best thing against infection. "I shall drink brandy," added Mr Vincy emphatically—as much as to say, this was not an occasion for firing with blank cartridges. "He's an uncommonly unfortunate lad, is Fred. He'd need have some luck by-and-by to make up for all this—else I don't know who'd have an eldest son."

"Don't say so, Vincy," said the mother, with a quivering lip, "if you don't want him to be taken from me."

"It will worret you to death, Lucy; that I can see," said Mr Vincy, more mildly.

"However, Wrench shall know what I think of the matter." (What Mr Vincy thought confusedly was, that the fever might somehow have been hindered if Wrench had shown the proper solicitude about his—the Mayor's—family.)

"I'm the last man to give in to the cry about new doctors or new parsons, either—whether they're Bulstrode's men or not. But Wrench shall know what I think, take it as he will."

Wrench did not take it at all well. Lydgate was as polite as he could be in his offhand way, but politeness in a man who has placed you at a disadvantage is only an additional exasperation, especially if he happens to have been an object of dislike beforehand. Country practitioners used to be an irritable species, susceptible on the point of honour; and Mr Wrench was one of the most irritable among them. He did not refuse to meet Lydgate in the evening, but his temper was somewhat tried on the occasion. He had to hear Mrs Vincy say—

"Oh, Mr Wrench, what have I ever done that you should use me so? —To go away, and never to come again! And my boy might have been stretched a corpse!"

Mr Vincy, who had been keeping up a sharp fire on the enemy Infection, and was a good deal heated in consequence, started up when he heard Wrench come in, and went into the hall to let him know what he thought.

"I'll tell you what, Wrench, this is beyond a joke," said the Mayor, who of late had had to rebuke offenders with an official air, and now broadened himself by putting his thumbs in his armholes. —"To let fever get unawares into a house like this. There are some things that ought to be actionable, and are not so—that's my opinion."

But irrational reproaches were easier to bear than the sense of being instructed, or rather the sense that a younger man, like Lydgate, inwardly considered him in need of instruction, for "in point of fact," Mr Wrench afterwards said, Lydgate paraded flighty, foreign notions, which would not wear. He swallowed his ire for the moment, but he afterwards wrote to decline further attendance in the case. The house might be a good one, but Mr Wrench was not going to truckle to anybody on a professional matter. He reflected, with much probability on his side, that Lydgate would by-and-by be caught tripping too, and that his ungentlemanly attempts to discredit the sale of drugs by his professional brethren would by-and-by recoil on himself. He threw out biting remarks on Lydgate's tricks, worthy only of a quack, to get himself a factitious reputation with credulous people. That cant about cures was never got up by sound practitioners.

This was a point on which Lydgate smarted as much as Wrench could desire. To be puffed by ignorance was not only humiliating, but perilous, and not more enviable than the reputation of the weather prophet. He was impatient of the foolish expectations amidst which all work must becarried on, and likely enough to damage himself as much as Mr Wrench could wish, by an unprofessional openness.

However, Lydgate was installed as medical attendant on the Vincys, and the event was a subject of general conversation in Middlemarch. Some said, that the Vincys had behaved scandalously, that Mr Vincy had threatened Wrench, and that Mrs Vincy had accused him of poisoning her son. Others were of opinion that Mr Lydgate's passing by was providential, that he was wonderfully clever in fevers, and that Bulstrode was in the right to bring him forward. Many people believed that Lydgate's coming to the town at all was really due to Bulstrode; and Mrs Taft, who was always counting stitches and gathered her information in misleading fragments caught between the rows of her knitting, had got it into her head that Mr Lydgate was a natural son of Bulstrode's, a fact which seemed to justify

第三章 文学与医学(Literature and Medicine)

her suspicions of evangelical laymen.

She one day communicated this piece of knowledge to Mrs Farebrother, who did not fail to tell her son of it, observing—

"I should not be surprised at anything in Bulstrode, but I should be sorry to think it of Mr Lydgate."

"Why, mother," said Mr Farebrother, after an explosive laugh, "you know very well that Lydgate is of a good family in the North. He never heard of Bulstrode before he came here."

"That is satisfactory so far as Mr Lydgate is concerned, Camden," said the old lady, with an air of precision. "But as to Bulstrode—the report may be true of some other son."

[...]

Chapter XLV

"It is the humour of many heads to extol the days of their forefathers, and declaim against the wickedness of times present. Which notwithstanding they cannot handsomely do, without the borrowed help and satire of times past; condemning the vices of their own times, by the expressions of vices in times which they commend, which cannot but argue the community of vice in both. Horace, therefore, Juvenal, and Persius, were no prophets, although their lines did seem to indigitate and point at our times."—Sir Thomas Browne: *Pseudodoxia Epidemica.*

That opposition to the New Fever Hospital which Lydgate had sketched to Dorothea was, like other oppositions, to be viewed in many different lights. He regarded it as a mixture of jealousy and dunderheaded prejudice. Mr Bulstrode saw in it not only medical jealousy but a determination to thwart himself, prompted mainly by a hatred of that vital religion of which he had striven to be an effectual lay representative—a hatred which certainly found pretexts apart from religion such as were only too easy to find in the entanglements of human action. These might be called the ministerial views. But oppositions have the illimitable range of objections at command, which need never stop short at the boundary of knowledge, but can draw for ever on the vasts of ignorance. What the opposition in Middlemarch said about the New Hospital and its administration had certainly a great deal of echo in it, for heaven has taken care that everybody shall not be an originator; but there were differences which represented every social shade between the polished moderation of Dr Minchin and the trenchant assertion of Mrs Dollop, the landlady of the Tankard in Slaughter Lane.

Mrs Dollop became more and more convinced by her own asseveration, that Doctor Lydgate meant to let the people die in the Hospital, if not to poison them, for the sake of cutting them up without saving by your leave or with your leave; for it was a known "fac" that he had wanted to cut up Mrs Goby, as respectable a woman as any in Parley Street, who had money in trust before her marriage—a poor tale for a doctor, who if he was good for anything should know what was the matter with you before you died, and not want to pry into your inside after you were gone. If that was not reason, Mrs Dollop wished to know what was; but there was a prevalent feeling in her audience that her opinion was a bulwark, and that if it were overthrown there would be no limits to the cutting-up of bodies, as had been well seen in Burke and Hare with their pitch plaisters—such a hanging business as that was not wanted in Middlemarch!

And let it not be supposed that opinion at the Tankard in Slaughter Lane was unimportant to the medical profession: that old authentic public house—the original Tankard, known by the name of Dollop's —was the resort of a great Benefit Club, which had some months before put to the vote whether its longstanding medical man, "Doctor Gambit," should not be cashiered in favour of "this Doctor Lydgate," who was capable of performing the most astonishing cures, and rescuing people altogether given up by other practitioners. But the balance had been turned against Lydgate by two members, who for some private reasons held that this power of resuscitating persons as good as dead was an equivocal recommendation, and might interfere with providential favours. In the course of the year, however, there had been a change in the public sentiment, of which the unanimity at Dollop's was an index.

A good deal more than a year ago, before anything was known of Lydgate's skill, the judgments on it had naturally been divided, depending on a sense of likelihood, situated perhaps in the pit of the stomach or in the pineal gland, and differing in its verdicts, but not the less valuable as a guide in the total deficit of evidence. Patients who had chronic diseases or whose lives had long been worn threadbare, like old Featherstone's, had been at once inclined to try him; also, many who did not like paying their doctor's bills, thought agreeably of opening an account with a new doctor and sending for him without stint if the children's temper wanted a dose, occasions when the old practitioners were often crusty; and all persons thus inclined to employ Lydgate held it likely that he was clever. Some considered that he might do more than others "where there was liver;"—at least there would be no harm in getting a few bottles of "stuff" from him, since if these proved useless it would still be possible to return to the Purifying Pills, which kept you alive, if they did not remove the yellowness. But these were people of minor importance. Good Middlemarch families were of course not going to change their doctor without reason shown; and everybody who had employed Mr Peacock did not feel obliged to accept a new man merely in the character of his successor, objecting that he was "not likely to be equal to Peacock."

But Lydgate had not been long in the town before there were particulars enough reported of him to breed much more specific expectations and to intensify differences into partisanship; some of the particulars being of that impressive order of which the significance is entirely hidden, like a statistical amount without a standard of comparison, but with a note of exclamation at the end. The cubic feet of oxygen yearly swallowed by a full-grown man—what a shudder they might have created in some Middlemarch circles! "Oxygen! nobody knows what that may be—is it any wonder the cholera has got to Dantzic? And yet there are people who say quarantine is no good!"

One of the facts quickly rumoured was that Lydgate did not dispense drugs. This was offensive both to the physicians whose exclusive distinction seemed infringed on, and to the surgeon apothecaries with whom he ranged himself; and only a little while before, they might have counted on having the law on their side against a man who without calling himself a London-made M. D. dared to ask for pay except as a charge on drugs. But Lydgate had not beenexperienced enough to foresee that his new course would be even more offensive to the laity; and to Mr Mawmsey, an important grocer in the Top Market, who, though not one of his patients, questioned him in an affable manner on the subject, he was injudicious enough to give a hasty popular explanation of his reasons, pointing out to Mr Mawmsey that it must lower the character of practitioners, and be a constant injury to the public, if their only mode of getting paid for their work was by their making out long bills for draughts, boluses, and mixtures.

"It is in that way that hard-working medical men may come to be almost as mischievous as quacks," said Lydgate, rather thoughtlessly. "To get their own bread they must overdose the king's lieges; and that's a bad sort of treason, Mr Mawmsey—undermines the constitution in a fatal way."

Mr Mawmsey was not only an overseer (it was about a question of outdoor pay that he was having an interview with Lydgate), he was also asthmatic and had an increasing family: thus, from a medical point of view, as well as from his own, he was an important man; indeed, an exceptional grocer, whose hair was arranged in a flame-like pyramid, and whose retail deference was of the cordial, encouraging kind—jocosely complimentary, and with a certain considerate abstinence from letting out the full force of his mind. It was Mr Mawmsey's friendly jocoseness in questioning him which had set the tone of Lydgate's reply. But let the wise be warned against too great readiness at explanation: it multiplies the sources of mistake, lengthening the sum for reckoners sure to go wrong.

Lydgate smiled as he ended his speech, putting his foot into the stirrup, and Mr Mawmsey laughed more than he would have done if he had known who the king's lieges were, giving his "Good morning, sir, good morning, sir," with the air of one who saw everything clearly enough. But in truth his views were perturbed. For years he had been paying bills with strictly-made items, so that for every half-crown and eighteen pence he was certain something measurable had been delivered. He had done this with satisfaction, including it among his responsibilities as a husband and father, and regarding a longer bill than usual as a dignity worth mentioning. Moreover, in addition to the massive benefit of the drugs to "self and family," he had enjoyed the pleasure of forming an acute judgment as to their immediate effects, so as to give an intelligent statement for the guidance of Mr Gambit—a practitioner just a little lower in status than Wrench or Toller, and especially esteemed as an accoucheur, of whose ability Mr Mawmsey had the poorest opinion on all other points, but in doctoring, he was wont to say in an undertone, he placed Gambit above any of them.

Here were deeper reasons than the superficial talk of a new man, which appeared still flimsier in the drawing-room over the shop, when they were recited to Mrs Mawmsey, a woman accustomed to be made much of as a fertile mother,—generally under attendance more or less frequent from Mr Gambit, and occasionally having attacks which required Dr Minchin.

第三章 文学与医学(Literature and Medicine)

"Does this Mr Lydgate mean to say there is no use in taking medicine?" said Mrs Mawmsey, who was slightly given to drawling. "I should like him to tell me how I could bear up at Fair time, if I didn't take strengthening medicine for a month beforehand. Think of what I have to provide for calling customers, my dear!"—here Mrs Mawmsey turned to an intimate female friend who sat by— "a large veal pie—a stuffed fillet—a round of beef—ham, tongue, et cetera, et cetera! But what keeps me up best is the pink mixture, not the brown. I wonder, Mr Mawmsey, with your experience, you could have patience to listen. I should have told him at once that I knew a little better than that."

"No, no, no," said Mr Mawmsey; "I was not going to tell him my opinion. Hear everything and judge for yourself is my motto. But he didn't know who he was talking to. I was not to be turned on his finger. People often pretend to tell me things, when they might as well say, 'Mawmsey, you're a fool.' But I smile at it: I humour everybody's weak place. If physic had done harm to self and family, I should have found it out by this time."

The next day Mr Gambit was told that Lydgate went about saying physic was of no use.

"Indeed!" said he, lifting his eyebrows with cautious surprise. (He was a stout husky man with a large ring on his fourth finger.) "How will he cure his patients, then?"

"That is what J say," returned Mrs Mawmsey, who habitually gave weight to her speech by loading her pronouns. "Does he suppose that people will pay him only to come and sit with them and go away again?"

Mrs Mawmsey had had a great deal of sitting from Mr Gambit, including very full accounts of his own habits of body and other affairs; but of course he knew there was no innuendo in her remark, since his spare time and personal narrative had never been charged for. So he replied, humorously—

"Well, Lydgate is a good-looking young fellow, you know."

"Not one that I would employ," said Mrs Mawmsey. "Others may do as they please."

Hence Mr Gambit could go away from the chief grocer's without fear of rivalry, but not without a sense that Lydgate was one of those hypocrites who try to discredit others by advertising their own honesty, and that it might be worth some people's while to show him up. Mr Gambit, however, had a satisfactory practice, much pervaded by the smells of retail trading which suggested the reduction of cash payments to a balance. And he did not think it worth his while to show Lydgate up until he knew how. He had not indeed great resources of education, and had had to work his own way against a good deal of professional contempt; but he made none the worse accoucheur for calling the breathing apparatus "longs."

Other medical men felt themselves more capable. Mr Toller shared the highest practice in the town and belonged to an old Middlemarch family: there were Tollers in the law and everything else above the line of retail trade. Unlike our irascible friend Wrench, he had the easiest way in the world of taking things which might be supposed to annoy him, being a well-bred, quietly facetious man, who kept a good house, was very fond of a little sporting when he could get it, very friendly with Mr Hawley, and hostile to Mr Bulstrode. It may seem odd that with such pleasant habits he should have been given to the heroic treatment, bleeding and blistering and starving his patients, with a dispassionate disregard to his personal example; but the incongruity favoured the opinion of his ability among his patients, who commonly observed that Mr Toller had lazy manners, but his treatment was as active as you could desire: —no man, said they, carried more seriousness into his profession: he was a little slow in coming, but when he came, he did something. He was a great favourite in his own circle, and whatever he implied to any one's disadvantage told doubly from his careless ironical tone.

He naturally got tired of smiling and saying, "Ah!" when he was told that Mr Peacock's successor did not mean to dispense medicines; and Mr Hackbutt one day mentioning it over the wine at a dinner-party, Mr Toller said, laughingly, "Dibbitts will get rid of his stale drugs, then. I'm fond of little Dibbitts—I'm glad he's in luck."

"I see your meaning, Toller," said Mr Hackbutt, "and I am entirely of your opinion. I shall take an opportunity of expressing myself to that effect. A medical man should be responsible for the quality of the drugs consumed by his patients. That is the rationale of the system of charging which has hitherto obtained; and nothing is more offensive than this ostentation of reform, where there is no real amelioration."

"Ostentation, Hackbutt?" said Mr Toller, ironically. "I don't see that. A man can't very well be ostentatious of what nobody believes in. There's no reform in the matter: the question is, whether the profit on the drugs is paid to the medical man by the druggist or by the patient, and whether there shall be extra pay under the name of attendance."

"Ah, to be sure; one of your damned new versions of old humbug," said Mr Hawley, passing the decanter to Mr Wrench.

Mr Wrench, generally abstemious, often drank wine rather freely at a party, getting the more irritable in consequence.

"As to humbug, Hawley," he said, "that's a word easy to fling about. But what I contend against is the way medical men are fouling their own nest, and setting up a cry about the country as if a general practitioner who dispenses drugs couldn't be a gentleman. I throw back the imputation with scorn. I say, the most ungentlemanly trick a man can be guilty of is to come among the members of his profession with innovations which are a libel on their time-honoured procedure. That is my opinion, and I am ready to maintain it against anyone who contradicts me." Mr Wrench's voice had become exceedingly sharp.

"I can't oblige you there, Wrench," said Mr Hawley, thrusting his hands into his trouser pockets.

"My dear fellow," said Mr Toller, striking in pacifically, and looking at Mr Wrench, "the physicians have their toes trodden on more than we have. If you come to dignity it is a question for Minchin and Sprague."

"Does medical jurisprudence provide nothing against these infringements?" said Mr Hackbutt, with a disinterested desire to offer his lights. "How does the law stand, eh, Hawley?"

"Nothing to be done there," said Mr Hawley. "I looked into it for Sprague. You'd only break your nose against a damned judge's decision."

"Pooh! No need of law," said Mr Toller. "So far as practice is concerned the attempt is an absurdity. No patient will like it—certainly not Peacock's, who have been used to depletion. Pass the wine."

Mr Toller's prediction was partly verified. If Mr and Mrs Mawmsey, who had no idea of employing Lydgate, were made uneasy by his supposed declaration against drugs, it was inevitable that those who called him in should watch a little anxiously to see whether he did "use all the means he might use" in the case. Even good Mr Powderell, who in his constant charity of interpretation was inclined to esteem Lydgate the more for what seemed a conscientious pursuit of a better plan, had his mind disturbed with doubts during his wife's attack of erysipelas, and could not abstain from mentioning to Lydgate that Mr Peacock on a similar occasion had administered a series of boluses which were not otherwise definable than by their remarkable effect in bringing Mrs Powderell round before Michaelmas from an illness which had begun in a remarkably hot August. At last, indeed, in the conflict between his desire not to hurt Lydgate and his anxiety that no "means" should be lacking, he induced his wife privately to take Widgeon's Purifying Pills, an esteemed Middlemarch medicine, which arrested every disease at the fountain by setting to work at once upon the blood. This co-operative measure was not to be mentioned to Lydgate, and Mr Powderell himself had no certain reliance on it, only hoping that it might be attended with a blessing.

But in this doubtful stage of Lydgate's introduction he was helped by what we mortals rashly call good fortune. I suppose no doctor ever came newly to a place without making cures that surprised somebody—cures which may be called fortune's testimonials, and deserve as much credit as the written or printed kind. Various patients got well while Lydgate was attending them, some even of dangerous illnesses; and it was remarked that the new doctor with his new ways had at least the merit of bringing people back from the brink of death. The trash talked on such occasions was the more vexatious to Lydgate, because it gave precisely the sort of prestige which an incompetent and unscrupulous man would desire, and was sure to be imputed to him by the simmering dislike of the other medical men as an encouragement on his own part of ignorant puffing. But even his proud outspokenness was checked by the discernment that it was as useless to fight against the interpretations of ignorance as to whip the fog; and "good fortune" insisted on using those interpretations.

Mrs Larcher having just become charitably concerned about alarming symptoms in her charwoman, when Dr Minchin called, asked him to see her then and there, and to give her a certificate for the Infirmary; whereupon after examination he wrote a statement of the case as one of tumour, and recommended the bearer Nancy Nash as an outpatient. Nancy, calling at home on her way to the Infirmity, allowed the staymaker and his wife, in whose attic she lodged, to read Dr Minchin's paper, and by this means became a subject of compassionate conversation in the neighbouring shops of Churchyard Lane as being afflicted with a tumour at first declared to be as large and hard as a duck's egg, but later in the day to be about the size of "your fist." Most hearers agreed that it would have to be cut out, but one had known of oil and another of "squitchineal" as adequate to soften and reduce any lump in the body when taken enough of into the inside—the oil by gradually "soopling," the squitchineal by eating away.

Meanwhile when Nancy presented herself at the Infirmary, it happened to be one of Lydgate's days there. After questioning and examining her, Lydgate said to the house-surgeon in an undertone, "It's not tumour: it's cramp." He ordered her a blister and some steel mixture, and told her to go home and rest, giving her at the same time a note to Mrs Larcher, who, she said, was her best employer, to testify that she was in need of good food.

But by-and-by Nancy, in her attic, became portentously worse, the supposed tumour having indeed given way to the blister, but only wandered to another region with angrier pain. The staymaker's wife went to fetch Lydgate, and he continued for a fortnight to attend Nancy in her own home, until under his treatment she got quite well and went to work again. But the case continued to be described as one of tumour in Churchyard Lane and other streets—nay, by Mrs Larcher also; for when Lydgate's remarkable cure was mentioned to Dr Minchin, he naturally did not like to say, "The case was not one of tumour, and I was mistaken in describing it as such," but answered, "Indeed! Ah! I saw it was a surgical case, not of a fatal kind." He had been inwardly annoyed, however, when he had asked at the Infirmary about the woman he had recommended two days before, to hear from the house-surgeon, a youngster who was not sorry to vex Minchin with impunity, exactly what had occurred: he privately pronounced that it was indecent in a general practitioner to contradict a physician's diagnosis in that open manner, and afterwards agreed with Wrench that Lydgate was disagreeably inattentive to etiquette. Lydgate did not make the affair a ground for valuing himself or (very particularly) despising Minchin, such rectification of misjudgments often happening among men of equal qualifications. But report took up this amazing case of tumour, not clearly distinguished from cancer, and considered the more awful for being of the wandering sort; till much prejudice against Lydgate's method as to drugs was overcome by the proof of his marvellous skill in the speedy restoration of Nancy Nash after she had been rolling and rolling in agonies from the presence of a tumour both hard and obstinate, but nevertheless compelled to yield.

How could Lydgate help himself? It is offensive to tell a lady when she is expressing her amazement at your skill, that she is altogether mistaken and rather foolish in her amazement. And to have entered into the nature of diseases would only have added to his breaches of medical propriety. Thus he had to wince under a promise of success given by that ignorant praise which misses every valid quality.

In the case of a more conspicuous patient, Mr Borthrop Trumbull, Lydgate was conscious of having shown himself something better than an everyday doctor, though here too it was an equivocal advantage that he won. The eloquent auctioneer was seized with pneumonia, and having been a patient of Mr Peacock's, sent for Lydgate, whom he had expressed his intention to patronise. Mr Trumbull was a robust man, a good subject for trying the expectant theory upon—watching the course of an interesting disease when left as much as possible to itself, so that the stages might be noted for future guidance; and from the air with which he described his sensations Lydgate surmised that he would like to be taken into his medical man's confidence, and be represented as a partner in his own cure. The auctioneer heard, without much surprise, that his was a constitution which (always with due watching) might be left to itself, so as to offer a beautiful example of a disease with all its phases seen in clear delineation, and that he probably had the rare strength of mind voluntarily to become the test of a rational procedure, and thus make the disorder of his pulmonary functions a general benefit to society.

Mr Trumbull acquiesced at once, and entered strongly into the view that an illness of his was no ordinary occasion for medical science.

"Never fear, sir; you are not speaking to one who is altogether ignorant of the *vis medicatrix*," said he, with his usual superiority of expression, made rather pathetic by difficulty of breathing. And he went without shrinking through his abstinence from drugs, much sustained by application of the thermometer which implied the importance of his temperature, by the sense that he furnished objects for the microscope, and by learning many new words which seemed suited to the dignity of his secretions. For Lydgate was acute enough to indulge him with a little technical talk.

It may be imagined that Mr Trumbull rose from his couch with a disposition to speak of an illness in which he had manifested the strength of his mind as well as constitution; and he was not backward in awarding credit to the medical man who had discerned the

第三章 文学与医学(Literature and Medicine)

quality of patient he had to deal with. The auctioneer was not an ungenerous man, and liked to give others their due, feeling that he could afford it. He had caught the words "expectant method," and rang chimes on this and other learned phrases to accompany the assurance that Lydgate "knew a thing or two more than the rest of the doctors—was far better versed in the secrets of his profession than the majority of his compeers."

This had happened before the affair of Fred Vincy's illness had given to Mr Wrench's enmity towards Lydgate more definite personal ground. The new comer already threatened to be nuisancein the shape of rivalry, and was certainly a nuisance in the shape of practical criticism or reflections on his hard-driven elders, who had had something else to do than to busy themselves with untried notions. His practice had spread in one or two quarters, and from the first the report of his high family had led to his being pretty generally invited, so that the other medical men had to meet him at dinner in the best houses; and having to meet a man whom you dislike is not observed always to end in a mutual attachment. There was hardly ever so much unanimity among them as in the opinion that Lydgate was an arrogant young fellow, and yet ready for the sake of ultimately predominating to show a crawling subservience to Bulstrode. That Mr Farebrother, whose name was a chief flag of the anti-Bulstrode party, always defended Lydgate and made a friend of him, was referred to Farebrother's unaccountable way of fighting on both sides.

Here was plenty of preparation for the outburst of professional disgust at the announcement of the laws Mr Bulstrode was laying down for the direction of the New Hospital, which were the more exasperating because there was no present possibility of interfering with his will and pleasure, everybody except Lord Medlicote having refused help towards the building, on the ground that they preferred giving to the Old Infirmary. Mr Bulstrode met all the expenses, and had ceased to be sorry that he was purchasing the right to carry out his notions of improvement without hindrance from prejudiced coadjutors; but he had had to spend large sums, and the building had lingered. Caleb Garth had undertaken it, had failed during its progress, and before the interior fittings were begun had retired from the management of the business; and when referring to the Hospital he often said that however Bulstrode might ring if you tried him, he liked good solid carpentry and masonry, and had a notion both of drains and chimneys. In fact, the Hospital had become an object of intense interest to Bulstrode, and he would willingly have continued to spare a large yearly sum that he might rule it dictatorially without any Board; but he had another favourite object which also required money for its accomplishment: he wished to buy some land in the neighbourhood of Middlemarch, and therefore he wished to get considerable contributions towards maintaining the Hospital. Meanwhile he framed his plan of management. The Hospital was to be reserved for fever in all its forms; Lydgate was to be chief medical superintendent, that he might have free authority to pursue all comparative investigations which his studies, particularly in Paris, had shown him the importance of, the other medical visitors having a consultative influence, but no power to contravene Lydgate's ultimate decisions; and the general management was to be lodged exclusively in the hands of five directors associated with Mr Bulstrode, who were to have votes in the ratio of their contributions, the Board itself filling up any vacancy in its numbers, and no mob of small contributors being admitted to a share of government.

There was an immediate refusal on the part of every medical man in the town to become a visitor at the Fever Hospital.

"Very well," said Lydgate to Mr Bulstrode, "we have a capital house-surgeon and dispenser, a clear-headed, neat-handed fellow; well get Webbe from Crabsley, as good a country practitioner as any of them, to come over twice a week, and in case of any exceptional operation, Protheroe will come from Brassing. I must work the harder, that's all, and I have given up my post at the Infirmary. The plan will flourish in spite of them, and then they'll be glad to come in. Things can't last as they are: there must be all sorts of reform soon, and then young fellows may be glad to come and study here." Lydgate was in high spirits.

"I shall not flinch, you may depend upon it, Mr Lydgate," said Mr Bulstrode. "While I see you carrying out high intentions with vigour, you shall have my unfailing support. And I have humble confidence that the blessing which has hitherto attended my efforts against the spirit of evil in this town will not be withdrawn. Suitable directors to assist me I have no doubt of securing. Mr Brooke of Tipton has already given me his concurrence, and a pledge to contribute yearly: he has not specified the sum—probably not a great one. But he will be a useful member of the Board."

A useful member was perhaps to be defined as one who would originate nothing, and always vote with Mr Bulstrode.

The medical aversion to Lydgate was hardly disguised now. Neither Dr Sprague nor Dr Minchin said that he disliked Lydgate's knowledge, or his disposition to improve treatment: what they disliked was his arrogance, which nobody felt to be altogether deniable. They implied that he was insolent, pretentious, and given to that reckless innovation for the sake of noise and show which was the essence of the charlatan.

…

思考题

1. According to Mrs. Cadwallader and Lady Chettam, how is health related to constitution? What does this indicate about the medical profession in Middlemarch, especially so far as the dispensation of medicine is concerned?
2. How do the Middlemarchers respond to Mr Lydgate's medical experiment of "cutting-up" patients' bodies and his ideas of the New Hospital?
3. Why is Mr Lydgate the object of dislike in Middlemarch for doctors like Mr. Wrench, Mr Toller, Mr Hackbut, Dr Minchin and some others? What does this suggest about the outcome of Lydgate's medical reform?

第三节　补充阅读《古舟子咏》

阅读英国浪漫主义诗人柯勒律治的叙事长诗《古舟子咏》("The Rime of Ancient Mariner", 1798)的选段,结合其中对疾病的描写,思考作者对生命和疾病的态度,进而探究该诗所表达的人文精神,特别是其中所探讨的人和自然之间的关系。

The Rime of Ancient Mariner[①]
Samuel Taylor Coleridge

PART I

It is an ancient Mariner,

---

① COLERIDGE S T. "The Rime of the Ancient Mariner"[Z/OL]. https://www.poetryfoundation.org/poems/43997/the-rime-of-the-ancient-mariner-text-of-1834.

And he stoppeth one of three.
'By thy long grey beard and glittering eye,
Now wherefore stopp'st thou me?

The Bridegroom's doors are opened wide,
And I am next of kin;
The guests are met, the feast is set:
May'st hear the merry din.'

He holds him with his skinny hand,
'There was a ship,' quoth he.
'Hold off! unhand me, grey-beard loon!'
Eftsoons his hand dropt he.

He holds him with his glittering eye—
The Wedding-Guest stood still,
And listens like a three years' child:
The Mariner hath his will.

The Wedding-Guest sat on a stone:
He cannot choose but hear;
And thus spake on that ancient man,
The bright-eyed Mariner.

'The ship was cheered, the harbour cleared,
Merrily did we drop
Below the kirk, below the hill,
Below the lighthouse top.

The Sun came up upon the left,
Out of the sea came he!

第三章 文学与医学(Literature and Medicine)

And he shone bright, and on the right
Went down into the sea.

Higher and higher every day,
Till over the mast at noon—'
The Wedding-Guest here beat his breast,
For he heard the loud bassoon.

The bride hath paced into the hall,
Red as a rose is she;
Nodding their heads before her goes
The merry minstrelsy.

The Wedding-Guest he beat his breast,
Yet he cannot choose but hear;
And thus spake on that ancient man,
The bright-eyed Mariner.

And now the STORM-BLAST came, and he
Was tyrannous and strong:
He struck with his o'ertaking wings,
And chased us south along.

With sloping masts and dipping prow,
As who pursued with yell and blow
Still treads the shadow of his foe,
And forward bends his head,
The ship drove fast, loud roared the blast,
And southward aye we fled.

And now there came both mist and snow,

And it grew wondrous cold:
And ice, mast-high, came floating by,
As green as emerald.

And through the drifts the snowy clifts
Did send a dismal sheen:
Nor shapes of men nor beasts we ken—
The ice was all between.

The ice was here, the ice was there,
The ice was all around:
It cracked and growled, and roared and howled,
Like noises in a swound!

At length did cross an Albatross,
Thorough the fog it came;
As if it had been a Christian soul,
We hailed it in God's name.

It ate the food it ne'er had eat,
And round and round it flew.
The ice did split with a thunder-fit;
The helmsman steered us through!

And a good south wind sprung up behind;
The Albatross did follow,
And every day, for food or play,
Came to the mariner's hollo!

In mist or cloud, on mast or shroud,
It perched for vespers nine;

Whiles all the night, through fog-smoke white,
Glimmered the white Moon-shine.'

'God save thee, ancient Mariner!
From the fiends, that plague thee thus! —
Why look'st thou so?'—With my cross-bow
I shot the ALBATROSS.

PART II

The Sun now rose upon the right:
Out of the sea came he,
Still hid in mist, and on the left
Went down into the sea.

And the good south wind still blew behind,
But no sweet bird did follow,
Nor any day for food or play
Came to the mariner's hollo!

And I had done a hellish thing,
And it would work 'em woe:
For all averred, I had killed the bird
That made the breeze to blow.
Ah wretch! said they, the bird to slay,
That made the breeze to blow!

Nor dim nor red, like God's own head,
The glorious Sun uprist:
Then all averred, I had killed the bird
That brought the fog and mist.
'Twas right, said they, such birds to slay,

That bring the fog and mist.

The fair breeze blew, the white foam flew,
The furrow followed free;
We were the first that ever burst
Into that silent sea.

Down dropt the breeze, the sails dropt down,
'Twas sad as sad could be;
And we did speak only to break
The silence of the sea!

All in a hot and copper sky,
The bloody Sun, at noon,
Right up above the mast did stand,
No bigger than the Moon.

Day after day, day after day,
We stuck, nor breath nor motion;
As idle as a painted ship
Upon a painted ocean.

Water, water, every where,
And all the boards did shrink;
Water, water, every where,
Nor any drop to drink.

The very deep did rot: O Christ!
That ever this should be!
Yea, slimy things did crawl with legs
Upon the slimy sea.

About, about, in reel and rout
The death-fires danced at night;
The water, like a witch's oils,
Burnt green, and blue and white.

And some in dreams assurèd were
Of the Spirit that plagued us so;
Nine fathom deep he had followed us
From the land of mist and snow.

And every tongue, through utter drought,
Was withered at the root;
We could not speak, no more than if
We had been choked with soot.

Ah! Well a-day! What evil looks
Had I from old and young!
Instead of the cross, the Albatross
About my neck was hung.

PART Ⅲ

There passed a weary time. Each throat
Was parched, and glazed each eye.
A weary time! A weary time!
How glazed each weary eye,

When looking westward, I beheld
A something in the sky.

At first it seemed a little speck,

And then it seemed a mist;
It moved and moved, and took at last
A certain shape, I wist.

A speck, a mist, a shape, I wist!
And still it neared and neared:
As if it dodged a water-sprite,
It plunged and tacked and veered.

With throats unslaked, with black lips baked,
We could nor laugh nor wail;
Through utter drought all dumb we stood!
I bit my arm, I sucked the blood,
And cried, A sail! A sail!

With throats unslaked, with black lips baked,
Agape they heard me call:
Gramercy! They for joy did grin,
And all at once their breath drew in,
As they were drinking all.

See! See! (I cried) She tacks no more!
Hither to work us weal;
Without a breeze, without a tide,
She steadies with upright keel!

The western wave was all a-flame.
The day was well nigh done!
Almost upon the western wave
Rested the broad bright Sun;
When that strange shape drove suddenly

第三章 文学与医学(Literature and Medicine)

Betwixt us and the Sun.

And straight the Sun was flecked with bars,
(Heaven's Mother send us grace!)
As if through a dungeon-grate he peered
With broad and burning face.

Alas! (thought I, and my heart beat loud)
How fast she nears and nears!
Are those *her* sails that glance in the Sun,
Like restless gossameres?

Are those her *ribs* through which the Sun
Did peer, as through a grate?
And is that Woman all her crew?
Is that a DEATH? and are there two?
Is DEATH that woman's mate?

Her lips were red, *her* looks were free,
Her locks were yellow as gold:
Her skin was as white as leprosy,
The Night-mare LIFE-IN-DEATH was she,
Who thicks man's blood with cold.

The naked hulk alongside came,
And the twain were casting dice;
'The game is done! I've won! I've won!'
Quoth she, and whistles thrice.

The Sun's rim dips; the stars rush out;
At one stride comes the dark;

With far-heard whisper, o'er the sea,
Off shot the spectre-bark.

We listened and looked sideways up!
Fear at my heart, as at a cup,
My life-blood seemed to sip!
The stars were dim, and thick the night,
The steersman's face by his lamp gleamed white;
From the sails the dew did drip—
Till clomb above the eastern bar
The hornèd Moon, with one bright star
Within the nether tip.

One after one, by the star-dogged Moon,
Too quick for groan or sigh,
Each turned his face with a ghastly pang,
And cursed me with his eye.

Four times fifty living men,
(And I heard nor sigh nor groan)
With heavy thump, a lifeless lump,
They dropped down one by one.

The souls did from their bodies fly,—
They fled to bliss or woe!
And every soul, it passed me by,
Like the whizz of my cross-bow!

PART IV

'I fear thee, ancient Mariner!
I fear thy skinny hand!

And thou art long, and lank, and brown,
As is the ribbed sea-sand.

I fear thee and thy glittering eye,
And thy skinny hand, so brown.'—
Fear not, fear not, thou Wedding-Guest!
This body dropt not down.

Alone, alone, all, all alone,
Alone on a wide wide sea!
And never a saint took pity on
My soul in agony.

The many men, so beautiful!
And they all dead did lie:
And a thousand thousand slimy things
Lived on; and so did I.

I looked upon the rotting sea,
And drew my eyes away;
I looked upon the rotting deck,
And there the dead men lay.

I looked to heaven, and tried to pray;
But or ever a prayer had gusht,
A wicked whisper came, and made
My heart as dry as dust.

I closed my lids, and kept them close,
And the balls like pulses beat;
For the sky and the sea, and the sea and the sky

Lay dead like a load on my weary eye,
And the dead were at my feet.

The cold sweat melted from their limbs,
Nor rot nor reek did they:
The look with which they looked on me
Had never passed away.

An orphan's curse would drag to hell
A spirit from on high;
But oh! more horrible than that
Is the curse in a dead man's eye!
Seven days, seven nights, I saw that curse,
And yet I could not die.

The moving Moon went up the sky,
And no where did abide:
Softly she was going up,
And a star or two beside—

Her beams bemocked the sultry main,
Like April hoar-frost spread;
But where the ship's huge shadow lay,
The charmèd water burnt alway
A still and awful red.

Beyond the shadow of the ship,
I watched the water-snakes:
They moved in tracks of shining white,
And when they reared, the elfish light
Fell off in hoary flakes.

第三章 文学与医学(Literature and Medicine)

Within the shadow of the ship
I watched their rich attire:
Blue, glossy green, and velvet black,
They coiled and swam; and every track
Was a flash of golden fire.

O happy living things! no tongue
Their beauty might declare:
A spring of love gushed from my heart,
And I blessèd them unaware:
Sure my kind saint took pity on me,
And I blessed them unaware.

The self-same moment I could pray;
And from my neck so free
The Albatross fell off, and sank
Like lead into the sea.

第四章

文学与遗传学（Literature and Genetics）

第一节　遗传学的文学表征

📖 背景知识

遗传学（genetics）是生命科学领域的一门重要学科，是研究生物遗传和变异的科学。学界一般将1900年奥地利生物学家孟德尔（Gregor Mendel，1822—1884）的遗传定律被重新发现认定为遗传学诞生的标志[①]。而遗传学作为一个学科的名称，则是1905年英国学者贝特森（William Bateson，1861—1926）在将孟德尔的论文译成英语时首次提出[②]。

早在数千年前的新石器时代，人们就对遗传的奥秘展开了有意无意的探索。最早有迹可循的遗传理论来自古希腊医生希波克拉底和古希腊哲学家亚里士多德。希波克拉底的"泛生论"认为，遗传物质来自身体的各个部分。而亚里士多德却认为，遗传物质存在于精液之中[③]。18世纪末，达尔文的祖父伊拉兹马斯·达尔文（Erasmus Darwin，1731—1802）在他的著作《动物规律》（*Zoönomia*，1794—1796）中提出十项原则，包括获得性遗传、性的选择、保护色等，但比较含混，不很明确[④]。1809年，法国博物学家拉马克（Jean-Baptiste Lamarck，1744—1829）在其《动物哲学》（*Philosophie Zoologique*）中，对伊拉兹马斯·达尔文的思想进一步阐释，提出了"用进废退"和"获得性状遗传"等理论。他认为随着环境的变化，生物个体会出于生存的需要而随之发生变化，那些有用的器官会得到进化，而那些不用的器官就会发生退化，且这种获得性状可以遗传给后代。1868年，英国生物学家、进化论奠基人达尔文在《动物与植物在家养下的变异》（*Variation of Animals and Plants Under Domestication*）一书中，举例说明了"用进废退"的现象，指出"泛生粒"（pangenes）普遍存在于动物的每个器官，

[①] 郭玉华. 遗传学[M]. 北京：中国农业大学出版社，2014：1-7.
[②] ROOF J. Genetics[C]//CLARKE B, ROSSINI M. The Routledge companion to literature and science. London: Routledge, 2011: 125.
[③] Ideas of Hippocrates and Aristotle [Z/OL]. https://biocyclopedia.com/index/genetics/genetics_an_overview/ideas_of_hippocrates_and_aristotle.php. 另参见陆俏颖. 获得性遗传有望卷土重来吗？[J]. 自然辩证法通讯，2017(6)：30-36.
[④] 童第周. 简谈生物学上的理论学说及其发展史[J]. 哲学研究，1978(9)：2-14.

第四章 文学与遗传学（Literature and Genetics）

收集遗传特征，并随血液的循环流动汇合于生殖细胞。德国动物学家魏斯曼（August Weismann, 1834—1914）是达尔文之后在生物科学领域产生重大影响的学者，是新达尔文主义的创立者。他接受和支持达尔文进化论中的选择理论，但否定获得性状遗传，反对拉马克主义和泛生论。魏斯曼认为，生物体由种质和体质两部分组成，种质在世代间保持连续，因而生物的遗传就在于种质的连续。环境只能影响体质，不能影响种质，因此获得性状不能遗传[1]。被誉为"现代遗传学之父"的孟德尔利用豌豆作为试材，通过系列实验发现了遗传学的两大基本定律——分离定律和自由组合定律。1866年，孟德尔发表论文《植物杂交实验》（"Experiments on Plant Hybridization"），由于刊载在名不见经传的期刊上，它一直未获得学界的重视。直到1900年，荷兰的弗里斯（Hugo de Vries, 1848—1935）、德国的柯伦斯（Carl Correns, 1864—1933）和奥地利的柴马克（Erich von Tschermak, 1871—1962）三个植物学家，经过不同试材的植物杂交实验，得出了与孟德尔相同的遗传规律，孟德尔的论文才引起广泛关注，这也标志着遗传学作为独立的科学分支的诞生[2]。

遗传学是一门发展极为迅猛的科学，几乎每隔十年，就会经历一次重大的研究突破。如：1910年以后，美国科学家摩尔根（Thomas Hunt Morgan, 1866—1945）通过对果蝇的研究确立了遗传学中的"染色体理论"，证明基因位于染色体上，并因此获得了1933年的诺贝尔生理医学奖。1953年，美国科学家詹姆斯·沃森（James Watson, 1928—）和英国科学家弗朗西斯·克里克（Francis Crick, 1916—2004）根据英国女科学家罗莎琳·富兰克林（Rosalind Franklin, 1920—1958）拍到的DNA结构的X射线晶体衍射照片，提出了DNA分子的双螺旋结构模式理论。沃森和克里克因此获得1962年的诺贝尔生理医学奖。20世纪70年代，科学家们已经掌握了人工合成和分离基因的技术，基因工程开始成为分子遗传学研究的新领域。1990年，美国政府宣布启动人类基因组计划（Human Genome Project），该计划与曼哈顿原子弹计划、阿波罗登月计划并称为20世纪自然科学史上的三大里程碑。迄今为止，现代遗传学已发展出细胞遗传学、进化遗传学、群体遗传学、医学遗传学、分子遗传学、基因组学和遗传工程等众多分支。"分子遗传学和基因组学已经成为生物科学中最活跃和最有生命力的学科之一；而遗传工程将是分子遗传学中最重要的方向[3]。"

沃森和克里克发现DNA的分子结构后，遗传学开始引起一些大众的兴趣，面向大众读者的遗传学作品也开始出现。例如：沃森于1969年出版《双螺旋》（The Double Helix），以第一人称视角记述了发现DNA双螺旋结构的经历。克里克也于1990年出版《狂热的追求》（What Mad Pursuit），主要记录作者本人1953—1966年的个人经历。霍勒斯·贾德森

---

[1] 郭玉华. 遗传学[M]. 北京：中国农业大学出版社，2014：1-7. 另参见朱军. 遗传学[M]. 北京：中国农业出版社，2002：1-5.
[2] 宗宪春，施树良. 遗传学[M]. 武汉：华中科技大学出版社，2014：1-4.
[3] 朱军. 遗传学[M]. 北京：中国农业出版社，2002：4.

(Horace Freeland Judson,1931—2011)通过对多位科学家的访谈和大量的调查,在《创世纪的第八天》(The Eighth Day of Creation,1979)中通俗但严谨地记录了分子生物学历史上的众多重要工作。1990 年,人类基因组计划开启之后,更多此类的作品大量涌现,凯文·戴维斯(Kevin Davies,1960—)的《破解基因组》(Cracking the Genome,2001)和詹姆斯·史瑞福(James Shreeve)的《基因组之战》(The Genome War,2004),从不同角度记述了公共和私人测序机构间的合作与竞争①。随着遗传学研究的深入,人们在越来越多地享受到基因技术、生命科学带来的巨大益处的同时,也越来越多地关注到它们在伦理、法律等方面可能导致的风险与危机,例如"优生学"(eugenics)、基因筛查、基因编辑、克隆等技术的误用可能会引发的灾难性后果。这些关注广泛见诸非虚构和虚构类的文学作品中。

文学和科学的互动由来已久。一方面,科学的发展影响和指引着文学创作的方向,另一方面,文学创作也预示未来的科学发展②。早在沃森和克里克发现 DNA 的结构和基因的复制模式之前,利用基因技术改造人类的场景就已出现在小说之中了。H. G. 威尔斯(Herbert George Wells,1866—1946)的《莫罗博士岛》(The Island of Dr. Moreau,1896)和阿道司·赫胥黎(Aldous Huxley,1894—1963)的《美丽新世界》(Brave New World,1932)就是其中的代表。随着设计婴儿、器官移植、基因编辑、克隆技术的进一步普及,更多小说家开始以克隆及克隆人为素材,对科技伦理、生命伦理、社会问题展开严肃深刻的反思。如:奥克塔维娅·巴特勒(Octavia Butler,1947—2006)的《异种繁殖》三部曲(The Xenogenesis Trilogy)、娜奥米·密歇森(Naomi Mitchison,1897—1999)的《三号解决方案》(Solution Three,1975)、艾拉·莱文(Ira Levin,1929—2007)的《巴西来的男孩》(The Boys from Brazil,1976)等。除了克隆人,变种人形象也屡屡出现在像艾萨克·阿西莫夫(Isaac Asimov,1920—1992)的《基地与帝国》(Foundation and Empire,1952)、亨利·库纳特(Henry Kuttner,1915—1958)的《变种》(Mutant,1953)、A. E. 范·沃格特(Alfred Elton van Vogt,1912—2000)的《斯兰》(Slan,1946)之类的科幻小说里③。

描绘主人公经过基因改造、基因变异等技术而获得超能力的漫画作品也大受读者欢迎,比如漫威公司的《蜘蛛侠》(Spider-Man)、《X 战警》(X-Men)等,这些漫画大多成功被搬上大银幕。除超级英雄题材的电影外,以遗传学的相关技术和科学发现为背景的科幻电影数量也十分可观,如:《异种》(Species,1995)、《银翼杀手》(Blade Runner,1982)、《星战前传二——克隆

---

① ROOF J. Genetics[C]//CLARKE B, ROSSINI M. The Routledge companion to literature and science. London: Routledge, 2011: 125 - 126.
② HANSON C. Genetics and the literary imagination[M]. Oxford: Oxford University Press, 2020: 5.
③ 同①128 - 130.

人的进攻》(*Star Wars: Episode Ⅱ—Attack of the Clones*, 2002)、《变种异煞》(*Gattaca*, 1997)等①。

文献传真

阅读《遗传学》("Genetics"),思考文末问答题。本文节选自《劳特利奇指南:文学与科学》②。

Genetics

Judith Roof

There has been a literature of genetics ever since philosophers and scientists began considering the mechanisms of heredity by which physical traits passed from generation to generation. Empirical observation gave rise to various theories about how that transmission occurred. Generally, these ideas were bound up with theories of human reproduction. The ancient Greek philosopher Aristotle believed that semen was responsible for passing on traits, while the Greek physician of that same classical era, Hippocrates, developed a theory of pangenesis in which the material enabling heredity was collected from throughout the body. Amr ibn Bahr Al-Jahiz, ninth-century North African philosopher and zoologist, considered species' struggles to survive in their environments.

Enlightenment considerations of heredity still reflected these notions. The observation and classification of varieties of organic beings raised questions about how species maintained consistency from generation to generation and how changes might be introduced as part of a more comprehensive set of questions about evolution. In the late eighteenth century, Erasmus Darwin's *Zoönomia* (1794 – 1796) advanced the ideas that mammals derived from a single source or "filament" and that they acquired and passed on new traits developed in response to their environments. Jean-Baptiste Lamarck elaborated these ideas in *Philosophie Zoologique* (1809), asserting that individuals develop new, useful traits, lose useless traits, and pass these alterations on to their progeny. In his *Variation of Animals and Plants Under Domestication*, published in

---

① ROOF J. Genetics [C]//CLARKE B, ROSSINI M. The Routledge companion to literature and science. London: Routledge, 2011: 130 – 131.

② 同①124 – 128.

1868, nine years after *On the Origin of Species* (1859), Charles Darwin set out a mechanism of heredity in which an individual's "pangenes," circulating throughout the organism, gather traits and migrate to the reproductive cells. That Darwin's theory of evolution needed some mechanism for the transmission of traits sparked greater interest in issues of heredity, producing some opposition to Lamarck's ideas, especially on the part of August Weismann, a German evolutionary biologist. Weismann disagreed with Lamarckism and pangenesis, positing instead that germ cells were unaffected by the environment and, thus, that an individual's acquired traits were not passed to the next generation.

The plant breeding experiments of Gregor Mendel produced an account of heredity that worked according to sets of statistical rules. Through experiments with pea plants, Mendel hypothesized that the basic unit of heredity was an "allele," and that alleles passed on definable traits (such as plant size and blossom color) in statistically measurable proportions. Providing a set of concepts that would enable biologists to infer the processes of heredity underlying the appearance of phenotypical traits (those expressed in bodily forms), Mendel's paper, "Experiments on plant hybridization," was published in an obscure journal in 1866. The paper's rediscovery in 1900 by Hugo DeVries and Carl Correns invigorated work on the connections between reproductive biology and genetics that had continued after Darwin. William Bateson, who translated Mendel's paper into English, coined the term "genetics" in 1905.

Genetics spawned its own literatures, including the scientific literatures devoted to discoveries about genetic science; popularizations and histories; discussions of ethical issues; critiques of genetics and its popularizations; and fiction and literary criticism that employ concepts from genetics as either subject matter or a major trope. The scientific literature of genetics worked through increasingly complex observations and statistical models based on Mendel's findings. Thomas Hunt Morgan, who worked with fruit flies, demonstrated that genes, responsible for the transmission of traits, are located on chromosomes. With several colleagues, Morgan published the first major work of scientific genetics, *The Mechanisms of Mendelian Heredity* (1915). While research continued on the operation of genes, mutations, and traits, others such as Linus Pauling, James Watson, Francis Crick, Rosalind Franklin, and Maurice Wilkins tried to discern the structure and mechanisms of deoxyribonucleic acid (DNA), a substance first identified in the late nineteenth century, and then identified by biochemist Oswald Avery as the chemical that made up genetic material. Using X-ray diffraction images of DNA produced by Rosalind Franklin, Watson and Crick were able to describe the DNA molecule's double helical structure. They published their findings in two essays in Nature in 1953. After the discovery of the structure and function of DNA, the scientific literature of genetics focused on mapping DNA, tracking the mechanisms by which genes managed organic processes, and determining the distribution of genes in populations. In 1990 genetic research took up the highly visible project of attempting to map the entire human genome.

Histories and popularizations

After Watson and Crick described the structure of DNA and genetics evolved into a field with a certain popular appeal, descriptions of genetics aimed at the general public began to appear. One of the first was Watson's autobiographical account of his work with DNA, *The Double Helix* (1969). Crick followed twenty years later with his own account, *What Mad Pursuit* (1990). Horace Judson produced the first popular history of the DNA "revolution" in biology in *The Eighth Day of Creation* (1979). Following governmental genome mapping initiatives begun in the late 1980s, more histories and popular accounts of genetic research appeared in the 1990s. Jonathan Weiner traces the career of behavioral geneticist Seymour Benzer in *Time, Love, Memory* (1999); Matt Ridley produced *Genome* (1999). Lily Kay's comprehensive academic history, *Who Wrote the Book of Life?* (2000), was followed by A. H. Sturtevant's *A History of Genetics* (2001), and Michel Morange's *The Misunderstood Gene* (2001). The latter shifts attention to the complexities of genetic operation as well as genes' cooperation with other processes. Morange also suggests that the promises of medical breakthroughs made on behalf of genetic research are neither so simple nor one-sided as they may seem.

As the Human Genome Project was officially established in 1990, more accounts aimed at a broad audience appeared. James Watson, the initial head of the Human Genome Project, published additional memoirs and essays arguing for the importance of genetic research—a collection of essays he wrote after 1953, *A Passion for DNA* (2000), and a new history and overview of post-DNA genetic research, *DNA: The Secret of Life*

(2003). Robert Cook-Deegan traces the interactions of the Department of Energy (the original sponsor of genetic research in the United States), the National Institute of Health, and various private corporations established to aid and profit from genetic research in *The Gene Wars* (1994), as does Kevin Davies in *Cracking the Genome* (2001). In *The Genome War* (2004), James Shreeve focuses on the ways that genetic researcher Craig Venter transformed genetic research into a profitable corporate enterprise.

Other literature focuses on more specific ethical issues about the interrelation between public knowledge and private profit or on the palliative possibilities of genetic research. Watson's promotional essays were anticipated by collections of essays that consider the ethical issues of genetic research, such as Daniel Kevles and Leroy Hood's *The Code of Codes* (1992), which raises questions about how genetic information is to be used in forensics, its effects on reproductive policies and insurance, how to protect individual privacy and prevent the possibility of discrimination, and how to marshal equitably the distribution of resources in relation to potential medical uses of genetic information. Timothy Murphy and Marc Lappé's essay collection, *Justice and the Human Genome Project* (1994), focuses on such social issues as how genetic information will alter our understandings of racial and class difference and pressure towards certain standards or norms represented by genetic profiles. Barbara Rothman's *The Book of Life* (2001) considers the potential eugenic practices genetic science enables.

Critiques

In the 1970s, critiques of the claims of genetic science began to appear, to be followed by analyses and assessments of its popularizations as well as of the hype surrounding the Human Genome Project. Richard Dawkins published *The Selfish Gene* (1976), which suggested shifting the frame of reference by which we understood the activities of genes from the scale of the organism to the gene itself. Dawkins argued that what genes preserve and replicate, rather than organisms or their traits, are the genes themselves. Humans are merely one vector among many engaged in this process. Others countered Dawkins by extending their critique to the assumptions underlying the broader field of genetics. In *Biology as Ideology* (1991), Richard Lewontin questioned genetics' assumptions about genetic cause and somatic effect, pointing out that the assumption that genes govern all life processes reduces the totality of the living organism to a mechanical

第四章 文学与遗传学(Literature and Genetics)

process. He continued to question the assumptions and claims of genetics in *It Ain't Necessarily So* (2000). In *Exploding the Gene Myth* (1999), Ruth Hubbard and Elijah Wald also raised questions about the ways genetic science is disseminated, especially where popular simplifications make hyperbolic claims about what genetic science may be able to do. Offering correctives to such media claims, Hubbard and Wald recast genetic science in more accurate terms and reconsidered several key public issues of genetic research: eugenics, gene screening, the link between genes and behaviors, the manipulation of genes, DNA identifications, and genetic discrimination.

In the mid-1990s, in addition to scientists themselves, science historians, sociologists, and humanities scholars began analyzing the larger assumptions of the discourse used to describe genetics in the public sphere. Taking up Richard Lewontin's questions, Evelyn Fox Keller, in *Refiguring Life* (1995), demonstrated the ways the linguistic figurations of genes influenced both public perceptions of genetic research's possibilities and the directions of research itself. In *The Century of the Gene* (2000), she seconded Hubbard and Wald, focusing on the problems created when genetic science is represented through a reductive, one-cause-to-one-effect relationship. Arguing for a far more complex understanding of science, Keller urged against seeing genes as the answer to all biological questions. In *What It Means to be 98% Chimpanzee* (2002), Jonathan Marks also critiqued reductive versions of genetic science and questioned what distinctions and commonalities genes and the genome enable us to make.

Sociologists and humanists also began analyzing the rhetoric, metaphors, and images deployed in representations of genes and genetic science for the popular audience. Dorothy Nelkin and M. Susan Lindee examined what they called "the DNA mystique"—the sets of ideas enabling DNA and genetics to become the symbols by which questions of family, individual character, causality, and the future of medicine are understood. In *Imagenation: Popular Images of Genetics* (1998), José van Dijck also examined the images through which genetic science has been represented in the public sphere, showing, like Keller, how such representations actually influence the directions of scientific thought, and how genes have become an "imaginary" force dislocated from genetic science itself. In *The Meanings of the Gene* (1999), Celeste Condit analyzes the public stories told about genes, discerning the anxieties they represent, and identifying worries about genetic determinism and discriminatory eugenics. She studies the tension between a reductive genetics—in which genes are presented as dominating biological causality—and properly complex biological ideas—in which genes are appreciated as one element among the many others involved in living systems.

思考题

1. What advances in genetics have provoked much public concern?
2. Aldous Huxley's Brave New World was written in 1931 and published in 1932. What are the factors leading to the creation of this dystopian novel?
3. What are the significant technological advances predicted by Aldous Huxley in Brave New World?
4. Explore how genetics finds expression in various literary texts.

第二节　《美丽新世界》与基因工程

作品导读

1. 作者简介

《美丽新世界》是英国著名作家阿道司·赫胥黎的作品。阿道司·赫胥黎出身名门。祖父是《天演论》(Evolution and Ethics, 1893)的作者、著名生物学家托马斯·亨利·赫胥黎(Thomas Henry Huxley, 1825—1895)。父亲莱纳德·赫胥黎(Leonard Huxley, 1860—1933)曾担任高水准文学期刊《康希尔杂志》(Cornhill Magazine)的编辑。母亲茱莉亚·阿诺德(Julia Arnold, 1862—1908)是英国著名诗人、文学评论家马修·阿诺德的侄女。兄长朱利安·索瑞尔·赫胥黎(Julian Sorrell Huxley, 1887—1975)也是一位著名生物学家,他深受生物进化论的影响,强调人种方面的自然选择和优生优育思想。1908年,十四岁的阿道司·赫胥黎入学伊顿公学,立志成为像祖父和兄长一样杰出的生物学家、医生,但两年后却因罹患眼疾被迫辍学。在接下来的两年里,他双目失明,但努力学习布莱叶盲文,在左眼恢复部分视力后,于1913年入读牛津大学贝利奥尔学院,攻读英语文学专业。1915年时,他与奥托琳·莫雷尔夫人(Lady Ottoline Morrell, 1873—1938)相识。在她的加辛顿庄园,赫胥黎结识了劳伦斯、罗素(Bertrand Russell, 1872—1970)、艾略特(Thomas Stearns Eliot, 1888—1965)、伍尔芙(Virginia Woolf, 1882—1941)、曼斯菲尔德(Katherine Mansfield, 1888—1923),以及后来成为他第一任妻子的玛莉亚·尼斯(Maria Nys, 1919—1955)。1923—1937年,赫胥黎与

第四章　文学与遗传学(Literature and Genetics)

妻儿旅居意大利和法国,广泛游历欧洲大陆。在法国居住期间,创作出版了《针锋相对》(Point Counter Point, 1928)和《美丽新世界》。1937年,由于欧洲时局日益紧张,赫胥黎携妻儿前往美国,并在加利福尼亚州定居,直到1963年因癌症去世。

赫胥黎一生著有五十多部作品,包括小说、短篇小说集、诗歌、戏剧、游记、散文集等。除《针锋相对》《美丽新世界》之外,赫胥黎的小说作品还包括《克鲁姆庄园》(Crome Yellow, 1921)、《滑稽的环舞》(Antic Hay, 1923)、《那些不结果的叶子》(Those Barren Leaves, 1925)、《加沙的盲人》(Eyeless in Gaza, 1936)、《夏去夏来天鹅死》(After Many a Summer Dies the Swan, 1939)、《时间须停止》(Time Must Have a Stop, 1944)、《猿与本质》(Ape and Essence, 1948)、《天才与女神》(The Genius and the Goddess, 1955)、《岛》(Island, 1962)。短篇小说集有《俗世牵绊》(Mortal Coils, 1922)、《小墨西哥人》(Little Mexican, 1924)等。诗歌集包括《焚烧之轮》(The Burning Wheel: Poems, 1916)、《诗歌选集》(Selected Poems, 1925)、《蝉》(The Cicadas, 1931)等。戏剧有《光明世界》(The World of Light, 1931)。游记包括《爱开玩笑的彼拉多》(Jesting Pilate, 1926)和《墨西哥湾之外》(Beyond the Mexique Bay, 1934)。散文作品有《在边缘》(On the Margin, 1923)、《新旧文集》(Essays New and Old, 1926)、《目的与手段》(Ends and Means, 1937)、《科学、自由与和平》(Science, Liberty and Peace, 1946)、《重访美丽新世界》(Brave New World Revisited, 1958)、《论艺术和艺术家》(On Art and Artists, 1960)等等。

赫胥黎的作品虽在语言和技巧上与现代主义小说相去甚远,其主题特征及人文思想却与劳伦斯和伍尔芙等人的作品有诸多共通之处,探讨了现代个体的孤独和困惑,批判了资本主义社会的政治制度和价值体系。比如,其处女作《克鲁姆庄园》与伍尔芙的《黛洛维夫人》(Mrs. Dalloway, 1925)一样,以一战后英国社会的对立与冲突——理性与癫狂、自然社会的和谐与工业社会的无序、物质的富足与精神的空虚——为主题对象,探讨20世纪初科学新发现与旧有社会体系及宗教文明冲突背景下现代个体的生存困境[①]。因此,赫胥黎从创作伊始,就一直关注科技文明对人类精神信仰造成的冲击。除了《克鲁姆庄园》外,其他小说如《滑稽的环舞》《那些不结果的叶子》《针锋相对》《时间须停止》《美丽新世界》及其续篇也都反思了现代科技给人类带来的影响,特别是科技的发展给人类生存造成的困境。通过揭示

---

① VERČKO R. Existential concerns and narrative techniques in the novels of Ford Madox Ford, Virginia Woolf and Aldous Huxley[J]. Acta Neophilologica, 2005, 38(1-2): 49-59. 另参见 DUNLAP S. "One must be scientific": natural history and ecology in Mrs. Dalloway[C]//MARTIN A, HOLLAND K. Interdisciplinary/multidisciplinary Woolf. Liverpool: Liverpool University Press, 2013: 127-131. 实际上,赫胥黎在创作该小说时也参考了布鲁姆斯伯里社团成员(The Bloomsbury Group, or Bloomsbury Set),小说中的人物安妮(Anne)与伍尔芙存在诸多相似之处。另参见 Aldous Huxley against the Bloomsbury Group [Z/OL]. https://huxleyandthebloomsberries.wordpress.com/other-similarities-between-bloomsbury-group-members-crome-yellow-characters/.

技术文明带来的"恐怖与肮脏"以及"科学的无用性"(futility of science)[1],赫胥黎和劳伦斯一样,力图在"科学统治下的恐怖世界之外"[2],造就一个"从某种程度上来说不同于现代社会的小世界"[3]。在《科学、自由与和平》(*Science, Liberty and Peace*, 1946)、《人类对太空的征服是提升还是降低其地位?》("*Has Man's Conquest of Space Increased or Diminished His Stature?*", 1963)等非虚构著述中,他鼓励人们从不同的视角来审视人类对自然的征服:科学进步带来的不只是物质的繁荣和生活的便捷,相反,它也造成了人类的贪婪、"思维惯性"、"情感空虚"以及精神上的贫瘠[4]。第一次世界大战的爆发以及战后英国上层社会的糜烂生活无不反映了现代科技的负面作用。在他看来,科学与技术被牢牢地捆绑在战争的车辆上。因此,在批评现代科技的同时,赫胥黎也试图以东方佛教背后的哲学思想为基础,建构和平主义思想及替代性精神信仰。本章将节选《美丽新世界》部分章节,探讨作者如何在表征遗传基因方面的科学成就的同时,反思技术文明并试图建构某种精神信仰。

2. 作品介绍

《美丽新世界》的故事背景设置在福帝纪元632年的世界国,福帝纪元始于福特T型汽车投入量产的1908年。那里的居民享受着高度的"文明",科技空前发达,远离衰老疾病,生活无忧无虑。而居住在世界国之外保留地的印第安人却过着截然不同的日子。世界国的伯纳德·马克思(Bernard Marx)在和女伴列宁娜·克朗(Lenina Crowne)前往保留地度假时,巧遇原世界国居民琳达(Linda)和她的儿子"野蛮人"约翰(John),并将他俩带回新世界。在保留地出生长大的约翰始终无法认同新世界的行为模式和价值理念,积极反抗,但最后失败,自杀身亡。小说共十八章,按场景的变化可以分成三个部分,前六章发生在新世界,第六章末尾到第九章转到新墨西哥保留地,第十章到十八章又转回新世界。随着故事地点的转换,小说的主人公也随之变化。前九章的故事主要围绕伯纳德·马克思展开,而后九章主要讲述"野蛮人"约翰被带回新世界后的经历。

小说采用第三人称叙事视角。故事开篇,一座三十四层的"低矮"大楼出现在读者面前,这里是"中央伦敦孵化与条件训练中心",中心主任(the Director)和他的助手亨利·福斯特(Henry Foster)正在带领一群青年学生参观,讲授如何通过流水线克隆生产不同等级的胚胎来达到最佳的人口比例,维持社会的稳定。这些胚胎被人为设定成阿尔法、贝塔、伽马、德尔塔、埃普西隆五大"种姓"(caste),分别代表五个社会等级,长大成人后从事不同种类的工作。如:等级最高的阿尔法们体健貌美,头脑聪颖,擅长脑力劳动,而等级最低的埃普西隆们

---

[1] ROBERTS J H. Huxley and Lawrence[J]. The Virginia Quarterly Review, 1937(4): 547, 553.
[2] 同[1]553.
[3] PARKES A. Logics of disintegration in Lawrence and Huxley[EB/OL]. https://journals.openedition.org/lawrence/2471.
[4] 同[1]547.

第四章　文学与遗传学（Literature and Genetics）

则长相丑陋，容貌相同，智力低下，只能承担体力劳动。在受精室、装瓶室、社会命运预定室、换瓶车间参观结束后，一行人来到育婴房，观看德尔塔种姓的婴儿接受新巴普洛夫条件反射训练，护士们通过噪音和电击来训练婴儿们对书本和鲜花产生"本能"的厌恶。主任还向学生们介绍了睡眠教育法的重要性。

从育婴房出来，主任和学生们在花园遇到控制官穆斯塔法·蒙德（Mustapha Mond）。穆斯塔法与学生们交谈，严厉批判了历史、家庭和一夫一妻制。与此同时，女主人公列宁娜·克朗正在更衣室与朋友范妮·克朗（Fanny Crowne）聊起以性格古怪、行为乖张闻名的伯纳德·马克思。伯纳德是心理局的睡眠教育专家，虽然身为阿尔法+，但身材却比同种姓的人矮小许多，因而受到身边人的轻视。有传言说他的缺陷是因为工作人员在他还是胚胎的时候，错把酒精加到了他的代血剂里的缘故。伯纳德本人也因此自卑，对世界国和身边人的行为有诸多不满。伯纳德敏感的性格引起了列宁娜的青睐，她答应伯纳德的邀约，愿意同他一起前去新墨西哥的原始保留地度假。在伯纳德请主任审批旅行证件时，主任一时失神，突然提起自己二十多年前也曾和一位贝塔种姓的女伴去过保留地，因为遭遇暴风雨，女伴走失，从此便没了踪迹。回过神来的主任焦虑异常，警告伯纳德谨言慎行，如果再有离经叛道的表现就要遣送他去冰岛受苦。

来到保留地的伯纳德和列宁娜对那里污秽、肮脏的环境大为震惊，无法接受原住民衰老、病弱、丑陋的形象。在这里，他们遇到约翰及其母亲琳达。伯纳德很快猜到琳达就是主任失散的女伴，而约翰则是其儿子。胎生在世界国可是惊天丑闻。出于报复主任的目的，伯纳德将约翰和琳达带回新世界，并在受精室所有工作人员的面前让约翰和主任父子相认。主任羞愧难当，辞去了职务。此后，"野蛮人"约翰在城中大受欢迎，伦敦高种姓的人们都迫不及待地想和他见上一面。伯纳德不仅保住了工作，也因约翰"监护人"的身份大受追捧。

在保留地出生和长大的约翰接受的教育主要有两大来源：一是母亲琳达教他诵读的来自新世界的《胚胎的化学和细菌学条件设置——胚胎库贝塔人员使用说明书》；二是琳达在保留地的情人柏培（Popé）带来的《莎士比亚全集》。在新鲜感退去之后，对新世界有了更深入了解的约翰越来越发现自己的爱情观、价值理念与这里格格不入。虽然与列宁娜相互吸引，但却因为双方对爱情理解的不同而备受煎熬。约翰通过伯纳德结识了赫姆霍尔兹·华生（Helmholtz Watson），一位因个人能力出众、思想超前而倍感孤独的阿尔法+。赫姆霍尔兹在情绪工程学院写作系工作，擅长写睡眠教育的歌谣和感官电影的剧本，一心想要写出像X光一样具有穿透力的作品。赫姆霍尔兹与约翰趣味相投，一见如故，但即便如此，当约翰为他朗读《罗密欧与朱丽叶》里凯普莱特夫妇逼迫朱丽叶与帕里斯伯爵结婚的那段剧本时，还是忍不住哈哈大笑，因为他觉得这样的情节实在过于荒诞。不久，约翰接到医院的电话，通知他琳达病危的消息。自从回到世界国，琳达一直在医生的默许下过量吸食唆麻迷幻剂，以远离现实，解除痛苦。约翰赶往医院见到了母亲最后一面。沉浸在丧母之痛中的约翰，离开病房,恰巧看到一群在医院从事体力工作的德尔塔在集中领取每天定量发放的唆麻。怒不可遏的他夺下装唆麻的药盒,扔出窗外,引发了德尔塔们的暴动。最终警察到场,用唆麻气体和麻药平息了这场暴乱,并将约翰、赫姆霍尔兹和伯纳德带到了控制官穆斯塔法面前。

穆斯塔法和约翰针对艺术、科学、宗教和稳定幸福等话题展开激烈的争论。穆斯塔法坚称,为了幸福和稳定,这些都可以被牺牲,而约翰则认为没有这些,生命便失去意义。随后,伯纳德和赫姆霍尔兹被流放到孤岛。为了提高写作水平,赫姆霍尔兹自愿前往环境恶劣的福克兰岛。穆斯塔法不允许约翰跟伙伴们一起去往海岛,约翰只能在伦敦找了一个人迹罕至的灯塔住了下来,种菜打猎,自给自足。为了洁净心灵,消除杂念,抵御新世界"文明"的侵袭,他时常用绳子抽打自己,自我惩罚。这个场景碰巧被三个德尔塔看到。此后,不仅记者争相报道,还引来大批世界国的居民,列宁娜也在前来围观的人群中。她的到来令约翰彻底失控。在这场集体狂欢之后,从唆麻药力中清醒过来的约翰因为羞愧、愤怒、绝望自缢身亡。

3. 作品赏析

《美丽新世界》是20世纪伟大的"反乌托邦"(dystopian)经典,传达了阿道司·赫胥黎对"社会、政治和技术秩序中某些令人担忧的趋势"的反思①,蕴含着赫胥黎对"科学进步对人类个体的影响"的严肃思考②。有学者认为,《美丽新世界》"可能是20世纪最富影响力的小说",因为它的影响力不仅仅局限在文学领域,小说中赫胥黎对"社会、政治、经济、心理、科学、哲学"等问题的关注③,是这部"概念小说"(novel of ideas)有别于其他通俗科幻小说之处。

小说写作于1931年,出版于1932年。彼时的欧洲尚未从第一次世界大战的余波中恢复,又遭受了经济衰退的重击,政局动荡,社会问题尖锐,第二次世界大战也在酝酿之中。《美丽新世界》即诞生在"大规模的工业化生产、经济大萧条,再加上法西斯势力逐渐抬头"的复杂历史背景下④。另外,随着生物技术、遗传学的快速发展,越来越多的科学家表现出对于"优生学"的兴趣和支持,英国遗传学家约翰·霍尔丹(John Burdon Sanderson Haldane, 1892—1964)就是当中的代表人物。霍尔丹家族和赫胥黎家族是世交,约翰·霍尔丹与阿道司·赫胥黎从小相识。1923年,年轻的霍尔丹在剑桥大学发表了题为《代达罗斯,或科学与未来》("Daedalus, or Science and the Future")的演讲,引起很大的社会反响,其中提到"生殖与性爱的分离""体外培育胎儿""通过生殖选择改造民族性格"等观点⑤。此外,在该演讲中

---

① 艾布拉姆斯. 文学术语辞典[M]. 吴松江,译. 北京:北京大学出版社,2009:657.
② HUXLEY A. Brave new world[M]. New York:Harper & Brothers,1946.
③ BLOOM H. Bloom's guides:brave new world(new edition)[M]. New York:Infobase Publishing,2011:100.
④ 同③14.
⑤ 霍尔丹,戴开元. 代达罗斯,或科学与未来[J]. 科学文化评论,2011,8(2):29-50.

第四章 文学与遗传学（Literature and Genetics）

霍尔丹还提倡"迷幻药物的临床应用"①。小说《美丽新世界》中，在世界国的极权统治下，统治阶级利用体外受精和基因技术，工业化、按比例生产克隆人，用唆麻进行情绪控制等假想，无疑流露出赫胥黎对科学技术被滥用的担忧：包括优生学在内的科学技术存在被邪恶政权滥用的可能性；基因筛选和改造会抹杀人类的多样性，触发种族歧视等众多恶果。这些态度在很大程度上与罗素一致②。

小说中滥用科学技术造成的另一大灾难是人性的丧失。世界国崇尚"集体、同一、稳定""人人属于彼此"，没有家庭、没有父母、没有固定的伴侣、没有爱情、没有伦理道德。世界国的居民在睡眠教育、新巴普洛夫条件反射训练等技术的摧残下，失去了思考的能力，失去了对美和真的渴望，失去了体验生活酸甜苦辣的权利。小说书名出自莎士比亚的悲喜剧《暴风雨》（The Tempest）。"啊！神奇呀，这里有这么多美好的人！人类有多么美！啊！美丽的新世界，有这样的人在里头！"这是自幼随父亲米兰公爵普洛斯彼罗（Prospero）流落孤岛、从未见过生人的女主人公米兰达（Miranda）在第一次见到岛外来客时发出的赞叹。当然，未经世故的她不明白这些来客华丽的外表之下隐藏的丑陋灵魂，正如《美丽新世界》中初入世界国的"野蛮人"约翰一样。莎士比亚的戏剧体现了人性的方方面面，展现了人类种种的复杂情感，教会约翰了解世界、表达情感的方式。但这些正是世界国为了追求"幸福"和"稳定"必须禁止和抛弃的。因此，满怀憧憬而来的约翰，最终选择以自杀作为对这个技术泛滥、享乐至上的"美丽新世界"的终极反抗。

《美丽新世界》的故事情节并不复杂，思想却十分深邃。下面请阅读小说节选部分，并回答相关问题。选文第一章讲述世界国如何利用科技对胚胎进行设定，来制造不同种姓的克隆人。选文第十六章是"野蛮人"约翰和世界国控制官穆斯塔法就美、艺术、科学、幸福、稳定等话题展开的争论。

作品选读

Brave New World

Aldous Huxley

Chapter 1

A SQUAT grey building of only thirty-four stories. Over the main entrance the words, CENTRAL LONDON HATCHERY AND CONDITIONING CENTRE, and, in a shield, the World State's motto, COMMUNITY, IDENTITY, STABILITY.

---

① 刘钝."两种文化"视野下的霍尔丹与罗素之争[J]. 浙江大学学报（人文社会科学版），2016,46(1)：3.
② 罗素,戴开元,刘钝. 伊卡洛斯，或科学的未来[J]. 科学文化评论，2014,11(4)：5-18.

The enormous room on the ground floor faced towards the north. Cold for all the summer beyond the panes, for all the tropical heat of the room itself, a harsh thin light glared through the windows, hungrily seeking some draped lay figure, some pallid shape of academic goose-flesh, but finding only the glass and nickel and bleakly shining porcelain of a laboratory. Wintriness responded to wintriness. The overalls of the workers were white, their hands gloved with a pale corpse-coloured rubber. The light was frozen, dead, a ghost. Only from the yellow barrels of the microscopes did it borrow a certain rich and living substance, lying along the polished tubes like butter, streak after luscious streak in long recession down the work tables.

"And this," said the Director opening the door, "is the Fertilizing Room."

Bent over their instruments, three hundred Fertilizers were plunged, as the Director of Hatcheries and Conditioning entered the room, in the scarcely breathing silence, the absent-minded, soliloquizing hum or whistle, of absorbed concentration. A troop of newly arrived students, very young, pink and callow, followed nervously, rather abjectly, at the Director's heels. Each of them carried a notebook, in which, whenever the great man spoke, he desperately scribbled. Straight from the horse's mouth. It was a rare privilege. The D. H. C. for Central London always made a point of personally conducting his new students round the various departments.

"Just to give you a general idea," he would explain to them. For of course some sort of general idea they must have, if they were to do their work intelligently—though as little of one, if they were to be good and happy members of society, as possible. For particulars, as everyone knows, make for virtue and happiness; generalities are intellectually necessary evils. Not philosophers but fret-sawyers and stamp collectors compose the backbone of society.

"To-morrow," he would add, smiling at them with a slightly menacing geniality, "you'll be settling down to serious work. You won't have time for generalities. Meanwhile …"

Meanwhile, it was a privilege. Straight from the horse's mouth into the notebook. The boys scribbled like mad.

Tall and rather thin but upright, the Director advanced into the room. He had a long chin and big rather prominent teeth, just covered, when he was not talking, by his full,

第四章 文学与遗传学(Literature and Genetics)

floridly curved lips. Old, young? Thirty? Fifty? Fifty-five? It was hard to say. And anyhow the question didn't arise; in this year of stability, A. F. 632, it didn't occur to you to ask it.

"I shall begin at the beginning," said the D. H. C. and the more zealous students recorded his intention in their notebooks: *Begin at the beginning.* "These," he waved his hand, "are the incubators." And opening an insulated door he showed them racks upon racks of numbered test-tubes. "The week's supply of ova. Kept," he explained, "at blood heat; whereas the male gametes," and here he opened another door, "they have to be kept at thirty-five instead of thirty-seven. Full blood heat sterilizes." Rams wrapped in theremogene beget no lambs.

Still leaning against the incubators he gave them, while the pencils scurried illegibly across the pages, a brief description of the modern fertilizing process; spoke first, of course, of its surgical introduction—"the operation undergone voluntarily for the good of Society, not to mention the fact that it carries a bonus amounting to six months' salary"; continued with some account of the technique for preserving the excised ovary alive and actively developing; passed on to a consideration of optimum temperature, salinity, viscosity; referred to the liquor in which the detached and ripened eggs were kept; and, leading his charges to the work tables, actually showed them how this liquor was drawn off from the test-tubes; how it was let out drop by drop onto the specially warmed slides of the microscopes; how the eggs which it contained were inspected for abnormalities, counted and transferred to a porous receptacle; how (and he now took them to watch the operation) this receptacle was immersed in a warm bouillon containing free-swimming spermatozoa—at a minimum concentration of one hundred thousand per cubic centimetre, he insisted; and how, after ten minutes, the container was lifted out of the liquor and its contents re-examined; how, if any of the eggs remained unfertilized, it was again immersed, and, if necessary, yet again; how the fertilized ova went back to the incubators; where the Alphas and Betas remained until definitely bottled; while the Gammas, Deltas and Epsilons were brought out again, after only thirty-six hours, to undergo Bokanovsky's Process.

"Bokanovsky's Process," repeated the Director, and the students underlined the words in their little notebooks.

One egg, one embryo, one adult-normality. But a bokanovskified egg will bud, will proliferate, will divide. From eight to ninety-six buds, and every bud will grow into a perfectly formed embryo, and every embryo into a full-sized adult. Making ninety-six human beings grow where only one grew before. Progress.

"Essentially," the D. H. C. concluded, "bokanovskification consists of a series of arrests of development. We check the normal growth and, paradoxically enough, the egg responds by budding."

Responds by budding. The pencils were busy.

He pointed. On a very slowly moving band a rack-full of test-tubes was entering a large metal box, another, rack-full was emerging. Machinery faintly purred. It took eight minutes for the tubes to go through, he told them. Eight minutes of hard X-rays being about as much as an egg can stand. A few died; of the rest, the least susceptible divided into two; most put out four buds; some eight; all were returned to the incubators, where the buds began to develop; then, after two days, were suddenly chilled, chilled and checked. Two, four, eight, the buds in their turn budded; and having budded were dosed almost to death with alcohol; consequently burgeoned again and having budded—bud out of bud out of bud—were thereafter—further arrest being generally fatal—left to develop in peace. By which time the original egg was in a fair way to becoming anything from eight to ninety-six embryos—a prodigious improvement, you will agree, on nature. Identical twins-but not in piddling twos and threes as in the old viviparous days, when an egg would sometimes accidentally divide; actually by dozens, by scores at a time.

"Scores," the Director repeated and flung out his arms, as though he were distributing largesse. "Scores."

But one of the students was fool enough to ask where the advantage lay.

"My good boy!" The Director wheeled sharply round on him. "Can't you see? Can't you see?" He raised a hand; his expression was solemn. "Bokanovsky's Process is one of the major instruments of social stability!"

Major instruments of social stability.

Standard men and women; in uniform batches. The whole of a small factory staffed with the products of a single bokanovskified egg.

"Ninety-six identical twins working ninety-six identical machines!" The voice was

第四章 文学与遗传学 (Literature and Genetics)

almost tremulous with enthusiasm. "You really know where you are. For the first time in history." He quoted the planetary motto. "Community, Identity, Stability." Grand words. "If we could bokanovskify indefinitely the whole problem would be solved."

Solved by standard Gammas, unvarying Deltas, uniform Epsilons. Millions of identical twins. The principle of mass production at last applied to biology.

"But, alas," the Director shook his head, "we *can't* bokanovskify indefinitely."

Ninety-six seemed to be the limit; seventy-two a good average. From the same ovary and with gametes of the same male to manufacture as many batches of identical twins as possible—that was the best (sadly a second best) that they could do. And even that was difficult.

"For in nature it takes thirty years for two hundred eggs to reach maturity. But our business is to stabilize the population at this moment, here and now. Dribbling out twins over a quarter of a century—what would be the use of that?"

Obviously, no use at all. But Podsnap's Technique had immensely accelerated the process of ripening. They could make sure of at least a hundred and fifty mature eggs within two years. Fertilize and bokanovskify—in other words, multiply by seventy-two—and you get an average of nearly eleven thousand brothers and sisters in a hundred and fifty batches of identical twins, all within two years of the same age.

"And in exceptional cases we can make one ovary yield us over fifteen thousand adult individuals."

Beckoning to a fair-haired, ruddy young man who happened to be passing at the moment. "Mr. Foster," he called. The ruddy young man approached. "Can you tell us the record for a single ovary, Mr. Foster?"

"Sixteen thousand and twelve in this Centre," Mr. Foster replied without hesitation. He spoke very quickly, had a vivacious blue eye, and took an evident pleasure in quoting figures. "Sixteen thousand and twelve; in one hundred and eighty-nine batches of identicals. But of course they've done much better," he rattled on, "in some of the tropical Centres. Singapore has often produced over sixteen thousand five hundred; and Mombasa has actually touched the seventeen thousand mark. But then they have unfair advantages. You should see the way a negro ovary responds to pituitary! It's quite astonishing, when you're used to working with European material. Still," he added, with a laugh (but the light of combat was in his eyes and the lift of his chin was challenging), "still, we mean to beat them if we can. I'm working on a wonderful Delta-Minus ovary at this moment. Only just eighteen months old. Over twelve thousand seven hundred children already, either decanted or in embryo. And still going strong. We'll beat them yet."

"That's the spirit I like!" cried the Director, and clapped Mr. Foster on the shoulder. "Come along with us, and give these boys the benefit of your expert knowledge."

Mr. Foster smiled modestly. "With pleasure." They went.

In the Bottling Room all was harmonious bustle and ordered activity. Flaps of fresh sow's peritoneum ready cut to the proper size came shooting up in little lifts from the Organ Store in the sub-basement. Whizz and then, click! the lift-hatches hew open; the bottle-liner had only to reach out a hand, take the flap, insert, smooth-down, and before the lined bottle had had time to travel out of reach along the endless band, whizz, click! another flap of peritoneum had shot up from the depths, ready to be slipped into yet another bottle, the next of that slow interminable procession on the band.

Next to the Liners stood the Matriculators. The procession advanced; one by one the eggs were transferred from their test-tubes to the larger containers; deftly the peritoneal lining was slit, the morula dropped into place, the saline solution poured in... and already the bottle had passed, and it was the turn of the labellers. Heredity, date of fertilization, membership of Bokanovsky Group—details were transferred from test-tube to bottle. No longer anonymous, but named, identified, the procession marched slowly on; on through an opening in the wall, slowly on into the Social Predestination Room.

"Eighty-eight cubic metres of card-index," said Mr. Foster with relish, as they entered.

"Containing *all* the relevant information," added the Director.

"Brought up to date every morning."

"And co-ordinated every afternoon."

"On the basis of which they make their calculations."

"So many individuals, of such and such quality," said Mr. Foster.

"Distributed in such and such quantities."

"The optimum Decanting Rate at any given moment."

第四章 文学与遗传学(Literature and Genetics)

"Unforeseen wastages promptly made good."

"Promptly," repeated Mr. Foster. "If you knew the amount of overtime I had to put in after the last Japanese earthquake!" He laughed good-humouredly and shook his head.

"The Predestinators send in their figures to the Fertilizers."

"Who give them the embryos they ask for."

"And the bottles come in here to be predestined in detail."

"After which they are sent down to the Embryo Store."

"Where we now proceed ourselves."

And opening a door Mr. Foster led the way down a staircase into the basement.

The temperature was still tropical. They descended into a thickening twilight. Two doors and a passage with a double turn insured the cellar against any possible infiltration of the day.

"Embryos are like photograph film," said Mr. Foster waggishly, as he pushed open the second door. "They can only stand red light."

And in effect the sultry darkness into which the students now followed him was visible and crimson, like the darkness of closed eyes on a summer's afternoon. The bulging flanks of row on receding row and tier above tier of bottles glinted with innumerable rubies, and among the rubies moved the dim red spectres of men and women with purple eyes and all the symptoms of lupus. The hum and rattle of machinery faintly stirred the air.

"Give them a few figures, Mr. Foster," said the Director, who was tired of talking.

Mr. Foster was only too happy to give them a few figures.

Two hundred and twenty metres long, two hundred wide, ten high. He pointed upwards. Like chickens drinking, the students lifted their eyes towards the distant ceiling.

Three tiers of racks: ground floor level, first gallery, second gallery.

The spidery steel-work of gallery above gallery faded away in all directions into the dark. Near them three red ghosts were busily unloading demijohns from a moving staircase.

The escalator from the Social Predestination Room.

Each bottle could be placed on one of fifteen racks, each rack, though you couldn't see it, was a conveyor traveling at the rate of thirty-three and a third centimetres an hour. Two hundred and sixty-seven days at eight metres a day. Two thousand one hundred and thirty-six metres in all. One circuit of the cellar at ground level, one on the first gallery, half on the second, and on the two hundred and sixty-seventh morning, daylight in the Decanting Room. Independent existence—so called.

"But in the interval," Mr. Foster concluded, "we've managed to do a lot to them. Oh, a very great deal." His laugh was knowing and triumphant.

"That's the spirit I like," said the Director once more. "Let's walk around. You tell them everything, Mr. Foster."

Mr. Foster duly told them.

Told them of the growing embryo on its bed of peritoneum. Made them taste the rich blood surrogate on which it fed. Explained why it had to be stimulated with placentin and thyroxin. Told them of the *corpus luteum* extract. Showed them the jets through which at every twelfth metre from zero to 2040 it was automatically injected. Spoke of those gradually increasing doses of pituitary administered during the final ninety-six metres of their course. Described the artificial maternal circulation installed in every bottle at Metre 112; showed them the resevoir of blood-surrogate, the centrifugal pump that kept the liquid moving over the placenta and drove it through the synthetic lung and waste product filter. Referred to the embryo's troublesome tendency to anæmia, to the massive doses of hog's stomach extract and foetal foal's liver with which, in consequence, it had to be supplied.

Showed them the simple mechanism by means of which, during the last two metres out of every eight, all the embryos were simultaneously shaken into familiarity with movement. Hinted at the gravity of the so-called "trauma of decanting," and enumerated the precautions taken to minimize, by a suitable training of the bottled embryo, that dangerous shock. Told them of the test for sex carried out in the neighborhood of Metre 200. Explained the system of labelling—a T for the males, a circle for the females and for those who were destined to become freemartins a question mark, black on a white ground.

"For of course," said Mr. Foster, "in the vast majority of cases, fertility is merely a nuisance. One fertile ovary in twelve hundred—that would really be quite sufficient for our purposes. But we want to have a good choice. And of course one must always have an enormous margin of safety. So we allow as many as thirty per cent of the female embryos to develop normally. The others get a dose of male sex-hormone every twenty-four metres for

第四章 文学与遗传学(Literature and Genetics)

the rest of the course. Result: they're decanted as freemartins—structurally quite normal (except," he had to admit, "that they do have the slightest tendency to grow beards), but sterile. Guaranteed sterile. Which brings us at last," continued Mr. Foster, "out of the realm of mere slavish imitation of nature into the much more interesting world of human invention."

He rubbed his hands. For of course, they didn't content themselves with merely hatching out embryos: any cow could do that.

"We also predestine and condition. We decant our babies as socialized human beings, as Alphas or Epsilons, as future sewage workers or future..." He was going to say "future World controllers," but correcting himself, said "future Directors of Hatcheries," instead.

The D. H. C. acknowledged the compliment with a smile.

They were passing Metre 320 on Rack 11. A young Beta-Minus mechanic was busy with screw-driver and spanner on the blood-surrogate pump of a passing bottle. The hum of the electric motor deepened by fractions of a tone as he turned the nuts. Down, down... A final twist, a glance at the revolution counter, and he was done. He moved two paces down the line and began the same process on the next pump.

"Reducing the number of revolutions per minute," Mr. Foster explained. "The surrogate goes round slower; therefore passes through the lung at longer intervals; therefore gives the embryo less oxygen. Nothing like oxygen-shortage for keeping an embryo below par." Again he rubbed his hands.

"But why do you want to keep the embryo below par?" asked an ingenuous student.

"Ass!" said the Director, breaking a long silence. "Hasn't it occurred to you that an Epsilon embryo must have an Epsilon environment as well as an Epsilon heredity?"

It evidently hadn't occurred to him. He was covered with confusion.

"The lower the caste," said Mr. Foster, "the shorter the oxygen." The first organ affected was the brain. After that the skeleton. At seventy per cent of normal oxygen you got dwarfs. At less than seventy eyeless monsters.

"Who are no use at all," concluded Mr. Foster.

Whereas (his voice became confidential and eager), if they could discover a technique for shortening the period of maturation what a triumph, what a benefaction to

Society!

"Consider the horse."

They considered it.

Mature at six; the elephant at ten. While at thirteen a man is not yet sexually mature; and is only full-grown at twenty. Hence, of course, that fruit of delayed development, the human intelligence.

"But in Epsilons," said Mr. Foster very justly, "we don't need human intelligence."

Didn't need and didn't get it. But though the Epsilon mind was mature at ten, the Epsilon body was not fit to work till eighteen. Long years of superfluous and wasted immaturity. If the physical development could be speeded up till it was as quick, say, as a cow's, what an enormous saving to the Community!

"Enormous!" murmured the students. Mr. Foster's enthusiasm was infectious.

He became rather technical; spoke of the abnormal endocrine co-ordination which made men grow so slowly; postulated a germinal mutation to account for it. Could the effects of this germinal mutation be undone? Could the individual Epsilon embryo be made a revert, by a suitable technique, to the normality of dogs and cows? That was the problem. And it was all but solved.

Pilkington, at Mombasa, had produced individuals who were sexually mature at four and full-grown at six and a half. A scientific triumph. But socially useless. Six-year-old men and women were too stupid to do even Epsilon work. And the process was an all-or-nothing one; either you failed to modify at all, or else you modified the whole way. They were still trying to find the ideal compromise between adults of twenty and adults of six. So far without success. Mr. Foster sighed and shook his head.

Their wanderings through the crimson twilight had brought them to the neighborhood of Metre 170 on Rack 9. From this point onwards Rack 9 was enclosed and the bottle performed the remainder of their journey in a kind of tunnel, interrupted here and there by openings two or three metres wide.

"Heat conditioning," said Mr. Foster.

Hot tunnels alternated with cool tunnels. Coolness was wedded to discomfort in the form of hard X-rays. By the time they were decanted the embryos had a horror of cold.

第四章 文学与遗传学(Literature and Genetics)

They werepredestined to emigrate to the tropics, to be miner and acetate silk spinners and steel workers. Later on their minds would be made to endorse the judgment of their bodies. "We condition them to thrive on heat," concluded Mr. Foster. "Our colleagues upstairs will teach them to love it."

"And that," put in the Director sententiously, "that is the secret of happiness and virtue—liking what you've got to do. All conditioning aims at that: making people like their unescapable social destiny."

In a gap between two tunnels, a nurse was delicately probing with a long fine syringe into the gelatinous contents of a passing bottle. The students and their guides stood watching her for a few moments in silence.

"Well, Lenina," said Mr. Foster, when at last she withdrew the syringe and straightened herself up.

The girl turned with a start. One could see that, for all the lupus and the purple eyes, she was uncommonly pretty.

"Henry!" Her smile flashed redly at him—a row of coral teeth.

"Charming, charming," murmured the Director and, giving her two or three little pats, received in exchange a rather deferential smile for himself.

"What are you giving them?" asked Mr. Foster, making his tone very professional.

"Oh, the usual typhoid and sleeping sickness."

"Tropical workers start being inoculated at Metre 150," Mr. Foster explained to the students. "The embryos still have gills. We immunize the fish against the future man's diseases." Then, turning back to Lenina, "Ten to five on the roof this afternoon," he said, "as usual."

"Charming," said the Director once more, and, with a final pat, moved away after the others.

On Rack 10 rows of next generation's chemical workers were being trained in the toleration of lead, caustic soda, tar, chlorine. The first of a batch of two hundred and fifty embryonic rocket-plane engineers was just passing the eleven hundred metre mark on Rack 3. A special mechanism kept their containers in constant rotation. "To improve their sense of balance," Mr. Foster explained. "Doing repairs on the outside of a rocket in mid-air is a ticklish job. We slacken off the circulation when they're right way up, so that they're half starved, and double the flow of surrogate when they're upside down. They learn to associate topsy-turvydom with well-being; in fact, they're only truly happy when they're standing on their heads."

"And now," Mr. Foster went on, "I'd like to show you some very interesting conditioning for Alpha Plus Intellectuals. We have a big batch of them on Rack 5. First Gallery level," he called to two boys who had started to go down to the ground floor.

"They're round about Metre 900," he explained. "You can't really do any useful intellectual conditioning till the foetuses have lost their tails. Follow me."

But the Director had looked at his watch. "Ten to three," he said. "No time for the intellectual embryos, I'm afraid. We must go up to the Nurseries before the children have finished their afternoon sleep."

Mr. Foster was disappointed. "At least one glance at the Decanting Room," he pleaded.

"Very well then." The Director smiled indulgently. "Just one glance."

[...]

Chapter 16

THE ROOM into which the three were ushered was the Controller's study.

"His fordship will be down in a moment." The Gamma butler left them to themselves.

Helmholtz laughed aloud.

"It's more like a caffeine-solution party than a trial," he said, and let himself fall into the most luxurious of the pneumatic arm-chairs. "Cheer up, Bernard," he added, catching sight of his friend's green unhappy face. But Bernard would not be cheered; without answering, without even looking at Helmholtz, he went and sat down on the most uncomfortable chair in the room, carefully chosen in the obscure hope of somehow deprecating the wrath of the higher powers.

The Savage meanwhile wandered restlessly round the room, peering with a vague superficial inquisitiveness at the books in the shelves, at the sound-track rolls and reading machine bobbins in their numbered pigeon-holes. On the table under the window lay a massive volume bound in limp black leather-surrogate, and stamped with large golden T's. He picked it up and opened it. MY LIFE AND WORK, BY OUR FORD. The book had

第四章 文学与遗传学(Literature and Genetics)

been published at Detroit by the Society for the Propagation of Fordian Knowledge. Idly he turned the pages, read a sentence here, a paragraph there, and had just come to the conclusion that the book didn't interest him, when the door opened, and the Resident World Controller for Western Europe walked briskly into the room.

Mustapha Mond shook hands with all three of them; but it was to the Savage that he addressed himself. "So you don't much like civilization, Mr. Savage," he said.

The Savage looked at him. He had been prepared to lie, to bluster, to remain sullenly unresponsive; but, reassured by the good-humoured intelligence of the Controller's face, he decided to tell the truth, straightforwardly. "No." He shook his head.

Bernard started and looked horrified. What would the Controller think? To be labelled as the friend of a man who said that he didn't like civilization—said it openly and, of all people, to the Controller—it was terrible. "But, John," he began. A look from Mustapha Mond reduced him to an abject silence.

"Of course," the Savage went on to admit, "there are some very nice things. All that music in the air, for instance…"

"Sometimes a thousand twangling instruments will hum about my ears and sometimes voices."

The Savage's face lit up with a sudden pleasure. "Have you read it too?" he asked. "I thought nobody knew about that book here, in England."

"Almost nobody. I'm one of the very few. It's prohibited, you see. But as I make the laws here, I can also break them. With impunity, Mr. Marx," he added, turning to Bernard. "Which I'm afraid you *can't* do."

Bernard sank into a yet more hopeless misery.

"But why is it prohibited?" asked the Savage. In the excitement of meeting a man who had read Shakespeare he had momentarily forgotten everything else.

The Controller shrugged his shoulders. "Because it's old; that's the chief reason. We haven't any use for old things here."

"Even when they're beautiful?"

"Particularly when they're beautiful. Beauty's attractive, and we don't want people to be attracted by old things. We want them to like the new ones."

"But the new ones are so stupid and horrible. Those plays, where there's nothing but helicopters flying about and you *feel* the people kissing." He made a grimace. "Goats and monkeys!" Only in Othello's word could he find an adequate vehicle for his contempt and hatred.

"Nice tame animals, anyhow," the Controller murmured parenthetically.

"Why don't you let them see *Othello* instead?"

"I've told you; it's old. Besides, they couldn't understand it."

Yes, that was true. He remembered how Helmholtz had laughed at *Romeo and Juliet*. "Well then," he said, after a pause, "something new that's like *Othello*, and that they could understand."

"That's what we've all been wanting to write," said Helmholtz, breaking a long silence.

"And it's what you never will write," said the Controller. "Because, if it were really like *Othello* nobody could understand it, however new it might be. And if were new, it couldn't possibly be like *Othello*."

"Why not?"

"Yes, why not?" Helmholtz repeated. He too was forgetting the unpleasant realities of the situation. Green with anxiety and apprehension, only Bernard remembered them; the others ignored him. "Why not?"

"Because our world is not the same as Othello's world. You can't make flivvers without steel—and you can't make tragedies without social instability. The world's stable now. People are happy; they get what they want, and they never want what they can't get. They're well off; they're safe; they're never ill; they're not afraid of death; they're blissfully ignorant of passion and old age; they're plagued with no mothers or fathers; they've got no wives, or children, or lovers to feel strongly about; they're so conditioned that they practically can't help behaving as they ought to behave. And if anything should go wrong, there's soma. Which you go and chuck out of the window in the name of liberty, Mr. Savage. *Liberty*!" He laughed. "Expecting Deltas to know what liberty is! And now expecting them to understand *Othello*! My good boy!"

The Savage was silent for a little. "All the same," he insisted obstinately, "*Othello*'s good, *Othello*'s better than those feelies."

第四章 文学与遗传学(Literature and Genetics)

"Of course it is," the Controller agreed. "But that's the price we have to pay for stability. You've got to choose between happiness and what people used to call high art. We've sacrificed the high art. We have the feelies and the scent organ instead."

"But they don't mean anything."

"They mean themselves; they mean a lot of agreeable sensations to the audience."

"But they're... they're told by an idiot."

The Controller laughed. "You're not being very polite to your friend, Mr. Watson. One of our most distinguished Emotional Engineers..."

"But he's right," said Helmholtz gloomily. "Because it is idiotic. Writing when there's nothing to say..."

"Precisely. But that require the most enormous ingenuity. You're making fiivvers out of the absolute minimum of steel—works of art out of practically nothing but pure sensation."

The Savage shook his head. "It all seems to me quite horrible."

"Of course it does. Actual happiness always looks pretty squalid in comparison with the over-compensations for misery. And, of course, stability isn't nearly so spectacular as instability. And being contented has none of the glamour of a good fight against misfortune, none of the picturesqueness of a struggle with temptation, or a fatal overthrow by passion or doubt. Happiness is never grand."

"I suppose not," said the Savage after a silence. "But need it be quite so bad as those twins?" He passed his hand over his eyes as though he were trying to wipe away the remembered image of those long rows of identical midgets at the assembling tables, those queued-up twin-herds at the entrance to the Brentford monorail station, those human maggots swarming round Linda's bed of death, the endlessly repeated face of his assailants. He looked at his bandaged left hand and shuddered. "Horrible!"

"But how useful! I see you don't like our Bokanovsky Groups; but, I assure you, they're the foundation on which everything else is built. They're the gyroscope that stabilizes the rocket plane of state on its unswerving course." The deep voice thrillingly vibrated; the gesticulating hand implied all space and the onrush of the irresistible machine. Mustapha Mond's oratory was almost up to synthetic standards.

"I was wondering," said the Savage, "why you had them at all—seeing that you can get whatever you want out of those bottles. Why don't you make everybody an Alpha Double Plus while you're about it?"

Mustapha Mond laughed. "Because we have no wish to have our throats cut," he answered. "We believe in happiness and stability. A society of Alphas couldn't fail to be unstable and miserable. Imagine a factory staffed by Alphas—that is to say by separate and unrelated individuals of good heredity and conditioned so as to be capable (within limits) of making a free choice and assuming responsibilities. Imagine it!" he repeated.

The Savage tried to imagine it, not very successfully.

"It's an absurdity. An Alpha-decanted, Alpha-conditioned man would go mad if he had to do Epsilon Semi-Moron work—go mad, or start smashing things up. Alphas can be completely socialized—but only on condition that you make them do Alpha work. Only an Epsilon can be expected to make Epsilon sacrifices, for the good reason that for him they aren't sacrifices; they're the line of least resistance. His conditioning has laid down rails along which he's got to run. He can't help himself; he's foredoomed. Even after decanting, he's still inside a bottle—an invisible bottle of infantile and embryonic fixations. Each one of us, of course," the Controller meditatively continued, "goes through life inside a bottle. But if we happen to be Alphas, our bottles are, relatively speaking, enormous. We should suffer acutely if we were confined in a narrower space. You cannot pour upper-caste champagne-surrogate into lower-caste bottles. It's obvious theoretically. But it has also been proved in actual practice. The result of the Cyprus experiment was convincing."

"What was that?" asked the Savage.

Mustapha Mond smiled. "Well, you can call it an experiment in rebottling if you like. It began in A. F. 473. The Controllers had the island of Cyprus cleared of all its existing inhabitants and re-colonized with a specially prepared batch of twenty-two thousand Alphas. All agricultural and industrial equipment was handed over to them and they were left to manage their own affairs. The result exactly fulfilled all the theoretical predictions. The land wasn't properly worked; therewere strikes in all the factories; the laws were set at naught, orders disobeyed; all the people detailed for a spell of low grade work were perpetually intriguing for high-grade jobs, and all the people with high-grade jobs were counter-intriguing at all costs to stay where they were. Within six years they

第四章 文学与遗传学 (Literature and Genetics)

were having a first-class civil war. When nineteen out of the twenty-two thousand had been killed, the survivors unanimously petitioned the World Controllers to resume the government of the island. Which they did. And that was the end of the only society of Alphas that the world has ever seen."

The Savage sighed, profoundly.

"The optimum population," said Mustapha Mond, "is modelled on the iceberg—eight-ninths below the water line, one-ninth above."

"And they're happy below the water line?"

"Happier than above it. Happier than your friend here, for example." He pointed.

"In spite of that awful work?"

"Awful? *They* don't find it so. On the contrary, they like it. It's light, it's childishly simple. No strain on the mind or the muscles. Seven and a half hours of mild, unexhausting labour, and then the *soma* ration and games and unrestricted copulation and the feelies. What more can they ask for? True," he added, "they might ask for shorter hours. And of course we could give them shorter hours. Technically, it would be perfectly simple to reduce all lower-caste working hours to three or four a day. But would they be any the happier for that? No, they wouldn't. The experiment was tried, more than a century and a half ago. The whole of Ireland was put on to the four-hour day. What was the result? Unrest and a large increase in the consumption of *soma*; that was all. Those three and a half hours of extra leisure were so far from being a source of happiness, that people felt constrained to take a holiday from them. The Inventions Office is stuffed with plans for labour-saving processes. Thousands of them." Mustapha Mond made a lavish gesture. "And why don't we put them into execution? For the sake of the labourers; it would be sheer cruelty to afflict them with excessive leisure. It's the same with agriculture. We could synthesize every morsel of food, if we wanted to. But we don't. We prefer to keep a third of the population on the land. For their own sakes—because it takes *longer* to get food out of the land than out of a factory. Besides, we have our stability to think of. We don't want to change. Every change is a menace to stability. That's another reason why we're so chary of applying new inventions. Every discovery in pure science is potentially subversive; even science must sometimes be treated as a possible enemy. Yes, even science."

Science? The Savage frowned. He knew the word. But what it exactly signified he could not say. Shakespeare and the old men of the pueblo had never mentioned science, and from Linda he had only gathered the vaguest hints: science was something you made helicopters with, something that caused you to laugh at the Corn Dances, something that prevented you from being wrinkled and losing your teeth. He made a desperate effort to take the Controller's meaning.

"Yes," Mustapha Mond was saying, "that's another item in the cost of stability. It isn't only art that's incompatible with happiness; it's also science. Science is dangerous; we have to keep it most carefully chained and muzzled."

"What?" said Helmholtz, in astonishment. "But we're always saying that science is everything. It's a hypnopædic platitude."

"Three times a week between thirteen and seventeen," put in Bernard.

"And all the science propaganda we do at the College…"

"Yes; but what sort of science?" asked Mustapha Mond sarcastically. "You've had no scientific training, so you can't judge. I was a pretty good physicist in my time. Too good—good enough to realize that all our science is just a cookery book, with an orthodox theory of cooking that nobody's allowed to question, and a list of recipes that mustn't be added to except by special permission from the head cook. I'm the head cook now. But I was an inquisitive young scullion once. I started doing a bit of cooking on my own. Unorthodox cooking, illicit cooking. A bit of real science, in fact." He was silent.

"What happened?" asked Helmholtz Watson.

The Controller sighed. "Very nearly what's going to happen to you young men. I was on the point of being sent to an island."

The words galvanized Bernard into violent and unseemly activity. "Send *me* to an island?" He jumped up, ran across the room, and stood gesticulating in front of the Controller. "You can't send *me*. I haven't done anything. It was the others. I swear it was the others." He pointed accusingly to Helmholtz and the Savage. "Oh, please don't send me to Iceland. I promise I'll do what I ought to do. Give me another chance. Please give me another chance." The tears began to flow. "I tell you, it's their fault," he sobbed. "And not to Iceland. Oh please, your fordship, please…" And in a paroxysm of abjection he threw himself on his knees before the Controller. Mustapha Mond tried to make him get up; but Bernard persisted in his grovelling; the stream of words poured out inexhaustibly. In the end the Controller had to ring for his fourth secretary.

"Bring three men," he ordered, "and take Mr. Marx into a bedroom. Give him a good *soma* vaporization and then put him to bed and leave him."

The fourth secretary went out and returned with three green-uniformed twin footmen. Still shouting and sobbing. Bernard was carried out.

"One would think he was going to have his throat cut," said the Controller, as the door closed. "Whereas, if he had the smallest sense, he'd understand that his punishment is really a reward. He's being sent to an island. That's to say, he's being sent to a place where he'll meet the most interesting set of men and women to be found anywhere in the world. All the people who, for one reason or another, have got too self-consciously individual to fit into community-life. All the people who aren't satisfied with orthodoxy, who've got independent ideas of their own. Everyone, in a word, who's anyone. I almost envy you, Mr. Watson."

Helmholtz laughed. "Then why aren't you on an island yourself?"

"Because, finally, I preferred this," the Controller answered. "I was given the choice: to be sent to an island, where I could have got on with my pure science, or to be taken on to the Controllers' Council with the prospect of succeeding in due course to an actual Controllership. I chose this and let the science go." After a little silence, "Sometimes," he added, "I rather regret the science. Happiness is a hard master—particularly other people's happiness. A much harder master, if one isn't conditioned to accept it unquestioningly, than truth." He sighed, fell silent again, then continued in a brisker tone, "Well, duty's duty. One can't consult one's own preference. I'm interested in truth, I like science. But truth's a menace, science is a public danger. As dangerous as it's been beneficent. It has given us the stablest equilibrium in history."

思考题

1. What is Bokanovsky's Process? In what sense would Bokanovsky's Process help create and maintain social stability in the World State?
2. Is it ethical to employ genetic engineering to produce "the optimum population"?
3. What do people in the World State sacrifice for stability and happiness?
4. Why is Shakespeare prohibited in the World State?

5. According to Mustapha Mond, what makes science dangerous? What limits are imposed on scientific inquiry in the World State?

6. Why is the World State dystopian rather than utopian?

7. What is your view about the future of genetic engineering?

第三节　补充阅读:莎士比亚十四行诗两首

阅读莎士比亚十四行诗第一和第十四首。诗中诗人劝告自己的"俊美朋友"(the Fair Friend)早日结婚,生育后代,以对抗时间,战胜死亡。思考莎士比亚对遗传的理解。

Sonnet 1[①]

From fairest creatures we desire increase,
That thereby beauty's rose might never die,
But as the riper should by time decease,
His tender heir might bear his memory:
But thou, contracted to thine own bright eyes,
Feed'st thy light's flame with self-substantial fuel,
Making a famine where abundance lies,
Thyself thy foe, to thy sweet self too cruel.
Thou that art now the world's fresh ornament
And only herald to the gaudy spring,
Within thine own bud buriest thy content
And, tender churl, mak'st waste in niggarding.
Pity the world, or else this glutton be,
To eat the world's due, by the grave and thee.

---

① SHAKESPEARE W. "Sonnet 1: From fairest creatures we desire increase"[Z/OL]. https://nosweatshakespeare.com/sonnets/1/.

第四章 文学与遗传学(Literature and Genetics)

Sonnet 14[1]

Not from the stars do I my judgment pluck,
And yet methinks I have Astronomy,
But not to tell of good or evil luck,
Of plagues, of dearths, or seasons' quality;
Nor can I fortune to brief minutes tell,
Pointing to each his thunder, rain, and wind,
Or say with princes if it shall go well
By oft predict that I in heaven find:
But from thine eyes my knowledge I derive,
And, constant stars, in them I read such art
As truth and beauty shall together thrive,
If from thyself to store thou wouldst convert;
Or else of thee this I prognosticate:
Thy end is truth's and beauty's doom and date.

---

[1] SHAKESPEARE W. "Sonnet 14: Not from the stars do I my judgement pluck" [Z/OL]. https://nosweatshakespeare.com/sonnets/14/.

第五章

文学与信息通信技术(Literature and ICT)

第一节 信息通信技术及其文学表征

背景知识

信息通信技术(information and communications technology, ICT)是指处理和传递信息的技术。人们通常将它视作信息技术(information technology, IT)或通信技术(communication technology, CT)的拓展和延伸,但实际上其范畴更加宽广,是两者融合的结果。信息技术是使用计算机来储存或获取数据和信息的技术,它着重于信息的编码或解码,以及它在通信载体上的传输方式,因而也有学者认为信息技术本身包含了信息技术和通信技术[1]。通信技术,有时也称信息技术,主要指用来加工处理和传递信息的设备和软件,它侧重于信息的传送[2]。随着技术的发展,特别是网络的快速发展,信息技术和通信技术紧密结合在一起,形成一个新的范畴。学界将这两个技术融合而成的新概念和技术领域称为信息通信技术,将信息技术和通信技术视作其分支领域,认为其研究范畴包括因特网、无线网络、电话、计算机、软件、中间设备、电视会议、社交网络以及其他所有能用来获取、检索、储存、传递和处理信息的媒体应用硬件、软件及服务等[3]。由于相关概念、方法和工具在不断地演变,目前并不存在统一或被普遍接受的定义[4]。

人类信息通信古已有之,大致经历了如下几个形态的演变:史前壁画、古希腊的羊皮书信、古埃及的陶片书信、古波斯及古罗马时期的信鸽、中国古代的烽火、快马驿站、18 世纪末

---

[1] Information technology[Z/OL]. [2023-07-09]. https://en.wikipedia.org/wiki/Information_technology. 关于信息技术与信息通信技术的关系,参见 KENSHŪJO K K S. Approaches for systematic planning of development projects information and communication technology[M]. Dowagiac: Institute for International Cooperation, 2004: 2.

[2] ROGERS E M. Communication technology: the new media in society[M]. New York: The Free Press, 1986: 2.

[3] CARTELLI A, PALMA M. Encyclopedia of information communication technology[M]. Hershey: Information Science Reference, 2009: xxiv.

[4] 各个时期通信形式的演变参见 MEADOW C T. Making connections: communication through the ages[M]. Lanham: Scarecrow Press, 2002. 另参见 History of telecommunication[Z/OL]. [2023-07-25]. https://en.wikipedia.org/w/index.php?title=History_of_telecommunication&oldid=1035411188.

第五章　文学与信息通信技术(Literature and ICT)

法国的信号旗、19世纪30年代开始的电报、19世纪中期美国的快马邮递、19世纪后期的电话、19世纪末的无线电、20世纪20年代的电视、20世纪50年代末的卫星通信、20世纪60年代开始的计算机网络通信，以及20世纪80年代开始的数字媒体通信，而ICT作为专业术语则是从20世纪80年代开始在学界流行起来①。在《信息通信技术：社会中的新媒体》(*Communication Technology: The New Media in Society*，1986)一书中，罗杰斯(Everett M. Rogers，1931—2004)将当下数字革命前的信息通信技术的发展史划分为四个时期，它们是分别是早期的图像、符号通信，文艺复兴以来的印刷术通信，19世纪中期以来的电信通信，20世纪中后期开始的计算机交互式通信②。当然，每个时期都有一些标志性的发明，它们不仅加快了信息流通的速度，而且拓展了信息流通的范围，促进了社会经济和文明的发展。欧洲工业革命以来，每个阶段的繁荣都由关键技术的革新引领或推动，而信息与通信技术的发明或变革显得更为重要。比如，19世纪电报的发明使得即时通信成为可能，除了用于私人通信，还被广泛用于欧美各主要市场大宗商品的贸易、股票交易、铁路运输信息的调度等，毕竟电报实现了文字信息转变成电流信号进行传播，提高了信息传播的速度和效率，促进了当时经济的发展。20世纪初的无线电通信技术、20世纪中期的计算机通信技术以及当前的数字化信息通信技术也都极大推动了经济的发展。目前，ICT已成为引领社会经济和文化发展的重要力量，相关产业已成为全球最具活力、规模最大的产业之一③。

现代信息通信技术的发展离不开以计算机为代表的信息技术特别是互联网技术。计算机科学的重要组成部分是数学算法，信息的处理、转换与传输就是信息的编码、储存、传输和解码，在这个过程中，各种信息被转换成计算机能识别和计算的数据。当前，计算机上储存和运算的数据都采用二进制进行编码。香农(Claude Shannon，1916—2001)1937年撰写的论文《继电器与开关电路的符号分析》("A Symbolic Analysis of Relay and Switching Circuits")奠定了数字电路理论的基础。在撰写论文的过程中，香农使用继电器实现了二进制运算，成为世界上最早将二进制引入数字电路控制方面的实例。同年底，斯蒂比兹(George Stibitz，1904—1995)发明了世界上第一台二进制电子计算机，它也采用了继电器来表示二进制④。在利用二进制进行编码时，存在不同的标准。为了避免混乱，美国电气和电子工程师协会在1967年制定了美国信息交换标准代码ASCII，并于1969年发布了用于网络信息交换的ASCII格式(ASCII Format for Network Interchange)。由于ASCII的前身为摩尔

---

① Information and communication technology (ICT) [Z/OL]. https://www.techopedia.com/definition/24152/information-and-communications-technology-ict. 另参见 Information and communications technology [Z/OL]. [2023-07-06]. https://en.wikipedia.org/wiki/Information_and_communications_technology.
② ROGERS E M. Communication technology: the new media in society[M]. New York: The Free Press, 1986: 23-66.
③ 罗兰贝格中国ICT产业营商环境白皮书[Z/OL]. [2020-04-23]. https://www.vzkoo.com/read/b52e2328f9761ff5677e9c8d6e1be710.html.
④ 二进制[Z/OL]. [2023-02-12]. https://zh.wikipedia.org/zh-cn/二进制.

斯电报码,19世纪电报的发明常被视作现代通信开始的标志,而当时遍布世界的电报网络也被称为现代网络的鼻祖。

奠定现代信息通信理论技术基础的是香农的另一篇论文《通信的数学理论》("A Mathematical Theory of Communication",1948),它通过讨论信息通道频宽以及信号、噪声比如何影响信息通道的容量,探讨如何有效地编码传递的信息①。成功的信息通信要求收到的信息与传输的信息完全一致,其检验标准就是,一方面它能够复现信息传送者的意图,另一方面"噪声不是有意附加到信号上的任何东西":尽管噪声无法让受众理解,它却是通信内容最丰富的信号——"与其说信息与你所说的相关,不如说它与你所能说的相关。换言之,信息(information)就是衡量个体选择所欲传达的消息(message)时的自由的标准"——"选择自由越大,不确定性越大,传递的信息也就越丰富"②。若结合热力学中的"熵"(entropy)这一概念来看,香农的定义就更明白易懂了:"在信息通信理论中,若记得信息与建构消息时的自由度相关,用熵来衡量就再自然不过了。因此,就如判断热力学综合系统一样,我们可以说'高度有序的通信不以高度的任意性或自由度为标志,亦即信息(或熵)'水平低③。"据此可判断,噪声是信息最大化的信号,而完全可预测的信号则不传递任何信息。由于噪声包含大量无用信息,香农关注如何将其降至最低以便最大效度地传递有用信息。香农的合作者韦弗(Warren Weaver,1894—1978)对噪声提出了不同的看法,强调不应当把信息与意义混淆起来,认为"通信的意义层面与工程层面无关",指出"语义接受者会对消息进行二次解码,这就要求消息在统计学上的语义特征必须与全部受众或构成受众整体的各小组在统计学上的语义能力保持一致"④。由此可看出,信息传递者的意图并不是意义的唯一来源。另外,信息传递中除了工程方面的噪声,还存在语义方面的噪声。韦弗认为,这种信息熵增不仅不会损害意义的传递,它反而有助于意义的接受。韦弗的观点无疑"赋予了噪声某种有益的成分"⑤。经过韦弗的介绍和改进,香农的信息论变得更加明白易懂。它不仅影响了信息通信理论的发展,也对人文和社会科学产生了重要影响。

在《信息理论》("Information Theory")一文中,施韦格豪斯(Philipp Schweighauser,

---

① VERDÚ S. Fifty years of Shannon theory[J]. IEEE transactions on information theory, 1998, 44(6):2057. 另参见 SCHWEIGHAUSER P. Information theory[C]//CLARKE B, ROSSINI M. The Routledge companion to literature and science. London: Routledge, 2011: 145 – 154.

② SHANNON C, WEAVER W. The mathematical theory of communication[M]. Urbana: University of Illinois Press, 1963: 7 – 9, 19.

③ 同②13.

④ 同②26.

⑤ SCHWEIGHAUSER P. Information theory[C]//CLARKE B, ROSSINI M. The Routledge companion to literature and science. London: Routledge, 2011: 150.

第五章 文学与信息通信技术(Literature and ICT)

1971—)概述了人文社科领域信息通信研究的成果①。其中包括海尔斯(Nancy Katherine Hayles,1943—)对香农和韦弗信息通信模型与罗兰巴特在《S/Z》中提出的信息通信模型的对比研究、塞雷斯(Michel Serres,1930—2019)在《寄生虫》(*The Parasite*,1980)中对被主流文化所排斥的他者的信息噪音的哲学讨论、阿塔里(Jacques Attali,1943—)在《噪音:音乐的政治经济学》(*Noise: The Politic Economy of Music*,1977)中提出的制造"噪音"的颠覆性作曲实践、保尔森(William R. Paulson,1955—)在《文化噪音:信息世界的文学文本》(*The Noise of Culture: Literary Texts in a World of Information*,1988)中就信息时代处于边缘地位的文学作品在建构"文化噪音"方面所起的社会功能的讨论,以及施韦格豪斯自身在《美国文学噪音:1890—1985》(*The Noises of American Literature*,1890-1895,2006)一书中为研究"作为文化生产及噪音表征之场"的美国文学而建构的"文学声学"(literary acoustics)。同时,施韦格豪斯还介绍了德国人文社科领域在该方面的成果,特别是基特勒(Friedrich A. Kittler,1943—2011)在建构媒体考古学方面的两本专著《话语网络:1800/1900》(*Discourse Networks 1800/1900*,1985)和《留声机、电影和打字机》(*Gramophone, Film, Typewriter*,1999)。另外,他还提及了与基特勒立场相同的"柏林流派"(Berlin School)的代表西格特(Bernhard Siegert)的理论专著《中继站:文学作为邮政系统的一个时代》(*Relays: Literature as an Epoch of the Postal Systems*,1999)、基特勒之前的"斯图加特流派"的开创者本斯(Max Bense,1910—1990)的技术媒体理论。

施韦格豪斯的论文还介绍了信息通信理论在文学创作层面的影响。他指出,许多现当代作家如约瑟夫·海勒(Joseph Heller,1923—1999)、威廉姆·吉布森(William Gibson,1948—)、唐·德里罗(Don Delillo,1936—)、戴维·佛斯特·华勒斯(David Foster Wallace,1962—2008)、理查德·鲍尔斯等的作品或多或少地都受到信息通信理论的影响,认为最经典的例子当属托马斯·品钦(Thomas Pynchon,1937—)的《拍卖第四十九批》(*The Crying of Lot 49*,1966),强调该作品如早期作家H. G. 威尔斯和亨利·亚当斯(Henry Adams,1838—1918)在各自的作品《时间机器》(*The Time Machine*,1895)和《亨利·亚当斯的教育》(*The Education of Henry Adams*,1907)中所做的那样,都使用了热力学中的熵这一概念,描述了地球走向热寂(heat death)时的悲观景象。在施韦格豪斯看来,小说《拍卖第四十九批》不仅在情节结构层面模拟了信息通信中信息与噪声的关系,而且在形式上也通过碎片式叙事、多重不确定性、复杂的互文性指涉、开放式结尾等策略,质疑了传统语言的用法,进而在文化交流体系中注入噪声②。

---

① SCHWEIGHAUSER P. Information theory[C]//CLARKE B, ROSSINI M. The Routledge companion to literature and science. London: Routledge, 2011: 151-154.
② 同①154.

无论是理论研究,还是文学表征,施韦格豪斯的论文及研究专著都反映了人文社科领域信息通信研究方面的成果。由于其侧重点是信息通信理论中探讨的信息与噪声的关系,他的研究无法揭示该研究领域的全貌。比如,他的讨论没有涉及信息编码原理、信息通信的伦理维度等对人文社会科学的影响,特别是文学创作又是如何反映此类问题的。另外,正如前文表明的那样,人类信息通信古已有之,通信技术不仅包含由计算机、网络等组成的数字媒体,还包括电话、无线电、电报、信号旗等,这些技术也或多或少地影响了所在时代的文化活动。比如,狄更斯、盖斯凯尔夫人(Elizabeth Cleghorn Gaskell, 1810—1865)、乔治·艾略特、安东尼·特罗洛普(Anthony Trollope, 1815—1882)、亨利·詹姆斯(Henry James, 1843—1916)等维多利亚时代的作家都在各自作品中探讨过电报这一信息通信技术对社会文化生活的影响。批评家门克(Richard Menke)在其几部专著中也讨论了现实主义文学在主题、情节结构和叙事等层面如何受到电报技术的影响[1]。本章作品选读部分将以亨利·詹姆斯的小说《在笼中》(*In the Cage*, 1898)中的几个章节为例,说明 19 世纪的电报通信技术的文学表征及其影响。

文献传真

阅读《信息理论》("Information Theory"),思考文末问答题。本文节选自《劳特利奇指南:文学与科学》[2]。

Information Theory

Philipp Schweighauser

Claude E. Shannon's publication of "A Mathematical Theory of Communication" in the *Bell System Technical Journal* of July and October 1948 marks the beginning of information theory and can be considered "the Magna Carta of the information age".[3] Shannon's work brought into being a research field that is both an important sub-discipline of mathematics and an applied science relevant to a multiplicity of fields, including but not restricted to computer science, cryptology, philosophy, psychology, (functional) linguistics, statistics, engineering, physics, biology (especially

---

[1] MENKE R. Telegraphic realism: Victorian fiction and other information systems[M]. Stanford, California: Stanford University Press, 2008. 另参见 MENKE R. Literature, print culture and media technologies, 1880-1900[M]. Cambridge: Cambridge University Press, 2019.

[2] SCHWEIGHAUSER P. Information theory[C]//CLARKE B, ROSSINI M. The Routledge companion to literature and science. London: Routledge, 2011: 145-154.

[3] VERDÚ S. Fifty years of Shannon theory[J]. IEEE transactions on information theory, 1998, 44(6): 2057.

genetics), and economics. But Shannon could not have written his seminal paper without the work done by important precursors: the Bell Lab engineers Harry Nyquist and Ralph Hartley[①]; the mathematicians John von Neumann and Norbert Wiener[②]; and the physicists Ludwig Boltzmann[③], J. Willard Gibbs[④], and Leó Szilard (1929)[⑤]. In contemporary information theory, much of this early work still plays an important role. More recent research has either elaborated on Shannon's original insights or followed the different path of algorithmic information theory outlined by Gregory J. Chaitin, Andrey Nikolaevich Kolmogorov, and Ray Solomonoff in the 1960s.[⑥]

[...]

Despite these limitations, Shannon and Weaver's mathematical theory of communication has had profound effects on cybernetics and systems theory. However, in their later development, these disciplines abandon the older transmission model of communication for one that describes processes of information exchange or cognitive construction taking place at several hierarchically distinct levels within highly complex systems such as computers, the human body, and society. Apart from these further developments, Shannon and Weaver's theorems themselves had a strong impact on the humanities and social sciences. In what follows, I will sketch some of their most prominent uses, with a special emphasis on theoretical and literary reflections on noise.

Katherine Hayles (1987) compares Shannon and Weaver's model of communication to Roland Barthess as developed in S/Z. Starting from the assumption that science and literature are isomorphic manifestations of a shared culture, Hayles contrasts the different

---

① NYQUIST H. Certain factors affecting telegraph speed[J]. Bell system technical journal, 1924(3): 324–346. 另参见 HARTLEY R. Transmission of information[J]. Bell system technical journal, 1928(7): 535–563.

② NEUMANN J. Matchmatische gundlagen der quantenmechanik[M]. Berlin: Springer, 1932. 另参见 WIENER N. Cybernetics or control and communication in the animal and the machine[M]. Cambridge: MIT Press, 1948.

③ BOLTZMANN L. Vorlesungen uber gastheorie[M]. Leipzig: Johann Ambrosius Barth, 1896–1898.

④ GIBBS J W. On the equilibrium of heterogenous substances[J]. Transactions of the connecticut academy of sciences, 1878(3): 108–248, 343–524.

⑤ SZILARD L. Uber die entropieveminderung in einem thermodynamischen system bei eingriffen intelligenter wesen[J]. Zeitschrift fur pysik, 1929, 53(11–12): 840–56.

⑥ CHAITIN G. Algoritchmic information theory[M]. Cambridge: Cambridge University Press, 1987.

"economies of explanation" at work in Shannon and Barthes.① Both theorists note that noise contains a surplus of information. But while Shannon's work is embedded in a capitalist-scientific economy that demands the reduction of the many to the few and tries to mute noise by designing it as useless, Barthes's work is embedded in a literary economy that demands the expansion of the few to the many, values playfulness over usefulness, and celebrates noise. Thus, "similar concepts emerge with radically different values when they are embedded within different economies".② Hayles's observation applies to many of the uses information theory has been put to in literary, cultural, and media theory. This is especially the case for reflections on the innovative and subversive potential of noise.

For instance, Michel Serres, in *The Parasite*, *Genesis*, and a variety of essays, appropriates *le parasite*—informatic "noise" in technical French—as a figure for the excluded third, i. e. for all those objects and people that dualist thinking seeks to exclude:

> Science is not necessarily a matter of the one or of order, the multiple and noise are not necessarily the province of the irrational. This can be the case, but it is not always so. The whole set of these divisions delineates the space of noise, the clash of these dichotomies overruns it with noise, simple and naïve, repetitive, strategies of the desire for domination. To think in terms of pairs is to make ready some dangerous weapon, arrows, darts, dovetails, whereby to hold space and kill. To think by negation is not to think. Dualism tries to start a ruckus [chercher noise], make noise, it relates to death alone. It puts to death and it maintains death. Death to the parasite, someone says, without seeing that a parasite is put to death only by a stronger parasite.③

It is in line with these observations that Jacques Attali, in *Noise*: *The Political Economy of Music*, champions the improvisational sounding practices of what he calls

---

① HAYLES K. Information or noise? Economy of explanation in Barthes's S/Z and Shannon's information theory[C]// LEVINE G. One culture: essays in science and literature. Madison: University of Wisconsin Press, 1987: 119–120.
② 同①131.
③ SERRES M. Genesis[M]. Ann Arbor: University of Michigan Press, 1997: 131.

第五章　文学与信息通信技术（Literature and ICT）

"composition": "the conquest of the right to make noise, in other words, to create one's own code and work, without advertising its goal in advance".① For Attali, such practices are prophetic; they herald "the emergence of a formidable subversion, one leading to a radically new organization never yet theorized".②

In *The Noise of Culture: Literary Texts in a World of Information*, William R. Paulson draws on Serres's work, information theory, and theoretical biology, as well as Russian and Belgian formalism to reflect on the function of literature in a world that is structured increasingly around the production, circulation, and exchange of machine-readable, clear information. Acknowledging the marginality of literature in the information age, Paulson contends that the social function of literature today may best be described as "the noise of culture":

> Literature is not and will not ever again be at the center of culture, if indeed it ever was. There is no use in either proclaiming or debunking its central position. Literature is the noise of culture, the rich and indeterminate margin into which messages are sent off, never to return the same, in which signals are received not quite like anything emitted.③

In *The Noises of American Literature, 1890–1985*, I build on Paulson's insights as well as soundscape studies and Frankfurt School aesthetics to propose a history of literary acoustics that explores American literary texts from the late nineteenth to the late twentieth century as "sites of both the cultural production and the representation of noise".④

Other uses of information theory in the humanities and social sciences can be traced in Friedrich A. Kittler's media archeology, which starts from the assumption that "media determine our situation" and finds its most influential expression in two of Kittler's major books, *Discourse Networks 1800/1900* and *Gramophone, Film,*

---

① ATTALI J J. Noise: the political economy of music[M]. Minneapolis: University of Minnesota Press, 1985: 132.
② 同①6.
③ PAULSON W R. The noise of culture: literary texts in a world of information[M]. Ithaca: Cornell University Press, 1988: 180.
④ PHLLIP S. The noise of American literature, 1890–1985: toward a history of literary acoustics[M]. Gainesville: University Press of Florida, 2006: 19.

Typewriter.① Kittler's "informational-theoretical materialism" is shared by a host of other German media theorists—the so-called "Berlin School" of media theory—among them Bernhard Dotzler, Wolfgang Ernst, and Bernhard Siegert, whose *Relays: Literature as an Epoch of the Postal System*(1999) is one of the most fascinating books to come out of that tradition. Well before Kittler, Max Bense inaugurated another German tradition of technology-centered media theory, the "Stuttgart School." Bense's informational aesthetics considers acts of selection as the most fundamental link between art and mathematics and is particularly interested in the interplay of order and complexity in works of art.

So far, I have sketched the basic assumptions of Shannon's theory of communication and some of its uses in literary, cultural, and media theory. Concerning the intersections of information theory and literature, there is, however, a second avenue to explore, if only very briefly: the impact of information theory on the literary imagination. Many writers have drawn on information theory: Joseph Heller in *Something Happened*(1974), William Gibson in *Neuromancer*(1984), Don DeLillo in *White Noise*(1985), David Foster Wallace in *The Broom of the System*(1987), Richard Powers in *The Gold Bug Variations*(1991), Neal Stephenson in *Snow Crash*(1992) and *Cryptonomicon*(1999), and Greg Bear in *Dead Lines: a novel of life... after death*(2004), to name but a few. Yet Thomas Pynchon's *The Crying of Lot* 49 (1966) remains the most prominent example of such a text, and the remainder of this chapter discusses that novel as a paradigmatic case.

Like earlier writers such as H. G. Wells in *The Time Machine*(1895) and Henry Adams in *The Education of Henry Adams* (1907/1918), Pynchon draws on the thermodynamic notion of entropy to draw a gloomy picture of the Earth as moving toward heat death, i.e. to the gradual but complete dissipation of energy predicted by the nineteenth-century physicist Hermann von Helmholtz, who considered the world a closed thermodynamic system subject to the irreversible increase in entropy postulated by the second law of thermodynamics.② But in Pynchon's fictional world, thermodynamic

---

① FRIEDRICH K A. Discourse networks 1800/1900[M]. Stanford: Stanford University Press, 1990: xxxix.

② PETER F. From apocalypse to entropy and beyond: the second law of thermodynamics in post-war American fiction[M]. Essen: Die Blaude Eule, 1997: 99 – 105.

entropy is counteracted by a second type of entropy: informational entropy. While the thermodynamic world of von Helmholtz and Henry Adams knew entropy only as dissipation of energy, the informational world of Shannon and Pynchon has learned to distinguish between two types of entropy with contrary connotations. In Pynchon's novel, an encounter between informational entropy and thermodynamic entropy is played out in a machine built by John Nefastis. Nefastis claims that his apparatus reverses the process of entropic increase and thus refutes the second law of thermodynamics. Thus, the Nefastis Machine would make James Clerk Maxwell's thought experiment come true: the idea that a Demon who sorts out the slower- and faster-moving molecules within a closed system could halt entropic degradation and produce a perpetual motion machine. Nefastis's apparatus requires a psychic who can communicate with Maxwell's Demon:

> "Communication is the key," cried Nefastis. "The Demon passes his data on to the sensitive, and the sensitive must reply in kind. There are untold billions of molecules in that box. The Demon collects data on each and every one. At some deep psychic level, he must get through. The sensitive must receive that staggering set of energies, and feedback something like the same quantity of information. To keep it all cycling."①

In Nefastis's scheme, an exchange of information between a sensitive and the Demon allows it to wage a battle against the increase in thermodynamic entropy. While Pynchon casts the viability of Nefastis's apparatus into doubt, the competition staged in it between thermodynamic and informational entropy plays out on a larger scale throughout Pynchon's novel. The cultural inertia of Southern California depicted at the beginning of the narrative, its "unvarying gray sickness", corresponds to a state near thermodynamic equilibrium or maximum entropy, at which the system has come to an almost complete standstill.② But in the course of the novel the movement toward entropic degradation is countered by repeated injections of informational entropy or noise into the system: the Paranoids' "shuddering deluge of thick guitar sounds"③, the cryptic

---

① PYNCHON T. The crying of lot 49[M]. London: Picador, 1966: 72-73.
② 同①14.
③ 同①25.

messages relayed by the underground mail delivery system W. A. S. T. E., and the communication networks of the 1960s counter-culture more generally. The outcome of the battle between thermodynamic and informational entropy ends indecisively in Pynchon's novel, but in its staging of that battle, *The Crying of Lot 49* stands as a powerful monument to the energy that the fusion of literature and science can release. What enables Pynchon's novel to do that, though, is not only its negotiation of information and noise at the plot level, but also its recalcitrant literary form—its fragmented plot structure, multiple indeterminacies, complex system of intertextual references, and refusal of narrative closure—which challenges conventionalized language uses and thus injects noise into the system of cultural communication.

思考题

1. According to Shannon, what is noise? How does noise affect the successful conveyance of the sender's intended message in communication?
2. What is entropy? In what ways does Thomas Pynchon's novel *The Crying of Lot 49* justify an interpretation of its thematic concerns in terms of the concept of information entropy?

第二节 《在笼中》与电报通信

作品导读

1. 作者简介

小说《在笼中》的作者是美裔英国作家亨利·詹姆斯,他是欧美现实主义向现代主义过渡阶段的一位重要作家、评论家,其父老亨利·詹姆斯(Henry James Sr., 1811—1882)是神学家,哥哥威廉姆·詹姆斯(William James, 1842—1910)是著名的哲学家及心理学家,妹妹爱丽丝·詹姆斯(Alice James, 1848—1892)是一名日记作家。不到1岁时,亨利·詹姆斯就随家人移居伦敦,然后于1845年回到美国,并在位于奥尔巴尼(Albany)的祖母家度过大部分童年时期。1855—1860年,詹姆斯全家旅居欧洲,去过英国、法国、瑞士等多个国家。由于旅行,他的教育杂乱无章,其父有意让他接受多种因素的影响,其中最主要的是哲学和科学。回到美国后的第二年,他便前往哈佛大学攻读法学。由于并不喜欢法律,他开始发展文学爱

第五章　文学与信息通信技术(Literature and ICT)

好,结识了作家豪厄尔斯(William Dean Howells,1837—1920)和诺顿(Charles Eliot Norton,1827—1908),并与出版商菲尔兹(James Thomas Fields,1817—1881)夫妇成为终身朋友,而他们则成为亨利·詹姆斯早期创作的职业向导。

亨利·詹姆斯的创作大致可分为三个阶段[①]。第一阶段(1863—1881年)早期,他受美国浪漫主义作家霍桑的影响,创作了《时刻戒备》(Watch and Ward,1871)、《热衷游历的人》(A Passionate Pilgrim,1871)和《罗德里克·赫德森》(Roderick Hudson,1875)等小说。1875年,他移居法国,结识了左拉(Émile Zola,1840—1902)、屠格涅夫等作家。次年,他到英国定居,前后将近三十年,创作了《美国人》(The American,1877)、《欧洲人》(The Europeans,1878)、《黛西·米勒》(Daisy Miller,1878)、《华盛顿广场》(Washington Square,1880)和《贵妇画像》(The Portrait of a Lady,1881)等作品,其间,霍桑对其影响日渐式微,取而代之的是乔治·艾略特、屠格涅夫和左拉等人的影响。在第一阶段,奠定詹姆斯英美文学界地位的是其国际主题题材小说,通过美国女性的视角,展现欧美新旧文明之间的差异。第二阶段(1884—1897年)为过渡阶段,詹姆斯创作了《波士顿人》(The Bostonians,1886)、《卡萨玛西玛公主》(The Princess Casamassima,1886)和《悲惨的缪斯》(The Tragic Muse,1890)三部小说。此后,他开始了戏剧实验,但是,在剧作《盖伊多姆维尔》(Guy Domville,1895)首映失败后,再次转向小说创作,发表了《阿斯本文稿》(The Aspern Papers,1888)、《波音顿的收藏品》(The Spoils of Poynton,1896)、《梅西之所知》(What Maisie Knew,1897)、《拧紧螺丝》(The Turn of the Screw,1898)、《在笼中》等作品。在叙事技巧上,这些作品深受舞台艺术影响,强调人物内心的展示,而不是讲述;在人物及主题方面,侧重于英国文化背景中儿童的内心意识及其道德教育。

在第三阶段(1900—1916年),詹姆斯发表了《圣泉》(The Sacred Fount,1901)、《鸽翼》(The Wings of the Dove,1902)、《使节》(The Ambassador,1903)、《金碗》(The Golden Bowl,1904)等小说,出版了《英国风情》(English Hours,1905)、《美国景象》(The American Scene,1907)、《意大利时光》(Italian Hours,1909)等游记,创作了《童年及其他》(A Small Boy and Others,1913)、《作为儿子和兄弟》(Notes of a Son and Brother,1914)和《中年岁月》(The Middle Years,1917)三部自传。最后阶段也是最重要的阶段,《鸽翼》《使节》和《金碗》等小说中的叙事技巧,特别是展示人物内心意识的叙述视角及叙事语言日臻成熟,它们突破了狄更斯等人开创的现实主义小说传统,指明了现代主义小说的发展方向,对意识流小说的发展有着重要影响。鉴于其创作成果及艺术成就,詹姆斯被公认为心理现实小说之父,他是英语文学领域最伟大的小说家之一。

[①] 关于亨利·詹姆斯创作阶段的划分,参见 EDEL L. Henry James[Z/OL]. [2023-04-11]. https://www.britannica.com/biography/Henry-James-American-writer.

19世纪的现实主义小说不仅反映了维多利亚时期的科学发现或科学进步,而且也参与建构了当时的科学话语①。亨利·詹姆斯的心理现实主义小说也同样如此,不仅在表现技巧上通过借用当时作为社会科学分支的心理科学知识来更客观地反映人物的内心世界,而且在题材内容上也反映了当时的科学发明,如电报、打字机、电话、幻灯机等。比如,在《贵妇画像》小说开篇,詹姆斯借助身在欧洲的小说人物在理解来自美国的电报信息上的困难,直接切入小说主题,即探讨欧美两种文化之间的矛盾与冲突②。在《华盛顿广场》中,故事内容与情节结构都受到当时医学科学和生物学的影响,特别是达尔文进化论影响下的优生学③。小说《在笼中》不仅在题材和内容上反映了电报这一信息通信技术在维多利亚时期英国社会的商用发展及其影响,而且在叙事结构和叙事语言上都呈现出电报信息的特征。另外,该小说的创作缘起及动机也与电报技术有着紧密的关系。借助该小说的创作,詹姆斯试图阐明科技进步如何改变人类的生活方式、认知方式以及人伦价值观。本章选择此作品作为教学内容,不仅能阐明19世纪的信息通信技术给当时社会造成的影响,而且能说明文学在表征和解决相关问题方面的功能。

2. 作品介绍

《在笼中》出版于1898年,主要讲述女电报员如何借工作之便,以阅读小说的方式来窥探并参与到客户的恋情中去的故事。女电报员姓名不详,工作所在地考科(Cocker)邮局位于伦敦富人聚集地梅菲尔(Mayfair)街区。由于电报价格高昂,其客户非富即贵,他们借助电报订购日常生活用品、安排约会、购买火车票、预订宾馆等。女电报员则穷困潦倒,与寡母租住在邮局附近,每天午饭后阅读廉价的言情小说,借此消磨时光。未婚夫马吉(Mudge)是邮局隔壁杂货店的伙计,最近刚升为领班,被调往伦敦北部去负责查而克农场(Chalk Farm)区的店铺。在她看来,马吉为人无趣,将来婚姻生活必定让人无聊绝望,因而暂时拒绝了让其调至他所负责区域邮局的请求。更重要的是,梅菲尔邮局的工作让其窥见了伦敦上流社会生活的点滴,这不仅给其生活带来一些乐趣,而且让其无限憧憬,幻想自己有朝一日能被某贵族看上,成为所阅读小说中的幸福女主人公。

在工作中,女电报员发现有些客户会一次发送多封电报,而且每份电报的落款各不相同。这激发了她的好奇心,推测电报客户的隐私,想象处于事态发展高潮的情景。最牵动其想象力的是埃弗拉德(Everard)与布拉迪恩(Bradeen)太太之间的电报。起初,布拉迪恩太

---

① SMITH J. The novel and science[C]//LISA R. The Oxford handbook of the Victorian novel. Oxford: Oxford University Press, 2013: 441-458. 另参见 OTIS L. Literature and science in the nineteenth century[M]. Oxford: Oxford University Press, 2002.

② MENKE R. Telegraphic realism: Henry James's in the cage[J]. PMLA, 2000(5): 975-990.

③ SCHEIBER A J. Eugenic anxiety in Henry James's Washington square[J]. Literature and medicine, 1996(2): 244-262.

第五章　文学与信息通信技术(Literature and ICT)

太在电报中一会儿自称西西,一会儿自称玛丽,或其他什么名字。电报接收人中除了一些贵族太太外,经常指向一位名叫埃弗拉德的先生。据此,女电报员推测埃弗拉德与布拉迪恩之间必有私情,不久后他俩一起来发电报时的亲密情景证实了她的猜想。埃弗拉德的社会地位和英俊外貌让女电报员怦然心动,根据布拉迪恩与其偷情电报中的信息,她拼凑出他所住宾馆的位置,经常在深夜到其宾馆周围徘徊,制造出与其偶然相遇的场景,然后与其手牵手散步,承诺愿意为其做一切。由于一直关注埃弗拉德,女电报员记住了他与布莱迪恩之间电报的所有内容,帮助布拉迪恩修正了一封电报的内容,帮助埃弗拉德回忆一封很久前他发给布拉迪恩但却被人拦截的偷情电报,进而帮助他们避免了私情被暴露的风险。在她看来,埃弗拉德肯定也爱上了她,他来发电报是因为她的存在。让其失望的是,埃弗拉德并没有因为她的帮助而爱她或与她结婚,进而实现其改变社会地位的梦想。相反,在布拉迪恩的丈夫去世后不久,他为了偿还债务而被迫与布拉迪恩结婚。小说结尾,女电报员回到现实,准备前往未婚夫所在地区的邮局工作并与其结婚。

女电报员的爱情故事反映了维多利亚时期下层女性的生活现实和职业理想。就如其阅读的廉价小说一样,它构成了19世纪末快餐文化的一部分,为下层职业女性提供了供其阅读和消遣的对象,但同时也对之进行了道德教育。另外,由于以电报为媒介,该小说在内容上、情节安排上以及叙事语言上都紧扣电报,再现了电报建构的社会文化,即建构了门克所强调的"电报现实主义"①。通过阅读该小说,可以在一定层面上了解电报技术如何影响了19世纪末英国社会各阶层的生活状况,特别是挣扎于阶层牢笼里的下层百姓②。

3. 作品赏析

小说《在笼中》并非简单地复制现实。相反,通过"电报化"现实的表征,不仅说明电报信息通信的工作原理、信息传播过程中影响信息传播效率的主要因素,而且思考了信息传播与资本主义经济和社会文化之间的关系,探讨了电报这一新信息通信技术对人伦价值的影响,因而在更深层次上建构了社会现实,并对技术文化做出一定的批判。

电报交流的原理就是将语言符号进行编码,然后通过电报装置将信息编码转化成电流符号,再将载有电报信息的电流符合还原成语言符号。电报传送的过程就是由电报员控制并传输电流变化、记载电流变化、将记载电流变化的符号还原成语言符号。记载电流变化的方式有针孔印刷、声音辨读和字母印刷。电报通信最初依靠摩斯码自动记录器(morse register)来接收电报信息,当文字通过编码转换成电流时,电报接收器上的电磁片就会运动,

---

① MENKE R. Telegraphic realism: Henry James's in the cage[J]. PMLA, 2000(5): 975–990.
② 关于该小说中反映的阶级的牢笼,阶级剥削与压迫,参见 GÓMEZ P M R. An archetypal reading of the cage symbol in Henry James's major phase[J]. Revista Canaria De Estudios Ingleses, 2007(54): 69–86. 另参见 NICOLA N. The reading gaol of Henry James's "In the Cage"[J]. ELH, 1999(1): 179–201.

进而带动连接在电磁片上的金属针,与此同时,另一电磁片会接通电源,带动装有纸带的滚轴,当纸带从金属针下走过,上面会记下点号(dot)和破折号(dash),而这两种符号的不同排列组合则代表了不同文字。电报信息接收后,须由经过专门培训的电报员将摩斯码还原成语言,然后再反馈给电报接收者。由于摩斯接收器会经常卡纸,加上熟练掌握摩斯码的电报员会直接根据电报接收器电流变化时发出的滴答声来辨读电报内容,纸带就显得多余了。《在笼中》发表于19世纪末,摩斯接收器早已被通过声音来辨读电报内容的"音响器"(sounder)所取代,小说中的女电报员的工作就是坐在电报笼子里来"操作并监视音响器",传递并辨读记载电报信息的"各种各样的电流脉冲造成的声音"。

由于电报信息的传递必须转换成机器可以识别和传递的摩尔斯电码,电报的发送和接收都离不开经受过职业训练的电报员。小说中埃弗拉德与布拉迪恩之间的偷情电报以及他们与朋友家人之间的电报通信都离不开女电报员这一信息中介。电报员不是信息内容的受众或发出者,他们的存在使得电报发送者和接收者的隐私直接暴露在邮局这一个公共空间内,在协助电报发送者和接收者进行信息通信的同时,电报员窥探了他人的隐私,在一定程度上制造并传播了谣言。为了防止信息泄露,电报发送者往往使用与电报接受者都熟悉的暗号、短语甚至代码来传递信息。当然,使用突破语法结构的简洁话语可以节省费用,毕竟电报是以字数来收费的,但更重要的是,这种语言的使用可以保护个人隐私。正是出于这种考虑,埃弗拉德和布拉迪恩在电报传情的过程中偏爱支离破碎的短语,他们这么做自然不是为了省钱。在女电报员看来,贵族"乐意用足可以让她受贫穷煎熬的父母、失踪的兄弟、饿死的姐姐开销一辈子的钱来发送一则内容为'更多的爱'或'很抱歉'的电报"。为了确保私情不被发现,埃弗拉德的多封电报"只是一些数字,它们什么都不能说明"。女电报员发现,发送这种纯数字构成的电报后,"除了暧昧甜美的声音,她什么都没听到,没有听到一个名字,没有听到一个地址,没有听到任何有意义的话语"。尽管如此,她还是从这些数字中拼凑一个有意义的整体,发现了埃弗拉德和布拉迪恩之间的电报恋情,发现了他们各自住处所在的位置,了解了他们的朋友圈。因此,无论电报信息如何加密,只要存在电报员这个第三者,电报通信就有可能泄密。除了电报员,还有另外一些因素造成了电报信息的泄密。尽管电报使得即时通信成为可能,但是电报接收者不可能与电报发送者同时处在电报线路的两端。这就表明,除了电报员,通信主体还需要借助代理人来发送或接收电报讯息。在维多利亚社会,达官贵人往往让佣人去邮电局收取或发送信息。或许,正是由于这个原因,小说中埃弗拉德发送的一封电报情书在传送过程中被他人截取了,进而使得他与布拉迪恩之间的恋情差点因此而暴露在公众视野中。

电报员不仅传递和接收电报信息,而且会干预信息,成为噪声的来源,造成了信息传播链闭环中的熵增现象。《在笼中》的女电报员不仅用她所阅读的言情小说的叙事逻辑来解读或推测客户的电报内容,进而满足其追踪上层社会风尚的欲望,同时还借助其强大的记忆力

第五章 文学与信息通信技术(Literature and ICT)

在脑海中保存客户的电报信息,并在必要的时候不经客户允许,修正在她看来内容存在问题的电报信息,并因此得到客户的赞许。比如,当埃弗拉德的私情暴露且危及他的性命时,女电报员先前未征得布拉迪恩小姐同意而修改了内容的一封电报使得埃弗拉德保住了性命和名声,并在布拉迪恩的丈夫去世后与布拉迪恩结婚。通过这一插曲可以看出,电报员在信息通信过程中扮演了重要的角色,影响了信息的有效传播。

电报发明作为人类思想的产物不可能是中性的,在进入商品流通领域时带上了使用者的价值和意志。《在笼中》的电报笼子地处伦敦上流社会聚集地,电报是贵族日常交流的工具,建构了上层社会的文化价值。按照哈贝马斯技术文化的逻辑,如果技术的使用不促进社会所必需的交流,那么技术就会带来危害①。《在笼中》里的电报尽管促进了埃弗拉德和布拉迪恩小姐之间的偷情,但由于偷情并非道德社会的必要交流,这种电报有伤社会风化,加速了世纪末上层社会道德的腐化。另外,电报技术阻断了交流主体之间信息直接传播的通道,这使得电报员可以自由获取他人的信息,从而在一定程度上危害了电报交流主体的隐私。尽管埃弗拉德和布拉迪恩在电报中使用暗号,但女电报员仍推测出他们间的私情,并根据电报上的地址找到埃弗拉德的宾馆,然后下班后到该宾馆外不断徘徊,蓄意制造意外相遇的假象。随后,女电报员对未婚夫说"一切在我掌控之中"。在脑海中,女电报员狂想到:"一个坏女孩可能会怎么做呢?……我不得不告诉你我已经掌握足够的信息,因此非常值得你来收买我!"显然,女电报员已经意识到自己所掌握的贵族隐私的价值,并在一定程度上传递了绯闻。另外,女电报员告诉未婚夫说她"愿尽一切来帮助埃弗拉德",但却不愿答应未婚夫的要求搬到他工作所在的场所以节省开支。可以看出,女电报员的道德观念在电报的干预下发生了扭曲,她的行为让埃弗拉德和布拉迪恩感到"迷惑、不安和恐惧"。

通过展现电报技术对主体的影响,詹姆斯旨在批判现代科学技术对自己小说创作以及生活的影响。在写作《在笼中》时,詹姆斯"已经购买了昂贵且奇妙的打字机,并雇佣私人打字员处理文稿和日常信件"②。在这种写作模式下,詹姆斯向打字员口授文稿,然后打字员用打字机记述文稿并向读者或其他目标群体传递信息。显然,打字机具有电报技术一样的属性,使得客户的信息暴露公共空间里。在詹姆斯看来,"打字员粗俗,品德绝不高尚"③。在1895年王尔德同性恋审判中,到法庭举证王尔德有罪的正是那些和电报员、打字员属于同一阶层的电话接线员、文书和服务生等。在这一丑闻后,詹姆斯把这一阶层比作"一窝几乎和婴儿一样幼稚的敲诈勒索者",然后指出"我们必须感激那些我们可以攫取的任何遮盖物,因为如今人的质朴和诚实都暴露在公众视野下"④。因此,詹姆斯与《在笼中》的贵族一

---

① 转引自 FEENBERG A. Questioning technology[M]. New York: Routledge, 1996: 156.
② EDEL L. The life of Henry James[M]. vol. 4. New York: Avon, 1978: 176.
③ EDEL L. The letters of Henry James[M]. vol. 4. Cambridge: Harvard University Press, 1984: 75.
④ 同②12.

样有足够的理由来惧怕这些以现代技术为工具的职业阶层。为保护自己的隐私,詹姆斯在打字员处理过的信件上往往加上隐秘的附言,这类似于《在笼中》偷情贵族所用的暗号和多重身份。可以说,詹姆斯在打字员处理过的信件中的秘密附言就是他所感激的"遮盖物",它在一定程度上能够给予詹姆斯一个完整的主体。从这个意义上来讲,《在笼中》反映了詹姆斯对技术文化下主体完整性和社会价值观念的担忧,表明了他建构和发展突破消费文化逻辑的现代主体和道德的愿望。

如何提高通信效率、通信安全、通信过程中人的主体性及道德是当下数字通信媒体建设和发展过程中必须解决的重要问题。因此,《在笼中》关于电报通信技术的讨论对于当下以电脑、网络等为载体的数字化媒体通信的建设和发展有着重要的启示。选文第四章、第五章是维多克自述如何创造怪物以及见到怪物后的恐惧心理。选文第Ⅰ~Ⅴ章讨论了电报通信的原理,电报通信对个体行为、语言和道德的影响。选文第XXII~XXIII章则讨论了电报员如何利用自己的技能帮助电报客服摆脱困境,反映了电报员如何影响信息流通和信息接受。

作品选读

In the Cage

Henry James

Chapter I

It had occurred to her early that in her position—that of a young person spending, in framed and wired confinement, the life of a guinea-pig or a magpie—she should know a great many persons without their recognizing the acquaintance. That made it an emotion the more lively—though singularly rare and always, even then, with opportunity still very much smothered—to see anyone come in whom she knew outside, as she called it, anyone who could add anything to the meanness of her function. Her function was to sit there with two young men—the other telegraphist and the counter-clerk; to mind the "sounder," which was always going, to dole out stamps and postal-orders, weigh letters, answer stupid questions, give difficult change and, more than anything else, count words as numberless as the sands of the sea, the words of the telegrams thrust, from morning to night, through the gap left in the high lattice, across the encumbered shelf that her forearm ached with rubbing. This transparent screen fenced out or fenced in, according to the side of the narrow counter on which the human lot was cast, the duskiest corner of a shop pervaded not a little, in winter, by the poison of perpetual gas, and at all times by the presence of hams, cheese, dried fish, soap, varnish, paraffin and other solids and fluids that she came to know perfectly by their smells without consenting to know them by their names.

The barrier that divided the little post-and-telegraph-office from the grocery was a frail structure of wood and wire; but the social, the professional separation was a gulf that fortune, by a stroke quite remarkable, had spared her the necessity of contributing at all publicly to bridge. When Mr. Cocker's young men stepped over from behind the other counter to change a five-pound note—and Mr. Cocker's situation, with the cream of the "Court Guide" and the dearest furnished apartments, Simpkin's, Ladle's, Thrupp's, just round the corner, was so select that his place was quite pervaded by the crisp rustle of these emblems—she pushed out the sovereigns as if the applicant were no more to her than one of the momentary, the practically featureless, appearances in the great procession; and this perhaps all the more from the very fact of the connection (only recognized outside indeed) to which she had lent herself with ridiculous inconsequence. She recognized the others the less because she had at last so unreservedly, so irredeemably, recognized Mr. Mudge. However that might be, she was a little ashamed of having to admit to herself that Mr. Mudge's removal to a higher sphere—to a more commanding position, that is, though to a much lower neighborhood—would have been described still better as a luxury than as the mere simplification, the corrected awkwardness, that she contented herself with calling it. He had at any rate ceased to be all day long in her eyes, and this left something a little fresh for them to rest on of a Sunday. During the three months of his happy survival at Cocker's after her consent to their engagement she had often asked herself what it was marriage would be able toadd to a familiarity that seemed already to have scraped the platter so clean. Opposite there, behind the counter of which his superior stature, his whiter apron, his more clustering curls and more present, too present, *h's* had been for a couple of years the principal ornament, he had moved to and fro before her as on the small sanded floor of their contracted future. She was conscious now of the improvement of not having to take her present and her future at once. They were about as much as she could manage when taken separate.

She had, none the less, to give her mind steadily to what Mr. Mudge had again written her about, the idea of her applying for a transfer to an office quite similar—she couldn't yet hope for a place in a bigger—under the very roof where he was foreman, so that, dangled before her every minute of the day, he should see her, as he called it, "hourly," and in a part, the far N. W. district, where, with her mother, she would save on their two rooms alone nearly three shillings. It would be far from dazzling to exchange Mayfair for Chalk Farm, and it wore upon her much that he could never drop a subject; still, it didn't wear as things *had* worn, the worries of the early times of their great misery, her own, her mother's and her elder sister's—the last of whom had succumbed to all but absolute want when, as conscious and incredulous ladies, suddenly bereft, betrayed, overwhelmed, they had slipped faster and faster down the steep slope at the bottom of which she alone had rebounded. Her mother had never rebounded any more at the bottom than on the way; had only rumbled and grumbled down and down, making, in respect of caps, topics and "habits," no effort whatever—which simply meant smelling much of the time of whiskey.

Chapter II

It was always rather quiet at Cocker's while the contingent from Ladle's and Thrupp's and all the other great places were at luncheon, or, as the young men used vulgarly to say, while the animals were feeding. She had forty minutes in advance of this to go home for her own dinner; and when she came back and one of the young men took his turn there was often half an hour during which she could pull out a bit of work or a book—a book from the place where she borrowed novels, very greasy, in fine print and all about fine folks, at a ha'penny a day. This sacred pause was one of the numerous ways in which the establishment kept its finger on the pulse of fashion and fell into the rhythm of the larger life. It had something to do, one day, with the particular flare of importance of an arriving customer, a lady whose meals were apparently irregular, yet whom she was destined, she afterwards found, not to forget. The girl was blasée; nothing could belong more, as she perfectly knew, to the intense publicity of her profession; but she had a whimsical mind and wonderful nerves; she was subject, in short, to sudden flickers of antipathy and sympathy, red gleams in the grey, fitful needs to notice and to "care," odd caprices of curiosity. She had a friend who had invented a new career for women—that of being in and out of people's houses to look after the flowers. Mrs. Jordan had a manner of her own of sounding this allusion; "the flowers," on her lips, were, in fantastic places, in happy

第五章 文学与信息通信技术(Literature and ICT)

homes, as usual as the coals or the daily papers. She took charge of them, at any rate, in all the rooms, at so much a month, and people were quickly finding out what it was to make over this strange burden of the pampered to the widow of a clergyman. The widow, on her side, dilating on the initiations thus opened up to her, had been splendid to her young friend, over the way she was made free of the greatest houses—the way, especially when she did the dinner-tables, set out so often for twenty, she felt that a single step more would transform her whole social position. On its being asked of her then if she circulated only in a sort of tropical solitude, with the upper servants for picturesque natives, and on her having to assent to this glance at her limitations, she had found a reply to the girl's invidious question. "You've no imagination, my dear!"—that was because a door more than half open to the higher life couldn't be called anything but a thin partition. Mrs. Jordan's imagination quite did away with the thickness.

Our young lady had not taken up the charge, had dealt with it good-humouredly, just because she knew so well what to think of it. It was at once one of her most cherished complaints and most secret supports that people didn't understand her, and it was accordingly a matter of indifference to her that Mrs. Jordan shouldn't; even though Mrs. Jordan, handed down from their early twilight of gentility and also the victim of reverses, was the only member of her circle in whom she recognised an equal. She was perfectly aware that her imaginative life was the life in which she spent most of her time; and she would have been ready, had it been at all worth while, to contend that, since her outward occupation didn't kill it, it must be strong indeed. Combinations of flowers and greenstuff, forsooth! What she could handle freely, she said to herself, was combinations of men and women. The only weakness in her faculty came from the positive abundance of her contact with the human herd; this was so constant, it had so the effect of cheapening her privilege, that there were long stretches in which inspiration, divination and interest quite dropped. The great thing was the flashes, the quick revivals, absolute accidents all, and neither to be counted on nor to be resisted. Some one had only sometimes to put in a penny for a stamp and the whole thing was upon her. She was so absurdly constructed that these were literally the moments that made up—made up for the long stiffness of sitting there in the stocks, made up for the cunning hostility of Mr. Buckton and the importunate sympathy of the counter-clerk, made up for the daily deadly flourishy letter from Mr.

Mudge, made up even for the most haunting of her worries, the rage at moments of not knowing how her mother did "get it."

She had surrendered herself moreover of late to a certain expansion of her consciousness; something that seemed perhaps vulgarly accounted for by the fact that, as the blast of the season roared louder and the waves of fashion tossed their spray further over the counter, there were more impressions to be gathered and really—for it came to that—more life to be led. Definite at any rate it was that by the time May was well started the kind of company she kept at Cocker's had begun to strike her as a reason—a reason she might almost put forward for a policy of procrastination. It sounded silly, of course, as yet, to plead such a motive, especially as the fascination of the place was after all a sort of torment. But she liked her torment; it was a torment she should miss at Chalk Farm. She was ingenious and uncandid, therefore, about leaving the breadth of London a little longer between herself and that austerity. If she hadn't quite the courage in short to say to Mr. Mudge that her actual chance for a play of mind was worth any week the three shillings he desired to help her to save, she yet saw something happen in the course of the month that in her heart of hearts at least answered the subtle question. This was connected precisely with the appearance of the memorable lady.

Chapter III

She pushed in three bescribbled forms which the girl's hand was quick to appropriate, Mr. Buckton having so frequent a perverse instinct for catching first any eye that promised the sort of entertainment with which she had her peculiar affinity. The amusements of captives are full of a desperate contrivance, and one of our young friend's ha' pennyworths had been the charming tale of *Picciola*. It was of course the law of the place that they were never to take no notice, as Mr. Buckton said, whom they served; but this also never prevented, certainly on the same gentleman's own part, what he was fond of describing as the underhand game. Both her companions, for that matter, made no secret of the number of favourites they had among the ladies; sweet familiarities in spite of which she had repeatedly caught each of them in stupidities and mistakes, confusions of identity and lapses of observation that never failed to remind her how the cleverness of men ends where the cleverness of women begins. "Marguerite, Regent Street. Try on at six. All Spanish lace. Pearls. The full length." That was the first; it had no signature. "Lady Agnes

第五章 文学与信息通信技术(Literature and ICT)

Orme, Hyde Park Place. Impossible to-night, dining Haddon. Opera to-morrow, promised Fritz, but could do play Wednesday. Will try Haddon for Savoy, and anything in the world you like, if you can get Gussy. Sunday Montenero. Sit Mason Monday, Tuesday. Marguerite awful. Cissy." That was the second. The third, the girl noted when she took it, was on a foreign form: "Everard, Hôtel Brighton, Paris. Only understand and believe. 22nd to 26th, and certainly 8th and 9th. Perhaps others. Come. Mary."

Mary was very handsome, the handsomest woman, she felt in a moment, she had ever seen—or perhaps it was only Cissy. Perhaps it was both, for she had seen stranger things than that—ladies wiring to different persons under different names. She had seen all sorts of things and pieced together all sorts of mysteries. There had once been one—not long before—who, without winking, sent off five over five different signatures. Perhaps these represented five different friends who had asked her—all women, just as perhaps now Mary and Cissy, or one or other of them, were wiring by deputy. Sometimes she put in too much—too much of her own sense; sometimes she put in too little; and in either case this often came round to her afterwards, for she had an extraordinary way of keeping clues. When she noticed she noticed; that was what it came to. There were days and days, there were weeks sometimes, of vacancy. This arose often from Mr. Buckton's devilish and successful subterfuges for keeping her at the sounder whenever it looked as if anything might arouse; the sounder, which it was equally his business to mind, being the innermost cell of captivity, a cage within the cage, fenced oft from the rest by a frame of ground glass. The counter-clerk would have played into her hands; but the counter-clerk was really reduced to idiocy by the effect of his passion for her. She flattered herself moreover, nobly, that with the unpleasant conspicuity of this passion she would never have consented to be obliged to him. The most she would ever do would be always to shove off on him whenever she could the registration of letters, a job she happened particularly to loathe. After the long stupors, at all events, there almost always suddenly would come a sharp taste of something; it was in her mouth before she knew it; it was in her mouth now.

To Cissy, to Mary, whichever it was, she found her curiosity going out with a rush, a mute effusion that floated back to her, like a returning tide, the living colour and splendour of the beautiful head, the light of eyes that seemed to reflect such utterly other things than the mean things actually before them; and, above all, the high curt consideration of a manner that even at bad moments was a magnificent habit and of the very essence of the innumerable things—her beauty, her birth, her father and mother, her cousins and all her ancestors—that its possessor couldn't have got rid of even had she wished. How did our obscure little public servant know that for the lady of the telegrams this was a bad moment? How did she guess all sorts of impossible things, such as, almost on the very spot, the presence of drama at a critical stage and the nature of the tie with the gentleman at the Hôtel Brighton? More than ever before it floated to her through the bars of the cage that this at last was the high reality, the bristling truth that she had hitherto only patched up and eked out—one of the creatures, in fine, in whom all the conditions for happiness actually met, and who, in the air they made, bloomed with an unwitting insolence. What came home to the girl was the way the insolence was tempered by something that was equally apart of the distinguished life, the custom of a flowerlike bend to the less fortunate—a dropped fragrance, a mere quick breath, but which in fact pervaded and lingered. The apparition was very young, but certainly married, and our fatigued friend had a sufficient store of mythological comparison to recognise the port of Juno. Marguerite might be "awful," but she knew how to dress a goddess.

Pearls and Spanish lace—she herself, with assurance, could see them, and the "full length" too, and also red velvet bows, which, disposed on the lace in a particular manner (she could have placed them with the turn of a hand) were of course to adorn the front of a black brocade that would be like a dress in a picture. However, neither Marguerite nor Lady Agnes nor Haddon nor Fritz nor Gussy was what the wearer of this garment had really come in for. She had come in for Everard—and that was doubtless not his true name either. If our young lady had never taken such jumps before it was simply that she had never before been so affected. She went all the way. Mary and Cissy had been round together, in their single superb person, to see him—he must live round the corner; they had found that, in consequence of something they had come, precisely, to make up for or to have another scene about, he had gone off—gone off just on purpose to make them feel it; on which they had come together to Cocker's as to the nearest place; where they had put in the three forms partly in order not to put in the one alone. The two others in a manner, covered it, muffled it, passed it off. Oh yes, she went all the way, and this was a specimen of how she often went. She would know the hand again any time. It was as handsome and as everything else as the woman herself. The woman herself had, on learning his flight, pushed past Everard's servant and into his room; she had written her missive at his table and with his pen. All this, every inch of it, came in the waft that she blew through and left behind her, the influence that, as I have said, lingered. And among the things the girl was sure of, happily, was that she should see her again.

Chapter IV

She saw her in fact, and only ten days later; but this time not alone, and that was exactly a part of the luck of it. Not unaware—as how could her observation have left her so? —of the possibilities through which it could range, our young lady had ever since had in her mind a dozen conflicting theories about Everard's type; as to which, the instant they came into the place, she felt the point settled with a thump that seemed somehow addressed straight to her heart. That organ literally beat faster at the approach of the gentleman who was this time with Cissy, and who, as seen from within the cage, became on the spot the happiest of the happy circumstances with which her mind had invested the friend of Fritz and Gussy. He was a very happy circumstance indeed as, with his cigarette in his lips and his broken familiar talk caught by his companion, he put down the half-dozen telegrams it would take them together several minutes to dispatch. And here it occurred, oddly enough, that if, shortly before the girl's interest in his companion had sharpened her sense for the messages then transmitted, her immediate vision of himself had the effect, while she counted his seventy words, of preventing intelligibility. *His* words were mere numbers, they told her nothing whatever; and after he had gone she was in possession of no name, of no address, of no meaning, of nothing but a vague sweet sound and an immense impression. He had been there but five minutes, he had smoked in her face, and, busy with his telegrams, with the tapping pencil and the conscious danger, the odious betrayal that would come from a mistake, she had had no wandering glances nor roundabout arts to spare. Yet she had taken him in; she knew everything; she had made up her mind.

He had come back from Paris; everything was re-arranged; the pair were again shoulder to shoulder in their high encounter with life, their large and complicated game. The fine soundless pulse of this game was in the air for our young woman while they remained in the shop. While they remained? They remained all day; their presence continued and abode with her, was in everything she did till nightfall, in the thousands of other words she counted, she transmitted, in all the stamps she detached and the letters she weighed and the change she gave, equally unconscious and unerring in each of these particulars, and not, as the run on the little office thickened with the afternoon hours, looking up at a single ugly face in the long sequence, nor really hearing the stupid questions that she patiently and perfectly answered. All patience was possible now, all questions were stupid after his, all faces were ugly. She had been sure she should see the lady again; and even now she should perhaps, she should probably, see her often. But for him it was totally different; she should never never see him. She wanted it too much. There was a kind of wanting that helped—she had arrived, with her rich experience, at that generalisation; and there was another kind that was fatal. It was this time the fatal kind; it would prevent.

Well, she saw him the very next day, and on this second occasion it was quite different; the sense of every syllable he paid for was fiercely distinct; she indeed felt her progressive pencil, dabbing as if with a quick caress the marks of his own, put life into every stroke. He was there a long time—had not brought his forms filled out but worked them off in a nook on the counter; and there were other people as well—a changing pushing cluster, with every one to mind at once and endless right change to make and information to produce. But she kept hold of him throughout; she continued, for herself, in a relation with him as close as that in which, behind the hated ground glass, Mr. Buckton luckily continued with the sounder. This morning everything changed, but rather to dreariness; she had to swallow the rebuff to her theory about fatal desires, which she did without confusion and indeed with absolute levity; yet if it was now flagrant that he did live close at hand—at Park Chambers—and belonged supremely to the class that wired everything, even their expensive feelings (so that, as he never wrote, his correspondence cost him weekly pounds and pounds, and he might be in and out five times a day) there was, all the same, involved in the prospect, and by reason of its positive excess of light, a perverse melancholy, a gratuitous misery. This was at once to give it a place in an order of feelings on which I shall presently touch.

Meanwhile, for a month, he was very constant. Cissy, Mary, never re-appeared with him; he was always either alone or accompanied only by some gentleman who was lost in the blaze of his glory. There was another sense, however—and indeed there was more than one—in which she mostly found herself counting in the splendid creature with whom she had originally connected him. He addressed this correspondent neither as Mary nor as Cissy; but the girl was sure of whom it was, in Eaten Square, that he was perpetually wiring to—and all so irreproachably! —as Lady Bradeen. Lady Bradeen was Cissy, Lady Bradeen was Mary, Lady Bradeen was the friend of Fritz and of Gussy, the customer of Marguerite, and the close ally in short (as was ideally right, only the girl had not yet found a descriptive term that was) of the most magnificent of men. Nothing could equal the frequency and variety of his communications to her ladyship but their extraordinary, their abysmal propriety. It was just the talk—so profuse sometimes that she wondered what was left for their real meetings—of the very happiest people. Their real meetings must have been constant, for half of it was appointments and allusions, all swimming in a sea of other allusions still, tangled in a complexity of questions that gave a wondrous image of their life. If Lady Bradeen was Juno it was all certainly Olympian. If the girl, missing the answers, her ladyship's own outpourings, vainly reflected that Cocker's should have been one of the bigger offices where telegrams arrived as well as departed, there were yet ways in which, on the whole, she pressed the romance closer by reason of the very quantity of imagination it demanded and consumed. The days and hours of this new friend, as she came to account him, were at all events unrolled, and however much more she might have known she would still have wished to go beyond. In fact she did go beyond; she went quite far enough.

But she could none the less, even after a month, scarce have told if the gentlemen who came in with him recurred or changed; and this in spite of the fact that they too were always posting and wiring, smoking in her face and signing or not signing. The gentlemen who came in with him were nothing when he was there. They turned up alone at other times—then only perhaps with a dim richness of reference. He himself, absent as well as present, was all. He was very tall, very fair, and had, in spite of his thick preoccupations, a good-humour that was exquisite, particularly as it so often had the effect of keeping him on. He could have reached over anybody, and anybody—no matter who—would have let him; but he was so extraordinarily kind that he quite pathetically waited, never waggling things at her out of his turn nor saying "Here!" with horrid sharpness. He waited for pottering old ladies, for gaping slaveys, for the perpetual Buttonses from Thrupp's; and the thing in all this that she would have liked most unspeakably to put to the test was the possibility of her having for him a personal identity that might in a particular way appeal. There were moments when he actually struck her as on her side, as arranging to help, to support, to spare her.

But such was the singular spirit of our young friend that she could remind herself with a pang that when people had awfully good manners—people of that class,—you couldn't tell. These manners were for everybody, and it might be drearily unavailing for any poor particular body to be overworked and unusual. What he did take for granted was all sorts of facility; and his high pleasantness, his relighting of cigarettes while he waited, his unconscious bestowal of opportunities, of boons, of blessings, were all a part of his splendid security, the instinct that told him there was nothing such an existence as his could ever lose by. He was somehow all at once very bright and very grave, very young and immensely complete; and whatever he was at any moment it was always as much as all the rest the mere bloom of his beatitude. He was sometimes Everard, as he had been at the Hôtel Brighton, and he was sometimes Captain Everard. He was sometimes Philip with his surname and sometimes Philip without it. In some directions he was merely Phil, in others he was merely Captain. There were relations in which he was none of these things, but a quite different person—"the Count." There were several friends for whom he was William. There were several for whom, in allusion perhaps to his complexion, he was "the Pink 'Un'." Once, once only by good luck, he had, coinciding comically, quite miraculously, with another person also near to her, been "Mudge." Yes, whatever he was, it was a part of his happiness—whatever he was and probably whatever he wasn't. And his happiness was a part—it became so little by little—of something that, almost from the first of her being at Cocker's, had been deeply with the girl.

Chapter V

This was neither more nor less than the queer extension of her experience, the double life that, in the cage, she grew at last to lead. As the weeks went on there she lived more and more into the world of whiffs and glimpses, she found her divinations work faster and stretch further. It was a prodigious view as the pressure heightened, a panorama fed with facts and figures, flushed with a torrent of colour and accompanied with wondrous world-music. What it mainly came to at this period was a picture of how London could amuse itself; and that, with the running commentary of a witness so exclusively a witness, turned for the most part to a hardening of the heart. The nose of this observer was brushed by the bouquet, yet she could never really pluck even a daisy. What could still remain fresh in her daily grind was the immense disparity, the difference and contrast, from class to class, of every instant and every motion. There were times when all the wires in the country seemed to start from the little hole-and-corner where she plied for a livelihood, and where, in the shuffle of feet, the flutter of "forms," the straying of stamps and the ring of change over the counter, the people she had fallen into the habit of remembering and fitting together with others, and of having her theories and interpretations of, kept up before her their long procession and rotation. What twisted the knife in her vitals was the way the profligate rich scattered about them, in extravagant chatter over their extravagant pleasures and sins, an amount of money that would have held the stricken household of her frightened childhood, her poor pinched mother and tormented father and lost brother and starved sister, together for a lifetime. During her first weeks she had often gasped at the sums people were willing to pay for the stuff they transmitted—the "much love"s, the "awful" regrets, the compliments and wonderments and vain vague gestures that cost the price of a new pair of boots. She had had a way then of glancing at the people's faces, but she had early learnt that if you became a telegraphist you soon ceased to be astonished. Her eye for types amounted nevertheless to genius, and there were those she liked and those she hated, her feeling for the latter of which grew to a positive possession, an instinct of observation and detection. There were the brazen women, as she called them, of the higher and the lower fashion, whose squanderings and graspings, whose struggles and secrets and love-affairs and lies, she tracked and stored up against them till she had at moments, in private, a triumphant vicious feeling of mastery and ease, a sense of carrying their silly guilty secrets in her pocket, her small retentive brain, and thereby knowing so much more about them than they suspected or would care to think. There were those she would have liked to betray, to trip up, to bring down with words altered and fatal; and all through a personal hostility provoked by the lightest signs, by their accidents of tone and manner, by the particular kind of relation she always happened instantly to feel.

[...]

Chapter XXII

Eighteen days elapsed, and she had begun to think it probable she should never see him again. He too then understood now: he had made out that she had secrets and reasons and impediments, that even a poor girl at the P. O. might have her complications. With the charm she had cast on him lightened by distance he had suffered a final delicacy to speak to him, had made up his mind that it would be only decent to let her alone. Never so much as during these latter days had she felt the precariousness of their relation—the happy beautiful untroubled original one, if it could only have been restored—in which the public servant and the casual public only were concerned. It hung at the best by the merest silken thread, which was at the mercy of any accident and might snap at any minute. She arrived by the end of the fortnight at the highest sense of actual fitness, never doubting that her decision was now complete. She would just give him a few days more to come back to her on a proper impersonal basis—for even to an embarrassing representative of the casual public a public servant with a conscience did owe something—and then would signify to Mr. Mudge that she was ready for the little home. It had been visited, in the further talk she had had with him at Bournemouth, from garret to cellar, and they had especially lingered, with theirrespectively darkened brows, before the niche into which it was to be broached to her mother that she must find means to fit.

He had put it to her more definitely than before that his calculations had allowed for that dingy presence, and he had thereby marked the greatest impression he had ever made on her. It was a stroke superior even again to his handling of the drunken soldier. What she considered that in the face of it she hung on at Cocker's for was something she could only have described as the common fairness of a last word. Her actual last word had been, till it should be superseded, that she wouldn't forsake her other friend, and it stuck to her through thick and thin that she was still at her post and on her honour. This other friend had shown so much beauty of conduct already that he would surely after all just re-appear long enough to relieve her, to give her something she could take away. She saw it, caught it, at times, his parting present; and there were moments when she felt herself sitting like a beggar with a hand held out to almsgiver who only fumbled. She hadn't taken the sovereigns, but shewould take the penny. She heard, in imagination, on the counter, the ring of the copper. "Don't put yourself out any longer," he would say, "for so bad a

第五章 文学与信息通信技术 (Literature and ICT)

case. You've done all there is to be done. I thank and acquit and release you. Our lives take us. I don't know much—though I've really been interested—about yours, but I suppose you've got one. Mine at any rate will take *me*—and where it will. Heigh-ho! Good-bye." And then once more, for the sweetest faintest flower of all: "Only, I say—see here!" She had framed the whole picture with a squareness that included also the image of how again she would decline to "see there," decline, as she might say, to see anywhere, see anything. Yet it befell that just in the fury of this escape she saw more than ever.

He came back one night with a rush, near the moment of their closing, and showed her a face so different and new, so upset and anxious, that almost anything seemed to look out of it but clear recognition. He poked in a telegram very much as if the simple sense of pressure, the distress of extreme haste, had blurred the remembrance of where in particular he was. But as she met his eyes a light came; it broke indeed on the spot into a positive conscious glare. That made up for everything, since it was an instant proclamation of the celebrated "danger"; it seemed to pour things out in a flood. "Oh yes, here it is—it's upon me at last! Forget, for God's sake, my having worried or bored you, and just help me, just *save* me, by getting this off without the loss of a second!" Something grave had clearly occurred, a crisis declared itself. She recognized immediately the person to whom the telegram was addressed—the Miss Dolman of Parade Lodge to whom Lady Bradeen had wired, at Dover, on the last occasion, and whom she had then, with her recollection of previous arrangements, fitted into a particular setting. Miss Dolman had figured before and not figured since, but she was now the subject of an imperative appeal. "Absolutely necessary to see you. Take last train Victoria if you can catch it. If not, earliest morning, and answer me direct either way."

"Reply paid?" said the girl. Mr. Buckton had just departed and the counter-clerk was at the sounder. There was no other representative of the public, and she had never yet, as it seemed to her, not even in the street or in the Park, been so alone with him.

"Oh yes, reply paid, and as sharp as possible, please."

She affixed the stamps in a flash. "She'll catch the train!" she then declared to him breathlessly, as if she could absolutely guarantee it.

"I don't know—I hope so. It's awfully important. So kind of you. Awfully sharp, please." It was wonderfully innocent now, his oblivion of all but his danger. Anything else that had ever passed between them was utterly out of it. Well, she had wanted him to be impersonal!

There was less of the same need therefore, happily, for herself; yet she only took time, before she flew to the sounder, to gasp at him: "You're in trouble?"

"Horrid, horrid—there's a row!" But they parted, on it, in the next breath; and as she dashed at the sounder, almost pushing, in her violence, the counter-clerk off the stool, she caught the bang with which, at Cocker's door, in his further precipitation, he closed the apron of the cab into which he had leaped. As he rebounded to some other precaution suggested by his alarm, his appeal to Miss Dolman flashed straight away.

But she had not, on the morrow, been in the place five minutes before he was with her again, still more discomposed and quite, now, as she said to herself, like a frightened child coming to its mother. Her companions were there, and she felt it to be remarkable how, in the presence of his agitation, his mere scared exposed nature, she suddenly ceased to mind. It came to her as it had never come to her before that with absolute directness and assurance they might carry almost anything off. He had nothing to send—she was sure he had been wiring all over—and yet his business was evidently huge. There was nothing but that in his eyes—not a glimmer of reference or memory. He was almost haggard with anxiety and had clearly not slept a wink. Her pity for him would have given her any courage, and she seemed to know at last why she had been such a fool. "She didn't come?" she panted.

"Oh yes, she came; but there has been some mistake. We want a telegram."

"A telegram?"

"One that was sent from here ever so long ago. There was something in it that has to be recovered. Something very, very important, please—we want it immediately."

He really spoke to her as if she had been some strange young woman at Knightsbridge or Paddington; but it had no other effect on her than to give her the measure of his tremendous flurry. Then it was that, above all, she felt how much she had missed in the gaps and blanks and absent answers—how much she had had to dispense with: it was now black darkness save for this little wild red flare. So much as that she saw, so much her mind dealt with. One of the lovers was quaking somewhere out of town, and the other was quaking just where he stood. This was vivid enough, and after an instant she knew it was all she wanted. She wanted no detail, no fact—she wanted no nearer vision of discovery or shame. "When was your telegram? Do you mean you sent it from here?" She tried to do the young woman at Knightsbridge.

"Oh yes, from here—several weeks ago. Five, six, seven"—he was confused and impatient—"don't you remember?"

"Remember?" she could scarcely keep out of her face, at the word, the strangest of smiles.

But the way he didn't catch what it meant was perhaps even stranger still. "I mean, don't you keep the old ones?"

"For a certain time."

"But how long?"

She thought; she *must* do the young woman, and she knew exactly what the young woman would say and, still more, wouldn't. "Can you give me the date?"

"Oh God, no! It was some time or other in August—toward the end. It was to the same address as the one I gave you last night."

"Oh!" said the girl, knowing at this the deepest thrill she had ever felt. It came to her there, with her eyes on his face, that she held the whole thing in her hand, held it as she held her pencil, which might have broken at that instant in her tightened grip. This made her feel like the very fountain of fate, but the emotion was such a flood that she had to press it back with all her force. That was positively the reason, again, of her flute-like Paddington tone. "You can't give us anything a little nearer?" Her "little" and her "us" came straight from Paddington. These things were no false note for him—his difficulty absorbed them all. The eyes with which he pressed her, and in the depths of which she read terror and rage and literal tears, were just the same he would have shown any other prim person.

"I don't know the date. I only know the thing went from here, and just about the time I speak of. It wasn't delivered, you see. We've got to recover it."

Chapter XXIII

She was as struck with the beauty of his plural pronoun as she had judged he might be with that of her own; but she knew now so well what she was about that she could almost play with him and with her new-born joy. "You say 'about the time you speak of.' But I don't think you speak of an exact time—*do* you?"

He looked splendidly helpless. "That's just what I want to find out. Don't you keep the old ones? —can't you look it up?"

Our young lady—still at Paddington—turned the question over. "It wasn't delivered?"

"Yes, it *was*; yet, at the same time, don't you know? it wasn't." He just hung back, but he brought it out. "I mean it was intercepted, don't you know? and there was something in it." He paused again and, as if to further his quest and woo and supplicate success and recovery, even smiled with an effort at the agreeable that was almost ghastly and that turned the knife in her tenderness. What must be the pain of it all, of the open gulf and the throbbing fever, when this was the mere hot breath? "We want to get what was in it—to know what it was."

"I see—I see." She managed just the accent they had at Paddington when they stared like dead fish. "And you have no clue?"

"Not at all—I've the clue I've just given you."

"Oh the last of August?" If she kept it up long enough she would make him really angry.

"Yes, and the address, as I've said."

"Oh the same as last night?"

He visibly quivered, as with a gleam of hope; but it only poured oil on her quietude, and she was still deliberate. She ranged some papers. "Won't you look?" he went on.

"I remember your coming," she replied.

He blinked with a new uneasiness; it might have begun to come to him, through her difference, that he was somehow different himself. "You were much quicker then, you know!"

"So were you—you must do me that justice," she answered with a smile. "But let me see. Wasn't it Dover?"

"Yes, Miss Dolman—"

"Parade Lodge, Parade Terrace?"

"Exactly—thank you so awfully much!" He began to hope again. "Then you *have* it—the other one?"

She hesitated afresh; she quite dangled him. "It was brought by a lady?"

"Yes; and she put in by mistake something wrong. That's what we've got to get hold of!" Heavens, what was he going to say? —flooding poor Paddington with wild betrayals! She couldn't too much, for her joy, dangle him, yet she couldn't either, for his dignity, warn or control or check him. What she found herself doing was just to treat herself to the middle way. "It was intercepted?"

"It fell into the wrong hands. But there's something in it," he continued to blurt out, "that *may* be all right. That is, if it's wrong, don't you know? It's all right if it's wrong," he remarkably explained.

What *was* he, on earth, going to say? Mr. Buckton and the counter-clerk were already interested; no one would have the decency to come in; and she was divided between her particular terror for him and her general curiosity. Yet she already saw with what brilliancy she could add, to carry the thing off, a little false knowledge to all her real. "I quite understand," she said with benevolent, with almost patronizing quickness. "The lady has forgotten what she did put."

"Forgotten most wretchedly, and it's an immense inconvenience. It has only just been found that it didn't get there; so that if we could immediately have it—"

"Immediately?"

"Every minute counts. You *have*," he pleaded, "surely got them on file?"

"So that you can see it on the spot?"

"Yes, please—this very minute." The counter rang with his knuckles, with the knob of his stick, with his panic of alarm. "Do, *do* hunt it up!" he repeated.

"I dare say we could get it for you," the girl weetly returned.

"Get it?"—he looked aghast. "When?"

"Probably by to-morrow."

"Then it isn't here?"—his face was pitiful.

She caught only the uncovered gleams that peeped out of the blackness, and she wondered what complication, even among the most supposable, the very worst, could be bad enough to account for the degree of his terror. There were twists and turns, there were places where the screw drew blood, that she couldn't guess. She was more and more glad she didn't want to. "It has been sent on."

"But how do you know if you don't look?"

She gave him a smile that was meant to be, in the absolute irony of its propriety, quite divine. "It was August 23rd, and we've nothing later here than August 27th."

Something leaped into his face. "27th – 23rd? Then you're sure? You know?"

She felt she scarce knew what—as if she might soon be pounced upon for some lurid connection with a scandal. It was the queerest of all sensations, for she had heard, she had read, of these things, and the wealth of her intimacy with them at Cocker's might be supposed to have schooled and seasoned her. This particular one that she had really quite lived with was, after all, an old story; yet what it had been before was dim and distant beside the touch under which she now winced. Scandal? —it had never been but a silly word. Now it was a great tense surface, and the surface was somehow Captain Everard's wonderful face. Deep down in his eyes a picture, a scene—a great place like a chamber of justice, where, before a watching crowd, a poor girl, exposed but heroic, swore with a quavering voice to a document, proved an alibi, supplied a link. In this picture she bravely took her place. "It was the 23rd."

"Then can't you get it this morning—or some time to-day?"

She considered, still holding him with her look, which she then turned on her two companions, who were by this time unreservedly enlisted. She didn't care—not a scrap, and she glanced about for a piece of paper. With this she had to recognize the rigor of official thrift—a morsel of blackened blotter was the only loose paper to be seen. "Have you got a card?" she said to her visitor. He was quite away from Paddington now, and the next instant, pocket-book in hand, he had whipped a card out. She gave no glance at the name on it—only turned it to the other side. She continued to hold him, she felt at present, as she had never held him; and her command of her colleagues was for the moment not less marked. She wrote something on the back of the card and pushed it across to him.

He fairly glared at it. "Seven, nine, four—"

"Nine, six, one"—she obligingly completed the number. "Is it right?" she smiled.

He took the whole thing in with a flushed intensity; then there broke out in him a visibility of relief that was simply a tremendous exposure. He shone at them all like a tall lighthouse, embracing even, for sympathy, the blinking young men. "By all the powers—it's wrong!" And without another look, without a word of thanks, without time for anything or anybody, he turned on them the broad back of his great stature, straightened his triumphant shoulders, and strode out of the place.

She was left confronted with her habitual critics. "'If it's wrong it's all right!'" she extravagantly quoted to them.

The counter-clerk was really awe-stricken. "But how did you know, dear?"

"I remembered, love!"

Mr. Buckton, on the contrary, was rude. "And what game is that, miss?"

No happiness she had ever known came within miles of it, and some minutes elapsed before she could recall herself sufficiently to reply that it was none of his business.

思考题

1. What has motivated Henry James to create a novel about the usage of telegraph in late 19th-century?
2. Why did the telegraph girl persist in using letters to communicate with her fiancé while telegraph had tremendously narrowed the distance between places and greatly reduced the time spent on the communication of message?
3. Please use Shannon's communication model with Weaver's proposed changes to explain the function of noise added by the telegraph girl to the communication of secret love between Everard and Lady Bradeen.
4. For what reasons does Everard use lots of numbers in his message sent to his lover Lady Bradeen?
5. In what ways has the use of telegraph affected the telegraph girl's morality? Why should she refuse to transfer to a post-and-telegraph office near the place where her fiancé works?

第三节 补充阅读《终结的意义》

阅读英国当代作家朱利安·巴恩斯(Julian Barnes, 1946—)的小说《终结的意义》(*The Sense of an Ending*, 2011)中的选段,思考电子邮件这一信息通信技术如何影响现代个体的生活。小说主人公托尼(Tony)在退休后的某天突然收到前女友维罗妮卡(Veronica)母亲的律师信函,信中说维罗妮卡母亲去世后给他留下一笔500英镑的遗产以及托尼中学好友艾德里安(Adrian)的日记本。托尼认为,这500英镑似乎是维罗妮卡的母亲替女儿给他的补偿费,然而他却无法理解为何多年前已自杀身亡的艾德里安的日记本会落到维罗妮卡母亲的手上。当然,艾德里安自杀前曾经和维罗妮卡交往过,而这恰恰是在她抛弃托尼之后。托尼对此耿耿于怀,曾在他们公开恋情之后给艾德里安发了一封绝交信,信中诅咒他和维罗妮卡的爱情。当托尼联系律师索要属于自己的遗产时,得知艾德里安的日记本却被前女友维罗妮卡拿走了,尽管他通过律师反复向其索要它,她就是不愿给他。于是,托尼恳请律师征得前女友维罗妮卡的哥哥杰克(Jack)的同意,将杰克的电子邮箱给他,试图让杰克帮助其斡旋。选文就是关于托尼如何在获得杰克的电子邮箱后通过杰克获取了前女友的电子邮箱,以及他如何反复发电子邮件给前女友,试图要回艾德里安的日记本。

The Sense of an Ending

Julian Barnes

Mrs. Marriott was able, two weeks later, to provide me with an email address for Mr. John Ford. Miss Veronica Ford had declined to allow her contact details to be passed on. And Mr. John Ford was clearly being cautious himself: no phone number, no postal address.

I remembered Brother Jack sitting back on a sofa, careless and confident. Veronica had just ruffled my hair and was asking, "He'll do, won't he?" And Jack had winked at me. I hadn't winked back.

I was formal in my email. I offered my condolences. I pretended to happier memories of Chislehurst than was the case. I explained the situation and asked Jack to use what influence he had to persuade his sister to hand over the second "document," which I understood to be the diary of my old schoolfriend Adrian Finn.

About ten days later Brother Jack turned up in my inbox. There was a long preamble about travelling, and semi-retirement, and the humidity of Singapore, and Wi-Fi and cybercafés. And then: "Anyway, enough chit-chat. Regret I am not my sister's keeper—never have been, just between ourselves. Stopped trying to change her mind years ago. And frankly, my putting in a good word for you could easily have the opposite effect. Not that I don't wish you well on this particular sticky wicket. Ah—here comes my rickshaw—must dash. Regards, John Ford."

Why did I feel there was something unconvincing about all this? Why did I immediately picture him sitting quietly at home—in some plush mansion backing on to a golf course in Surrey—laughing at me? His server was aol. com, which didn't tell me anything. I looked at his email's timing, which was plausible for both Singapore and Surrey. Why did I imagine BrotherJack had seen me coming and was having a bit of fun? Perhaps because in this country shadings of class resist time longer than differentials in age. The Fords had been posher than the Websters back then, and they were jolly well going to stay that way. Or was this mere paranoia on my part?

Nothing to be done, of course, but email back politely and ask if he could let me have Veronica's contact details.

...

A week or so passed, and Brother Jack's name was there in my inbox again. "Here's Veronica's email, but don't let on you got it from me. Hell to pay and all that. Remember the 3 wise monkeys—see no evil, hear no evil, speak no evil. That's my motto, anyway. Blue skies, view of Sydney Harbour Bridge, almost. Ah, here comes my rickshaw. Regards, John F."

I was surprised. I'd expected him to be unhelpful. But what did I know of him or his life? Only what I'd extrapolated from memories of a bad weekend long before. I'd always assumed that birth and education had given him an advantage over me that he'd effortlessly maintained until the present day. I remembered Adrian saying that he'd read about Jack in some undergraduate magazine but didn't expect to meet him (but nor had he expected to go out with Veronica). And then he'd added, in a different, harsher tone, "I hate the way the English have of not being serious about being serious." I never knew—because stupidly I never asked—what that had been based on.

They say time finds you out, don't they? Maybe time had found out Brother Jack and punished him for his lack of seriousness. And now I began to elaborate a different life for Veronica's brother, one in which his student years glowed in his memory as filled with happiness and hope—indeed, as the one period when his life had briefly achieved that sense of harmony we all aspire to. I imagined Jack, after graduation, being nepotistically placed into one of those large multinational companies. I imagined him doing well enough to begin with and then, almost imperceptibly, not so well. A clubbable fellow with decent manners, but lacking the edge required in a changing world. Those cheery sign-offs, in letter and conversation, came after a while to appear not sophisticated but inept. And though he wasn't exactly given the push, the suggestion of early retirement combined with occasional bits of ad hoc work was clear enough. He could be a kind of roving honorary consul, a backup for the local man in big cities, a troubleshooter in smaller ones. So he remade his life, and found some plausible way to present himself as a success. "View of Sydney Harbour Bridge, almost." I imagined him taking his laptop to café terraces with Wi-Fi, because frankly that felt less depressing than working from the room of a hotel with fewer stars than he'd been previously used to.

I've no idea if this is how big firms work, but I'd found a way of thinking about Brother Jack which brought no discomfort. I'd even managed to dislodge him from that mansion overlooking the golf course. Not that I would go so far as to feel sorry for him. And—this was the point—not that I owed him anything either.

"Dear Veronica," I began. "Your brother has very kindly given me your email address..."

It strikes me that this may be one of the differences between youth and age: when we are young, we invent different futures for ourselves; when we are old, we invent different pasts for others.

Her father drove a Humber Super Snipe. Cars don't have names like that any more, do they? I drive a Volkswagen Polo. But Humber Super Snipe—those were words that eased off the tongue as smoothly as "the Father, the Son and the Holy Ghost." Humber Super Snipe. Armstrong Siddeley Sapphire. Jowett Javelin. Jensen Interceptor. Even Wolseley Farina and Hillman Minx.

Don't get me wrong. I'm not interested in cars, old or new. I'm vaguely curious why you might name a large saloon after such a small game bird as the snipe, and whether a Minx had a tempestuous female nature. Still, I'm not curious enough to find out. At this stage I prefer not to know.

第五章 文学与信息通信技术（Literature and ICT）

But I've been turning over in my mind the question of nostalgia, and whether I suffer from it. I certainly don't get soggy at the memory of some childhood knickknack; nor do I want to deceive myself sentimentally about something that wasn't even true at the time—love of the old school, and so on. But if nostalgia means the powerful recollection of strong emotions—and a regret that such feelings are no longer present in our lives—then I plead guilty. I'm nostalgic for my early time with Margaret, for Susie's birth and first years, for that road trip with Annie. And if we're talking about strong feelings that will never come again, I suppose it's possible to be nostalgic about remembered pain as well as remembered pleasure. And that opens up the field, doesn't it? It also leads straight to the matter of Miss Veronica Ford.

"Blood money?"

I looked at the words and couldn't make sense of them. She'd erased my message and its heading, not signed her reply, and just answered with a phrase. I had to call up my sent email and read it through again to work out that grammatically her two words could only be a reply to my asking why her mother had left me five hundred pounds. But it didn't make any sense beyond this. No blood had been spilt. My pride had been hurt, that was true. But Veronica was hardly suggesting that her mother was offering money in exchange for the pain her daughter had caused me, was she? Or was she?

At the same time, it made sense that Veronica didn't give me a simple answer, didn't do or say what I hoped or expected. In this she was at least consistent with my memory of her. Of course, at times I'd been tempted to set her down as the woman of mystery, as opposed to the woman of clarity I married in Margaret. True, I hadn't known where I was with her, couldn't read her heart or her mind or her motivation. But an enigma is a puzzle you want to solve. I didn't want to solve Veronica, certainly not at this late date. She'd been a bloody difficult young woman forty years ago, and—on the evidence of this two-word, two-finger response—didn't seem to have mellowed with age. That's what I told myself firmly.

Though why should we expect age to mellow us? If it isn't life's business to reward merit, why should it be life's business to give us warm, comfortable feelings towards its end? What possible evolutionary purpose could nostalgia serve?

I had a friend who trained as a lawyer, then became disenchanted and never practised. He told me that the one benefit of those wasted years was that he no longer feared either the law or lawyers. And something like that happens more generally, doesn't it? The more you learn, the less you fear. "Learn" not in the sense of academic study, but in the practical understanding of life.

Perhaps all I'm really saying is that, having gone out with Veronica all those years ago, I wasn't afraid of her now. And so I began my email campaign. I was determined to be polite, unoffendable, persistent, boring, friendly: in other words, to lie. Of course, it only takes a microsecond to delete an email, but then it doesn't take much longer to replace the one deleted. I would wear her down with niceness, and I would get Adrian's diary. There was no "undoused firein my breast"—I had assured Margaret of this. And as for her more general advice, let's say that one advantage of being an ex-husband is that you no longer need to justify your behaviour. Or follow suggestions.

I could tell Veronica was perplexed by my approach. Sometimes she answered briefly and crossly, often not at all. Nor would she have been flattered to know the precedent for my plan. Towards the end of my marriage, the solid suburban villa Margaret and I lived in suffered a little subsidence. Cracks appeared here and there, bits of the porch and front wall began to crumble. (And no, I didn't think of it as symbolic.) The insurance company ignored the fact that it had been a famously dry summer, and decided to blame the lime tree in our front garden. It wasn't an especially beautiful tree, nor was I fond of it, for various reasons: it screened out light from the front room, dropped sticky stuff on the pavement, and overhung the street in a way that encouraged pigeons to perch there and crap on the cars parked beneath. Our car, especially.

My objection to cutting it down was based on principle: not the principle of maintaining the country's stock of trees, but the principle of not kowtowing to unseen bureaucrats, baby-faced arborists, and current faddy theories of blame adduced by insurance companies. Also, Margaret quite liked the tree. So I prepared a long defensive campaign. I queried the arborist's conclusions and requested the digging of extra inspection pits to confirm or disprove the presence of rootlets close to the house's foundations; I argued over weather patterns, the great London clay belt, the imposition of a region-wide hosepipe ban, and so on. I was rigidly polite; I aped my opponents' bureaucratic language; I annoyingly attached copies of previous correspondence to each new letter; I invited further site inspections and suggested extra use for their manpower. With each letter, I managed to come up with another query they would have to spend their time considering; if they failed to answer it, my next letter, instead of repeating the query, would refer them to the third or fourth paragraph of my communication of the 17th inst, so that they would have to look up their ever-fattening file. I was careful not to come across as a loony, but rather as a pedantic, unignorable bore. I liked to imagine the moaning and groaning as yet another of my letters arrived; and I knew that at a certain point it would make bean-counting sense for them to just close the case. Eventually, exasperatedly, they proposed a thirty per cent reduction in the lime tree's canopy, a solution I accepted with deep expressions of regret and much inner exhilaration.

Veronica, as I'd anticipated, didn't enjoy being treated like an insurance company. I'll spare you the tedium of our exchanges and cut to its first practical consequence. I received a letter from Mrs. Marriott enclosing what she described as "a fragment of the disputed document." She expressed the hope that the next months might bring a full restitution of my legacy. I thought this showed a lot of optimism.

第六章

文学与人工智能/生命（Literature and AI/AL）

第一节 人工智能与人工生命的文学表征

■ 背景知识

人工智能（artificial intelligence，AI），亦称机器智能、机器智慧，是科学与工程方面最新的研究领域。通常，它是指通过计算机程序来研究、开发用于模拟、延伸和拓展人类智能的理论、方法、技术以及应用系统的新技术。1995 年，约翰·麦卡锡（John McCarthy，1927—2011）将其定义为"制造智能机器的科学与工程"。安德烈亚斯·卡普兰（Andreas Kaplan）和迈克尔·海恩莱因（Michael Haenlein）则将之定义为"系统正确地解释并学习外部数据，利用获取的知识，通过灵活适应来实现特定的目标和任务的能力"。当前，主流教材将其定义为"智能主体"，即任何观察周围环境并采取行动以最大化成功实现特定目的的系统[1]。

作为一门学科，人工智能的确立以 1956 年麦卡锡·明斯基（Marvin Minsky，1927—2016）、香农等科学家在达特茅斯大学召开的会议为标志。在此次大会上，"人工智能"这一概念首次被提出。从 20 世纪 50 年代至今，人工智能研究大致经历了三个发展阶段。第一阶段（20 世纪 50—80 年代），人工智能刚诞生，基于抽象数学推理的可编程数字计算机已经出现，符号主义（symbolism）快速发展，但由于很多事物不能形式化表达，建立的模型存在一定局限性。此外，随着计算任务的复杂性不断加大，人工智能发展一度遇到瓶颈。第二阶段（20 世纪 80—90 年代末），专家系统得到快速发展，数学模型有重大突破，但由于专家系统在知识获取、推理能力等方面的不足，以及开发成本高等原因，人工智能的发展又一次进入低谷期。第三阶段（21 世纪初至今），随着大数据的积聚、理论算法的革新、计算能力的提升，人工智能在很多应用领域取得了突破性进展，迎来了又一个繁荣时期[2]。

人工智能以图灵（Alan Turing）的理论假设和测试方法为基础，涵盖了计算机科学、信息工程、数学、心理学、神经生理学、仿生学、语言学、哲学等多个领域，其主要研究问题包括推

---

[1] Artificial intelligence [Z/OL]. [2020-08-27]. https://en.wikipedia.org/w/index.php?title=Artificial_intelligence&oldid=975177933.
[2] 全国信息安全标准化技术委员会. 人工智能标准化白皮书[S]. 北京：中国电子技术标准化研究院，2018.

第六章　文学与人工智能/生命（Literature and AI/AL）

理、知识表示、规划、学习、自然语言处理、知觉、移动和控制物体等方面。而人工智能的核心则是计算机科学技术，其目的就是来验证图灵的假设，用机器来复制或模拟人类智能。图灵认为，"如果一台机器能够像人类那样做出智能反应，那么它就像人类那样有智慧"①。1956年的达特茅斯会议则指出，人类学习的每一个方面或智力的任何特征都能被精确地描述，这样，机器就可以来模拟它②。可以看出，人工智能的基本构成要素包括思维、行为和理性三个方面，它们相互作用组成"像人一样思考"、"像人一样行为"、"理性地思考"和"理性地行为"四个层面。与此对应的是人工智能研究的四个途径，它们分别是"像人一样思考：认知模型方法"、"像人一样行为：图灵测试法"、"理性地思考：'思维法则'方法"和"理性地行为：理性主体方法"③。

人工生命（artificial life，AL or ALife），指通过计算机模型、机器人技术和生物化学等方法来模拟具有自然生命系统特征的人造系统，研究生命系统的基本领域、生命系统的变化过程及其进化，它是人工智能产生的概念。虽然人工生命研究领域与人工智能研究领域有重叠部分，但它们的初衷和演变历史却截然不同。人工智能主要研究是否能够以及如何实现智能模拟，在计算机诞生初期就开始兴起。人工生命研究以澄清自然行为的本质为目的，其研究者们一直孤军作战，直至20世纪80年代末第一届人工生命大会的召开，他们才合力共探如何模拟人工生命系统。

人工生命的历史可追溯至20世纪40—50年代冯·诺依曼（John von Neumann，1903—1957）的细胞自动机。他撇开生物学结构，试图用数学和逻辑方法来揭示生命的本质，并将自我繁衍的特征应用于人造系统。诺依曼认为，无论是自然生命系统，还是人工生命系统，都应该具有两个功能：其一是算法，相当于计算机的程序，它能够在繁衍下一代过程中运行；其二是描述，相当于被加工的数据，它能够复制和传到下一代。以此为基础，他提出了细胞自动机的假设，并证明确实存在自我繁殖的细胞自动机。这表明，若将自我繁衍看成生命独有的功能，机器也能做到这点。同时，人工智能之父图灵于1952年发表论文，提出了一些关于人工生命萌芽的思想。受限于当时计算机的计算能力，诺依曼和图灵关于人工生命的研究并未引起足够重视。1970年，康韦（John Conway，1937—2020）编写了"生命游戏"（The Game of Life）程序，提出了一些细胞自动机无法预测的复杂模式，如延伸、变形和停止等，这吸引了大批学者，其中包括托弗·兰顿（Christophe Langton，1949—）④。1987年，兰顿以

---

① Turing test [Z/OL]. [2023-07-03]. https://en.wikipedia.org/wiki/Turing_test. 另参见 TURING A. Computing machinery and intelligence[J]. Mind, 1950(263): 433-460.

② NEAPOLITAN R E, JIANG X. Artificial intelligence: with an introduction to machine learning[M]. 2nd ed. Boca Raton: CRC Press, 2018: 2.

③ RUSSELL S J, NORVIG P. Artificial intelligence: a modern approach[M]. 3rd ed. London: Pearson, 2016: 1-4.

④ Conway's game of life [Z/OL]. [2023-07-12]. https://en.wikipedia.org/wiki/Conway%27s_Game_of_Life. 另参见 IZHIKEVICH E M. Game of life[J]. Scholarpedia, 2015(6): 1816.

"生成以及模拟生命系统"为主题,在洛斯阿拉莫斯组织召开了第一届人工生命国际大会,自此人工生命作为一门新的学科正式成立。兰顿认为,如果人造系统具有繁衍、进化、生存、死亡等生命特征,那么,它也应该被看作一种生命形式,而不是将目光囿于已知的生命形式①。根据其研究方法及手段,人工生命可以分为基于硬件的强人工生命(hard AL)、基于软件的软人工生命(soft AL)和基于化学生物学的弱人工生命(wet AL)三种类型②。

研究并制造模仿人类智能的机器引起了学界关于人类大脑的哲学争论,以及创造具有人类一样智慧的"人工存在或生命"(Artificial Being/Life)相关伦理问题。神话、小说和哲学自古以来就讨论过这些问题。另外,具有思维能力的人工存在或人工生命古已有之。作为叙事技巧,它们广泛存在于虚构作品中,比如玛丽·雪莱的《弗兰肯斯坦》或者卡勒尔·卡佩克(Karel Capek, 1890—1938)的《罗瑟姆万能机器人》(Rossum's Universal Robots, 1920)。正如约翰·斯通(John Johnston)指出的那样,早在人工智能和人工生命出现之前,富有想象力的作家就已经开始关注人工生命,毕竟历来生命被认为是智慧存在的先决条件。随着18世纪末及19世纪初生物学的出现及发展,生命成为科学研究的对象,这就使得虚构作品开始关注人工生命。除了《弗兰肯斯坦》和《罗瑟姆万能机器人》,关注人工生命的经典作品还包括威尔斯的《莫洛博士岛》、赫胥黎的《美丽新世界》、迪克(Philip K. Dick, 1928—1982)的《模拟造人》(We Can Build You, 1972)等。这些生命及其命运提出了当今人工智能领域一些广为讨论的热点问题,比如人工生命的伦理问题、人工生命对人类存在的威胁等③。

人工智能正式成为文学作品探讨的对象则是在计算机诞生后,这恰与人工智能和人工生命这两门学科出现的先后时间顺序相反。然而,使人工生命和人工智能成为虚构作品重要主题的背景因素,不仅包括计算机技术,而且包括控制论、信息理论和现代基因技术(特别是关于基因作用的发现)等学科给生物学和生命科学带来的巨大变革。随着计算机技术的快速发展,越来越多虚构作品以人工智能为素材,探讨焦虑或问题类主题,这在流行体裁科幻小说和电影方面更是如此。尽管人工生命和人工智能可以视作两门不同的科学,作家们并没有将它们视作两个不同的话题。相反,它们经常有趣地交织在一起。比如:特勒(Astro Teller, 1970—)的小说《训诂》(Exegesis, 1997)、克里奇顿(Michael Crichton, 1942—2008)的《猎物》(Prey, 2002)以及麦克尤恩(Ian McEwan, 1948—)的《像我一样的机器》(Machines Like Me, 2019)。

---

① ROZENBERG G, BACK T, KOK J N. Handbook of natural computing[M]. vol. 4. Berlin: Springer, 2012: 1806-1822.

② Artificial life[Z/OL]. [2023-06-06]. https://en.wikipedia.org/wiki/Artificial_life.

③ MAMBROL N. Artificial intelligence and artificial life[Z/OL]. (2018-07-29). https://literariness.org/2018/07/29/artificial-intelligence-and-artificial-life/. 另参见 CLARKE B, ROSSINI M. The Routledge companion to literature and science[M]. London: Routledge, 2011: 4-16.

第六章 文学与人工智能/生命（Literature and AI/AL）

文献传真

阅读《人工智能与人工生命》（"AI and ALife"），思考文末问答题。本文节选自《劳特利奇指南：文学与科学》①。

AI and ALife

John Johnston

I

What is life, and what makes human life unique? With the rise of the life sciences and Darwin's theory of evolution by natural selection in the nineteenth century, new answers to these questions were proposed that were deeply at odds with traditional understandings and beliefs. With the advent in the twentieth century of new, life-altering technologies like genetic engineering, and life-simulating sciences like Artificial Life (ALife), these questions became even more insistent. Moreover, after World War II, efforts to build fast, intelligent machines and the subsequent development of the computer made the assumption of human intellectual superiority seem uncertain and sure to be challenged, especially since the new science of Artificial Intelligence seemed to lead inexorably to the construction of superhuman machine intelligence. Indeed, both ALife and Artificial Intelligence (AI) dramatically encouraged the thought that the opposition between the natural and the artificial, the born and the made—an opposition dating back to that of *physis* versus *techne*—in ancient Greek culture—was no longer so hard and fast, and certainly not inevitable. Yet this philosophical conundrum was hardly the central issue or worry. Rather, it was the nagging possibility that henceforth the evolutionary dynamic might begin to act on a biosphere soon active with non-natural life forms and that its crowning achievement—namely humanity itself—might eventually be displaced and superseded by its own technical invention. In short, many feared that the future would be determined by some cyborgian, post-biological form of the posthuman, or that the human species might be eclipsed altogether as evolution's torch of life and intelligence passed to its artificial progeny.

It was inevitable, therefore, that the possibilities of both ALife and AI would begin to

---

① JOHNSTON J. AI and ALife[C]//CLARKE B, ROSSINI M. The Routledge companion to literature and science. London: Routledge, 2011: 4-7.

be explored, variously and even idiosyncratically, by literary writers. Here, "ALife" will simply refer to new and non-natural forms of life brought into existence through external and technical means at least initially under human control; similarly, "AI" will refer to some kind of human-constructed machine intelligence (usually an advanced computer) capable of performing actions of such complexity that they require a level of intelligence comparable to that of humans.① As we might expect—given that life has always been assumed to be a precondition for intelligence—ALife was of interest to imaginative writers long before AI.

Specifically, ALife became possible as a fictional interest with the beginnings of the properly scientific study of life, that is, with the emergence of biology in the late eighteenth and early nineteenth centuries, whereas AI, with rare exceptions, became a serious fictional interest only after the birth of the computer.② Interestingly, the official births of the professional scientific disciplines devoted to ALife and AI—in 1987 and 1956, respectively—reverse this chronological order. However, in regard to ALife and AI as fictional themes, the most important background influence was not only the computer but also the immense transformation of biology and the life sciences by cybernetics, information theory, and modern genetics (specifically, the discovery in 1953 of how DNA functions). For many readers, in fact, the contemporary emergence of these themes in fiction will be associated with the historical amalgamation of technics and science in what has become known as technoscience and its more recent condensation, cyborg science.③

No doubt the first modern narrative about ALife is Mary Shelley's novel *Frankenstein*. It was followed by a number of well-known literary classics that, from the contemporary perspective that now post-dates the official inauguration of the new science of ALife, could well be said to be concerned with ALife avant la lettre. Specific examples would include H. G. Wells's *The Island of Dr. Moreau*, Karel Capek's *R. U. R.*, Aldous Huxley's *Brave*

---

① For further discussion of these two new sciences, see: JOHNSTON J. The allure of machinic life: cybernetics, artificial life, and the new AI[M]. Cambridge: MIT Press, 2008.

② Edgar Allen Poe's 1836 essay about "The Turk," a fake mechanical chess player that was exhibited in Europe and the U. S., may well be the first time a literary writer has expressed interest in AI.

③ For technoscience, see: HOTTOIS G. Le signe et la technique. La philsophie a l'epreuve de la technique[M]. Paris: Aubier, 1984. LATOUR B. Laboratory life: the construction of scientific facts[M]. Princeton: Princeton, 1985. For cyborg science, see: HARAWAY D J. Simians, cyborgs and women[M]. New York: Routledge, 1991. MIROWSKI P. Machine dreams: economics become a cyborg science[M]. Cambridge: Cambridge University Press, 2002.

第六章 文学与人工智能/生命(Literature and AI/AL)

New World, and Philip K. Dick's *We Can Build You*. However, with the accelerated development of computer technology, machine intelligence as a source of worry or "problem" theme becomes more prominent, particularly in the rapidly growing new popular genres of science fiction and film. Nevertheless, although ALife and AI can be clearly distinguished as two new sciences of the artificial, they do not always operate as distinctly different fictional interests, but are often intricately related in a number of interesting ways. For example, in Astro Teller's novel *Exegesis* (1997) a computer program—specifically, a data miner called "Edgar"—unaccountably becomes "smart"; in the special terms of AI, he or "it" is smart enough to pass the Turing test. However, the protagonist Alice, the human with whom Edgar regularly communicates, openly doubts that he is in any real or biological sense "alive." ① Conversely, Michael Crichton's novel *Prey* (2002) combines both ALife and AI: the nano-swarms engineered by the company Xymos Technology, while clearly of unnatural origin, seem "alive" by any standard biological definition—they require food, reproduce, and evolve—and thus are a form of ALife. But they are not especially intelligent. In fact, their intelligence is based exclusively on a few algorithms that model simple predatory and learning behaviors. Thus the swarms never display anything approaching human intelligence and remain a very limited form of AI. ②

In what follows I examine in more detail the specific ways in which ALife and AI are related, intermixed, or remain separate, albeit sometimes only implicitly, in a range of examples from contemporary fiction. But before doing so I want to consider *Frankenstein* as a first rough template for what I shall call ALife fiction's characteristic "thematic"—in what sense can it be said that this non-natural form or entity is "alive"? —as well as its accompanying and necessary "problematic"—does this life-form participate in or have anything to do with a life cycle? Does it grow, learn, die, and, most importantly, reproduce? Within this framework, we shall then consider what happens with the entrance

---

① Significantly, Edgar later self-terminates, repeating a pattern evident in Richard Powers's earlier AI novel, *Galatea 2.2* (1995), in which "Helen," an intelligent neural net machine, self-terminates after she learns that she is not fully "alive."

② However, to enhance the plot's drama, Crichton has the swarm enter into a "symbiotic" relationship with both the narrator's wife and her co-worker. Since Crichton draws extensively on ALife and AI science, even including a lengthy bibliography, this produces a weakening or at least an anomalous effect, since there is no credible explanation for how this could have happened, in contrast to the production of the swarms themselves and their rapid evolution.

of AI into fiction, and how these relations are variously re-articulated, specifically in relation to the body and the question of death.

II

First published in 1818, Mary Shelley's *Frankenstein* is usually read as a novel about a scientist's continuing refusal to assume responsibility for his Promethean creation. Shelley's narrative also manifests two thematic interests that will become central not only to the official new science of ALife, but also to a significant body of contemporary fiction that bears the latter's stamp or ethos even when there is no evidence of direct influence. This first interest is not simply in the creation—or re-creation—of a life form, but also in the definition of life and how it is to be distinguished from non-life or inert matter. In Shelley's novel this interest is inscribed in the "spark" that reanimates and thus brings to a living, self-aware state the assemblage of human bones, tissue, and organs that Victor Frankenstein has brought together on what is probably the first entrance of the dissecting table into fictional discourse; but it is also evident in the network of subtle references to the scientific debate between vitalism and materialism that had raged in London from 1814 to 1819 (much of it publicly staged) and in which Percy Shelley's (and Byron's) personal physician, William Lawrence, had participated.①

The second interest is reproduction and the attendant possibility of evolution, which enter the plot of Shelley's novel at a later turning point. This occurs when Frankenstein promises the Monster—as he comes to refer to the Creature on whom he believes he has bestowed life—that he will fabricate for him a female partner if the Monster will cease hounding him and depart for South America with his new mate. Frankenstein, however, reneges on his side of the bargain. That Frankenstein will not repeat the act of creation both intensifies and leaves open to interpretation exactly how that act should be understood: as a human mimicking of divine creation or—in what amounts to a very different understanding of both human and vital agency—a setting up of the specific material conditions necessary for life's emergence.

Throughout *Frankenstein* we are often made aware of the Creature's frightful body and unbearable physical presence. The Creature is alive, but will always remain outside the

---

① On this aspect of the novel, see: BUTLER M. Frankenstein and radical science[C]//SHELLEY M. Frankenstein: the Norton critical edition. New York: Norton, 1996: 302-313.

life cycle. Contrarily, there is never any question of the Creature's intelligence. Similarly, in Capek's play *R. U. R.* the intelligence of the robots is not at all an issue; it is, rather, the fact that they cannot and do not know how to reproduce. This is the secret that their human makers withhold from them. Thus in both *Frankenstein* and *R. U. R.*, intelligence follows "naturally" from the fact of having a body, a living body, even if it originates in wholly artificial conditions. And here we can observe an absolute continuity with Huxley's genetically and chemically engineered humans in *Brave New World*: in both play and novels, levels of intelligence stem merely from different chemical gradients. However, all of this will change dramatically with the birth of the electronic or digital computer. Whereas the very concept of life requires a body, henceforth intelligence will seem to require only a computer or computational apparatus, which is usually made of inert matter. For the first time in human history, intelligence is divorced from life, thus making it possible to be intelligent but not alive.

思考题

1. What fears has the development of AI and ALife brought to human beings?
2. What factors have prompted Mary Shelley to create the first modern narrative about ALife?
3. What significances does Mary Shelley's *Frankenstein* have for Johnston's discussion of AI and ALife?
4. What's the relationship between AI and ALife?

第二节 《弗兰肯斯坦》与人工生命

作品导读

1. 作者简介

《弗兰肯斯坦:现代普罗米修斯》(*Frankenstein; or, The Modern Prometheus*, 1818)简称《弗兰肯斯坦》,是英国浪漫主义女作家玛丽·雪莱的作品。玛丽·雪莱原名玛丽·沃尔斯通克拉福特·葛德文(Mary Wollstonecraft Godwin),母亲玛丽·沃尔斯通克拉福特(Mary Wollstonecraft, 1759—1797)是著名的女权主义者,《女权辩护》(*A Vindication of the Rights of*

Woman,1792)的作者,父亲威廉·葛德文(William Godwin,1756—1836)是自由思想家和小说家,《政治正义论》(Political Justice,1793)的作者。玛丽出生后不久,母亲因产后发热去世。玛丽对此十分自责,在其父亲再婚后,与继母关系十分紧张,在情感上也与父亲日渐疏远。由于继母不允许她上学,玛丽在家里接受教育,博览群书,包括其父母的著作。在16岁时,玛丽与浪漫主义诗人珀西·雪莱(Percy Bysshe Shelley,1792—1822)正式相识。不顾雪莱已婚的事实,玛丽与其相恋,并于1814年私奔到欧洲游历6周。直至1816年雪莱妻子自杀后,他们才正式结婚。1814—1823年,玛丽经历了各种人生变故。她前后共生了四个孩子,其中三个夭折;她多次流产,差点因此丧命。更不幸的是,丈夫雪莱在一次远航中溺水身亡。此后,玛丽回到英国,依靠写作和雪莱父亲微薄的资助维持生计,直至1851年逝世于伦敦家中。

玛丽·雪莱一生共著有《弗兰肯斯坦》、《玛蒂尔达》(Mathilda,1959)、《最后的人》(The Last Man,1826)、《珀沃贝克的财富》(The Fortunes of Perkin Warbeck,1830)、《洛朵》(Lodore,1835)、《福克纳》(Falkner,1837)等12部小说,游记《六周旅行史》(History of a Six Weeks' Tour,1817)和《德国、意大利游记:1840、1842和1843年》(Rambles in Germany and Italy,in 1840,1842,and 1843,1844)两卷,儿童诗剧《冥后》(Proserpine,1832)和《迈达斯》(Midas,1922)两部,短篇小说集一部。除此之外,她还编辑出版了雪莱诗歌集,撰写了多个人物的传记。在这些作品中,最具影响力的当推《弗兰肯斯坦》和《最后的人》这两部被当前学界称为科幻小说鼻祖的哥特式作品,而她本人也因此被誉为科幻小说之母[1]。

然而,玛丽·雪莱生前影响有限,原因如下:一方面,她一生笼罩在父母以及其丈夫的光环下,其作品没有引起学界足够的关注。另一方面,其作品因为关注女性的权利,探讨人造生命,展望未来人类命运,其思想性和人文性远远走在时代前列,甚至在一定程度上与她身处的维多利亚社会的保守主义价值观背道而驰,因而备受争议。加上雪莱父亲为了保护家族名声,禁止她在雪莱去世后编辑出版任何与之相关的东西,其所有小说,包括《弗兰肯斯坦》和《最后的人》,最初都匿名出版,且在出版前费尽周折。正是由于这几方面的原因,玛丽·雪莱的创作成就生前没有得到公认。相反,由于她早年与雪莱私奔,并在同父异母的姐姐以及雪莱前妻自杀后不久,不顾众人反对,与雪莱结婚并游历欧洲,因而在当时文学圈内臭名昭著。毕竟,她不仅是一位作家,而且是一名女性,其举止为维多利亚社会不齿[2]。直至20世纪70年代,随着女性主义文学批评理论的兴起,学界才重新发现玛丽·雪莱的作品,研

---

[1] FREEMAN C. Hail Mary: on the author of *Frankenstein* and the origins of science fiction[J]. Science fiction studies,2002:29:253-264.

[2] SAMPSON F. Frankenstein at 200: why hasn't Mary Shelley been given the respect she deserves?[Z/OL].(2018-01-13).[2023-05-16]. https://www.theguardian.com/books/2018/jan/13/frankenstein-at-200-why-hasnt-mary-shelley-been-given-the-respect-she-deserves-.

第六章 文学与人工智能/生命（Literature and AI/AL）

究其女性作家的身份，探讨其作品所关注的女性社会问题，如家庭、教育、婚姻和生育。特别是《弗兰肯斯坦》和《最后的人》中探讨的非自然生育，即人工生命问题。在一些批评家看来，玛丽·雪莱不仅关注女性的命运，更关注自然科学快速发展背景下的人类命运，思考科学技术的进步对人性和人类存在带来的挑战。鉴于这个原因，本章将节选《弗兰肯斯坦》部分内容，讨论小说如何表现人工生命相关的社会问题，进而思考文学在解决此类问题、建构和传承人文价值方面的作用。

2. 作品介绍

《弗兰肯斯坦》主要讲述了被学界誉为"科学怪人"的维多克·弗兰肯斯坦（Victor Frankenstein）通过实验创造有生命的怪物以及该怪物带给他的悲剧。在小说中，维多克的悲剧主要以框架故事（frame story）的形式，嵌入航海冒险家沃尔顿（Robert Walton）船长与其姐姐玛格丽特（Margaret Walton Saville）的通信中。沃尔顿是名落魄的作家，试图通过到北极探险来丰富自己的科学知识、提高自己的名声。在航海过程中，沃尔顿及其手下发现一个由一名巨人驱赶的狗拉雪橇飞驰而过，不久后便救下一直拼命追赶巨人的维多克，此时他几乎奄奄一息。在船员的照顾下，他渐渐恢复体力。在他看来，沃尔顿似乎与他一样，对科学十分执着，而这恰恰造成了他自己的苦难。为了告诫沃尔顿，他讲述了自己的遭遇。此前，小说叙事都是以沃尔顿的书信展现出来。

维多克的叙事从其童年展开。他来自日内瓦的一个富裕家庭，堂妹伊丽莎白（Elizabeth）自母亲去世后就与他们生活在一起。维多克自幼就对科学理论感兴趣，父母也一直鼓励他及弟弟厄尼斯特（Ernest）和威廉姆（William）通过化学来了解世界。就在他准备前往德国上大学时，伊丽莎白不幸染上猩红热。更不幸的是，母亲卡洛琳（Caroline）在照顾伊丽莎白时染病去世。他备受打击，心性大变，决定在大学期间探索生命的奥秘，特别是如何结合化学、解剖学和炼丹术来恢复死者的生命或创造新生命。通过多年的努力，他终于成功了。他将解剖实验室剩余下来的尸块拼凑成人体形状，最后利用电击使其获得生命。但是，由于未掌握如何复制人体细节部分的技术，所创造出来的生命不仅庞大，而且相貌令人厌恶。在巨怪醒来前，维多克逃离了实验室。当他游走在大街上时，他惊恐的神情吓到了意外相遇的好友亨利·克勒瓦尔（Henry Clerval）。当他们回到其住所时，怪物消失了，随后他大病一场。经过亨利的精心照料，维多克逐渐恢复健康。然而噩耗传来，弟弟威廉姆被谋杀了。他赶回日内瓦，发现真凶不是威廉姆的保姆贾斯汀（Justine Moritz），而是他创造出来的怪物。然而，他无法阻止贾斯汀被处绞刑的厄运，因为他知道没有人会相信他的故事。维多克感到无比的悲伤、内疚，独自躲进山里。同时，怪物找到了他，恳请他听听它的故事。

小说由此转向怪物的自述。他的丑陋相貌让人极其害怕，于是，他白天四处藏匿，夜间外出寻找食物。当他躲在一个废弃的房间过冬时，他通过偷听失明的房主及其一对儿女间的日常对话学会了说话。另外,他靠捡来的《失乐园》(*Paradise Lost*, 1667)、《少年维特的烦恼》(*Sorrows of Werther*, 1774)等书籍,学会了识字和阅读,认识到自己的孤独。当他发现是贫穷以及卑微的社会地位造成这家人神情忧郁、生活艰苦,他非常同情他们,决定不再偷他们的食物和柴火。并且,他夜里出去帮他们捡木材、修葺篱笆,希望能够感化他们。趁盲人房主的儿女外出后,他走出来与房主相认。或许,因为什么都看不见,房主对他比较友善。然而,当房主的儿女回来见到其容貌后,他们十分惊恐,把他赶走了。意识到人类永远"无法将其纳入人类的道德共同体",怪物开始将人类视作敌人①。无法压抑内心的绝望、孤独和愤怒,怪物找到了维多克的家人,谋杀了他的弟弟威廉姆,并嫁祸于保姆贾斯汀。随后,怪物找到山里,逼迫维多克给他创造一个女性伴侣,这样,他就会与她去遥远的美国生活,否则,他会逐一杀死维多克剩下的朋友和家人。

此后,小说作者将叙事再次交给维多克。为了满足怪物的要求,他独自乘船到苏格兰的一个海岛上做实验。由于担心造出来的女性生命会与怪物一样邪恶,他们的后代甚至会危及全人类,维多克毁坏了自己的实验对象,这让一直跟踪他的怪物暴跳如雷。当怪物威胁说会出现在他的新婚之夜时,维多克误以为其报仇对象是自己而不是家人,便不再担心。不料,灾难接踵而来。在出海处置实验仪器时,暴风将他乘坐的船吹至爱尔兰海岸。而此时,怪物谋杀了身在爱尔兰的亨利,并设计陷害维多克。因此,维多克一上岸就被投入监狱。在家人、朋友的帮助下,维多克洗脱罪名,并回到日内瓦,准备和堂妹伊丽莎白结婚。由于一直以为怪物想谋杀自己,维多克未对伊丽莎白做出一些保护措施,而这便给了怪物谋杀她的机会。当维多克意识到伊丽莎白身处险境时,为时已晚。怪物勒死了伊丽莎白,并有意嘲弄维多克。难以接受伊丽莎白死亡的现实,维多克的父亲在几天后便因过度伤心去世了。为了报仇,维多克到处追寻怪物,直到最后在北极被沃尔顿船长及其水手救起。

小说最后回到沃尔顿与姐姐的通信这一外在叙事框架。遇见怪物后没几天,沃尔顿的探险船陷入冰块的包围,一些船员被冻死。在突围后,沃尔顿为了船员的安危,开始返航回英国。而维多克却想独自去追赶怪物,由于他太过虚弱,不久便去世了。弥留之际,他告诫沃尔顿不要野心过大,相反,应该追求平静生活中的快乐。随后,怪物出现在船上,他十分伤心,因为维多克的死未能够给他带来任何心安。他发誓,再也不会给人类带来任何祸害,因为他要自我了断,不想让人知道他曾经存在过。然后,他彻底消失了。小说至此结束,留给读者的则是无限的思考,其中包括科学发展带给人类的危害、生命的本质及其繁衍方式、人工生命相关的伦理问题、人工生命的权利等。即便在200多年后的今天,小说中维多克复活由多具尸体碎片拼凑起来的人体的故事依然骇人听闻和让人着迷。

---

① JOHNSTON J. Traumatic responsibility: Victor Frankenstein as creator and casualty[C]//GUSTON D H, ROBERTS J. Annotated for scientists, engineers and creators of all kinds. Cambridge: The MIT Press, 2017: 300.

3. 作品赏析

《弗兰肯斯坦》关于人工生命的想象并非空穴来风,解读该小说首先应了解其创作的时代背景、创作动机及创作主旨。欧洲浪漫主义文学的兴起,其中一个重要原因就是对18世纪科学理性和古典主义的一次反扑:反对机械、教条的启蒙运动时期的自然哲学,崇尚个性的张扬和自我的表达,强调个体想象和创新,追求个体自我与自然的有机结合。受此影响,浪漫主义时期的科学家认为观察和研究自然必然包含着理解自我,指出不应该依靠暴力来获取关于自然的知识。在他们看来,启蒙思想鼓励滥用科学,因此,他们试图寻求一种获取知识的新途径,这不仅有利于人类的进步,而且有利于自然①。小说借助维多克的临终遗言,也表达了这种浪漫主义科学观,反对滥用科学,强调个体在自然中的宁静。

玛丽·雪莱选择人工生命这一题材,既有其偶然性,也有其必然性。表面看来,《弗兰肯斯坦》的创作起因在于1816年玛丽和雪莱在日内瓦湖度假时与拜伦之间的一场写作比赛,看谁写的鬼怪故事最好。当其他人都动笔后,玛丽对到底写什么仍然一头雾水,直至某次傍晚听到拜伦和雪莱讨论生命的本质,特别是能否用电流来复活尸体,她灵光一闪②。至于生命的本质、电学和解剖学,玛丽并不陌生。遇见雪莱之前,她早受到父母自由思想的熏陶,不仅认识伊斯拉姆斯·达尔文、哈姆福瑞·戴夫(Humphry Davy,1778—1829)、威廉姆·尼克尔森(William Nicholson,1753—1815)和约瑟夫·普瑞斯特里(Joseph Priestley,1733—1804)等父亲小圈子里的科学家,而且熟悉他们关于生命的科学理论,比如说,伊斯拉姆斯提出的"自然发生论"③,戴夫和尼克尔森关于生命和化学之间关系的论断④,普瑞斯特里关于生命与电学和气体之间关系的主张等⑤。另外,雪莱对电学实验特别感兴趣,学过解剖学,研究过气体的属性和食物的化学构造。认识玛丽后,他的科学热情在一定程度上影响了玛丽,他的科学知识也丰富和拓展了玛丽的知识视野,特别是他从私人医生劳伦斯(William Lawrence,1783—1867)那里了解到的关于生命本质的论述⑥。这些理论和知识都为她写作《弗兰肯斯坦》打下坚实的基础。所以,当听到雪莱与拜伦讨论生命本质和用电流来复活尸

---

① POGGI S, BOSSI M. Romanticism in science: science in Europe, 1790-1840[M]. Dordrecht: Kluwer Academic Publishers, 1994: xii.
② ibid.
③ SIMILI R. Erasmus Darwin, galvanism, and the principle of life[Z/OL]. https://www.lilec.it/romanticismo/erasmus-darwin-galvanism-and-the-principle-of-life/.
④ BALL P. The making of modern Prometheus[Z/OL]. https://www.chemistryworld.com/opinion/how-frankenstein-left-chemistry-with-a-monstrous-reputation/1017377.article.
⑤ ROBINSON C E. Introduction[A]//GUSTON D H, ROBERTS J. Annotated for scientists, engineers and creators of all kinds. Cambridge: The MIT Press, 2017: 3.
⑥ BUTLER M. Introduction[A]//SHELLEY M. Frankenstein or the modern Prometheus. Oxford: Oxford University Press, 2008: xv-xvii.

体时，她自然而然地就开始构思维多克的形象，探讨他如何通过实验来复活尸体。

借助"科学狂人"维多克的悲剧，玛丽·雪莱表达了浪漫主义时期人们对科学发明抱有的恐惧，而维多克的怪物也像幽灵一样，一直萦绕在人们记忆的深处。甚至在很多时候，学界常将"科学狂人"等同于怪物。毕竟，小说涉及的伦理问题，不仅关系到人造生命对其创造者乃至整个人类的伦理责任，而且关乎人类对所创造物（不管是人造生命，还是其他任何事物）的伦理责任，因此，这个责任是相互的、对等的。诚然，怪物暴戾、凶残，但是，造成其乖张性格的恰恰是人类自己。首先，维多克作为怪物的创造者或父亲，他没有履行父亲对儿女应尽的社会责任，相反，他在见到其丑陋相貌后逃跑了，完全漠视其存在。他的失责让怪物感到孤独，让他无法了解如何处世，如何生存。人们对其丑陋相貌所持有的恐惧及厌恶让其倍感失望。尽管如此，他还是希望能得到人类的同情，希望通过自己的善举融入人类社会。结果，得到其帮助的穷人兄妹非但没有领情，反而将其逐出门外。人类的冷漠和歧视让其彻底绝望，因此他希望通过谋杀维多克的弟弟来引起其关注，甚至希望维多克给自己创造一个伴侣，借此克服自己情感和生理上的孤独。当他发现永远无法实现自己的愿望后，他彻底癫狂。为了复仇，他杀死了维多克的好友亨利以及维多克的新婚妻子伊丽莎白，而伊丽莎白的死亡也使得维多克父亲因为过度悲恸撒手人寰。最后，维多克也死在报仇路上，而他的死亡则让怪物失去其内心与人类之间的最后一根纽带，因而决定自杀。这个结局，无论对于读者，还是对于小说中的其他幸存者，都应该是人心所向。如维多克临终告诫的那样，在追求科学知识的过程中，不应野心过大，否则会造成悲剧。

《弗兰肯斯坦》中利用电流来复活尸体的做法对浪漫主义时期的欧洲人来说并不陌生。当时，路易吉·加尔瓦尼（Luigi Galvani，1737—1798）用电流让死去青蛙的腿运动的电流实验已经逐渐为大众所熟知[1]。另外，其侄儿在伦敦用动物和罪犯的尸体做实验，证实电流可以让死尸做出某种动作。所以，当读者阅读到小说中电流给予怪物生命的情节时并未感到太震惊，小说中的哥特式场景及事件对于浪漫主义时期的大众来说也并不稀奇。最让人费解的是怪物自学语言的场面及其复杂的内心世界。小说发表后不久，司格特（Walter Scott，1771—1832）批评说这一情节"不可能且太过牵强"[2]。因此，该小说让读者不禁思考，人工生命是否具有语言和认知能力？是否具有思维和情感？是否具有道德责任心？或者，人工生命是否应该存在？制造他们的科学家是否违背了人伦秩序？在人工智能及人工生命快速发展的今天，这些问题依然非常重要。英国当代作家麦克尤恩在2019年发表的《像我一样的机器人》也试图回答这些问题，探讨人工生命带来的伦理挑战。

---

[1] CALDWELL J M. Literature and medicine in nineteenth-century Britain: from Mary Shelley to George Eliot [M]. Cambridge: Cambridge University Press, 2004: 40.

[2] Literary influences and reception [Z/OL]. [2023-07-11]. https://sites.udel.edu/britlitwiki/literary-influences-and-reception/.

第六章 文学与人工智能/生命(Literature and AI/AL)

在写作《弗兰肯斯坦》时,玛丽·雪莱也许并未考虑到上述伦理问题。如一些女性主义和精神分析文论家指出的那样,她关注生命复活这一科学实验是由于其内心的痛苦。她自幼失去了母亲,感到自己被遗弃了。通过让怪物体验被其创造者抛弃后的孤独和仇恨,玛丽似乎想抚平内心因为母爱的缺失带来的伤痛。另外,玛丽多次流产,其早产的女儿也在十几天后夭折。在她看来,女儿的死亡在一定程度上是由于雪莱没有尽到父亲的责任。在女儿去世后,她一度梦见女儿复活,甚至和雪莱讨论过如何让生命复活。也有证据表明,玛丽和雪莱相信死者可以复活,死亡和生命可以逆转①。从这些因素来看,玛丽在小说中通过探讨电流复活生命的科学实验,除了思考现代科学带给人类的危害,还带有自己个人的考虑,即如何借助人工生命来联结生者和死者,以缓解内心的苦楚。所以,至于玛丽虚构人工生命的目的到底是什么,就见仁见智了。但是,小说所设想的关于人工生命带来的系列问题在200多年后的今天仍具有现实意义,值得我们深入探讨。下面请阅读小说节选部分,并回答相关问题。选文第四章、第五章是维多克自述如何创造怪物以及见到怪物后的恐惧心理。选文第十二章、第十三章是怪物的自述,主要讲他被遗弃后如何渴望被人类认同、如何自学人类的语言。

作品选读

Frankenstein; or, The Modern Prometheus
Mary Shelley

[...]

Chapter 4

From this day natural philosophy, and particularly chemistry, in the most comprehensive sense of the term, became nearly my sole occupation. I read with ardour those works, so full of genius and discrimination, which modern inquirers have written on these subjects. I attended the lectures and cultivated the acquaintance of the men of science of the university, and I found even in M. Krempe a great deal of sound sense and real information, combined, it is true, with a repulsive physiognomy and manners, but not on that account the less valuable. In M. Waldman I found a true friend. His gentleness was never tinged by dogmatism, and his instructions were given with an air of frankness and good nature that banished every idea of pedantry. In a thousand ways he smoothed for

---

① RUSTON S. The science of life and death in Mary Shelley's Frankenstein[Z/OL]. https://www.bl.uk/romantics-and-victorians/articles/the-science-of-life-and-death-in-mary-shelleys-frankenstein.

me the path of knowledge and made the most abstruse inquiries clear and facile to my apprehension. My application was at first fluctuating and uncertain; it gained strength as I proceeded and soon became so ardent and eager that the stars often disappeared in the light of morning whilst I was yet engaged in my laboratory.

As I applied so closely, it may be easily conceived that my progress was rapid. My ardour was indeed the astonishment of the students, and my proficiency that of the masters. Professor Krempe often asked me, with a sly smile, how Cornelius Agrippa went on, whilst M. Waldman expressed the most heartfelt exultation in my progress. Two years passed in this manner, during which I paid no visit to Geneva, but was engaged, heart and soul, in the pursuit of some discoveries which I hoped to make. None but those who have experienced them can conceive of the enticements of science. In other studies you go as far as others have gone before you, and there is nothing more to know; but in a scientific pursuit there is continual food for discovery and wonder. A mind of moderate capacity which closely pursues one study must infallibly arrive at great proficiency in that study; and I, who continually sought the attainment of one object of pursuit and was solely wrapped up in this, improved so rapidly that at the end of two years I made some discoveries in the improvement of some chemical instruments, which procured me great esteem and admiration at the university. When I had arrived at this point and had become as well acquainted with the theory and practice of natural philosophy as depended on the lessons of any of the professors at Ingolstadt, my residence there being no longer conducive to my improvements, I thought of returning to my friends and my native town, when an incident happened that protracted my stay.

One of the phenomena which had peculiarly attracted my attention was the structure of the human frame, and, indeed, any animal endued with life. Whence, I often asked myself, did the principle of life proceed? It was a bold question, and one which has ever been considered as a mystery; yet with how many things are we upon the brink of becoming acquainted, if cowardice or carelessness did not restrain our inquiries. I revolved these circumstances in my mind and determined thenceforth to apply myself more particularly to those branches of natural philosophy which relate to physiology. Unless I had been animated by an almost supernatural enthusiasm, my application to this study would have been irksome and almost intolerable. To examine the causes of life, we must

第六章 文学与人工智能/生命（Literature and AI/AL）

first have recourse to death. I became acquainted with the science of anatomy, but this was not sufficient; I must also observe the natural decay and corruption of the human body. In my education my father had taken the greatest precautions that my mind should be impressed with no supernatural horrors. I do not ever remember to have trembled at a tale of superstition or to have feared the apparition of a spirit. Darkness had no effect upon my fancy, and a churchyard was to me merely the receptacle of bodies deprived of life, which, from being the seat of beauty and strength, had become food for the worm. Now I was led to examine the cause and progress of this decay and forced to spend days and nights in vaults and charnel-houses. My attention was fixed upon every object the most insupportable to the delicacy of the human feelings. I saw how the fine form of man was degraded and wasted; I beheld the corruption of death succeed to the blooming cheek of life; I saw how the worm inherited the wonders of the eye and brain. I paused, examining and analysing all the minutiae of causation, as exemplified in the change from life to death, and death to life, until from the midst of this darkness a sudden light broke in upon me—a light so brilliant and wondrous, yet so simple, that while I became dizzy with the immensity of the prospect which it illustrated, I was surprised that among so many men of genius who had directed their inquiries towards the same science, that I alone should be reserved to discover so astonishing a secret.

Remember, I am not recording the vision of a madman. The sun does not more certainly shine in the heavens than that which I now affirm is true. Some miracle might have produced it, yet the stages of the discovery were distinct and probable. After days and nights of incredible labour and fatigue, I succeeded in discovering the cause of generation and life; nay, more, I became myself capable of bestowing animation upon lifeless matter.

The astonishment which I had at first experienced on this discovery soon gave place to delight and rapture. After so much time spent in painful labour, to arrive at once at the summit of my desires was the most gratifying consummation of my toils. But this discovery was so great and overwhelming that all the steps by which I had been progressively led to it were obliterated, and I beheld only the result. What had been the study and desire of the wisest men since the creation of the world was now within my grasp. Not that, like a magic scene, it all opened upon me at once: the information I had obtained was of a nature rather to direct my endeavours so soon as I should point them towards the object of my search than to exhibit that object already accomplished. I was like the Arabian who had been buried with the dead and found a passage to life, aided only by one glimmering and seemingly ineffectual light.

I see by your eagerness and the wonder and hope which your eyes express, my friend, that you expect to be informed of the secret with which I am acquainted; that cannot be; listen patiently until the end of my story, and you will easily perceive why I am reserved upon that subject. I will not lead you on, unguarded and ardent as I then was, to your destruction and infallible misery. Learn from me, if not by my precepts, at least by my example, how dangerous is the acquirement of knowledge and how much happier that man is who believes his native town to be the world, than he who aspires to become greater than his nature will allow.

When I found so astonishing a power placed within my hands, I hesitated a long time concerning the manner in which I should employ it. Although I possessed the capacity of bestowing animation, yet to prepare a frame for the reception of it, with all its intricacies of fibres, muscles, and veins, still remained a work of inconceivable difficulty and labour. I doubted at first whether I should attempt the creation of a being like myself, or one of simpler organization; but my imagination was too much exalted by my first success to permit me to doubt of my ability to give life to an animal as complex and wonderful as man. The materials at present within my command hardly appeared adequate to so arduous an undertaking, but I doubted not that I should ultimately succeed. I prepared myself for a multitude of reverses; my operations might be incessantly baffled, and at last my work be imperfect, yet when I considered the improvement which every day takes place in science and mechanics, I was encouraged to hope my present attempts would at least lay the foundations of future success. Nor could I consider the magnitude and complexity of my plan as any argument of its impracticability. It was with these feelings that I began the creation of a human being. As the minuteness of the parts formed a great hindrance to my speed, I resolved, contrary to my first intention, to make the being of a gigantic stature, that is to say, about eight feet in height, and proportionably large. After having formed this determination and having spent some months in successfully collecting and arranging my materials, I began.

第六章 文学与人工智能/生命(Literature and AI/AL)

No one can conceive the variety of feelings which bore me onwards, like a hurricane, in the first enthusiasm of success. Life and death appeared to me ideal bounds, which I should first break through, and pour a torrent of light into our dark world. A new species would bless me as its creator and source; many happy and excellent natures would owe their being to me. No father could claim the gratitude of his child so completely as I should deserve theirs. Pursuing these reflections, I thought that if I could bestow animation upon lifeless matter, I might in process of time (although I now found it impossible) renew life where death had apparently devoted the body to corruption.

These thoughts supported my spirits, while I pursued my undertaking with unremitting ardour. My cheek had grown pale with study, and my person had become emaciated with confinement. Sometimes, on the very brink of certainty, I failed; yet still I clung to the hope which the next day or the next hour might realize. One secret which I alone possessed was the hope to which I had dedicated myself; and the moon gazed on my midnight labours, while, with unrelaxed and breathless eagerness, I pursued nature to her hiding-places. Who shall conceive the horrors of my secret toil as I dabbled among the unhallowed damps of the grave or tortured the living animal to animate the lifeless clay? My limbs now tremble, and my eyes swim with the remembrance; but then a resistless and almost frantic impulse urged me forward; I seemed to have lost all soul or sensation but for this one pursuit. It was indeed but a passing trance, that only made me feel with renewed acuteness so soon as, the unnatural stimulus ceasing to operate, I had returned to my old habits. I collected bones from charnel-houses and disturbed, with profane fingers, the tremendous secrets of the human frame. In a solitary chamber, or rather cell, at the top of the house, and separated from all the other apartments by a gallery and staircase, I kept my workshop of filthy creation; my eyeballs were starting from their sockets in attending to the details of my employment. The dissecting room and the slaughter-house furnished many of my materials; and often did my human nature turn with loathing from my occupation, whilst, still urged on by an eagerness which perpetually increased, I brought my work near to a conclusion.

The summer months passed while I was thus engaged, heart and soul, in one pursuit. It was a most beautiful season; never did the fields bestow a more plentiful harvest or the vines yield a more luxuriant vintage, but my eyes were insensible to the charms of nature.

And the same feelings which made me neglect the scenes around me caused me also to forget those friends who were so many miles absent, and whom I had not seen for so long a time. I knew my silence disquieted them, and I well remembered the words of my father: "I know that while you are pleased with yourself you will think of us with affection, and we shall hear regularly from you. You must pardon me if I regard any interruption in your correspondence as a proof that your other duties are equally neglected."

I knew well therefore what would be my father's feelings, but I could not tear my thoughts from my employment, loathsome in itself, but which had taken an irresistible hold of my imagination. I wished, as it were, to procrastinate all that related to my feelings of affection until the great object, which swallowed up every habit of my nature, should be completed.

I then thought that my father would be unjust if he ascribed my neglect to vice or faultiness on my part, but I am now convinced that he was justified in conceiving that I should not be altogether free from blame. A human being in perfection ought always to preserve a calm and peaceful mind and never to allow passion or a transitory desire to disturb his tranquility. I do not think that the pursuit of knowledge is an exception to this rule. If the study to which you apply yourself has a tendency to weaken your affections and to destroy your taste for those simple pleasures in which no alloy can possibly mix, then that study is certainly unlawful, that is to say, not befitting the human mind. If this rule were always observed; if no man allowed any pursuit whatsoever to interfere with the tranquility of his domestic affections, Greece had not been enslaved, Caesar would have spared his country, America would have been discovered more gradually, and the empires of Mexico and Peru had not been destroyed.

But I forget that I am moralizing in the most interesting part of my tale, and your looks remind me to proceed. My father made no reproach in his letters and only took notice of my silence by inquiring into my occupations more particularly than before. Winter, spring, and summer passed away during my labours; but I did not watch the blossom or the expanding leaves—sights which before always yielded me supreme delight—so deeply was I engrossed in my occupation. The leaves of that year had withered before my work drew near to a close, and now every day showed me more plainly how well I had succeeded. But my enthusiasm was checked by my anxiety, and I appeared rather like one

第六章 文学与人工智能/生命（Literature and AI/AL）

doomed by slavery to toil in the mines, or any other unwholesome trade than an artist occupied by his favourite employment. Every night I was oppressed by a slow fever, and I became nervous to a most painful degree; the fall of a leaf startled me, and I shunned my fellow creatures as if I had been guilty of a crime. Sometimes I grew alarmed at the wreck I perceived that I had become; the energy of my purpose alone sustained me: my labours would soon end, and I believed that exercise and amusement would then drive away incipient disease; and I promised myself both of these when my creation should be complete.

[…]

Chapter 5

It was on a dreary night of November that I beheld the accomplishment of my toils. With an anxiety that almost amounted to agony, I collected the instruments of life around me, that I might infuse a spark of being into the lifeless thing that lay at my feet. It was already one in the morning; the rain pattered dismally against the panes, and my candle was nearly burnt out, when, by the glimmer of the half-extinguished light, I saw the dull yellow eye of the creature open; it breathed hard, and a convulsive motion agitated its limbs.

How can I describe my emotions at this catastrophe, or how delineate the wretch whom with such infinite pains and care I had endeavoured to form? His limbs were in proportion, and I had selected his features as beautiful. Beautiful! Great God! His yellow skin scarcely covered the work of muscles and arteries beneath; his hair was of a lustrous black, and flowing; his teeth of a pearly whiteness; but these luxuriances only formed a more horrid contrast with his watery eyes, that seemed almost of the same colour as the dun-white sockets in which they were set, his shrivelled complexion and straight black lips.

The different accidents of life are not so changeable as the feelings of human nature. I had worked hard for nearly two years, for the sole purpose of infusing life into an inanimate body. For this I had deprived myself of rest and health. I had desired it with an ardour that far exceeded moderation; but now that I had finished, the beauty of the dream vanished, and breathless horror and disgust filled my heart. Unable to endure the aspect of the being I had created, I rushed out of the room and continued a long time traversing my bedchamber, unable to compose my mind to sleep. At length lassitude succeeded to the tumult I had before endured, and I threw myself on the bed in my clothes, endeavouring to seek a few moments of forgetfulness. But it was in vain; I slept, indeed, but I was disturbed by the wildest dreams. I thought I saw Elizabeth, in the bloom of health, walking in the streets of Ingolstadt. Delighted and surprised, I embraced her, but as I imprinted the first kiss on her lips, they became livid with the hue of death; her features appeared to change, and I thought that I held the corpse of my dead mother in my arms; a shroud enveloped her form, and I saw the grave-worms crawling in the folds of the flannel. I started from my sleep with horror; a cold dew covered my forehead, my teeth chattered, and every limb became convulsed; when, by the dim and yellow light of the moon, as it forced its way through the window shutters, I beheld the wretch—the miserable monster whom I had created. He held up the curtain of the bed; and his eyes, if eyes they may be called, were fixed on me. His jaws opened, and he muttered some inarticulate sounds, while a grin wrinkled his cheeks. He might have spoken, but I did not hear; one hand was stretched out, seemingly to detain me, but I escaped and rushed downstairs. I took refuge in the courtyard belonging to the house which I inhabited, where I remained during the rest of the night, walking up and down in the greatest agitation, listening attentively, catching and fearing each sound as if it were to announce the approach of the demoniacal corpse to which I had so miserably given life.

Oh! No mortal could support the horror of that countenance. A mummy again endued with animation could not be so hideous as that wretch. I had gazed on him while unfinished; he was ugly then, but when those muscles and joints were rendered capable of motion, it became a thing such as even Dante could not have conceived.

I passed the night wretchedly. Sometimes my pulse beat so quickly and hardly that I felt the palpitation of every artery; at others, I nearly sank to the ground through languor and extreme weakness. Mingled with this horror, I felt the bitterness of disappointment; dreams that had been my food and pleasant rest for so long a space were now become a hell to me; and the change was so rapid, the overthrow so complete!

Morning, dismal and wet, at length dawned and discovered to my sleepless and aching eyes the church of Ingolstadt, its white steeple and clock, which indicated the sixth hour. The porter opened the gates of the court, which had that night been my asylum, and I issued into the streets, pacing them with quick steps, as if I sought to avoid the wretch

第六章 文学与人工智能/生命(Literature and AI/AL)

whom I feared every turning of the street would present to my view. I did not dare return to the apartment which I inhabited, but felt impelled to hurry on, although drenched by the rain which poured from a black and comfortless sky.

I continued walking in this manner for some time, endeavouring by bodily exercise to ease the load that weighed upon my mind. I traversed the streets without any clear conception of where I was or what I was doing. My heart palpitated in the sickness of fear, and I hurried on with irregular steps, not daring to look about me:

> Like one who, on a lonely road,
> Doth walk in fear and dread,
> And, having once turned round, walks on,
> And turns no more his head;
> Because he knows a frightful fiend
> Doth close behind him tread.
> [Coleridge's "Ancient Mariner."]

Continuing thus, I came at length opposite to the inn at which the various diligences and carriages usually stopped. Here I paused, I knew not why; but I remained some minutes with my eyes fixed on a coach that was coming towards me from the other end of the street. As it drew nearer I observed that it was the Swiss diligence; it stopped just where I was standing, and on the door being opened, I perceived Henry Clerval, who, on seeing me, instantly sprung out. "My dear Frankenstein," exclaimed he, "how glad I am to see you! How fortunate that you should be here at the very moment of my alighting!"

Nothing could equal my delight on seeing Clerval; his presence brought back to my thoughts my father, Elizabeth, and all those scenes of home so dear to my recollection. I grasped his hand, and in a moment forgot my horror and misfortune; I felt suddenly, and for the first time during many months, calm and serene joy. I welcomed my friend, therefore, in the most cordial manner, and we walked towards my college. Clerval continued talking for some time about our mutual friends and his own good fortune in being permitted to come to Ingolstadt. "You may easily believe," said he, "how great was the difficulty to persuade my father that all necessary knowledge was not comprised in the noble art of book-keeping; and, indeed, I believe I left him incredulous to the last, for his constant answer to my unwearied entreaties was the same as that of the Dutch schoolmaster in *The Vicar of Wakefield*: 'I have ten thousand florins a year without Greek, I eat heartily without Greek.' But his affection for me at length overcame his dislike of learning, and he has permitted me to undertake a voyage of discovery to the land of knowledge."

"It gives me the greatest delight to see you; but tell me how you left my father, brothers, and Elizabeth."

"Very well, and very happy, only a little uneasy that they hear from you so seldom. By the by, I mean to lecture you a little upon their account myself. But, my dear Frankenstein," continued he, stopping short and gazing full in my face, "I did not before remark how very ill you appear; so thin and pale; you look as if you had been watching for several nights."

"You have guessed right; I have lately been so deeply engaged in one occupation that I have not allowed myself sufficient rest, as you see; but I hope, I sincerely hope, that all these employments are now at an end and that I am at length free."

I trembled excessively; I could not endure to think of, and far less to allude to, the occurrences of the preceding night. I walked with a quick pace, and we soon arrived at my college. I then reflected, and the thought made me shiver, that the creature whom I had left in my apartment might still be there, alive and walking about. I dreaded to behold this monster, but I feared still more that Henry should see him. Entreating him, therefore, to remain a few minutes at the bottom of the stairs, I darted up towards my own room. My hand was already on the lock of the door before I recollected myself. I then paused, and a cold shivering came over me. I threw the door forcibly open, as children are accustomed to do when they expect a spectre to stand in waiting for them on the other side; but nothing appeared. I stepped fearfully in: the apartment was empty, and my bedroom was also freed from its hideous guest. I could hardly believe that so great a good fortune could have befallen me, but when I became assured that my enemy had indeed fled, I clapped my hands for joy and ran down to Clerval.

We ascended into my room, and the servant presently brought breakfast; but I was unable to contain myself. It was not joy only that possessed me; I felt my flesh tingle with excess of sensitiveness, and my pulse beat rapidly. I was unable to remain for a single instant in the same place; I jumped over the chairs, clapped my hands, and laughed aloud. Clerval at first attributed my unusual spirits to joy on his arrival, but when he observed me more attentively, he saw a wildness in my eyes for which he could not account, and my loud, unrestrained, heartless laughter frightened and astonished him.

"My dear Victor," cried he, "what, for God's sake, is the matter? Do not laugh in that manner. How ill you are! What is the cause of all this?"

"Do not ask me," cried I, putting my hands before my eyes, for I thought I saw the dreaded spectre glide into the room; "HE can tell. Oh, save me! Save me!" I imagined that the monster seized me; I struggled furiously and fell down in a fit.

Poor Clerval! What must have been his feelings? A meeting, which he anticipated with such joy, so strangely turned to bitterness. But I was not the witness of his grief, for I was lifeless and did not recover my senses for a long, long time.

This was the commencement of a nervous fever which confined me for several months. During all that time Henry was my only nurse. I afterwards learned that, knowing my father's advanced age and unfitness for so long a journey, and how wretched my sickness would make Elizabeth, he spared them this grief by concealing the extent of my disorder. He knew that I could not have a more kind and attentive nurse than himself; and, firm in the hope he felt of my recovery, he did not doubt that, instead of doing harm, he performed the kindest action that he could towards them.

But I was in reality very ill, and surely nothing but the unbounded and unremitting attentions of my friend could have restored me to life. The form of the monster on whom I had bestowed existence was forever before my eyes, and I raved incessantly concerning him. Doubtless my words surprised Henry; he at first believed them to be the wanderings of my disturbed imagination, but the pertinacity with which I continually recurred to the same subject persuaded him that my disorder indeed owed its origin to some uncommon and terrible event.

By very slow degrees, and with frequent relapses that alarmed and grieved my friend, I recovered. I remember the first time I became capable of observing outward objects with any kind of pleasure, I perceived that the fallen leaves had disappeared and that the young buds were shooting forth from the trees that shaded my window. It was a divine spring, and the season contributed greatly to my convalescence. I felt also sentiments of joy and affection revive in my bosom; my gloom disappeared, and in a short time I became as cheerful as before I was attacked by the fatal passion.

"Dearest Clerval," exclaimed I, "how kind, how very good you are to me. This whole winter, instead of being spent in study, as you promised yourself, has been consumed in my sick room. How shall I ever repay you? I feel the greatest remorse for the disappointment of which I have been the occasion, but you will forgive me."

"You will repay me entirely if you do not discompose yourself, but get well as fast as you can; and since you appear in such good spirits, I may speak to you on one subject, may I not?"

I trembled. One subject! What could it be? Could he allude to an object on whom I dared not even think? "Compose yourself," said Clerval, who observed my change of colour, "I will not mention it if it agitates you; but your father and cousin would be very happy if they received a letter from you in your own handwriting. They hardly know how ill you have been and are uneasy at your long silence."

"Is that all, my dear Henry? How could you suppose that my first thought would not fly towards those dear, dear friends whom I love and who are so deserving of my love?"

"If this is your present temper, my friend, you will perhaps be glad to see a letter that has been lying here some days for you; it is from your cousin, I believe."

[...]

Chapter 12

"I lay on my straw, but I could not sleep. I thought of the occurrences of the day. What chiefly struck me was the gentle manners of these people, and I longed to join them, but dared not. I remembered too well the treatment I had suffered the night before from the barbarous villagers, and resolved, whatever course of conduct I might hereafter think it right to pursue, that for the present I would remain quietly in my hovel, watching and endeavouring to discover the motives which influenced their actions.

"The cottagers arose the next morning before the sun. The young woman arranged the cottage and prepared the food, and the youth departed after the first meal.

"This day was passed in the same routine as that which preceded it. The young man was constantly employed out of doors, and the girl in various laborious occupations within. The old man, whom I soon perceived to be blind, employed his leisure hours on his instrument or in contemplation. Nothing could exceed the love and respect which the younger cottagers exhibited towards their venerable companion. They performed towards him every little office of affection and duty with gentleness, and he rewarded them by his benevolent smiles.

"They were not entirely happy. The young man and his companion often went apart and appeared to weep. I saw no cause for their unhappiness, but I was deeply affected by it. If such lovely creatures were miserable, it was less strange that I, an imperfect and solitary being, should be wretched. Yet why were these gentle beings unhappy? They possessed a delightful house (for such it was in my eyes) and every luxury; they had a fire to warm them when chill and delicious viands when hungry; they were dressed in excellent clothes; and, still more, they enjoyed one another's company and speech, interchanging each day looks of affection and kindness. What did their tears imply? Did they really express pain? I was at first unable to solve these questions, but perpetual attention and time explained to me many appearances which were at first enigmatic.

"A considerable period elapsed before I discovered one of the causes of the uneasiness of this amiable family: it was poverty, and they suffered that evil in a very distressing degree. Their nourishment consisted entirely of the vegetables of their garden and the milk of one cow, which gave very little during the winter, when its masters could scarcely procure food to support it. They often, I believe, suffered the pangs of hunger very poignantly, especially the two younger cottagers, for several times they placed food before the old man when they reserved none for themselves.

"This trait of kindness moved me sensibly. I had been accustomed, during the night, to steal a part of their store for my own consumption, but when I found that in doing this I inflicted pain on the cottagers, I abstained and satisfied myself with berries, nuts, and roots which I gathered from a neighbouring wood.

"I discovered also another means through which I was enabled to assist their labours. I found that the youth spent a great part of each day in collecting wood for the family fire, and during the night I often took his tools, the use of which I quickly discovered, and brought home firing sufficient for the consumption of several days.

"I remember, the first time that I did this, the young woman, when she opened the door in the morning, appeared greatly astonished on seeing a great pile of wood on the outside. She uttered some words in a loud voice, and the youth joined her, who also expressed surprise. I observed, with pleasure, that he did not go to the forest that day, but spent it in repairing the cottage and cultivating the garden.

"By degrees I made a discovery of still greater moment. I found that these people possessed a method of communicating their experience and feelings to one another by articulate sounds. I perceived that the words they spoke sometimes produced pleasure or pain, smiles or sadness, in the minds and countenances of the hearers. This was indeed a godlike science, and I ardently desired to become acquainted with it. But I was baffled in every attempt I made for this purpose. Their pronunciation was quick, and the words they uttered, not having any apparent connection with visible objects, I was unable to discover any clue by which I could unravel the mystery of their reference. By great application, however, and after having remained during the space of several revolutions of the moon in my hovel, I discovered the names that were given to some of the most familiar objects of discourse; I learned and applied the words, 'fire,' 'milk,' 'bread,' and 'wood.' I learned also the names of the cottagers themselves. The youth and his companion had each of them several names, but the old man had only one, which was 'father.' The girl was called 'sister' or 'Agatha,' and the youth 'Felix,' 'brother,' or 'son.' I cannot describe the delight I felt when I learned the ideas appropriated to each of these sounds and was able to pronounce them. I distinguished several other words without being able as yet to understand or apply them, such as 'good,' 'dearest,' 'unhappy.'

"I spent the winter in this manner. The gentle manners and beauty of the cottagers greatly endeared them to me; when they were unhappy, I felt depressed; when they rejoiced, I sympathized in their joys. I saw few human beings besides them, and if any other happened to enter the cottage, their harsh manners and rude gait only enhanced to me the superior accomplishments of my friends. The old man, I could perceive, often endeavoured to encourage his children, as sometimes I found that he called them, to cast off their melancholy. He would talk in a cheerful accent, with an expression of goodness that bestowed pleasure even upon me. Agatha listened with respect, her eyes sometimes filled with tears, which she endeavoured to wipe away unperceived; but I generally found

第六章 文学与人工智能/生命（Literature and AI/AL）

that her countenance and tone were more cheerful after having listened to the exhortations of her father. It was not thus with Felix. He was always the saddest of the group, and even to my unpractised senses, he appeared to have suffered more deeply than his friends. But if his countenance was more sorrowful, his voice was more cheerful than that of his sister, especially when he addressed the old man.

"I could mention innumerable instances which, although slight, marked the dispositions of these amiable cottagers. In the midst of poverty and want, Felix carried with pleasure to his sister the first little white flower that peeped out from beneath the snowy ground. Early in the morning, before she had risen, he cleared away the snow that obstructed her path to the milk-house, drew water from the well, and brought the wood from the outhouse, where, to his perpetual astonishment, he found his store always replenished by an invisible hand. In the day, I believe, he worked sometimes for a neighbouring farmer, because he often went forth and did not return until dinner, yet brought no wood with him. At other times he worked in the garden, but as there was little to do in the frosty season, he read to the old man and Agatha.

"This reading had puzzled me extremely at first, but by degrees I discovered that he uttered many of the same sounds when he read as when he talked. I conjectured, therefore, that he found on the paper signs for speech which he understood, and I ardently longed to comprehend these also; but how was that possible when I did not even understand the sounds for which they stood as signs? I improved, however, sensibly in this science, but not sufficiently to follow up any kind of conversation, although I applied my whole mind to the endeavour, for I easily perceived that, although I eagerly longed to discover myself to the cottagers, I ought not to make the attempt until I had first become master of their language, which knowledge might enable me to make them overlook the deformity of my figure, for with this also the contrast perpetually presented to my eyes had made me acquainted.

"I had admired the perfect forms of my cottagers—their grace, beauty, and delicate complexions; but how was I terrified when I viewed myself in a transparent pool! At first I started back, unable to believe that it was indeed I who was reflected in the mirror; and when I became fully convinced that I was in reality the monster that I am, I was filled with the bitterest sensations of despondence and mortification. Alas! I did not yet entirely know the fatal effects of this miserable deformity.

"As the sun became warmer and the light of day longer, the snow vanished, and I beheld the bare trees and the black earth. From this time Felix was more employed, and the heart-moving indications of impending famine disappeared. Their food, as I afterwards found, was coarse, but it was wholesome; and they procured a sufficiency of it. Several new kinds of plants sprang up in the garden, which they dressed; and these signs of comfort increased daily as the season advanced.

"The old man, leaning on his son, walked each day at noon, when it did not rain, as I found it was called when the heavens poured forth its waters. This frequently took place, but a high wind quickly dried the earth, and the season became far more pleasant than it had been.

"My mode of life in my hovel was uniform. During the morning I attended the motions of the cottagers, and when they were dispersed in various occupations, I slept; the remainder of the day was spent in observing my friends. When they had retired to rest, if there was any moon or the night was star-light, I went into the woods and collected my own food and fuel for the cottage. When I returned, as often as it was necessary, I cleared their path from the snow and performed those offices that I had seen done by Felix. I afterwards found that these labours, performed by an invisible hand, greatly astonished them; and once or twice I heard them, on these occasions, utter the words 'good spirit,' 'wonderful'; but I did not then understand the signification of these terms.

"My thoughts now became more active, and I longed to discover the motives and feelings of these lovely creatures; I was inquisitive to know why Felix appeared so miserable and Agatha so sad. I thought (foolish wretch!) that it might be in my power to restore happiness to these deserving people. When I slept or was absent, the forms of the venerable blind father, the gentle Agatha, and the excellent Felix flitted before me. I looked upon them as superior beings who would be the arbiters of my future destiny. I formed in my imagination a thousand pictures of presenting myself to them, and their reception of me. I imagined that they would be disgusted, until, by my gentle demeanour and conciliating words, I should first win their favour and afterwards their love.

"These thoughts exhilarated me and led me to apply with fresh ardour to the acquiring the art of language. My organs were indeed harsh, but supple; and although my voice was very unlike the soft music of their tones, yet I pronounced such words as I understood with tolerable ease. It was as the ass and the lap-dog; yet surely the gentle ass whose intentions were affectionate, although his manners were rude, deserved better treatment than blows and execration.

"The pleasant showers and genial warmth of spring greatly altered the aspect of the earth. Men who before this change seemed to have been hid in caves dispersed themselves and were employed in various arts of cultivation. The birds sang in more cheerful notes, and the leaves began to bud forth on the trees. Happy, happy earth! Fit habitation for gods, which, so short a time before, was bleak, damp, and unwholesome. My spirits were elevated by the enchanting appearance of nature; the past was blotted from my memory, the present was tranquil, and the future gilded by bright rays of hope and anticipations of joy."

Chapter 13

"I now hasten to the more moving part of my story. I shall relate events that impressed me with feelings which, from what I had been, have made me what I am.

"Spring advanced rapidly; the weather became fine and the skies cloudless. It surprised me that what before was desert and gloomy should now bloom with the most beautiful flowers and verdure. My senses were gratified and refreshed by a thousand scents of delight and a thousand sights of beauty.

"It was on one of these days, when my cottagers periodically rested from labour—the old man played on his guitar, and the children listened to him—that I observed the countenance of Felix was melancholy beyond expression; he sighed frequently, and once his father paused in his music, and I conjectured by his manner that he inquired the cause of his son's sorrow. Felix replied in a cheerful accent, and the old man was recommencing his music when someone tapped at the door.

"It was a lady on horseback, accompanied by a country-man as a guide. The lady was dressed in a dark suit and covered with a thick black veil. Agatha asked a question, to which the stranger only replied by pronouncing, in a sweet accent, the name of Felix. Her voice was musical but unlike that of either of my friends. On hearing this word, Felix came up hastily to the lady, who, when she saw him, threw up her veil, and I beheld a countenance of angelic beauty and expression. Her hair of a shining raven black, and curiously braided; her eyes were dark, but gentle, although animated; her features of a regular proportion, and her complexion wondrously fair, each cheek tinged with a lovely pink.

"Felix seemed ravished with delight when he saw her, every trait of sorrow vanished from his face, and it instantly expressed a degree of ecstatic joy, of which I could hardly have believed it capable; his eyes sparkled, as his cheek flushed with pleasure; and at that moment I thought him as beautiful as the stranger. She appeared affected by different feelings; wiping a few tears from her lovely eyes, she held out her hand to Felix, who kissed it rapturously and called her, as well as I could distinguish, his sweet Arabian. She did not appear to understand him, but smiled. He assisted her to dismount, and dismissing her guide, conducted her into the cottage. Some conversation took place between him and his father, and the young stranger knelt at the old man's feet and would have kissed his hand, but he raised her and embraced her affectionately.

"I soon perceived that although the stranger uttered articulate sounds and appeared to have a language of her own, she was neither understood by nor herself understood the cottagers. They made many signs which I did not comprehend, but I saw that her presence diffused gladness through the cottage, dispelling their sorrow as the sun dissipates the morning mists. Felix seemed peculiarly happy and with smiles of delight welcomed his Arabian. Agatha, the ever-gentle Agatha, kissed the hands of the lovely stranger, and pointing to her brother, made signs which appeared to me to mean that he had been sorrowful until she came. Some hours passed thus, while they, by their countenances, expressed joy, the cause of which I did not comprehend. Presently I found, by the frequent recurrence of some sound which the stranger repeated after them, that she was endeavouring to learn their language; and the idea instantly occurred to me that I should make use of the same instructions to the same end. The stranger learned about twenty words at the first lesson; most of them, indeed, were those which I had before understood, but I profited by the others.

"As night came on, Agatha and the Arabian retired early. When they separated Felix kissed the hand of the stranger and said, 'Good night sweet Safie.' He sat up much longer, conversing with his father, and by the frequent repetition of her name I conjectured that their lovely guest was the subject of their conversation. I ardently desired

第六章 文学与人工智能/生命(Literature and AI/AL)

to understand them, and bent every faculty towards that purpose, but found it utterly impossible.

"The next morning Felix went out to his work, and after the usual occupations of Agatha were finished, the Arabian sat at the feet of the old man, and taking his guitar, played some airs so entrancingly beautiful that they at once drew tears of sorrow and delight from my eyes. She sang, and her voice flowed in a rich cadence, swelling or dying away like a nightingale of the woods.

"When she had finished, she gave the guitar to Agatha, who at first declined it. She played a simple air, and her voice accompanied it in sweet accents, but unlike the wondrous strain of the stranger. The old man appeared enraptured and said some words which Agatha endeavoured to explain to Safie, and by which he appeared to wish to express that she bestowed on him the greatest delight by her music.

"The days now passed as peaceably as before, with the sole alteration that joy had taken place of sadness in the countenances of my friends. Safie was always gay and happy; she and I improved rapidly in the knowledge of language, so that in two months I began to comprehend most of the words uttered by my protectors.

"In the meanwhile also the black ground was covered with herbage, and the green banks interspersed with innumerable flowers, sweet to the scent and the eyes, stars of pale radiance among the moonlight woods; the sun became warmer, the nights clear and balmy; and my nocturnal rambles were an extreme pleasure to me, although they were considerably shortened by the late setting and early rising of the sun, for I never ventured abroad during daylight, fearful of meeting with the same treatment I had formerly endured in the first village which I entered.

"My days were spent in close attention, that I might more speedily master the language; and I may boast that I improved more rapidly than the Arabian, who understood very little and conversed in broken accents, whilst I comprehended and could imitate almost every word that was spoken.

"While I improved in speech, I also learned the science of letters as it was taught to the stranger, and this opened before me a wide field for wonder and delight.

"The book from which Felix instructed Safie was Volney's *Ruins of Empires*. I should not have understood the purport of this book had not Felix, in reading it, given very minute explanations. He had chosen this work, he said, because the declamatory style was framed in imitation of the Eastern authors. Through this work I obtained a cursory knowledge of history and a view of the several empires at present existing in the world; it gave me an insight into the manners, governments, and religions of the different nations of the earth. I heard of the slothful Asiatics, of the stupendous genius and mental activity of the Grecians, of the wars and wonderful virtue of the early Romans—of their subsequent degenerating—of the decline of that mighty empire, of chivalry, Christianity, and kings. I heard of the discovery of the American hemisphere and wept with Safie over the hapless fate of its original inhabitants.

"These wonderful narrations inspired me with strange feelings. Was man, indeed, at once so powerful, so virtuous and magnificent, yet so vicious and base? He appeared at one time a mere scion of the evil principle and at another as all that can be conceived of noble and godlike. To be a great and virtuous man appeared the highest honour that can befall a sensitive being; to be base and vicious, as many on record have been, appeared the lowest degradation, a condition more abject than that of the blind mole or harmless worm. For a long time I could not conceive how one man could go forth to murder his fellow, or even why there were laws and governments; but when I heard details of vice and bloodshed, my wonder ceased and I turned away with disgust and loathing.

"Every conversation of the cottagers now opened new wonders to me. While I listened to the instructions which Felix bestowed upon the Arabian, the strange system of human society was explained to me. I heard of the division of property, of immense wealth and squalid poverty, of rank, descent, and noble blood."

"The words induced me to turn towards myself. I learned that the possessions most esteemed by your fellow creatures were high and unsullied descent united with riches. A man might be respected with only one of these advantages, but without either he was considered, except in very rare instances, as a vagabond and a slave, doomed to waste his powers for the profits of the chosen few! And what was I? Of my creation and creator I was absolutely ignorant, but I knew that I possessed no money, no friends, no kind of property. I was, besides, endued with a figure hideously deformed and loathsome; I was not even of the same nature as man. I was more agile than they and could subsist upon coarser diet; I bore the extremes of heat and cold with less injury to my frame; my stature far exceeded theirs. When I looked around I saw and heard of none like me. Was I, then, a monster, a blot upon the earth, from which all men fled and whom all men disowned?

"I cannot describe to you the agony that these reflections inflicted upon me; I tried to dispel them, but sorrow only increased with knowledge. Oh, that I had forever remained in my native wood, nor known nor felt beyond the sensations of hunger, thirst, and heat!

"Of what a strange nature is knowledge! It clings to the mind when it has once seized on it like a lichen on the rock. I wished sometimes to shake off all thought and feeling, but I learned that there was but one means to overcome the sensation of pain, and that was death—a state which I feared yet did not understand. I admired virtue and good feelings and loved the gentle manners and amiable qualities of my cottagers, but I was shut out from intercourse with them, except through means which I obtained by stealth, when I was unseen and unknown, and which rather increased than satisfied the desire I had of becoming one among my fellows. The gentle words of Agatha and the animated smiles of the charming Arabian were not for me. The mild exhortations of the old man and the lively conversation of the loved Felix were not for me. Miserable, unhappy wretch!

"Other lessons were impressed upon me even more deeply. I heard of the difference of sexes, and the birth and growth of children, how the father doted on the smiles of the infant, and the lively sallies of the older child, how all the life and cares of the mother were wrapped up in the precious charge, how the mind of youth expanded and gained knowledge, of brother, sister, and all the various relationships which bind one human being to another in mutual bonds.

"But where were my friends and relations? No father had watched my infant days, no mother had blessed me with smiles and caresses; or if they had, all my past life was now a blot, a blind vacancy in which I distinguished nothing. From my earliest remembrance I had been as I then was in height and proportion. I had never yet seen a being resembling me or who claimed any intercourse with me. What was I? The question again recurred, to be answered only with groans.

"I will soon explain to what these feelings tended, but allow me now to return to the cottagers, whose story excited in me such various feelings of indignation, delight, and wonder, but which all terminated in additional love and reverence for my protectors (for so I loved, in an innocent, half-painful self-deceit, to call them)."

思考题

1. What has motivated Victor Frankenstein to create the artificial life? In what ways has Victor Frankenstein's creation challenged conventional understandings about the birth of a life?
2. According to Victor Frankenstein, what's the most important thing a scientist has to consider in the creation of artificial life?
3. What ethical responsibility do you think Victor Frankenstein should take for the monster he has created? If you were Victor Frankenstein, what would you do with the monster?
4. How do you understand the monster's endeavor to learn human language? Do you think artificial life should be endowed with the same ability as humans, especially the ability to think, speak and write?
5. How shall we look at the monster's need for love and recognition from human beings? Should he be given the equal rights as those enjoyed by humans?
6. Should human beings create artificial life and artificial intelligence? What's your view about the future of artificial life and artificial intelligence?

第三节　补充阅读《机器中的达尔文》

阅读萨缪尔·巴特勒(Samuel Butler, 1835—1902)发表于1863年的散文《机器中的达尔文》("Darwin among the Machines"),思考人工智能/智能机器对人类社会的影响。

Darwin among the Machines[①]

Samuel Butler

SIR—There are few things of which the present generation is more justly proud than of the wonderful improvements which are daily taking place in all sorts of mechanical

---

① "A first year in Canterbury settlement with other early essays"[Z/OL].[2023-07-25]. https://nzetc.victoria.ac.nz/tm/scholarly/tei-ButFir-t1-g1-t1-g1-t4-body.html.

appliances. And indeed it is matter for great congratulation on many grounds. It is unnecessary to mention these here, for they are sufficiently obvious; our present business lies with considerations which may somewhat tend to humble our pride and to make us think seriously of the future prospects of the human race. If we revert to the earliest primordial types of mechanical life, to the lever, the wedge, the inclined plane, the screw and the pulley, or (for analogy would lead us one step further) to that one primordial type from which all the mechanical kingdom has been developed, we mean to the lever itself, and if we then examine the machinery of the Great Eastern, we find ourselves almost awestruck at the vast development of the mechanical world, at the gigantic strides with which it has advanced in comparison with the slow progress of the animal and vegetable kingdom. We shall find it impossible to refrain from asking ourselves what the end of this mighty movement is to be. In what direction is it tending? What will be its upshot? To give a few imperfect hints towards a solution of these questions is the object of the present letter.

We have used the words "mechanical life," "the mechanical kingdom," "the mechanical world" and so forth, and we have done so advisedly, for as the vegetable kingdom was slowly developed from the mineral, and as in like manner the animal supervened upon the vegetable, so now in these last few ages an entirely new kingdom has sprung up, of which we as yet have only seen what will one day be considered the antediluvian prototypes of the race.

We regret deeply that our knowledge both of natural history and of machinery is too small to enable us to undertake the gigantic task of classifying machines into the genera and sub-genera, species, varieties and sub-varieties, and so forth, of tracing the connecting links between machines of widely different characters, of pointing out how subservience to the use of man has played that part among machines which natural selection has performed in the animal and vegetable kingdoms, of pointing out rudimentary organs which exist in some few machines, feebly developed and perfectly useless, yet serving to mark descent from some ancestral type which has either perished or been modified into some new phase of mechanical existence. We can only point out this field for investigation; it must be followed by others whose education and talents have been of a much higher order than any which we can lay claim to.

Some few hints we have determined to venture upon, though we do so with the profoundest diffidence. Firstly, we would remark that as some of the lowest of the vertebrata attained a far greater size than has descended to their more highly organised living representatives, so adiminution in the size of machines has often attended their development and progress. Take the watch for instance. Examine the beautiful structure of the little animal, watch the intelligent play of the minute members which compose it; yet this little creature is but a development of the cumbrous clocks of the thirteenth century— it is no deterioration from them. The day may come when clocks, which certainly at the present day are not diminishing in bulk, may be entirely superseded by the universal use of watches, in which case clocks will become extinct like the earlier saurians, while the watch (whose tendency has for some years been rather to decrease in size than the contrary) will remain the only existing type of an extinct race.

The views of machinery which we are thus feebly indicating will suggest the solution of one of the greatest and most mysterious questions of the day. We refer to the question: What sort of creature man's next successor in the supremacy of the earth is likely to be. We have often heard this debated; but it appears to us that we are ourselves creating our own successors; we are daily adding to the beauty and delicacy of their physical organisation; we are daily giving them greater power and supplying by all sorts of ingenious contrivances that self-regulating, self-acting power which will be to them what intellect has been to the human race. In the course of ages we shall find ourselves the inferior race. Inferior in power, inferior in that moral quality of self-control, we shall look up to them as the acme of all that the best and wisest man can ever dare to aim at. No evil passions, no jealousy, no avarice, no impure desires will disturb the serene might of those glorious creatures. Sin, shame, and sorrow will have no place among them. Their minds will be in a state of perpetual calm, the contentment of a spirit that knows no wants, is disturbed by no regrets. Ambition will never torture them. Ingratitude will never cause them the uneasiness of a moment. The guilty conscience, the hope deferred, the pains of exile, the insolence of office, and the spurns that patient merit of the unworthy takes —these will be entirely unknown to them. If they want "feeding" (by the use of which very word we betray our recognition of them as living organism) they will be attended by patient slaves whose business and interest it will be

第六章 文学与人工智能/生命（Literature and AI/AL）

to see that they shall want for nothing. If they are out of order they will be promptly attended to by physicians who are thoroughly acquainted with their constitutions; if they die, for even these glorious animals will not be exempt from that necessary and universal consummation, they will immediately enter into a new phase of existence, for what machine dies entirely in every part at one and the same instant?

We take it that when the state of things shall have arrived which we have been above attempting to describe, man will have become to the machine what the horse and the dog are to man. He will continue to exist, nay even to improve, and will be probably better off in his state of domestication under the beneficent rule of the machines than he is in his present wild state. We treat our horses, dogs, cattle, and sheep, on the whole, with great kindness; we give them whatever experience teaches us to be best for them, and there can be no doubt that our use of meat has added to the happiness of the lower animals far more than it has detracted from it; in like manner it is reasonable to suppose that the machines will treat us kindly, for their existence is as dependent upon ours as ours is upon the lower animals. They cannot kill us and eat us as we do sheep; they will not only require our services in the parturition of their young (which branch of their economy will remain always in our hands), but also in feeding them, in setting them right when they are sick, and burying their dead or working up their corpses into new machines. It is obvious that if all the animals in Great Britain save man alone were to die, and if at the same time all intercourse with foreign countries were by some sudden catastrophe to be rendered perfectly impossible, it is obvious that under such circumstances the loss of human life would be something fearful to contemplate—in like manner were mankind to cease, the machines would be as badly off or evenworse. The fact is that our interests are inseparable from theirs, and theirs from ours. Each race is dependent upon the other for innumerable benefits, and, until the reproductive organs of the machines have been developed in a manner which we are hardly yet able to conceive, they are entirely dependent upon man for even the continuance of their species. It is true that these organs may be ultimately developed, inasmuch as man's interest lies in that direction; there is nothing which our infatuated race would desire more than to see a fertile union between two steam engines; it is true that machinery is even at this present time employed in begetting machinery, in becoming the parent of machines often after its own kind, but the days of flirtation, courtship, and matrimony appear to be very remote, and indeed can hardly be realised by our feeble and imperfect imagination.

Day by day, however, the machines are gaining ground upon us; day by day we are becoming more subservient to them; more men are daily bound down as slaves to tend them, more men are daily devoting the energies of their whole lives to the development of mechanical life. The upshot is simply a question of time, but that the time will come when the machines will hold the real supremacy over the world and its inhabitants is what no person of a truly philosophic mind can for a moment question.

Our opinion is that war to the death should be instantly proclaimed against them. Every machine of every sort should be destroyed by the well-wisher of his species. Let there be no exceptions made, no quarter shown; let us at once go back to the primeval condition of the race. If it be urged that this is impossible under the present condition of human affairs, this at once proves that the mischief is already done, that our servitude has commenced in good earnest, that we have raised a race of beings whom it is beyond our power to destroy, and that we are not only enslaved but are absolutely acquiescent in our bondage.

For the present we shall leave this subject, which we present gratis to the members of the Philosophical Society. Should they consent to avail themselves of the vast field which we have pointed out, we shall endeavour to labour in it ourselves at some future and indefinite period.

I am, Sir, etc.,
CELLARIUS

第七章

文学与农学(Literature and Agriculture)

第一节　农业科学的文学表征

背景知识

　　农业在汉语中一般是指栽培农作物和饲养牲畜的生产事业。在国民经济中,农业还包括林业、畜牧业、渔业和农村副业等生产在内。所以,又有"农学""农业科学"等表达。所谓"农学",是指研究农业生产的科学,内容包括作物栽培、育种、土壤、气象、肥料、农业病虫害等①。"农业科学"通常是指研究农业发展自然规律和经济规律的科学,涉及面较广,如:农业环境,农作物、畜牧生产,农业工程和农业经济等多种科学,因此具有综合性,并且,广义的农业科学也包括林业科学和水产科学等。而在英语中,农业"agriculture"一词,原出自拉丁文,"agri"是土地,"culture"是耕作栽培之意,农业本身就被定义为一门科学或艺术,它是指耕作土壤、收获作物和饲养牲畜的科学或艺术;亦即生产对人类有用的植物和动物,以及在不同程度上制备这些产品供人类使用和处置(如通过营销)的科学或艺术②。总之,农业是人类社会最古老、最基本的生产活动,它是人类利用自然环境提供的条件,通过促进和控制生物体(包括植物、动物和微生物)的生命活动来取得人类社会所需要的产品的活动③。

　　人类历史可追溯到300多万年前,而农业则在新石器时代初期才出现,距今约有1万多年的历史。在农业出现前的数百万年岁月里,人类祖先依靠采集、狩猎维生活,在这漫长的历史过程中,逐渐积累了某些有用植物生长发育的知识,同时也观察到丢弃在居住地周围的野生种子和果实残余可以发芽、生长、开花、结实,此后人们就在住所附近种植植物,并不断地重复这一过程,最终把可食用的野生植物驯化为农作物。这就是最简单、最原始的农业——种植业的开始。随着农业的出现,家畜的饲养在狩猎的基础上也产生了。

　　中国是世界上最早从事农业生产的地区之一,也是世界农作物起源中心之一。农业的

---

① 中国社会科学院语言研究所词典编辑室. 现代汉语词典[M]. 5版. 北京:商务印书馆,2005:1005.
② GOVE P B. Webster's third new international dictionary of the English language[M]. Springfield:G & C Merriam Co,1961:44.
③ 徐文修,万素梅,刘建国. 农学概论[M]. 北京:中国农业大学出版社,2018:2.

出现是在不同地区各自独立发生的。凡是有人居住的地方,在条件成熟以后,都不可避免地由采集、狩猎向农业转变。目前学术界一般认为,东亚、西亚(中东)和中美洲等是世界农业起源的三个中心。东亚最早的农业地区是黄河流域和长江流域。黄河流域土壤疏松肥沃,气候温暖干燥,为以种植谷子、大豆为特色的原始旱地农业的发生、发展提供了良好的自然条件;长江流域气候温暖湿润、雨量充沛,为以水稻种植为特色的原始水田农业的发展创造了条件。西亚的底格里斯河和幼发拉底河流域,还有古埃及的尼罗河流域也是世界农业最早的发生地。当欧洲还处在中石器时代时,西亚就已进入新石器时代,出现了农业的萌芽,并逐步转向种植和饲养。中美洲的墨西哥除驯化玉米外,还培育了甘薯、马铃薯、花生、向日葵、辣椒、南瓜等一大批在当今世界上受到广泛利用的作物。

农业的发展大都经历了以下三个阶段:(1) 原始农业(原始社会末期和奴隶社会时期)。原始农业阶段指的是人类摆脱了采集、狩猎生活并能依靠自己的劳动来增加食物的农业发展阶段。(2) 传统农业(封建社会时期)。传统农业阶段指的是从畜力和铁制农具出现以后,到大机器使用以前这一时期的农业发展阶段。在西方开始于希腊、罗马时期,在我国则产生于春秋战国时期。这一阶段经历了大约2000年的时间,农业生产主要是为满足生产者的需要,所以是一种封闭或半封闭自给自足的自然经济。但也正是传统农业的发展,进一步增加了农业剩余产品的数量,从而可以维持更多的非农人口,因而在更大的范围内促进了手工业和商业的发展。随着手工业和商业的不断发展,非农人口数量不断增加,而且向中心地带集中,从而形成了城市,更为重要的是传统农业的发展导致国家的兴起,并为工业革命准备了必要条件。(3) 现代农业(始于19世纪中叶)。现代农业是指工业化以来高资本、高能量、高技术投入,并以商品生产为主要特征的农业生产体系,首先发生于欧洲和北美洲,又可分为三个时期:19世纪到20世纪初,是传统农业向现代农业转变的过渡时期;20世纪初到20世纪50年代,是现代农业的确立时期;20世纪50年代后,是现代农业的发展时期。现代农业与传统农业相比,即整个生产过程都是建立在现代科学技术基础之上的,机械工业、能源工业和化学工业的迅猛发展为农业生产提供了新的、更大规模的物质、能量来源,它不仅满足了人口加速增长对食物数量方面的需求和经济增长导致的对食物质量和花色品种的需求,同时还提供了日益增多的工业原料。现代农业取得巨大成就的同时,也给社会的进一步发展带来了严重的问题,并使人类面临着严峻的挑战,例如能源危机、环境污染、土地退化等问题。对于这些问题,人类应客观地分析,并积极寻找解决问题的有效途径[①]。

文学与农业科学虽是不同的概念,但却有着不可分割的联系。从广义上而言,文学是关于人的学问,具体来说,文学是"以语言文字为工具形象化地反映客观现实的艺术,包括戏

[①] 徐文修,万素梅,刘建国. 农学概论[M]. 北京:中国农业大学出版社,2018:2-3.

剧、诗歌、小说、散文等"①。如透过我国最早的一部诗歌总集《诗经》，就不难了解公元前11世纪到公元前6世纪(西周初年至春秋中叶)社会生活的方方面面，如劳动与爱情、风俗与婚姻、祭祖与宴会，甚至天象、地貌、动物、植物等。本章认为那些关于农业的书籍，从广义上而言，都可以被视为文学作品，特别是在西方现代学科划分之前，尤其如此。从这个角度来看，我国关于农业科学的语言文字成果，不仅产出较早，而且相当丰硕。如：大约成书于北魏末年(533—544)的《齐民要术》，其作者贾思勰就在书中构建了"较为完整的农业科学体系"②。其实，早在该书成书之前，就有《氾胜之书》和《四民月令》等的存在。《氾胜之书》是西汉(前206—公元25)晚期氾胜之汇录的一部农学著作，这本书一般被认为是我国"现存最早的农书"③。《齐民要术》对《氾胜之书》和《四民月令》等书都有所引用，其中引用《氾胜之书》为最多。总之，我国的这些农书都是中国劳动人民数千年耕作经验的总结，这些成果体现了我国劳动人民顺四时、识寒暑，遵循自然规律；向自然索要劳动成果时，不仅取之有节，而且用之有度，充分体现了"天人合一"的思想。

西方早期，也可见歌颂农业劳作、描绘淳朴的乡村风景的文学作品。如公元前8世纪末至7世纪初的古希腊诗人赫西俄德的作品《工作与时日》，这不仅是一部有关劝诫的道德格言集，还是一部农业历书。再如古罗马诗人维吉尔(Publius Vergilius Maro, 70—19 BCE)为鼓励人民务农，在公元前29年发表的《农事诗》(Georgics)。早期美国文学多推崇重农思想(agrarianism)，如克里夫库尔(J. Hector St. John de Crèvecoeur, 1735—1813)在《一位美国农夫的来信》(Letters from an American Farmer, 1782)中把自耕农生活描绘成理想化生活。

随着城市化和工业革命的发展，尽管西方传统农耕文明逐渐解体，但是关于土地、自然、乡村等的文学并未因此而衰亡。一方面，讲述土地故事、为自然代言的文学传统始终有着历史的传承；另一方面，还出现了许多讴歌传统农业方式、怀念乡村文明，反对工业化社会，主张保持农业传统的文学流派及作品等。据统计，20世纪末英国最流行的两位19世纪英国作家是简·奥斯汀和托马斯·哈代，他们作品的借阅量总是居于图书馆借阅量的榜首。人们对此根源也进行了探究。尽管奥斯汀代表的是一个逝去的世界，在这当中逝去的是优雅、宫廷风格的服装、端庄的举止、广泛意义上的仕女风度和绅士风度，以及漂亮的房屋；与此同时，哈代所代表的是对树篱灌木、干草堆和健壮的英国乡村简朴、诚实、田园风格生活方式的怀念。尽管前者代言较高的阶层，后者心系较低的阶级，两者间不乏共同特点，即都代表了对理想的生活的向往，在这两个阶级的世界中都没有汽车活动的空间。总之，他们所表现的是英国

---

① 中国社会科学院语言研究所词典编辑室. 现代汉语词典[M]. 5版. 北京：商务印书馆，2005：1428-1429页.
② 王瑞文，柳松，黄凤芝. 中国传统文化概论[M]. 北京：北京工业大学出版社，2019：180.
③ 李会影. 世界古代科技发明创造大全[M]. 北京：北京工业大学出版社，2015：113.

乡村的树荫、草坪和小路的精神,展示了比较理想的人与自然和谐相处的生活,而这种生活随着工业化、城市化的不断推进,正在逝去,因而也深为多数人所眷念,正如英国诗人菲利普·拉金(Philip Larkin,1922—1985)在《去了,去了》一诗中所写的那样:

> 英国的这一切都将逝去,
> 树荫、草坪、小路,
> 会馆、雕刻在教堂上的唱诗班。
> 将要留下的是书;它将在各种画廊里
> 流连;但现在为我们所留下的
> 将是混凝土和轮胎①。

在美国,与农业较为接近、讲述土地故事、为自然代言的文学,即美国自然文学,虽然自20世纪下半叶在文坛兴起,但其实这种对自然的书写,可追溯到早期的美国文学。"它是一种讲述土地的故事并从中探索人类心灵的图谱与地理图谱相依附的文学,是将自然史与人类发展史融合在一起的文学②。"梭罗的《瓦尔登湖》(Walden,1854)、惠特曼的诗、苏珊·库珀(Susan F. Cooper,1813—1894)的《乡村时光》(Rural Hours,1850)等无不体现了这种书写。20世纪30年代,美国出现经济危机,各种矛盾日趋激化,南方出现了"重农学派",他们反对工业化社会,提倡维护南方传统的乡土文学,主张南方继续保持农业传统。他们还创办了《南方评论》(Southern Review)和《基农评论》(Kenon Review)两本杂志作为自己的阵地,这对美国"新批评派"(New Criticism)文艺理论的形成起到很大的作用。

其实,反映工业化对农业影响的文学作品,并不罕见。托马斯·哈代的《德伯家的苔丝》(Tess of the d'Urbervilles,1891)和约翰·斯坦贝克(John Steinbeck,1902—1968)的《愤怒的葡萄》(The Grapes of Wrath,1939)就都反映了现代化对农民的不良影响。哈代在《德伯家的苔丝》中塑造的主人公一家经历了由自给自足的经济状态向受雇于人、被人剥削的农业工人的转变,最后结局悲惨。斯坦贝克《愤怒的葡萄》则揭露了农业机械化背景下农民的生存困境以及生态被严重破坏的危机。

总之,如果说西方20世纪以前,许多文学作品字里行间主要表达了对农业和土地的深切歌颂,那么20世纪以后,情况开始发生变化,随着人们逐渐发现农业生产也会对环境造成破坏,农业不再是环境友好型的,甚至对环境具有毒害作用③,于是通过创作相关文学作品,将相关认识表达了出来。如:雷彻尔·卡逊(Rachel Carson,1907—1964)的《寂静的春天》(Silent Spring,1962)以及简·斯迈利(Jane Smiley,1949—)的长篇小说《千亩农庄》(A

---

① BATE J. Culture and environment: from Austen to Hardy[J]. New Literary History,1999(30):541-560.
② 程虹. 美国自然文学三十讲[M]. 上海:外语教学与研究出版社,2014:i.
③ WUNDERLICH G. Hues of American agrarianism[J]. Agriculture and human values,2000(17):195-196.

Thousand Acres, 1991)就都揭露了农药等农业科技滥用给人类和环境带来的极大危害。随着农业工业化和商品化,食物的生产越来越依赖农药、化肥和添加剂,随之而来的食品安全问题也越发受到人们的关注,如:麦克·波伦(Michael Pollan,1955—)的《杂食动物的困境》(*The Omnivore's Dilemma*,2006)和《食物无罪》(*In Defense of Food*,2008)等就揭露了食品与土地、食品与人类关系的异化现象①,透露出对食物与土地之间纽带松动的担忧。

文献传真

阅读《农业研究》("Agricultural Studies"),并回答文末思考题。本文节选自《劳特利奇指南:文学与科学》②。

Agricultural Studies

Susan M. Squier

Agrarian studies is explicit in its intention to include the humanities in its social sciences centered area of investigation. Yet unlike agrarian studies' attention to "rural life and society" broadly conceived, agricultural studies displays an explicit focus on agriculture. Moreover, while agrarian studies (despite its intentions) draws its strength predominantly from the social sciences, agricultural studies enroll scholars in several emergent (and often interconnecting) areas of literary studies including science studies, animal studies, ecocriticism and environmental studies, women and gender studies, and science fiction. Literature-and-science scholars have begun to use specifically literary methods to assess the impact of agricultural innovations on the individual and society. For example, science studies scholars are forging a critical literature that explores the role of scientized agriculture in the production of the human being as citizen. [...]

What is the agricultural studies method in practice, then? We can see its outlines by comparing Broglio's approach to Romantic literature and art with William Conlogue's treatment of nineteenth- and twentieth-century American farm texts, *Working the Garden: American Writers and the Industrialization of Agriculture*(2001). Both studies consider an aesthetic category and set of cultural practices in relation to an agricultural

---

① 杨颖育.谁动了我们的"食物":当代美国生态文学中的食物书写与环境预警[J].当代文坛,2011(2):113.
② SQUIER S M. Agricultural studies[C]//CLARKE B, ROSSINI M. The Routledge companion to literature and science. London: Routledge, 2011: 242-252.

innovation: whether it is the new practice of cross-breeding cattle (Broglio) or the restructuring of American wheat farming (Conlogue). In both studies, the juxtaposition of art and agricultural science results in a reevaluation of customary aesthetic judgments: a reassessment of the picturesque for the former, and for the latter a challenge to the literary reliance on the pastoral mode as the appropriate prism through which to interpret the "farm text" (Conlogue 2001).① And essential to each study is a thick description of changing agricultural practices: the new impetus to improve British beef by selective breeding, and the new huge bonanza wheat farms that emerged in the 1880s in the Dakotas' Red River Valley.

Exploring farm literature as a site of intense debate over the changes in American agriculture resulting from industrialization, Conlogue argues against using the literary model of the pastoral to approach these texts. Virgil's *Georgics* offer a better lens: the *georgic* addresses issues of "how work, community, technological restraint, and human uses of nature changed with the introduction of an urban-defined industrial agriculture that has erased the pastoral's central tension between city and country". ②Conlogue's study distinguishes between the Old Agriculture, infused with the values of yeoman-like integrity, community, and the worth of inherited farm knowledge, and the New Agriculture, characterized by a rationalized, industrialized business model with profit at the core. Challenging an earlier formulation of the genre as any form of fiction that deals with farm life, that accurately portrays the details of farming in a vernacular style and reflects the essentially conservative attitudes and values of farming people, Conlogue reveals what differentiates an agricultural studies perspective, which responds to actually occurring changes in farming structure and practice, from a simple focus on agricultural themes. Viewed from his engaged perspective, with a focus on the relations between culture and the production of individual subjects, he defines farm fiction as that which attends to the interrelationships of the natural world and the world of human work, the force and importance of history, the relation between the well-being of individual farm

---

① CONLOGUE W. Working the garden: American writers and the industrialization of agriculture [M]. Chapel Hill: University of North Carolina Press, 2001.
② SQUIER S M. Agricultural studies[C]//CLARKE B, ROSSINI M. The Routledge companion to literature and science. London: Routledge, 2011: 9.

第七章 文学与农学(Literature and Agriculture)

families and the broader community, and the effect of technologies (particularly but not exclusively agricultural technologies) on human beings and the environment.

Conlogue's agricultural studies analysis of farm fiction is attentive to gender, ethnicity, and race, categories which have all been intimately shaped by, and have left their mark on, the structure and practice of agriculture in the United States. Offering chapters assessing the visibility (or lack thereof) of women in the New Agriculture; the relationship between class and the transformation of agriculture from a way of life to a business; and the relationship between racism and industrial farming, Conlogue's study exemplifies the agricultural studies method of giving equal attention to the epistemological practices of widely divergent disciplines, including both a chart drawn from rural sociology that provides a detailed comparison of conventional and alternative agriculture, and also Conlogue's own autobiographical narrative. This strategic openness to both modes of knowledge exemplifies agricultural studies' commitment to analyzing the meaning of agriculture at all scales and magnitudes.

We have seen that agricultural studies characteristically gives us new ways to think about literary analysis as well as an understanding of changes in agricultural science. Janet Galligani Casey's *A New Heartland: Women, Modernity, and the Agrarian Ideal in America* exemplifies this method by reviewing modernism/modernity through the lens of agriculture. Casey argues that rural texts are modernist in that they challenge the dominant ideologies of agrarian life, ranging from its conservative positions on gender and race to its radical embrace of agricultural rationalization.[①] Turning to popular bestsellers, the early twentieth-century agricultural periodical *The Farmer's Wife*, and the work of two women rural photographers, this study, too, incorporates non-canonical texts, arguing that in their resistance to the categories of the pastoral and the agrarian ideal, these rural texts constitute a distinctly modern kind of aesthetic production.

Returning, in closing, to Raymond Williams's glimpse out of his window, we can consider how this paragraph exemplifies agricultural studiesabove. As we begin reading, we sense the scene's distinctly English tone. The elms, the white horse, and the may or hawthorn tree carry resonances of ancient Druid festivals and village celebrations of the

---

① CASEY J G. A new heartland: women, modernity, and the agrarian ideal in America[M]. Oxford: Oxford University Press, 2002.

maypole, as well as echoes of Alfred Tennyson's "immemorial elms" (1847) and G. K Chesterton's *Ballad of the White Horse*(1911). We can follow Williams's vision of the country as it expands from the simply botanical and naturalist perspective to the explicitly agricultural, as he acknowledges that "there is a deep contrast in which so much feeling is held: between what seems an unmediated nature—a physical awareness of trees, birds, the moving shapes of land—and a working agriculture, in which so much of nature is in fact being produced". ①

This awareness of deep contrast is essential to agricultural studies, a method of analysis attentive to the role of technique in all aspects of the agricultural endeavor. It understands technology not only as the pruning shears which the farm laborers carry, but also the technology of gender that differentiates male from female farm workers, so that the men in their typical khaki coats and the women in their kerchiefs do different kinds of work at different times. ② The men prune while the women harvest; the men work from morning to evening while the women can only hire themselves out as harvesters during school hours when the children are out of the home. And unlike the men, women's agricultural work is not only productive, but reproductive. As with the livestock (the pigs and the sheep), for women their share of farm work includes the bearing of and caring for children, as well as keeping the household.

Reading this passage from an agricultural studies perspective, we notice the rhythm of animal birth and death that forms the core of agriculture; we explore the texture and imprint of technology upon the land (those serrated tracks in the mud); and we see time passing—both the passage of a day (that small hours light in the pigsty as the farmer helps with a litter of pigs), and an era (as good farm land gives way to a crop of new plots of sour boulder clay, sold on speculation for suburban housing). And we can formulate the essential qualities of an agricultural studies perspective. It will be situated in space and place, aware of the forces of gender and class, and sensitive not only to myth and folk knowledge, but to technology, economics and culture as well. While such complex, simultaneous, and often clashing experiences and meanings by no means

---

① WILLIAMS R. The country and the city[M]. Oxford: Oxford University Press, 1973: 3.
② TERESA D L. Technologies of gender: essays on theory, film, and fiction[M]. Bloomington: Indiana University Press, 1987.

exhaust its potential, they at least suggest some of the intellectual and cultural importance of the field of agricultural studies.

思考题

1. What is the purpose of agricultural research in the field of literature?
2. What is the core of agricultural research in the field of literature?
3. How does agricultural research relate to gender, race and ideology?

第二节 《德伯家的苔丝》与农业科学

作品导读

1. 作者简介

《德伯家的苔丝》简称《苔丝》，是英国著名诗人、小说家托马斯·哈代的代表作。哈代是横跨两个世纪的作家，早期和中期的创作以小说为主，继承和发扬了维多利亚时代的文学传统；晚年以其出色的诗歌开拓了英国20世纪的文学。1840年6月2日，哈代出生在多塞特郡（Dorset）多尔切斯特（Dorchester）郊外的上伯克汉普顿（Higher Bockhampton）。他的父亲是一个承包建筑业务的小建筑师，爱好音乐；母亲杰迈玛·汉德（Jemima Hand，1813—1904）重视知识与教育，擅长讲民间故事。哈代是他们的长子①。多塞特郡是农业郡，在哈代青少年时期，几乎没有近代工业。多塞特郡又毗邻大荒原。哈代8岁开始在本村上小学，后来转到郡城的一所学校学习拉丁语言和文学。1856年哈代离开学校，来到多尔切斯特，跟随一个教堂建筑师做学徒。在此期间，他结识了多塞特郡著名的语言学家和田园诗人威廉·巴恩斯（William Barnes，1801—1886），并受其影响。其间，哈代开始研读文学和哲学著作，并自学希腊文，阅读《圣经》和其他神学著作。由于此时哈代一直生活在农业郡的氛围之中，他对农民的生活、性格、风俗、语言等极为熟悉。1862年，哈代离开多尔切斯特，前往伦敦，开始在阿瑟·布洛姆菲尔德（Arthur Blomfield，1829—1899）的建筑师事务所工作。在伦敦的五年，是哈代思想形成过程中的最重要时期。哈代在名建筑师布洛姆菲尔德手下当绘图员，曾在建筑论文比赛中获奖。同时继续钻研文学和哲学，并在伦敦大学皇家学院进修近代语言，特别是法语。当时《物种起源》刚发表不久，哈代接受了达尔文的进化论。叔本华的"唯意志论"哲学和赫胥黎的不可知论对哈代的思想也产生了较大的影响。这一切促使他

---

① 何宁. 哈代研究史[M]. 南京：译林出版社，2011：314.

放弃了在家乡初步形成的基督教观念而成为一名自由主义者。特别是他在城市生活的实践,使他进一步看清了城市与农村在思想、道德、风俗、习惯上的巨大差异。1867 年,哈代因身体不能适应伦敦的气候,返回故乡多塞特,从事建筑工作,同时开始文学创作。哈代的文学生涯开始于诗歌,后因无缘发表,改试小说创作。1874 年,哈代与爱玛·吉福德(Emma Lavinia Gifford, 1840—1912)结婚,1912 年爱玛去世。1914 年 2 月,哈代与其秘书达格戴尔(Florence Emily Dugdale, 1879—1937)结婚,同年 11 月发表了纪念爱玛的《1912—13 组诗》(Poems of 1912-13)。哈代晚年开始编写自传。1928 年 1 月哈代逝世,其骨灰被安放在西敏寺的诗人角,而心脏被葬在故乡斯廷斯福德(Stinsford)墓园。

  托马斯·哈代,不管是作为小说家还是诗人,其创作成就都比较高。在小说创作方面,他不仅被认为是英国现实主义时期文学(19 世纪 30 年代—1918)的杰出代表,而且还被认为是英国现代主义小说的先驱之一。他的诗歌创作同样影响深远。例如,诗人奥登把他看成济慈(John Keats, 1795—1821)和卡尔·桑德堡(Carl Sandburg, 1878—1967),认为哈代是其诗歌之父,而唐纳德·戴维(Donald Davie, 1922—1995)则认为:对二十世纪英国诗歌产生重大影响的是哈代,而不是叶芝或艾略特[①]。

  哈代的小说基本以农村为题材,与农业科学关系密切。他一生共发表了近 20 部长篇小说,早期作品《绿荫树下》(Under the Greenwood Tree, 1872)、《一双湛蓝的眼睛》(A Pair of Blue Eyes, 1873)和《远离尘嚣》(Far from the Madding Crowd, 1874)描写了农村恬静明朗的田园生活。《还乡》(The Return of the Native, 1878)的出版确立了其作为重要作家的地位,标志着他开始转向人物的悲剧,此类作品有《卡斯特桥市长》(The Mayor of Casterbridge, 1886)、《德伯家的苔丝》和《无名的裘德》(Jude the Obscure, 1895)等。《无名的裘德》出版后,受到社会上各种批评责难,哈代转而全力从事诗歌创作,除了近千首短小的抒情诗外,还著有以拿破仑战争为题材的三卷本诗剧《列王》(The Dynasts, 1904—1908)。此外,哈代还创作了许多以"威塞克斯(Wessex)故事"为总名的中短篇小说。

  事实上,这些小说都以他的故乡多塞特郡及其附近的农村地区为背景,但他没有用家乡的真名"多塞特",而是统一用了"威塞克斯"这个名称。在小说里,"威塞克斯"是英国南部农村残留下来的一个家长统治的宗法社会。工业革命后的英国,资产阶级虽在全国取得了统治地位,但威塞克斯依然是一个没有经受"现代文明"洗礼的地方。它保持着旧有传统风习,敌视资产阶级现代文明,企图消除由于资产阶级的影响而出现的动荡不安。哈代后期作品明显变得阴郁低沉,其主题思想是无法控制的外部力量和内心冲动决定着个人命运,并造成悲剧。毕竟,资产阶级不断侵蚀着威塞克斯地区,传统习俗和旧有秩序遭到破坏,威塞克斯社会的主要阶级——农民阶级的命运发生了悲剧性变化。《德伯家的苔丝》和《无名的裘

[①] 聂珍钊. 托马斯·哈代小说研究:悲戚而刚毅的艺术家[M]. 武汉:华中师范大学出版社,1992:12.

第七章 文学与农学（Literature and Agriculture）

德》就讲述了威塞克斯农村青年男女走投无路、陷于绝望的悲剧故事①。

哈代的小说创作可以分为三个阶段。第一阶段的作品包括《绿荫下》《远离尘嚣》等，带有浪漫主义的风格，是田园理想的颂歌。第二阶段的作品主要描写威塞克斯社会的悲剧，如《还乡》《卡斯特桥市长》等。第三阶段的作品有《德伯家德苔丝》《无名的裘德》等，主要描写威塞克斯破产农民的前途和命运。总之，哈代的小说以优秀的艺术形象记叙了十九世纪英国南部宗法制农村社会毁灭的历史，表现了英国农村社会的历史变迁②。他笔下的小说关注维多利亚时代工业革命的发展对英国传统农业社会的侵蚀，展现了农业科技的变化对农民的影响，关注到了技术高速发展下人类的命运，思考其对底层农民带来的危机和身份转变。因此本章将节选《苔丝》部分内容，讨论小说如何展现农业科学的发展给人们带来的影响，进而思考文学在揭露社会变化带来的问题、引发人们思考方面所起到的作用。

2. 作品介绍

《德伯家的苔丝》主要讲述了一位美丽、善良、纯洁的农家姑娘的悲剧故事。在群山环抱、美丽而幽静的布蕾谷（the Vale of Blackmoor）居住着德北菲尔德（Durbeyfield）一家，他们家境十分贫寒，老德北是一个乡下小贩，做着一点小买卖。5月末的一个傍晚，在通往马勒村的路上，牧师特林厄姆（Parson Tringham）告诉德北，说他考证发现德北原是当地古老的武士世家德伯氏（D'Urbervilles）的嫡系子孙。德北生性懒惰，又好喝酒，得知自己出身名门的当天晚上，他又喝得酩酊大醉。由于父亲喝醉不能去送货，德北17岁的女儿苔丝（Tess）勇敢地承担了替父亲赶集卖蜂窝的担子。谁知在赶集路上，她赶的马车与邮车相撞，结果，家里的老马被撞死，全家的生活来源没了着落。苔丝为此感到痛苦和羞愧，为了帮助家庭摆脱生活困境，她听从了母亲的安排，去纯瑞脊（Trantridge）一个有钱的德伯老太太那里认亲。德伯先生是英国北方的一个商人。他发财后，一心想在南方安家立业，做个乡绅。因此，他从博物馆里挑了"德伯"这个古老姓氏，冒充世族乡绅。这些情形，苔丝和她的父母一点也不知道。德伯太太是个性格怪僻的瞎眼老太婆。她的儿子亚雷（Alec）是个花花公子。他一看见美丽的苔丝，便打了占有她的主意，于是让苔丝去他家养鸡场养鸡。在纯瑞脊养鸡，苔丝充满疑惧，处处拒绝他的殷勤，却无法回避他。9月里一个星期六的晚上，苔丝被亚雷诱奸，苔丝又气又恨，一个月后，挎着一个沉重的篮子，毅然离开了纯瑞脊。苔丝回家后，把这件可怕的事情告诉了母亲，母亲唯一不安的只是亚雷不打算娶她，苔丝欲哭无泪，很快村里传开了有关苔丝的消息，并遭到了村里人的讥笑和背后议论，她躲在家里不敢出门。更糟糕的是，苔丝发现自己怀孕了，但孩子出生不久后便夭折了。

春天来临后，苔丝第二次离开家，前往风景如画的塔尔勃塞牛奶厂（Talbothays Dairy）当

---

① 王守仁. 英国文学选读[M]. 3版. 北京：高等教育出版社，2011：8.
② 聂珍钊. 托马斯·哈代小说研究：悲戚而刚毅的艺术家[M]. 武汉：华中师范大学出版社，1992：9.

挤奶工。苔丝在这里心情十分愉悦,认识了年轻的克莱(Angel Clare)。克莱的父亲是低教派(Low Church)牧师,但克莱不愿子承父业,一心想当农场主。在牛奶厂学习挤奶技术时,克莱发现不爱言语的苔丝与其他乡下姑娘有许多不同之处,并很快钟情于她。在共同的劳动生活中,他俩渐生恋情,且像火一样炽热。爱情改变了克莱对生活的设想,他放弃了家里为他安排的门当户对的婚姻,娶苔丝这个内心充满诗意的大自然的女儿为妻。新婚之夜,苔丝说出自己的遭遇。克莱无法原谅她,于是遗弃了苔丝,独自一人去了巴西。

被克莱抛弃后,苔丝独自前往棱窟槐(Flintcomb-Ash)的农场,在那里受尽白眼和欺凌,被东家派到地里干男人的粗重活。在风驰电掣般的打麦机前,苔丝不停地解麦捆,累得喘不过气来,但她一直忍耐着,希望有一天克莱能与自己重归于好。一年后的12月30日,苔丝听到一个教徒在讲道,发现他竟是亚雷:四年前他还是满口秽言秽语,如今却满口仁义道德。见到苔丝后,亚雷再次纠缠不休。为摆脱父亲去世后母亲和5个弟妹无处安身、无经济来源的困境,苔丝不得不和亚雷同居。远在巴西的克莱吃尽苦头,开始追悔过去,认识到自己的过错,于是返回英国,决心与苔丝重归旧好,但在一所海滨公寓找到她时却为时已晚。克莱的归来使苔丝万分痛苦,她觉得自己的一生都被亚雷毁了。在绝望中,她杀死亚雷,然后与克莱逃亡。为躲避官府的追捕,他们避开大路,在荒野的一所空房子里度过婚后最幸福的几天。后来他们来到石柱林立的异教神坛。疲乏的苔丝躺在祭坛上,最后被警察抓住,处以绞刑。在这部小说中,哈代透过貌似简单的农村生活,揭示了复杂的历史变化,生动再现了维多利亚时期尤其是19世纪末英国农民的境遇,表达了他对自耕农悲惨遭遇的同情。

3. 作品赏析

《苔丝》的故事内容与作者所处的时代背景息息相关,解读该小说首先应了解其创作的时代背景、创作动机及创作主旨。19世纪,工业革命席卷英国,资本主义机器化生产以不可阻挡的势头迅速发展起来,英国广大农村旧的生活方式逐渐瓦解了,机器进入农村,大量农民涌入城市和工矿区成为雇佣工人。哈代在《苔丝》中艺术地再现了一幅破产农民被迫不断迁徙、背井离乡的情景,真实地反映了当时工业革命对整个社会的影响。英国工业革命后,大量农民和农业工人处于悲惨的境地,他们失去了土地、失去了工作和他们热爱的简单的农业生活方式。工业革命对英国自然环境的影响更为突出,茂盛肥沃的山野变成了铁路和中心城市,美丽的乡村风光遭到破坏①。

哈代非常关注美丽的乡村在这一巨变中如何走向没落,因为他的信仰主要建立在田园农耕文明的基础之上,认为自然是一切生活方式的核心,对自然的谋杀将会造成人性的丧失。哈代的观念与其经历有关。他来自大自然,22岁之前一直待在故乡伯克汉普顿。这是

---

① 郭辉,陈倩.《德伯家的苔丝》对工业革命的批判意识[J]. 长城,2010(4):141-142.

第七章 文学与农学(Literature and Agriculture)

英格兰南部多塞特郡一个美丽的村庄,远离工业文明,保持着传统的宗法制,是一个难得的世外桃源。哈代自小热爱大自然,经常随父亲一起走进荒原,感悟大自然的美。他对这片土地的热爱几近痴迷,这在其作品中也有所反映。哈代小说中被称为"威塞克斯"的地方其实就是他的故乡,这是多塞特郡的一个古称,他以这片古老而神奇的土壤为背景创作了多部作品。尽管成名后经常出入伦敦上流社会,并多次去欧洲大陆旅游,哈代一生中的大部分时间还是在故乡度过的。所以哈代在《苔丝》中把苔丝的生活场地布蕾谷和工作场地大牛奶厂都描述成像他的故乡多塞特郡一样,是远离工业文明的净土,是世外桃源,是未受任何污染的纯净的大自然。而这部小说深切反映了作者对南方传统乡村的没落这一现象的悲叹与惋惜。

在19世纪的最后25年,一个复杂的新型饮食经济开始出现。在这种经济中,某些农产品的工业化生产使许多农村的食品加工及其附属的生活方式变得过时。农业萧条促使人们广泛地从种植业转向畜牧业,从农田的耕种转向牲畜的养殖,从小规模的混合型农场转变成大规模、专业化农场。这些新的经营活动是我们今天所认为的工厂化农场的第一次迭代:高度机械化,由剩余生产驱动,由流动劳动力推动。从德北一家被迫迁徙到苔丝在各种农业活动中的辗转,都生动地体现了这些发展[①]。此外,交通的便利更是加速了农业的工业化,如小说中塔尔勃塞农场的牛奶厂通过四通八达的铁路网络和快速的火车这种现代化的交通工具运送牛奶,因此生产的牛奶第二天一早就能送到伦敦这样的大城市的饭桌上,而不再是靠着慢悠悠的马车和狭窄的乡间小道,这样鲜明的对比也暗示着小农经济灭亡的必然性。

当然,这并不意味着农业机械化是极其错误的。哈代的小说更多地是对新的生产体系中出现的不平等现象的一种考察,《苔丝》对农村剥削导致的日益失衡的关系体系提出了重要的批判[②]。哈代笔下的脱粒机不知满足地吞食着麦子,暗示了资产阶级的贪得无厌,把乡村隐喻成被消费的对象[③]。小说中农业资本家的代理人为了节省租钱,尽快归还租来的打麦机,迫使雇工们同机器人一样从早到晚不停地做着艰苦又繁重的体力活。手工业生产被机械生产代替了。这些雇工们大都是村里的失地农民,他们对打麦机充满了厌恶却又别无选择,只好不停地做工以便跟上机器的速度。苔丝的工作是不停地把麦捆解开,递给下一个雇工,由他把麦子扔进打麦机。因为机器不停地工作,所以雇工们也要长时间超负荷劳动。但即使是这样,在资本主义的疯狂剥削下,极其艰苦的劳动也不能使苔丝摆脱家庭贫困。《苔丝》与其说是带有反科学思想,不如说它深刻地反映了新旧社会交替下底层农民的隐痛,有力抨击了以农业科学的发展为契机残酷剥削农村劳动力的资产阶级。

---

① MARTELL J. The Dorset dairy, the pastoral, and Thomas Hardy's *Tess of the d'Urbervilles*[J]. Nineteenth-century literature, 2013(1):6.
② 同①67.
③ SALMONS K. Food in the novels of Thomas Hardy[M]. London: Palgrave Macmillan, 2017:87.

除了揭露社会现实外,《苔丝》中关于农业的描写还对小说的本身情节发展或主题暗示起到一定的作用。如苔丝在墓前祭奠夭折的孩子时,把花放在一个小水罐里以保持它们的鲜活。罐子外面的标签是"基尔韦尔的果酱"(Keelwell's Marmalade),这是一种受欢迎的食品品牌,由加工过的水果制成,象征着一种新的资本体系。在这种体系中,农村的产品成为品牌商业产品。讽刺的是,苔丝的孩子正是这个新市场经济的受害者。但苔丝看不到这种烙印。取而代之的是,在她的眼里,这些花成了她早夭的孩子的象征。苔丝用商业食品罐子祭奠孩子的场景描写,起到了很好的反讽效果。小说中的农业科学有时也起到象征作用。如《苔丝》中的草莓场景代表了真实版和理想版乡村之间的冲突,在这场冲突中,女主人公被渲染成"资本的被动受害者",亚雷把草莓放在苔丝嘴里的行为代表着对妇女的剥削,亚雷扮演着食物的提供者,苔丝扮演着被动接受者的角色。草莓生长在温室里,还未到季节便成熟了。苔丝虽然喜欢草莓,但只喜欢应季的品种①。苔丝被迫吃下亚雷喂的早熟草莓,象征着农业科技的发展对传统农民的迫害,也暗示着他们无法逃脱这样的命运。下面请阅读小说节选部分,并回答相关问题。选文第四十七章、第四十八章是苔丝在棱窟槐农场干活的场景。

作品选读

Tess of the d'Urbervilles

Thomas Hardy

Chapter 47

It is the threshing of the last wheat-rick at Flintcomb-Ash Farm. The dawn of the March morning is singularly inexpressive, and there is nothing to show where the eastern horizon lies. Against the twilight rises the trapezoidal top of the stack, which has stood forlornly here through the washing and bleaching of the wintry weather.

When Izz Huett and Tess arrived at the scene of operations only a rustling denoted that others had preceded them; to which, as the light increased, there were presently added the silhouettes of two men on the summit. They were busily "unhaling" the rick, that is, stripping off the thatch before beginning to throw down the sheaves; and while this was in progress Izz and Tess, with the other women-workers in their whitey-brown pinners, stood waiting and shivering, Farmer Groby having insisted upon their being upon the spot thus early, to get the job over if possible by the end of the day. Close under the eaves of

---

① SALMONS K. Food in the novels of Thomas Hardy[M]. London: Palgrave Macmillan, 2017: 91 – 93.

第七章 文学与农学(Literature and Agriculture)

the stack, and as yet barely visible was the red tyrant that the women had come to serve—a timber-framed construction, with straps and wheels appertaining—the threshing-machine, which, whilst it was going, kept up a despotic demand upon the endurance of their muscles and nerves.

A little way off there was another indistinct figure; this one black, with a sustained hiss that spoke of strength very much in reserve. The long chimney running up beside an ash-tree, and the warmth which radiated from the spot, explained without the necessity of much daylight that here was the engine which was to act as the primum mobile of this little world. By the engine stood a dark motionless being, a sooty and grimy embodiment of tallness, in a sort of trance, with a heap of coals by his side: it was the engine-man. The isolation of his manner and colour lent him the appearance of a creature from Tophet, who had strayed into the pellucid smokelessness of this region of yellow grain and pale soil, with which he had nothing in common, to amaze and to discompose its aborigines.

What he looked he felt. He was in the agricultural world, but not of it. He served fire and smoke; these denizens of the fields served vegetation, weather, frost, and sun. He travelled with his engine from farm to farm, from county to county, for as yet the steam threshing-machine was itinerant in this part of Wessex. He spoke in a strange northern accent, his thoughts being turned inwards upon himself, his eye on his iron charge; hardly perceiving the scenes around him, and caring for them not at all; holding only strictly necessary intercourse with the natives, as if some ancient doom compelled him to wander here against his will in the service of his Plutonic master. The long strap which ran from the driving-wheel of his engine to the red thresher under the rick was the sole tie-line between agriculture and him.

While they uncovered the sheaves he stood apathetic beside his portable repository of force, round whose hot blackness the morning air quivered. He had nothing to do with preparatory labour. His fire was waiting incandescent, his steam was at high-pressure, in a few seconds he could make the long strap move at an invisible velocity. Beyond its extent the environment might be corn, straw, or chaos; it was all the same to him. If any of the autochthonous idlers asked him what he called himself, he replied shortly "an engineer."

The rick was unhaled by full daylight; the men then took their places, the women mounted, and the work began. Farmer Groby—or, as they called him, "he"—had arrived ere this, and by his orders Tess was placed on the platform of the machine, close to the man who fed it; her business being to untie every sheaf of corn handed on to her by Izz Huett who stood next, but on the rick, so that the feeder could seize it and spread it over the revolving drum which whisked out every grain in one moment.

They were soon in full progress, after a preparatory hitch or two, which rejoiced the hearts of those who hated machinery. The work sped on till breakfast-time, when the thresher was stopped for half-an-hour; and on starting again after the meal the whole supplementary strength of the farm was thrown into the labour of constructing the straw-rick which began to grow beside the stack of corn. A hasty lunch was eaten as they stood, without leaving their positions; and then another couple of hours brought them near to dinner-time; the inexorable wheels continuing to spin, and the penetrating hum of the thresher to thrill to the very marrow all who were near the revolving wire cage.

The old men on the rising straw-rick talked of the past days when they had been accustomed to thresh with flails on the oaken barn-floor; when everything, even to the winnowing, was effected by hand-labour, which to their thinking, though slow, produced better results. Those, too, on the corn-rick, talked a little; but the perspiring ones at the machine, including Tess, could not lighten their duties by the exchange of many words. It was the ceaselessness of the work which tried her so severely, and began to make her wish that she had never come to Flintcomb-Ash. The women on the corn-rick, Marian, who was one of them, in particular, could stop to drink ale or cold tea from the flagon now and then, or to exchange a few gossiping remarks while they wiped their faces or cleared the fragments of straw and husk from their clothing; but for Tess there was no respite; for, as the drum never stopped, the man who fed it could not stop, and she, who had to supply the man with untie sheaves, could not stop either, unless Marian changed places with her, which she sometimes did for half an hour in spite of Groby's objection that she was too slow-handed for a feeder.

For some probably economical reason it was usually a woman who was chosen for this particular duty, and Groby gave as his motive in selecting Tess that she was one of those who best combined strength with quickness in untying, and both with staying power; and this may have been true. The hum of the thresher, which prevented speech, increased to a raving whenever the supply of corn fell short of the regular quantity. As Tess and the

第七章　文学与农学（Literature and Agriculture）

man who fed could never turn their heads, she did not know that just before the dinner-hour a person had come silently into the field by the gate, and had been standing under a second rick watching the scene, and Tess in particular. He was dressed in a tweed suit of fashionable pattern, and he twirled a gay walking-cane.

"Who is that?" said Izz Huett to Marian. She had at first addressed the inquiry to Tess, but the latter could not hear it.

"Somebody's fancy-man, I s'pose," said Marian laconically.

"I'll lay a guinea he's after Tess."

"O no. 'Tis a ranter pa'son who's been sniffing after her lately—not a dandy like this."

"Well—this is the same man."

"The same man as the preacher? But he's quite different?"

"He hev left off his black coat and white neckercher, and hev cut off his whiskers; but he's the same man for all that."

"D'ye really think so. Then I'll tell her," said Marian.

"Don't. She'll see him soon enough, good-now."

"Well, I don't think it at all right for him to join his preaching to courting a married woman, even though her husband mid be abroad, and she, in a sense, a widow."

"Oh—he can do her no harm," said Izz drily. "Her mind can no more be heaved from that one place where it do bide than a stooded waggon from the hole he's in. Lord love 'ee, neither courtpaying, nor preaching, nor the seven thunders themselves, can wean a woman when 'twould be better for her that she should be weaned."

Dinner-time came, and the whirling ceased, whereupon Tess left her post, her knees trembling so wretchedly with the shaking of the machine that she could scarcely walk. "You ought to het a quart o' drink into 'ee, as I've done," said Marian. "You wouldn't look so white then. Why, souls above us, your face is as if you'd been hag-rode!"

It occurred to the good-natured Marian that, as Tess was so tired, her discovery of her visitor's presence might have the bad effect of taking away her appetite; and Marian was thinking of inducing Tess to descend by a ladder on the further side of the stack when the gentleman came forward and looked up.

Tess uttered a short little "Oh!" and a moment after she said quickly, "I shall eat my dinner here—right on the rick."

Sometimes, when they were so far from their cottages, they all did this; but as there was rather a keen wind going to-day Marian and the rest descended, and sat under the straw-stack.

The new-comer was, indeed, Alec d'Urberville the late evangelist, despite his changed attire and aspect. It was obvious at a glance that the original *Weltlust* had come back; that he had restored himself, as nearly as a man could do who had grown three or four years older, to the old jaunty, slap-dash guise under which Tess had first known her admirer, and cousin so-called. Having decided to remain where she was Tess sat down among the bundles out of sight of the ground, and began her meal; till by and by she heard footsteps upon the ladder, and immediately after Alec appeared upon the stack—now an oblong and level platform of sheaves. He strode across them, and sat down opposite to her without a word.

Tess continued to eat her modest dinner, a slice of thick pancake which she had brought with her: the other workfolk were by this time all gathered under the rick, where the loose straw formed a comfortable retreat.

"I am here again, as you see," said d'Urberville.

"Why do you trouble me so!" she cried, reproach flashing from her very finger-ends.

"I trouble you? I think I may ask, why do you trouble me?"

"Sure, I don't trouble you any-when!"

"You say you don't? But you do! You haunt me. Those very eyes that you turned upon me with such a bitter flash a moment ago, they come to me, just as you showed them then, in the night and in the day. Tess, ever since you told me of that child of ours, it is just as if my feelings, which have been flowing in a strong puritanical stream, had suddenly found a way open in the direction of you and had all at once gushed through. The religious channel is left dry forthwith; and it is you who have done it!"

She gazed in silence. "What—you have given up your preaching entirely?" she asked. She had gathered from Angel sufficient of the incredulity of modern thought to despise flash enthusiasms; but as a woman she was somewhat appalled.

In affected severity d'Urberville continued: "Entirely. I have broken every engagement since that afternoon I was to address the drunkards at Casterbridge Fair. The

第七章 文学与农学(Literature and Agriculture)

deuce only knows what I am thought of by the brethren. Ah-ha! The brethren! No doubt they pray for me, weep for me; for they are kind people in their way. But what do I care? How could I go on with the thing when I had lost my faith in it? —it would have been hypocrisy of the basest kind! Among them I should have stood like Hymenæus and Alexander, who were delivered over to Satan that they might learn not to blaspheme. What a grand revenge you have taken! I saw you innocent, and I deceived you. Four years after, you find me a Christian enthusiast; you then work upon me, perhaps to my complete perdition... But Tess, my coz, as I used to call you, this is only my way of talking, and you must not look so horribly concerned. Of course you have done nothing except retain your pretty face and shapely figure. I saw it on the rick before you saw me—that tight pinafore-thing sets it off, and that wing-bonnet—you field-girls should never wear those bonnets if you wish to keep out of danger." He regarded her silently for a few moments, and with a short cynical laugh resumed: "I believe that if the bachelor apostle, whose deputy I thought I was, had been tempted by such a pretty face, he would have let go the plough for her sake as I do."

Tess attempted to expostulate, but at this juncture all her fluency failed her, and without heeding he added: "Well, this paradise that you supply is perhaps as good as any other, after all. But to speak seriously, Tess." D'Urberville rose and came nearer, reclining sideways amid the sheaves and resting upon his elbow. "Since I last saw you I have been thinking of what you said that he said. I have come to the conclusion that there does seem rather a want of common-sense in these threadbare old propositions: how I could have been so fired by poor Parson Clare's enthusiasm, and have gone so madly to work, transcending even him, I cannot make out. As for what you said last time, on the strength of your wonderful husband's intelligence—whose name you have never told me—about having what they call an ethical system without any dogma; I don't see my way to that at all."

"Why, you can have the religion of loving-kindness and purity at least, if you can't have—what do you call it—dogma."

"O no. I'm a different sort of fellow from that! If there's nobody to say, 'Do this, and it will be a good thing for you after you are dead; do that, and it will be a bad thing for you', I can't warm up. Hang it, I am not going to feel responsible for my deeds and passions if there's nobody to be responsible to; and if I were you, my dear, I wouldn't either."

She tried to argue, and tell him that he had mixed in his dull brain two matters, theology and morals, which in the primitive days of mankind had been quite distinct. But owing to Angel Clare's reticence, to her absolute want of training, and to her being a vessel of emotions rather than reasons, she could not get on.

"Well—never mind"—he resumed, "here I am, my love, as in the old times!"

"Not as then—never as then—'tis different!" she entreated. "And there was never warmth with me. O why didn't you keep your faith, if the loss of it has brought you to speak to me like this!"

"Because you've knocked it out of me; so the evil be upon your sweet head. Your husband little thought how his teaching would recoil upon him. Ha-ha—I'm awfully glad you have made an apostate of me, all the same... Tess I am more taken with you than ever. And I pity you, too. For all your closeness I see you are in a bad way—neglected by one who ought to cherish you."

She could not get her morsels of food down her throat; her lips were dry, and she was ready to choke. The voices and laughs of the workfolk eating and drinking under the rick came to her as if they were a quarter of a mile off.

"It is cruelty to me!" she said. "How—how can you treat me to this talk, if you care ever so little for me?"

"True, true," he said, wincing a little. "I did not come to reproach you for my deeds. I came, Tess, to say that I don't like you to be working like this, and I have come on purpose for you. You say you have a husband who is not I. Well, perhaps you have; but I've never seen him, and you've not told me his name; and altogether he seems rather a mythological personage. However, even if you have one, I think I am nearer to you than he is. I, at any rate, try to help you out of trouble, but he does not, bless his invisible face! The words of the stern prophet Hosea that I used to read come back to me. Don't you know them, Tess? —'And she shall follow after her lover, but she shall not overtake him; and she shall seek him, but shall not find him: then shall she say, I will go and return to my first husband; for then was it better with me than now.' ...Tess, my trap is waiting just under the hill, and—darling mine, not his! —you know the rest."

第七章 文学与农学(Literature and Agriculture)

Her face had been rising to a dull crimson fire while he spoke; but she did not answer.

"You have been the cause of my backsliding," he continued, stretching his arm towards her waist; "you should be willing to share it, and leave that mule you call husband for ever."

One of her leather gloves, which she had taken off to eat her skimmer-cake, lay in her lap, and without the slightest warning she passionately swung the glove by the gauntlet directly in his face. It was heavy and thick as a warrior's, and it struck him flat on the mouth. Fancy might have regarded the act as the recrudescence of a trick in which her armed progenitors were not unpractised. Alec fiercely started up from his reclining position. A scarlet oozing appeared where her blow had alighted, and in a moment the blood began dropping from his mouth upon the straw. But he soon controlled himself, calmly drew his handkerchief from his pocket, and mopped his bleeding lips.

She too had sprung up; but she sank down again. "Now punish me!" she said, turning up her eyes to him with the hopeless defiance of the sparrow's gaze before its captor twists its neck. "Whip me, crush me; you need not mind those people under the rick. I shall not cry out. Once victim, always victim: that's the law."

"O no, no, Tess," he said blandly. "I can make full allowance for this. Yet you most unjustly forget one thing, that I would have married you if you had not put it out of my power to do so. Did I not ask you flatly to be my wife—hey? —answer me."

"You did."

"And you cannot be. But remember one thing:" his voice hardened as his temper got the better of him with the recollection of his sincerity in asking her, and her present ingratitude; and he stepped across to her side and held her by the shoulders, so that she shook under his grasp: "Remember, my lady, I was your master once; I will be your master again. If you are any man's wife you are mine!"

The threshers now began to stir below. "So much for our quarrel," he said, letting her go. "Now I shall leave you; and shall come again for your answer during the afternoon. You don't know me yet. But I know you."

She had not spoken again, remaining as if stunned. D'Urberville retreated over the sheaves and descended the ladder, while the workers below rose and stretched their arms, and shook down the beer they had drunk. Then the threshing-machine started afresh; and amid the renewed rustle of the straw Tess resumed her position by the buzzing drum as one in a dream, untying sheaf after sheaf in endless succession.

Chapter 48

In the afternoon the farmer made it known that the rick was to be finished that night, since there was a moon by which they could see to work, and the man with the engine was engaged for another farm on the morrow. Hence the twanging and humming and rustling proceeded with even less intermission than usual.

It was not till "nammet"-time, about three o'clock, that Tess raised her eyes and gave a momentary glance round. She felt but little surprise at seeing that Alec d'Urberville had come back, and was standing under the hedge by the gate. He had seen her lift her eyes, and waved his hand urbanely to her, while he blew her a kiss. It meant that their quarrel was over. Tess looked down again, and carefully abstained from gazing in that direction.

Thus the afternoon dragged on. The wheat-rick shrank lower, and the straw-rick grew higher, and the corn-sacks were carted away. At six o'clock the wheat-rick was about shoulder-high from the ground. But the unthreshed sheaves remaining untouched seemed countless still, notwithstanding the enormous numbers that had been gulped down by the insatiable swallower, fed by the man and Tess, through whose two young hands the greater part of them had passed; and the immense stack of straw where in the morning there had been nothing appeared as the fæces of the same buzzing red glutton. From the west sky a wrathful shine—all that wild March could afford in the way of sunset—had burst forth after the cloudy day flooding the tired and sticky faces of the threshers, and dyeing them with a coppery light, as also the flapping garments of the women, which clung to them like dull flames.

A panting ache ran through the rick. The man who fed was weary, and Tess could see that the red nape of his neck was encrusted with dirt and husks. She still stood at her post, her flushed and perspiring face coated with the corn-dust, and her white bonnet embrowned by it. She was the only woman whose place was upon the machine, so as to be shaken bodily by its spinning, and the decrease of the stack now separated her from Marian and Izz, and prevented their changing duties with her as they had done. The

第七章　文学与农学(Literature and Agriculture)

incessant quivering in which every fibre of her frame participated had thrown her into a stupefied reverie, in which her arms worked on independently of her consciousness. She hardly knew where she was, and did not hear Izz Huett tell her from below that her hair was tumbling down.

By degrees the freshest among them began to grow cadaverous and saucer-eyed. Whenever Tess lifted her head she beheld always the great upgrown straw-stack, with the men in shirt-sleeves upon it against the grey north sky: in front of it the long red elevator like a Jacob's ladder, on which a perpetual stream of threshed straw ascended; a yellow river running up-hill, and spouting out on the top of the rick.

She knew that Alec d'Urberville was still on the scene, observing her from some point or other, though she could not say where. There was an excuse for his remaining, for when the threshed rick drew near its final sheaves a little ratting was always done, and men unconnected with the threshing sometimes dropped in for that performance—sporting characters of all descriptions, gents with terriers and facetious pipes, roughs with sticks and stones.

But there was another hour's work before the layer of live rats at the base of the stack would be reached; and as the evening light in the direction of the Giant's Hill by Abbot's-Cernel dissolved away, the white-faced moon of the season arose from the horizon that lay towards Middleton Abbey and Shottsford on the other side. For the last hour or two Marian had felt uneasy about Tess, whom she could not get near enough to speak to; the other women having kept up their strength by drinking ale, and Tess having done without it through traditional dread, owing to its results at her home in childhood. But Tess still kept going: if she could not fill her part she would have to leave, and this contingency, which she would have regarded with equanimity, and even with relief, a month or two earlier, had become a terror since d'Urberville had begun to hover round her.

The sheaf-pitchers and feeders had now worked the rick so low that people on the ground could talk to them. To Tess's surprise Farmer Groby came up on the machine to her, and said that if she desired to join her friend he did not wish her to keep on any longer, and would send somebody else to take her place. The "friend" was d'Urberville, she knew, and also that this concession had been granted in obedience to the request of that friend, or enemy. She shook her head, and toiled on.

The time for the rat-catching arrived at last, and the hunt began. The creatures had crept downwards with the subsidence of the rick till they were all together at the bottom, and being now uncovered from their last refuge they ran across the open ground in all directions, a loud shriek from the by-this-time half-tipsy Marian informing her companions that one of the rats had invaded her person—a terror which the rest of the women had guarded against by various schemes of skirt-tucking and self-elevation. The rat was at last dislodged, and amid the barking of dogs, masculine shouts, feminine screams, oaths, stampings, and confusion as of pandæmonium Tess untied her last sheaf; the drum slowed, the whizzing ceased, and she stepped from the machine to the ground.

Her lover—who had only looked on at the rat-catching—was promptly at her side.

"What—after all? —my insulting slap too?" said she in an under-breath. She was so utterly exhausted that she had not strength to speak louder.

"I should indeed be foolish to feel offended at anything you say or do," he answered in the seductive voice of the Trantridge time. "How the little limbs tremble! You are as weak as a bled calf, you know you are; and yet you need have done nothing since I arrived. How could you be so obstinate! However, I have told the farmer that he has no right to employ women at steam-threshing. It is not proper work for them, and on all the better class of farms it has been given up, as he knows very well. I will walk with you as far as your house."

"O yes," she answered with a jaded gait. "Walk wi' me if you will! I do bear in mind that you came to marry me, before you knew o' my state. Perhaps—perhaps you are a little better and kinder than I have been thinking you were. Whatever is meant as kindness I am grateful for; whatever is meant in any other way I am angered at... I cannot sense your meaning sometimes."

"If I cannot legitimize our former relations at least I can assist you. And I will do it with much more regard for your feelings than I formerly showed. My religious mania, or whatever it was, is over. But I retain a little good-nature; I hope I do. Now, Tess; by all that's tender and strong between man and woman, trust me. I have enough and more than enough to put you out of anxiety, both for yourself and your brothers and sisters. I can make them all comfortable, if you will only show confidence in me."

"Have you seen 'em lately?" she quickly inquired.

第七章 文学与农学(Literature and Agriculture)

"Yes. They didn't know where you were. It was only by chance that I found you here."

The cold moon looked aslant upon Tess's fagged face between the twigs of the garden-hedge, as she paused outside the cottage which was her temporary home, d'Urberville pausing beside her. "Don't mention my little brothers and sisters—don't make me break down quite!" she said. "If you want to help them—God knows they need it—do it without telling me. But no, no!" she cried. "I will take nothing from you, either for them or for me."

He did not accompany her further, since as she lived with the household all was public indoors. No sooner had she herself entered, laved herself in a washing-tub, and shared supper with the family, than she fell into thought, and, withdrawing to the table under the wall, by the light of her own little lamp wrote in a passionate mood:—

My own husband! Let me call you so—I must—even if it makes you angry to think of such an unworthy wife as I. I must cry to you in my trouble—I have no one else. I am so exposed to temptation, Angel! I fear to say who it is, and I do not like to write about it at all. But I cling to you in a way you cannot think. Can you not come to me now, at once, before anything terrible happens? O I know you cannot, because you are so far away. I think I must die if you do not come soon, or tell me to come to you. The punishment you have measured out to me is deserved—I do know that—well deserved, and you are right and just to be angry with me. But Angel, please, please, not to be just—only a little kind to me, even if I do not deserve it, and come to me. If you would come I could die in your arms. I would be well content to do that if so be you had forgiven me.

Angel, I live entirely for you. I love you too much to blame you for going away, and I know it was necessary you should find a farm. Do not think I shall say a word of sting or bitterness. Only come back to me. I am desolate without you, my darling, O so desolate! I do not mind having to work; but if you will send me one little line and say, I am coming soon, I will bide on, Angel: O so cheerfully!

It has been so much my religion ever since we were married, to be faithful to you in every thought and look that even when a man speaks a compliment to me before I am aware, it seems wronging you. Have you never felt one little bit of what you used to feel when we were at the dairy? If you have, how can you keep away from me? I am the same woman, Angel, as you fell in love with; yes, the very same! not the one you disliked, but never saw. What was the past to me as soon as I met you? It was a dead thing altogether. I became another woman, filled full of new life from you. How could I be the early one? Why do you not see this? Dear, if you would only be a little more conceited, and believe in yourself so far as to see that you were strong enough to work this change in me, you would perhaps be in a mind to come to me, your poor wife.

How silly I was in my happiness when I thought I could trust you always to love me! I ought to have known that such as that was not for poor me. But I am sick at heart, not only for old times, but for the present. Think, think how it do hurt my heart not to see you ever, ever! Ah, if I could only make your dear heart ache one little minute of each day as mine does every day and all day long, it might lead you to show pity to your poor lonely one.

People still say that I am rather pretty, Angel (handsome is the word they use, since I wish to be truthful). Perhaps I am what they say. But I do not value my good looks: I only like to have them because they belong to you, my dear, and that there may be at least one thing about me worth your having. So much have I felt this that when I met with annoyance on account of the same I tied up my face in a bandage as long as people would believe in it. O Angel, I tell you all this not from vanity—you will certainly know I do not—but only that you may come to me.

If you really cannot come to me will you let me come to you? I am, as I say, worried, pressed to do what I will not. It cannot be that I shall yield one inch, yet I am in terror as to what an accident might lead to, and I so defenceless on account of my first error. I cannot say more about this—it makes me too miserable. But if I break down by falling into some fearful snare my last state will be worse than my first. O God—I cannot think of it! Let me come at once, or at once come to me!

I would be content, ay glad, to live with you as your servant, if I may not as your wife; so that I could only be near you, and get glimpses of you, and think of you as mine.

The daylight has nothing to show me, since you are not here, and I don't like to see the rooks and starlings in the fields, because I grieve and grieve to miss you who used to see them with me. I long for only one thing in heaven or earth or under the earth, to meet you, my own dear. Come to me, come to me, and save me from what threatens me!

Your faithful heartbroken TESS.

思考题

1. How does the agricultural machinery develop in the excerpts? Please list at least two agricultural machines mentioned above.
2. What kind of way does Hardy use in Chapter 47 when describing the agriculture machine? What's the function of it?
3. How do you understand "For some probably economical reason it was usually a woman who was chosen for this particular duty" in the ninth paragraph of Chapter 47?
4. After reading, what do you think are the pros and cons of the development of agricultural science? Does the use of machines increase or lighten the labor intensity of the workers?
5. How does the utilization of machines affect the relationship between human and agriculture? Who is the biggest beneficiary of the use of agriculture machine?
6. What's the reason for the tragedy of Tess? Do you think it has any relationship to do with the development of agricultural science? Why?

第三节　补充阅读《愤怒的葡萄》

阅读约翰·斯坦贝克的小说《愤怒的葡萄》的第五章,结合佃农与拖拉机驾驶员的对话,思考人与土地、人与机器的关系。

The Grapes of Wrath[①]
John Steinbeck
Chapter Five

The owners of the land came onto the land, or more often a spokesman for the owners came. They came in closed cars, and they felt the dry earth with their fingers, and sometimes they drove big earth augers into the ground for soil tests. The tenants, from

---

① STEINBECK J. The grapes of wrath[M]. New York: The Viking Press, 1958.

their sun-beaten dooryards, watched uneasily when the closed cars drove along the fields. And at last the owner men drove into the dooryards and sat in their cars to talk out of the windows. The tenant men stood beside the cars for a while, and then squatted on their hams and found sticks with which to mark the dust.

In the open doors the women stood looking out, and behind them the children— corn-headed children, with wide eyes, one bare foot on top of the other bare foot, and the toes working. The women and the children watched their men talking to the owner men. They were silent.

Some of the owner men were kind because they hated what they had to do, and some of them were angry because they hated to be cruel, and some of them were cold because they had long ago found that one could not be an owner unless one were cold. And all of them were caught in something larger than themselves. Some of them hated the mathematics that drove them, and some were afraid, and some worshiped the mathematics because it provided a refuge from thought and from feeling. If a bank or a finance company owned the land, the owner man said, The Bank—or the Company—needs—wants—insists—must have—as though the Bank or the Company were a monster, with thought and feeling, which had ensnared them. These last would take no responsibility for the banks or the companies because they were men and slaves, while the banks were machines and masters all at the same time. Some of the owner men were a little proud to be slaves to such cold and powerful masters. The owner men sat in the cars and explained. "You know the land is poor. You've scrabbled at it long enough, God knows."

The squatting tenant men nodded and wondered and drew figures in the dust, and yes, they knew, God knows. If the dust only wouldn't fly. If the top would only stay on the soil, it might not be so bad.

The owner men went on leading to their point: "You know the land's getting poorer. You know what cotton does to the land; robs it, sucks all the blood out of it."

The squatters nodded—they knew, God knew. If they could only rotate the crops they might pump blood back into the land.

Well, it's too late. And the owner men explained the workings and the thinkings of the monster that was stronger than they were. "A man can hold land if he can just eat and pay taxes; he can do that."

第七章 文学与农学(Literature and Agriculture)

"Yes, he can do that until his crops fail one day and he has to borrow money from the bank."

"But—you see, a bank or a company can't do that, because those creatures don't breathe air, don't eat side-meat. They breathe profits; they eat the interest on money. If they don't get it, they die the way you die without air, without side-meat. It is a sad thing, but it is so. It is just so."

The squatting men raised their eyes to understand. "Can't we just hang on? Maybe the next year will be a good year. God knows how much cotton next year. And with all the wars—God knows what price cotton will bring. Don't they make explosives out of cotton? And uniforms? Get enough wars and cotton'll hit the ceiling. Next year, maybe." They looked up questioningly.

"We can't depend on it. The bank—the monster has to have profits all the time. It can't wait. It'll die. No, taxes go on. When the monster stops growing, it dies. It can't stay one size."

Soft fingers began to tap the sill of the car window, and hard fingers tightened on the restless drawing sticks. In the doorways of the sun-beaten tenant houses, women sighed and then shifted feet so that the one that had been down was now on top, and the toes working. Dogs came sniffing near the owner cars and wetted on all four tires one after another. And chickens lay in the sunny dust and fluffed their feathers to get the cleansing dust down to the skin. In the little sties the pigs grunted inquiringly over the muddy remnants of the slops.

The squatting men looked down again. "What do you want us to do? We can't take less share of the crop—we're half starved now. The kids are hungry all the time. We got no clothes, torn an' ragged. If all the neighbors weren't the same, we'd be ashamed to go to meeting."

And at last the owner men came to the point. "The tenant system won't work any more. One man on a tractor can take the place of twelve or fourteen families. Pay him a wage and take all the crop. We have to do it. We don't like to do it. But the monster's sick. Something's happened to the monster."

"But you'll kill the land with cotton."

"We know. We've got to take cotton quick before the land dies. Then we'll sell the land. Lots of families in the East would like to own a piece of land."

The tenant men looked up alarmed. "But what'll happen to us? How'll we eat?"

"You'll have to get off the land. The plows'll go through the dooryard."

And now the squatting men stood up angrily. "Grampa took up the land, and he had to kill the Indians and drive them away. And Pa was born here, and he killed weeds and snakes. Then a bad year came and he had to borrow a little money. An' we was born here. There in the door—our children born here. And Pa had to borrow money. The bank owned the land then, but we stayed and we got a little bit of what we raised."

"We know that—all that. It's not us, it's the bank. A bank isn't like a man. Or an owner with fifty thousand acres, he isn't like a man either. That's the monster."

"Sure," cried the tenant men, "but it's our land. We measured it and broke it up. We were born on it, and we got killed on it, died on it. Even if it's no good, it's still ours. That's what makes it ours—being born on it, working it, dying on it. That makes ownership, not a paper with numbers on it."

"We're sorry. It's not us. It's the monster. The bank isn't like a man."

"Yes, but the bank is only made of men."

"No, you're wrong there—quite wrong there. The bank is something else than men. It happens that every man in a bank hates what the bank does, and yet the bank does it. The bank is something more than men, I tell you. It's the monster. Men made it, but they can't control it."

The tenants cried, "Grampa killed Indians, Pa killed snakes for the land. Maybe we can kill banks—they're worse than Indians and snakes. Maybe we got to fight to keep our land, like Pa and Grampa did."

And now the owner men grew angry. "You'll have to go."

"But it's ours," the tenant men cried. "We—"

"No. The bank, the monster owns it. You'll have to go."

"We'll get our guns, like Grampa when the Indians came. What then?"

"Well—first the sheriff, and then the troops. You'll be stealing if you try to stay, you'll be murderers if you kill to stay. The monster isn't men, but it can make men do what it wants."

"But if we go, where'll we go? How'll we go? We got no money."

第七章　文学与农学(Literature and Agriculture)

"We're sorry," said the owner men. "The bank, the fifty-thousand-acre owner can't be responsible. You're on land that isn't yours. Once over the line maybe you can pick cotton in the fall. Maybe you can go on relief. Why don't you go on west to California? There's work there, and it never gets cold. Why, you can reach out anywhere and pick an orange. Why, there's always some kind of crop to work in. Why don't you go there?" And the owner men started their cars and rolled away.

The tenant men squatted down on their hams again to mark the dust with a stick, to figure, to wonder. Their sunburned faces were dark, and their sun-whipped eyes were light. The women moved cautiously out of the doorways toward their men, and the children crept behind the women, cautiously, ready to run. The bigger boys squatted beside their fathers, because that made them men. After a time the women asked, What did he want?

And the men looked up for a second, and the smolder of pain was in their eyes. "We got to get off. A tractor and a superintendent. Like factories."

"Where'll we go?" the women asked.

"We don't know. We don't know."

And the women went quickly, quietly back into the houses and herded the children ahead of them. They knew that a man so hurt and so perplexed may turn in anger, even on people he loves. They left the men alone to figure and to wonder in the dust.

After a time perhaps the tenant man looked about—at the pump put in ten years ago, with a goose-neck handle and iron flowers on the spout, at the chopping block where a thousand chickens had been killed, at the hand plow lying in the shed, and the patent crib hanging in the rafters over it.

The children crowded about the women in the houses. What we going to do, Ma? Where we going to go?

The women said, We don't know, yet. Go out and play. But don't go near your father. He might whale you if you go near him. And the women went on with the work, but all the time they watched the men squatting in the dust—perplexed and figuring.

The tractors came over the roads and into the fields, great crawlers moving like insects, having the incredible strength of insects. They crawled over the ground, laying the track and rolling on it and picking it up. Diesel tractors, puttering while they stood idle; they thundered when they moved, and then settled down to a droning roar. Snub-nosed monsters, raising the dust and sticking their snouts into it, straight down the country, across the country, through fences, through dooryards, in and out of gullies in straight lines. They did not run on the ground, but on their own roadbeds. They ignored hills and gulches, water courses, fences, houses.

The man sitting in the iron seat did not look like a man; gloved, goggled, rubber dust mask over nose and mouth, he was a part of the monster, a robot in the seat. The thunder of the cylinders sounded through the country, became one with the air and the earth, so that earth and air muttered in sympathetic vibration. The driver could not control it—straight across country it went, cutting through a dozen farms and straight back. A twitch at the controls could swerve the cat', but the driver's hands could not twitch because the monster that built the tractor, the monster that sent the tractor out, had somehow got into the driver's hands, into his brain and muscle, had goggled him and muzzled him— goggled his mind, muzzled his speech, goggled his perception, muzzled his protest. He could not see the land as it was, he could not smell the land as it smelled; his feet did not stamp the clods or feel the warmth and power of the earth. He sat in an iron seat and stepped on iron pedals. He could not cheer or beat or curse or encourage the extension of his power, and because of this he could not cheer or whip or curse or encourage himself. He did not know or own or trust or beseech the land. If a seed dropped did not germinate, it was nothing. If the young thrusting plant withered in drought or drowned in a flood of rain, it was no more to the driver than to the tractor.

He loved the land no more than the bank loved the land. He could admire the tractor—its machined surfaces, its surge of power, the roar of its detonating cylinders; but it was not his tractor. Behind the tractor rolled the shining disks, cutting the earth with blades—not plowing but surgery, pushing the cut earth to the right where the second row of disks cut it and pushed it to the left; slicing blades shining, polished by the cut earth. And pulled behind the disks, the harrows combing with iron teeth so that the little clods broke up and the earth lay smooth. Behind the harrows, the long seeders—twelve curved iron penes erected in the foundry, orgasms set by gears, raping methodically, raping without passion. The driver sat in his iron seat and he was proud of the straight lines he did not will, proud of the tractor he did not own or love, proud of the power he could not control. And when that crop grew, and was harvested, no man had crumbled a hot clod in

第七章 文学与农学（Literature and Agriculture）

his fingers and let the earth sift past his fingertips. No man had touched the seed, or lusted for the growth. Men ate what they had not raised, had no connection with the bread. The land bore under iron, and under iron gradually died; for it was not loved or hated, it had no prayers or curses.

At noon the tractor driver stopped sometimes near a tenant house and opened his lunch: sandwiches wrapped in waxed paper, white bread, pickle, cheese, Spam, a piece of pie branded like an engine part. He ate without relish. And tenants not yet moved away came out to see him, looked curiously while the goggles were taken off, and the rubber dust mask, leaving white circles around the eyes and a large white circle around nose and mouth. The exhaust of the tractor puttered on, for fuel is so cheap it is more efficient to leave the engine running than to heat the Diesel nose for a new start. Curious children crowded close, ragged children who ate their fried dough as they watched. They watched hungrily the unwrapping of the sandwiches, and their hunger-sharpened noses smelled the pickle, cheese, and Spam. They didn't speak to the driver. They watched his hand as it carried food to his mouth. They did not watch him chewing; their eyes followed the hand that held the sandwich. After a while the tenant who could not leave the place came out and squatted in the shade beside the tractor.

"Why, you're Joe Davis's boy!"

"Sure," the driver said.

"Well, what you doing this kind of work for—against your own people?"

"Three dollars a day. I got damn sick of creeping for my dinner—and not getting it. I got a wife and kids. We got to eat. Three dollars a day, and it comes every day."

"That's right," the tenant said. "But for your three dollars a day fifteen or twenty families can't eat at all. Nearly a hundred people have to go out and wander on the roads for your three dollars a day. Is that right?"

And the driver said, "Can't think of that. Got to think of my own kids. Three dollars a day, and it comes every day. Times are changing, mister, don't you know? Can't make a living on the land unless you've got two, five, ten thousand acres and a tractor. Crop land isn't for little guys like us any more. You don't kick up a howl because you can't make Fords, or because you're not the telephone company. Well, crops are like that now. Nothing to do about it. You try to get three dollars a day someplace. That's the only way."

The tenant pondered. "Funny thing how it is. If a man owns a little property, that property is him, it's part of him, and it's like him. If he owns property only so he can walk on it and handle it and be sad when it isn't doing well, and feel fine when the rain falls on it, that property is him, and some way he's bigger because he owns it. Even if he isn't successful he's big with his property. That is so."

And the tenant pondered more. "But let a man get property he doesn't see, or can't take time to get his fingers in, or can't be there to walk on it—why, then the property is the man. He can't do what he wants, he can't think what he wants. The property is the man, stronger than he is. And he is small, not big. Only his possessions are big—and he's the servant of his property. That is so, too." The driver munched the branded pie and threw the crust away. "Times are changed, don't you know? Thinking about stuff like that don't feed the kids. Get your three dollars a day, feed your kids. You got no call to worry about anybody's kids but your own. You get a reputation for talking like that, and you'll never get three dollars a day. Big shots won't give you three dollars a day if you worry about anything but your three dollars a day."

"Nearly a hundred people on the road for your three dollars. Where will we go?"

"And that reminds me," the driver said, "you better get out soon. I'm going through the dooryard after dinner."

"You filled in the well this morning."

"I know. Had to keep the line straight. But I'm going through the dooryard after dinner. Got to keep the lines straight. And—well, you know Joe Davis, my old man, so I'll tell you this. I got orders wherever there's a family not moved out—if I have an accident—you know, get too close and cave the house in a little—well, I might get a couple of dollars. And my youngest kid never had no shoes yet."

"I built it with my hands. Straightened old nails to put the sheathing on. Rafters are wired to the stringers with baling wire. It's mine. I built it. You bump it down—I'll be in the window with a rifle. You even come too close and I'll pot you like a rabbit."

"It's not me. There's nothing I can do. I'll lose my job if I don't do it. And look—suppose you kill me? They'll just hang you, but long before you're hung there'll be another guy on the tractor, and he'll bump the house down. You're not killing the right guy."

"That's so," the tenant said. "Who gave you orders? I'll go after him. He's the one

第七章　文学与农学 (Literature and Agriculture)

to kill."

"You're wrong. He got his orders from the bank. The bank told him, 'Clear those people out or it's your job.'"

"Well, there's a president of the bank. There's a board of directors. I'll fill up the magazine of the rifle and go into the bank."

The driver said, "Fellow was telling me the bank gets orders from the East. The orders were, 'Make the land show profit or we'll close you up.'"

"But where does it stop? Who can we shoot? I don't aim to starve to death before I kill the man that's starving me."

"I don't know. Maybe there's nobody to shoot. Maybe the thing isn't men at all. Maybe like you said, the property's doing it. Anyway I told you my orders."

"I got to figure," the tenant said. "We all got to figure. There's some way to stop this. It's not like lightning or earthquakes. We've got a bad thing made by men, and by God that's something we can change." The tenant sat in his doorway, and the driver thundered his engine and started off, tracks falling and curving, harrows combing, and the phalli of the seeder slipping into the ground. Across the dooryard the tractor cut, and the hard, foot-beaten ground was seeded field, and the tractor cut through again; the uncut space was ten feet wide. And back he came. The iron guard bit into the house-corner, crumbled the wall, and wrenched the little house from its foundation so that it fell sideways, crushed like a bug. And the driver was goggled and a rubber mask covered his nose and mouth. The tractor cut a straight line on, and the air and the ground vibrated with its thunder. The tenant man stared after it, his rifle in his hand. His wife was beside him, and the quiet children behind. And all of them stared after the tractor.

第八章

文学与气候科学（Literature and Climate Science）

第一节　气候的文学表征

背景知识

气候科学（climate science）是研究气候的一门科学。"气候"（climate）一词源于古希腊文 κλίμα，意为倾斜（inclination），指各地气候的冷暖同太阳光线的倾斜程度有关。气候是"某一特定地点漫长时期的大气的状况，是短时期内构成天气的那些大气因子（及其变化）的长期概况。这些因子是：太阳辐射、温度、湿度、降水（类型、频率、数量）、气压、风（风速和风向）[1]。"气象要素（气温、降水、光照、风力等）的各种统计量（均值、极值、概率等）是表述气候的基本依据。根据世界气象组织（WMO）的规定，一般气候的计算时间为 30 年[2]。气候作为自然环境的重要组成部分，与人类社会息息相关。任何气候变化都会对自然生态环境以及社会经济系统产生影响，甚至危及人类社会未来的生存与发展。

自 21 世纪以来，全球变暖、冰川融化、极端气候等频发，气候变化已成为当今全球社会的重要话题。气候变化导致生物多样性受到威胁、海平面上升、水资源分布不均等问题，对一些国家以及沿海地区造成威胁，同时也对农、林、牧、渔等经济社会活动产生了不利影响。愈演愈烈的极端气候事件也正在成为人们需要面对的新常态，在《联合国气候变化框架公约》（UNFCCC）第二十七次缔约方大会（COP27）上，科学家们发布了 2021 年气候科学的 10 大新见解（10 New Insights in Climate Science）报告，指出当前气候变化的影响已经超出预期，仅靠人们去适应气候已经无法应对气候变化带来的损失和损害。亚当·特雷克斯勒（Adam Trexler）认为："气候变化超越了本地地方，到达全球空间[3]。"诚然，气候变化已经成为影响全人类和地球上所有物种的全球性事件，其主要根源在于西方发达资本主义国家在

---

[1] 美国不列颠百科全书公司. 不列颠百科全书：第 4 卷[M]. 中国大百科全书出版社《不列颠百科全书》编辑部，译. 北京：中国大百科全书出版社，2007：291.

[2] 气候[Z/OL]. [2023-07-25]. https://baike.baidu.com/item/气候/384697.

[3] TREXLER A. Anthropocene fictions: the novel in a time of climate change[M]. Charlottesville: University of Virginia Press, 2015: 237.

第八章 文学与气候科学（Literature and Climate Science）

工业化历史上的过量温室气体排放。由气候变化引发的恶果对不同国家、不同地区、不同物种的影响程度不一。极端气候产生的洪涝、高温、山火等自然灾害让人们甚为忧虑，由此引发的社会问题层出不穷。气候变化导致的各种自然灾害，不仅加剧了贫富分化，还会催生性别歧视、社会不公等现实问题，甚至引发暴力犯罪等恶性事件。面对全球极端气候变化的威胁，人们逐渐意识到，仅仅依靠科学并不能从根本上解决气候变化危机，因为科学本身无法触及与气候变化相关的人对自然的压迫、性别政治和环境正义等意识形态问题[1]。气候变化这一前所未有的复杂现象不仅需要在科学的范畴内进行探讨，更应在广阔的社会背景和文化语境中进行研究，以便开展生态教育，牢固树立生态文明观，帮助引导人们探寻解决气候问题的出路。在文学艺术领域，关于气候变化的文学作品和电影创作逐渐成为传播环保知识、增强生态意识的重要手段，"气候变化小说"（climate change fiction）应运而生。

"气候变化小说"又称"气候小说"（climate fiction），是21世纪出现的新兴小说流派。"气候变化小说"并不是一个全新的概念，早在19世纪，法国小说家儒勒·凡尔纳（Jules Verne）就在科幻小说《北冰洋的幻想》（*The Purchase of the North Pole*, 1889）中探讨过气候变化和温度骤降问题。美国作家丹·布隆（Dan Bloom）在接受《大西洋月刊》采访时首次正式提出，应将文学范畴内的"气候小说"改称为"气候变化小说"，以警醒社会各界重视全球变暖等气候变化问题。2013年，"气候变化小说"一词被首次使用，当时美国国家公共电台（National Public Radio，NPR）用Cli-Fi指代那些涉及人为因素导致气候变化的文艺作品。作品中的气候变化现象不仅为故事情节发展提供背景，同时也是小说叙事的固有部分，对小说的人物设定和情节构思有着极大影响。如今，气候变化小说已经由科幻小说的一个子类演变为一种具有自身特色的文学流派。与传统科幻小说不同，气候变化小说很少聚焦于虚构星球或未来科技，而是在大气污染、海平面上升、全球变暖等环境危机话语中，阐述气候变化对人类文明的影响[2]，"以一系列现实主义和非现实主义的形式处理深刻而复杂的气候问题"[3]。

文学与气候的研究起点是人类社会所面临的气候变化危机，批评家通过分析批判人类中心主义，引导读者关注日益严峻的气候变化危机，号召人们采取措施来保护地球大气，从而凸显文学研究的现实意义。关于文学与气候的研究起步虽早，但数量零星，成果较为零散。直到2000年，学界才开始在"人类世"和生态批评的框架下对文学中的气候书写进行系统研究。"人类世"一词最早出现在20世纪80年代，由美国密歇根大学海洋生物学家尤金·斯托莫（Eugene F. Stoermer, 1934—2012）创造。2000年，诺贝尔化学奖获得者保罗·

---

[1] GAARD G. Ecofeminism and climate change[J]. Women's studies international forum, 2015(49)：20-33.
[2] 来岑岑. 气候变化小说的主题意蕴[N]. 中国社会科学报, 2021-08-02.
[3] JOHNS-PUTRA A. Climate and literature[M]. Cambridge：Cambridge University Press, 2019：245.

克鲁岑和斯托莫正式提出"人类世"概念,用这一术语表示以全球气候变化为表征的"人类主导的地质时期"①。随着文学与气候研究的兴起,人类世概念逐渐由自然科学传播至人文社会科学,在哲学、历史学、人类学、社会学等领域受到高度关注。特雷克斯勒的《人类世小说:气候变化时代的小说》(Anthropocene Fictions: The Novel in a Time of Climate Change, 2015)是第一部专门研究气候变化小说的专著。特雷克斯勒从气候学、社会学、地理学和环境经济学等方面出发,梳理了百余部直接指涉人为气候变化的小说,其中不乏亚瑟·赫索格(Arthur Herzog, 1927—2010)的《热浪》(Heat, 1977)、金·斯坦利·罗宾逊(Kim Stanley Robinson, 1952—)的"首都三部曲"(Science in the Capital Trilogy)、保罗·巴奇加卢皮(Paolo Bacigalupi, 1972—)的《发条女孩》(The Windup Girl, 2009)、伊恩·麦克尤恩的《追日》(Solar, 2010)等经典之作。这些文学作品具有强烈的现实观照,已经成为气候变化时代中构建生态意义的重要工具。克莱尔·科尔布鲁克(Claire Colebrook, 1965—)在展望人类世文学未来的同时,重新审视了"灭绝"(extinction)的概念。"气候变化和人类世与灭绝和结局的转变意识联系在一起;变异性不再被认为是生命的壮丽,结局也不再是为了未来而扫除死寂的世界②。"德国学者安东尼娅·梅纳特(Antonia Mehnert)的《气候变化小说:美国文学中的全球变暖表征》(Climate Change Fictions: Representations of Global Warming in American Literature, 2016)是聚焦美国气候变化小说的第一部专著。梅纳特选取了美国当代12个气候变化叙事文本,结合全球气候变化语境,剖析了其中的时空变换、气候风险和环境正义等核心主题,呼吁人类社会增强生态危机意识。作为最早开展气候小说研究的生态批评学者之一,英国和爱尔兰文学与环境协会(ASLE-UKI)前主席阿德琳·约翰斯-普特拉(Adeline Johns-Putra, 1973—)认为,气候变化文学研究是一种跨学科研究,可以将其称作"气候变化批评"(climate change criticism)或"批判性气候变化"(critical climate change)③。约翰斯-普特拉在最新出版的《剑桥文学指南:文学与气候》(The Cambridge Companion to Literature and Climate, 2022)中分析了文学与气候之间的相互作用,反映了南北半球、土著居民和非白人社区不同的天气经历,以全球气候实例丰富读者对于气候的多样理解。

气候变化小说作为文学与气候研究的新兴文学流派,具有鲜明的时代特色,能够帮助读者了解气候变化作为一种人为过程的科学。气候变化小说不是为了描写世界末日或地球文明终结,而是注重启发读者深入挖掘导致气候灾难的深层原因,以此强调生态危机的严峻性、紧迫性及全球性。正如姜礼福所说:"人类世是政治事件……人类世中的气候变化是人类生存的严重挑战,意味着地球进入'事件'多发期,这些事件会造成地区性或全球性影响,

---

① CRUTZEN P J. Geology of mankind[J]. Nature, 2002, 415(1): 23.
② JOHNS-PUTRA A. Climate and literature[M]. Cambridge: Cambridge University Press, 2019: 280.
③ JOHNS-PUTRA A. Climate change in literature and literary studies: from Cli-Fi, climate change theater and ecopoetry to ecocriticism and climate change criticism[J]. WIREs climate change, 2012, 7(2): 266-282.

第八章 文学与气候科学(Literature and Climate Science)

需要国家多个机构或国际社会共同应对,需要发挥政治势力的核心作用①。"究其根本,气候危机是一场社会危机,关乎人类普遍利益,需要全球秉持人类命运共同体理念合力应对。气候变化小说通过对气候灾难等环境问题的书写,呼吁人类重新思考人与自然的辩证关系,共同应对气候变化带来的危机和挑战。

文献传真

阅读《气候科学》("Climate Science"),思考文末问答题。本文节选自《劳特利奇指南:文学与科学》②。

Climate Science
Robert Markley

Beyond Anthropogenic Time

Embodied time is written in terms of memory. In his study of meteorology in the late seventeenth and eighteenth centuries, Jan Golinski calls attention to the ways in which amateur naturalists who observed and described weather patterns struggled with the limitations of language. The author of the anonymous Worcestershire diary called his daily weather register "my Ephemeris or Historical Remarques on vicissitudes of the weather, with a narrative of its course & Tracing it in its various winding meanders round ye year" but complained that "our Language is exceeding scanty & barren of words to use & express ye various notions I have of Weather &c".③ This "scanty & barren" language restricts the ability to turn the daily experience of the weather into a theory of climate. Without a causal, scientific narrative to explain changes in the weather, such records drift toward the theological semiotics of catastrophe and apocalypse: the experience of embodied responses to the weather tends to be cast in providentialist terms.

In his account of the devastating wind storm that struck England and Wales in late 1703, a once-in-500-years extra-tropical cyclone, Daniel Defoe describes his fears as the storm approached: "the Night would be very tempestuous," he recognized, because "the

---

① 姜礼福,孟庆粉. 人类世:从地质概念到文学批评[J]. 湖南科技大学学报(社会科学版),2018,21(6):45.
② MARKLEY R. Climate science[C]//CLARKE B, ROSSINI M. The Routledge companion to literature and science. London: Routledge, 2011: 63-76.
③ GOLINSKI J. British weather and the climate of enlightenment[M]. Chicago: University of Chicago Press, 2007: 19.

Mercury [in his barometer] sunk lower than ever I had observ'd it on any Occasion whatsoever." But the plunging readings seemed so anomalous that they "made [him] suppose that the Tube had been handled and disturb'd by [his] Children".① The full force of the storm dilates the time between midnight and dawn, both in distracting Defoe from his observations and in threatening to end both experiential and historical time: after midnight, he admits of the barometer that his "Observations… are not regular enough to supply the Reader with a full Information, the Disorders of that Dreadful Night having found me other imployment, expecting every Moment when the House I was in would bury us all in its own Ruins".② This sense of impending destruction becomes an emblem of God's vengeance on England for its sins. Defoe sees time in dialectic and emblematic terms; his peril and salvation are also England's. In this sense, the gaps left by imperfect languages and unattended barometers mark the ruptures within history and experience that structure Protestant theology during the early eighteenth century: divine power always threatens to end kronos, chronological time, and to redefine kairos as divine vengeance.

By the end of the eighteenth century, the "empty" time of mathematical simulation and climatological reconstruction began to assert its explanatory power by disembodying climate, that is, by treating climatic change not as the catastrophic irruption of divine judgment but as a non-anthropogenic time that transcends both individual and historical experience. At the end of the eighteenth century, climatological time emerges as a distinct ontological challenge to theological time in three interlocking sets of developments. All three sought to redefine the scientific basis for understanding time and, in the process, recast traditional ideas about Nature. In the 1790s, the nebular hypothesis of planetary formation advanced by Pierre Simon de Laplace, the "discovery" of geological time by James Hutton, and the argument for species extinction put forth by Georges Cuvier transformed conceptions of climate by decoupling history from human experience and memory.

The nebular hypothesis anthropomorphized the life cycle of planets in terms of youth, maturity, old age, and heat-death, offering a model of climatic change as the consequence

---

① DEFOE D. The storm[M]. London: Allen Lane, 2003: 24.
② 同①25.

第八章 文学与气候科学（Literature and Climate Science）

of irreversible, universal processes.① Laplace removed Newton's God from the mathematical equations that produced a compelling model of the origins, evolution, and fate of the solar system. Hutton's vision of geological time with "no vestige of a beginning, no prospect of an end" presented a cyclical history of erosion and upheaval that continually reshaped earth.② This continual reshaping both went beyond and challenged the theological catastrophism that ascribed evidence such as drowned cities and toppled buildings to the vengeance of an angry God. Eighty years after Defoe had echoed a near-universal sentiment among early natural philosophers—"Nature plainly refers us beyond her Self, to the Mighty Hand of Infinite Power, the Author of Nature, and Original of all Causes"—Hutton's geological history challenged perceptions of the reliability of experiential notions of duration, history③, nature, and causality. The Earth itself threatened to become a sublime, non-human environment. Cuvier's account of the extinction of fossilized species raised profound questions about the limits of Mosaic history and the ways in which past environments differed from present conditions.④ The fascination with the skeletal remains of dinosaurs, giant sloths, and mastodons that gripped London, Paris, Philadelphia, and New York in 1800 suggested that Nature bred entire species that required primeval ecologies no human ever had seen. The emphasis throughout the nineteenth century on the savage violence of prehistoric carnivores indicates the extent to which it was difficult to imagine the ecological conditions that provided forage for gigantic species of plant-eaters.

Even before Darwin published *The Origin of Species*, then, scientific thought had begun to challenge the biblical monopoly on conceptions of history and had provided competing models of climatological time, the creation and reshaping of the earth and its natural environment, and humankind's future. The fad in Victorian science fiction for end-of-the-universe stories, many riffing on Mary Shelley's *The Last Man*, testifies to the ways

---

① ROLAND N L. Creation by natural law: Laplace's nebular hypothesis in American thought [M]. Seattle: University of Washington Press, 1977.
② HUTTON J. Theory of the earth, with proofs and illustrations, 2 vols [M]. Edinburgh: Printed for Messers Cadell, Junior, Davis, and Creech, 1795: 200.
③ DEFOE D. The storm [M]. London: Allen Lane, 2003: 2.
④ RUDWICK M S J. Bursting the limits of time: the reconstruction of geohistory in the age of revolution [M]. Chicago: University of Chicago Press, 2005.

in which the specter of species extinction could be reimagined on a massive, planetary scale. Extinction thus haunts the tendency in late eighteenth- and early nineteenth-century science to chart, measure, and quantify both the natural world and the social regimes of economics and politics. In this sense, the understanding of long-term change, of a climatological time that exists beyond human experience, gestures paradoxically toward embracing and resisting the mathematically determined universe imagined by Laplace. A time that transcends and beggars human experience, however, can be conceived only differentially, and paradoxically, in its relation to phenomenological perceptions of time and existence. If mathematical reductionism locks humankind and climate into intractable processes that lead to extinction, it also provokes redefinitions of ideas of divinity and therefore of the complex relationships of humankind to experience, Nature, and time.

Nineteenth-century transcendentalism suggests that the ruptures between microcosm and macrocosm, between humankind's experience of time and Nature's time, are produced by the self-generating alienation of custom or ideology. In his essay "Nature," Ralph Waldo Emerson recasts the threat of extinction within phenomenological notions of time, Nature, and experience:

> The knowledge that we traverse the whole scale of being, from the centre to the poles of nature, and have some stake in every possibility, lends that sublime lustre to death, which philosophy and religion have too outwardly and literally striven to express in the popular doctrine of the immortality of the soul. The reality is more excellent than the report. Here is no ruin, no discontinuity, no spent ball. The divine circulations never rest nor linger. Nature is the incarnation of a thought, and turns to a thought again, as ice becomes water and gas. The world is mind precipitated, and the volatile essence is forever escaping again into the state of free thought... That power which does not respect quantity, which makes the whole and the particle its equal channel, delegates its smile to the morning, and distils its essence into every drop of rain. Every moment instructs, and every object: for wisdom is infused into every form.①

---

① EMERSON R W. Nature [A]//PORTE J. Essays and lectures by Ralph Waldo Emerson. New York: Library of America, 1983: 542.

第八章 文学与气候科学(Literature and Climate Science)

In gesturing toward the reflexivity of microcosm and macrocosm, Emerson yokes Hutton's geological or Laplace's universal time to experiential moments and perceptions that defy scientific reductionism. Human life, like the planet itself, is "no spent ball," but a web of complex, proliferating, and dynamic energies.① Emerson locates "perfection" and "harmony" in individual days. He begins this essay by observing:

> There are days which occur in this climate, at almost any season of the year, wherein the world reaches its perfection, when the air, the heavenly bodies, and the earth, make a harmony, as if nature would indulge her offspring; when, in these bleak upper sides of the planet, nothing is to desire that we have heard of the happiest latitudes, and we bask in the shining hours of Florida and Cuba; when everything that has life gives sign of satisfaction... These halcyons may be looked for with a little more assurance in that pure October weather, which we distinguish by the name of the Indian Summer. The day, immeasurably long, sleeps over the broad hills and warm wide fields. To have lived through all its sunny hours, seems longevity enough.②

In contrast to nineteenth-century scientists later struggling to explain the prospect of an Earth succumbing to the heat-death ostensibly predicted by the second law of thermodynamics, Emerson finds time both focused and dilated, intimations of immortality distilled into the "sunny hours" of "pure October weather" that bring to the climate of northern New England the kind of "satisfaction" ostensibly experienced in the tropical sunshine of the Caribbean. Emerson's "halcyons" locate embodied human experience within a matrix of "harmony," in which multiplying complexities produce greater intimations and emotive understandings of Nature as "the circumstance which dwarfs every other circumstance," an unalienated universal composed of, and generating, infinite experiences of "that power which does not respect quantity, which makes the whole and the particle its equal channel."

Transcendentalism can thus be seen as one response to the fundamental paradoxes

---

① BUELL L. The environmental imaginations: Thoreau, nature writing, and the formation of American culture [M]. Cambridge: Harvard University Press, 1995: 219-251.

② EMERSON R W. Nature [A]//PORTE J. Essays and lectures by Ralph Waldo Emerson. New York: Library of America, 1983: 540.

posed by climatological time. Rather than a mathematically determined universe that exists beyond the limits of perception and experience, and therefore that can be imagined only in terms of the irrelevance or negation of embodied experience, the world becomes open to the interweaving of mind and matter. In Emerson's "Nature," the transcendental imperative that "does not respect quantity" encourages humankind to embrace the processes of an ongoing reintegration of self and environment rather than succumb to the profound ontological as well as epistemological displacements of what Emerson terms "custom." To turn away from "our life of solemn trifles," humankind must recognize that Nature can be described only as a kind of double negative, a negation of a natural world already alienated by "the ambitious chatter of the schools [that] would persuade us to despise" material existence in favor of metaphysical abstractions. Nature's time therefore exists as the primeval negation of humankind's efforts to measure and institutionalize time: "Here no history, or church, or state, is interpolated on the divine sky and the immortal year." In an important sense, the threat to traditional structures of thought and belief posed by Laplace and Cuvier is subsumed by Emerson's encompassing change within an organic regeneration of both mind and climate—"We come to our own, and make friends with matter." Dynamic and unpredictable change is transformed into the energies of self-renewal.

Yet the ethics of individualism that Emerson is typically credited with (or accused of) constitutes only one half of a dialectic in the nineteenth century. In *Late Victorian Holocausts*, Mike Davis charts the devastating human and environmental consequences of European imperialism and its hallucinogenic optimism that colonial proprietors could plough under complex ecologies throughout the underdeveloped world to grow cash crops (cotton, opium, tea, tobacco, and rice) for export to Europe and North America.① Unrestrained imperial expansion and robber-baron capitalism trumpeted the view that the climates of India, Africa, and the America could be "improved" by large-scale monoculture. This view of Nature as an infinite storehouse focuses less on what Karl Marx calls exchange value than on the infinite elasticity of use-value: the belief that John Locke advanced in the *Two Treatises of Government* (1690) that the infinite productivity of the natural world forms a consensual basis for individual and property

---

① DAVIS M. Late Victorian holocausts: el nino famines and the making of the third world[M]. London: Verso, 2001.

第八章 文学与气候科学（Literature and Climate Science）

rights—and property, in turn, secures the basis of political and social identity.

Locke invokes explicitly the classical ideal of a "golden age" when humanity, or at least specific populations, reaped the benefits of a beneficent Nature.[①] In such a world of abundant resources and a stable climate, as he argues in the second treatise, labor offers the prospect of limitless productivity rather than marking, as it does in the Judeo-Christian tradition, humankind's banishment from Eden. "In the beginning," Locke declares, "all the World was *America*"—that is, all the world was open to an unending exploitation guaranteed by the fecundity of nature.[②] In this formulation, labor is divorced from a material world of life-and-death calculations (when to plant, when to harvest, how much seed to conserve for next year's planting, whether to kill the cow to feed one's family during a harsh winter, and so forth) that defined agricultural existence during the Little Ice Age in much of early modern Europe.[③]

By the later eighteenth century, neo-Lockean liberalism had turned bodies into reliable machines, capable of increasing their useful labor, and the land into a repository of potential value that could be mined, refashioned, and exploited without suffering any diminution in either extent or productivity. By the nineteenth century, as Davis suggests, the Lockean argument that the fruits of one's labor theoretically cannot exceed a normative notion of bodily sufficiency had been corrupted into the conversion of humans into interchangeable units of labor, and the natural world consequently becomes an *effect* of humankind's use. The time of the world thus becomes the time of economic calculation. In the long tradition of apocalyptic science fiction that emerges in the nineteenth century, it is precisely this world of humankind's dominion that, to quote H. G. Wells in *The War of the Worlds*, begins "losing coherency, losing shape and efficiency, guttering, softening, running at last in that swift liquefaction of the social body".[④] These apocalyptic scenarios, the "Grotesque gleam of a time no history will ever fully describe!"[⑤], invariably have ecological overtones because, in their playful cultural necrosis, they offer a way of imagining a time after human history: the end of

---

① MARKLEY R. "Land enough in the world": Locke's golden age and the infinite extensions of "use"[J]. South atlantic quarterly, 1999, 98: 817-837.
② LOCKE J. Two treatises of government[M]. Cambridge: Cambridge University Press, 1960: 2-3.
③ FAGAN B. The Little Ice Age: how climate made history: 1300-1850[M]. New York: Basic Books, 2000.
④ WELLS H G. The war of the worlds[M]. Geduld: Indiana University Press, 1984: 82.
⑤ 同②145.

kronos and the aftermath of *kairos*.

思考题

1. How does the limitation of language impact the representation of climate in literature, particularly in terms of capturing the daily experiences of weather patterns and turning them into a theory of climate?

2. How do literary accounts, such as Daniel Defoe's description of a devastating wind storm, reflect the interplay between embodied human experience of climate and theological interpretations of weather events?

3. In what ways does literature respond to the scientific developments in understanding climatological time and its decoupling from human experience and memory? How does this response shape the portrayal of climate and time in literary works?

第二节　《零下五十度》与气候变化

作品导读

1. 作者简介

《零下五十度》(*Fifty Degrees Below*, 2005)是美国科幻小说大师金·斯坦利·罗宾逊的作品。1952年,金·斯坦利·罗宾逊出生于美国伊利诺伊州,幼年随父母搬迁到南加州橘县。1974年,罗宾逊获加利福尼亚大学圣迭戈分校文学学士学位,并于1975年获波士顿大学英语文学硕士学位。在美国文学评论家、马克思主义学者弗雷德里克·詹姆逊(Fredric Jameson, 1934—)的影响下,罗宾逊在加利福尼亚大学圣迭戈分校攻读英语博士期间开始阅读菲利普·迪克的作品。他的博士论文《菲利普·迪克的长篇小说》(*The Novels of Philip K. Dick*)于1984年出版,针对迪克作品的类型传统和创新提出了诸多创见,至今仍是学界研究迪克的重要著作之一。罗宾逊具有深厚的英语文学研究背景和杰出的写作能力,他的作品文学性强,语言优美,叙事结构精巧,细节丰富。他曾经在加利福尼亚大学戴维斯分校教授写作课,也曾受邀担任号角工作坊(Clarion Workshop)的写作老师[①]。在近半个世纪的

[①] 杨琼. 学者型科幻作家:金·斯坦利·罗宾逊[Z/OL]. https://sw.kpcswa.org.cn/Catalog/201703/import/2018/0127/78.html.

第八章　文学与气候科学(Literature and Climate Science)

科幻文学写作生涯里,罗宾逊多次斩获科幻小说界最高荣誉雨果奖(Hugo Award for Best Novel)和星云奖(Nebula Award for Best Novel),更曾六次摘取轨迹奖(Locus Award)桂冠,可谓获奖无数。

罗宾逊的作品多以生态可持续性、气候变化和全球变暖为主题,时常关注生态环境、科技与人类之间的辩证关系。他在早年间出版的"加州三部曲"(Three Californias trilogy),或称"橘县三部曲"(Orange County trilogy)就从不同层面预设了美国加利福尼亚州的三种未来。第一部长篇小说《蛮荒海岸》(The Wild Shore,1984)以第一人称回忆录的形式讲述了美国核战争幸存者在被联合国严密封锁63年的与世隔绝的环境中,为了生存、发展乃至复兴昔日辉煌而走过的一段艰难而悲壮的历程①。在《黄金海岸》(The Gold Coast,1988)中,2027年的南加州充斥着以汽车为导向的文化和生活方式,公寓、高速公路和购物中心随处可见。年轻人沉浸在跑车、性行为和毒品世界中无法自拔,却陷入了工业恐怖主义(industrial terrorism)的圈套。《太平边缘》(Pacific Edge,1990)展望了2065年的生态乌托邦(utopian)世界,绿党(Greens)与新联邦党(New Federals)就最后一片荒野的开发问题产生激烈冲突,保护"绿色"环境免遭荼毒成为社区居民的当务之急。"火星三部曲"(Mars trilogy)的出版使罗宾逊名声大振,一举成为当代美国最受好评的科幻作家之一。作为一系列关于火星移民的奠基之作,《红火星》(Red Mars,1992)、《绿火星》(Green Mars,1993)和《蓝火星》(Blue Mars,1996)堪称史诗般的科幻巨著。书中的故事跨越百年,讲述了从2026—2128年,首批地球移民在登陆火星之后如何克服种种困境,将火星改造为适合居住的家园。三部作品包罗万象,从自然百科到高新科技,从火星地理到地球哲学,从政治到宗教,从人性到数学,火星中的自然景观、天地巨变和人性纷争等气势恢宏的场景,都在罗宾逊无与伦比的想象力中一一展现②。在罗宾逊笔下,火星与地球的生存现状呈现出鲜明的对比。平等主义(egalitarianism)、社会学和科学在火星上取得飞速进步,而地球却仍然遭受着人口过剩、资源匮乏等生态灾难。通过对乌托邦和反乌托邦的主题建构,"火星三部曲"结合现实科技,对首批移民在火星所做的地球化改造进行了具有可行性的假设,开创了广阔而合理的火星全景,奠定了后续火星科幻题材的基调。"首都三部曲"的影响力也同样不容小觑。《雨的四十种征兆》(Forty Signs of Rain,2004)、《零下五十度》和《生死六十天》(Sixty Days and Counting,2007)着眼于日益严峻的全球变暖危机,强调从国家政策和国际关系两个层面共同应对生态紧急事件的必要性,具有强烈的人文关怀。罗宾逊近年出版的几部独立长篇小说依旧延续着对气候变化的关注。在《纽约2140》(New York 2140,2017)设想的未来中,倘

---

① 蛮荒海岸[Z/OL].[2023-07-25].https://book.douban.com/subject/3024740/.
② 金·斯坦利·罗宾逊[Z/OL].[2023-07-25].https://baike.baidu.com/item/金·斯坦利·罗宾逊?fromModule=lemma_search-box.

若人类放任全球气候变暖现象持续发展,两极冰川消融导致全球海平面上升,纽约市将会没入水下。然而,罗宾逊并未止步于灾难的预告,而是把重点放在描述人们如何在巨变的世界中重建家园的励志故事。最新的长篇小说《未来部》(*The Ministry for the Future*, 2020)一经出版,便在西方世界引起了巨大轰动,更是荣登美国前总统巴拉克·奥巴马(Barack Obama, 1961—)2020年的最爱书单。在小说开头,一股巨型"湿球"温度("wet-bulb" temperature)热浪在一周内席卷了印度一角,给小镇居民的生命带来了致命威胁。罗宾逊以一个外来白人社区援助者的视角,在沉浸式的讲述中为全球贫困社区主张正义,瓦解全球生态恐怖主义(eco-terrorism)的阴谋。

2. 作品介绍

《零下五十度》是罗宾逊代表作品"首都三部曲"的第二部小说,此时的华盛顿特区气温异常,生态环境空前恶化,人们陷入了科学技术与气候突变的冲突中。《零下五十度》延续了《雨的四十种征兆》的故事剧情,在华盛顿特区被世纪风暴淹没之后,科学家弗兰克·温德华(Frank Vanderwal)决定在国家科学基金会(National Science Foundation, NSF)再待一年,致力于研究如何积极解决日益紧张的气候变化问题。公寓租约已经到期,华盛顿的房地产市场也有所收紧,弗兰克最终决定在石溪公园(Rock Creek Park)内建造一个树屋以供休息。在此期间,弗兰克还加入了野生观察小组(Feral Observation Group, FOG),日常追踪四处游荡的野生动物。基金会的"温德华委员会"(Vanderwal committee)开始着手应对气候变化现状,由于工作原因,弗兰克和老板黛安(Diane)的关系突飞猛进,却只能碍于职位差距保持表面距离。与此同时,在《雨的四十种征兆》中与弗兰克一起被困电梯的神秘女人卡罗琳(Caroline)再次出现,与弗兰克再续前缘。弗兰克在向卡罗琳表达爱意的同时,却意外得知卡罗琳已婚的事实,尽管这段婚姻并不遂人愿。不仅如此,卡罗琳和丈夫都在政府内部从事秘密的间谍活动,负责监控包括弗兰克在内的诸多科研人士,时间长达一年之久。两人相互告别后,弗兰克重新投入了工作,和黛安前往基金会针对全球环境和能源问题提供解决方案,并指出隐藏背后的政治阻力。随后他们一行人途经日本和孟加拉湾,最后来到了肯巴隆。在一段流落街头的经历后,尼克(Nick)发现季风即将到来,紧随其后的降雨使大家兴奋不已。第二天下午,他们参观了西北部的一个动物园,度过了轻松愉快的一天。许多大型猫科动物被卷入海水,后被巡逻艇救出。黎明前一小时,他们被告知季风重来,但这次却伴随着有史以来最严重的洪涝灾难。沿途的许多村庄被洪水淹没,弗兰克等人得幸于直升机救助,安全离开。

厄尔尼诺等极端气候使地球生态环境脆弱不堪,小说主人公们也在不断避难的过程中寻找应对措施。在生存条件日趋恶劣的情况下,人们逐渐意识到气候变化对周遭环境的威胁,开始为人类未来感到担忧。来自国家海洋和大气管理局的研究小组对于气候突变案例

第八章 文学与气候科学（Literature and Climate Science）

做了具体建模分析,得出了一些气候变化的具体数据。为了对气候现象进行细致观察,弗兰克在公园外的森林里开展研究。在试图捕获野生动物的过程中,弗兰克不幸遭遇意外,但好在没有危及生命。出院后,弗兰克依旧坚持实验,在寒冷的冬夜与自然对抗,以严谨的态度对待工作任务。整个冬天,强风如天气预报所示再次来袭,气温连续12天创历史新低。一个星期六的早晨,弗兰克接尼克去动物园,他们在动物园参与的第一项活动就是学习把石头敲成刀刃和箭头,完成后他们去看长臂猿和暹罗猿。在那一刻,弗兰克意识到自己作为灵长类动物的地位,同时对自己的爱情感到惋惜,再加上与藏传佛教徒的邂逅,让他下定决心过一种更真实的生活。夏天逐渐过去,气候突然开始好转。弗兰克和黛安一起去冰岛欣赏了美丽的风景;卡罗琳如愿与丈夫分开;菲尔（Phil）也成功赢得了美国总统选举:所有人都沉浸在欢乐的气氛中。

3. 作品赏析

当今世界,人类文明是如此不可思议。人类在取得巨大的科学、技术和经济进步的同时,由于自身不当行为引起的气候变化和物种灭绝等生态问题都给自然秩序带来了巨大的冲击,人类环境已经危机四伏。气候变化主要表现在三方面:全球气候变暖、酸雨以及臭氧层破坏,其中全球气候变暖是当前最为迫切的问题。人类在近一个世纪以来,大量使用矿物燃料,排放出大量温室气体,导致在二十世纪世界平均温度攀升。全球气候变暖导致冰川和积雪融化加速,引起海平面上升,不少国家以及临海地区面临被淹没的危险。此外,全球气候变暖还导致各种气候灾害频发,如干旱、洪水、暴风雪等,对人类的经济社会活动产生了不利影响。为阻止全球变暖趋势,1992年联合国专门制定了《联合国气候变化框架公约》（United Nations Framework Convention on Climate Change, UNFCCC）,旨在引起全球居民对气候变暖现象的重视。人类世概念也逐渐成为人文社会科学领域的热门话题,引起了文学研究者对气候变化文学的广泛关注。《零下五十度》正是罗宾逊在这一背景下创作出的科幻小说,力图通过文学的方式警醒人类社会意识到气候问题的紧迫性及其带来的灾难性后果。小说展现了因气候突变导致的世界末日图景,着重探讨自然秩序失衡之下的一系列环境危机。在当今的生态话语体系下,自然秩序对于保护地球环境具有不可替代的重要性。自然秩序的失衡成为人类与自然环境产生冲突的本质原因,全面引发生态危机。

《零下五十度》以主人公弗兰克的视角展开,以气候问题贯穿全文,描述了气候变化带来的影响,促使人们思考气候变化问题。小说开篇描写了华盛顿特区被洪水所迫,表面看似恢复,实则伤痕累累,以一种沉闷的氛围突出洪水带给这个国家的伤害,更是为后面全球变暖的气候问题做出铺垫。小说运用调侃、诙谐、反讽的语气,采用大量的对话描写,条理十分清晰。小说中的对话符合人物各自的身份,加强了人物性格的刻画,一方面使人物形象更加丰满,另一方面也增加了小说的趣味性和可读性。在语言上没有太过于复杂的词汇和长难句,十分口语化,浅显易懂,让读者产生了极大的阅读兴趣。小说中对人物的细致描写巧妙运用了多种修辞手法。在形容安娜(Anna)睡觉的状态时,罗宾逊写道:"Anna stitched the meandering border between sleep and dreams, in and out, up and down."。读者从中不难看出,安娜睡得并不安稳。此时的她在为乔(Joe)的身体健康担心,也在为他们的未来命运担忧。描写日出美景时,罗宾逊用比喻的修辞手法将黎明时分的阳光比作银币:"He looked back; Joe's watery prints caught little chips of the dawn light, looking like silver coins.",使乔的形象更加真实活泼。当季风再次来临,面对灾难,前来营救的直升机也因为大风在空中飘忽不定。罗宾逊将直升机比喻为一片被吹落的树叶:"The helo flew off like a blown leaf.",生动形象地描绘出人类在毁灭性自然灾害面前的渺小,也暗示了弗兰克一行人前路的坎坷。小说中有大量关于恶劣天气的描述,而弗兰克却因为各种原因流离失所,无家可归,坚持在户外环境生活下去。这种情节设置不仅表现了弗兰克作为科学研究人员艰苦奋斗的坚强意志,也从侧面反映出小说的气候变化主题。小说除了从个人生活方面构建人物形象,还从政治角度切入,以总统选举等激烈场面再现当时的社会环境。为了更加凸显人物的立体感,罗宾逊通过语言、动作和心理等多视角描写,以细节为抓手,生动全面地展现了不同人物的个性和特点,使读者产生共鸣。

《零下五十度》是一部科幻小说,也是一部科幻乌托邦文学作品。提到乌托邦,人们可能会最先想到英国托马斯·莫尔(Thomas More,1478—1535)的小说《乌托邦》(*Utopia*,1516)。莫尔在小说中创造了一个名为"乌托邦"的小岛,本义是"美好的不存在的地方",后成为虚构的美好世界的代名词。因为超越性,乌托邦想象承载着大众对苦痛现实的批判和对幸福生活的期盼①。19世纪科幻小说产生,由于科幻小说与乌托邦文学对现实的关注一致,两者关系密切,而随着科技的迅速发展,"古典类型的乌托邦在机器大工业时代逐渐失去了它的生命力,科幻乌托邦文学的发展已经成为历史的必然趋势"②。在《零下五十度》中,我们也能看到作者的乌托邦思想。罗宾逊描绘了弗兰克及其同事们希望借助科技力量来实现对气候变化的干预,为减缓全球变暖不停尝试各种办法,将解决气候问题这一乌托邦式的转变聚焦于人类的地球责任,他设想将科学付诸行动,作为一种替代手段,取代资本主义晚期的政治主导力量,即利己主义、超个人主义以及竞争③。

《零下五十度》的开篇便描绘了洪水后的城市现状以及主人公弗兰克的生活和心理状态。洪水之后,城市残破不堪,房价、物价飞涨,向读者展现了气候变化带来的苦痛现实。弗兰克虽然经历了低谷和迷茫,却还是在洪水冲击后的公园中搭建起木屋,回到国家科学基金

---

① 黄敏. 西方科幻小说中的时空乌托邦思想[D]. 济南:山东大学,2019:8.
② 王小菲. 科幻小说与乌托邦文学[J]. 山花,2013(9):161.
③ ROBERT M. "How to go forward": catastrophe and comedy in Kim Stanley Robinson's Science in the Capital trilogy [J]. Configurations, 2012(1):11.

第八章 文学与气候科学(Literature and Climate Science)

会工作,并为解决气候变化问题努力。通过描写弗兰克解决气候问题时遇到各种困难和挑战但还是不放弃的心理,表达了作者对解决气候问题的愿景,同时描写弗兰克和其他组织利用科技力量来预测气候变化以及找出应对办法,表现出作者认为人类拥有能够应对气候问题的能力,认为这一乌托邦追求也有其现实可能性。科幻小说的乌托邦书写通过对现实可能性的追求使得读者能够意识到现实的局限,让读者明白不存在不经努力就能到达的美好未来。科幻小说展现美好的现实可能性的同时,也表明实现这一可能性的过程是艰难的[①]。而现在,在气候问题愈发严重的背景下,解决气候问题这一愿景不仅只是小说中的乌托邦,而是现实中整个社会的愿景。生存环境越来越恶劣,人类面临的压力越来越大,这种乌托邦不再是一个美好的想法,而是一种生存必需品[②]。罗宾逊希望通过科学来实现气候问题的解决,有其合理性。首先,如今科学发展迅速,以前很多不能解决的问题现在利用科学后得到了解决。科学的力量十分强大,但是人们的意识还不够,罗宾逊认为:"许多人,尤其是我的许多左派同事,认为科学只是权力的工具,我认为这是错误的。于我而言,我们实际处于可以被称为是'科学对抗资本主义'的世界,在这个世界里,诸如环境主义、环境正义、社会正义、民主等更小的进步概念都将被一起击败,除非它们与一个仍有可能成功反对完全资本主义未来的力量——科学——结盟[③]。"其次,罗宾逊的妻子便是一位科学家,他在日常生活中时常与妻子交流,有时会听妻子与其他科学家讨论问题。此外,他还常与一些科学家朋友闲聊或者提问。在写书之前,他会收集一堆书以及网上的资料,通读一遍,然后打电话给科学家、朋友或是陌生人,一边写一边问问题[④]。气候问题带来的精神以及社会问题引人深思。小说中主人公弗兰克在遭受气候问题之后,精神上也产生了创伤。他在洪水之后无家可归,变得日渐迷茫。在得知自己受到监视之后,弗兰克无法全身心地投入工作,逐渐产生了自我认同危机。久而久之,弗兰克很难区分梦想和现实,无法像正常人一样生活。在很长一段时间里,他的创伤记忆把他塑造成了一个外星人,甚至感到自己身处一个内部分裂的世界[⑤]。这些都是气候问题对他的精神所造成的影响。此外,小说中还描写了弗兰克受到了监视以及极端气候发生之后社会出现动荡,气候问题造成了社会问题。监视本是一种违法行为,但是由于气候危机,小说中卡罗琳对弗兰克的监视只是由于她所在的公司能够在气候危机中获取利益,并不在乎采用何种手段。当前气候问题愈发严峻,而人们似乎还并未完全对其产生意识,或是已经意识到但却没有采取行动。借助弗兰克生活方式的转变,小说表达了人与

---

① 刘霖杰. 乌托邦作为科幻小说中现实可能性的书写[J]. 荆楚学刊, 2021, 22(6): 23-29.
② ROBINSON K S. Remarks on utopia in the age of climate change[J]. Utopian Studies, 2016(1): 10.
③ 同②6.
④ DOUG D, LISA Y. "Science's consciousness": an interview with Kim Stanley Robinson[J]. Configurations, 2012(1): 188.
⑤ 盛曹睿. 金·斯坦利·罗宾逊"首都三部曲"中的危机书写研究[D]. 南京: 南京航空航天大学, 2019: 39.

自然密不可分的关系。小说中弗兰克在遭受洪水之后,无家可归,而他出于本能,在公园里搭建树屋,过上了一种回归本真的生活。由此可见,"人类最终与自然不可分割,无论如何被周围环境改变"①。这些都让罗宾逊对科学有了一定的了解,让他对科学充满信心。此外,在罗宾逊看来,当前的资本主义政治并不能解决气候问题。小说中弗兰克在国家基金会开会时,看见安娜找到方法但不能行动,同事们为了缓解环境问题而四处碰壁,这都反映出当前资本主义政治的缺陷。作者在小说最后以菲尔的当选为结局,通过人物之间的一系列精彩对话,以及选举中敌对势力的不断博弈为我们展现了一个政治与环境问题紧密相连的社会。一方面,气候问题事关国家人民的生命财产安全,这是弗兰克一直为之付出努力并保护的东西。另一方面,气候问题也是政治家们用于攻击敌对势力的手段。不难看出,环境问题在与人类生活紧密联系的同时,又与政治野心密不可分。小说的最后也是作者想要表述的观点:"对一些人来说,你是这样的,对另一些人来说,你是那样的。有时会有幽灵降临。声音控制了你的内心。人们拿走他们看到的东西,他们认为那就是全部。有时你就想用这种方式愚弄他们。但不管你想不想愚弄他们。他们愚弄了你!这样下去——每个人都过着自己的生活,每个人都在愚弄别人——不!过多种生活很容易!难的是做一个完整的人。"换句话说,气候问题需要在一种能与科学和谐相处的政治体制中加以深思。

从气候视角来看,《零下五十度》无疑具有丰富的全球化意蕴,融合了生态与政治、伦理与正义、想象与反思,极具启发性和号召性。小说所展示的气候变化危机,目的就是为了将人类从操控自然的陶醉中唤醒。或许罗宾逊在小说中对气候变化的后果有所夸大,但他始终致力于激励读者思考生态危机的本质,并积极探索可能的解决方案。通过描写人与自然的关系,罗宾逊暗示了人们需要转变思维。如果弗兰克没有转变思维去公园,而是选择继续在城市中生活,他也不会感受到回归自然的快乐,体验全新的低碳生活方式。因为"当我们最健康的时候,我们是最快乐的;当我们以一种相当低碳的方式,如在户外散步、交谈、偶尔奔跑或跌倒等,生活在物质世界中时,我们是最健康的"②。地球上的资源是有限的,并且分布不均,有些资源富裕的地方人们会过度消费,缺少保护意识。罗宾逊借《零下五十度》提倡增强对生态环境的保护意识,为后代留下生存空间。应对气候问题不仅仅是国家、机构的责任,个人的行动也十分重要。

罗宾逊认为,当今人类生活在一个多元价值观的世界里。当社会危机是由生态问题引发时,规范人类行为的道德已经稀缺,人类对待自然的态度在政治和经济的纠葛中不断变化。不同的兴趣主体有不同的兴趣需求。而人类利益是"全人类"利益的体现,是关系到人类生存、发展和福祉的最根本利益,是与全人类命运密切相关的各种利益的总和。但在现实

---

① ROBINSON K S. Remarks on utopia in the age of climate change[J]. Utopian Studies, 2016(1): 14.
② 同②12.

第八章 文学与气候科学（Literature and Climate Science）

层面上，人类和国家的利益往往相互冲突。对于每个国家来说，所谓的人类利益必然是虚幻的，国家利益永远高于一切。在巨大的国家利益面前，人类的利益往往被牺牲。然而，为了在全球化时代共同生活在地球上，人们在处理生态事件时应该考虑到人类的利益。各国应该超越民族主义，抛开利益短视，以国际社会的共同利益解决环境问题。人类要不断提高对气候，对自然的关注意识，正如小说里所讲，气候变化不仅是自然的，也是社会的，关系到个人、社会、国家，以及全人类。罗宾逊在小说中探讨解决气候危机所涉及的社会和技术复杂性的同时也为读者提供了可持续性的未来国家的形象。小说中表示解决紧迫而具有破坏性的气候变化的唯一可能方案在于国际力量的团结，或者本质上是构建人类命运共同体，这为人类的未来指明了方向，即中国所倡导的人类命运共同体理念。

作品选读

Fifty Degrees Below

Kim Stanley Robinson

Chapter Two ABRUPT CLIMATE CHANGE

The ground is mud. There are a few sandstone rocks scattered here and there, and some river-rounded chunks of amber quartzite, but for the most part, mud. Hard enough to walk on, but dismal to sit or lie on.

The canopy stands about a hundred feet overhead. In the summer it is a solid green ceiling, with only isolated shafts and patches of sunlight slanting all the way to the ground. The biggest trees have trunks that are three or four feet in diameter, and they shoot up without thinning, putting out their first major branches some forty or fifty feet overhead. There are no evergreens, or rather, no conifers. No needles on the ground, no pinecones. The annual drift of leaves disintegrates entirely, and that's the mud: centuries of leaf mulch.

The trees are either very big or very small, the small ones spindly and light-starved, doomed-looking. There are hardly any medium-sized trees; it is hard to understand the succession story. Only after Frank joined FOG did he learn from one of his associates that the succession was in fact messed up, its balance thrown off by the ballooning population of white-tailed deer, whose natural predators had all been eradicated. No more wolf or puma; and so for generations now the new young trees had been mostly eaten by deer.

Big or small, all the trees were second or third growth; the whole watershed had been clearcut before the Civil War, and during the war the guns of Fort DeRussey, at the high point of the park near Military Road and Oregon Avenue, had a clear shot in all directions, and had once fired across the gorge at a Confederate scouting party.

The park was established in 1890, and developed with the help of the great designer Frederick Law Olmstead; his sons' firm wrote a plan at the end of the First World War that guided the park through the rest of the twentieth century. Now, in the wake of the flood, it appeared to have reverted to the great hardwood forest that had blanketed the eastern half of the continent for millions of years.

The muddy forest floor was corrugated, with any number of small channels appearing in the slope down to Rock Creek. Some of these channels cut as deep as thirty feet, but they always remained mud troughs, with no stony creekbeds down their middles. Water didn't stay in them after a rain.

The forest appeared to be empty. It was easy to hike around in, but there was little to see. The animals, both native and feral, seemed to make efforts to stay concealed.

There was trash all over. Plastic bottles were the most common item, then glass bottles, then miscellaneous: boxes, shoes, plastic bag scraps... one plastic grocery bag hung in a branch over Rock Creek like a prayer flag. Another high-water mark.

There were many more signs of the flood. Most of the park's roads, paths, and picnic areas had been located down by the creek, and so were now buried in mud or torn away. The gorge walls were scarred by landslides. Many trees had been uprooted, and some of these had been caught by the Boulder Bridge, forming a dam there that held a narrow lake upstream. The raw sandstone walls undercut by this lake were studded with boulders emerging from a softer matrix. All over the forest above these new cliff, windrows of downed trees, root balls, branches, and trash dotted the forest floor.

The higher roads and trails had survived. The Western Ridge Trail extended the length of the park on its eponymous ridge, and was intact. The nine numbered cross-trails running down from the ridge trail into the gorge now all ended abruptly at some point. Up north near the Maryland border, the Pinehurst Branch Trail was gone, its creekbed ripped like the main gorge.

Before the flood there had been thirty little picnic areas in the park, ten of them

第八章 文学与气候科学（Literature and Climate Science）

reserved for use by permit. The higher ones were damaged, the dozen on the creek gone. Almost all of them had been paltry things, as far as Frank could determine in the aftermath—small clearings with picnic tables, fireplaces, a trashcan. Site 21 was the worst in the park, two old tables in perpetual gloom, stuck at the bottom of a damp hollow that ran right onto Ross Drive. With that road closed to traffic, of course, it had gained some new privacy. Indeed in the mud under one table Frank found a used condom and a pair of women's pink underwear, Disney brand, picture of Ariel on waistband, tag saying Sunday. Hopefully they had had a blanket with them. Hopefully they had had fun. The condom seemed a good sign.

Hast of site 21 the drop to the creek was steep. The big trees that had survived overhung the water. Sandstone boulders as big as cars stood in the stream. There was no sign of the gravel path the map indicated had run up the western bank, and only short stretches of Beach Drive, a two-lane car road which had paralleled it on the eastern side. Above a flat-walled boulder, set crosswise in the stream, tall trees canted out over the creek into the open air. Across the ravine was a steep wall of green. Here the sound of the creek was louder than the sound of the city. If Beach Drive stayed closed to traffic, as it looked like it would, then water would remain the loudest sound here, followed by insects. Some birds were audible. The squirrels had gray fluffy backs, and stomachs covered with much finer fur, the same gold-copper color as the lion tamarins still missing from the zoo. There were lots of deer, white-tailed in name and fact, big-eared, quick through the trees. It was a trick to move quietly through the forest after them, because small branches were everywhere underfoot, ready to snap in the mud. People were easier to track than deer. The windrows were the only good place to hide; the big tree trunks were broad enough to hide behind, but then you had to look around them to see, exposing yourself to view.

What would the forest look like in the autumn? What would it look like in winter? How many of the feral animals could survive a winter out?

IT TURNED OUT THAT HOME DEPOT sold a pretty good tree-house kit. Its heavy-duty hardware allowed one to collar several floor beams securely to trunk or major branches, and after that it was a simple matter of two-by-fours and plywood, cut to whatever dimensions one wanted. The rest of the kit consisted mostly of fripperies, the gingerbread fill making a Swiss Family allusion that caused Frank to smile, remembering his own childhood dreams: he had always wanted a treehouse. But these days he wanted it simple.

Getting that was complicated. For a while he left work as early as he could and drove to one edge of the park or another, testing routes and parking places. Then it was off into the park on foot, using a Potomac Appalachian Trail Club map to learn it. He hiked all the trails that had survived, but usually these were just jumping-off points for rambles in the forest and scrambles in the gorge.

At first he could not find a tree he liked. He had wanted an evergreen, preferably in a stand of other evergreens. But almost every tree in Rock Creek Park was deciduous. Beech, oak, sycamore, ash, poplar, maple—he couldn't even tell which was which. All of them had tall straight trunks, with first branches very high, and crowns of foliage above that. Their bark had different textures, however, and by that sign—bark corrugated in a vertical diamond pattern—he decided that the best trees were probably chestnut oaks.

There were many of these upstream from site 21. One of them canted out and overhung the creek. It looked as if its upper branches would have a nice view, but until he climbed it he wouldn't know.

While making his reconnaissances he often ran into the frisbee golfers, and when he did he usually joined them. In running the course they always passed site 21, and if the homeless guys were there the second vet, whose name was Andy, would shout his abrasive welcome: "Who's *winning*? Who's *winning*?" The frisbee players usually stopped to chat for a moment. Spencer, the player with the dreadlocks, would ask what had happened lately, and sometimes get an earful in response. Then they were off again, Spencer in the lead, dreadlocks flying under bandanna, Robin and Robert following at speed. Robin sounded like some kind of deist or animist, everything was alive to him, and after his throws he always shouted instructions to his frisbee or begged for help from the trees. Robert spoke more in the style of a sports announcer commenting on the play. Spencer spoke only in shrieks and howls, some kind of shaman language; but he was the one who chatted with the homeless guys.

During one of these pass-bys Frank saw that Chessman was there, and under Zeno's baleful eye he offered to come back and play him for money. Chessman nodded, looking

第八章 文学与气候科学(Literature and Climate Science)

pleased.

So after the run Frank returned, toting a pizza in a box and a sixpack of Pabst. "Hey the doctor's here," Zeno said in his heavy joking tone. Frank ignored that, sat down and lost ten dollars to the boy, playing the best he could but confirming his impression that he was seriously outclassed. He said little, left as soon as it seemed okay.

The first time he climbed his candidate chestnut oak he had to use crampons, ice axe, and a telephone lineman's pole-climbing kit that he had from his window-washing days, dug out of the depths of his storage locker. Up the tree at dawn, kicking in like a telephone lineman, slinging up the strap and leaning back in his harness, up and up, through the scrawny understory and into the fork of the first two big branches. It was nice to be able to sink an ice axe in anywhere one liked; an awkward climb, nevertheless. It would be good to confirm a tree and install a ladder.

Up here he saw that one major branch curved out over the creek, then divided into two. That fork would provide a foundation, and somewhat block the view from below. He only needed a platform a bit bigger than his sleeping bag, something like a ledge bivouac on a wall climb. There was a grand view of the ravine wall opposite him, green to a height considerably higher than he was. Glimpses of the burbling creek downstream, but no view of the ground directly below. It looked good.

After that he parked and slept in the residential neighborhood to the west, and got up before dawn and hiked into the forest carrying lumber and climbing gear. This was pretty conspicuous, but at that time of day the gray neighborhood and park were completely deserted. It was only a ten-minute hike in any case, a drop through forest that would usually be empty even at the busiest time of a Sunday afternoon.

He only needed two dawn patrols to install a climbing ladder, wound on an electric winch that he reeled up and down using a garage-door remote he found at Radio Shack. After that the two-by-sixes, the two-by-fours, and two three-by-five sheets of half-inch plywood could be hauled up using the ladder as a winch cable. Climb the ladder with the miscellaneous stuff, ice axing into the trunk for balance, backpack full of hardware and tools.

Collar around trunk; beams on branches; plywood floor; low railing, gapped for the ladder. He maneuvered slowly around the trunk as he worked, slung in a self-belay from a piton nailed above him. Cirque du Soleil meets Home Improvement. Using woodscrews rather than nails reduced the sound of construction, while also making the thing stronger.

Every day an hour's work in the green horizontal light, and all too soon it was finished, and then furnished. A clear plastic tarp stapled and glued to the trunk overhead served as a see-through roof, tied out to branches on a slant to let the rain run off. The opening in the rail, the winch screwed down to the plywood just inside it. Duffel bag against the trunk holding rolled foam mattress, sleeping bag, pillow, lantern, gear.

Standing on the platform without his sling one morning, in the slanting light that told him it was time to drive to work, he saw that the thing was built. Too bad! He would have liked the project to have lasted longer.

Driving across town that morning, he thought, "Now I have two bedrooms, in a modular home distributed throughout the city. One bedroom was mobile, the other in a tree. How cool was that? How perfectly rational and sane?"

Over in Arlington he drove to the NSF basement parking lot, then walked over to Optimodal Health Club to shower.

Big, new, clean, blazingly well-lit; it was a shocking contrast to the dawn forest, and he always changed at his locker feeling a bit stunned. Then it was off to the weight room.

His favorite there was a pull-down bar that gave his lats a workout they otherwise would not get. Low weight, high reps, the pull like something between swimming and climbing. A peaceful warm-up, on his knees as if praying.

Then over to the leg press. Here too he was a low-weight high-rep kind of guy, although since joining the club it had occurred to him that precisely the advantage of a weight room over the outdoors was the chance to do strength work. So now he upped the weight for a few hard pushes at the end of the set.

Up and down, back and forth, push and pull, all the while taking in the other people in the room: watching the women, to be precise. Without ever actually focusing on them. Lifting, running, rowing, whatever they did Frank liked it. He had a thing for jock women that long predated his academic interest in sociobiology. Indeed it seemed likely that he had gotten into the latter to explain the former—because for as long as he could remember, women doing sports had been the ultimate stimulus to his attraction. He loved

第八章 文学与气候科学(Literature and Climate Science)

the way sports moves became female when women did them—more graceful, more like dance—and he loved the way the moves revealed the shapes of their bodies. Surely this was another very ancient primate pleasure.

At Optimodal this all remained true even though there was not a great deal of athleticism on display. Often it was a case of nonathletes trying to "get in shape," so that Frank was covertly observing women in various stages of cardiovascular distress. But that was fine too: sweaty pink faces, hard breathing; obviously this was sexy stuff. None of that bedroom silliness for Frank—lingerie, make-up, even dancing—all that was much too intentional and choreographed, even somehow confrontational. Lovelier by far were women unselfconsciously exerting themselves in some physical way.

"Oh hi Frank."

He jumped a foot.

"Hi Diane!"

She was sitting in a leg press seat, now grinning: "Sorry, I startled you."

"That's all right."

"So you did join."

"Yes, that's right. It's just like you said. Very nice. But don't let me interrupt you."

"No, I was done."

She took up a hand towel and wiped her brow. She looked different in gym clothes, of course. Short, rounded, muscular; hard to characterize, but she looked good. She drew the eye. Anyway, she drew Frank's eye; presumably everyone was different that way.

She sat there, barefoot and sweaty. "Do you want to get on here?"

"Oh no, no hurry. I'm just kind of waking myself up, to tell the truth."

"Okay."

She blew a strand of hair away from her mouth, kicked out against the weight ten times, slowing down in the last reps. She smelled faintly of sweat and soap. Presumably also pheromones, estrogens, estrogenlike compounds, and perfumes.

"You've got a lot on the stack there."

"Do I?" She peered at the weights. "Not so much."

"Two hundred pounds. Your legs are stronger than mine."

"I doubt that."

But it was true, at least on that machine. Diane pressed the two hundred ten more times; then Frank replaced her and keyed down the weights. Diane picked up a dumbbell and did some curls while he kicked in his traces. She had very nice biceps. Firm muscles under flushed wet skin. Absence of fur made all this so visible. On the savannah they would have been watching each other all the time, aware of each other as bodies.

He wondered if he could make an observation like that to Diane, and if he did, what she would say. She had surprised him often enough recently that he had become cautious about predicting her.

She was looking at the line of runners on treadmills, so Frank said, "Everyone's trying to get back to the savannah."

Diane smiled and nodded. "Easy to do."

"Is it?"

"If you know that's what you're trying for."

"Hmmm. Maybe so. But I don't think most people know."

"No. Hey, are you done there? Will you check me on the bench press? My right elbow kind of locks up sometimes."

So Frank held the handlebar outside her hand. A young woman, heavily tattooed on her arms, waited for the machine to free up.

Diane finished and Frank held out a hand to help her. She took it and hauled herself up, their grips tightening to hold. When she was up the young woman moved in to replace her, but Diane took up a towel and said, "Wait a second, let me wipe up the wet spot."

"Oh I hate the wet spot," the young woman said, and immediately threw a hand to her mouth, blushing vividly. Frank and Diane laughed, and seeing it the young woman did too, glowing with embarrassment. Diane gave the bench a final flourish and handed it over, saying, "There, if only it were always that easy!"

They laughed again and Frank and Diane moved to the next machine. Military press, leg curls; then Diane looked at her watch and said, "Oops, I gotta get going," and Frank said "Me too," and without further ado they were off to their respective locker rooms. "See you over there."

第八章 文学与气候科学(Literature and Climate Science)

"Yeah, see you."

Into the men's room, the shower, ahhhh. Hot water must have been unusual in the hominid world. Hot springs, the Indian Ocean shallows. Then out on the street, the air still cool, feeling as benign as he had in a long time. And Diane emerged at the same time from the women's locker room, transformed into work mode, except wetter. They walked over to NSF together, talking about a meeting they were scheduled to attend later in the day. Frank arrived in his office at eight a.m. as if it were any ordinary morning. He had to laugh.

The meeting featured a presentation by Kenzo and his team to Diane, Frank's committee, and some of the members of the National Science Board, the group that oversaw the Foundation in somewhat a board-of-directors style, if Frank understood it correctly. By the time Frank arrived, a large false-color map of the North Atlantic was already on the screen. On it the red flows marking the upper reaches of the Gulf Stream broke apart and curled like new ferns, one near Norway, one between Iceland and Scotland, one between Iceland and Greenland, and one extending up the long channel between Greenland and Labrador.

"This is how it used to look," Kenzo said. "Now here's the summer's data from the Argos buoy system."

They watched as the red tendrils shrank in on themselves until they nearly met, at about the latitude of southern Ireland. "That's where we're at now, in terms of temperature. Here's surface height." He clicked to another false-colored map that revealed what were in effect giant shallow whirlpools, fifty kilometers wide but only a few centimeters deep.

"This is another before map. We think these downwelling sites were pretty stable for the last eight thousand years. Note that the Coriolis force would have the currents turning right, but the land and sea-bottom configurations make them turn left. So they aren't as robust as they might be. And then, here's what we've got now—see? The downwelling has clearly shifted to southwest of Ireland."

"What happens to the water north of that now?" Diane asked.

"Well—we don't know yet. We've never seen this before. It's a fresh-water cap, a kind of lens on the surface. In general, water in the ocean moves in kind of blobs of relative freshness or salinity, you might say, blobs that mix only slowly. One team identified and tracked the great salinity anomaly of 1968 to '82, that was a huge fresher blob that circled in the North Atlantic on the surface. It made one giant circuit, then sank on its second pass through the downwelling zone east of Greenland. Now with this freshwater cap, who knows? If it's resupplied from Greenland or the Arctic, it may stay there."

Diane stared at the map. "So what do you think happened to cause this freshwater cap?"

"It may be a kind of Heinrich event, in which icebergs float south. Heinrich found these by analyzing boulders dropped to the sea floor when the icebergs melted. He theorized that anything that introduces more fresh water than usual to the far North Atlantic will tend to interfere with downwelling there. Even rain can do it. So, we've got the Arctic sea ice breakup as the main suspect, plus Greenland is melting much more rapidly than before. The poles are proving to be much more sensitive to global warming than anywhere else, and in the north the effects look to be combining to freshen the North Atlantic. Anyway it's happened, and the strong implication is that we're in for a shift to the kind of cold-dry-windy climate that we see in the Younger Dryas."

"So." Diane looked at the board members in attendance. "We have compelling evidence for an ocean event that is the best-identified trigger event for abrupt climate change."

"Yes," Kenzo said. "A very clear case, as we'll see this winter."

"It will be bad?"

"Yes. Maybe not the full cold-dry-windy, but heck, close enough. The Gulf Stream used to combine with Greenland to make a kind of jet-stream anchor, and now the jet stream is likely to wander more, sometimes shooting straight down the continents from the Arctic. It'll be cold and dry and windy all over the northern hemisphere, but especially in the eastern half of North America, and all over Europe." Kenzo gestured at the screen. "You can bet on it."

"And so... the ramifications? In terms of telling Congress about the situation?"

Kenzo waved his hands in his usual impresario style. "You name it! You could reference that Pentagon report about this possibility, which said it would be a threat to national security, as they couldn't defend the nation from a starving world."

第八章　文学与气候科学（Literature and Climate Science）

"Starving?"

"Well, there are no food reserves to speak of. I know the food production problem appeared to be solved, at least in some quarters, but there were never any reserves built up. It's just been assumed more could always be grown. But take Europe—right now it pretty much grows its own food. That's six hundred and fifty million people. It's the Gulf Stream that allows that. It moves about a petawatt northward, that's a million billion watts, or about a hundred times as much energy as humanity generates. Canada, at the same latitude as Europe, only grows enough to feed its thirty million people, plus about double that in grain. They could up it a little if they had to, but think of Europe with a climate suddenly like Canada's—how are they going to feed themselves? They'll have a four- or five-hundred million—person shortfall."

"Hmm," Diane said. "That's what this Pentagon report said?"

"Yes. But it was an internal document, written by a team led by an Andrew Marshall, one of the missile defense crowd. Its conclusions were inconvenient to the administration and it was getting buried when someone on the team slipped it to *Fortune* magazine, and they published it. It made a little stir at the time, because it came out of the Pentagon, and the possibilities it outlined were so bad. It was thought that it might influence a vote at the World Bank to change their investment pattern. The World Bank's Extractive Industries Review Commission had recommended they cut off all future investment in fossil fuels, and move that same money into clean renewables. But in the end the World Bank board voted to keep their investment pattern the same, which was ninety-four percent to fossil fuels and six percent to renewables. After that the Pentagon report experienced the usual fate."

"Forgotten."

"Yes."

"We don't remember our reports either," Edgardo said. "There are several NSF reports on this issue. I've got one here called 'Environmental Science and Engineering for the twenty first Century, The Role of the National Science Foundation.' It called for quadrupling the money NSF gave to its environmental programs, and suggested everyone else in government and industry do the same. Look at this table in it—forty-five percent of Earth's land surface transformed by humans—fifty percent of surface fresh water used—

two-thirds of the marine fisheries fully exploited or depleted. Carbon dioxide in the atmosphere thirty percent higher than before the industrial revolution. A quarter of all bird species extinct. He looked up at them over his reading glasses. "All these figures are worse now."

Diane looked at the copy of the page Edgardo had passed around. "Clearly ignorance of the situation has not been the problem. The problem is acting on what we know. Maybe people will be ready for that now. Better late than never."

"Unless it is too late," Edgardo suggested.

Diane had said the same thing to Frank in private, but now she said firmly, "Let's proceed on the assumption that it is never too late. I mean, here we are. So let's get Sophie in, and prepare something for the White House and the congressional committees. Some plans. Things we can do right now, concerning both the Gulf Stream and global warming more generally."

"We'll need to scare the shit out of them," Edgardo said.

"Yes. Well, the marks of the flood are still all over town. That should help."

"People are already fond of the flood," Edgardo said. "It was an adventure. It got people out of their ruts."

"Nevertheless," Diane said, with a grimace that was still somehow cheerful or amused. Scaring politicians might be something she looked forward to.

Given all that he had to do at work, Frank didn't usually get away as early as he would have liked. But the June days were long, and with the treehouse finished there was no great rush to accomplish any particular task. Once in the park, he could wander up the West Ridge Trail and choose where to drop deeper to the east, looking for animals. Just north of Military Road the trail ran past the high point of the park, occupied by the site of Fort DeRussey, now low earthen bulwarks. One evening he saw movement inside the bulwarks, froze: some kind of antelope, its russet coloring not unlike the mounded earth, its neck stretched as it pulled down a branch with its mouth to strip off leaves. White stripes running diagonally up from its white belly. An exotic for sure. A feral from the zoo, and his first nondescript!

It saw him, and yet continued to eat. Its jaw moved in a rolling, side-to-side mastication; the bottom jaw was the one that stayed still. It was alert to his movements,

第八章　文学与气候科学(Literature and Climate Science)

and yet not skittish. He wondered if there were any general feral characteristics, if escaped zoo animals were more trusting or less than the local natives. Something to ask Nancy.

Abruptly the creature shot away through the trees. It was big! Frank grinned, pulled out his FOG phone and called it in. The cheap little cell phone was on something like a walkie-talkie or party line system, and Nancy or one of her assistants usually picked up right away. "Sorry, I don't really know what it was." He described it the best he could. Pretty lame, but what could he do? He needed to learn more. "Call Clark on phone 12," Nancy suggested, "he's the ungulate guy." No need to GPS the sighting, being right in the old fort.

He hiked down the trail that ran from the fort to the creek, paralleling Military Road and then passing under its big bridge, which had survived but was still closed. It was nice and quiet in the ravine, with Beach Drive gone and all the roads crossing the park either gone or closed for repairs. A sanctuary.

Green light in the muggy late afternoon. He kept an eye out for more animals, thinking about what might happen to them in the abrupt climate change Kenzo said they were now entering. All the discussion in the meeting that day had centered on the impacts to humans. That would be the usual way of most such discussions; but whole biomes, whole ecologies would be altered, perhaps devastated. That was what they were saying, really, when they talked about the impact on humans: they would lose the support of the domesticated part of nature. Everything would become an exotic; everything would have to go feral.

He walked south on a route that stayed on the rim of the damaged part of the gorge as much as possible. When he came to site 21 he found the homeless guys there as usual, sitting around looking kind of beat.

"Hey, Doc! Why aren't you playing frisbee? They ran by just a while ago."

"Did they? Maybe I'll catch them on their way back."

Frank regarded them; hanging around in the steamy sunset, smoking in their own fire, empties dented on the ground around them. Frank found he was thirsty, and hungry.

"Who'll eat pizza if I go get one?"

Everyone would. "Get some beer too!" Zeno said, with a hoarse laugh that falsely insinuated this was a joke.

Frank hiked out to Connecticut and bought thin-crusted pizzas from a little stand across from Chicago's. He liked them because he thought the owner of the stand was mocking the thick pads of dough that characterized the pizzas in the famous restaurant. Frank was a thin crust man himself.

Back into the dusky forest, two boxes held like a waiter. Then pizza around the fire, with the guys making their usual desultory conversation. The vet always studying the *Post's* federal news section did indeed appear well-versed in the ways of the federal bureaucracy, and he definitely had a chip on his shoulder about it. "The left hand don't know what the right one is doing," he muttered again. Frank had already observed that they always said the same things; but didn't everybody? He finished his slice and crouched down to tend their smoky fire. "Hey someone's got potatoes burning in here."

"Oh yeah, pull those out! You can have one if you want."

"Don't you know you can't cook no potato on no fire?"

"Sure you can! How do you think?"

Frank shook his head; the potato skins were charred at one end, green at the other. Back in the paleolithic there must have been guys hanging out somewhere beyond the cave, guys who had offended the alpha male or killed somebody by accident or otherwise fucked up—or just not been able to understand the rules—or failed to find a mate (like Frank)—and they must have hunkered around some outlier fire, eating lukewarm pizza and making crude chitchat that was always the same, laughing at their old jokes.

"I saw an antelope up in the old fort," he offered.

"I saw a tapir," the Post reader said promptly.

"Come on Fedpage, how you know it was a tapir."

"I saw that fucking jaguar, I swear."

Frank sighed. "If you report it to the zoo, they'll put you in their volunteer group. They'll give you a pass to be in the park."

"You think we need a pass?"

"We be the ones giving them a pass!"

"They'll give you a cell phone too." That surprised them.

Chessman slipped in, glancing at Frank, and Frank nodded unenthusiastically; he

第八章 文学与气候科学(Literature and Climate Science)

had been about to leave. And it was his turn to play black. Chessman set out the board between them and moved out his king's pawn.

Suddenly Zeno and Andy were arguing over ownership of the potatoes. It was a group that liked to argue. Zeno was among the worst of these; he would switch from friendly to belligerent within a sentence, and then back again. Abrupt climate change. The others were more consistent. Andy was consistently abrasive with his unfunny humor, but friendly. Fedpage was always shaking his head in disgust at something he was reading. The silent guy with the silky dark red beard was always subdued, but when he spoke always complained, often about the police. Another regular was older, with faded blond-gray hair, pockmarked face, not many teeth. Then there was Jory, an olive-skinned skinny man with greasy black hair and a voice that sounded so much like Zeno's that Frank at first confused them when listening to their chat. He was if anything even more volatile than Zeno, but had no friendly mode, being consistently obnoxious and edgy. He would not look at Frank except in sidelong glances that radiated hostility.

Last among the regulars was Cutter, a cheery, bulky black guy, who usually arrived with a cut of meat to cook on the fire, always providing a pedigree for it in the form of a story of petty theft or salvage. Adventures in food acquisition. He often had a couple of buddies with him, knew Chessman, and appeared to have a job with the city park service, judging by his shirts and his stories. He more than the others reminded Frank of his window-washing days, also the climbing crowd—a certain rowdy quality—life considered as one outdoor sport after the next. It seemed as if Cutter had somewhere else as his base; and he had also given Frank the idea of bringing by food.

Chessman suddenly blew in on the left flank and Frank resigned, shaking his head as he paid up. "Next time," he promised. The fire guttered out, and the food and beer were gone. The potatoes smoldered on a table top. The guys slowed down in their talk. Redbeard slipped off into the night, and that made it okay for Frank to do so as well. Some of them made their departures into a big production, with explanations of where they were going and why, and when they would likely return again; others just walked off, as if to pee, and did not come back. Frank said, "Catch you guys," in order not to appear unfriendly, but only as he was leaving, so that it was not an opening to any inquiries.

Off north to his tree. Ladder called down, the motor humming like the sound of his brain in action. The thing is, he thought as he waited, nobody knows you. No one can. Even if you spent almost the entirety of every day with someone, and there were people like that—even then, no. Everyone lived alone in the end, not just in their heads but even in their physical routines. Human contacts were parcellated, to use a term from brain science or systems theory; parcelled out. There were:

1. the people you lived with, if you did; that was about a hundred hours a week, half of them asleep;

2. the people you worked with, that was forty hours a week, give or take;

3. the people you played with, that would be some portion of the thirty or so hours left in a week;

4. then there were the strangers you spent time with in transport, or eating out or so on. This would be added to an already full calendar according to Frank's calculations so far, suggesting they were all living more hours a week than actually existed, which felt right. In any case, a normal life was split out into different groups that never met; and so no one knew you in your entirety, except you yourself.

One could, therefore:

1. pursue a project in paleolithic living,

2. change the weather,

3. attempt to restructure your profession, and

4. be happy,

all at once, although *not* simultaneously, but moving from one thing to another, among differing populations; behaving as if a different person in each situation. It could be done, because *there were no witnesses*. No one saw enough to witness your life and put it all together.

Through the lowest leaves of his tree appeared the aluminum-runged nylon rope ladder. One of his climbing friends had called this kind of ice-climbing ladder a "Miss Piggy," perhaps because the rungs resembled pig iron, perhaps because Miss Piggy had stood on just such a ladder for one of her arias in The Muppets' Treasure Island. Frank grabbed one of the rungs, tugged to make sure all was secure above, and started to climb, still pursuing his train of thought. The parcellated life. Fully optimodal. No reason not to enjoy it; and suddenly he realized that he was enjoying it. It was like being a versatile

第八章 文学与气候科学(Literature and Climate Science)

actor in a repertory theater, shifting constantly from role to role, and all together they made up his life, and part of the life of his time.

Cheered by the thought, he ascended the upper portion of his Miss Piggy, swaying as little as possible among the branches. Then through the gap, up and onto his plywood floor.

He hand-turned the crank on the ladder's spindle to bring the ladder up after him without wasting battery power. Once it was secured, and the lubber's hole filled with a fitted piece of plywood, he could relax. He was home.

Against the trunk was his big duffel bag under the tarp, all held in place by bungee cords. From the duffel he pulled the rolled-up foam mattress, as thick and long as a bed. Then pillows, mosquito net, sleeping bag, sheet. On these warm nights he slept under the sheet and mosquito net, and only used his down bag as a blanket near dawn.

Lie down, stretch out, feel the weariness of the day bathe him. Slight sway of the tree: yes, he was up in a tree house.

The idea made him happy. His childhood fantasy had been the result of visits to the big concrete treehouse at Disneyland. He had been eight years old when he first saw it, and it had bowled him over: the elaborate waterwheel-powered bamboo plumbing system, the bannistered stairs spiraling up the trunk, the big living room with its salvaged harmonium, catwalks to the separate bedrooms on their branches, open windows on all four sides…

His current aerie was a very modest version of that fantasy, of course. Just the basics: a ledge bivouac rather than the Swiss family mansion, and indeed his old camping gear was well-represented around him, augmented by some nifty car-camping extras, like the lantern and the foam mattress and the pillows from the apartment. Stuff scavenged from the wreckage of his life, as in any other Robinsonade.

The tree swayed and whooshed in the wind. He sat on his thick foam pad, his back holding it up against the trunk. Luxurious reading in bed. Around him laptop, cell phone, a little cooler; his backpack held a bathroom bag and a selection of clothing; a Coleman battery-powered lantern. In short, everything he needed. The lamp cast a pool of light onto the plywood. No one would see it. He was in his own space, and yet at the same time right in the middle of Washington, D. C. One of the ferals in the ever-encroaching forest. "*Oooop, oop oop ooooop*!" His tree swayed back and forth in the wind. He switched off his lamp and slept like a babe.

Except his cell phone rang, and he rolled over and answered it without fully waking. "Hello?"

"Frank Vanderwal?"

"Yes? What time is it?" And where am I?

"It's the middle of the night. Sorry, but this is when I can call." As he was recognizing her voice, she went on: "We met in that elevator that stuck."

Already he was sitting up. "Ah yeah of course! I'm glad you called."

"I said I would."

"I know."

"Can you meet?"

"Sure I can. When?"

"Now."

"Okay."

Frank checked his watch. It was three in the morning.

"That's when I can do it," she explained. "That's fine. Where?"

"There's a little park, near where we first met. Two blocks south of there, a block east of Wisconsin. There's a statue in the middle of the park, with a bench under it. Would that be okay?"

"Sure. It'll take me, I don't know, half an hour to get there. Less, actually."

"Okay. I'll be there."

The connection went dead.

Again he had failed to get her name, he realized as he dressed and rolled his sleeping gear under the tarp. He brushed his teeth while putting on his shoes, wondering what it meant that she had called now. Then the ladder finished lowering and down he went, swaying hard and holding on as he banged into a branch. Not a good time to fall, oh no indeed.

On the ground, the ladder sent back up. Leaving the park the streetlights blazed in his eyes, caged in blue polygons or orange globes; it was like crossing an empty stage set. He drove over to Wisconsin and up it, then turned right onto Elm Street. Lots of parking here. And there was the little park she had mentioned. He had not known it existed. It was dark except for one orange streetlight at its north end, near a row of tennis courts. He parked and got out.

Midpark a small black statue of a female figure held up a black hoop. The streetlight and the city's noctilucent cloud illuminated everything faintly but distinctly. It reminded Frank of the light in the NSF building on the night of his abortive b-and-e, and he shook his head, not wanting to recall that folly; then he recalled that that was the night they had met, that he had broken into the NSF building specifically because he had decided to stay in D.C. and search for this woman.

And there she was, sitting on the park bench. It was 3:34 a.m. and there she sat, on a park bench in the dark. Something in the sight made him shiver, and then he hurried to her.

She saw him coming and stood up, stepped around the bench. They stopped face to face. She was almost as tall as he was. Tentatively she reached out a hand, and he touched it with his. Their fingers intertwined. Slender long fingers. She freed her hand and gestured at the park bench, and they sat down on it.

"Thanks for coming," she said.

"Oh hey. I'm so glad you called."

"I didn't know, but I thought…"

"Please. Always call. I wanted to see you again."

"Yes." She smiled a little, as if aware that seeing was not the full verb for what he meant. Again Frank shuddered: who was she, what was she doing?

"Tell me your name. Please."

"… Caroline."

"Caroline what?"

"Let's not talk about that yet."

Now the ambient light was too dim; he wanted to see her better. She looked at him with a curious expression, as if puzzling how to proceed.

"What?" he said.

She pursed her lips.

"What?"

She said, "Tell me this. Why did you follow me into that elevator?"

Frank had not known she had noticed that. "Well! I… I liked the way you looked."

She nodded, looked away. "I thought so." A tiny smile, a sigh: "Look," she said, and stared down at her hands. She fiddled with the ring on her left ring finger.

"What?"

"You're being watched." She looked up, met his gaze. "Do you know that?"

"No! But what do you mean?"

"You're under surveillance."

Frank sat up straighter, shifted back and away from her. "By whom?"

She almost shrugged. "It's part of Homeland Security."

"What?"

"An agency that works with Homeland Security."

"And how do you know?"

"Because you were assigned to me."

Frank swallowed involuntarily. "When was this?"

"About a year ago. When you first came to NSF."

Frank sat back even further. She reached a hand toward him. He shivered; the night seemed suddenly chill. He couldn't quite come to grips with what she was saying. "Why?"

She reached farther, put her hand lightly on his knee. "Listen, it's not like what you're thinking."

"I don't know what I'm thinking!"

She smiled. The touch of her hand said more than anything words could convey, but right now it only added to Frank's confusion.

She saw this and said, "I monitor a lot of people. You were one of them. It's not really that big of a deal. You're part of a crowd, really. People in certain emerging technologies. It's not direct surveillance. I mean no one is watching you or anything like that. It's a matter of tracking your records, mostly."

"That's all?"

"Well—no. E-mail, where you call, expenditures—that sort of thing. A lot of it's automated. Like with your credit rating. It's just a kind of monitoring, looking for patterns."

第八章 文学与气候科学(Literature and Climate Science)

"Uh huh," Frank said, feeling less disturbed, but also reviewing things he might have said on the phone, to Derek Gaspar for instance. "But look, why me?"

"I don't get told why. But I looked into it a little after we met, and my guess would be that you're an associational."

"Meaning?"

"That you have some kind of connection with a Yann Pierzinski."

"Ahhhhh?" Frank said, thinking furiously.

"That's what I think, anyway. You're one of a group that's being monitored together, and they all tend to have some kind of connection with him. He's the hub."

"It must be his algorithm."

"Maybe so. Really I don't know. I don't make the determinations of interest."

"Who does?"

"People above me. Some of them I know, and then others above those. The agency is pretty firewalled."

"It must be his algorithm. That's the main thing he's worked on ever since his doctoral work."

"Maybe so. The people I work for use an algorithm themselves, to identify people who should be tracked."

"Really? Do you know what kind?"

"No. I do know that they're running a futures market. You know what those are?"

Frank shook his head. "Like that Poindexter thing?"

"Yes, sort of. He had to resign, and really he should have, because that was stupid what he was doing. But the idea of using futures markets itself has gone forward."

"So they're betting on future acts of terrorism?"

"No no. That was the stupid part, putting it like that. There's much better ways to use those programs. They're just futures markets, when you design them right. They're like any other futures market. It's a powerful way to collate information. They outperform most of the other predictive methods we use."

"That's hard to believe."

"Is it?" She shrugged. "Well, the people I work for believe in them. But the one they've set up is a bit different than the standard futures market. It's not open to anyone, and it isn't even real money. It's like a virtual futures market, a simulation. There are these people at MIT who think they have it working really well, and they've got some real-world results they can point to. They focus on people rather than events, so really it's a people futures market, instead of commodities or ideas. So Homeland Security and associated agencies like ours have gotten interested. We've got this program going, and now you're part of it. It's almost a pilot program, but it's big, and I bet it's here to stay."

"Is it legal?"

"It's hard to say what's legal these days, don't you think? At least concerning surveillance. A determination of interest usually comes from the Justice Department, or is approved by it. It's classified, and we're a black program that no one on the outside will ever hear about. People who try to publish articles about idea futures markets, or people futures markets, are discouraged from doing so. It can get pretty explicit. I think my bosses hope to keep using the program without it ever causing any fuss."

"So there are people betting on who will do innovative work, or defect to China, or like that?"

"Yes. Like that. There are lots of different criteria."

"Jesus," Frank said, shaking his head in amazement. "But, I mean—who in the hell would bet on me?"

She laughed. "I would, right?"

Frank put his hand on top of hers and squeezed it.

"But actually," she said, turning her hand and twining her fingers with his, "at this point, I think most of the investors in the market are various kinds of diagnostic programs."

Now it was Frank's turn to laugh. "So there are computer programs out there, betting I am going to become some kind of a security risk."

She nodded, smiling at the absurdity of it. Although Frank realized, with a little jolt of internal surprise, that if the whole project were centered around Pierzinski, then the programs might be getting it right. Frank himself had judged that Pierzinski's algorithm might allow them to read the proteome directly from the genome, thus giving them any number of new gene therapies, which if they could crack the delivery problem had the potential of curing outright many, many diseases. That would be a good in itself, and

第八章 文学与气候科学 (Literature and Climate Science)

would also be worth billions. And Frank had without a doubt been involved with Yann's career, first on his doctoral committee and then running the panel judging his proposal. He had impacted Yann's career in ways he hadn't even intended, by sabotaging his application so that Yann had gone to Torrey Pines Generique and then Small Delivery Systems, where he was now.

Possibly the futures market had taken notice of that.

Caroline was now looking more relaxed, perhaps relieved that he was not outraged or otherwise freaked out by her news. He tried to stay cool. What was done was done. He had tried to secure Pierzinski's work for a company he had ties to, yes; but he had failed. So despite his best (or worst) efforts, there was nothing now he needed to hide.

"You said MIT," he said, thinking things over. "Is Francesca Taolini involved with this?"

A surprised look, then: "Yes. She's another subject of interest. There's about a dozen of you. I was assigned to surveil most of the group."

"Did you, I don't know... do you record what people say on the phone, or in rooms?"

"Sometimes, if we want to. The technology has gotten really powerful, you have no idea. But it's expensive, and it's only fully applied in some cases. Pierzinski's group—you guys are still under a much less intrusive kind of thing."

"Good." Frank shook his head, like a dog shaking off water. His thoughts were skittering around in all directions. "So... you've been watching me for a year. But I haven't done anything."

"I know. But then..."

"Then what?"

"Then I saw you on that Metro car, and I recognized you. I couldn't believe it. I had only seen your photo, or maybe some video, but I knew it was you. And you looked upset. Very... intent on something."

"Yes," Frank said. "That's right."

"What happened? I mean, I checked it out later, but it seemed like you had just been at NSF that day."

"That's right. But I went to a lecture, like I told you."

"That's right, you did. Well, I didn't know that when I saw you in the Metro. And there you were, looking upset, and so—I thought you might be trailing me. I thought you had found out somehow, done some kind of back trace— that's another area I've been working on, mirror searching. I figured you had decided to confront me, to find out what was going on. It seemed possible, anyway. Although it was also possible it was just one of those freak things that happen in D.C. I mean, you do run into people here."

"But then I followed you." Frank laughed briefly.

"Right, you did, and I was standing there waiting for that elevator, thinking: What is this guy going to do to me?" She laughed nervously, remembering it.

"You didn't show it."

"No? I bet I did. You didn't know me. Anyway, then the elevator stuck—"

"You didn't stop it somehow?"

"Heck no, how would I do that? I'm not some kind of a…"

"James Bond? James Bondette?"

She laughed. "It is not like that. It's just surveillance. Anyway there we were, and we started talking, and it didn't take long for me to see that you didn't know who I was, that you didn't know about being monitored. It was just a coincidence."

"But you said you knew I had followed you."

"That's right. I mean, it seemed like you had. But since you didn't know what I was doing, then it had to be, I don't know…"

"Because I liked the way you looked."

She nodded.

"Well, it's true," Frank said. "Sue me."

She squeezed his hand. "It's okay. I mean, I liked that. I'm in a kind of a bad… Well anyway, I liked it. And I already liked you, see? I wasn't monitoring you very closely, but closely enough so that I knew some things about you. I—I had to monitor some of your calls. And I thought you were funny."

"Yes?"

"Yes. You are funny. At least I think so. Anyway, I'm sorry. I've never really had to think about what I do, not like this, not in terms of a person I talk to. I mean—how horrible it must sound."

第八章 文学与气候科学(Literature and Climate Science)

"You spy on people."

"Yes. It's true. But I've never thought it has done anybody any harm. It's a way of looking out for people. Anyway, in this particular case, it meant that I knew you already. I liked you already. And there you were, so, you know… it meant you liked me too." She smiled crookedly. "That was okay too. Guys don't usually follow me around."

"Yeah right."

"They don't."

"Uh huh. The man who knew too little, watched by the spy who knew even less."

She laughed, pulled her hand away, punched him lightly on the arm. He caught her hand in his, pulled her to him. She leaned into his chest and he kissed the top of her head, as if to say, I forgive you your job, I forgive the surveillance. He breathed in the scent of her hair. Then she looked up, and they kissed, very briefly; then she pulled away. The shock of it passed through him, waking him up and making him happy. He remembered how it had been in the elevator; this wasn't like that, but he could tell she remembered it too.

"Yes," she said thoughtfully. "Then we did that. You're a handsome man. And I had figured out why you had followed me, and I felt—oh, I don't know. I liked you."

"Yes," Frank said, still remembering the elevator. Feeling the kiss. His skin was glowing.

She laughed again, looking off at her memories. "I worried afterward that you would think I was some kind of a loose woman, jumping you like I did. But at the time I just went for it."

"Yes you did," Frank said.

They laughed, then kissed again.

When they stopped she smiled to herself, pushed her hair off her forehead. "My," she murmured.

Frank tried to track one of the many thoughts skittering back into his head. "You said you were in a kind of a bad?"

"Ah. Yes. I did."

The corners of her mouth tightened. She pulled back a bit. Suddenly Frank saw that she was unhappy; and this was so unlike the impression he had gained of her in the elevator that he was shocked. He saw he did not know her, of course he did not know her. He had been thinking that he did, but it wasn't so. She was a stranger.

"What?" he said.

"I'm married."

"Ahh."

"And, you know. It's bad."

"Uh oh." But that was also good, he thought.

"I... don't really want to talk about it. Please. But there it is. That's where I'm at."

"Okay. But... you're out here."

"I'm staying with friends tonight. They live nearby. As far as anyone knows, I'm sleeping on their couch. I left a note in case they get up, saying I couldn't sleep and went out for a run. But they won't get up. Or even if they do, they won't check on me."

"Does your husband do surveillance too?"

"Oh yeah. He's much further up than I am."

"I see."

Frank didn't know, what to say. It was bad news. The worst news of the night, worse than the fact that he was under surveillance. On the other hand, there she was beside him, and they had kissed.

"Please." She put a hand to his mouth, and he kissed her fingertips. He tried to swallow all his questions.

But some of these questions represented a change of subject, a move to safer ground. "So—tell me what you mean exactly when you say surveillance? What do you do?"

"There are different levels. For you, it's almost all documentary. Credit cards, phone bills, e-mail, computer files."

"Whoah."

"Well, hey. Think about it. Physical location too, sometimes. Although mostly that's at the cell-phone—records level. That isn't very precise. I mean, I know you're staying over off of Connecticut somewhere, but you don't have an address listed right now. So, maybe staying with someone else. That kind of stuff is obvious. If they wanted to, they could chip you. And your new van has a transponder, it's GPS-able."

"Shit."

第八章 文学与气候科学(Literature and Climate Science)

"Everyone's is. Like transponders in airplanes. It's just a question of getting the code and locking on."

"My lord."

Frank thought it over. There was so much information out there. If someone had access to it, they could find out a tremendous amount. "Does NSF know this kind of stuff is going on with their people?"

"No. This is a black-black."

"And your husband, he does what?"

"He's at a higher level."

"Uh oh."

"Yeah. But look, I don't want to talk about that now. Some other time."

"When?"

"I don't know. Some other time."

"When we meet again?"

She smiled wanly. "Yes. When we meet again. Right now," lighting up her watch and peering at it, "shit. I have to get back. My friends will be getting up soon. They go to work early."

"Okay... You'll be okay?"

"Oh yeah. Sure."

"And you'll call me again?"

"Yes. I'll need to pick my times. I need to have a clear space, and be able to call you from a clean phone. There's some protocols we can establish. We'll talk about it. We'll set things up. But now I've gotta go."

"Okay."

A peck of a kiss and she was off into the night.

He drove his van back to the edge of Rock Creek Park, sat in the driver's seat thinking. There was still an hour before dawn. For about half an hour it rained. The sound on the van's roof was like a steel drum with only two notes, both hit all the time.

Caroline. Married but unhappy. She had called him, she had kissed him. She knew him, in some sense; which was to say, she had him under surveillance. Some kind of security program based on the virtual wagers of some MIT computers, for Christ's sake.

Perhaps that was not as bad as it first sounded. A pro forma exercise. As compared to a bad marriage. Sneaking out at three in the morning. It was hard to know what to feel.

With the first grays of dawn the rain stopped, and he got out and walked into the park. Bird calls of various kinds: cheeps, trills; then a night thrush, its little melodies so outrageous that at first they seemed beyond music, they were to human music as dreams were to art—stranger, bolder, wilder. Birds singing in the forest at dawn, singing, *The rain has stopped*! *The day is here*! *I am here*! *I love you*! *I am singing*!

It was still pretty dark, and when he came to the gorge overlook he pulled a little infrared scope he had bought out of his pocket, and had a look downstream to the waterhole. Big red bodies, shimmering in the blackness; they looked like some of the bigger antelopes to Frank, maybe the elands. Those might bring the jaguar out. A South American predator attacking African prey, as if the Atlantic had collapsed back to this narrow ravine and they were all in Gondwanaland together. Far in the distance he could hear the siamangs' dawn chorus, he assumed; they sounded very far away. Suddenly something inside his chest ballooned like a throat pouch, puffed with happiness, and to himself (to Caroline) he whispered, "ooooooooop! ooooooop!"

He listened to the siamangs, and sang under his breath with them, and fitted his digital camera to the night scope to take some IR photos of the drinking animals for FOG. In the growing light he could see them now without the scope. Black on gray. He wondered if the same siamang or gibbon made the first call every morning. He wondered if its companions were lying on branches in comfort, annoyed to be awakened; or if sleeping in the branches was uncomfortable, and all of them thus ready and waiting to get up and move with the day. Maybe this differed with animal, or circumstance—as with people—so that sometimes they snoozed through those last precious moments, before the noise became so raucously operatic that no one could sleep through it. Even at a distance it was a thrilling sound; and now it was the song of meeting Caroline, and he quit trying not to spook the big ungulates at the waterhole and howled. "OOOOOOOOP! OooooooooOOOOOOOP OOP! OOP!"

He felt flooded. He had never felt like this before, it was some new emotion, intense and wild. No excess of reason for him, not anymore! What would the guru say about this? Did the old man ever feel like this? Was this love, then, and him encountering it for the

第八章 文学与气候科学(Literature and Climate Science)

first time, not ever knowing before what it was? It was true she was married. But there were worse entanglements. It didn't sound like it was going to last. He could be patient. He would wait out the situation. He would have to wait for another call, after all.

Then he saw one of the gibbons or siamangs, across the ravine and upstream, swinging through branches. A small black shape, like a big cat but with very long arms. The classic monkey shape. He caught sight of white cheeks and knew that it was one of the gibbons. White-cheeked gibbons. The whoops had sounded miles away, but they might have been closer all along. In the forest it was hard to judge.

There were more of them, following the first. They flew through the trees like crazy trapeze artists, improvising every swing. Brachiation: amazing. Frank photographed them too, hoping the shots might help the FOG people get an ID. Brachiating through the trees, no plan or destination, just free-forming it through the branches. He wished he could join them and fly like Tarzan, but watching them he knew just what an impossible fantasy that was. Hominids had come down out of the trees, they were no longer arboreal. Tarzan was wrong, and even his tree house was a throwback.

Upstream the three elands looked up at the disturbance, then continued to drink their fill. Frank stood on the overlook, happily singing his rising glissando of animal joy, "oooooooooop!"

And speaking of animals, there was a party at the re-opened National Zoo, scheduled for later that very morning.

THE NATIONAL ZOO, PERCHED AS IT was on a promontory overlooking a bend in the Rock Creek gorge, had been hammered by the great flood. Lipping over from the north, the surge had rushed down to meet the rise of the Potomac, and the scouring had torn a lot of the fencing and landscaping away. Fortunately most of the buildings and enclosures were made of heavy concrete, and where their foundations had not been undercut, they had survived intact. The National Park system had been able to fund the repairs internally, and given that most of the released animals had survived the flood, and been rounded up afterward rather easily (indeed some had returned to the zoo site as soon as the water subsided), repairs had proceeded with great dispatch. The Friends of the National Zoo, numbering nearly two thousand now, had pitched in with their labor and their collective memory of the park, and the reconstructed version now opening to the public looked very like the original, except for a certain odd rawness.

The tiger and lion enclosure, at the southern end of the park, was a circular island divided into four quadrants, separated by a moat and a high outer wall from the human observers. The trees on the island had survived, although they looked strangely sparse and bedraggled for June.

On this special morning the returning crowd was joined by the Khembali legation, on hand to repeat their swimming tigers' welcoming ceremony, so ironically interrupted by the flood. The Quiblers were there too, of course; one of the tigers had spent two nights in their basement, and now they felt a certain familial interest.

Anna enjoyed watching Joe as he stood in his backpack on Charlie's back, happy to be up where he could see properly, whacking Charlie on the sides of the head and shouting "Tiger? Tiger?"

"Yes, tiger," Charlie agreed, trying blindly to catch the little fists pummeling him. "Our tigers! Swimming tigers!"

A dense crowd surrounded them, ooohing together when the door to the tigers' inner sanctum opened and a few moments later the big cats strode out, glorious in the morning sun.

"Tiger! Tiger!"

The crowd cheered. The tigers ignored the commotion. They padded around on the washed grass, sniffing things. One marked the big tree in their quadrant, protected from claws if not from pee by a new wooden cladding, and the crowd said "Ah." Nick Quibler explained to the people around him that these were Bengal tigers that had been washed out to sea in a big flood of the Brahmaputra, not the Ganges; that they had survived by swimming together for an unknown period of time, and that the Brahmaputra's name changed to the Tsangpo after a dramatic bend upstream. Anna asked if the Ganges too hadn't een flooding at least a little bit. Joe jumped up and down in his backpack, nearly toppling forward over Charlie's head. Charlie listened to Nick, as did Frank Vanderwal, standing behind them among the Khembalis.

Rudra Cakrin gave a small speech, translated by Drepung, thanking the zoo and all its people, and then the Quiblers.

"Tiger tiger tiger!"

第八章 文学与气候科学(Literature and Climate Science)

Frank grinned to see Joe's excitement. "Ooooop!" he cried, imitating the gibbons, which excited Joe even more. It seemed to Anna that Frank was in an unusually good mood. Some of the FONZies came by and gave him a big round button that said FOG on it, and he took another one from them and pinned it to Nick's shirt. Nick asked the volunteers a barrage of questions about the zoo animals still on the loose, at the same time eagerly perusing the FOG brochure they gave him. "Have any animals gotten as far as Bethesda?"

Frank replied for the FONZies, allowing them to move on in their rounds. "They're finding smaller ones all over. They seem to be radiating out the tributary streams from Rock Creek. You can check the website and get all the latest sightings, and track the radio signals from the ones that have been tagged. When you join FOG, you can call in GPS locations for any ferals that you see."

"Cool! Can we go and look for some?"

"I hope so," Frank said. "That would be fun." He looked over at Anna and she nodded, feeling pleased. "We could make an expedition of it."

"Is Rock Creek Park open yet?"

"It is if you're in the FOG."

"Is it safe?" Anna asked.

"Sure. I mean there are parts of the gorge where the new walls are still unstable, but we would stay away from those. There's an overlook where you can see the torn-up part and the new pond where a lot of them drink."

"Cool!"

The larger of the swimming tigers slouched down to the moat and tested the water with his huge paw.

"Tiger tiger tiger!"

The tiger looked up. He eyed Joe, tilted back his massive head, roared briefly at what had to be the lowest frequencies audible to humans, or even lower. It was a sound mostly felt in the stomach.

"Ooooooh," Joe said. The crowd said the same.

Frank was grinning with what Anna now thought of as his true smile. "Now that's a vocalization," he said.

Rudra Cakrin spoke for a while in Tibetan, and Drepung then translated.

"The tiger is a sacred animal, of course. He stands for courage. When we are at home, his name is not to be said aloud; that would be bad luck. Instead he is called King of the Mountain, or the Big Insect."

"The Big Insect?" Nick repeated incredulously. "That'd just make him mad!"

The larger tiger, a male, padded over to the tree and raked the new cladding, leaving a clean set of claw marks on the fresh wood. The crowd ooohed again.

Frank hooted. "Hey, I'm going to go see if I can set the gibbons off. Nick, do you want to join me?"

"To do what?"

"I want to try to get the gibbons to sing. I know they've recaptured one or two."

"Oh, no thanks. I think I'll stay here and keep watching the tigers."

"Sure. You'll be able to hear the gibbons from here, if they do it."

Eventually the tigers flopped down in the morning shade and stared into space. The zoo people made speeches as the crowd dispersed through the rest of the zoo. Some pretty vigorous whooping from the direction of the gibbons' enclosure nevertheless did not sound quite like the creatures themselves. After a while Frank rejoined them, shaking his head. "There's only one gibbon couple mat's been recovered. The rest are out in the park. I've seen some of them. It's neat," he told Nick. "You'll like it."

Drepung came over. "Would you join our little party in the visitors' center?" he asked Frank.

"Sure, thanks. My pleasure."

They walked up the zoo paths together to a building near the entry on Connecticut. Drepung led the Quiblers and Frank to a room in back, and Rudra Cakrin guided them to seats around a round table under a window. He came over and shook Frank's hand: "Hello, Frank. Welcome. Please to meet you. Please to sit. Eat some food, drink some tea."

Frank looked startled. "So you *do* speak English!"

The old man smiled. "Oh yes, very good English. Drepung make me take lessons."

Drepung rolled his eyes and shook his head. Padma and Sucandra joined them as they passed out sample cups of Tibetan tea. The cross-eyed expression on Nick's face when

第八章 文学与气候科学（Literature and Climate Science）

he smelled his cup gave Drepung a good laugh. "You don't have to try it," he assured the boy.

"It's like each ingredient has gone bad in a completely different way," Frank commented after a taste.

"Bad to begin with," Drepung said.

"Good!" Rudra exclaimed. "Good stuff."

He hunched forward to slurp at his cup. He did not much resemble the commanding figure who had given the lecture at NSF, Anna thought, which perhaps explained why Frank was regarding him so curiously.

"So you've been taking English lessons?" Frank said. "Or maybe it's like Charlie said? That you spoke English all along, but didn't want to tell us?"

"Charlie say that?"

"I was just joking," Charlie said.

"Charlie very funny."

"Yes... so you are taking lessons?"

"I am scientist. Study English like a bug."

"A scientist!"

"I am always scientist."

"Me too. But I thought you said, at your lecture, that rationality wasn't enough. That an excess of reason was a form of madness."

Rudra consulted with Drepung, then said, "Science is more than reason. More stronger." He elbowed Drepung, who elaborated:

"Rudra Cakrin uses a word for science that is something like devotion. A kind of devotion, he says. A way to honor, or worship."

"Worship what, though?"

Drepung asked Rudra, got a reply. "Whatever you find," he said. "Devotion is a better word than worship, maybe."

Rudra shook his head, looking frustrated by the limited palette of the English language. "You *watch*" he said in his gravelly voice, fixing Frank with a glare. "Look. If you can. Seems like healing."

He appealed again to Drepung. A quick exchange in Tibetan, then he forged on.

"Look and heal, yes. Make better. Make worse, make better. For example, take a *walk*. Look *in*. In, out, around, down, up. Up and down. Over and under. Ha ha ha."

Drepung said, "Yes, his English lessons are coming right along."

Sucandra and Padma laughed at this, and Rudra scowled a mock scowl, so unlike his real one.

"He seldom sticks with one instructor for long," Padma said.

"Goes through them like tissues," Sucandra amplified.

"Oh my," Frank said.

The old man returned to his tea, then said to Frank, "You come to our home, please?"

"Thank you, my pleasure. I hear it's very close to NSF."

Rudra shook his head, said something in Tibetan.

Drepung said, "By home, he means Khembalung. We are planning a short trip there, and the rimpoche thinks you should join us. He thinks it would be a big instruction for you."

"I'm sure it would," Frank said, looking startled. "And I'd like to see it. I appreciate him thinking of me. But I don't know how it could work. I'm afraid I don't have much time to spare these days."

Drepung nodded. "True for all. The upcoming trip is planned to be short for this very reason. That is what makes it possible for the Quibler family also to join us."

Again Frank looked surprised.

Drepung said, "Yes, they are all coming. We plan two days to fly there, four days on Khembalung, two days to get back. Eight days away. But a very interesting week, I assure you."

"Isn't this monsoon season there?"

The Khembalis nodded solemnly. "But no monsoon, this year or two previous. Big drought. Another reason to see."

Frank nodded, looked at Anna and Charlie: "So you're really going?"

Anna said, "I thought it would be good for the boys. But I can't be away from work for long."

"Or else her head will explode," Charlie said, raising a hand to deflect Anna's elbow from his ribs. "Just joking! Anyway," addressing her, "you can work on the plane and I'll watch Joe. I'll watch him the whole way."

"Deal," Anna said swiftly.

"Charlie very funny," Rudra said again.

Frank said, "Well, I'll think it over. It sounds interesting. And I appreciate the invitation," nodding to Rudra.

"Thank you," Rudra said.

Sucandra raised his glass. "To Khembalung!"

"No!" Joe cried.

思考题

1. What did the changing color of the sky mean?
2. Why was Phil persuaded to run for president of the United States?
3. "Homeless" has occurred many times and what can we infer from it?
4. "Primate" is mentioned many times and what's the purposes of them?
5. After Frank handed in his resignation letter, why did he try to withdraw his resignation and go back to NFS?

第三节　补充阅读《人生四季》

阅读济慈的诗歌《人生四季》("The Human Seasons"),思考人类与气候的辩证关系。

The Human Seasons[①]

John Keats

Four Seasons fill the measure of the year;
There are four seasons in the mind of man:
He has his lusty Spring, when fancy clear
Takes in all beauty with an easy span;

---

① KEATS J. "The Human Seasons" [Z/OL]. https://www.poetryfoundation.org/poems/44472/the-human-seasons.

He has his Summer, when luxuriously
Spring's honied cud of youthful thought he loves
To ruminate, and by such dreaming high
Is nearest unto heaven: quiet coves
His soul has in its Autumn, when his wings
He furleth close; contented so to look
On mists in idleness—to let fair things
Pass by unheeded as a threshold brook.
He has his Winter too of pale misfeature,
Or else he would forego his mortal nature.

参考文献

艾布拉姆斯,2009. 文学术语辞典[M]. 吴松江,译. 北京:北京大学出版社:657.

不列颠百科全书公司,2008. 不列颠简明百科全书(英文版)[M]. 上海:上海外语教育出版社.

曹巍,魏晓红,2014. 乔治·艾略特小说的创作思想[J]. 大家(12):1.

常宇,蔡敏,2020. 以叙事医学为突破口,诠释医者人文情怀:打造医学非虚构文学文本提升医院品牌形象[J]. 叙事医学(2):98-100.

程虹,2014. 美国自然文学三十讲[M]. 上海:外语教学与研究出版社.

地质学发展史[Z/OL]. [2018-07-24]. https://www.sohu.com/a/242923299_650579.

地质学发展简史[Z/OL]. [2023-07-05]. https://www.zgbk.com/ecph/words?SiteID=1&ID=49148&SubID=78317.

段军霞,2016. 鲍尔斯小说的道德回归[J]. 殷都学刊(1):84.

二进制[Z/OL]. [2023-02-12]. https://zh.wikipedia.org/zh-cn/二进制.

高晞,2020. 医学与历史[M]. 上海:复旦大学出版社.

郭辉,陈倩,2010.《德伯家的苔丝》对工业革命的批判意识[J]. 长城(4):141-142.

郭莉萍,2013. 从"文学与医学"到"叙事医学"[J]. 科学文化评论(3):5-22.

郭玉华,2014. 遗传学[M]. 北京:中国农业大学出版社.

何宁,2011. 哈代研究史[M]. 南京:译林出版社.

胡铁生,2009. 生态批评的理论焦点与实践[J]. 吉林大学社会科学学报(5):79-86.

黄敏,2019. 西方科幻小说中的时空乌托邦思想[D]. 济南:山东大学.

霍尔丹,2011. 代达罗斯,或科学与未来[J]. 科学文化评论(2):29-50.

姜礼福,孟庆粉,2018. 人类世:从地质概念到文学批评[J]. 湖南科技大学学报(社会科学版)(6):45.

金·斯坦利·罗宾逊[Z/OL].[2024-03-25].https://baike.baidu.com/item/金·斯坦利·罗宾逊?fromModule=lemma_search-box.

卡尔格-德克尔,2004.医药文化史[M].姚燕,周惠,译.北京:生活·读书·新知三联书店.

卡斯蒂廖尼,2003.医学史[M].程之范,译.桂林:广西师范大学出版社.

卡特赖特,弗雷德里克,2020.疾病改变历史[M].陈仲丹,译.北京:华夏出版社.

拉更斯,塔巴克,2017.地球科学导论[M].7版.徐学纯,梁琛岳,郑琦,等译.北京:电子工业出版社.

来岑岑,2021.气候变化小说的主题意蕴[N].中国社会科学报,2021-08-02.

李会影,2015.世界古代科技发明创造大全[M].北京:北京工业大学出版社.

李媛,2013.医学与文学的相遇[J].云南行政学院学报(6):182-183.

李增,2017.英国维多利亚时期的医学伦理小说:以乔治·爱略特的《米德尔马契》为中心[J].江西社会科学(4):86-96.

刘钝,2016."两种文化"视野下的霍尔丹与罗素之争[J].浙江大学学报(人文社会科学版)(1):3.

刘霖杰,2021.乌托邦作为科幻小说中现实可能性的书写[J].荆楚学刊(6):23-29.

罗兰贝格中国ICT产业营商环境白皮书[Z/OL].[2020-04-23].https://www.vzkoo.com/read/b52e2328f9761ff5677e9c8d6e1be710.html.

骆谋贝,2021.医学人文学视角下《灰色马,灰色的骑手》中的疾病叙事[J].外国文学研究(2):153-164.

罗素,2014.伊卡洛斯,或科学的未来[J].科学文化评论(4):5-18.

陆俏颖,2017.获得性遗传有望卷土重来吗?[J].自然辩证法通讯(6):30-36.

马建军,2007.乔治·艾略特研究[M].武汉:武汉大学出版社.

蛮荒海岸[Z/OL].[2023-07-25].https://book.douban.com/subject/3024740/.

毛卫强,2022.《奇妙的生物》中的博物学书写[J].国外文学(4):141-149.

美国不列颠百科全书公司,2007. 不列颠百科全书:第4卷[M]. 中国大百科全书出版社《不列颠百科全书》编辑部,译. 北京:中国大百科全书出版社.

聂珍钊,1992. 托马斯·哈代小说研究:悲戚而刚毅的艺术家[M]. 武汉:华中师范大学出版社.

帕克,2019. DK医学史:从巫术、针灸到基因编辑[M]. 李虎,译. 北京:中信出版集团.

气候[Z/OL].[2023-07-25]. https://baike.baidu.com/item/气候/384697.

全国信息安全标准化技术委员会,2018. 人工智能标准化白皮书[S]. 北京:中国电子技术标准化研究院.

舒良树,2010. 普通地质学[M]. 3版. 北京:地质出版社.

沈胜娟,王悦,2010. 医学导论[M]. 上海:第二军医大学出版社.

盛曹睿,2019. 金·斯坦利·罗宾逊"首都三部曲"中的危机书写研究[D]. 南京:南京航空航天大学.

苏佳灿,黄标通,许金廉,等,2020. 医学起源与发展简史[M]. 上海:上海大学出版社.

孙玮志,2018. 中国传统医学与古典文学[N]. 光明日报,2018-08-13(13).

天工开物[Z/OL].[2023-01-07]. https://zh.wikipedia.org/wiki/天工开物.

童第周,1978. 简谈生物学上的理论学说及其发展史[J]. 哲学研究(9):2-14.

王瑞文,柳松,黄凤芝,2019. 中国传统文化概论[M]. 北京:北京工业大学出版社.

王守仁,2011. 英国文学选读[M]. 3版. 北京:高等教育出版社.

王小菲,2013. 科幻小说与乌托邦文学[J]. 山花(9):161.

温晶晶,2015. 19世纪英国女性文学生态伦理批评[M]. 北京:国防工业出版社.

邢润川,1990. 关于化学史的分期[J]. 科学技术与辩证法(5):32.

徐文修,万素梅,刘建国,2018. 农学概论[M]. 北京:中国农业大学出版社.

薛守瑞,2021. 文学与医学的天然亲近感:兼论鼠疫题材小说中的医疗书写[J]. 中国医学人文(2):16-19.

杨琼,2017. 学者型科幻作家:金·斯坦利·罗宾逊[Z/OL].[2023-07-25].

https://sw.kpcswa.org.cn/Catalog/201703/import/2018/0127/78.html

杨颖育,2011. 谁动了我们的"食物":当代美国生态文学中的食物书写与环境预警[J]. 当代文坛(2):113.

赵匡华,1990. 化学通史[M]. 北京:高等教育出版社.

张运明,2002. 化学·社会·生活[M]. 南宁:广西科学技术出版社.

郑民,王亭,2015. 文学与医学文化[M]. 济南:山东大学出版社.

中国社会科学院语言研究所词典编辑室,2005. 现代汉语词典[M]. 5版. 北京:商务印书馆.

朱军,2002. 遗传学[M]. 北京:中国农业出版社.

宗宪春,施树良,2014. 遗传学[M]. 武汉:华中科技大学出版社.

"A FIRST YEAR IN CANTERBURY SETTLEMENT WITH OTHER EARLY ESSAYS"[Z/OL]. [2023-07-25]. https://nzetc.victoria.ac.nz/tm/scholarly/tei-ButFir-t1-g1-t1-g1-t4-body.html.

Al-Biruni[Z/OL]. [2023-06-24]. https://en.wikipedia.org/wiki/Al-Biruni.

Aldous Huxley against the Bloomsbury Group[Z/OL]. [2023-07-25]. https://huxleyandthebloomsberries.wordpress.com/other-similarities-between-bloomsbury-group-members-crome-yellow-characters/.

ALFRED T,2021. In memoriam[Z/OL]. [10-11]. https://en.wikisource.org/wiki/In_Memoriam_(Tennyson).

ANGELO J A,2006. Encyclopedia of space and astronomy[M]. New York: Facts on File Inc.

ARCHIBALD G,1898. Types of scenery and their influence on literature: the Romanes lecture 1898[M]. New York: Kennikat Press.

Artificial intelligence [Z/OL]. [2020-08-27]. https://en.wikipedia.org/w/index.php?title=Artificial_intelligence&oldid=975177933.

Artificial life [Z/OL]. [2023-06-06]. https://en.wikipedia.org/wiki/Artificial_life.

ASHWORTH W B,2018. Science of the day: George-Louis Leclerc, Comte de Buffon[Z/OL]. [09-07]. https://www.lindahall.org/about/news/scientist-of-the-day/georges-louis-leclerc-comte-de-buffon-2.

ATTALI J J, 1985. Noise: the political economy of music[M]. Minneapolis: University of Minnesota Press.

AUDEN W H, 1948. "In Praise Of Limestone"[Z/OL]. [2023-07-25]. https://allpoetry.com/In-Praise-Of-Limestone.

BALL P, 2007. Chemistry and power in recent American fiction[C]// SCHUMMER J. The public image of chemistry. Hackensack: World Scientific.

BALL P, 1948. The making of modern Prometheus[Z/OL]. [2023-07-25]. https://www.chemistryworld.com/opinion/how-frankenstein-left-chemistry-with-a-monstrous-reputation/1017377.article.

BATE J, 1999. Culture and environment: from Austen to Hardy[J]. New Literary History(30): 541-560.

BARNES J, 2011. The sense of an ending[M]. London: Knopf.

BHARATDWAJ K, 2006. Physical geography: introduction to earth[M]. New Delhi: Discovery Publishing House.

BLOOM H, 2011. Bloom's guides: brave new world: new edition[M]. New York: Infobase Publishing.

BOLTZMANN L, 1896-1898. Vorlesungen uber gastheorie[M]. Leipzig: Johann Ambrosius Barth.

BRAZIER M, 2008. Exploitation and enrichment: the paradox of medical experimentation[J]. Journal of medical ethics(34): 180-181.

BRUNO A, 2016. A eurasian mineralogy: Aleksandr Fersman's conception of the natural world[J]. Isis, 107(3): 518-539.

BROWN T L, 2015. Chemistry: the central science[M]. 13th ed. London: Pearson.

BROWN V A, BRYANT C, 2021. Cooperative evolution: reclaiming Darwin's vision[M]. Canberra: Australian National University Press.

BUCKLAND A, 2013. Novel science: fiction and the invention of nineteenth-century geology[M]. Chicago: The University of Chicago Press.

BUELL L, 1995. The environmental imaginations: Thoreau, nature writing, and the formation of American culture[M]. Cambridge: Harvard University Press.

BUTLER M, 1996. Frankenstein and radical science[C]//Frankenstein, Mary Shelley-the Norton critical edition. New York: Norton.

BUTLER M, 2008. Introduction[A]//SHELLEY M. Frankenstein or the modern Prometheus. Oxford: Oxford University Press.

CALDWELL J M, 2004. Literature and medicine in nineteenth-century Britain: from Mary Shelley to George Eliot[M]. Cambridge: Cambridge University Press.

CARTELLI A, PALMA M, 2009. Encyclopedia of information communication technology[M]. Hershey: Information Science Reference.

CASEY J G, 2002. A new heartland: women, modernity, and the agrarian ideal in America[M]. Oxford: Oxford University Press.

CASTREE N, 2014. The anthropocene and the environmental humanities: extending the conversation[J]. Environmental humanities, 5(1): 233-260.

CECELIA T, 1987. Shifting gears: technology, literature, culture in modernist America[M]. Chapel Hill: University of North Carolina Press.

CHARON R, BANKS J T, 1995. Literature and medicine: contributions to clinical practice[J]. Annals of internal medicine(8): 599-606.

CHAITIN G. Algoritchmic information theory[M]. Cambridge: Cambridge University Press, 1987.

CHAUHAN L K, 2017. Basics of geophysics[M]. Lunawada: Redshine International Press.

CHRISTIE A, 1962. Poirot loses a client[M]. New York: Dodd Mead and Co.

CLARKE B, ROSSINI M, 2011. The Routledge companion to literature and science[M]. London: Routledge.

COBB A B, 2009. Earth chemistry[M]. New York: Chelsea House Publishers.

COLERIDGE S T, 1798. "The Rime of the Ancient Mariner"[Z/OL]. [2023-07-25]. https://www.poetryfoundation.org/poems/43997/the-rime-of-the-ancient-mariner-text-of-1834.

CONLOGUE W, 2001. Working the garden: American writers and the industrialization of agriculture[M]. Chapel Hill: University of North Carolina Press.

Contemporaryscience in John Donne's poetry[Z/OL]. [2023-07-25]. https://

www. englishliterature. info/2021/06/science-in-john-donnes-poetry. html.

Conway's game of life [Z/OL]. [2023-07-12]. https://en. wikipedia. org/wiki/Conway%27s_Game_of_Life.

CORNFIELD P J, 1995. Power and the professions in Britain between 1700 and 1850[M]. London: Routledge.

COSANS C E, 2009. Owen's ape and Darwin's bulldog: beyond Darwinism and creationism[M]. Bloomington: Indiana University Press.

CROSS J, 1885. George Eliot's life[M]. London: Blackwood.

CRUTZEN P J, 2002. Geology of mankind[J]. Nature, 415(1): 23.

DAVIS M, 2001. Late Victorian holocausts: el nino famines and the making of the third world[M]. London: Verso.

DAWSON G, 2016. Show me the bone: reconstructing prehistoric monsters in nineteenth century[M]. Chicago: University of Chicago Press.

DEFOE D, 2003. The storm[M]. London: Allen Lane.

DEWEY J, 2002. Richard Powers [Z/OL]. [2023-07-25]. https://www. richardpowers. net/biography/.

DEWEY J, 2002. Understanding Richard Powers[M]. Columbia: University of South Carolina Press.

DOUG D, LISA Y, 2012. "Science's consciousness": an interview with Kim Stanley Robinson[J]. Configurations(1): 188.

DJERASSI C, 1998. NO[M]. Athens: University of Georgia Press.

DJERASSI C, HOFFMANN R, 2001. Oxygen[M]. Weinheim: Wiley-VCH Verlag.

DUNLAP S, 2013. "One must be scientific": natural history and ecology in Mrs. Dalloway[C]//MARTIN A, HOLLAND K. Interdisciplinary/multidisciplinary Woolf. Liverpool: Liverpool University Press.

EDEL L, 2023. Henry James[Z/OL]. [04-11]. https://www. britannica. com/biography/Henry-James-American-writer.

EDEL L, 1984. The letters of Henry James[M]. vol. 4. Cambridge: Harvard University Press.

EDEL L, 1978. The life of Henry James[M]. vol. 4. New York: Avon.

EDGAR I I, 1935. Shakespeare's psychopathological knowledge: a study in criticism and interpretation[J]. The journal of abnormal and social psychology(1): 70-83.

ELIOT G, 2000. Middlemarch: an authoritative text, backgrounds, criticism [M]. New York: W. W. Norton & Company.

EMERSON R W, 1983. Nature[A]//PORTE J. Essays and lectures by Ralph Waldo Emerson. New York: Library of America.

FAGAN B, 2000. The little Ice Age: how climate made history: 1300-1850 [M]. New York: Basic Books.

FEENBERG A, 1996. Questioning technology[M]. New York: Routledge.

FREDERICK P L, 1979. The geology of sense and sensibility[J]. Yearbook of English studies, 9: 246-255.

FREEMAN C, 2002. Hail Mary: On the author of Frankenstein and the origin of science fiction[J]. Science fiction studies, 29: 253-264.

FRIEDMAN G M, 1978. Classification of sediments and sedimentary rocks[C]// FAIRBRIDGE R W. Encyclopedia of sedimentology. Dordrecht: Springer.

FRIEDRICH K A, 1990. Discourse networks 1800/1900[M]. Stanford: Stanford University Press.

GAARD G, 2015. Ecofeminism and climate change [J]. Women's studies international forum(49): 20-33.

Gain[Z/OL]. [2023-07-25]. https://medhum.med.nyu.edu/view/1451.

GARRISON F H, 1917. An introduction to the history of medicine [M]. Philadelphia: W. B. Saunders Company.

GeoHumanities forum[Z/OL]. [2023-07-10]. https://geohumanitiesforum.org/about/.

Geology[Z/OL]. [2023-06-22]. https://en.wikipedia.org/wiki/Geology.

George Eliot[Z/OL]. [2023-07-10]. https://en.wikipedia.org/wiki/George_Eliot.

GEORGE L, 1998. The novel as scientific discourse: the example of Conrad[J].

Novel: a forum on fiction, 21: 220-227.

GIBBS J W, 1878. On the equilibrium of heterogenous substances [J]. Transactions of the Connecticut academy of sciences(3): 108-248, 343-524.

GLASBY G, 2007. Goldschmidt in Britain[J/OL]. Geoscientist, 17(13): 22-27. https://www.geolsoc.org.uk/Geoscientist/Archive/March-2007/Goldschmidt-in-Britain.

GLENDENING J, 2013. Science and religion in neo-Victorian novels: eye of the ichthyosaur[M]. New York: Routledge.

GOHAU G, 1990. A history of geology[M]. New Brunswick: Rutgers University Press.

GOLINSKI J, 2007. British weather and the climate of enlightenment[M]. Chicago: University of Chicago Press.

GÓMEZ P M R, 2007. An archetypal reading of the cage symbol in Henry James's major phase[J]. Revista Canaria De Estudios Ingleses(54): 69-86.

GOTHE J W V, 1963. Elective affinities[M]. Washington, D.C.: Henry Regnery.

GUPTA H, 1989. Encyclopedia of solid earth geophysics[M]. Dordrecht: Springer.

HAGEN M, SKAGEN M V, 2013. Literature and chemistry: effective affinities [M]. Nordre Ringgade: Aarhus University Press.

HANSON C, 2020. Genetics and the literary imagination[M]. Oxford: Oxford University Press.

HARAWAY D J, 1991. Simians, cyborgs and women[M]. New York: Routledge.

HARDY B, 1982. Readings in George Eliot[M]. London: Peter Owen Limited.

HARRISON T, 1992. Square rounds[M]. London: Faber and Faber.

HARTLEY R, 1928. Transmission of information[J]. Bell system technical journal(7): 535-563.

HAWKINS A, 1993. Reconstructing illness: studies in pathography[M]. West Lafayette: Purdue University Press.

HAWTHORNE N, 1970. The birth-mark[C]//WAGGONER H H. Nathaniel Hawthorne: selected tales and sketches. 3rd ed. New York: Holt, Rinehart and Winston.

HAYLES K, 1987. Information or noise? Economy of explanation in Barthes's S/Z and Shannon's information theory[C]//LEVINE G. One culture: essays in science and literature. Madison: University of Wisconsin Press.

HEISE U, 2002. Toxin, drugs, and global system: risk and narrative in the contemporary novel[J]. American literature(4): 747-778.

HERINGMAN N, 2004. Romantic rocks, aesthetic geology[M]. New York: Cornell University Press.

History of geology[Z/OL]. [2023-07-25]. https://en.wikipedia.org/wiki/History_of_geology#17th_century.

History of telecommunication[Z/OL]. [2023-07-25]. https://en.wikipedia.org/w/index.php?title=History_of_telecommunication&oldid=1035411188.

HOFFMANN R, 1995. The same and not the same[M]. New York: Columbia University Press.

HOTTOIS G, 1984. Le signe et la technique. La philsophie a l'epreuve de la technique[M]. Paris: Aubier.

HUTTON J, 1795. Theory of the earth, with proofs and illustrations, 2 vols[M]. Edinburgh: Printed for Messers, Cadell, Junior, Davis, and Creech.

HUDSON J, 1992. The history of chemistry[M]. New York: The Macmillan Press Ltd.

HUXLEY A, 1946. Brave new world[M]. New York: Harper & Brothers.

Ideas of Hippocrates and Aristotle [Z/OL]. [2023-07-25]. https://biocyclopedia.com/index/genetics/genetics_an_overview/ideas_of_hippocrates_and_aristotle.php.

Information and communications technology[Z/OL]. [2023-07-06]. https://en.wikipedia.org/wiki/Information_and_communications_technology.

Information and communication technology (ICT) [Z/OL]. [2023-07-25]. https://www.techopedia.com/definition/24152/information-and-communications-technology-ict.

Information technology[Z/OL]. [2023-07-09]. https://en. wikipedia. org/wiki/Information_technology.

IZHIKEVICH E M, 2015. Game of life[J]. Scholarpedia(6): 1816.

JAN Z, 2018. Geology: a very short introduction[M]. Adobe Digital ed. New York: Oxford University Press.

JOHN M, 1898. The mountains of California[M]. New York: The Century Co.

JOHN R, 2011. Missing links: in search of human origins[M]. New York: Oxford University Press.

JONES G, 1985. Book reviews: Darwin's plot: evolutionary narrative in Darwin, George Eliot and nineteenth-century fiction[J]. Isis, 76(1): 93–94.

JONES J, 2011. Leonardo da Vinci's earth-shattering insights about geology[Z/OL]. [11-23]. https://www. theguardian. com/artanddesign/jonathanjonesblog/2011/nov/23/leonardo-da-vinci-earth-geology.

JONES R F, 1940. Science and criticism in the neo-classical age of English literature[J]. Journal of the history of ideas(4): 381-412.

John Woodward[Z/OL]. [2022-09-05]. https://en. wikipedia. org/wiki/John_Woodward_(naturalist).

JOHNS-PUTRA A, 2019. Climate and literature[M]. Cambridge: Cambridge University Press.

JOHNS-PUTRA A, 2012. Climate change in literature and literary studies: from Cli-Fi, climate change theater and ecopoetry to ecocriticism and climate change criticism[J]. WIREs climate change, 7(2): 266–282.

JOHNSTON J, 2011. AI and ALife[C]//CLARKE B, ROSSINI M. The Routledge companion: literature and science. London: Routledge.

JOHNSTON J, 2008. The allure of machinic life: cybernetics, artificial life, and the new AI[M] Cambridge: The MIT Press.

JOHNSTON J, 2017. Traumatic responsibility: Victor Frankenstein as creator and casualty[C]//GUSTON D H, ROBERTS J. Annotated for scientists, engineers and creators of all kinds. Cambridge: The MIT Press.

KARNICKY J, 2007. Fascinated disgust in Richard Powers[J]. Contemporary Fiction and the Ethics of Modern Culture.

KEATS J, 1818. "The Human Seasons"[Z/OL]. [2023-07-25]. https://www.poetryfoundation.org/poems/44472/the-human-seasons.

KENNEDY M, 2010. Revising the clinic: vision and representation in Victorian medical narrative and the novel[M]. Columbus: The Ohio State University Press.

KENSHŪJO K K S. Approaches for systematic planning of development projects information and communication technology[M]. Dowagiac: Institute for International Cooperation, 2004.

KLAVER J M I, 2014. Charles Lyell's churches and the erosion of faith in Matthew Arnold's "Dover Beach"[J]. Linguae &-Rivista di lingue e culture monderne, 13(1): 21-34.

KNIGHT D M, 1970. The physical sciences and the romantic movement[J]. History of science(9): 54-75.

KUSKY T M, CULLEN K E, 2010. Encyclopedia of earth and space science[M]. New York: Facts on File Inc.

LABINGER J, 2011. Chemistry[C]//CLARKE B, ROSSINI M. The Routledge companion to literature and science. London: Routledge.

LARSEN T B, 2018. A Review of anthropocene reading: literary history in geological times, edited by Tobias Menley and Jesse Oak Taylor[J]. Universitas: journal of research, scholarship, and creative activity, 13(1): 1-8.

LASZLO P, 2007. On the self-image of chemists, 1950-2000[C]//SCHUMMER J. The publicimage of chemistry. Hackensack: World Scientific.

LATOUR B, 1985. Laboratory life: the construction of scientific facts[M]. Princeton: Princeton.

LEAVIS F R, 1963. Two cultures? The significance of C. P. Snow[M]. Richmond: Pantheon.

LEVINE G, 1987. One culture: essays in science and literature[M]. Madison: University of Wisconsin Press.

LEVI P, 1984. The periodic table[M]. New York: Schocken Books.

Literary influences and reception[Z/OL].[2023-07-11]. https://sites.udel.edu/britlitwiki/literary-influences-and-reception/.

LOCKE J, 1960. Two treatises of government[M]. Cambridge: Cambridge University Press.

LOGAN P M, 1991. Conceiving the body: realism and medicine in Middlemarch[J]. History of the human sciences(2): 207.

LOWE D B, 2016. The chemistry book[M]. New York: Sterling Publishing.

LOXTERKAMP D, 1997. A measure of my days: the journal of a country doctor[M]. Hanover: University Press of New England.

MA C, RUBIN A E, 2021. Meteorite mineralogy[M]. Cambridge: Cambridge University Press.

MAMBROL N. Artificial intelligence and artificial life[Z/OL].(2018-07-29). https://literariness.org/2018/07/29/artificial-intelligence-and-artificial-life/.

MARKLEY R, 1999. "Land enough in the world": Locke's golden age and the infinite extensions of "use"[J]. South Atlantic quarterly, 98: 817-837.

MARSHAK S, 2009. Plate tectonics[M]. New York: Chelsea House Publishers.

MARTELL J, 2013. The Dorset dairy, the pastoral, and Thomas Hardy's *Tess of the d'Urbervilles*[J]. Nineteenth-century literature(1): 6.

MCCORMACK K, 2000. George Eliot and Victorian intoxication: dangerous drugs for the condition of England[M]. Berlin: Springer.

MCPHEE J. Assembling California-I[Z/OL].[1992-08-30]. https://www.newyorker.com/magazine/1992/09/07/assembling-california-part-i.

MEADOW C T, 2002. Making connections: communication through the ages[M]. Lanham: Scarecrow Press.

MENELY T, TAYLOR J O, 2017. Anthropocene reading: literary history in geological times[M]. University Park: The Pennsylvania State University Press.

MENKE R, 2019. Literature, print culture and media technologies, 1880–1900[M]. Cambridge: Cambridge University Press.

MENKE R, 2008. Telegraphic realism: Victorian fiction and other information systems[M]. Stanford, California: Stanford University Press.

MIROWSKI P, 2002. Machine dreams: economics become a cyborg science[M]. Cambridge: Cambridge University Press.

MONROE J S, WICANDER R, 2010. Historical geology[M]. 6th ed. Belmont: Brooks/Cole.

MORSE K, 1920. Milton's ideas of science as shown in "Paradise Lost"[J]. The scientific monthly(2): 150-156.

MULVEY M, PORTER R, 1993. Literature and medicine during the eighteenth century[M]. London: Routledge.

NEAPOLITANR E, JIANG X, 2018. Artificial intelligence: with an introduction to machine learning[M]. 2nd ed. Boca Raton: CRC Press.

Nebular hypothesis [Z/OL]. [2023-06-21]. https://en.wikipedia.org/wiki/Nebular_hypothesis.

NEUMANN J, 1932. Matchematische gundlagen der quantenmechanik [M]. Berlin: Springer.

NICOLA N, 1999. The reading gaol of Henry James's "In the Cage"[J]. ELH (1): 179-201.

NICOLAUS S. Tag archives: Leonardo da Vinci fossils[Z/OL]. [2020-07-13]. https://www.geological-digressions.com/tag/leonardo-da-vinci-fossils/.

NORWICK S A, 2011. Geology[C]//CLARKE B, ROSSINI M. The Routledge companion: literature and science. London: Routledge.

NYQUIST H, 1924. Certain factors affecting telegraph speed[J]. Bell system technical journal (3): 324-346.

O'CONNOR R, 2007. The earth on show: fossils and the poetics of popular science [M]. Chicago: The University of Chicago Press.

O'CONNOR R, 2020. Geology and paleontology [C]//DENISOFF D, SCHAFFER T. The Routledge companion to Victorian literature. Abingdon: Routledge.

O'HARA K D, 2018. A brief history of geology[M]. Cambridge: Cambridge University Press.

OTIS L, 2002. Literature and science in the nineteenth century[M]. Oxford:

Oxford University Press.

PARKES A, 2021. Logics of disintegration in Lawrence and Huxley[EB/OL]. [2023-07-25]. https://journals.openedition.org/lawrence/2471.

PATRICIA I, 1980. Hardy and the wonders of geology[J]. Review of English studies, 31: 60-61.

PAULSON W R, 1988. The noise of culture: literary texts in a world of information[M]. Ithaca: Cornell University Press.

PETER F, 1997. From apocalypse to entropy and beyond: the second law of thermodynamics in post-war American fiction[M]. Essen: Die Blaude Eule.

PHLLIP S, 2006. The noise of American literature, 1890-1985: toward a history of literary acoustics[M]. Gainesville: University Press of Florida.

Physical astronomy for the mechanistic universe[Z/OL]. [2023-07-10]. https://www.loc.gov/collections/finding-our-place-in-the-cosmos-with-carl-sagan/articles-and-essays/modeling-the-cosmos/physical-astronomy-for-the-mechanistic-universe.

Planetary geology[Z/OL]. [2023-06-17]. https://en.wikipedia.org/wiki/Planetary_geology.

PLUMMER C C, CARLSON D, 2016. Physical geology[M]. 15th ed. New York: McGraw-Hill Education.

POGGI S, BOSSI M, 1994. Romanticism in science: science in Europe, 1790-1840[M]. Dordrecht: Kluwer Academic Publishers.

PORTER R, 1997. The greatest benefit to mankind: a medical history of humanity[M]. New York: W. W. Norton & Company.

POWERS R, 1998. Gain[M]. New York: Farrar, Straus and Giroux.

PYNCHON T, 1966. The crying of lot 49[M]. London: Picador.

RABBITT M C, 1980. Minerals, lands, and geology for the common defence and general welfare[M]. United States Government Printing Office.

RAFFERTY J P, 2012. Geological sciences[M]. London: Britannica Educational Publishing.

RICHARDSON A, 2001. British romanticism and the science of the mind[M]. Cumbridge: Cambridge University Press.

ROBERTS J H, 1937. Huxley and Lawrence[J]. The Virginia quarterly review (4): 547, 553.

ROBINSON C E, 2017. Introduction [A]//GUSTON D H, ROBERTS J. Annotated for scientists, engineers and creators of all kinds. Cambridge: The MIT Press.

ROBINSON K S, 2016. Remarks on utopia in the age of climate change[J]. Utopian studies(1): 10.

ROBERT M, 2012. "How to go forward": catastrophe and comedy in Kim Stanley Robinson's Science in the Capital trilogy[J]. Configurations(1): 11.

ROGERS E M, 1986. Communicationtechnology: the new media in society[M]. New York: The Free Press.

ROLAND N L, 1977. Creation by natural law: Laplace's nebular hypothesis in American thought [M]. Seattle: University of Washington Press.

ROOF J, 2011. Genetics [C]//CLARKE B, ROSSINI M. The Routledge companion to literature and science. London: Routledge.

ROSE M, 2018. "Anthropocentric signatures": writing natures in Doctor Faustus [J]. Early modern culture, 13:188 – 198.

ROUSSEAU G, 2011. Medicine[C]//CLARKE B, ROSSINI M. The Routledge companion: literature and science. London: Routledge.

ROZENBERG G, BACK T, KOK J N, 2012. Handbook of natural computing [M]. vol. 4. Berlin: Springer.

RUDWICK M S J, 2005. Bursting the limits of time: the reconstruction of geohistory in the age of revolution[M]. Chicago: University of Chicago Press.

RUDWICK M J S, 1997. George Cuvier, fossil bones, and geological catastrophes: new translations and interpretations of the primary texts[M]. London: The University of Chicago Press.

RUSSELL S J, NORVIG P, 2016. Artificial intelligence: a modern approach [M]. 3rd ed. London: Pearson.

RUSTON S, 2015. The science of life and death in Mary Shelle's Frankenstein[Z/OL]. [2023-07-25]. https://www. bl. uk/romantics-and-victorians/articles/the-science-of-life-and-death-in-mary-shelleys-frankenstein.

SALMONS K, 2017. Food in the novels of Thomas Hardy[M]. London: Palgrave Macmillan.

SAMPSON F, 2018. Frankenstein at 200-why hasn't Mary Shelley been given the respect she deserves?[Z/OL].(2018-01-13)[2023-05-16]. https://www.theguardian.com/books/2018/jan/13/frankenstein-at-200-why-hasnt-mary-shelley-been-given-the-respect-she-deserves-.

SARAMAGO J, PONTIERO G, 1985. Blindness: a novel[M]. London: Harvill.

SAYERS D L, EUSTACE R, 1995. The documents in the case[M]. New York: Harper Paper Backs.

SCARRY E, 1995. The body in pain: the making and unmaking of the world[M]. New York: Oxford University Press.

SCHACTER D L, SCARRY E, 2000. Memory, brain, and belief[M]. Cambridge, Mass.: Harvard University Press.

SCHATZBERG W, WAITE R A, JOHNSON J K, 1987. The relations of literature and science: an annotated bibliography of scholarship, 1880−1980[M]. New York: Modern Language Association.

SCHEIBER A J, 1996. Eugenic anxiety in Henry James's Washington square[J]. Literature and medicine(2): 244−262.

SCHUMMER J, 2006. Historical roots of the "mad scientist": chemists in nineteenth-century literature[J]. Ambix(2): 99−127.

SCHRAMM J, 2013. George Eliot and the law[C]//ANDERSON A, SHAW H E. A companion to George Eliot. Hoboken: Wiley-Blackwell.

SCHWEIGHAUSER P, 2011. Information theory[C]//CLARKE B, ROSSINI M. The Routledge companion: literature and science. London: Routledge.

SEN S, 2007. Earth: the planet extraordinary[M]. New Delhi: Allied Publishers.

SERRES M, 1997. Genesis[M]. Ann Arbor: University of Michigan Press.

Shakespearethrough the eyes of a chemist[Z/OL].[2023-07-25]. https://nextmovesoftware.com/blog/2013/10/28/shakespeare-through-the-eyes-of-a-chemist/.

SHAKESPEARE W, 1609. "Sonnet 1: From fairest creatures we desire increase" [Z/OL]. [2023-07-25]. https://nosweatshakespeare.com/sonnets/1/.

SHAKESPEARE W, 1609. "Sonnet 14: Not from the stars do I my judgement pluck"[Z/OL]. [2023-07-25]. https://nosweatshakespeare.com/sonnets/14/.

SHANNON C, WEAVER W, 1963. The mathematical theory of communication [M]. Urbana: University of Illinois Press.

SHARROCK R, 1962. The chemist and the poet: sir Humphrey Davy and the preface to Lyrical Ballads[J]. Notes and records of the royal society of London (17): 76.

SHAW D, 2018. Anthropocene [Z/OL]. [2018-10-10]. https://criticalposthumanism.net/anthropocene/.

SIEDLECKI B, 1985. Two scientific manifestos: discourses on science in Jonson's the alchemist and Marlowe's doctor Faustus [D]. Edmonton: The University of Alberta.

SIMILI R. Erasmus Darwin, galvanism, and the principle of life[Z/OL]. [2023-07-25]. https://www.lilec.it/romanticismo/erasmus-darwin-galvanism-and-the-principle-of-life/.

SMITH J, 2013. The novel and science[C]//LISA R. The Oxford handbook of the Victorian novel. Oxford: Oxford University Press.

SONTAG S. Illness as metaphor[M]. New York: Random House, 1979.

SQUIER S M, 2011. Agricultural studies[C]//CLARKE B, ROSSINI M. The Routledge companion: literature and science. London: Routledge.

STEINBECK J. The grapes of wrath[M]. New York: The Viking Press, 1958.

SUSAN G, 1975. Early Victorian science writers and Tennyson's "In Memoriam": a study in cultural exchange: part II[J]. Victorian studies, 18(4): 444.

SZILARD L, 1929. Uber die entropieveminderung in einem thermodynamischen system bei eingriffen intelligenter wesen[J]. Zeitschrift fur pysik, 53(11-12): 840-56.

TANNER V, 1937. Jakob Johannes Sederholm[M]. Helsinki: Tilgmann.

TALLIS R, 1995. Newton's sleep: the two cultures and the two kingdoms[M], Basingstoke: Macmillan.

TERESA D L, 1987. Technologies of gender: essays on theory, film, and fiction [M]. Bloomington: Indiana University Press.

The geological observation of Robert Hook [Z/OL]. [2016-01-18]. https://paleonerdish. wordpress. com/2016/01/18/the-geological-observations-of-robert-hooke/.

THOMAS N. Geology corresponds with Homer's of ancient Tory [Z/OL]. [2003-03-03]. https://www1. udel. edu/PR/UDaily/2003/troy030303. html.

TRACY C, 2010. Remarkable creatures [M]. London: Harper Collins Publishers: 126–127.

TREXLER A, 2015. Anthropocene fictions: the novel in a time of climate change [M]. Charlottesville: University of Virginia Press.

TURING A, 1950. Computing machinery and intelligence [J]. Mind(263): 433–460.

Turing test [Z/OL]. [2023-07-03]. https://en. wikipedia. org/wiki/Turing_test.

VAI G B, 2009. The scientific revolution and Nicolas Steno's twofold conversion [J]. Memoir of the geological society of America (203): 187–208.

VARVOGLI, A, VARVOGLIS A, 1995. Chemists as characters and as authors in literature [J]. The chemical intelligencer(2): 43-46, 55.

VEITH W, 2002. The genesis conflict [M]. Delta: Amazing Discoveries.

VERDÚ S, 1998. Fifty years of Shannon theory [J]. IEEE transactions on information theory, 44(6): 2057.

VERČKO R, 2005. Existential concerns and narrative techniques in the novels of Ford Madox Ford, Virginia Woolf and Aldous Huxley [J]. Acta Neophilologica, 38(1-2): 49–59.

VICKERS N, 2004. Coleridge and the doctors, 1795–1806 [M]. Oxford: Clarendon Press.

Victorians were obsessed with the idea that George Eliot had two different-sized hands [Z/OL]. [2023-07-25]. https://crimereads. com/victorians-george-eliot-hands/.

VONNEGUT K, 1963. Cat's cradle [M]. New York: Holt, Rinehart & Winston.

WALTERS C C, 2006. The origin of petroleum[C]//HSU C S, ROBINSON P R. Practical advances in petroleum processing. Vol. 1. New York: Springer.

WELLS H G, 1984. The war of the worlds[M]. Geduld: Indiana University Press.

WHITINGTON J. Geological humanism[Z/OL]. [2020-09-22]. https://culanth.org/fieldsights/geological-humanism.

WHITROW G J. Pierre-Simon, marquis de Laplace[Z/OL]. [2023-05-29]. https://www.britannica.com/biography/Pierre-Simon-marquis-de-Laplace#ref29401.

WIENER N, 1948. Cybernetics or control and communication in the animal and the machine[M]. Cambridge: MIT Press.

William Whiston[Z/OL]. [2023-07-08]. https://en.wikipedia.org/wiki/William_Whiston.

WILLIAMS R, 1973. The country and the city[M]. Oxford: Oxford University Press.

WUNDERLICH G, 2000. Hues of American agrarianism[J]. Agriculture and human values(17): 195-196.

YASUHARA K, 2007. Development of new geomaterials[J]. Tsuchi to Kiso, 54(12): 6-7.

YOUNG D, 2003. Mind over magma: the story of igneous petrology[M]. Princeton: Princeton University Press.